THE
CIRCLE
OF
CERIDWEN

BOOK ONE

THE CIRCLE OF
CERIDWEN SAGA

THE
CIRCLE
OF
CERIDWEN

OCTAVIA RANDOLPH

PYEWACKET PRESS

The Circle of Ceridwen is
the first book in The Circle of Ceridwen Saga by
Octavia Randolph.

Copyright 1995 Octavia Randolph.
Pyewacket Press

ISBN: 978-1-942044-17-8 (Hardback)
ISBN: 978-0-985458-24-9 (Paperback)

Book design by DesignForBooks.com

Photo credits: Castle, iStockphoto©vcstimeless, swords:
iStockphoto©foolonthehill. Textures, graphics,
photo manipulation, and map by Michael Rohani.

The Circle of Ceridwen Saga employs British spellings, alternate spellings,
archaic words, and oftentimes unusual verb to subject placement. This is
intentional. A Glossary of Terms will be found at the end of the novel.

LIST OF
CHARACTERS

Ceridwen, daughter of a dead warlord of the Kingdom of Mercia, aged fifteen

Ælfwyn, a lady of Wessex residing in Lindisse, now controlled by the Danes

Yrling, a Dane

Toki, a Dane, nephew to Yrling

Sidroc, a Dane, nephew to Yrling

Gyric, son of Godwulf of Kilton in the Kingdom of Wessex

Cadmar, once a warrior of Wessex, now a monk

Godwin, Gyric's older brother

Modwynn, Lady of Kilton, mother to Gyric and Godwin

Godwulf, Lord of Kilton, an ealdorman of Wessex, husband to Modwynn

Edgyth, wife to Godwin

Ælfred, King of Wessex

THE
CIRCLE
OF
CERIDWEN
THE YEAR 871

NORThUMBRIA

Jorvic
Four Stones
R. Trent
R. Dee   LINDISSE
Ceridwen's Village   EAST
MERCIA ANGLICA
WELSH
KINGDOMS Cirenceaster
Cippenham
Glastonbuch
Kilton WESSEX Witanceaster
Æthelina
Swanawic

Frankland

CONTENTS

THE
CIRCLE
OF
CERIDWEN

Me þæt wyrd gewæf ond gewyrht forgeaf
For Me Fate Wove This, Gave This To Do

PREFACE

I was born in 856, a time when the Island of Britain was divided into many Kingdoms. As I was later taught, the very first people of Britain were the Old People, the small, dark-haired folk who survive in the wilds of Gwynedd and the lands North of Northumbria. Later came the raving, red-haired Lovers of Stones, who drove the Old People into the fastnesses they still occupy. Then came the many swift ships of Cæsar, and in the year 43 his warriors conquered much of Britain. The people of the Cæsars were great builders, and most learned, and for 400 years the folk of Britain prospered. Then my own people, the fair-haired and light-eyed Angles and Saxons, came from their marshy lands across the North Sea. My folk were fierce and war-like, and burnt the cities of the Cæsars. We lived instead off the rich Earth of Britain, for the forests ran with deer and pig, and the soil yielded up every good thing to our ploughs. We ruled almost all of Britain, and the greatest of our warriors became our Kings. But peace was rare, for these Kings fought always with each other.

Then, within our grandsire's memory, a new people began to visit our shores. They were seamen unlike any we had ever seen, and raiders so skilled they took whatever they wanted and fled before our warriors could catch them.

These were the Danes.

WHAT I SAW AND LIVED

I was daughter to two men, but no woman claimed me as hers. My dead sire was an ealdorman, the chief of our shire. He had long fallen in a skirmish with the wild Welsh beyond our river Dee, and his stony lands taken by the same. I was thus alone when I was wee, and Cedd, brother of my father Cerd, took me. Cedd became ealdorman, for my father had no son, and his ceorls, his armed men, came and pledged to him, and he gave them rings and bracelets to seal their love. Cedd had also freeborn cottars and slaves to farm his land, as an ealdorman should. Cedd's wife had died in childbed with her firstborn, and he had not taken another wife. So he took me as his daughter to the hall of upright timber he had built as a young man, and I lived with him until my ninth Summer.

My mother was dead, said my kinsman; or nameless, said his serving-women; I heard both tales. Cedd became as father to me, and each night I sat at his left at the great oak table in his hall. My father's brother was tall, and in his arms was still much force and brawn, but he could no longer walk aright. During the same skirmish where my father had been killed Cedd had been grievously wounded, and his knees still carried the scars of the spear-thrusts. In the damp Winter he would drink and drink again to dull their ache, and still throw down his cup and howl with rage at his Fate. At these times I was scarce, for he could not be comforted. But I did not fear him, for he was my kinsman, and good to me.

In early Fall when the woods ran with game, Cedd would mount his best and boldest horse and ride out at dawn with his ceorls, their horses stamping, bits jingling, and return at dusk laughing and shouting with stag or boar to fill the firepit. The men would join together in the timber hall, and place at rest against the wall their iron-tipped, barbed spears. The torches in their iron stands would blaze out, casting their light upon the gold rings and silver bracelets and arm-rings the men wore, and the light glittered also from bronze cup to cup. The hall would fill with the smells of smoke and the singeing of meat, and the sounds of the spitting fat flying into the coals. My kinsman, his ceorls about him, would tell of the hunt just run, and of the hunt before, and of the hunt of many seasons past. And tho' child as I was, I would sit blinking in the brilliant torch light and feel that the Gods had blest no place so much as this snug warm hall.

At other times Cedd would lift me up upon his saddle, and we would ride out to the trackway that bordered his lands, and skirt the grove and river marshes that made up the boundaries. These were my favourite times, sitting before him, gladsome and proud; his thick strong arm about me. Beyond his lands lay the village, and so came my first memory of it, seeing from over the horse's mane the round huts of willow wattle and daub with their bushy thatch.

In the village centre stood the stone preaching cross where the Prior spoke to the villagers. The cross was old, older than Cedd's memory, and had on both sides figures carved in the runes of our people. One side told stories of the Holy Book, of which I was yet ignorant. The other bore a tale of the hero Weland, weapon-smith of the Gods, which I knew well. Cedd would stop and point out the marks to me, and tell me again the tale of the great warrior, and in this way did I first learn the runes.

Beyond the village lay the Priory of the Black Monks, as we called the raven-clothed Benedictines. Sometimes on our ride we would come across the Prior himself. Cedd would call out to him, laughing, and in reply the grave thin-lipped Prior would turn and look up. He would sometimes speak to Cedd, gesturing to me as he did, but my father's brother would only laugh the more and turn our horse and trot off.

But the time came when Cedd did not ride out to hunt, and stayed in his hall. He walked about but little, and grasped at his chest and throat in pain. Came the day when he did not rise from his pallet, and his ceorls went to him and did not leave. For two days the hall was filled with his groans, and I was kept away. All grew quiet, and at noon I was at last brought to him. Tho' it was high Summer, the firepit was bright with flame, for the ceorls had brought Cedd's pallet before it, that he might be kept warm. There I looked upon the face of my kinsman for the last time. His breath came in gasping sighs, and his staring eyes looked far beyond the hall. His brow was damp, and his hand when I touched it, cold. Thus we sat, the ceorls and a serving woman and I, until the room grew still of

Cedd's breathing; and as the dusk came on, the life left him. I was led away, dry-eyed but hollow within.

Then it was night, but there was no sleep in the house, for all through the dark hours I heard the voices of the ceorls and the movement of the serving people. At dawn the ceorls rode out to the grove, and cleared the heart of it of trees, and with the help of the cottars rolled stones the size of sheep into a circle. Within this circle they laid a mass of charcoal, and then cut boughs from every tree which grew in the grove, save lady willow; from oak, beech, elder, and apple was the needfire built.

Then at dusk a wain was driven, pulled by a horse and carrying the body of Cedd. And the ceorls came after it, bearing torches which they thrust into the ground to make a circle of light against the darkening sky. They carried off the body of Cedd from the wain, and as they lifted the pallet I saw my kinsman wore his ring shirt and fine helmet, and that across his chest was placed his sword, for he had no son to wield it and learn its name and ways. The ceorls lay the pallet upon the pyre, and placed by my kinsman's side his round shield of alder wood, and his iron-tipped ash spear. They placed also at his side bronze drinking cups. I stood watching this with the serving women, and behind us were the slaves that were Cedd's, and beyond them the gathering cottars of the village.

The chiefest of the ceorls lit a new oil torch and turned to face the pyre, and held the torch uplifted in salute. Then did he walk about the needfire, thrusting the torch between the branches. Smoke came, and more smoke, and there was no sound save the sudden crying of a rook watching in an oak tree. I raised my head to his call, and then of an instant did the flames spring forth from the needfire, licking at the pallet in its hunger. The flames burnt with brilliant light against the Summer night sky, and the ash of the sacred fire mixed with the ash of the dead. Then the ceorls began to walk in circle around the pyre, chanting the praises of he who was dead, and they did not cease praising my kinsman until the ashes were cold with the dawn.

For a little time after that I lived alone at the hall with the serving people. Then the Prior made appeal to the King that my kinsman's land, which was Folkland, and held in Cedd's own right, should now be made Bookland and given to the Priory for its maintenance. And it was made so, and the ceorls went away, and the household dispersed, and the hall that was once bright with fire and the voices of men was turned into a granary for the Prior. And the Prior took me to live with him in that, my ninth Summer, and I was baptised.

THE PRIORY

S O my life changed greatly after this, for the Prior was a grave man and not given to laughter. And tho' I did not rise in the black of night for Matins or spend the days in ceaseless prayer and work as the monks did, I was kept much occupied, for the Prior said the work of redemption was ceaseless.

The place where the Priory stood was old out of mind, worshipped by the Lovers of Stones, and the huge circles of rock still thrust up their faces to keen at the Moon and Sun. The Prior planted his crops around them, and in their shade the scraggy sheep nibbled the grasses. The land went to marsh towards the river, the forests rose up behind, and in the narrow margin between Spring flood and dark wood the Priory scraped out such a living as it might.

At the Priory I was well treated, and I got sums and chanting, and chart-reading from the hands of the Prior himself, for he was fond of such things, and kept a roll of map parchments carefully from damp and rot. These showed upon them the great roads of cut stone built by the Cæsars, and also the tracks of rivers, so that travellers might pass from shire to shire, and in times of peace, from Kingdom to Kingdom. I looked upon these lines with wonder, thinking of all the other folk that lived at the ends of those slender lines on parchment. But my greatest learning was to read, and then to write, most surely in my own tongue, but a little also of the Holy Tongue of Rome, for by far the greater number of books at the Priory were in this sacred speech. And the Prior did not disallow it, for the Black Monks are great for learning; and besides, I knew it would increase my bride-price, which the Prior would collect, when I was wed.

From Sulla the serving woman I learnt the womanly tasks of yarn-spinning and weaving, for that is always woman's first task, high born or low. She and I spent much of each morning at spindle or loom. But the arts of fine stitching with needle and coloured thread I taught myself, for I had few adornments and always marvelled over any bits of fancy work the Prior might receive to dress the blessed altar. In this way I made bright many linens to cover the holy books, and made for myself gay designs of fanciful beasts and birds upon my gowns and sashes. Likewise I was given to braiding and plaiting my long hair in all manner of designs of my devising, until Sulla said never horse had witch's knots woven in its mane as I wove in mine.

The Prior had always said that after I reached my fifteenth Summer – for I was a Summer's child – I would come into my portion, and what was left of my father's fortune would be mine. Since the night the Prior told me this, already in my thirteenth Summer, and just become a woman by Nature's curious ways, I lived every hour for my fifteenth birthday. That I might take the veil had been his first wish, but I had no calling: it was clear in my heart, and clear, too to the Prior when he looked into my green eyes. Neither would I wed the few choices I might have amongst ceorls, young or old, in the shire. For I was restless, and wished for more, and it rankled. I chafed, and walked at times in anger in the woods, and stood at night gazing speechless at the heavens, where starry messengers streaked and were gone. Like them, I desired to quit the place of my raising.

As the date approached I grew uneasy, for the Prior began to press me to choose amongst two men for my husband; for I was too great a girl, he said, to continue living there, and it was well time I was wed. Both men were ceorls, well-landed, having slaves, and houses of timber. The first was old, and had daughters older than me, and he was widowed not long ago. Him I did not like as he was miserly and begrudged his poor daughters every comfort, hating them for being girls, and wanting a new wife only to get sons upon. The second was young, but so uncouth and clumsy that even the serving-women laughed behind his back. I made so bold to scold the Prior once for wishing me upon men who could not read nor write, who signed only with the cross of St Andrew when they paid their tribute to the King. At this the Prior grew wroth, and chastised me for pride in my learning of letters, when he had taught me only for the glory of God. For I was so ignorant then that I knew not that few men of high birth could read and write as their grandsires could. Such had been the terror of the raiding Danes, that all men strove only to repel them, so that even as the invaders slaughtered the holy monks at Lindisfarne and Jarrow the sons of Mercia and Northumbria and Wessex and Anglia would forget the tools of learning and know only the tools of war.

But if I had pride in my learning, I had more in my desire not to remain where there was naught for me but the fading memory of my father's name. So I resolved to take my portion, and my name, which was all I had if you do not count my face, and be off.

THE ARTFUL ONE

BUT that was all a secret, and I met the woman in the glade first. She lived far outside the circle of the village, in a tumbled-down stone mill. It was never used within anyone's memory, for the silted river was become a woods of hazel shrubs, with huge old willows barely recalling that they had once sunk their feet in flowing water. The mill was half crumbled, but the rest was kept up snug and dry, and marvellously furnished, for I went inside. Of course it was forbidden for me to go thus, and I never did — not for the forbidding of it, for I never paid that part of it much mind — but just that Fall day I found myself amongst the hazels and willows, with the old mill-house before me, and I did not turn.

I stood no farther than fifty paces from it, hidden by the trees of the glade, which still bore their leaves, tho' yellow and worn with age. The air was still there; passing still. No bird sang out, and the late Sun glinted off the water as if it alone was living there. Then the low door opened, and she appeared. She stood outside the door, looking over at me. So I stepped forward to show myself, and she lifted her hand.

She was not the old hag the Prior said she was; that I could see for certain, and I came towards her, and saw she was not a hag at all, but rather pinched in the face, but somehow comely, and more than comely.

When I had halved the distance between us, she spoke my name in a low voice without much sweetness, deep for a woman, but pleasing still.

"Ceridwen," she said, and her face held no expression.

I stopped and said, too loud for the silence of the glade, "You are the Woman who practices her Art."

She nodded, and held out her upraised hand, and I came to her, and took it.

We stood outside the mossy door, each looking at each. Tho' I was but fourteen, I stood already as tall as she. Her hair was long and dark, tied up in a ribband of bright yellow that made it look the darker. Just about the temples were a few hairs gone white, very few, but there. The skin on her face and arms was beautifully pale and clear, and the blue veins in her small hands made them seem even more delicate than they were. One held the throat of her mantle closed, and the other, adorned with a ring of carved gold, still rested in my right hand.

Then she said, "I bid you," and slipped her hand from mine and pushed open the door. In I went, and she followed me, shutting the door behind us.

The dimness stopped me in the centre of the room, and she took my arm and guided me to a bench with a table before it. I sat, and as my eyes grew strong again, she glided from shelf to chest, and came back with a pottery pitcher and two tiny silver beakers. One was set with white crystals, and the other worked in coils and spirals, both splendid with beauty. The pitcher was coarse and heavy, and she stood and poured out a browny liquid before sitting down. She raised her beaker, the one set all in crystals, and drank, and I lifted the other to my lips and also drank. It was mead, strong and sweet, and curiously spiced; delicious on the tongue.

I put down my cup, and looked about the dim insides of the place, for tho' she sat just before me, I was not bold enough to meet her eyes. The only light came from the smoke hole over the firepit which bore but the smallest of fires. I wished for more light to see the woven hangings which covered the walls, all different; and the covering of the bed, small and low, pieced together of stripes of finely woven wool, brightly coloured. On the floor was a wolf pelt of light grey, of wonderful thickness, and so large it was an island before the bed. A shelf held a rush burner of coarse iron, next to a candleholder of finely wrought bronze, and another of horn trimmed in silver.

At last I spoke for the funny richness of the place drove me to wish to hear my own voice.

"Where are the men?" I asked, and finally met her eyes.

A look like a smile but with a twisted lip came over her, but she did not look away. Again, with a voice too low she spoke. "When they come, they come only at dark."

I nodded my head, but I was stupid of it all. I said, "You know my name."

She nodded, that was all.

I went on, "The Prior says it is an awful heathen name."

Now she laughed, full and rich in the throat. I smiled too, not knowing why she laughed, but liking the sound of it.

Finally she said, "You are well treated?"

And not knowing what else to say, I nodded and answered, "They call me Lady."

It was nearing dusk, and a fair way back to the Priory. She did not take my hand at parting nor ask me to stop again, but only nodded. She pulled open the heavy door, and out I walked into the fading afternoon.

From that day on I came as I could to the glade. She was always there, and always alone. By and by we spoke more freely, and she told me how she came by her finer things, the beakers and candle holders, and linens and animal skins; which was from which man, and who they were and where they came from. In Winter I could not come as often, for that year was thick with snow and cold, which made the days I could come of more meaning to me; for my life was so without change that my visits to her became my greatest pleasure. I think, too, that she began to look for me.

I came always in the afternoon, for in the forenoon when I had finished my reading or writing I was at work spinning, or helping the monks prepare inks or parchment. I would tell her of all these things, of how the brother in charge of the scriptorium and I would gather whitethorn twigs, and soak and pound them with the gums from apple bark for black ink, and mix the simple colours he would allow me to do: red from the alder bark, green from its spring flowers, and brown from its twigs, and make also browny-black ink from oak galls. And tho' I helped make many a parchment from the chosen lambs, I did all my writing practice in my wax tablet, for parchment is far too precious for aught but the practised scribe. But I did have the trimmings from the quires the monks made to make tiny booklets of my own.

She cared about the writing, and so once I brought my tablet with me, and wrote in it with my brass stylus for her to see. I wrote first the alphabet, and then my name, 'Ceridwen daughter of Cerd'. She watched with wide eyes at this craft, and I, eager to show her more, softened the wax by the fire and spread it smooth again with the side of my stylus, so I could write again.

"This is Latin," I said, as I traced into the yellow wax the words 'In principio'. "It means, 'In the Beginning'".

She puzzled over the letters, and her brow furrowed. "Is it not just like what you had written first? For the marks are the same, or seem so."

I thought a moment. "The marks – the alphabet – is nearly the same, but this speech, Latin, is the speech of Rome. We use much the same alphabet to record the speech of our people, tho' with our own words."

She sat looking at the letters as she spoke.

"Is this our speech if it uses not our marks? Long before the men of Iona and the Black Monks came, our people wrote with sacred signs."

"The runes are sacred," I agreed; but not being able to answer her question, I finally said, "All writing is perhaps sacred."

Here she looked up at me and smiled. "Yes, that may be so, and it gladdens me this art is yours."

Sometimes when I came to the glade she spoke to me of the men, some of them well-born ceorls with rich gifts, and some simple freemen, who brought barley and vegetables and smoked pig. And once we had a true feast in the little mill house, finer by far than I had ever had at the Priory, even at Hlafmesse when the first harvest was brought in late Summer. For the night before a grand man had visited her, who had brought not only a bolt of linen but a fine dinner as well, and plenty of it, enough for them in the night, and we two in the afternoon. We ate squab and currants and drank good strong ale, and I laughed at the weight of it in my head. But she told me there was plenty of the other kind as well – men in high estate but with low minds and hearts.

These words touched me as if I was stone, for having no knowledge of the outside world, it seemed to me that the free and grand must be so to the heart as well as the eye.

DAWN INTO DAY

ONE dawn I came to her to bid Fare-well. Winter had passed twice since we had first spoken, and I fell fifteen.

Little the Prior guessed my scheme, for to steal away in the middle of the night was not what he had raised me to; but even less could I take the veil or marry, each a neat end to his trouble. A month after Yule had he delivered to me my portion, and I stood ready to depart.

My plan was this: to strike out North, and find the Cæsar's Road which ran East. Along this route lay lands rich with lead mines, and the athelings of the King, his very kin, owned these lands. There must be great house-holds there, and such need many a maiden to spin, to sew, to wait, and thus care for the divers wants of the family. I was good with needle; my manner fair passing; I knew a bit of the ordering of a household; I could learn more. To some good woman in such family, kin or old nursemaid to the Lord or Lady, would I apply.

Forty pieces of silver remained of my father's estate, and I had thought long of the best use of them. I set down five pieces – which is what I had once heard the smith say she was worth – when I led the mare Shagg from the Priory croft-house. I had also a pigskin bag, old and creased but sturdy, and still showing the mark of painted designs of spirals upon it, which had been my father's. Into this went my comb of carved bone, carefully wrapped since it was my favourite thing and of great worth, and my wax writing tablet. I rolled together my other linen shift, two pair of wool stockings, and my wool gown of russet colour, made gay by me with coloured thread work on the sleeves and hem. My only mantle I would wear, and tho' it was not of the finest weave it had a hood lined with squirrel that was warm and passing soft.

In a common hide bag I took also one small bronze cooking pot; hide food bags with barley and rye, also turnips, and a cabbage; a few pasties and loaves; a leathern flask with stopper for drink; a tinderbox with iron and flint; an old cow skin for a ground-sheet; and the two wool blankets from my bed. And for all these things I took from the Priory store I laid down five pieces of silver on the great work table in the scriptorium, where I knew no brother would come until after Lauds. And also I took a roll of hay for the first day's feed for Shagg. Around my waist I wrapped a sash and then knotted with a leathern cord my dead father's seax, the knife that gave its name to the Saxons; for though the blade was deeply nicked it was still precious in its silver handle and in meaning to me; and I would have need of a knife.

Thus arrayed I stole out of the Priory before dawn on a foggy, snowless day a week after Candlemas, under a waxing late Winter Moon. I tied my bags upon the saddle and mounted Shagg, and we walked as quiet as I could make her out of the Priory yard. We passed the low hedges that marked the yard, and I looked back just once.

I fancied the rooty apple trees reached toward me, their arms barren and twisted, and I crossed myself and kicked the mare, and trotted down the fen.

The Sun was barely risen when we reached the glade. Leading Shagg I picked my way to the house of the woman. I pounded on her door, and as I did I heard my own heart pounding, for I was sore afraid that someone might be up and after me. I heard her call out, "Who be it?" and I called, "Ceridwen," and the door opened. She stood squinting against the new light. Her dark hair was tumbled over her face, and she clasped a coverlet over her bare skin.

I stepped inside where the dim mossy walls lay cold under their weavings, and saw she had a visitor newly gone, for the fire which had been heaped up had not yet burnt low, and two cups stood on the low table by the bed. She closed the door behind me and leaned against it, and with a little laugh said, "Glad it be you, and no one else."

She pushed the long hair off her brow and looked at me, and at my dress, and began to speak again. I stopped her.

"I come to bid you Fare-well, as I am off and gone from this place." Perhaps my teeth were chattering a bit at this; I do not know, but I saw then that I was leaving her as well, and she, my only friend.

"Whither do you go?" she asked, and wrapped herself more tightly in the coverlet, for it was sharp cold.

Now I know my teeth chattered, but I said only, "I am quitting this place," for I would not confess my plan to even her.

"Aye," she said at last, after gazing on me. "Nothing will stay you – good!" And her voice thrilled.

Now she moved to the table by the bed, and I moved nearer her, glad for the darkness of the room.

"I want to say Good-bye to you, and good wishes . . ." I began, but could say no more.

She held her small hand over mine, and looked into my face, so deep I closed my eyes. Then she said, "Be gone, and be well."

I thought to kiss her, but did not. I could not move. She slipped her hand from mine, and into my own she pressed the rough silver coin which had lain on the table.

"Your mother still lives," she said, and in her voice was again a thrill. "Take this, and so remember her."

❧❧❧❧❧❧❧❧❧❧

I have learnt to be grateful for time, and the passage of it, and only wish I could put a hundred years between me and what I wish to forget. Stumbling through the woods, half-leading, half-riding Shagg, the Sun rose up that morning, and the hours passed. Not until, hungered and benumbed by cold, I found the road I sought, did I open my clenched hand, there to reveal the new-minted roughness of the silver coin given me by my mother. I looked upon it as one who has never gazed upon silver, and looked so until my eyes burned.

I was shy of riding the road for fear of discovery. We walked as quickly as we could beside it, coming out often to be sure I had not lost it. It was slow work, for the trees were close, and in places dense with the bare vines and stalks of undergrowth. At times I thought I heard a horseman coming up the road behind or before, and so would stop, for the dry leaves and brittle twigs beneath our feet seemed to snap to betray us. But we saw no one, not even a swineherd driving his pigs into the oak groves about us.

At last, when the Sun had dropped far down in its shallow rise, we came out of the trees. As no one had crossed our path the whole of the day, I rode on at a fair trot down the Northly Road. The road was poor and stony and hedged about with briars. My gloves were thin, and my mantle too light, but I leaned over Shagg's neck, and the steamy heat from her head brought me some warmth. We continued on in this wise an hour or two – I never knew which, my brain being at this point as numb as my body.

The day began to fade; the trees edged in on us, holding their shadows; and a wind rising at my back set the dead leaves to skittering. My mouth felt dry, but I had forgot to fill my flask before I left, so I put it out of my mind. I turned the mare off the path, for now was time to make my night's camp. The trees were thick and the brambles more so, but a bit of the way into the wood I spied a clump of rock. Claiming this as my camp, I pulled my bags from the saddle and set about to make a fire. Iron and flint I had in my brass tinderbox, and I knelt down by the rocky ledge and began to gather bits of bark. I struck the flint to the iron again and again, but the wind ever rising blew my poor sparks everywhere but to the tinder. At last a smouldering thread of smoke arose, and with me cupping my hands about it, up shot a little licking flame. I went to Shagg and took off her saddle and bridle, and with a rope round her neck tied her to a half grown tree. Out of my food bag I took another pastie, and warmed it over the fire, scorching my fingers. I took also a handful of dried apples, most of which I gave to Shagg, for I was still athirst despite the cold, and could not swallow them.

The night fell in, the stars torched on above us, and I spread the cow-hide on the ground by the base of rock. I wrapped myself in my blankets, my satchel as my pillow. The fire began to flicker, but I heard Shagg rustling and snorting nearby, and it gave me heart. I turned my face to Heaven, asking Our Lady to bless and forgive me.

CHAPTER THE FIFTH

THE BRIDE
OF FOUR STONES

SNICK! Snap! Snick! The stars sang out in tiny voices above me. They began to swirl and tumble, down, down, onto my face. But the stars were wet – wet and cold. Up I jumped, awake at last, the dawn just coming on, the stars wet flakes of snow. I shook my head and a shower of snowflakes tumbled from my hood. The sky was as spoiled ink, cloudy with cold, gathering brighter.

The dawn came on full, and with it the snow. But it fell straight down, in gentle flakes, and was no trouble. 'Til almost midday we went on at a good clip, and not until the Sun stood still and the snow had nearly stopped did we stop as well. I took two loaves out of my bag, and because I could not give her time to forage, I gave one to Shagg, and also two turnips. I ate the loaf with a piece of goat's cheese, and for drink I scooped up a handful of snow, and ate it too, but it made me so cold inside I was sorry for it.

Now the flakes grew small. A wind picked up, and commenced to blow first at our backs, then in our faces. It stung, and I touched my cheek and my glove came away wet. Sleet! It came wetter now, and the snow in Shagg's

23

mane frosted over with ice crystals, and I shook my mantle and hood of snow, but it was wet through.

I could see the Sun travelling away to her early bed. Dumbly, I stopped Shagg in the road. Where was shelter? There were but few haw trees near, all small, and the Winter-ragged oaks could not protect us. I slid off Shagg's back and led her to the haws. My feet were so numb I tripped upon the broken stones of the road. I moved in as well as I could under the slender trees, growing colder and more numb. I slapped my arms and cheeks, but I was chilled through, and it was no use. I cursed Fate that had given me snow and sleet on the second day of my journey, when the weather the fortnight past had been mild and dry. Then I prayed, and cried a bit too. I knew I could not stay there, but must find some shelter where I could build a fire and dry my clothes, lest I sicken with cold and wet.

I grasped Shagg's mane and she snorted and tossed her head, and I would have pulled myself up in her saddle, but I did not, for a great weariness seemed to settle over me, and I felt dizzy. I leaned against her wet neck and steadied myself. The dizziness did not pass tho', and as I stood clutching her wet mane and breathing in her steamy odour I seemed to hear at a great distance the clinking of bridle bits and the jostling of animals being driven side by side.

I wanted to go back into the wood, but somehow my feet were rooted to the ground, and I could not move them, for I felt if I tried I should surely fall. So I stood there as if elf-shot, mute, cold, and wet; waiting for who or what I could not know. The sounds grew nearer, and I saw a horseman, heavily cloaked and carrying a spear, and where the cloak opened I could see he wore over his leathern tunic another hammered over with rings. He rode alone before two large waggons, covered over with tarpaulins stretched on tall arches, pulled by doubled yokes of oxen. The horseman stopped before me, and called out, and the waggons stopped. He spoke something to me, in a tongue like that of the Mercians, but I do not remember what, for I felt strangely light and giddy. Then a woman's face, broad and plain, thrust out from the tarpaulin covering the first waggon and cried out sharp "Why have we stopped?", and I opened my mouth to speak to her, and then knew nothing.

<hr />

The next was all confused, for I felt warmth about me, and my wet mantle was taken away, and I heard women's voices. A warm hand lay upon my frosted face, and I opened my eyes. From the dim light of a brass cresset I beheld the face of the woman with the sharp voice, and I knew myself to be within the waggon.

"Be a good maid," she said, peering down at me, and her voice was thick with the accent of the Saxons of Wessex. Then she turned and thrust her face through the opening and bellowed, "Away! For the Lady is well," and the waggon jolted and lurched on its way.

Now I became aware of another woman, for she came forward with a cloth and a bronze cup. "Drink this first, before you speak," said the second woman, and over the rim of the cup I saw her to be young and rich and of great beauty. It was spiced ale, steaming warm, and I drank it all.

Then I lowered the cup and said, "Ladies, I thank you for your kindness," and the sharp voiced woman handed me the cloth and said in answer, "Now wipe your hair, for you be as wet as a new chick."

I rubbed my head, and felt the blood coming back, and with it my senses. I raised myself from the cushioned bench, and looked about me in the dimness of the crowded waggon. A bird cage made of willow wands was tied over our heads, and in it a silent linnet hopped from one perch to another. Near it hung pots and ewers of bronze and iron; also straw baskets, heavy with their contents, which swung into the pots and made a dull gong-like sound when the waggon rolled hard to right or left. On a piece of slate glowed a charcoal brazier, filling the tiny space with delicious warmth.

The two women let me look, and did not interrupt, but sat watching me from the bench upon which they sat. The sharp-voiced one was dressed in a smock of light brown wool, plain but of good make, tied at her shapeless waist with a wool sash. On her head was a wrap of undyed linen, from which a few strands of greying dark hair escaped. Her face was plump, but her features were as sharp as her voice, and her eyes were black and merry.

The other was perhaps no older than me, but with a bearing and carriage of a great Lady. She looked tall, and her face was rather thin, with a long, straight nose. Her eyes were a dark blue, like a fair Summer's sky at dusk, and her hair a pale flaxen gold, which gleamed even in the dim waggon light. A thin head-dress of cream coloured silk covered it, and hung down over the back of her finely spun gown of blue wool. At her throat was a brooch of beautifully worked silver, set with garnets.

The young woman spoke. "I am Ælfwyn, daughter of Ælfsige. Burginde, my nurse" – and here she looked at the sharp-voiced woman – "had you brought in our waggon, for you had swooned on the road. Tell me who you are, and why you travel alone this way."

Her voice was cool and calm, and that of a Lady used to being obeyed. I pushed back my hair and remembered my comb, and my precious leathern satchel, and all it carried, and then the mare. "O!" I cried instead. "Where is Shagg?"

And the nurse answered, laughing, "If by that you mean your raggedy pony, fear not, for she be tied behind the waggon, her nose in a bag, eating our oats." And there was a kindness in her laugh that made me smile. Likewise I saw safe at her feet my satchel, wet through, but sound.

"I thank you," I said, and then set to answer the Lady Ælfwyn's questions. "I am Ceridwen, daughter of Cerd. I am travelling to the Cæsar's Road, and thence East, to the burhs of the King's athelings, there to seek a station, for my father is dead."

The nurse Burginde clapped her hands and laughed, "A station! We too go to find new stations!"

"Keep back your tongue," Ælfwyn silenced her, and then turned again to me. "Lady, or rather child, for you look not more than thirteen, tell me from whence you came, and how you reached this pass, for you are clearly of good birth, and yet to find you in this wasteland, alone, bewilders me."

I answered quick, "This is no wasteland, Lady, but my home shire, for I was raised first by my father's brother, and then by the Black Monks at the Priory by the river Dee." Then I looked hard into her face and spoke again. "And I am not thirteen, but fully fifteen, and come into my portion, and my dead father was an ealdorman."

At this they were silent, and the Lady Ælfwyn said at
last, "You speak as bold as a boy." And I blushed, but she
said, "I did not say that to shame, but to praise."

I nodded my head, and felt easier. She smiled, and
said, "You are a gentlewoman, and you seek a station?"

I answered, "Yes, Lady, for I was raised by churchmen,
but am not called to take the veil as they had wished." She
nodded, and I added, "Neither would I wed their choices
for me."

Now Ælfwyn closed her eyes, but opened them again
and with a wave of her hand bid me to go on.

"At some atheling's keep," I continued, "I hope to serve
his Lady, for I am skilled with needle, and also read and
write." Ælfwyn raised her eyebrows, but I went on. "And I
can teach the Lady's children, and –".

She stopped me with her hand, and said, "Enough. I
understand."

Then we three sat in silence a moment, jostling over
the road so that we swayed hard upon the low benches,
but little did I care, for it was warm and dry in the waggon.
The one called Burginde leaned over and looked into my
empty cup, and rose and went to the back of the waggon.
There she opened a wood chest painted black and green,
and came back with the ewer in one hand and a few dry
leaves in the other. She filled my cup with ale, and ground
the leaves between her fingers and dusted them in after.
"'Tis sage," she said to me, "and warming. Drink it, for you
are still chilled through." And drink it I did.

We went on more smoothly for a bit, and Ælfwyn
spoke again, in a quiet voice. "I have less choice than you,
for I am the bride of Four Stones."

I gazed upon her, and she met my gaze, and it was I who looked first away, for her eyes burned. I knew naught of what she spoke, and could not tell if by my speech I had brought this sorrow in her. So I was silent, and the nurse Burginde as well, which I was to learn was a rarity.

"My home is far South in the Kingdom of Wessex," said Ælfwyn, "and my father is the reeve of Cirenceaster. He and my grandsire have made a Peace with the Danes, that they might stop their slaughter at our borders. I go as part of the Peace to Yrling the Dane, one of the jarls who now rules over conquered Lindisse. The keep of Four Stones is now his, and I, its bride."

And she drew breath, and said, "Burginde, bring us ale."

Burginde turned and took from a basket another goblet of bronze, and brought down the ewer of ale, foamy from the swing of the waggon, and poured the brown liquid into the Lady's cup, and then into the one I had drunk from.

Then Ælfwyn held aloft her cup and said, "Drink with me, Lady, and toast my marriage." But in her voice was great bitterness, and no joy. She tipped the cup and drank, and I drank also.

It grew dark, and Burginde pulled open the tarpaulin flap to speak to the drover. "We are half jolted to death, and it is night. Let us stop now."

The drover called something back which I could not hear, and another voice, the horseman's, also answered. "We have made poor time and must go on 'til Moonrise."

But before Burginde slapped down the flaps in reply, she sauced back, "Ach! We are not so much in a hurry as that!"

She turned back into the waggon, making angry clucking sounds. Ælfwyn sighed, and I did too, for the jolting waggon, tho' warm, was tiring in its constant heave and roll, and I yearned to be still.

So we sat, but did not have long to wait, for soon we heard the calling of the horsemen to the drover. The waggon lurched into a clearing so that we three clung to whatever was near for support. The willow cage holding the linnet rocked back so hard that at last the little bird chirped out as it fluttered in its prison.

Then we stopped, and the horseman came and unlaced the back flap. I went to Shagg and rubbed her chin, and she snorted and bobbed her head and nickered. The drover got to work unhitching the oxen, and the horsemen unsaddled their horses and led them to the trees and hobbled them. I watched these men with something like awe, for they had removed their wool cloaks, and all wore ring-shirts and belts and sword scabbards of far greater worth than ever I had seen, and it told me again that Ælfsige, father of Ælfwyn, must be a great reeve to so provide for his thegns. Their horses were such that made Shagg look truly like a pony, and the saddles and other trappings, which they put into the second waggon to keep from damp, were bright with coloured leather and brass ornaments that glinted in the torchlight.

I stood there under the growing Moon and looked on all this, and Ælfwyn stood silently at my side. The drover gathered stones for the fire-bed, and laid the fire with dry logs and cakes of charcoal brought out of the second waggon.

We took our supper in our waggon. Burginde carried in a bronze platter that held small wheaten loaves split and toasted with sheep's cheese, fragrant and delicious-smelling. The drover handed in a steaming pottery bowl with a wooden dipper. Within was a browis rich with shreds of dried pig, and made savoury with turnips, cabbages, and onion. Burginde pulled the flap closed behind us, and we three women addressed our supper.

Ælfwyn looked at me and laughed and said, "As you are so late of the Benedictines, perhaps you should say our blessing."

So I held my hands over the loaves and pottery, and said, "As Our Mother provides for our bodies, so Our Father sustains our souls. Eat and rejoice." And Ælfwyn answered, "Amen," and Burginde answered, "Blest Be," and in the comfort of that seeming feast, thus did we give thanks.

After this meal I began to feel so weary that I knew I must soon meet sleep. I went outside to use the necessary the drover had dug, and coming back to the waggon I stayed to look at the stars. I remembered how last night I had slept with them over my head, never knowing that tonight I would lie warm and dry on feather cushions. And I thought how far away was the Priory, and my life there, and wondered what was next for me.

Then Ælfwyn came out, and we stood together looking at the sky. The plough and wain was bright, as was the Dog-star. The slender Moon was nearly set.

"What do you think of?" asked Ælfwyn, when we had stood for a moment.

"O," I smiled, "I think of these stars and their ways; that they always know their path and wander not. I looked at her and she smiled, and then I asked, gesturing at the sky, "And you? What do you see when you look thus?"

But at this Ælfwyn cast down her face. "I see only our Northwards path away from my home, to wed a man who I must hate, and who may take me even farther from my people."

At this I knew not what to say, but at last spoke. "Your father is a powerful reeve, and I am sure your mother is of high birth to have given such beauty to her daughter. Surely they would not cast a jewel into a mire."

For answer she turned her face away. I began to be uncertain, but went on. "Other Danes have bartered for high-born wives amongst the Angles and Saxons. Perhaps this Lord –" I stopped, for Ælfwyn wept aloud, and she hid her face in her hands under the cold watch of the stars, and I could give her no comfort.

Here Burginde came around the end of the waggon, and with a look of mingled pity and rue, helped me guide her charge back to our waggon.

Once inside Ælfwyn grew quiet, and Burginde moved about the waggon with an extra cheer, setting up our sleeping places with added cushions, taking wool coverlets from chests, and humming aloud all the while. During this time I sat quietly by Ælfwyn, holding her hand in mine, and thinking of the things that might befall her, and me.

Now Burginde brought out a large copper basin and placed it next the brazier, and filled the basin with hot water.

Ælfwyn arose and began untying her sash, and taking off mantle and gown. I stood and took her clothes and smoothed them, and Burginde rolled them and lay them in one of the large wood chests. Ælfwyn pulled off her shift and stood naked by the basin. Her form was indeed lovely, with a long narrow waist, small breasts with the palest of nipples, and curly hair of dark blonde under her arms and between her legs. Her head was wrapped in undyed linen, and the fine bones of her face spoke together with the fine lines of her limbs. I thought her very beautiful.

She dipped a linen cloth in the basin's water, and carefully wiped herself from face to feet. Then Burginde gave her a towel of linen, and as she rubbed herself dry the colour came back into her pale flesh. She looked at me and with a movement of her head invited me to wash also.

I stripped off my gown and stockings and shift, aware of how different was my body from Ælfwyn's. I was nearly as tall, but much more compactly built; my breasts and hips rounder, and the shock of red-brown curls where my thighs met was a darker echo of my chestnut-gold hair. I knew that Ælfwyn looked at me, shyly, and I wondered if she thought me striking. My nose, I thought, was too strong to make my face pretty, but in my green eyes and chestnut-gold hair I had no shame.

The water was warm and the smooth linen wash cloth a pleasure. When I was done Burginde wrapped my shoulders in a towel, and then performed her own quick ablutions as Ælfwyn and I finished drying ourselves. The two benches would serve as beds to us, and Burginde would sleep upon the deer hides on the floor. Burginde opened the rear waggon flap to pour out the washing water, and we heard more clearly the voices of the thegns still gathered about the fire. Then the flap closed, shutting out voices and the cold, and Burginde pinched out the cressets. A tiny glow from the brazier still illumined the waggon, and made the crowded space confused with shadows.

In the stillness I heard Ælfwyn sigh, and I called out softly, "Sleep well, Lady." Her murmured reply mixed with my own soft breathing, and I fell into sleep.

LOOKING FORWARD
AND BACK

IN the morning Burginde woke me, for I slept as one dead – such was the warmth and comfort of my bed. It was a cold, but not bitter morning, grey-skyed. The snow had melted, showing sodden branches and clotted lumps of brown leaves through the woods. The drover, whose name I could tell was Osred from Burginde's constant scolding, had set about yoking the oxen, and the three thegns to saddle their horses. To break our fast we had wheaten loaves, and with them a piece of honey comb. We ate as we stood before the fire, and with weak ale washed it down.

Travel in a waggon, I suppose, is always tedious, and more so in the cold and mud of Winter; and by the way Ælfwyn composed herself on her bench I could see she was full tired of it. Hand-work is not possible, for the rolling and jolting do not allow it; and one grows weary and sore of jostling.

Ælfwyn gestured me to her side, and asked, "For how long did you journey?"

I thought a moment. "For almost two days from the Priory. But I could not come as quick on Shagg as I might, for I was not certain I would not be followed, so I came cautiously, and in the woods at times."

Her eyebrows went up, and I went on, "You are thinking I have run off! But I have not – at least, not wrongfully. Shagg I bought with my own silver, and for those things such as food and tinderbox and suchlike I also laid down silver."

Now Ælfwyn laughed out loud. "Do you think I suspect you to be a felon?"

And I laughed too, for I saw I was pleading my case for no reason.

"Besides," she went on calmly, "the Prior who raised you – did he not do so using the estate of your father and your father's brother? Even if your portion was not great, for the little trouble you must have caused him, I think the Prior was enriched, and not you, by your father's death."

I did not know what to say, for I was abashed by the thought. But no, I said to myself, it could not be: He was generous-hearted to the village folk, and not such a one to take from an orphan maiden. And of a sudden I thought of my mother, and her face flashed before me.

Finally I spoke again, for I would hear Ælfwyn's tale, and so felt bold to ask her for it. "Lady," I said, "you go to a burh, or keep called Four Stones, in Lindisse, which is now ruled by the Danes. And you are to wed a jarl named Yrling, and you do this thing as part of a treaty made by your father. Tell me how this came to be."

Some little time passed, but she closed her eyes and spoke. "Yrling is indeed a Dane, and a jarl, and the enemy of my father, and of myself, and of all I hold dear. My father Ælfsige holds such lands at Cirenceaster that a swift runner cannot cover in a week. Beyond that is East Anglia, which beyond the call of memory was ruled by ealdormen who were at peace with my father. These ealdormen are no more, for in the last few years the Danes have murdered and enslaved them and in their fierceness now rule that Kingdom as their own. Likewise the next Kingdom to the North, that of Lindisse, is now fallen to the Danes, and the jarl Yrling is powerful in it. My father has lived as he could against this threat, sometimes warring, sometimes conceding land, and other times bargaining with gold and silver to satisfy the lust of the Danes. But now my father is weary, and desires a lasting peace, for the Danes have got horses from Anglia, and now horseman from Four Stones in Lindisse trample our crops and kill our slaves and thus wreak havoc on all of us, so that no joy lives under our roofs."

She took a breath and began again, more quietly. "Last year came a great sickness to the Danes, and at Four Stones many died, and Yrling did not come forth to waste and destroy. And Yrling had a young wife who died in that same sickness. It was during this time that my father thought to act, for now the Danes will never depart our homeland, for they have grown rich on the fatness of our wealth. But still we must forge a Peace with these hated men, for if peace does not come, surely we shall all perish." She sighed deeply. "Thus say all the wise men."

She looked at me and finished. "I am a part of their plan, for by me and the contents of these waggons, my father and grandsire hope to buy peace."

After I had heard all this I spoke. "Your father has ordained this thing?"

And Ælfwyn nodded and answered, "My mother and sisters wept, but he would not be stayed." She looked away and said, "He is a hard man, and I am cursed in having no brothers. My father must use us as he can." Her head drooped, and she finished. "So I go, to marry a man I hate."

"Hate?" I asked, and glanced first at Ælfwyn and then at Burginde, who sat silent on the floor in the back of the waggon. "How can that be, when you have never yet seen him? He may yet be good to you, tho' he be a Dane." And here a chill struck me, but still I finished, "Or at least, not cruel."

"Ah!" she scorned. "A Dane not cruel?"

And to this I had no answer, for I knew naught what to say. "At least, Lady, do not hate your new Lord," I finally said.

But Ælfwyn's head fell lower, and she said, "Hate him I must, for I have met the man I love."

I was full alarmed. "You do not mean that you are betrothed amiss?"

"Amiss?" she answered. "I was born amiss, and cursed be that day, for I was born to look into the eyes of Gyric, and so love him."

For the past few moments Burginde had been watching her mistress as one distracted, wringing her hands this way and that. Now she sprang up from her cushion, and nearly falling over me, clasped her mistress' hands and implored her to stop.

"Lady! Lady! You speak death and treason! Never more must you name him, never more think on him! Girl, you are mad! What! Will you lie in your bridal bed and call on his name?" Here Burginde burst into violent weeping, but Ælfwyn did not weep, and only clung to her serving woman silently. I moved away from them, for their sorrow was their own, and together they must share it.

I went to the larder chest at the back of the waggon, and brought out an ewer of strong ale, and filled a bronze cup half full, and handed it to Ælfwyn, spilling not a little. For I trembled, and she also, and the road beneath us.

But she found voice, and drank, and caressed the head of her childhood nurse, and suffered her to drink from her own cup.

I sat on the bench next to Ælfwyn, and thought, What comfort I could bring? And I answered myself: No comfort, for I am but a maid and ignorant of men and of life, save but from the stories of the Holy Book and the tales of my people; and I know full well that many a bride goes unwilling to her husband, for the Prior, who had blest any number, often said so. And I had never felt the sting of love, and knew not such sweetness and such pain.

Then the eyes of Ælfwyn met mine, and her beauty and her bravery touched my heart. "Friend," I said, "if your father has decreed this thing, then it must be. But if by this deed you win for your family some respite, all your people will honour your name, for you shall be a peace-weaver. And Heaven above will be your guide in this your duty, and I and your faithful Burginde your friends."

Her eyes were water-still. "You will come with me to Four Stones?"

I took her hand. "Yes, to serve and befriend you there."

She clasped me in her arms, and kissed me on the cheek; and I kissed her, and so was sealed between us our friendship. Thus was I taken into the service and company

of Ælfwyn, daughter of Ælfsige of Cirenceaster, and
gained, before I ever reached the Cæsar's Road, the station I sought.

CHOOSE WELL

E made camp that night as we had before, and I slept well. It was the little linnet that awakened me, and for a moment hearing this birdsong I thought to be back at the Priory. I sat up and remembered where I was, and also that it was the Sabbath. The air was sharp with the chill of Winter, and I pulled my blanket about me. The little bird sang out again, and I rose and gave it a crumb of bread from the larder chest. Then Burginde stirred and yawned, and Ælfwyn awoke, and thus began our Sabbath.

After we were on our way I turned to the Lady and asked, "Ælfwyn, who will bless your marriage?"

She answered calmly, "No one shall bless it."

"But is your new Lord not a Christian?" I asked in my ignorance.

She looked at me wonderingly. "A Danish jarl a Christian? No Dane accepts Our Saviour."

At this I was greatly struck, for tho' I knew the Danes to be followers still of Woden, yet I assumed that when they wed the daughters of Wessex or of Mercia they became Christian. I said nothing, and listened.

"He is heathen, as they all are, and I would not by my request have this union blest."

"There are perhaps worse things than being heathen," I began, thinking of my early years and the laughter of my kinsman. "Would it not comfort you to have it blest? Surely your new Lord would not mind. And when there are children –"

Her raised hand bid my silence. Still I would continue, along a track less painful to think of.

"This jarl, Yrling – he speaks our tongue and also his own?"

"Yes," she answered slowly, "he speaks well enough. For my father and grandsire spoke with him, and he to them, when they met and made the Peace."

"But you have not seen him."

"No. I shall soon look on his face; that is enough."

Then she turned away and said, "Braid up my hair, for I am weary of it down."

I took her comb of pear-wood and combed out her hair smooth and even, and plaited it in two thick plaits. These I wrapped about her head as in a crown, and fastened them with hair pins of bronze. She lifted her mirror of pure silver before her and admired my work, and while still thus watching her reflection, said in a soft voice, "I would that he who praised my hair so well could see it now."

Hearing this I knew she hoped to speak again of the man she loved, and by my attentive silence I bid her to go on. For I did not see what harm it might do; I saw only her need to speak of him, and my interest in hearing.

Still looking into the mirror she said, "The first day we met he praised my hair; I cannot look at it and not think of his words." She turned to me with half-closed eyes and a smile on her pale lips, as if remembering.

"Ælfwyn," I asked, "is Gyric from your home of Cirenceaster? Did you grow up with him?"

She opened her eyes. "No, to both. He is Gyric of Kilton, son of Godwulf, the great ealdorman; and his home is on the seacoast of Wessex, far to the West of mine. I have never seen it, but he says his father's keep sits on a bluff, looking out across the sea to Wales."

"Then Kilton is a distance from Cirenceaster. How did you then meet?"

"Yes, it is a great distance, but Gyric is in the train of King Æthelred and the King's young brother, Ælfred; and so travels the breadth of Wessex."

"You do not mean he fights with the King himself?" I asked in some wonder, for all knew of the prowess of King Æthelred and Ælfred, sons of Æthelwulf, dead King of Wessex; and my own King Burgred of Mercia was allied with this royal house, for Æthelwulf had years ago given his daughter Æthelswith to be Burgred's wife.

She answered with pride. "He fights with Ælfred, the King's brother, and travels in his very train. And Gyric's own father and brother are mighty in their shire, for they are athelings of the King, and faithful and steadfast in their service. Godwulf, father of Gyric, was as a brother to King Æthelwulf, and that love between them continues now that his son Æthelred rules."

"Have you then seen the King?" I asked, for I would hear more.

"Yes, I have seen him, for he came twice to my home in Cirenceaster, once in Summer, and also in late Fall, and that last time, spoke at length with my father; and he and his men stayed with us three days." She fell suddenly silent, and cast down her eyes. "King Æthelred had come again to ask for aid from my father, wanting him to ride with him against the Danes. This time my father refused him, but armed ten thegns and sent them to Æthelred in his stead. This my father did because his mind was set on his own troubles, and he sought to end them his own way with a separate Peace."

I nodded and she went on.

"Æthelred had with him many ealdormen and thegns, of all the great families of Wessex, and some too of Mercia. Amongst those travelling with him was Gyric, and tho' we met but briefly, he owned my heart, and I gave it."

I felt I must know one thing more, and touched her hand as I spoke. "Ælfwyn, it is true that you must not think about him in this way. Tell me only this: did you exchange vows?"

Then the tears started from her eyes so that they dropped upon our clasped hands, and she answered, "No, that we did not, for he would not allow it. He said the time was not right; we could not do such a thing without our parents' knowledge and consent. He is twenty-two and so of a good age to marry, and I am nearly seventeen; and his only brother is older and well-married, and I felt certain that all our kin would welcome such a match as ours. He bid me wait until he might plead our case with my father, and with his, which he could not do until he returned to Kilton after Twelfthnight. I listened, and believed his goodness, for friend, if he had but said a word I would have been his, and damned be my maidenhood." Here her weeping choked her words. "But he is a man of virtue, and steadfast, and so I was safe. Little did we know of the plan my father secretly devolved, for now I am sold away from love, and may be, from life itself."

"No more of such talk!" I entreated, and chided myself for having encouraged it.

She sat huddled in my arms, sobbing. I tried to soothe her, but she wept on. Finally I squeezed her hands and said, "Stop now," as firm as I could. She leaned back upon the cushions and her tears did stop, but whether it was from my words or their own exhaustion I knew not. I went to the basin and poured in a little water from a crockery jug, and dipped in this a linen cloth. Ælfwyn lay quiet, her eyes closed, her face wet with tears.

I laid the cloth upon her hot brow, and said, "Ælfwyn, some time this week we reach your new home, and a day or two after you will be wed to the jarl there. Tho' he is a Dane, and tho' you may choose to hate him, he must be a great Lord, or your father would not yield you up to him. You may respect your new husband, and all may go well, and your people be free of the curse which they have suffered. He may be kind to you, or he may be cruel, and pray God he is kind; but if he is not you may escape to the veil, and all of this would have been for naught. If you go to him now with hatred and scorn, then he will scorn your father's gift, and so all will also be lost – you, the hope of peace, and your friends with you, who, tho' humble as we are, you take also into danger with you. Choose, and choose well." When I had finished this I felt my face flame, for then I knew the boldness of my words.

Ælfwyn sat up and looked at me and murmured, "Your words are the words of my father, and true counsel."

More she did not say, but only leaned to kiss my cheek.

DWELLINGS
OF THE DEAD

W HEN we stopped at midday the road was no longer flat, but crossed gentle hills and vales, flanked by meadows in their Winter-brown dress. At the top of one hill was a bend in the road, from which, across a marshy distance, the great mouth of my own river Dee could be seen. The lead thegn called out, and the wag-gons halted, and we all gazed down across the plain to the ancient settlement of the Cæsars, the city called by them Deva, and by us Legaceaster.

The first thing that stood out was the great wall of stone, bermed over in places with soil. There were breaks in the wall, some of them large, and through them we saw what remained of the city. No roofs survived, but from the great number of walls still standing, there must have been two score or more fine buildings. The walls were of white and of grey stone, and a great quantity of this stone sat tumbled about the bases of the walls. Doorways and win-dows could be seen throughout the walls, leading inside to where grasses grew under the roof of the sky. I had never seen so many stone buildings, even if they be in ruin, and I exclaimed over them, as did Ælfwyn and Burginde.

We looked long at the white walls as our waggons passed, and were silent.

Then Ælfwyn said, "Never before have I seen such buildings as those. The followers of Cæsar must have been both rich and powerful."

"Yes," I said, "they were rich, and clever in their learning, and kept great armies."

"And yet they are no more than these broken walls, now."

"Our people came here, and made war with them, and overran them, and took this land for their own," I said. "Just as the followers of Cæsar themselves came and overran the Lovers of Stones, who came and overran the Old People."

Ælfwyn looked at me, hard. "And just perhaps as the Danes do now to us." I stared at her as she went on. "Now this country is ours, but as we won it from those who came before us, so might the Danes win it from us, and we become no more or less than these ruins."

I felt cold inside at these words. "What makes you speak this way?" I asked.

"It is the way my father speaks, and my grandsire, and yes, even Gyric have I heard speak such words."

"Perhaps there is a way other than war to have peace," I said. "Perhaps the union of you and Yrling will help."

"Yes, and perhaps we shall soon be as the savage Welsh, in which the race of the Old People survive; and what we once were will be no more than that."

And this thought, that we might become to the Danes what the remnants of the Old People were to us, chilled me again. "No," I said with firmness, "I do not believe that.

We have made this country our home, and have walked its forests and farmed its fields and fished its rivers too long. We have cared for it, and it has fed us. It is ours."

Ælfwyn's voice was mild. "Do not speak with such heat. I meant nothing amiss, and want with all my heart to see our people thrive, and drive out the Danes."

I smiled as well, and said, "I did not mean to speak in heat. I have learnt much these past days, and begin to see how little I knew of such things. But I do not believe that we won this land from so great a people as Cæsar's, only to lose it to such as the Danes."

Now the thegn riding before us called out, and we looked forward and saw the pitted Earth of the Northly Road crossed by a stone road twice its width. We went to the right, East upon the Cæsar's Road, and the wheels of the waggon seemed to roll over the polished floor of a great house, such was the smoothness of the Cæsar's Road to the Northly Road.

I saw then, as did Ælfwyn and Burginde, that the thegns were more watchful than ever. They rode each hour with their spears laid across their saddles, and their sword sheaths hanging from the leathern baldrics over their shoulders uncovered by their cloaks. They switched positions often, with the thegn in front changing with one of the two that rode in back, so that their eyes might be fresh to danger hidden in the trees ahead. We women saw these things, but did not speak of them.

At dusk we made camp in the largest clearing we could find. For the first time the thegns kept watch, and two of them slept while one stood guard by the horses. I heard them at times moving outside, and then again when they awakened each other for relief.

The morning was not fair, but no rain fell, and we set out at the same good pace. At midmorning we saw a flock of spotted goats being herded across the road, and saw down the meadow the man who drove them. He looked up at the thegns in surprise, and they called out that he had nothing to fear. He stopped and came back to them, and the first thegn questioned him.

"Have you seen aught of Danes?" he asked.

The goatherd shrank back, and answered, "No, and so preserve us. Why do you search for them here?"

"They search for us," answered the thegn, and he moved his horse forward, leaving the goatherd gaping behind us.

At end of day we again made camp in a large clearing, which I knew the thegns chose for its difficulty of surprise, for no trees stood near to shelter the advance of those who might creep undetected to the camp.

During the night it rained, and did so with such force that the tarpaulin above us began to sweat water. At daybreak we three took turns wiping down the inside of the tarpaulin so that we caught the great drops before they fell upon our heads. It still rained on, and our wiping tasks, in which we clambered all over the tops of chests and benches to reach the tarpaulin before it dropped its wet issue upon us, put us by turns in both silly and ill humours. We knew without speaking that the trials of the bad weather took our minds off what may lie at the end of the road ahead.

It rained hard all morning, and the thegns delayed our start in hopes of it clearing; but it did not, and we set out. We felt some damp in the waggon, for despite our efforts it began to sprinkle rain upon us; but it was as nothing to the wet and cold of the thegns and of Osred.

At last in late morning the rain began to lessen, and then to stop. A breeze, nearly warm and Spring-like, picked up from the South, and helped to dry out our sodden tarpaulins.

We rolled on some way, and by and by came to a path which led off the road to a lone small hut. There was no one near it today, and the Halloo of the thegns echoed and went unanswered as we passed.

I began to wonder at how few folk we met upon this great road. I expected to find many to guide my passage to the houses of the athelings on this route, and began to see that it would not have been with ease that I would have found either guide or goal.

We could see hills before us now, the hills of lead, and I told Ælfwyn what I knew of these hills; that much wealth came out of them, and that the ealdorman and reeves of these parts were made rich by it. And Burginde said she would have a wee tunnel of gold before all the hills of lead in Mercia, but Ælfwyn said, and rightly so, that tho' gold be the more beautiful to look upon, that lead could make one rich just as sure. "For," she finished, "we have no gold from the ground in Cirenceaster, but much wool fleece that buys us gold just the same."

And we nodded at this, and then I thought of the men outside and their swords and spears, and thought also of my dead father and kinsman, and said inwardly, Yes, and yet those thegns will take cold iron every time, for by their iron is life or death.

The morning was clear again, which was good, for we were not yet as dry as we liked from the drenching of yesterday. We were in hills now, their growth thick with beeches; but in daylight it was a cheerful place, sweet-smelling and full of birds and squirrels that darted across the road. We heard the routing of wild boars, and the thegns spoke amongst themselves to determine if they should stop and try to follow them for fresh meat. I was glad when they did not, for we had no dogs, and what would we have done if they or one of their horses were hurt in doing so? For boars are treacherous, and I had seen many times the wounds their tusks could make in man and beast.

As the weather was fine we had the front flap open all this time, and sometimes got out of the waggon and walked alongside it, for when we went down steeply it was better to walk than to suffer the joltings of the waggon.

When we women had climbed in once more, Ælfwyn said, "I wish we were there." Then she sat down and said, "No. I wish we would never be there, but I wish it were over."

Burginde leaned back on her bench and said, "The closer we get, the closer it be."

"Nothing will be over, but just begun," said I. "Only this part – this waiting – will be over. The rest will be a beginning for you, and all of us." A new thought came to me. "What happens to your father's thegns? Do they remain with us at Four Stones, or return to Cirenceaster?"

"I do not believe three Saxon thegns would be long welcome at a Danish camp, even if they do bring treasure. And they are amongst my father's best men. They will make sure I am delivered safely, and then return to Wessex."

I had another question. "You say you bring treasure. I have seen naught but rich things since I joined you: your linens of a fineness like silk; your silver and garnet brooch; your mirror of bright silver; the many cups of closely worked bronze. Even Burginde wears wool of high quality, and the swords and ring-tunics of your thegns are far better than those my kinsman was burnt with. Have you much more of these good things?"

Now Burginde laughed at me, but her mistress checked her with a raised hand.

"These waggons carry much, and most of it would have been mine in my own right had I wed a Saxon. Some are things for me to make my household with, some are gifts from my mother so that I should be glad in their beauty, but most are tribute to the Dane, and will be his outright."

So there would be no bride-price paid by the Dane for Ælfwyn; all the payment was on her side, as part of the tribute.

"And the waggons themselves, and the oxen, and Osred?" I asked.

"The waggons and oxen are part of the tribute, and Osred stays on with me, as Burginde does, to serve me," she answered. "And now I have you as well."

She smiled, and I did too, and said to her, "It is said that two heads be better than one."

At this Burginde answered, "Two heads be more mischief than one, that be certain."

Then Ælfwyn pulled the hem of Burginde's head wrap so that it fell over her face, and we laughed at her grumbling.

THE ESCORT

THE following morning we went down a long slow hill, and no hill rose before us to take its place. The pines dropped away, and woods of trees still barren edged the road. Now we moved much faster, and the wheels rang out against the cut stones the Cæsars had laid.

At midday we stopped by the first of many small lakes, and after we had rested, the thegns went to the second waggon and opened it. They brought out three helmets, of iron covered over with bright brass so that they glinted; and these they put on, and mounted their horses, and we went off. This was the first time I had seen them wear their helmets, and as I watched the lead thegn with his spear across his saddle and his sword sheath uncovered by his cloak, I knew that they thought at any time to be met by the Danes we sought.

In the waggon we three began to prepare ourselves as well. Burginde straightened up the baskets, and put away into chests stray things we had been using. I unfolded my leathern satchel, and placed into it those things of mine which I had out, as if I was going away. Ælfwyn shifted from bench to bench; looked out the flap, back at the contents of the waggon, and then outside again. Then she spoke. "They may not come for days."

To which Burginde answered, never stopping her work, "And they may come in an hour."

Ælfwyn spoke again. "What if they come by dark, when we are asleep?"

"They will not spring upon us," replied Burginde. "They value their lives."

"Why must we meet like this on the road, without a fixed point to meet at?" continued Ælfwyn, twisting her hands. "It is too hard, not knowing when they shall come, or how many."

"Or who," finished Burginde.

"It is best to be ready at any rate," I said, "for whether it be in an hour or four days we can ourselves control this one thing. And I am sure that Burginde is right: they will not spring upon us at night, for they do value their lives, or at least I hope they do."

There was little else we could do to prepare, but speaking of the coming meeting and doing the slight tasks we could was enough. We sat together in the waggon, looking out at the thegn before us, watching his watchfulness.

Ælfwyn spoke after a long silence. "I never knew that I would yearn for hand-work as I do now. I would welcome even the chance to spin."

I turned to her and said, "I too, have never gone so long without spindle or weaving, or at least the coloured thread work that I most enjoy."

"Well," she said, "soon enough we shall have such work, and much more to do as well."

"Have you looms with you?" I asked.

"Yes," she replied, "two of them, and also enough newly spun yarn and thread to keep three more looms full, and many bags of carded fleece; for we heard that there are no good fleeces left in Lindisse, as the sheep are gone wild or been killed off."

"How do the people live without sheep and the fleece they give?"

"I do not know. But it was thought best that I take enough yarn at least for the weaving of new clothes as I may need this year."

I nodded. "I do not care to spin, but often I have thought weaving a pleasure, and so do it passing well."

"Good," she agreed, "we will have another loom made, so the three of us can work together each morning. It will make the time go pleasantly, and recall me to my life at home, when I sat each morning at work with my mother and sisters and this grumpy old nurse."

At this Burginde looked up from her work, which was at that moment removing a splinter from her finger, and said, "Grumpy or no, your stockings would be full of knots if I did not spin for you."

When we set off in the morning the road went smooth as a ribband, and we passed lakes and groves of trees. The good weather held, and at noon we stopped by a lake, and poured out all of our stale water, and filled our barrels with the soft lake water.

That afternoon the land began to rise again, and the Cæsar's Road began to show more ruts. Then the land went down, and there was marsh of rushes and willow and hazel. And the wind now came from the North, and tho' the Sun was still bright, it grew cold, and we closed the flap up against the damp wind.

At one point we heard the splash of water as the oxen plodded through it, and Burginde pulled open the flap and we saw the road was nearly fallen away into the marsh. She closed the flap and grumbled, and wondered aloud where we would find dry land to make our camp, for it was drawing on to dusk. We piled more charcoals into the brazier, and Ælfwyn and I put on our mantles against the cold.

We sat together in silence on one of the benches, warming our hands at the brazier's glow. Then the waggon stopped again, but instead of hearing Osred coaxing the oxen, we heard no voices. Burginde moved to open the flap, but Ælfwyn stopped her with an upraised hand. We sat, listening with intent, and heard at first nothing but the dripping of marsh water off the bottom of the waggon, and the flapping of the oxen's ears as they shook their heads.

Then we heard the voice of the chief thegn, loud and calm. "Come forward, and show yourselves."

Burginde moved once more to the flap, but again Ælfwyn stopped her, and held a finger to her lips, bidding her be quiet. I feared the pounding in my heart must surely be heard by all outside, and felt my eyes starting in my head.

We heard then some movement of horses and jingling of bridles that told us more horsemen stood before us in the road.

The thegn spoke again. "Toki, you have found what you search for. This is the tribute of Ælfsige to Yrling."

Again we heard the movement of horses, as if they turned before us on the sodden road, but heard no other man.

The thegn spoke again, impatience growing in his words. "I know it is you, Toki, by your helmet; for I regarded it well when I saw you with Yrling." The thegn paused, and then went on. "Perchance I am wrong. Perchance the great Toki has after all fallen in some squabble amongst his brethren and his better now wears his helmet."

At last we heard an answer, in a broad, flat voice with a strange flute-like tone, but in the tongue of our people: "Toki's better does not live." And these words were full of contempt.

Then we heard several men's voices at once, speaking in a strange tongue, with the same flat, broad tone, and I heard for the first time the native speech of the Danes.

The higher voice belonging to the man Toki spoke next. "You will now leave. We will take the waggons to Four Stones."

We heard the sounds of horsemen coming up behind us, as if the two thegns behind the second waggon had moved to join the first in front.

The chief thegn's voice rang out. "No, we will not. You and I both sat at table with Ælfsige and Yrling when this Peace was made. You know its terms. We return only when the waggons are delivered at Four Stones." Then he added, "I am sure your greatest concern is that Yrling receives all he expects?"

Toki's voice flashed out, "You anger me, Saxon, but I will laugh. Do you think I, Toki, would pilfer from my own jarl?"

The thegn seemed to speak carefully. "I think nothing but to fulfil my duty in delivering these waggons."

There was more of the strange speech of the Danes, some of it sounding close to anger amongst them.

Toki spoke again. "You will yield up your swords and spears until you reach Four Stones and are ready to leave again."

Now the thegn's voice was full of wrath. "We will yield our weapons to no one. Will you, Toki, break so soon the Peace that your jarl has made?"

There was more speech amongst the Danes, and movement of horses, and jingling of bridle bits.

Finally Toki spoke again to the thegn. "We will proceed then to Four Stones," he began, and his voice was free of anger and almost light. "First we will look in these waggons to be sure that the tribute you bear is not that of more Saxon thegns."

Then we in the waggon knew we would have to show ourselves to these men, and the thought made my throat dry, tho' the thegns of Ælfsige be around us.

We heard a horse move nearer, and Toki's voice call out, "Let us see first what is in this waggon."

And at these words – I think for fear that he would open the tarpaulin flap himself and look in – Burginde grasped the flap ends and thrust out her face to the horseman.

"Ah!" came Toki's voice. "The bride of Yrling." Then he spoke to the Danes, and there was much laughter amongst them.

Burginde was sputtering in anger, but she still held the flap closed tight about her face so we could not see out, or they, in.

Toki spoke again. "Perhaps not. Perhaps this waggon carries another Lady."

As one gesture Ælfwyn and I pulled our hoods up over our heads, as if they could in some slight way shelter us from the gaze of this man that was waiting outside.

We heard the thegn's voice. "Lady, show yourself so we may cut short this sport and be on our way."

Ælfwyn drew a breath and clasped my hand, but said in a firm voice, "Burginde, open the flap."

Burginde drew back her face, then stood and pulled open the flap as far as it would allow. The day was fading fast, and the horsemen before us were silhouetted against the failing light. There were four Danes, the one closest mounted on a large grey horse of great worth. He wore a ring tunic such as the thegns wore, but across his chest was a baldric and sheath of magnificence, for the belt itself was worked all over in bronze bosses, and the sword hilt gleamed with gold. On his head he wore a helmet of iron, covered over with thin copper or gold foil, polished bright, so that in the setting Sun it fairly flamed.

He looked down at us, and then pulled off his helmet and held it under his arm, and his long yellow hair fell down in two braids upon his shoulders. We saw that he was young, and had a face that bore no scar; and I thought him very handsome, but very cold; for his eyes were bright with greed, and his lip twisted in a smile that was filled with scorn.

His gaze moved from Ælfwyn to me, and back again, and though she cast down her eyes at his glare, I felt anger, and would be as brazen as he, and kept my eyes fixed upon him, look tho' he might.

He spoke at last. "You Saxons are generous. You bring two brides to Yrling, of equal beauty."

Then Ælfwyn raised her head and addressed him, her voice full of resentment. "I am Ælfwyn, daughter of Ælfsige. I do not believe that my new Lord would suffer to hear your rude speech to his wife."

"Rude?" asked Toki in a mocking tone. "To praise beauty?"

"It is not thus praise from your lips," breathed Ælfwyn, and she near trembled with fury.

Now Toki spoke flatly. "Take off your hoods, Ladies, that I might see you better."

And Ælfwyn and I pushed back our hoods, and I felt a thrill of hatred against this Dane Toki.

He leaned forward in his saddle and considered us. Then he spoke in a smooth, light voice. "Yes, Lady," he said to Ælfwyn, "you are clearly the daughter of Ælfsige, for I heard from Yrling that your hair was as silver melted with gold."

Then he looked to me, and grinned as he spoke. "I myself prefer my gold with more copper in it, for it blazes all the better in the dark."

I felt my face flush with heat, and tried to speak out, but heard instead the voice of the chief thegn, grim and tight.

"Come away, Toki; you have seen enough. I wonder you do not hasten to the second waggon, where lies the real treasure."

Toki twisted in his saddle to look at the thegn. "One moment. I have a gift to bring to the bride of Yrling."

And he pulled from beneath his bronze-studded knife belt a small pouch of bright red leather, and tossed it at Ælfwyn so she was obliged to catch it lest it strike her.

Then he turned his horse, and spoke to the other Danes, and they rode with the thegns to the second waggon. Burginde closed up the flap at once, and we three women stood together, I still red with heat, Ælfwyn pale as snow. Burginde muttered to herself but we two were silent.

Ælfwyn raised the leathern pouch and looked at it mutely.

"Open it, at least," prompted Burginde. "I cannot bear any more surprises."

Ælfwyn sat down and pulled the string on the pouch. She slipped her fingers in and drew out a finely wrought red-gold chain made up of many thin links joined together in a twisted rope. In the middle of the chain hung a single white pearl as large as a quail egg, pierced through with a gold stem and clasped at top and bottom by gold caps. It was a necklace, and of amazing beauty.

We all exclaimed; I myself could not help it. The size of the pearl, its whiteness and smoothness, the colour and workings of the chain that bore it, even the caps that held the pearl, were all of great beauty and great worth.

Burginde spoke first. "If this be your welcome gift on the road, only think what awaits you at Four Stones." She turned the chain over in her hand. "'Tis not our work, and must be Danish, or perhaps the work of the Franks."

Ælfwyn thought a moment. "Tho' it be so beautiful, I am glad it is not our work, for I hate to think of the Lady who lost it to such as the Danes."

"Still," I said, "it is a wondrous gift, truly fit for a queen."

"Or a jarl's wife," finished Burginde.

Ælfwyn nodded her head. "Perhaps Yrling, in sending such a gift, truly desires to please me."

Burginde's answer was quick. "Perhaps, in sending such a one as that Toki to deliver it, he is as thick as Osred."

Ælfwyn took up the necklace and slipped it back in the pouch. "No man," she concluded, "who sends such a gift to the woman he will wed is thick."

"Yes, and we should not think ill of it," I said. "Perhaps he does seek to please you."

But Ælfwyn passed the pouch to Burginde, and stood up and said, "Put it away now; I have seen enough of it."

During this time we heard the voices of the thegns and the Danes by the second waggon. At times Toki spoke in our tongue to the thegns, and at times in his own. Then we heard them ride back, and heard the laughter of the Danes mixed with the flat tone of their speech.

The waggon began to move, and we took our seats.

THE END
OF THE ROAD

IT was dark when we made camp, and hard to see just where we were. Osred lit a fire, and Burginde prepared the meal, but Ælfwyn and I stayed inside, and only went out just before sleep. The Danes talked to each other without ceasing, and the thegns, it seemed, not at all. Where they, or the Danes slept, I do not know.

In the morning we came out from the waggon and felt at once the eyes of the Danes upon us. Ælfwyn turned away to the other side of the waggon, as if she would speak to Osred, who was working on an ox yoke there. Before I followed her I looked over to the Danes as they stood before the fire. I did not do so to be bold, but rather to stop their own boldness; and if I could not stop their gaze I resolved that I should at least meet it.

They fell silent, and looked at me with narrowed eyes. Toki smiled his scornful smile, and lifted his hand in a salute to mock me. I turned, and holding myself tall, walked away. Toki said something to the other Danes in their own speech, and I heard much laughter.

Ælfwyn stood by Osred. "We are already prisoners, and not yet there," she complained.

"You are not a prisoner, nor shall you be," I began. "These men are to Yrling as the thegns are to your father; they are pledged to him, and thus to you. Tho' they be rude, do not forget that you in your way can command them."

Osred looked up from the cord he was braiding. "The goose rules the gander, and she be twice as quick," he said.

"I am no goose," said Ælfwyn, and she did not smile at his joke.

"No, Lady," he answered, not looking up, "but they that squawks as one can pass as one."

Now she smiled. "Perchance you shall yet hear me squawk," she said; and she turned, and we made our way back inside the waggon.

The day was not a bright one, and as we began a fog rose that swirled about us. The Danes did not ride in any fixed pattern, but rode sometimes all ahead of us, all behind, and sometimes alongside of us, laughing and talking all the while. The thegns kept as they always had: one man before, and two behind, and kept as well their grim silence.

We stopped only briefly at noon. The marsh gave way gradually to dry land, and the reeds and willows to hazels and elders. I saw these things because we resolved not to close the flap if it was not wet or cold, for as I reasoned to Ælfwyn, Why should she not see the lands that would now be her home?

We sat looking out of the waggon, and she said, "It is easier now that we have met with these men. To wait for them was the hardest part."

I agreed, and asked, "Why do you think Yrling did not come?"

"Perhaps he is shy," laughed Burginde, to which Ælfwyn paid no mind.

"Perhaps," Ælfwyn said, "he is too proud to come and meet me on the road."

"Even tho' you bring such treasure?" I asked.

"Perhaps my treasure is naught compared to his. The pearl he sent may be one of many he owns," she said.

"Only think of what may soon be yours, if he be as generous then as he is now," pondered Burginde aloud.

"I do not think of it," snapped Ælfwyn. "I am not here for treasure. What good will it do me? Whatever jewels await me, I would rather be back in Wessex." She ended more gently, "But it cannot be. It is decreed that I do this thing; and do it I must."

"That is so," I said, eager to agree to so reasonable a speech, "and the honour you will win amongst your people will perchance be great; and you may also win honour amongst the folk of Lindisse." She looked at me and I went on, "Think you of my own King, Burgred of Mercia, and that he be wed to the daughter of King Æthelwulf of Wessex, and that she be sister of King Æthelred who rules you now. Through this and other acts of Æthelwulf, a Peace was procured for both countries, after long years of war. And the Lady Æthelswith is loved throughout Mercia, for tho' we are not her native people, she has done many kindnesses to win our love."

"What has she done?" asked Ælfwyn. "Perhaps I in my small way may find a model in her."

I thought a moment. "Well, she has made Abbots and Abbesses to raise up churches; and founded hospices for lepers; and fed the poor; and –"

"Yes," Ælfwyn broke in. "I shall raise up churches in a place now heathen! And she doubtless had silver of her own. How can I help the sick and hungry without silver? All that is in these waggons goes to Yrling."

"I do not know," I said, and I was almost as impatient as she. "But I think there are always ways to do what you most desire."

"Perchance," nodded Ælfwyn, "but my lot is given, and yours is chosen."

To this I had no answer, and so was silent.

The dark came on, and we stopped and made camp. On the morrow we would arrive at Four Stones, and one life end and another begin for each of us. But we did not speak of this; it was too close.

At supper Burginde brought an ewer of strong ivy ale, and poured out full cups for we three. That was her way of saying, So be it.

The morning lacked all brightness, and as we made preparation to leave this final camp I looked at the Winter-clad plain and wished for strong Sun or even grey rain to give it colour.

Of my two gowns I chose my green travelling one, for it was the better, and with my squirrel trimmed grey mantle made fair show; and I pinned my large pewter brooch at my neck. Burginde wore as always brown wool, but added over it an apron and head wrap of light blue. But Ælfwyn looked with dull eyes from gown to gown, and it was not without our urgings that she at last chose one in which to arrive at Four Stones. It was of dark cobalt, running to purple, and had golden thread work all along the hem and sleeves. At her throat she pinned her silver and garnet brooch. Over this she put a mantle of red wool, lined with marten fur; and the beauty of Ælfwyn thus arrayed as a queen was beyond all womanly beauty I had ever seen. Her yellowy hair fell over her shoulders as a shimmering veil, but when she held up her silver mirror and saw it, her brow creased, and she turned to me.

"Braid up my hair; I would not show it thus today," she said.

I plaited her hair so that it fell in one long rope of yellow to her narrow waist. Upon her head she draped her sheer silk scarf, and lifted the hood of her mantle over all.

"How beautiful you are," I said with feeling. "No one could but love you."

With a nod of her head she turned away from me and sat down on the bench. We could hear the Danes outside mounting their horses, and their talk was all the louder in their impatience to be off.

The waggon jerked forward, and we settled in for the final hours of our journey. After a time we heard the Danes ride ahead, laughing and shouting, with joy, I imagined, to be so close to home. When we could no longer hear their shouts Burginde peeked through the flap, and then pulled it wide so that we might all look out on the countryside of Lindisse.

It was passing fair to look upon, with the same broad meadows we had seen the day before. The Danes were riding far in front of us, and tho' I knew I must soon learn to bear their gaze, was glad they left us now alone and in peace. We went on for the better part of the morning, and then the Cæsar's Road beneath us came to an end; and the waggons heaved along upon nothing more than a rutted earthen road.

We leaned forward, straining our eyes towards the distance. A light mist began to fall. It was fine, almost the fineness of dew. I looked to Ælfwyn, to see if she should command the tarpaulin flap pulled shut, but she did not. It was quiet, for the Danes had rode on, and the thegns of Ælfsige spoke not. The only noise was the snorting of oxen as they pulled against the yoke, the jangling of the thegns' bridle bits, and the dull thud of the iron-rimmed wheels over the brown road.

The road broadened now, and fell away in slow descent. We rounded a turn and came upon all at once the tumbled ruins of a cottar's hut, blacked by fire, and trampled down as if by horse's hooves. This sight was so sudden that Ælfwyn and I each caught our breath. Burginde looked at us with round eyes, but said nothing.

Ahead of us were a great number of village huts, but it seemed strange that from so few came forth the smoke of cook-fires that stained the grey sky. We grew nearer, and I saw the Danes gallop through the village and vanish from sight.

I could just see the moving forms of people, some of whom crossed close to the road, others who moved away. The mist in the air was now become a drizzle, but the flap stayed open before us, for somehow we seemed compelled to watch and to see.

Closer we rolled, and the forms of people grew large, and now lined the road to see us pass. There were at least three score of them, and from somewhere a dog began to howl, and was joined by another dog, and this was the only welcome we heard.

Now the first of the huts were perhaps only a hundred paces from us, but the drizzling rain had so sheltered them from our gaze that only now could we truly see them.

There were a goodly number of huts, sixty or more, all with crofts made up of stout wooden stakes. These crofts were now broken, with wide gaps unmended, and held no beasts at all. Many of the huts themselves lay in heaps, broken and trampled upon the ground, or burnt so that wisps of wet thatch lay around scorched and sodden wattles.

We drew still closer. Edging the road upon either side gathered those who lived in this place. They were ragged, as only the poorest cottars are, and their faces dirty; but these things struck me not. What I stared at was this: That they were all women, every one of them, save for one toothless man of ancient age who gaped open mouthed at us, and for a few small boys who with their sisters clutched at their mother's rags in fear.

I looked down upon them, and every face which met mine was that of a woman or her child, and in their faces was a look that stung me, but from which I could not turn. Their eyes were the eyes of utter hopelessness, and of weariness beyond grief. They did not beg, they did not speak, nor make any sound at all, but only looked upon us with the eyes of the dead. I could not move, and tho' I felt Ælfwyn's hand thrust itself into mine, I could not turn to her, for my eyes no longer obeyed me.

These women, of every age of life, with their tattered rags falling off their thin arms, stood silent as we passed. Then one who had a babe of only a few weeks pressed to her breast raised it up in her arms towards us, and the babe cried out; and the woman wailed. Then did every woman there hold some child up for us to view. Girls who were children held their children in their arms and lifted them, crying, to us. Girls who were children but with the swollen bellies of mothers clung to their own mothers and hid their faces and wailed.

As this cry of misery came forth from these women, they pressed closer to us, and a dog who was a living skeleton snapped at the feet of the oxen. Then did the chief thegn, who had ridden in silence all this time before us, shout out to the women and spur his horse so that it tossed its head and snorted. The women cried out again, a sharp bright cry, and scattered. The waggons passed on.

Before us the open fields of the village lay along the road, and they were unploughed and unplanted, barren of all life. I fixed my gaze upon these fields, but saw them not, for my eyes were filled with the wretchedness of the women, and the horror of their usage at the hands of the Danes. I could not turn my head to Ælfwyn or Burginde, nor did I speak, nor did they.

THE KEEP
OF FOUR STONES

THE waggon rolled on beyond the fields where sat grouped low buildings, dark and glistening in the drizzling rain. The buildings grew near and men on foot and on horseback moved in front of them. Some were working outside a thick palisade of wooden palings which ran circling outside the buildings. Others carried things about: planks of timber, bundles of palings, casks large and small, iron bars, and many other such things. All the men were Danes, I could see, for all, light-haired or dark, wore their hair long and in two braids, and all were clean-shaven, and all spoke to each other in the broad flat tongue of the others.

Our waggon started through the palisade gate, but the chief thegn did not go before it. He reined his horse to one side and stood with the other thegns as Toki led the way into the yard of the keep.

Before us was a group of timber buildings, none taller than two levels high. Some were roofed with lead sheets, and some with thatch, and some with a mixture of both. The largest of the structures was a stable, for its wide doors were open and horses could be seen within. This building looked massive and well built, and was roofed over with lead. Around it huddled half a score of small sheds, which shared a common wall with the great stable and leaned against it as if for shelter. There were also timber buildings which stood alone, and of what uses I could not guess. To one side along the palisade stood crofts which held penned goats, cattle, and a few sheep.

This yard was filled with men at work, for some walked by, carrying armfuls of spears to an open shed at which a smith worked at an anvil; and others rolled casks across the muddy ground; and still others carried buckets through narrow doorways to the men working outside.

Our waggons did not halt, but rather rolled on to another large structure. We stopped, and I looked for the first time upon the ruin of the Hall of Four Stones.

For that is what it was – a blacked and blasted ruin. Facing us lay the tumbled remnants of its four walls, the lower part of which had been built of stone, and the upper portion of heavy timber. The lower stone walls were mostly untouched, but within those walls lay naught but the charred rubble of the upper walls and roof beams. Tho' it was a ruin, it was huge, and the largest hall I had ever seen, far larger and taller than any building at the Priory. I was moved by its greatness, and wondered at its lost glory.

It was then that Ælfwyn finally spoke. "Is it to this desolation that I have been sold, father?" And in her voice was both fear and disgust.

Now many men approached our waggons. Toki and the rest of the escort swung off their horses and greeted the men, and then led their horses away to the great stable. Osred was told by another Dane, who also spoke our tongue, to unyoke the oxen. This man was tall and dark haired, but the thing I noticed most about him was a great scar which he bore upon his cheek. Osred got to work, and some other men came forward and unyoked those of the second waggon, so it was clear that the waggons were to be left as they stood.

We could not see the thegns, and I thought perhaps they did not come inside the palisade gate with us, but waited outside. Osred too was gone, as he followed the men who led the oxen off.

Many men were looking at us, but no one greeted us. No man seemed in greater estate or to have authority over them. So we three women sat in the waggon and waited.

Some of the men who had come closer to look at us began to move away, and still no one came forth to lead us to Yrling.

Then did Ælfwyn speak again, and fairly hissed with anger. "There is no one to greet us."

I did not know what to do. The choice was to sit there and be idly gaped at, or to close up the tarpaulin flap, and sit thus slighted in the yard before the ruined hall. I saw the tall Dane who in our tongue had told Osred to unyoke the oxen. "Sir," I called, as loudly and boldly as I could, yet I knew my voice quavered in my throat, "please to take my Lady and me to your Lord." For if he would not come to greet us, we needs must go to him.

The Dane looked up and grinned in such a way that a dreadful thought rushed into me: Perhaps this man himself was Yrling; and I caught my breath, fearful lest I gave insult.

But no, I had not begun with such an affront, for he answered, still grinning, "He is not here, but returns tonight, or tomorrow, or when he will."

He spoke rather well, and with not so great a broad-
ness as Toki. I felt grateful that we understood him, and he
us. Also, he did not seem over-bold, for his grin had softened into a smile, and as he stood before us, he drove off
the idlers with a word or two in his own tongue. He was
as plain to look at as Toki was handsome, for his dark hair
hung lankly from a narrow brow, and tho' he was young, his
face was gaunt and creased with the deep scar which ran
from his left cheek bone to his chin. His face was quiet, tho',
and his eyes had a thoughtfulness which Toki's never wore.

He turned to us, and gestured that we should come
down from the waggon. Burginde clambered out the front
flap and off the waggon, and held out her hand to help her
mistress down. But the Dane jumped up upon the waggon
ledge in an easy movement, and made to grasp Ælfwyn to
swing her down. Tho' she recoiled from him, she had no
choice, and he grasped her by her waist and lowered her
to the ground. Then was I suffered to be grasped in the
same way and set upon the clay of the keep yard.

Toki returned, and he and the other Dane spoke
together. The tall Dane called to two men, and I saw he
ordered them to watch the waggons. Osred and the thegns
still could not be seen, so with only the eyes of the Danes
upon us we were led away.

We passed the front of the ruined hall. The sodden
rubble of the huge beams gave off a faint smell of charred
wood, but I could not stop and stare, for the two men
strode on before us.

As we turned the corner of this ruin, I saw along one
wall a building intact; but whether it had somehow been
spared the fire, or been built later by the conquering Danes
I could not tell. It was of timber, two levels high, but part

of it was sunken into the ground, for you walked down a broad flight of six or eight steps to enter.

Down the stone steps the Danes walked, and pushed open the door, which looked to have been cut in size to fit this doorway. Its iron strappings were wrought with intertwined crosses, flowers, and hound's heads, and I thought it to be the work of the perished workmen of Lindisse, and not the Danes.

The men left the door open behind us. By the grey light of noon we could see a hall of perhaps thirty paces breadth, in the centre of which glowed a fire untended in a large firepit. Trestle tables and benches lay up against the walls, and a great amount of rushes on the floor, so many that I could not tell if it was wood or stone or beaten clay.

More than this I could not see, for the room held no windows, only the firepit opening in the roof. Toki and the other man turned and led us along a short passageway. A flight of wooden stairs ranged against the timber wall. They creaked noisily beneath us but seemed sturdy enough.

Daylight came from a window opening on the landing at the top. There were three doors, one of which was open and we all entered. It was a room of narrow but long shape, with two glassless windows with wooden shutters. The walls and floor were of wide wood boards. It was bare of furniture, having only two chairs, a small table, and a low, broad bed which looked to have a ticking stuffed with straw or fern. There was a rush holder of the rudest make upon the table. The ceiling showed the roof beams, so I knew we were at the top.

The men turned to us and the one who had taken us from the waggon said, "This is your room. If you have need, call for me, Sidroc."

Toki said something to him in their own tongue, and
Sidroc laughed. They turned and went out of the room
and down the steps, and left us in that dreary place.

Burginde went and closed the door at once behind
them, and Ælfwyn stood speechless staring at the room.
Then she roused herself and said to Burginde, "Follow
them, and find Osred, and have brought up to us those
necessaries as we shall need."

And Burginde, tho' I could see she was afraid, did go,
and we heard her creaking loudly down the stairs after the
men. When we were alone in the room, Ælfwyn turned to
me, and in her face was both anger and dismay.

I did not know if she would weep or fume, but her
anger won, and she cried out, "Never did I expect so great
a slight! No one to greet me, and then I am cast aside
into this monk's cell of a room to await him. I bring him
a dowry that many a King's daughter might envy, and am
thus welcomed!"

She sunk down in one of the chairs, and I looked at
her, and then at the bleak room. I felt that at least we had
arrived from our long journey, and were safe, and out of the
curious gaze of the Danes below. I said, "Lady, instead let us
be thankful that we are here, and alive and well." I looked
around the room again and said, "At least it is clean."

She looked as well and said, "Yes, clean because it is
so empty." But the anger was gone from her voice.

I took off my mantle and she also, and found some
pegs on the wall to hang them by. We stood at each of the
small windows and looked out past the iron that strapped
them. We saw the burnt ruins of the hall below and beyond
it a portion of the yard of the keep. We could look as well

over a part of the palisade to the village we had passed through. The road which had brought us here faded into the gloom beyond it.

We heard stamping upon the stairs, and Burginde's voice, and we opened the door and she came in staggering under a load of blankets and pillows and cushions. Behind her came Osred and another man, a Dane, heaving a huge clothes chest into the room. I took heart to see this, for the comfort they brought into the room was the familiar comfort of the waggon.

They put down their loads and went back for more, and Burginde brought in one hand my pigskin satchel, and in the other the willow cage that held the linnet. The Dane left, and Osred turned to go also, but Ælfwyn stopped him.

"Stay, Osred, for I would ask you a question or two," she said, and she moved to the door and closed it. "Sit down, Burginde, and rest."

Burginde plumped down on the stool which had just been carried up, and Osred stood next to her.

Ælfwyn sat in one of the chairs and asked, "Tell me what you have seen. Are all here Danes? Are there no others?"

Osred answered, "No, Mistress, we are not quite alone, for I have seen a few lads of ten or twelve years, boys of Lindisse, working in the stables."

"How did they greet you?" asked Ælfwyn.

Osred answered slowly. "I greeted them, rather, for I was glad to see some of my own kind. But they said not much, and who could chide them? For the Danes are everywhere."

At these words Ælfwyn went to the door and pulled it open, but we were alone.

Then I would ask a question, and turned to Osred. "What of my mare?"

Osred grinned. "She be well enough, tho' the stable master, a great brawny fellow of a Dane, made it clear she be more fit to eat than to ride."

My face spoke for me, and Osred went on. "Do not fear, Lady; if the Danes be too proud to ride her, she can always pull a cart."

I felt sunk in sadness at this, and realised Shagg was no longer mine, but had become part of the tribute to Yrling.

Ælfwyn watched, and then spoke. "Ceridwen, she is yours still. The Danes will not care about so humble a pony. I will see that all understand that she is yours outright." These words she spoke with such firmness and resolve that we three all looked at her, and Ælfwyn seemed to take heart from her own speech. She spoke to Osred again. "Do you know yet where you shall sleep?"

He pondered before he spoke. "No, Mistress; most likely in the stable, or some shed as near to the oxen as can be, for I made it plain I was born a drover and wish to end as one, and all can see the oxen are well known to me, and me to them."

Ælfwyn replied, "At least for tonight I would have you sleep outside my door. Burginde, go with Osred, and seek out once more that Dane Sidroc who brought us here, and tell him – no, ask him that it might be so."

Ælfwyn went to one of the small chests that had been brought in, and took out of it a purse with a silver mount. From it she took a silver coin, and pressed it into Burginde's hand. "Give him this as you ask him, but let no one see you."

Then Burginde and Osred left, and as they did so Osred said he would return as he could with more goods from the waggons, and if all went well, be back later that night.

ALL THAT'S LEFT

IT was growing cold, and we found the shutters on the windows did not close aright. Burginde set the brazier up and fed it with coals, and also filled and lit two cressets so we had both heat and light. Ælfwyn and I pushed the clothes chests where they would be most useful, and as we did so Osred called up from below. Soon we had the luxury of the deer hides from the waggon under foot. He brought also willow baskets and a bronze ewer of strong and bitter ivy ale, which he delivered into Burginde's care with a wink.

"Osred," asked Ælfwyn, "have you seen the thegns? I would speak to them before they go, and am fearful they will be kept away."

"No, Mistress," he answered, "I have not seen them, but I heard from a stable boy that the thegns are yet outside the walls of the keep, and will leave on the morrow."

Of a sudden I had a thought. "Lady," I said to Ælfwyn, "I would prepare a letter for the thegns to take, that you might speak yourself to your parents and tell them you are well."

"Yes," she replied, and a smile broke upon her lips. "It will give them great pleasure to have such a missive. How shall we do this?"

I looked around the room and thought before I spoke. "I do not suppose that we might find a piece of parchment here at Four Stones. Nor have we time to prepare a piece of linen."

Then I thought of my wax tablet, that it was sturdy and would well withstand the hardships of the thegn's journey on horseback.

I turned to Osred, glad of my idea. "Do you go, Osred, and bring back as soon as you can a joiner, and he will make for us a wax tablet box such as mine, for that will hold a letter that cannot easily be destroyed, nor suffer from wet; for the only enemy of wax is heat."

He returned with a ragged boy, whose brown hair and pale blue eyes stared out of a thin face smudged with grime.

The boy looked at us uncertainly, and shifted from one foot to another.

"Are you the joiner's boy?" I asked.

"No, m'Lady," he answered in our own tongue, and looked around the room in a restless way.

"Well, where is he?" I asked, and gestured to Ælfwyn. "This Lady is your new mistress, and requires work of him."

He rocked from foot to foot. "Joiner's dead, m'Lady. Cooper's dead too. I be the cooper's boy."

I looked at Ælfwyn and then back to the boy. He would not meet my eyes and I tried to speak as kindly as I could. "Well," I said, "does that make you the cooper now?"

He shrugged and looked down. "I be what's left," he answered.

I took a step towards him. "We have work for you. Do you think you could help us?"

He glanced up. "I could but try, m'Lady," he finally said.

"Look here," I offered, holding the tablet before the boy. "Do you think you could build by the morning such a box as this? The two sides must fit together well, for I will fill it with wax that must be protected. And you see there are hinges of brass, and a clasp that holds the sides together?"

The boy took the shallow tablet from my hands and opened it, closed it, and turned it over.

"You may take this with you as your model, but you must treat it with care," I said. The boy nodded his head. "Can you do such a task as this? And by the morrow?" I finished, eager to hear him speak.

He looked down at the box again, and then up to me, and shook his head. "No, m'Lady. I cannot get the hinges, m'Lady, nor the clasp. There is no metal-worker save the Dane's armourers and smiths."

"It is all right," I said. "We can do without them, and tie the tablet with leathern cords to keep the two halves together. But they must fit well. And bring as much bees-wax as you can find; tallow and candle stumps and such. Can you do it?"

He nodded his head, and turned to go.

"Stay," called Ælfwyn, and she went to the larder chest and opened it. She drew out two boiled eggs and two loaves. "Take these," she said, and held them out to the boy.

He clasped the tablet under his arm and stuffed the food into his tunic, his eyes wide with fear and thanks. He bobbed his head and fled out of the room, and Osred followed him down the stairs.

Ælfwyn had turned away and gone to the window with the ill fitting shutter, where a large chink in the wood showed the palisade and the village beyond.

Burginde stirred around behind us in the larder chest, muttering to herself. "The folk be starving, and the men all dead; and the women got with children from the Danes, and look half mad with it. And no one's come to greet us, not even to bring a cup of ale or bite to eat. And no one in the keep save children and the two smirking Danes know our speech. And the looms will never fit –"

Ælfwyn turned. "Burginde, enough. I have eyes and ears, and need you not to recount the grief of this land nor the slight we have received." Her voice was calm and measured. "I think there is other work you might do, such as bring us water that we might bathe our hands. And then let us ourselves eat, for it is far past noon and we have had nothing."

After Burginde had left the room, I too looked around for more tasks that would occupy me, for I had no desire just then to dwell on all that I had seen. The little linnet's cage sat upon the table, and I held it at arm's reach before me and said, "Perhaps a nail could be pounded into the ceiling beams, so that this cage might hang by a cord from it."

Ælfwyn looked over at me and nodded, and then said, "You did well with the cooper's boy. I am only sad that the first meeting with my new people shows them to be so wretched. I did not know what to expect; I have dwelt so long on my own grief in coming here that I could think of little else. But this is worse that I could have dreamt."

I put down the willow cage and the linnet chirped. "You are here now, and perhaps can make the way easier for this sad folk."

"I doubt it," she replied. "I am not schooled in acts of mercy."

"That is not true," I answered. "It was an act of mercy to feed that starving boy, which you did at once."

Our speech ended there, for Burginde came bumping up the steps with a bucket of warm water. As she poured some of it in a basin, she spoke of what she had seen.

"There be cooks and helpers, all folk of Lindisse, most nearly all of them women. They say they did not come up to us for the fear of it, but I had a good talking to them, and think now they might show themselves and be of some use."

As if summoned, footsteps were heard below, and Burginde flung open the door. Two women of about middle age came in, dressed in the rough and greasy aprons of their calling. They carried a platter of cold roasted meat and a jug. They set their burdens on the table, and with wide eyes looked at Ælfwyn and I. Burginde shooed them away, and down they went.

Burginde peered into the jug, and then dipped in a finger and tasted it. "Barley beer," she said with satisfaction. She studied the meat on the platter. "'Tis roast pig. When I asked if they had cheeses as well, they looked as if I had asked for dragon's eggs. Cheese they have not had for many a month, as there are no sheep left."

We opened our larder chest and took out the last of our cheeses, and also some boiled eggs and loaves. Then with Burginde sitting on the stool by the brazier, and Ælfwyn and I on the chairs at the table, we ate our first meal at Four Stones. The roast pig was good, and tho' a few pickled onions or roasted leeks would have set it off well, it was tender and full of flavour. Likewise the barley beer pleased me much. I praised the food, and Burginde laughed and said, "Yes, let us thank the wretches thither for it."

At this Ælfwyn bid her keep her tongue for swallowing only, and tho' the meal did not lose all its savour for me, again I recalled the faces of the women of the ruined village, and felt full.

CHAPTER THE THIRTEENTH

THE TROPHY
OF THE DANES

I awakened to the shouts of workmen in the yard outside. The room was dim, but when I went to the shuttered window I saw the Sun half risen. I pulled open the other shutter, and Ælfwyn and Burginde stirred.

"Ach! Miserable hole!" muttered Burginde as she stumbled, yawning to the window. "As dark as the lowest hut."

She joined me, and then Ælfwyn too. The day would be foggy, and the damp clinging to all we saw made the scene more barren to the eye.

Ælfwyn shrugged and we turned away from the window to wash and dress. I chose again my green gown, and Ælfwyn took from one of her clothes chests a blue gown with sleeves of dark red. She pinned this with a small gold brooch at her neck.

As Burginde smoothed the beds, we heard noise on the stair. I opened the door to find one of the kitchen women we had met yesterday upon the landing. She bore a platter of small loaves, split and toasted, upon which laid slices of roast pig. There was also a mound of dried apples

and pears, and another jug of barley beer. She looked at
me with the same wide eyes of the day before, and I said,
"I thank you," and smiled to try to make her speak. But I
could get nothing from her, and as soon as she had passed
the platter into my hands she turned and clattered down
the wooden stairs.

We ate and even Burginde could not begrudge a
word on the quality of the bread, for it was sweet and fine
grained and full of flavour. "They did not kill the baker,"
she said with her mouth full.

After we cleared away we wondered aloud when we
might receive the looms. Burginde thought the second
waggon was not to be touched until Yrling arrived. As the
looms were there as well we could not have them until he
had received the treasure.

This brought to mind the departure of the thegns.
Burginde was about to leave to find the cooper's boy when
he called out from the bottom of the stairs, "Lady!" in a
hissing whisper. In one hand he bore my wax tablet, and
in the other the simple copy he had made. I opened it and
saw there was a proper depth for the wax to fill, and also
that the two sides fit together tightly. He had even brought
a braided leathern cord with him. From his pockets he
pulled handsful of chary candle stumps and a lump of
tallow.

"You have done well. I thank you, and your new Lady
also is pleased," I said, for I wished to praise his efforts as
they deserved.

He bobbed his head and a shy smile passed quickly
over his thin little face. Ælfwyn spoke not, but moved to
the chest that held her purse, and took from it a silver
piece. She came before the boy and held it out, but he

stared at it and made no move to take it. At last I took it and pressed it into his hand.

"This is from your mistress. She bids you take it for your good service to her." I spoke firmly as I feared the boy might insult with his silence. He raised his eyes to Ælfwyn, and they were brimful of tears.

I said to him, "Tell me your name," and his lip trembled and the tears streamed down his face. At last he said, "Ecgwald."

"Ecgwald, will you do your mistress another service?" I asked. "Our man Osred has told us that the thegns we rode here with are staying outside the palisade of the keep. Do you go now and find them, or find one who knows where they are, and tell them that the Lady Ælfwyn wishes to see them."

He nodded his head so that the tears flew upon the floor. "My cousin Mul is a stable boy, and will help me find them," he said between little hiccoughs.

"Good," I said. "Have you also a mother?" He nodded. "Then you will take her your coin as soon as you have found the thegns?" Again he nodded, and bobbed his head, and backed out of the chamber to run his errand.

I set to work warming the wax and tallow mixture over the brazier so I could mould it. When it was soft I pressed it into one side of the wood frame the boy had made.

We began to think about how the letter should run. "First it should say who wrote the letter, for they will wonder about it," she decided.

"No need," I said, "for the thegns themselves will deliver it, and will tell them of me."

"Of course," she said.

"Who will read it to them?" I asked. "That will tell us something."

"The monks at the abbey outside Cirenceaster have in the past read to my father charters and the like. No one at my father's burh reads, so I think such a monk will be brought to do it."

"Good," I said. "Then we will begin, 'Holy Brother, send greetings to my good and loving parents from their daughter Ælfwyn.'"

"That is good," Ælfwyn said, "and sounds as rich as the charters that are read to my father."

I laughed and said, "We will make it rich, so they know all be well, and they get pleasure from the listening."

"What next?"

"Well, I think we should tell of the journey, for one is always asked how the journey went," I said.

"But will not the thegns tell them, as they will tell them of you?" she asked.

"Yes," I countered, "but I think they need to hear you say it went well, for what is well for the thegns may not be well for a maiden, and this they know."

"True," she nodded, and began to laugh. "We could have met ten bandits on the road, had a flood and a drought, and if the thegns had delivered me and the waggons just the same they would say 'All went well.'"

After we had stopped our laughter she said, "And I want to say I have the company of the new friend who writes this, so that I will not be alone here. And that we are all well, but that the countryside is much destroyed, and the people here want for much." She paused and looked at me. "What can I say of Yrling? Nothing yet."

"Say you go with good heart to do your duty. That will gladden them, for tho' the deed be done, they will want to hear that you are well in your mind about this."

"Ah, I am far better in my mind than in my heart," she said, with a long quiet sigh.

Ælfwyn stood near me and looked down upon my work, and I strived to form each letter as perfectly as I could. The message read:

HOLY BROTHER,

Send greetings to my good and loving Parents from their daughter Ælfwyn. By the Grace of God your daughter and her train travelled well and easily due to the many comforts my loving Parents provided me with. I have yet to meet my husband but go with good heart to do my duty. The folk of Lindisse are sore in want and I rejoice to think I may keep my people at home from this pass. I am well; the friend who forms these words will write again. Your obedient and loving daughter

ÆLFWYN

I read it aloud and she seemed well pleased.

"Here," I said, holding out the brass stylus, "make your mark by your name." And I pointed to the last word that spelt out 'Ælfwyn'.

She took the stylus and held it above the wax. "What mark shall I make?" she asked.

"Two lines crossed are good," I said, and she scratched lightly at the brown wax. "Harder, so that they may see it," I urged.

"There," she said, drawing a firm cross in the wax.

She looked at me and then lowered her eyes. "I would like to learn to write my name, so that when we send a parchment to them I might use the name they gave me."

"Of course," I said, and felt glad. "You will do that and more, for I think you will easily learn this art."

She smiled at me as I bound up the tablet with the cord. "This is speech that will last," she said.

"Yes," I agreed, "for even after one is dust, written words stay behind."

Burginde spoke. "Gold always stays behind, and speaks a rich tongue too," she said.

I laughed at her, "Who needs gold when we have you?"

In a few minutes we heard the light step of Ecgwald on the stair. I went out upon the landing and he hissed up, "Lady! The thegns may not come into the yard. Will I take the tablet to them?"

Ælfwyn thought not a moment. "No," she said to me, "For I would see them one last time. We will take it ourselves to them at the gate of the burh."

"The Lady comes herself," I called down to the boy. "Go back to the thegns and tell them we are on our way."

He sped off, and we three put on our mantles. Burginde looked down into the yard and said, "We must have clogs, or our boots suffer, for 'tis all over mud."

Ælfwyn took up the wax tablet, and I carried the clogs for we two down the wooden steps; and this was the first time since arriving that she and I had gone down the stair.

We did not stop to look into the hall, but pulled open the heavy door. It felt strange to walk up and out by the stone steps of the sunken hall, as if we were emerging from the den of an animal. To one side of the yard stood the second waggon, its tarpaulins tightly laced. A Dane leaned against it, as a guard to its treasure. He regarded us not, and we went on.

It was muddy in the yard, and our clogs made sucking sounds on the sodden Earth. In a knot of men at the gate we saw the thegns, and their horses, ready saddled. The Danes Toki and Sidroc stood with four others like them.

We paused just a moment and then Ælfwyn gathered her skirt up and walked rapidly towards them.

The thegns were facing us and nodded their heads in greeting. Of the Danes, Toki saw us first, and stepped aside to let us pass.

"Ah, the brides of Yrling!" he smirked, and he swept his hand before him.

Sidroc turned and looked at us, and tho' he smiled at Toki's jest, spoke to him in their own tongue so that Toki was still.

Ælfwyn looked not at either of them, but in pride kept her eyes fixed upon the chief thegn. "This is the letter I send to my parents," she said, and placed it in his hands. "Pray tell them I am well, despite the welcome I have received here."

He nodded again. "We leave now. I bid you well," he said, and his voice and face were grave.

Ælfwyn began to speak, but Toki said something to Sidroc that made him break in.

Sidroc held out his hand. "I would see the box before you take it," he said.

Now the Lady turned on him. "Why? It is aught but a letter to my parents. Do you think I send back some of the treasure I have brought?" Her voice flashed with anger. "And if I did, do you think I would send so small a portion?"

I caught my breath. The thegn looked at Ælfwyn, and then at Sidroc, and passed the tablet to him. He undid the cord while Ælfwyn looked with all defiance at him and Toki.

Sidroc opened the tablet, and looked at it, and as he held it on its side it was plain that tho' he spoke well the tongue of our people, he read it not.

He held it up that Toki might see it, and Toki squinted and scowled. Then Sidroc placed the two halves together, and tied up the tablet with the cord, and passed it to the thegn.

Ælfwyn spoke to the thegn. "Thank you for all your good service to me. I pray my father rewards you well."

I too was moved to speak. "I add my thanks, and swear to serve and love this Lady as a sister."

I saw that there were tears in Ælfwyn's eyes, and that she would turn away rather than let the Danes see them.

The thegn spoke. "I bid you health," he said, and with a nod turned to his horse, and slipped the tablet into one of his saddle bags. "Your father shall have this soon, Lady," he said, and he and the two other thegns swung themselves into their saddles and raised their hands in Fare-well.

Ælfwyn turned quickly away, but I stayed another moment to look after them. We walked across the yard towards the hall, but halfway Ælfwyn stopped and spoke. "I cannot return to that chamber. Let us look about us here and see what we may."

I was glad of this, for to spend all the day sitting without work in the chamber again awaiting Yrling was too hard.

We looked about us, but the ugliness of the place did not present much to tempt us. As I saw yesterday, most of the buildings were low and rude, ill-designed and hastily put together; and as it was Winter, all sat upon a sea of mud and trampled straw. Only the great stable stood out, that and the blacked ruins of charred oak and tumbled stone which lay attached to Yrling's hall.

"I have heard from the Prior that the Danes are no builders, and now I see with my own eyes how truly he spoke," I said as we stood looking on this.

"They are far more skilled at destruction," answered Ælfwyn.

"To think they spared the stable when they took Four Stones, and let the hall burn!" added Burginde in disgust.

"Like as not they had no choice, Burginde," I answered. "They may be no builders, but enjoy other's work well enough."

Ælfwyn turned and gazed upon the huge blacked beams. "They have not even cleared away this rubble," she said.

"It is kept as a trophy," said a man's voice, quite near. We turned to look into the scarred face of Sidroc. "For many months the head of Merewala, the Lord of Four Stones, was stuck on that pike," he said, pointing to a tall wooden shaft with a barbed tip like that of a spear's, "until the ravens had their fill, and the skull crumbled under their pecking. Thus did he learn of our skill at war."

We said nothing, for what could we say? I thought we would turn to go, but Ælfwyn stood looking at the pike and said, "He rests in honour still."

Now Sidroc spoke again. "Ha! You are a spirited one, Lady, and are made of good stuff, for you stand up well to the nephew of Yrling."

She took her eyes from the pike and looked at him. "You are his nephew?"

He smiled. "Yes, I, and also Toki; but he is not my brother." He looked to me. "This Lady is not your sister, but your cousin?"

"No," she said. "The Lady is my friend."

"She is a good friend, then, to come so far with you," he said, and considered this thought with care. He looked at me again. "You are then also from Wessex."

"No, I have not come so far as my Lady," I said, "for I am come from Mercia, by the river Dee."

"Ah," he said with a grin. "I would like to see that place. I hear there is great wealth there."

I answered at once. "Then you have heard a lie, for our lands are poor and marshy, and for many years we have fought the Welsh so that no store of grain remains from year to year."

He narrowed his eyes at me. "Who are you?" he asked.

"I am Ceridwen, daughter of Cerd, and my dead father was an ealdorman," I said with firmness.

He laughed. "You are a true shield-maiden. I will be careful of you."

He turned back to Ælfwyn. "Someone in this keep wrote the letter in wax for you, but I know that the monks of Lindisse are dead. Tell me who it was, for we at times have need of a man who writes."

It was Ælfwyn's turn to smile. "Then I cannot help you, for I know of no such man."

Sidroc's face grew hard. "I do not jest, Lady," he said, and I would not have her go on with her sport.

I stepped between them, tho' my heart pounded in my breast. "My Lady speaks the truth," I said. "She knows of no such man. I am the scribe that wrote the letter."

Sidroc stared at me. "You? I do not believe it," he answered.

"Then you do not believe the truth. I was raised by the Black Monks, and they gave me this art."

He smiled and said, "I believe you, shield-maiden." He looked at Ælfwyn. "You do indeed bring rich treasure to Yrling."

She searched his face, and without moving her eyes from his spoke to him quietly. "She is not treasure, nor is the cream coloured pony, for it is hers outright. Will you see that this is known, nephew of Yrling?"

A smile broke slowly over his face. "Yes, I will see that it is known." He glanced at me. "But I would rather see her on a stallion of Yrling's."

My face burned and I looked away, but I need not have, for he turned on his heel and strode off.

Burginde opened her astonished mouth.

"Silence, Burginde," breathed Ælfwyn.

We three turned and walked through the muddy straw. My face still stung. Ælfwyn spoke out loud as she walked. "We are insulted, and we are ignored," I could hear her say.

Still, she did not head for the hall and the meagre solace of her chamber, but continued through the yard of Four Stones.

DOBBE'S TALE

E neared the stone steps which led down to the door of the hall, but we passed them and went on. The noises of many animals told us we were approaching a kitchen yard. We passed through a narrow gate, left open, and saw an empty cattle shed, and next to it a circular pig sty, with a few great swine rooting through the strawy mud. Some tattered and bedraggled hens roosted in the ruins of a fowl house.

The bread ovens and roasting pits came in sight, and men and women worked at a long table dressing the carcass of a pig. They looked up in their stained aprons, their hands and arms blood-spattered, their eyes dull in their heads.

A woman above middle life came forward from amongst them. Her face was worn and weather-beaten, but it creased into a recollection of a smile. Her arms trembled as if from the palsy, and she held on to the edge of the table as she stood before us. Her voice was low and gravelly, almost a croak, but she spoke our own tongue, and so it was most welcome.

"Ladies, I bid you welcome," she began, and untied her apron and wiped her hands and arms upon it. "We heard tell of your coming. I hope you have not been too

displeased with our work so far." Here she held her hand
to the carcass on the table.

"Indeed no," answered Ælfwyn. "All you have sent up
has been worthy fare."

The face of the woman creased still deeper into a smile,
so that her eyes nearly vanished in the folds. Ælfwyn went
on. "I am the Lady Ælfwyn, and this, my Lady Ceridwen,
and this, my nurse, Burginde."

The woman's head bobbed up and down at hearing
our names, and those at the table looked on with open
mouths. "Aye, Mistress," croaked the woman, "call me
Dobbe, and a faithful woman to you, daughter as I am of
Wessex." She then turned to a man of her own age who
had been stacking wood for the roasting pits. "Eomer,
fetch my keys, that I might have some ale poured out for
these Ladies."

He wiped his hands on some straw and walked into a
closed shed and returned with a clutch of keys strung on
a huge iron ring. Dobbe held them but a few inches from
her face as she sorted through them. "Aye, this one," she
said, holding it fast in her hand. "Susa! Call Susa, Eomer,
she is clean –" she instructed, but before he could open his
mouth a young round-faced woman stepped to the door
which connected to the hall. She came out and took the
keys that were offered her, her eyes as round as her face.

"Susa, open the green chest and bring cups of brass.
These Ladies need ale." Dobbe turned back to us as Susa
vanished through the doorway. "I would ask you to sit,
Ladies, if it were not such an indignity that Ladies should
sit in a kitchen yard. Things are not as they should be."

"Good Dobbe, I thank you," I said heartily, "for aught
but you have greeted my Lady since we came to this place."

Now the woman Susa came back, balancing three brass cups of ale on a platter of wood.

"I thank you, good woman," said Ælfwyn, as we took up our cups. "Pray let your people proceed with their work while I speak to you."

We turned our backs on the bloody table and walked a few steps with Dobbe to the roasting pits. Ælfwyn put the cup to her lips and drank, and then spoke in a low voice. "Tell me, Dobbe, how is it that you are here? A woman from my own country, Wessex?"

With no table for support, Dobbe trembled even more. "Good Lady, I have been here since before your birth. Dobbe came herself as a young girl, to a happier place." She stopped, and did not go on.

Ælfwyn said, "Then you have seen much."

"Aye, Lady, far too much, for I came in the train of Elspeth, blest be that good Lady's memory, and came with her from Wessex, all the way from Basingas, which was her home; for she came to wed Merewala."

"The same that was slaughtered last year?" asked Ælfwyn.

Dobbe nodded. "Aye, the very same; and the Dane slaughtered also his two sons." Again she fell silent.

I recalled the barbed iron spear tip on the tall pike, and what Sidroc had told us of it.

Ælfwyn spoke again. "And Eomer? Is he a man of Lindisse or of Wessex?"

Dobbe's face creased. "He is my faithful husband, and a man of Wessex; for he too came in the train of Elspeth."

We sipped at our ale; it was awkward standing in the kitchen yard, drinking ale and listening to the old cook, and Dobbe seemed to sense this. "A poor greeting this,

Lady, to be met by a blood-smeared crone! Lady, I was not always such! Nor Eomer . . . When we were in the service of Merewala, Eomer was steward of the pantry, and I chief amongst seamstresses!" She held out her gnarled hands, as twisted and brown as the galls of a walnut tree. "Little did we know to what depths we might fall . . . aye, but we lived; through it all, we lived; tho' many did not, and our son was taken from us . . ." Her voice caught, and she trembled so that Burginde grasped her by the arm to steady her.

Ælfwyn glanced at me, and then at Dobbe's lowered head. She spoke kindly. "Tell me, Dobbe, did your Lady Elspeth perish in the Danish siege?"

Dobbe shook her head. "No, Lady, the good Elspeth died many years before, God grant her peace. She did not live to see this –" she raised her hands to the yard around us. "He married no more, for Elspeth, good woman, had given him three sons, and tho' one died in a fall from his horse, two lived on robustly. And now Merewala and sons all, are dead!"

"Were there any daughters?" I asked.

Dobbe held her knotty hands before her face. "Aye, Lady, one, as gentle as Elspeth herself; but in the siege she was despoiled by the Danes and threw herself from the roof of the hall."

We spoke not; tears were in my eyes for the pity of it all, but this time Dobbe went on unbidden.

"The whole family is dead, and the rest dead also, or else driven into the woods to live as wolves . . . all of us who resisted at the fall of the burh, even unto women and children, were slain, and those who lived now live as slaves . . . My son died, protecting the hall of his Lord, and he had neither sword nor spear, being a humble gentle lad and of the Lord's pantry, and schooled to the service of the table, and not the service of war." Here her voice broke, and she sobbed. From across the kitchen yard Eomer cast a sorrowful look at her. She wept not long, tho', and Burginde forced her to sip a bit of ale from her cup.

"Tell us of she who came before me," asked Ælfwyn slowly.

"Aye," said Dobbe, gulping down tears and ale. "A sweet maid, too tender for this rough charge. She was a maid of Lindisse, but from the East, and came here with little more than her priest and a few others, save much gold. She died not six months after she came; the fever carried her off, but she was wasting as it was, and would have gone off without it, I think."

"Tell me of Yrling," Ælfwyn said suddenly, and Dobbe's face twisted at the sound of his name.

"Ah! The Dane! He is Lord here; he slew my rightful Lord, and his men struck down my boy as if he were chaff..."

Her voice trailed off, and Ælfwyn asked no more.

We stood silently, gazing into the cold firepit. After a time Dobbe spoke again. "We do such cooking here as we can, and such baking as we find grain for. No one is left to plant wheat and barley, and so this Summer there will be no food save what is already in the ground, or can be gathered. The Danes killed and ate the sheep soon after they came, and the rest were driven off into the forests and are no more, and so we have no milk or cheese. How the shire will live without wool I do not know, and the Dane seems not to care. The few sheep in the burh yard are all that is left from countless herds."

Ælfwyn nodded at all this. "Thank you, good woman, for all you have told me," she said, and we three drained our cups and handed them back to Dobbe.

"Thank you, good Lady, and may God bless and keep you, all three," answered Dobbe.

She came with us as far as the open wicket, and bowed as we left. We walked around the side of the hall without speaking. My thoughts dwelt on the sufferings Dobbe had known, and of the women, now dead, whom she had served: Elspeth and the poor daughter of Elspeth; and then the maid of Lindisse who had come, as Ælfwyn did, to wed Yrling, and had not lived six months. And yet Dobbe, tho' old, still lived; as she said, she lived through it all.

I thought to myself, Four Stones is death to its mistresses; and as I thought this I wondered if Ælfwyn thought the same. I glanced at her grave face as we walked, and was again moved by her pride and beauty. She looked at me, and I smiled, and took her hand and squeezed it, and said again in my heart: I am for you, and will never desert you.

We came to the entrance and walked down the stone steps to the iron-bound door. We pushed it open, and stood blinking in the dark of the hall. No one was there except four serving men – slaves, they looked to be, and one of them badly lamed – who looked up at us from the firepit which they were cleaning. Without a greeting or nod they went on with their work at the huge pit in the centre of the space. We walked through the hall, its walls bare and smoke-stained, the wood ceiling lost in grime, the floor laying under a foot of straw filthy from discarded bones and nameless debris. At the farthest end was a wood partition with a door, and on it was drawn, in charcoal or some other ashy stuff, the outline of a great black bird, its wings spread, its beak gaping open. Ælfwyn raised her hand to it, and said, "The Raven. It is the sign of the Danes."

I was glad we still wore our clogs, for the straw seemed to crawl beneath our feet. Burginde's dark eyes darted here and there as we made our way into the place, and she snorted in disgust.

"Pigsty!" she hissed out, her hands on her hips. "Such as not seen a broom or a strewing herb for years!"

She turned and called in her shrillest voice to the slaves by the firepit, and finding they understood our speech, exhorted them to turn their efforts to the raking away of the begrimed straw under our feet. The men were thin, with ragged hair and beards, dressed in the meanest of tatters, barely enough to drape their scrawny limbs. They hesitated, and Burginde strode up and caught one by the ear, and shook him soundly.

"Well? Well?" she shrieked, tugging mercilessly, "This is your new Lady before you! Will you or will you not clean this Danish filth?"

The poor fellow, a slight stooped man of five and thirty or so, opened his mouth and grunted a gurgle, horrible to hear. His tongue had been ripped from his throat.

Ælfwyn turned her face away, and Burginde released his ear. The four men looked at us stupidly, the tongueless one shaking. Burginde propped her hands back on her ample hips and glared at them all.

I made bold to speak, for I saw our authority hung in the balance. "Go now, do as you are bid, and make this place fit for your new Lady, and for your Lord's return."

Ælfwyn found voice. "Yes, make it so," she said, waving her hand in dismissal.

Burginde barked, "Rake this filth away and burn it outside, or lay it for the swine, tho' I daresay they lie in better straw then do these Danes! Then, clear that whole firepit, everything out –" she glanced at Ælfwyn, who inclined her head in approval, "and bring all new timber and charcoal. When that is done, and see you do not take all day about it, you great louts, then, when that is done, have clean straw brought in and laid down. I daresay you have no herbs to lay in this savage place, eh?"

Two of the men shook their heads, the other two looked merely stunned.

"Ach!" Burginde ended. "Well?" and the men shuffled off to begin their task.

I caught her hand for a moment and said, "Well done!" and we three women laughed together in the midst of that filthy place.

We climbed the stairs to our chamber, and Ælfwyn went to her purse and drew out a silver piece and handed it to Burginde. "Take this to Dobbe, that she knows that I am pleased with her," she said.

"Ach! You will empty your purse before nightfall," scolded Burginde.

Ælfwyn answered at once. "A newcomer at any place buys with his coin a token of respect. It is fitting that those that shall serve me ever after should have this first small boon of me. Besides," she added, "each coin I give now is one less from the dowry chest."

Even Burginde could find no fault with this, and left on her errand.

JARL AND LORD

L ATE in the afternoon we went downstairs to check on the progress of the hall. The filthy straw was gone, and we gazed in wonder at the floor, newly revealed. It was made up of small pieces of stone coloured red and black, no larger than a man's hand, and set in a rippling pattern that made waves across the floor.

We were pleased, and Ælfwyn looked around the walls and said, "I would have these walls lime-washed that it might be brighter."

Burginde laughed at this, and said we should stay our hands at any further changes save for clearing away filth. But I was glad that Ælfwyn thought this way, for it showed her spirit and pride, and I felt she would not end as had the first bride of Yrling.

We went back up to our chamber, and shortly heard steps on the stair below. Our dinner was come, brought by the young woman Susa from the kitchen yard. We sat down to the meal, welcoming it more for remembering whose hands had made it. As we ate I said, "It is good, is it not, Ælfwyn, to have a friend here?"

Ælfwyn smiled at this, and Burginde said, "A friend in high places is always welcome, and what place be higher than the kitchen?"

Evening came. We heard the men fill the hall below. We had had no word nor message, no sign of when Yrling might come, and Ælfwyn, I knew, did not desire to ask either Sidroc or the smirking Toki. Perhaps he was come now, and even then feasting below. The evening wore on, and we lit more cressets against the dark. The noise and laughter went on below.

Ælfwyn began to pace the length of the room, and I wondered at the difference of her temperament by day and by night. Finally I begged her to sit with me and play, and I set up the gaming bones and we two played.

At length we resolved to sleep; it was too late, he would never come now. So we undressed, and unbraided our hair, and did it in a simple plait for sleeping. Burginde trimmed the cressets, tho' the noise from below was so loud we knew we could not sleep. Still, we got into our beds and bade each other Good-night, and lay in the darkness listening to the roar of the men beneath. It seemed if anything to be growing louder, and not quieting with the hours. I strained my ears, but could not make anything out. Burginde grumbled a complaint in the darkness over the noise and stuffed a pillow over her head. In a few minutes I heard her snore. Ælfwyn lay silently, but I felt surely, with her eyes open.

The noise was awful to hear because we did not know their speech or songs, and it was all the louder now that we ourselves were quiet. It was a mix of shouts, laughter, clattering plates, snatches of song, and oaths. But more than the racket kept me awake. I seemed to feel a rush of troubling fear from the featherbed on which Ælfwyn lay so quietly.

I sat up in the dark. "Ælfwyn?" I asked in a hushed voice, and at once she sat up, her eyes so wide that they showed even in the gloom of our unlit chamber.

At that moment the racket below rose to a furious pitch, and Burginde snorted and muttered. Then came great laughter and stamping sounds, and all three of us were now bolt upright. Heavy boots tramped up the wooden steps leading to our room; three or four men at least. I wrenched my eyes from the door to Ælfwyn's face. It was perfectly white.

"No," she said softly, in almost a whisper, "not now, no."

I threw off my coverlet. The men were now outside on the landing. There was no time to try and relight a cresset; I pulled our mantles from the wall pegs, slipped into mine, and threw Ælfwyn's and Burginde's to them as they clambered out of their beds. Ælfwyn stood with a stricken look by her bed, clutching the mantle around her, her long pale fingers digging into the soft wool. Now the men were just outside the door, laughing and pounding on the stout wood.

One of the voices called out, "Lady! Ælfwyn, Ælfsige's daughter, your Lord is here!" At this there was much laughter, broken off suddenly by a word from one of the men.

All was silent. Ælfwyn took a step towards me and stopped. I drew a breath and tried to still the racing of my heart as I crossed to the door. I called, "Who is it that comes so late to my Lady Ælfwyn's chamber?"

The silence outside the door was unbearable to me. It did not last long. A deep voice broke it, commanding, "Open to Yrling, Jarl and Lord."

What little colour that was left in Ælfwyn's cheeks now fled, but she stood straight and did not waiver. She gave the slightest of nods, and I, with trembling fingers, grasped the iron on the door and pulled it open. Torchlight spilled into the dark chamber, nearly blinding me with its brilliance, and I moved back by Ælfwyn's side.

Three men came into the room, and I saw that one was Toki, and one was Sidroc. The third amongst them strode into the heart of the narrow chamber. So did we first set eyes on Yrling, Lord of Four Stones.

He spoke not, but looked upon us, at the room, and mostly at Ælfwyn. He was perhaps a little above middle height, but not so tall as Sidroc. His chest and arms were of a man far larger, tho', and from his sleeveless leathern tunic the bare brawn of his arms gleamed as if oiled. From his neck hung a single ornament on a chain, and from that first night I never saw him without it. It was a curious design, like a shortened, blunt spearhead hung upside down. The silver from which it was worked shone brightly, and it was covered all over with spirals, like onto our own jewels.

What was most striking, tho', was his bare arms, for he wore this night no linen tunic under his leathern tunic. Coloured designs in red and blue of intertwining serpents were pricked into his arms, the first of such I had ever seen. His hands were large and gloved in short gloves of dark leather, and he wore leathern wrappings about his legs, as if he had returned from battle or the hunt.

His hair was light brown, and like many of the Danish warriors, worn long, past shoulder length and braided in two braids. His eyes were blue and bright and flashed out from a wide brow, and but for a nose which had been badly broken, he might have been a man of high good looks. He had no large scars upon his face, and was, like most of the Danes, clean-shaven. He was beyond youth; I thought him to be more than thirty years of age, but not much more.

His eyes had stopped moving around the room and rested solely on Ælfwyn. She met his gaze for a moment, and then her cheeks flushed crimson and she looked at the floor. He continued to stare at her, a look that was nearly a glare. He made no move towards her in welcome, nor did he speak.

At last she stepped forward, a small step, and without raising her eyes from the floor inclined her head in the smallest of bows.

"Ha!" he said, as if he had won a small challenge. "I see now you can move, but can you speak?" His speech was so heavy with the flat twang of the Danes that it was hard to understand.

"Of course I speak," began the Lady, and I saw that although her head was still down, she was trembling with anger and not fear. "What would you have me say?" she answered more softly.

He looked at her, and then at me. "Some word of welcome, perhaps, for your Lord? Your hus-band?" and he grinned and stressed this word so that Toki's voice rang out in laughter. Sidroc smiled as well, but stilled Toki.

Ælfwyn bowed lower, but spoke to the floor, and tho' her voice was low, in it was much resentment. "Welcome, Lord. I am Ælfwyn, daughter of Ælfsige, reeve of Cirenceaster of the Kingdom of Wessex."

Yrling was not amused this time. "Look at me," he ordered, and Ælfwyn did. "Now you will be Ælfwyn, wife to Yrling, Jarl and Lord." His voice was stern, and he took not his bright eyes from her face.

Ælfwyn's cheek blanched, and she did not move, but kept her eyes fixed on Yrling. Yet for all her steadiness of gaze, I wondered if she saw him at all, but did not rather look past him, as one sight-blinded by a charm.

I feared to speak, yet feared the silence more. I could not see Toki well, for it was he who held the torch, but I looked to Sidroc, who still stood in the doorway. He looked back at me, and then spoke in a measured voice.

"The Lady is tired, uncle, and we have burst upon her and her friends and frightened them, when you only wished to welcome them and thank them for the preparations they have made to greet you."

Yrling said something to Sidroc in their own tongue, and Sidroc answered, and when Yrling looked at us he was smiling once again.

"I will see you tomorrow," he said flatly, and he turned and walked past Toki and Sidroc. We heard his step on the stair before Toki turned to follow him. Sidroc turned last, and looked at me as I wrapped my arm around Ælfwyn's waist. I lowered my head, but felt gratitude just the same.

When all three had gone Burginde went to the door and flung it closed. Ælfwyn stood silently, and then pushed out of my embrace, and sunk down on the edge of the bed. Burginde lit a cresset from the brazier and the little flame danced wildly around the room.

Ælfwyn sat limply with her hands in her lap. I looked at Burginde, but she was still sputtering in anger. I sat down next to Ælfwyn, and as soon as I tried to speak, she flung herself upon the cushions and pounded them with her fists, weeping tears of rage. She went on until her tears came in little short sobs.

Burginde stood before us, wringing her hands, and then turned on her heel and went to the larder chest and brought back a cup of ale.

Ælfwyn looked up for a moment at Burginde's urging. When she saw the offered cup, she sobbed out, "Drink it yourself, or give it me if it be poison."

Burginde shot back, "If it were poison, I would give it to the Dane. But as I would not roast in Hell for the likes of him, we had better fortify ourselves."

And she took a sip of the ale, and handed it to me, and I took a sip, too.

Ælfwyn raised herself from the bed, and wiped her face with her hand. "You are too forward, Nurse, and now you drink from my own cup," she said, but she took it from my hand when I offered it and drank.

"Ach!" protested Burginde. "Me forward? When you greet a Danish jarl thus!" And she began to laugh her deep hearty laugh. "When I saw his face when you answered him! Ah! 'Twas rich!"

Ælfwyn did not smile, but she handed back the cup and pushed the hair out of her eyes. Burginde made much of little, but there was wisdom in her ways, I could see.

The noise below us had died down, but we would not return to our beds so soon. Burginde opened the window shutter and let the cold night air flood the room, and then closed the shutter and fed the hungry brazier with many pieces of charcoal. I combed out Ælfwyn's hair and braided it up again, and we fluffed out our cushions and pillows, and walked up and down the room. All of these things helped to rid the room of the presence of the Danes, and to calm our thoughts. When at last we slipped into our beds, it was late, and I at least was so tired that I fell quickly into the arms of sleep.

OF THE TRIBUTE

WE awakened slowly in the morning, and when Burginde finally rose and went for water the rising Sun slanted in our windows from over the top of the palisade wall. It was a fine day at last, and sharp shadows fell in the yard below. We had washed and were beginning to dress when Susa came up with a steaming bronze ewer.

She dropped a rough curtsey. "'Tis broth from Dobbe; she hopes it pleases you," she said. Her round eyes noted each touch of comfort and colour we had brought into the bare room. She looked back at Ælfwyn. "And the Lord Yrling is awaiting you below. 'Twill be a big day."

"Why do you say that?" asked Ælfwyn quickly.

Susa stared at her, then looked down at her own shoes and gulped. "'Tis the treasure day, Lady."

Ælfwyn nodded her head. I moved to the door. "Thank you, Susa. The broth is most welcome," I said, and Susa scuttled past me, bowing as she went.

Burginde was pouring the broth into cups as I returned to the table. It was rich with fat and had a wonderful savour. "We should start all our days with such good stuff," said Burginde, smacking her lips after the first taste.

"I do not know why we should not," I said. "Dobbe does well to so please you, Ælfwyn, and I think truly wishes to serve you with her heart."

"Aye, the poor soul," added Burginde, "to have anyone take notice of her skill would be a joy to her in this savage place."

Ælfwyn sipped her broth and did not answer.

I thought of what Susa had told us. If the tribute was unloaded, the second waggon would at last be emptied. "Perhaps we will have the looms today," I said.

"Aye, but there be no time for to set them or warp them, if 'tis the marriage day," answered Burginde.

Ælfwyn set down her cup. "There will be no marriage today," she said with firmness. She looked at us and said more gently, "There is no cause for haste. Another day will do as well."

"Aye," nodded Burginde, "tho' the groom be ready, there be no reason to rush." She set down her cup and rubbed her hands together. "But 'tis at least the treasure day, and we must dress."

I put on my russet gown, and tied around my waist the gayest of my thread-work sashes, which has on it pictures I drew in yellow and brown thread of pheasants flying. I combed my hair smooth, and pulled it back with a russet ribband, and lay a fine linen wrap given me by Ælfwyn over my head.

Ælfwyn sat in thought for a moment, and then told Burginde to bring the deep cobalt dress and red mantle from her chests. It was the same she wore the day we had arrived at Four Stones, with no one to look at us but Sidroc and Toki, whose eyes we did not want. She took from her jewel casket all her finest brooches and pins, and chose again the silver one covered with garnets, as it was largest and most beautiful. I combed out her hair so it flowed along her back like a river, and over it she placed her headdress of thin silk. She looked as close to a great queen as I could ever hope to see, but a young and sad one.

We began to hear sounds coming from the hall below; voices and the movement of tables. At last we were ready, and Burginde brought out the small red leathern pouch from where she had been keeping it.

"Here is your pearl; you must wear it," she said as she drew the golden chain from its bag. The pearl appeared, as magnificent again as it was on the evening Toki delivered it.

But Ælfwyn did not take it. "I would not honour his rudeness by wearing it," she said, and gathered up her skirt as if to descend.

Burginde was quick, and blocked the door. She crossed her arms over her breast, and the chain swung from her clenched hand. "Wear it you will, Lady, or you be no daughter of your good mother."

Ælfwyn furrowed her brow and made no move. I held out my hand and Burginde passed the chain to me. "You do not honour his rudeness by so wearing it, but his generosity," I said with stress, "and why then would you not wear a jewel of such beauty?" She seemed to consider this. I went on, "In wearing it, you will please him, but more, you show your own worth in deserving such a treasure."

She reached for the chain and slipped it over her neck. I drew her hair and head-wrap so it fell smoothly once again. Burginde opened the door, and we stepped out on the landing.

We could clearly hear the high fluting voice of Toki, and the calmer, flatter tones of Sidroc.

"Let me go first," I said, "and Burginde will come behind you, that you should enter in some state."

Ælfwyn nodded, and I took my place. We began slowly down the wood steps, and walked into the hall. The great door was open, and daylight came streaming in, and the good light of the Sun fell from the firepit hole. The rippling pattern of the coloured stone floor stood bold before me, and I felt that I stepped onto a red lake.

Toki and Sidroc were indeed in the hall, seated at a large trestle table. Between them sat Yrling, and around them hovered two of the serving men who had swept away the straw yesterday. Food and drink were on the table, and the three Danes were eating. As we walked in, all three looked up, and Toki and Sidroc stopped their talk. Tho' I knew Ælfwyn and Burginde were just behind me, I felt alone as I could not see them, only the steady gaze of the Danes and the dull gape of the serving men as they stood against the wall.

At last when I had almost gained the table I stopped, and Sidroc slowly rose. He stood silently, looking at us, and then Toki looked at Sidroc and rose also, and finally did Yrling rise as well.

It was clear from their dress that this was no common day. Each man wore a leathern tunic with many designs burnt into it, and colour rubbed upon it, and set with many bosses of bronze; and the bare arms of each were adorned with arm-rings and bracelets of silver, beautiful to the eye. On Yrling there were also arm-rings and bracelets of pure gold which dazzled when he moved. And thus arrayed in their strength and richness all three men were in their way wonderful to behold, and amongst them Toki with his yellow hair and darting eyes was the most beautiful, and I thought, the cruellest and worst man.

Now Ælfwyn took a step forward, and bowed her head, but did not speak. Yrling pushed back the bench and came around the table to where we stood. As he did, I saw his eye was caught by the great pearl which now hung freely down from the Lady's throat as she bowed. She straightened, and looked at him, but his first words surprised us all.

"The pearl – how did you get it?" he asked, and his brow creased.

Ælfwyn raised her eyebrows. "Why, I wear it as your gift. Toki delivered it to me on the road here." And she looked in Toki's face, in wonder of what it meant. Toki grinned, and looked at Sidroc, and Sidroc made a slight gesture as he looked back at Yrling.

Yrling nodded his head once, and looked at Ælfwyn. "I had forgot; it was many days ago that I sent Toki with that charge." He smiled broadly, so that his white teeth flashed. "My gift is worn well."

Ælfwyn bowed again and spoke not, and Yrling raised his hand to the table, as an invitation that she should sit with him. At this both Toki and Sidroc began to cross over the floor to where we stood, but Sidroc spoke to Toki and stopped him, and came alone to stand before me. And Ælfwyn sat next to Yrling upon the bench, and I next to Sidroc, and thus did we first sit at meat with the Danes.

Burginde went through a door to the kitchen passage way, and we saw her not until after we had eaten. The plate was fine, for every bowl was bronze, and every platter of bronze too. Yrling drank from a golden goblet, very precious, set all around with blue and green stones, and had placed before Ælfwyn a golden goblet set with rock crystal and stones of jet, so strange and beautiful that I could not take my eyes from it. Ælfwyn too looked much at this cup, and Yrling watched her looking.

Before Sidroc and Toki were placed goblets of silver, rimmed with gold, and also before me was such a goblet placed, and that was the first time I had drunk from gold.

We drank a dark pungent ale and ate porridge made of dried beans mashed; and roasted fowls stuffed with bread; and plates of honeyed dried fruits: apples, pears, and cherries. And through it all the three Danes talked to each other in their own tongue, and as Sidroc was seated between me and Ælfwyn we could not speak to each other in ours. But the food was good, and I ate well, and Ælfwyn ate of it too, but without much relish.

Then Yrling pushed back his cup, and turned to Ælfwyn, and spoke to her in our speech, careful and slow. "We go now to the waggon, and I will accept the tribute that you bring."

Then he spoke to Sidroc, and Sidroc and Toki rose and went out of the hall so that Ælfwyn and I were left alone with Yrling. It was still; the serving men had gone, and I wished that Burginde might come back.

Yrling turned on the bench and looked at us. Like all the Danes, his eye was bold, and he looked upon us with no regard for the boldness of it. But his boldness was more like that of Sidroc than of Toki; for Toki I think looked to shame us, but Yrling and Sidroc looked for the pleasure it gave them, as a man looks at a good horse.

Ælfwyn would not flinch under this stare, but kept her gaze steadily upon his face as he looked first at her and then at me. When his eyes fell upon me thus, I lowered them for just a moment, and then raised the goblet to my lips. From over its gold rim I looked back at him, and he grinned, and picked up his own cup.

"This Lady you have brought with you, she is brave," he said, looking at Ælfwyn. "My sisters' sons tell me of her. It is good you are not alone." He looked over to me. "Toki wants you, but he wants all women, and all women want Toki. Sidroc is a better choice."

Ælfwyn wrapped her fingers around the stem of her beautiful goblet and spoke. "The Lady seeks not a husband."

Yrling laughed. "And Toki seeks not a wife!" he said.

I felt my face burn, and Ælfwyn looked at me and back to Yrling. She spoke with care. "My Lord, this Lady is my friend, and came here of her own will. I desire her company, and do not wish to have her driven away. But I myself will send her away if she be not safe under my own husband's roof." These last words she said softly, and looking full into Yrling's face.

For reply he only smiled, and reached out and took the pearl in his hand. He held it, and looked at her, and I looked away.

"She will be safe, as you yourself are safe, for no one would touch that which is of Yrling," he said, and he let slip the pearl from his grasp so that it fell gently against Ælfwyn's breast.

Then he stood, and we stood with him, and followed him out of the hall and into the light of the yard. I looked with relief to see Burginde come around the corner from the kitchen yard, and she joined us on the stone step.

Sidroc and Toki stood before the waggon, and many Danes, both warriors and workmen, were standing all about. Yrling came to the waggon, and jumped in one move unto the waggon board. He raised his arms and spoke to the men, and they cheered and raised their arms to him. Then he spoke more, and turned and pointed to Ælfwyn, and she took a step forward and inclined her head, but did not smile. He turned back and pulled open the tarpaulin flaps, and a great cheer came forth from the men.

And this was the way the Dane accepted his tribute: he opened chest after chest within the waggon, and took out what was in it, and held it before the men so that they cheered and beat their hands against their thighs, and laughed the laugh of triumph. He held up dishes of silver; and bracelets of gold; and huge pots of bronze, gorgeously worked; and ewers which might hold rare oils or scents, I could not tell. He pulled out length after length of cloth of purple, and held it before the men so that they whistled and hooted; and then he lifted a small casket, and looked into it, and dipped his hand and showed what the hand held: pieces of gold, newly minted and very bright. At this the men whistled and cheered the more, and then Yrling turned to where we stood, and pointed again to Ælfwyn, and the men cheered. And I heard in his speech the names 'Ælfsige' and 'Ælfwyn', and that was all I could make out.

Then he jumped down, and came to where Sidroc and Toki stood, fresh-faced from laughter and cheers. Sidroc called to two men, and together with them Sidroc and Toki began to carry the treasure into the hall. Yrling stood by us as they did this, and as the waggon emptied, the gathered men drifted off. We saw the looms in the back of the waggon, and Ælfwyn turned to Yrling and said, "I would have my looms so that we might work."

Yrling nodded, and called to one of the men, pointing out the looms. As they were carried past us, Ælfwyn saw a large plain chest in the waggon. "And that chest, too; for it holds my wool and thread," she said.

Yrling spoke to the men, and the chest followed the looms into the hall and up the stairs.

When the waggon was emptied Yrling turned, and we trailed after into the hall. He strode across the floor to the wood partition at the far end, and the open door told us that this was where the treasure had been brought.

This then, would be the chamber in which Ælfwyn would sleep. Men were setting chests on the floor as we walked in, but soon they were done, and only Sidroc remained with Yrling. The room was square, and had a single window set high on one wall so that only the sky showed. The new chests were crowded up against each other, and I saw that there was already a number of wood chests and barrels before these had come. The walls were bare; one peg held Yrling's leathern baldric, and from it hung a carved wooden sheath stained black that carried a sword with a gold hilt.

There was a torch holder on the wall, and a round bronze mirror, highly polished, hung near it; and that was all that was upon the walls. There was no furniture save one bench and a low rush bed, hardly better than a pallet.

Yrling said, "Now we will wed."

Ælfwyn jerked her head. "I will not wed today," she said flatly, but her eyes flared as if in fear.

Sidroc shifted his position and looked at her. "You are come here to be wed," he said quietly.

She looked first at him, and then at me. She said, "I cannot wed without a holy man to bless me. I must have a priest."

Sidroc dropped his hands. "There are none of your priests here, nor for many miles. It cannot be done."

She raised her eyes and looked at Sidroc. "Then I cannot wed."

During all of this Yrling watched closely the face of Ælfwyn, and his own face showed his anger.

I stepped forward, and spoke to Sidroc. "Sir," I said, "there must be a monk or brother nearby. Please to find him so that my Lady's wedding may be a happy one." I felt I could barely speak these last words.

Sidroc looked into my face and smiled his slow smile, and then looked again at Ælfwyn.

Yrling spoke now, and spoke to Sidroc. "Look for such a man. If he can be found before tomorrow noon, let him be present." Then he turned to Ælfwyn. "If not, she will wed without him."

Ælfwyn stood without moving, as if she counted the hours. I bowed my head and murmured, "Thank you, my Lord, thank you, Sir." I touched Ælfwyn by the hand, and we turned and walked across the rippling stone floor to the steps leading up to our chamber.

THE TRIBUTE DINNER

WHEN we entered our room we found Burginde huffing and straining as she heaved her body against a large chest in the middle of the floor. "Simple heads!" she cried. "Why could they not put it against the wall as they did the looms?"

Together we pushed the chest out of the way. Ælfwyn sat down at the table, and Burginde brought us water so we might wash our hands; and brought ale too. The Sun came in strongly at the windows, and made the room bright; and with all the comforts from the waggon, it seemed at last a pleasant place.

We sat in silence for some time. At last Burginde spoke from her stool by the brazier. "If you are not wed today, then you will be tomorrow; what gown and mantle will you wear?"

Ælfwyn looked into her cup and shrugged her shoulders. "I do not care. The red, or yellow; it matters not."

Burginde clucked her tongue. "You cannot marry in yellow, 'tis bad luck and brings a stillborn child." Ælfwyn made no response, and Burginde went on, "Choose the red. Your mother did, and it brought her good luck, and at last good babies."

Again Ælfwyn was silent, but her lip trembled, and she lowered her eyes. Burginde was warming her hands over the brazier, and could not see that tears now flowed down her mistress' face.

I reached my hand across the table and touched her wrist. "Lady," I said, "how can I help you?"

She shook her head and kept her eyes steadfast on her cup, but her tears flowed faster than ever. Burginde turned on her stool and saw this, and looked at her with pity.

"I – I am afraid," whispered Ælfwyn, and she clenched her hands upon the table top, and her shoulders began to shake.

Burginde got up and came to the table. "If it be the wedding night that frights you, do not worry; 'twill be unpleasant, but 'tis soon over; and if it hurts too much, begin to cry, and he will take you more gently."

At these words Ælfwyn covered her face with her hands and began to sob, and the tears squeezed out from between her clenched fingers in little streams. She laid her head down upon the table and buried it in her shaking arms as she wept.

Burginde knelt down at her mistress' hem, and touched her shoulder, and said, "And if ye be not a maiden, do not fear; he will most likely be drunk, and men can never tell."

Ælfwyn lifted her face from her arms and said, "Of course I be a maid! I would I were not!" And her voice was choked with anger and with tears.

"Come, come," chided Burginde, but in her gentlest voice. "'Twill be as nothing, and we must all face it. And tho' the first time be bad, the others be much better." She sat back on her heels and went on. "I cared for a boy once, and met him in every hay rick as I could, for I grew to like it very much. But when I was got with his child, he would not wed me, for the smith's daughter had her eye on him too, and he wed her. So 'twas no loss to me, for he was false, and I could have married the baker's boy even then. But I did not wed at all, for up in the big house your good mother was carrying you, and she had had two babes before you, which had died, and with them she had a poor time getting milk enough, and so she took me in; and my little babe died when not two days old, so you had both your mother and me to suckle you."

Ælfwyn's sobs had quieted, and now she turned to where her nurse sat crouched. Tho' her face wore the stain of tears, she blinked her eyes in surprise at this story.

Burginde laughed and touched Ælfwyn's cheek. "And how else did you think I came to you with my paps full of milk, when you were first a babe?"

Ælfwyn blushed, and lowered her head.

"So you see," finished Burginde, "it all comes right in the end, or mostly so, if you give it half the chance."

Ælfwyn was silent, but Burginde saw that she had her mistress' ear and added, "And believe me, when you have a babe in your arms you will like your husband more, or at least not mind him so, for the babe will mean more to you than any one thing, so that all else fades."

We stayed in all that afternoon, tho' it continued fair, for Ælfwyn would not go down into the yard to be gawked at. No one came to tell us that a holy man had been found, and the day began to fade. Susa came back, and we three looked at her hard, and Ælfwyn caught her breath; but she had only come to say that Yrling wanted us at table that night.

After Susa left Ælfwyn said, "I will not go; tell him I am unwell."

Burginde was quick with her answer. "Ach! Go you will, and eat and drink, for would you show such weakness to the Dane?"

I too thought it best that she go down, and said, "Lady, she is right, and since you have come here you have shown nothing but pride and courage to these men. And in having started so well, it is best to see much of him, and so grow used to him, is it not?"

She looked at me and said, "I will go, since you make my pride the point of it." And she smiled, the first I had seen all day.

I laughed and said, "What was it that Osred said? 'The goose rules the gander, and she be twice as quick'? Today you have already squawked loud and well!"

When it had grown dark we heard the men come into the hall, and we went down together. There were many tables set up in the hall, at least eight long ones, at which sat ten or more men each; and the longest table was the one by the wall at which sat Yrling with Sidroc and Toki on either side. A great fire blazed up in the firepit, and all the torches upon the walls were lit. The food had not come yet, but the men were noisy with their ale, and leaned back from the benches to shout to those at other tables. One cuffed a serving man so that he dropped the ewer he was carrying, and the ale ran across the floor, wetting the straw and making the rippling pattern in the stone glisten.

We walked around this, and the men paid us no mind, and only when we reached the table of Yrling did anyone look up or greet us, for Sidroc once again rose. He smiled, and Toki glanced up from his cup and grinned, but did not rise. Then Yrling stood, and the other Danes, five or six, who sat also at this table rose; and so Toki also rose up to greet us. I was made glad by this, that the bold Toki was forced in this way to show us respect.

When we had come to the table, Burginde went out through the door, for there were no women in the hall of her rank, and it was clear she would not wish to stay with the serving men at the firepit. So she left us with a bow, and went on.

Again Ælfwyn sat by Yrling's side, and again was placed before her the beautiful gold goblet set with rock crystal and jet. It was filled with ale by a serving man, and she took it up at once, and drunk deep, and looked into the bottom of her cup. So I knew from this she would dull her pain by these means, and that the Dane saw this.

The hall was noisy with men, and I thought it the more so since the tribute had been shown that day. When the food came it quieted, and tho' I tried not to look at him Sidroc spoke to me as we ate.

He saw me looking at Ælfwyn, and he began, "Your Lady is beautiful; it is more than my uncle expected."

"Thank you," I said. I thought to be silent, but saw I might learn something of value. I looked at him, and he smiled, and the scar on his cheek went crooked as it always did when he smiled. "Then your uncle will be good to her," I said.

He smiled more. "She will have all she wants, if she be good in return," he answered, looking towards her.

"She is very good," I answered heartily. "I can tell you that."

But he only turned back to me and laughed as if I had said something of great humour. "Ha!" he said, and slapped the table with his hand. "I think she will be!"

Now my face grew hot for I thought I had misspoke. I felt anger at myself, but anger too at these sly men who seemed always to want to shame us.

I thought of the morning and of how Yrling had questioned the pearl that Ælfwyn wore. I looked up at Sidroc, and then lowered my eyes. "You gave Toki the pearl, did you not?" I asked.

His voice grew quiet. "Yes, I did. Yrling would never think of such a thing."

"Then it was given falsely," I said, and I raised my eyes to his for a moment.

"No, it was not, for she would have had it sooner or later by Yrling's hand. And it did much good, to come on the road as a welcome gift."

This angered me, and I turned to him. "A gift given falsely never does good."

"Ha!" he said, and tho' I looked down, he brought his face close to mine. "Did you not all remark over it when you saw it? Did you not squeal with delight? Did you not talk of the richness of it, or the generosity of Yrling?"

I said nothing, but he went on, and the scorn had left his voice. "Things cannot always be as we would have them, shield-maiden. Your Lady knows this, I know this, and even Yrling will one day know this."

I did not know what to say to such words; and I wondered why he spoke so of Yrling.

Then Toki called over to him, and the two began to speak in a jesting way in their own tongue, and Yrling spoke with them also. Ælfwyn and I looked at each other but did not speak, for the three Danes knew our tongue, so there was nothing we wished to say. Ælfwyn raised her goblet again, and I saw that she had eaten almost nothing. Yrling stopped his jesting and looked at Ælfwyn by his side. Then did he reach out his hand for the pearl as it lay upon her breast and take it up in his grasp and hold it. He smiled upon Ælfwyn so that her face flamed. I looked away and as I did, the shudder that ran through Ælfwyn ran through me as well.

When the platters of food were cleared away Ælfwyn asked Yrling that we might return to our chamber, for, she said, she was weary and would rest. He nodded his head without looking at her. The talk between he and Sidroc and Toki which had occupied them for many minutes continued as we rose and picked our way through the hall. This talk was not the jesting speech which the Danes so often used, but dark and grave in tone; and Sidroc talked much and Yrling listened, and Toki scoffed and said things in heat as he often did. The other men at the table listened and also spoke, but the drinking and jesting went on just the same throughout the hall.

We went up the steps and closed our door on the noise below. I fed the brazier with more coals, and we got into our beds, but we left a cresset burning. I lay in the dark watching it cast its dancing light upon the walls. Ælfwyn was quiet, and she had eaten little but drunk much ale, and I thought her to be weary and wanting sleep. I thought of all we had seen and heard that day; and I thought too how tomorrow Ælfwyn would not ascend to the chamber with me, but go at day's end with Yrling to the room behind the wooden partition, and there amidst all the treasure she had brought pass from being maiden to wife.

Then I slept, but did not know how much time passed. I awoke in the dark to hear Ælfwyn groan, and hear her panting and tossing. Burginde arose and went to her as I lit the cresset from the brazier coals. Ælfwyn moaned and lay with her head off the bed, calling that she would be sick, and I reached for a wash basin and gave it to Burginde as Ælfwyn began to retch. Burginde placed the basin on the floor beneath Ælfwyn's head, and Ælfwyn cried out and retched, and her nurse soothed her and stroked her hair.

"Ach! You poor lamb, 'tis all gone right to your stomach, the jitters and all. Let it all come out; you will soon be put to rights." Burginde turned to me and said, "She has always had a tender stomach, and likely to upset; 'tis nothing." She turned back to her mistress, cooing and soothing.

I thought to bring water, that Ælfwyn might rinse her mouth and wipe her face. I went to the bucket but there was scarce any left. I poured it into a cup and said to Burginde, "Here is a bit of water; I will go and bring more."

Burginde turned her head and said, "There be a drawing well in the passage between the hall and the kitchen yard; the same as you see me go through when you sit at table with the Danes."

I nodded my head, and pulled on the russet gown I had worn. I slipped on my felt night shoes, glad that they were quiet, for I did not look forward to going below to the hall where slept the Danes. I opened the door, and crept out of the room as quietly as I could.

No noise came from below. I could not tell what time it was, only that all was still. I groped my way down the steep stair. I began to turn into the hall and was jolted by the sight of two men stretched upon the very steps of the iron-wrapped door of the hall. They were sound asleep, and lying as they were, no one could enter the hall through the door unbidden and in surprise.

I collected my wits and entered the body of the hall. The blaze in the firepit had burnt down to coals which still flared brilliant red. Shadows were cast across the floor and upon the lower portions of the walls. Some of the Danes were lying near the fire, asleep on straw pallets. Other men lay along the sides of the walls, and some slept on benches. By their sides lay their swords in their sheaths. The sounds of their snores filled my ears, and covered, I hoped, the sound of my own breathing. Some of the men tossed and snorted in their sleep. I looked upon them. What if one should awaken and think me an intruder? What if one grabbed me?

I shook these thoughts out of my mind. I recalled the timber hall of Cedd, my father's brother, and how his men had slept with him in just this way. I took a breath and went on, stepping as carefully as I knew how.

Now I was close to the door of the passageway I sought, and close also to the table at which Yrling and Sidroc and Toki always sat. Along the wall I saw a pallet upon which Toki slept, for his yellow hair was bright even in the dimness of the hall. Next to him was a pallet upon which a man slept, perhaps Sidroc to guess from the length of his form; his face was turned away. I did not see Yrling, but only an empty pallet, and I grew fearful that he himself might return to the hall from the latrine or some such place and find me. I went with haste towards the passageway. As I was about to step into it, a creaking noise from the other side of the hall made me turn my head. The door to the treasure room of Yrling was opening, and out of it came the serving woman Susa. Her hair was mussed and she was dressed only in a shift. She left the door open behind her, and as she did so I ducked into the passageway.

I peeped out and saw her come directly towards me, and then saw Yrling, clad in a linen tunic, come out of the room behind her. He too came towards me where I hid, but stopped at the empty pallet and yawned as he lay himself down.

Then I pulled back, for Susa was nearly upon me. When she turned into the passage I pressed myself up against the wall and held my finger over my lips. She walked in and saw me and was startled, so that she gave a little gasp, but she did not cry out. She looked at me with her round eyes starting from her face, and then turned over her shoulder to see if her gasp had alerted anyone. No sound came. She turned back to me but would not raise her face, and only clutched her hands over her bare arms. She was very frightened, and I felt pity for her fear; and tho' I felt also anger and contempt, it was not for her, but for the Dane.

I touched her arm and gave her a little push. She fled through the passageway towards the kitchen yard. I stood still and listened. After many minutes had passed I looked out and saw that Yrling slept. I filled my bucket and passed back out of the hall of the sleeping Danes.

When I entered our room Burginde called out, "Good stars above! Where have you been?"

Ælfwyn was sitting up, and looked weak and pale, but her retching had stopped.

I brought the bucket to Burginde and said, "I am sorry; I went slowly so no one would wake." And as I said this I yearned to tell them of what I had seen, but knew I would not, for it would do no good, and perhaps much harm, to so betray Susa.

Ælfwyn bathed her face and hands, and said she felt better and sleepy, but asked that we might leave the cresset burning. We did so, and we all lay down again, and sleep came once more.

SHUTTLE AND SWORD

IN the morning another serving woman brought us broth, and not Susa; and Burginde remarked on this but I said nothing. Burginde brought forth for Ælfwyn the red gown she had spoken of. It was beautiful to see, for it was of silk, and had a fineness of weave and brightness of colour that made it shimmer before the eye. With this she wore her blue mantle trimmed with marten fur, and a thin yellow silk head-dress like the wing of a honeybee.

I combed her hair so it once again flowed down her back, and left it loose as a bride's should be. For her brooch she chose the plainest of her golden pins, but the choice was right, for the simple circle of gold sat upon the red cloth as if the silk itself was a great ruby. And she wore no rings upon her fingers, nor any bracelets upon her wrists, and somehow looked the richer for it.

I braided up my hair for today I did not want it loose; its colour was too bright. I put on my good green gown and grey mantle. As I fastened a pewter brooch at my neck, Ælfwyn went to her jewel casket and drew out a silver disk set with green stones, and pressed it into my hand, saying, "Take and wear this brooch as my gift to you, for the emerald stones suits your eyes, and I would have you wear it for love of me."

I kissed her and we embraced, and I wore the silver brooch henceforth.

We did not wait to be called into the hall, but went down soon as we were dressed. I again walked before Ælfwyn, but when we came into the hall, no tables were set up. No one was there save Toki and a few other Danes, and the serving men who were at work building up the fire.

I turned to Ælfwyn to see what she wished to do. Toki stood by a far wall, talking to the Danes, and took no notice of us.

"I would not go back up," she said. "Let us go outside and have some air."

We walked out through the open door of the hall. The bright day foretold Winter's end. I felt glad for it, and glad this wedding day was not a wet and dark one.

As we stood there Sidroc and Yrling appeared from around the corner which led towards the gate. They were walking fast. Yrling was speaking as if in anger, and Sidroc had his hand on Yrling's arm, as if trying to calm him. Both men spoke loudly, and Yrling stopped and turned to Sidroc and they spoke more quietly, and Sidroc spoke at length. Yrling seemed to consider, and then spoke slowly to Sidroc. Both men looked satisfied, and continued on towards us.

They were still talking when they came up to the door. Sidroc looked at us as if he had just seen us, and stopped.

"I have found a holy man. He will be here at noon," he said to Ælfwyn, and then he and Yrling brushed by us, still talking, as if we were not there. They disappeared down the steps and into the hall, and Ælfwyn closed her eyes and lifted her chin as if she had been slapped.

She stood for a moment, and then turned and went down the steps through the door, and up the wooden stair to our chamber. We were just behind her, but when we reached the landing outside our door I stopped, for Burginde had touched my hand. She peered in the room, and came out again, and together she and I walked down the stair.

"She needs to be alone a bit; 'tis a hard time for any bride, but most so for her, being unwilling," she said. "And of course the Dane be all agog over her one moment, and pays her no mind the next."

We stood at the bottom of the stair, and went to the doorway where we might stand in the Sun.

"Burginde," I said, for I felt someone must know, "last night when I went to fetch the water I saw the serving girl Susa with Yrling, and they came from the treasure room, and she wore naught but her shift."

Burginde clucked her tongue, but did not seem surprised. "Ach! Poor hussy; she has but little choice," she said, "and it will probably end tonight. I will not say a word, but I am glad you told me."

We walked back into the hall. "It must be close to the time," she said, and we went up the stairs.

The door to our chamber was still open, and Ælfwyn sat within at the table. The full skirt of her red gown fell about her feet like a crimson pool.

"Would you like me to see if the holy man is here?" I asked. "Perhaps you would like to speak to him alone?"

She answered without raising her eyes. "I do not care about the holy man. I only asked for him to delay what cannot be delayed."

"Yes, I know," I said, as gently as I could. "But perhaps he can give you some comfort or counsel."

"There is no comfort for me," she said, "and my only counsel is to do what must be done."

There was no answer to this, for she had already heard everything, first from her parents, then from Burginde, and then from me as well.

"Perhaps one day there will be comfort for you," I said at last. "No one will deserve it more."

We heard a step at the bottom of the stair, and I rose and looked from the landing. Yrling himself stood at the bottom, holding in his hands a small casket of some kind. He was dressed as he had been last night, with all manner of gold and silver bracelets and arm-rings. He wore his leathern tunic, but also his baldric, and the gold hilt of his sword shone above the black scabbard.

I was surprised to see him, and looked at him for a moment before I remembered myself, and dipped my head to him. He came up the stairs, and I did not know if I should stay or go.

I looked in the room and said to Ælfwyn, "It is the Lord Yrling," and Ælfwyn rose from her chair.

He stepped into the room, and looked about it, which was his way, and then looked at Ælfwyn. The casket in his hands was made of ivory or bone, and it was precious, for it was carved all around with figures and animals, and it carried runes upon it.

I looked on it and guessed that it was stolen, or perhaps come in the tribute from Ælfsige; and I wondered for a moment – I do not know why – if some terrible thing might be within it.

Ælfwyn bowed, and her pale cheek turned paler, but she raised her eyes to this man who she would soon wed. He held the casket out to her. She looked at him with questioning eyes, and looked also as if she were afraid to touch it.

He spoke to her at last. "I bring you my wedding gift," he said, and again held it out so that she was forced to take it.

She lifted it in her hands and set it upon the table. She looked down at it, and then at him, and tho' he did not smile or speak, he seemed to bid her, Open it.

She placed her hand upon the lid, and the ivory of the chest was the same as the ivory of her pale fingers. She lifted the lid and looked in and caught her breath.

I could see only a glimmer of gold, and took a step closer. She dipped her hands into the gold and brought forth a necklace that had many golden disks strung together with golden links, and each of the disks of gold had a different gem set in it, so that the whole necklace was alive with bright colour. And she brought forth also from this casket two bracelets, one for either wrist. Each had gem stones set in disks of gold and joined by golden links.

She held up these things and looked at Yrling, and it was clear she was moved by the worth of the jewels. "These are beautiful," she said softly. "The nephew of Yrling has chosen well." And she looked at him full in the face.

I did not believe her boldness. Yrling stepped towards her and I thought for a moment he would truly strike her.

He did not, tho' his blue eyes stormed; but just smiled a hard smile. He stared at her. "It was Sidroc who thought to send you the pearl; but the pearl was always mine. These also are mine, and it is I who give them freely to you." In his voice was a terrible warning, and threat. "Perhaps instead I should give you to Sidroc."

Ælfwyn still held the golden necklace and bracelets in her hands, and her fingers had clenched around them. She lowered her eyes, and then let fall the jewels back into the ivory casket.

"Forgive me, my Lord," she murmured, "I have been unwell, and most unwise."

She said no more, but knelt down in front of him and bowed her head.

I looked at him standing before her, and saw how in her beauty she had humbled herself before him; and I saw again the plain unkempt Susa, and thought that he who had pleasured himself with a serving woman last night would today wed a Lady such as Ælfwyn.

He kept his eyes fixed upon her bowed head, and she moved not. He raised his eyes from her and looked at me, and said hoarsely, "Bring a spindle, or a weaving comb of this Lady's."

I looked at Burginde, and she went with me to the wooden chest that had come with the looms. We opened it, and on the top was a basket with shuttles and combs. One of the bone shuttles was charged with a small amount of blue wool. I took it to Yrling, and held it out to show him.

"This is, I think, what is wanted, my Lord," I said.

He nodded and I lifted Ælfwyn by the hand so that she once again stood before him. I broke off a short length of the blue yarn it held, and then placed the shuttle in her right hand. She clutched it to her breast, but her hand was steady.

Yrling drew off the silver ornament he always wore, the one which looked like a blunted spear point, and placed it with its chain over the head of Ælfwyn. Then with both of his hands he pulled his gold-hilted sword out of the black sheath that held it. He turned the hilt so that she might grasp it, and the Lady took the heavy sword in her right hand. As she did she held out to Yrling the bone shuttle, and he took it in his right hand.

He reached out his left hand, and she reached out hers, and he clasped his large brown hand over her slender white one, and held together their joined hands before them. Then did I take the length of blue yarn, and bind it round their wrists twice, and in this simplest of ways were they Hand-fasted.

They spoke not; exchanged no vows, only the tools by which they lived, as was the ancient way of my people.

I unwound the yarn from their wrists, and gave it to Ælfwyn, as it is the woman's charge to preserve the thread unbroken; and she gave back to Yrling his sword, and he to her the shuttle.

When he had put his sword back into its sheath he took the silver ornament from off Ælfwyn's neck and placed it once again around his own. Then he turned to the jewel casket and drew out the golden necklace he had brought, and himself placed it around her throat. And she took up the bracelets and put them on, and the gold upon her glimmered and danced upon the brilliant red of her gown.

Then he turned and walked out of the room, and we three women followed him down the wooden stair.

LORD AND LADY

OUTSIDE upon the first stone step Sidroc and Toki stood. Between them was a stooped, bald man in a shabby brown surplice; a man of Lindisse, perhaps, for I could understand his speech; and by the looks of him a lay-preacher. Upon his chest a simple wooden cross hung from a leathern cord. He had a high pitched, sheep-like voice, and was talking ceaselessly to the two Danes. They regarded him not, and stood looking out over the yard. The man in the surplice turned to look at Yrling as he came through the open door, and finally fell silent.

Yrling spoke to Sidroc, and the three Danes spoke for several minutes while we women and the lay-preacher stood watching. Then Yrling stopped talking, and he and Sidroc turned around, and Yrling looked at the preacher.

"What do you want to say?" he demanded. "Say it."

The preacher began to splutter, and looked from Ælfwyn to Yrling. But Ælfwyn's voice was calm. "My Lord and I have Hand-fasted. I would that you bless me in this undertaking."

Yrling looked his approval upon her. The preacher stood before them, and said, "May you be blest in this

147

union, and your Lord be a source of protection and strength to you, and you to him. And may your children walk in the path of truth. Amen."

And save for this last word, he spoke no word of Latin, but did raise his arm over them and make a tolerable Sign of the Cross.

Yrling put his hand over Ælfwyn's, and led her back into the hall. Sidroc and Toki followed them, but I turned to the preacher still upon the step.

"Brother," said I, "If you will wait a moment, I will see that you have food and drink before you start on your way."

At this Burginde nodded her head, and walked in a brisk way towards the kitchen yard gate.

I regarded the man more carefully. He had watery blue eyes, and skin deeply creased from weather; and his cheeks were as stubbly with grey prickles as his head was bare. "Tell me where you are from, for my Lady and I were told that no holy man yet lived near here," I began.

"That is so," he answered in his quavering voice, "and the Abbey of Lindisse is no more rubble now than yonder chapel." Here he gestured across the yard.

"And yet you live," I said.

"Yes, I live; tho' better men by far did not. I be a simple Watcher, and have no learning as the monks of Lindisse were famed for; still, I hoped to serve by my solitude and prayer. 'Twas that solitude that saved me; I was in my forest retreat when the Danes laid siege to this place; only later did I see what had been wreaked upon the folk of this land. Now I must go out in the world, and wander, and do what good as I can, for the folk have no other, and too soon will slide into heathen ways if they have but heathen ways before them."

"Yet you fear not the Danes that killed so many Brothers?" I asked.

"I fear them, but the killing frenzy is over in them; they have won this place, and they fear not and know not the True Word, and so take as little notice of such as me as if we were flies upon their horses' backs."

I thought a moment. "And the folk of Lindisse, they be all Christian?"

He rubbed his bristly chin. "They be nearly all Christian, in some degree. Few still go to the groves, for the Holy Men worked hard and long to conquer that evil."

I could not stop my answer. "Do not call it evil. Those who go to the groves seek peace as much as those who worship in chapels and chantrys."

His jaw dropped, and I felt ashamed of my answer, for who was I to so speak to a Brother, even if he be a solitary?

"Forgive me, Brother, for my speech; I too once worshipped in the groves, and tho' I later lived with the Black Monks, I cannot believe that what I did was evil."

He looked at me closely, "No, 'twas not evil for you, being but a child. 'Twas the fault of those that led you to that error."

But here I wished he had said nothing, for I could allow no harsh word to pass against my kinsman; nor could I say aught against the Prior who had taken me in and taught me different prayers to say and given me the arts of wax and ink.

I was spared any further speech, for Burginde now came back, bearing a cloth tied up as a pack in one hand, and a pottery cup in the other.

"'Tis good strong ale, drink it down, good Brother," she said, passing him the cup, "and then best be on your way. Inside is supper for tonight and tomorrow too, for when the cook heard a man of the cloth wanted feeding, she stinted not."

The preacher bobbed his head and took a mouthful of the ale.

"O! And Dobbe, the cook, that is, asks that you regard her in your prayers," finished Burginde.

I glanced back at the open door to the hall. I could hear men's voices coming from within, and the scraping sounds of tables being set upon their trestles.

"I must go in and join my Lady," I said, and took the hand of the preacher. "I thank you for your blessing of her, and bid you to return here as you can, for she may find need of comfort such as you can bring."

"I will be back, and keep all three of you Ladies in my humble prayers, and the good Dobbe will know no end of my praise," he said, hoisting the pack to measure its heft.

So we said Fare-well, and Burginde and I went down the steps into the hall.

Ælfwyn and Yrling were seated at the long table, and serving men were heaping coals upon the fire, and carrying bronze ewers about. One of the Danes went into the passageway where the well was, and came back with a large brass gong, near as large as a shield, and held the gong in one hand and a wooden beater in another. He struck the gong, and it made a deep and yet bright sound that echoed through the hall, and all the Danes laughed as he struck it again and again

Burginde went and stood at the firepit, for she would not miss her mistress' wedding feast; and I walked to the table, and since Sidroc was not there, I knew I must sit next to Toki.

But before I sat I went to Ælfwyn, and leaned over her and kissed her on both cheeks, and she embraced me. My heart was filled with love for her, and since she had no kin here, I must alone let her know that I wanted her happiness in this thing. We clasped hands, and smiled at each other, and tears glistened in both our eyes, but I laughed and kissed her again.

I did not know what to say to Yrling, and so said simply, "My Lord, I wish you joy." I bowed, and he smiled on me a smile without scorn, and for the first time I saw him as a man and not just as a Dane.

Men began to come in from the yard, and the serving men ran to and fro. Toki leaned on the table with his elbows, and called out to the other men in the hall, and looked by turns amused and bored. When I sat next to him he brought his face close to mine and whispered, "Yrling has the first of his brides. I think Toki should have the second."

I resolved not to feel anger, for this was my Lady's wedding day; and I would treat all he or Sidroc said as an innocent jest. I turned to him in surprise. "You mean you do not know the Lady's twin sister comes to wed you tonight?"

He jerked his head back, and his mouth twisted.

"O yes," I went on, "Yrling has it all arranged."

His eyes bulged, but here I could not keep on with my jest, and began to laugh.

He narrowed his eyes, but laughed also. Then he covered my hand with his own. "You are good, Lady, and show the same spirit as does Yrling's mare."

I did not know if Ælfwyn was the mare he spoke of, but I liked not his speech nor his tone, and regretted my jest. I slipped my hand away and put it in my lap, where he would dare not follow it.

Sidroc came to the table, and I looked up and said to him, "Sir, come with me to bid my Lady joy in her marriage," and I rose and left Toki open-mouthed as I took the hand Sidroc offered.

As we stepped away Sidroc smiled down at me, and said, "Toki will be angry that you prefer my hand to his."

I said, "You do not fear his anger; and for Toki any woman's hand would do as well."

Sidroc tossed back his head and laughed. "Your eyes are as sharp as your tongue."

And tho' I could not like him, I was glad that I stood with Sidroc and not with Toki as we came before Yrling and Ælfwyn.

Now all cups were filled, and Yrling raised his golden goblet to the men, and spoke to them, and drank. They jumped to their feet, and cheered. He raised his goblet a second time, and held up the hand of Ælfwyn, and spoke her name, and the men cheered and drank again.

Ælfwyn took her golden goblet, and lifted it to Yrling, and the men cheered even more. And never had I heard spoken in any tale of a bride honouring her husband this way, but knew that Ælfwyn did this through her courage and her will to please him.

Please him it did, and please all the Danes; and Yrling looked at her with eyes full of light. We all sat, and Sidroc led me to sit next to Ælfwyn, so that Yrling was on one side of us and Sidroc the other, of which I was glad.

The food came, and it was this: wheaten loaves, split and hollowed, and served as trenchers filled with a golden stew of fowl, like onto browis; and whole sides of roast pig, set about with roasted onions and turnips; and then a sweet porridge of wheat and honey and ground apples.

And there were two kinds of ale, the nut brown kind of every day, and after we had eaten, a sweeter, stronger brew, almost like mead, but not. I asked Sidroc what it was and he said it was made from oats mixed with barley.

All through the meal I sat next to Ælfwyn, with Sidroc on my other side, and tho' the Lady and I did not speak often, I felt much pleasure in her company. Yrling spoke to her at times, and I felt all was not lost with her, and that she might know some content in this life.

Then Yrling called out to Toki, and Toki laughed and went to the treasure room. He came back with a small wooden harp in his hands. Toki sat upon the table by Yrling, and began to pluck at the strings. It gave a low, thrilling sound; and Toki began to sing, and his voice had in song a sweetness it never had in speech.

I did not know what he sang of, but the tune was tender and slow, and could not have been of war, but of love, or sorrow and loss. When he sang all looked at him and could not look away, for such was the beauty of his voice and face. I looked at him and saw why many women would want him, but seeing him so made me like him less and not more, for it seemed all part of his lie. I glanced at Ælfwyn and saw that her eyes were hardened as she watched, and that no song from Toki could overtake her hate for him. Then I looked at Yrling, and saw how he looked at Toki, with eyes full of pleasure, and felt for one instant a great fear of the danger that was in Toki.

The song ended, and my fear passed. Toki sang another tune, fast and gay, and then handed the harp to another, who sang, and then another. Many men sang, some with the harp and some without.

Then one man with fair hair was pushed and pulled by his fellows to stand before us. Laughing he took from out his tunic three flat rings of brass, about the size of apples, and tossed them one, two, and three into the air above his head, and touched them so lightly that they never fell to the floor but stayed in motion above him in a never-ending circle. This I liked much, and had never seen done before, and I laughed and clapped my hands. And he did the same with three sticks of wood, and the same also with three bronze cups; and then the men wanted him to toss three swords unsheathed, but the fair-haired man only laughed and took up one of the cups and filled it and drank deep for all his labours.

The Sun was now setting, and a few of the men left to perform some tasks in the yard in advance of night. But most of the Danes stayed in the hall, and gathered at two of the tables and began to play at dice. Yrling and Sidroc and Toki joined in these games, and Ælfwyn and I looked on for a while, and then went back to the table and sat together.

Burginde was at the firepit, and Ælfwyn gestured to her to join us, and the three of us raised our cups together. Burginde praised and petted Ælfwyn, and made much of the necklace and bracelets, and touched them over and over again, remarking on their beauty and worth.

We looked upon the men about us, and knew they were glad-hearted with ale and gaming. The torches flared upon the walls, and the firepit blazed forth its red warmth. And tho' the men were strange, and their tongue stranger, one of us was now wed to their Lord, and the other two of us were thus bound also to these men and their ways. And I myself, warm with ale and hope, thought: All will go well here; the Lady will find peace, and I a new life with her and her husband's people.

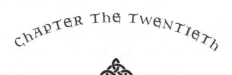

VALERIAN
FOR SWEETNESS

A T last Burginde rose from the table and said she must set to work to make up the marriage bed; and these words she said lightly to Ælfwyn that they might be borne lightly.

Burginde called Susa and the two went straight for the door of the treasure room, opened it and went inside.

The head of Yrling rose from his goblet, and he looked at the two as they went in, and turned his head back to where Ælfwyn and I sat. As he looked at her a slow smile spread across his face, and he wiped his mouth with his hand and called out to the men who were still gaming. Some of them grumbled, but they began to gather up the dice before them.

The serving men were clearing the last of the cups, and the Danes themselves began to take the tables off their trestles and to bring in the pallets from the passageway. Burginde and Susa were still within the treasure room, and Ælfwyn looked towards the open door.

"Shall I go in?" she whispered to me.

I did not want us to go in and find Burginde scolding Susa, yet it seemed better for her to go sooner, when the men were busy with their work, than later, when all eyes might be upon her.

"Yes," I answered, considering these things, "let us go now, and together, to make sure the room be as it should."

So we walked across the hall to the treasure room, and tho' my own eyes told me that the men scarcely regarded us, the warmth of my face made me feel as tho' every man stopped and stared.

I felt ashamed that my face was so red, and more so when I looked at Ælfwyn, for hers was white as snow. We gained the door, and stepped inside, and shut it behind us. Susa was setting and trimming the cressets, and Burginde just finishing making up the bed. The simple frame was now covered with feather mattresses, pillows, linen throws, and wool blankets. Over this Burginde was tossing a coverlet I had not yet seen, made entirely of wolf pelts, and backed with blue coloured linen. The thickness and lustre of the grey fur was such as might grace the bed of a queen. Burginde smiled as she patted it, and looked up into the surprised face of Ælfwyn.

"'Tis from your father; these be the wolves he took at Martinmas, and your own dear mother wove and sewed this backing; 'tis their wedding gift to you."

I thought Ælfwyn would cry at this reminder of her parent's love; but Burginde saved her from it by saying cheerfully, "You see, tho' they not be here, they have found a way to bless your wedding, and your bed."

Ælfwyn and Burginde embraced, and Burginde pointed out all the little comforts she had brought into the room, where the basin and ewer was, the Lady's night mantle, shoes, scent bottles, and such.

Then there was naught to do, and Susa had finished with the cressets and would take her leave. She came before Ælfwyn and made a deep curtsey, and Ælfwyn smiled down on her and said, "I am glad that you are here with us, Susa, for you are a good woman."

These words may have been the kindest Susa had heard in many months, and fitting for a Lady such as Ælfwyn to say on her wedding night to one who would serve her ever more, but Susa only burst out in tears so that Burginde hustled her out of the room.

"Susa be a flighty wench," said Burginde, coming back in and closing the door, "and weddings make such very odd."

But Ælfwyn was already thinking of other things, and turned to Burginde with a troubled look. "Shall I undress and be ready in the bed? Or should I wait here in my gown upon the bench?" she wanted to know.

Burginde laughed. "That be up to you. If you be ready in the bed, you will not have to undress before him this first night, and that might be a mercy; but then again, it might deprive him of the pleasure of watching you, and 'tis always a good thing to give your husband pleasure."

"I want it to be dark," said Ælfwyn, after thinking about this.

"Better to have a bit of light," said Burginde, "'twill be awkward enough without groping."

Burginde looked at Ælfwyn's face and laughed again. "Now, lamb, not to fright yourself. 'Tis the most natural thing in the world for a man and woman to do, and believe me, if your Lord has any sense about him, and I think he does, you will grow to welcome it, and look forward to the nights in his arms." She clasped her mistress to her for a moment. "And besides, you be a great healthy girl, and will soon bear a babe, and nothing will give you more joy than the first look into the little one's face."

Ælfwyn nodded her head, and began to take off her necklace. "I think I will be – in bed," she said softly.

Burginde went out to fetch some water hot from the kitchen yard, and came back with a bucket in one hand a sprig of dried herb in the other. She tucked the herb beneath the mattress of the bed. "Valerian," she said, "for sweetness between man and wife."

Ælfwyn bathed, and scented her skin with rose oil, so precious and rich in its scent that the room smelt like a day in June. I braided her hair, and made as lovely a plait as I could, and we told her over and over how beautiful she was.

Burginde pulled back the coverlets, and the one of wolf pelts fell in soft folds upon itself, and Ælfwyn got in upon the linen throw, and pulled it to her neck. We set the cressets as she liked them, and then it was time for us to leave her.

Burginde smiled down at her and said, "'Tis no loss we have no flowers in Wintertime to adorn your bed; the room is as filled with roses." She bent over and kissed her. "Be well, and be at ease."

I too bent over and kissed her. "I bid you Good-night, and will see you in the morning. You are very beautiful, and very good," I said, but it was not half the love I felt for her.

She clasped my hand and smiled, and said, "Good-night," and I opened the door and Burginde and I went out into the hall, and Burginde pulled the door closed behind her.

The hall was much darker now, for most of the torches were out, and the fire burned low. Some of the men were already snoring on their pallets. Yrling stood with Toki by the firepit, and Burginde went to them. She bobbed her head in her quick way to Yrling, and said, "My Lady be awaiting you, Lord," and the same smile I had seen before crept across Yrling's face; but Burginde would not stay to look at it, for she said, "And I bid you Good-night," and turned on her heel.

We turned and walked towards the stair, but Toki winked at me, and his face wore the grin it had the first night we had seen him, when he forced Ælfwyn and I to push back our mantles from our faces.

So did we go alone into the upper chamber, and the bed of Ælfwyn looked empty and bare as we walked in, and Burginde spread a coverlet over it so that its bareness was not so great.

We undressed and washed, and Burginde yawned again and again, for it was then late, and we had all drunk much ale; but tho' I got into my bed I did not feel sleepy. We bid each other Good-night, and Burginde was soon snoring her gentle snore. The sounds of the hall below died away, and all grew quiet, and as I lay in the dark I wondered if Yrling had yet gone into the treasure room.

THE LADY
OF FOUR STONES

IN the morning I was not fully awake when I heard a step on the stair outside. The room was still dim, but some streak of dawn came in from the shuttered windows. I sat up and the door opened, and there was Ælfwyn, dressed in her yellow gown, and with her hair loose about her shoulders and arms.

I ran from my bed to greet her. "Ælfwyn," I said, clasping her to me, "are you well? It is so early."

Burginde stirred in her bed and sat up, and saw us together, and Ælfwyn said, "Yrling has gone out with some of his men; he will be back soon and we will eat."

She seemed breathless, but she was not pale, and I could not tell how she fared. I said again, "Are you well?"

She smiled and then colour came to her cheeks. "Yes, I am well," she said, and I too felt colour come to my cheeks.

Burginde was up and bustling about dressing herself. She came over and looked closely at Ælfwyn's face. Then she pulled back and said, "You look well, Lady," in a tone with mock graveness that made Ælfwyn smile.

Ælfwyn wore a ring of gold set with blue stones upon her left hand. Never had I seen stones such as these, for they were clear like the best crystals, but a rich blue colour.

"Ah! How beautiful it is!" I exclaimed, and Ælfwyn also beheld the ring with pleasure.

"He has given it to me just now," said Ælfwyn softly.

Burginde laughed, and said, "Ach! Did I not say he esteemed you!" Ælfwyn smiled, but I saw for the first time that she looked tired, and Burginde must have seen it too. "'Tis good you are come so early," she said, "I want to make you a steeping bath of Lady's mantle; 'twill soothe you." And she went about gathering the bucket and left the room.

Ælfwyn crossed to the table and sat down on her chair. I dressed myself, but could not take my eyes from her. I sat down next to her, but could not speak; and she looked at me, and I blushed and looked down.

"Well," she said at last, "it is done."

I looked up at her. "Did it hurt?"

"Yes."

"Did you weep?"

"No, I did not weep. He was not – unkind."

I said nothing, for being ignorant of this Mystery, what could I say? I knew not even the right questions to ask.

"It was not what I expected," she said after a few moments.

"How so?" I asked quickly, for my mind was racing with all the things I had ever seen or heard about this Mystery, and I thought of all the animals I had seen mate in Fall, and the young they brought forth in Spring; and

I thought also of what my mother had told me. But none of this seemed to have much bearing on Ælfwyn as she passed from being maid to wife.

"I do not know exactly," she said, "it was not what I thought, but now it is done I no longer know what I thought it might be." She shook her head and shrugged her shoulders. "Do you understand?"

"I think I do," I said, but I did not. "Perhaps you will have a babe in the Fall," I suggested.

"Yes," she said, looking down at the table, "perhaps I will."

Burginde came back with the water, and set up the copper bathing tub, and took from the Simples chest a handful of shrivelled leaves, which she ground to a powder between her palms and shook into the tub. "The water is hot, and when you sit in it, 'twill reawaken the wound a bit, but the Lady's mantle will heal you up wonderfully, and tonight will go much easier."

Ælfwyn undressed and sat in the bath, and winced when she did, but Burginde teased her and made her smile. I felt glad for Ælfwyn and her new estate, and felt outside of it all.

I did her hair in braids wrapped about her head like a crown. She put on her yellow gown and also the great pearl, and her new gold ring set with blue stones glittered upon her hand.

We went downstairs into the hall, and she walked with measured step and without blushing to her husband's side at the table. And he stopped his talking to Toki, and looked upon her with pride, and I watched him and thought, He is not changed at all, but she is changed very much. But I recollected that he had had at least one wife before, and as Burginde said, many women, so one night would matter not to him; but to a maid one night was everything.

I sat next to Sidroc, and when we had begun to eat he said, "You make Toki jealous. He thinks you should sit one meal with me and one with him."

I looked at him as he said this. He smiled, but it was a quiet smile.

"Yesterday when I said you did not fear Toki's anger you laughed. Was I wrong in saying this?" I asked him.

He narrowed his eyes. "I do not fear Toki, tho' many men do," he said.

"No, you do not fear him, for you are a better man than he," I said, and tho' my words were bold, I tried to make them light.

I thought he might laugh, but he did not. "You think I am a better man than Toki?" he asked.

"Yes," I said, "I do, for you try to shame us less with your words and looks, and so you act more honourably to both my Lady and to Yrling." He looked at me with much interest, and I went on. "And it is clear that Yrling listens well to your words."

He smiled, and I went on again. "And I think you are also a better warrior than Toki, for the scar you bear must be from a great battle."

Now his face fell, and he looked down at the table and then at me with piercing eyes. "The scar I bear is from Toki, and he gave it to me when we were but boys."

I felt such a fool that I wished I could slip from the table. But I could not, so only said, "Perhaps he was jealous of you even then."

He snorted and said, "I think not," and then was silent.

I took a sip of ale and put down my goblet.

He said, "It is good that you think I am the better warrior, for I am."

I looked at him, glad that the moment was over.

He lowered his voice. "You are a true shield-maiden; you do not turn from a scar on a man's face."

I looked at him and did not lower my eyes. "My father was an ealdorman, and his brother ealdorman after him. He taught me that a scar is the badge of honour of the warrior, and this I believe."

He regarded me for a long moment. "I think I am glad we did not face your father and his brother in battle," he said, "for they were of better stuff than what we have found here."

In saying this, he gave my dead kinsmen much praise. I felt that praise came rarely from the Danes, and took a strange pleasure in hearing him say this.

I did not speak, but he lifted his cup to me, and I again took up mine.

After we had eaten Ælfwyn rose, and she and I went upstairs to our chamber. Burginde soon joined us, and when she came in found that Ælfwyn and I were already at work warping one of the looms.

"Ach!" she said, "'tis Distaff Day again, and Twelfthnight fun is over!" And we laughed at this jest, but it was a good one, for the wedding was over, and today our work would begin, just as Distaff Day signals the taking up of spinning and weaving after the holiday of Twelfthnight is past.

"Burginde, bring the warp weights; they must be in the new chest," said Ælfwyn as she held the tension tight on the first few threads.

Burginde went to the chest and opened it, and took out the basket of spindles and shuttles on top. She rummaged around, and then we heard her sharp whistle of surprise.

"What is it?" asked Ælfwyn. "Are they broken from the movement of the waggon?"

"No, Lady," she answered, and held out a handful of the clay rings. "They be fine. 'Tis something else I found."

Ælfwyn let go the warp threads, and we both went to where Burginde stood before the chest. Inside was a much smaller chest which she had just uncovered. The lid was open, and it was full of silver coins.

Ælfwyn touched the silver, and plunged her hand deep within the small chest. It was layers upon layers of small coins, all silver, some newly minted and rough, others worn and smooth, but all silver.

Ælfwyn pulled out a few of the pieces, and held them in her hand. "My mother told me to regard well my weaving . . . do you think she placed this here on purpose that it should be mine?"

I thought of the silver coin my own mother had pressed into my hand and said, "Yes, I do, Ælfwyn. She set it here without your knowledge, so you would find it later and it would be yours and not part of the tribute."

But Burginde's face was creased with worry. "Ach! Suppose the Dane find out, and find it he must! 'Twill look as tho' you stole from your own husband!"

"I do not think so," I said, "he missed nothing from the tribute, and I do not think this was part of it, but a gift in secret from your mother. To show it to your Lord will be perhaps to lose it."

Ælfwyn was deep in thought, and spoke not.

Burginde still scowled, and I turned to her. "What good will it do the Dane?" I asked. "She has brought him fifty times more than this already."

"Well, I would not see him get richer still," she grumbled. "But what if he find out?"

I looked back at Ælfwyn. "He will not find out, and if he does, then you must make it right with him. It will be like" – I searched for something fitting – "like the wolf skin spread, which he did not see until last night. He was not displeased that he had not seen it in the tribute waggon, was he? He was glad over it, was he not?"

Here Ælfwyn nodded her head, but Burginde was not convinced. "There be a big difference from a spread and silver," she said.

I looked again at Ælfwyn. "Then if he finds out, tell him it is our custom that newly-wed women receive much silver from their mothers. He does not know our ways."

Burginde began to laugh. "Ach!" she said, "and either do you!"

But Ælfwyn's mind was made up, and she need hear no more. "I shall keep this treasure, as I have given away so much," she said, and I rejoiced to hear it. She spoke slowly, but with great steadiness. "First, Burginde, I will give you seven pieces, for you have served me since I was born and came willingly into this new life with me."

And she counted out seven newly minted pieces into Burginde's hand. Burginde trembled and nearly dropped the pieces she held. Her mouth opened, but for once, nothing came out.

"Be silent, nurse; there is good cause to give you this, both for the past and for the future. For think of this: what if I should die of fever or in childbed? You would be left here alone, so far from Wessex. Seven pieces will buy your freedom from the household, if anyone contest your going; and give you enough to travel back to Cirenceaster."

Burginde still could not speak, for the tears welling in her eyes choked her. Ælfwyn's eyes, too, were moist, and the love between them was clear as they embraced.

Ælfwyn gently pushed herself away and again addressed the treasure box. "Next, I want every woman in the village to receive one silver piece at once. Since I have come here I have not been able to forget their misery, and now I have some way to aid them." She drew breath and let out a long sigh. "I give thanks I am not as one of them, and give thanks for the great kindness of my mother in providing this means to help them."

She turned to Burginde. "You will give it them, Burginde, for you can go without suspicion into their huts."

Burginde nodded her head, still too moved for speech.

Ælfwyn went on softly. "If you find women who have young daughters also got with babes by the Danes, give them two pieces," she said.

Burginde found voice. "I will go now, and take a basket with me as if I seek a village woman for herbs."

Ælfwyn nodded her head, and looked at the silver. "How many pieces shall I count out?" she asked.

"Start with fifty," I said. "Fifty will be light enough for Burginde to carry with no trouble. She will go hut to hut, and should she run out, she will return for more."

Burginde had been putting on her apron and mantle and gathering up a basket. She lined one of stout wicker with a linen cloth, and then slipped the silver into it. This she covered with another cloth, and then put a few handfuls of herb stalks over all.

"Come back as soon as you can, but use your time well to learn as much as you can of the women and their needs," said Ælfwyn as we walked Burginde to the door.

We bade her Fare-well, and went back and gazed at the silver gleaming in the chest.

THE WEAVING OF LIFE

"WE should count it all out," I said, picking up the silver pieces and letting them run through my fingers.

"To count it is to limit it," said Ælfwyn. "I would rather not, I think. It seems more this way."

"To count it is to know," I insisted. "There is plenty more left."

So we began the count. When we lifted the final piece out, I said, "Three hundred and eight."

"And Burginde has fifty with her, and seven of her own," added Ælfwyn.

I counted on my fingers. "That makes three hundred sixty five."

"One for every day of the year!" said Ælfwyn. "I am sure my mother planned it this way; she is quiet, but clever. Everything she does has meaning."

"When we write to her we will tell her you received her calendar," said I, laughing.

We took handfuls of the silver and put it all back into its chest, for as Ælfwyn said, It had come thus far safe, so there it should stay. We went to the loom and continued our work, as we knew Burginde would not return for some time.

"We will start with plain weave, and make it fine, for warm weather will soon be here, and we will want lighter cloth for clothes," said Ælfwyn.

I stroked one of the wound balls of yarn, and thought of all the good things of sheep: milk, and cheese, and greatest of all, wool; and I thought too of the making of parchment, and that without a lambskin I could not make any, and so could not send to Ælfwyn's parents the letter I had promised.

She seemed to read my thoughts, for she said, "Can it be true that no sheep are left here? How will the people live without sheep? How even will we live? If the Danes are to stay here and make Lindisse their home, surely they know they must farm and raise sheep."

"Yet they do not look to be farmers, or herdsmen," I said.

"No," she said, "all the men we have seen, save for smiths and the like, are warriors." She paused a moment. "They are used to take what they want, not grow it."

I thought of the empty fields of the village. "How shall we weave linen? I have seen no flax."

"Perhaps the people of Lindisse buy flax, and rett and hackle it here," said Ælfwyn. "If not, we shall have a retting pond dug, for I would have it all done close to the burh, as is done in Cirenceaster."

I wrinkled my nose at the thought of the retting pond. "Just do not have it dug too close to our windows!" I said, recalling the stench the decaying flax gives off.

She smiled and said, "Tho' linen thread be so much more work than wool, the pay back is in the weaving, for it is such a pleasure to the fingers." She looked over to the second loom frame. "Do you think Ecgwald can build us a third loom?"

"I think he could, if he studies these," I said. "But there must be a joiner here; how else could Yrling have rebuilt what he has?"

"I do not know," said Ælfwyn. "There are many things they seem to want. Women amongst them – there are no wives for these men."

"Do they have wives?" I asked. "If so, perhaps they are still in their homeland, and will come later."

"Perchance," mused Ælfwyn. "It is clear there are no women here, save the village women, and it does not seem that the Danes will take up with them, to marry them, I mean. Perhaps Burginde will tell us more."

"Ask Yrling. He will know if the men have wives or sweethearts in their homeland. After all, if this is to be the Danes' new home, they need wives."

She was silent a long time. "Yes. They cannot all come as part of a Peace."

I looked at her, but her head was lowered over her work, and I could not see her face.

"Are you well, Ælfwyn?" I asked.

"I am well," she answered, not looking up. "It is a strange day, that is all. To find my mother's silver, and also to receive so much richness from . . . him." And her voice trailed off.

"Why strange?" I asked, and tried to speak gently. "Your mother loves you, and the silver was of course a surprise, but a most happy one."

"Yes," she said, "and I give thanks for it." She looked over at me, and seemed to search for her words and the thoughts behind them. "But in contrast to her gift I think of all the gold he has given me, and the pearl, and . . ."

I touched her hand and looked at her most earnestly. "It is right that he gives you such things; you are his wife, and did you not bring him great treasure?"

"It is not that," she said, and looked down. "I had no choice in bringing him the treasure from Wessex. He has given me great riches, and he does not even know me."

I opened my mouth to speak, but she went on.

"He knows not what I am like, what makes me happy, what are my virtues and vices; I am an utter stranger to him, and if he regards me at all, it is because I brought him the tribute. To him, I could have been any maiden. He cares not."

I hardly knew what to say. "I cannot believe that is true. Even tho' you are new to each other, your beauty and goodness speak at once."

She smiled, but with no heartiness. "O! My face is pleasing to him, that I know; but yours pleases him equally."

I tried to jest. "Do you mean we could have tricked Toki on the road, and made me the bride?"

"Yes," she said, and I thought she would begin to weep, "or something close to it, for he does not know me, and I think does not even care to know me; so he cannot love me."

I took her hand. "That will come, will it not? He regards you well now, and true affection will follow. Any man would love you."

"I do not want the love of any man," she said, and her eyes were full.

I squeezed her hand and made her look at me. "Hush," I whispered. "Would you speak against your husband on the first day of your married life?"

She shook her head, and with her free hand brushed away the tears that now streaked her cheek. She said, "No; I will not speak against him. I only speak my heart."

"Ceridwen," said Ælfwyn after a little time, "I hope you will wed soon, so we can be married together."

I did not know if she was jesting, and began to laugh. "What! Two days ago you made it clear to Yrling that I did not seek a husband, and now you yourself seek one for me?"

She glanced down. "Well, it is different now; I am married, and it would be pleasant if you were too." She paused a moment. "We might have our babies at the same time."

I saw she did not jest, but I said nothing.

"You are always speaking to Sidroc, and he to you," she suggested.

"I speak to Sidroc because I choose to sit next to him rather than Toki," I said with some heat. "Besides," I added, trying to cool my words, "I am dowerless, and have nothing to bring to him or any other man."

"If you wed Sidroc, it would not matter, for he is rich enough, and Yrling would make a dowry for you, I think."

"I do not want to wed Sidroc, or any man," I said, and I felt alarm.

"Well, then you do not have to; you know that. I simply said it would be pleasant to be married at the same time." And she acted as if the subject was at an end.

"I am sorry if I was excited; I felt concern," I began. "You are right, it would be pleasant, and it is kind of you to think of me, but –" I did not finish, for we heard Susa upon the stair, and I was glad of it.

After we ate we went back to our work. We were tying the heddles of the first loom when we heard Burginde call up from below.

"'Tis me," she hissed, and we went to the doorway to meet her. Her face was red from fresh air and walking, and the basket in her arms overflowed with dried herbs and seed pods.

"You really did find goods for the Simples chest!" cried out Ælfwyn, as Burginde set down the basket on the table.

"Of course; for any tale's only as good as the proof," answered Burginde, and she took off her mantle and washed her hands.

"Sit down and eat before you tell us what you have seen," offered Ælfwyn. "You have been gone all morning."

"Thanks, Lady, but I can talk and eat, always could." And she took a mouthful of bread and began.

"Well," she said, "there be four pieces of silver left; I visited every hut. In some three or four women live together with their children, for all their husbands be dead, and many of them died defending their poor huts. So hut and husband both be gone. And to each of these women, whether they lived singly or in groups, I gave a piece of silver, and as it was clear to me there was need, such as daughters gotten with babes, I gave extra."

She paused to sip some ale, and Ælfwyn asked, "What did you tell them? How did they act towards you?"

"What I said in the first hut was pretty near to what I said in all the rest. They knew who I was, and I told them that I be sent from my mistress, that they might have some boon of her. And I said that she was a Lady of Cirenceaster in Wessex, and that she had come to cause peace in both her homeland and here, and that she took from her own treasury the gift that each of them would have. And then I gave them the coin."

"What did they do?" I asked. "Were they affright?"

"Some were affright; some wept; some just stared, and I had to push the silver into their hands. The ones my age took it better than the younger ones; they have lived more, and seen more sorrow, but talked more sense and sooner than the young. Some prayed aloud, but all, before I left, praised you," she said, looking at Ælfwyn.

"I am so glad," she murmured. "Tell us more. Did you learn aught of value?"

"Well," said Burginde, "there be a woman, a dyer by trade, and she be with child, about to bear; but her own mother be still alive. And the old woman be regarded as a healer and a leader amongst the women; 'twas she who filled my basket. I came to their hut towards the end, and so had talked to many women already; and began to think that some news was being kept from me; I knew not what."

She stopped to take another bite and swallowed hard. "I tell my tale to both of them, and before I am finished I am stopped by the old woman, who broke off a piece of mistletoe from a mess she had in her store, and makes me stick out my tongue so she can put the bit of leaf and berry upon it! Well, it did not jump off my tongue, so she knows I tell the truth; and so I went on, not a bit affronted, for my own grandmother did the same."

"Is that it?" asked Ælfwyn.

"No, no, there is more. So I take it in mind to ask this woman, in a quiet way, what is being held back from me, and think she would have said, but her daughter begged and pleaded with her not to; and I know the old wise woman did want to tell me; so perhaps she will, soon."

"Hmmm," said Ælfwyn. "I wonder what it can be? And why would they keep it from us?"

"I will try to learn more," said Burginde, "but I think the wise woman will tell; she sized me up pretty quick, mistletoe or not, and I think she knows she has no reason to fear."

I wondered to myself if the women were trying to protect not themselves, but Ælfwyn by their silence; but I did not know how this could be.

"Did anyone watch your coming or going?" asked Ælfwyn.

"No one cared. The big gate outside is closed, but I passed easily through one of the small doors, with little chaff from the Danes." She smiled her broad smile. "I took every chance to sauce them; 'tis a pity they knew not a word I said! But they cared not about my going, 'twas clear to them I headed right for the village, and I stepped lively."

"You have done well, Burginde," said Ælfwyn. "I knew you would."

"'Twas a pleasure to give pleasure," Burginde answered, fingering her own silver pieces.

We heard a heavy footfall at the bottom of the stair, but it did not do more than mount the first step. Burginde quickly hid her treasure beneath her pillow, and I stepped to the door and looked down the stairs.

At the bottom stood Yrling, and he looked at me but did not move. Then he said, "Send my Lady down to me," and turned and walked back as if he went into the hall.

I looked into the room at Ælfwyn, but she had heard him speak herself. She grew pale, but came forth without hesitation onto the landing. I walked before her, for I did not want her to go alone, and we went down the wooden steps together.

At the bottom we turned into the hall, and saw Yrling across the length of it, framed in the light of the open door to the treasure room. He looked at Ælfwyn and the smile grew across his face.

"Come," he said.

Ælfwyn left my side and hurried across the floor to where he stood waiting. She passed in front of him through the door, and without another glance at me he went in and closed it behind them.

THE MEETING
ON THE ROAD

I went back upstairs and told Burginde what had happened. She looked up and said, "Ach! He be a randy one. But he will have his fill sooner or later."

She went back to poring over her coin, and I sat at the table, but soon grew restless. "I think I will go out and take some air," I said to Burginde, "for all day I have been within, and I would see the Sun before it sets."

"You will want your clogs; the yard be muddy," she said, and I took the clogs and my mantle and went down the wooden steps.

Once I was out, I did not know quite what to do. I walked through the drear of the yard, and went around to the ruins of the great hall. I stood for some moments lost in thought as I gazed at the tumbled stones and charred beams. I looked too, at the staff which held the iron spear point, and recalled the story of Merewala and his fall. I thought of his young daughter and her Fate, and wondered if I stood upon the very spot she leapt to.

I turned away from the ruin, and tried to turn away also from my unquiet thoughts. I walked to the nearest door in the palisade, in front of which two Danes were lingering. They stepped aside, and I passed out briskly to the other side. Danes were about, but none stopped or questioned me. Soon the fields of the village were about me, and I looked again at last year's furrows, now choked and fouled with dead weeds when they should be sprouting green with new barley and peas. I bent down and scooped up a bit of the moist Earth and took a pinch of it between my fingers and touched it to my tongue. It was not salt, but sweet and rich and full of such things that would bring strong crops. I let fall the Earth from my hands and gazed down at the ragged furrows and sorrowed that this good soil lay fallow.

Across the field, far from the road, I saw two women working alone, scratching at the soil with stripped tree branches. They had no spade, no ox, no plough; and they who had last Spring walked behind their husbands, breaking up with their ploughbats the fresh clods their men had turned over with oxen, now scratched the Earth alone and in misery.

And I thought: Tonight each of these women will sleep with a silver pence beneath them; but how much more would they give to have their husbands and sons alive again. I thought of the goodness of she who gave the silver. I thought of him who she was forced to wed, and that it was his hand that had wrought all this grief upon so many women. I thought too of Ælfwyn's own pleasant land, and how she hoped the giving of her hand and the tribute she bore would keep her people from the terrors of war.

And so my thoughts came back again in circle, and I turned and looked back at the roofs of Four Stones. I took in at a glance its low and ugly forms, and felt glad to be outside of it and free from its shadow.

As I walked, I saw two horsemen appear from over a low hill and follow a trackway that skirted one of the fields. Both horses were large and grey, and the lighter one was ridden by a man whose yellow hair shone brightly in the Sun. I knew it to be Toki, and was not pleased to think that soon he would ride past me, teasing and making jests.

I pulled the hood of my mantle more firmly over my head and walked on, hoping they would pass without remark. As they grew nearer they did not slow, but rather began to race their horses. They called out to each other, and beat their horses with their rein ends, and the horses burst into long galloping strides. First Toki took the lead, but then the other man urged his horse forward, and Toki fell behind.

Now they were nearly upon me and I needs must move to keep myself from the mud flying off the hooves of their beasts. I walked into the neglected field, and Toki surged by on his great grey horse, whooping and beating him about the neck. The other man was just behind him, but Toki had reined his horse in, so for him at least the race was over, and he the winner.

I regained the road and started walking towards the village, glad that they were gone. I had not taken more than a few steps when I heard the champing of bits and jingling of bridle fittings behind me. I turned about, and there was the grinning Toki and the other Dane, panting and out of breath as were their mounts. Their horses danced under them, and Toki wheeled round and round calming his.

Toki moved his horse past me and blocked my path, and the other Dane brought his horse in behind me, so that I was subject to be struck by a hoof if one of the beasts should fright.

I would not look at them, but stepped into the muddy field and began to make my way through it.

The other Dane spoke to Toki, and Toki answered. My back was turned, but I heard one of the men move their horse, and ride away down the road at a trot.

"Greetings, shield-maiden," said Toki, and his light voice was full of mockery.

I did not turn to look at him, but he went on. "Or are you angered that I use the name Sidroc gave you?" I picked up the hem of my gown and began to move through the field away from him.

"He has all but spoken for you, so perhaps he will be angered at my words," called out Toki.

I would not answer, but he would not be deterred. He urged his horse forward, and soon overtook me. He leaned down from his horse and said, "Why do you not answer me, Lady? It is better sport when you do."

I looked up at him. "Why should I pleasure you then, when your sport is such a poor one? Do you take pleasure in trampling a woman on the road? Or in shaming her and her Lady at every chance? Is this what Danes value in their men?" My words were hot, but I did not care, and could not have cooled them if I tried.

I stared him full in the face, and his grin faded. He swung himself down from his horse, and stood next to me upon the unploughed Earth.

Now that the distance was closed between us, I did not feel so bold, but my anger was still hot in my veins, and I would not flinch.

"We value many things in our men; and in our women too," he said, and his speech was more quiet than any he had yet used with me. "Hardiness and spirit we value very much in our women, and if beauty and riches be found there as well, then the man who claims such a woman has claimed also the favour of the Gods."

I could not let this chance go by me, for I saw what path his words were taking. I spoke again, with as much firmness as I could. "Then you and every other man here should know at once that I am a poor choice for your testing-games, for I have no riches."

He began to laugh. "Ha! You think much of yourself, as all your kind do."

I thought the colour would rush into my face, but perhaps I was already red from anger. I spoke not, but looked away.

"Not to fear, Lady," he said in an easy tone. "You should think much of yourself, for you are worth much."

He paused, and shifted the bridle reins from one hand to another. "Any man here will pay Yrling a good bride-price for you."

I jerked my head and looked at him. "I will not be sold away like livestock at your Lord's pleasure," I said.

He laughed the more. "But you are such a prize!" he answered. "Hissing and spitting like a beautiful cat." He looked at me closely and lowered his voice. "I think, like most cats, you can be tamed."

I did not speak, but began to move away. He reached out and grasped my arm, and the strength in his fingers made me stop. I turned and looked at him, and spoke as steadily as I could. "Please to let me go. I want to return."

His hand dropped away, and he walked with me out of the field. We reached the road, and he did not remount his horse, but walked on with me.

After a few moments he said, "I am sorry I cannot marry you myself."

I did not know how to take these words; there was no mockery in them. I glanced at him.

"I already have a wife, but I do not like her very much," he said.

"You are already wed?" I asked, hoping that I had not walked into another jest.

"Yes," he answered, "but she is home, so I have not seen her for two Winters."

I believed these words, and asked, "Have you children?"

He nodded his head. "Two. One of them is a boy."

"Then perhaps your wife will come soon and join you here," I suggested.

"I do not know," he said, and he looked across the fields. "She dislikes the sea, and is fearful of ships."

I did not know what to say, so I said, "I am sorry."

"That is all right," he answered, "As I said, I do not like her much."

"Why then did you wed?" I asked. "You could have had a great choice amongst women, I think." I said this not for the praise of it, but because it was true.

"Before my father died he made this match for me, and the woman was rich, so I had to wed." He turned and looked at me and gave a short laugh. "Sometimes men have no choice either," he said.

"Yes," I said, but in truth it seemed to me that men had all the choice in life, and women very little.

I looked down, and we walked on in silence. I wished every moment he would mount his horse and ride away.

I looked at him from the tail of my eye, and thought to speak once more. "Why even tell me you are wed, if you are not bound by the Hand-fasting bonds? A man who is married to one, yet takes his pleasure with every woman as will have him, is not truly wed."

He only laughed. "You speak much, but you know little," he said.

I went on, and he walked by my side, leading his horse. "Why did you come out?" he asked. "There is nothing to see." He raised his arm to the landscape.

"I wanted air," I said. "I am not used to being shut up."

We walked along. "I never walk when I can ride," he said, not looking at me.

"Why then do you not ride?" I asked in a short voice.

He began to laugh, and I walked the faster.

"I would rather walk with you than ride, but most of all I want to ride with you," he said. I was silent, but he went on. "I would like to take you to the camp where we keep our horses. I have just come from there; it is not far."

"Perhaps another time," I answered. "When my Lady and I ride together, you can take us there."

"I would rather take you alone," he said. I was not looking at him, so I do not know if he grinned as he spoke.

"I think not," I said, and kept moving.

He grasped my arm again and stopped me. I would not look at him, but kept my eyes fixed on the fields. He said nothing, but I felt his staring eyes. At last I turned my head, and looked into his face.

"Sleipnir is strong," he said, inclining his head toward his horse. "He will carry us swiftly. We will be gone and back before dark." His voice was quiet and low.

"No," I said, "I will not ride with you." I began to feel true fright. We were still far from the palisade; I did not think anyone would hear me if I cried out.

His fingers tightened around my arm, and he brought his face close to mine. His blue eyes flashed. "I also am strong, and could lift you upon the saddle and ride off with you," he said, and his voice was almost a whisper.

I wanted to speak, but knew I must choose carefully what to say. I could not believe that he would try to carry me off; I recalled the words of Yrling when he said that I would be safe, for no one would touch that which was his. But he looked at me in such a way that his wildness struck me with fear.

"Your own Lord told my Lady that I would be safe here at Four Stones. Would you dishonour him by breaking his word?" I asked, and I tried to stem my fear as I looked at him. "And do not think that Yrling would never know if you used force upon me. I would go to him at once and tell him."

He stepped closer to me and our bodies touched. "Perhaps after once with me, you would not wish to tell him," he breathed.

I pulled my arm away so hard that I broke his grasp. "I would never go to you willingly! My father and kinsman would kill you if you despoiled me, but they themselves have joined the dead. Do you take pride in your threat against a maid with no one to defend her?"

He did not answer, and I went on; I could not stop my words. "I would not rest until I had revenge against you, even if I myself must do it alone, and no man came forth to punish you."

He looked at the ground and then spat upon it. "I do not want you," he said. "Sidroc can have all."

And he turned and grasped his horse's mane and swung himself into the saddle. He dug his heels hard into the animal's side, and the beast reared and then plunged down the road towards the palisade of Four Stones.

FRIGHT AND FIGHT

AS he rode off I closed my eyes tight to keep the tears from them, but my tears flowed just the same. I was trembling with anger and hatred and with fear, and at that moment if I could have struck Toki from his horse with a thunderbolt I would have done it, and rejoiced.

Then I felt the force of my wickedness in thinking this, but felt even stronger the force of the wickedness that was in Toki. I walked fast, and the tears streamed down my cheeks, and as I walked I spoke aloud in my anger and fear. I gained the palisade, and then the hall, and burst into our chamber.

Burginde was alone, sitting on her stool over some mending.

She came to my side in a moment and clasped her arm about me. "Lady, what troubles you?" she asked, and touched my wet face with her hand.

"It is Toki," I cried. "I met him on the village road, and he would not leave me alone."

She drew back. "He did not touch you!"

"No, no," I choked through my tears. "Only pinched my wrist in holding me. I broke away, and told him that I would kill him if he touched me."

"Good!" she said. "And yet he tried to catch you up, and grasped you by the wrist?"

"Yes."

"Did you strike him?"

"No, I only pulled away, and tried to shame him."

"You should have kneed him in the cods," said Burginde decisively. "Like this." And she lifted her skirt and raised her knee in a quick motion.

Despite my anger and upset I laughed a little, and Burginde brought the basin and poured out water. I splashed my face, and Burginde went on talking. "Never be afraid to strike out against a man if he will not listen to the word No. 'Tis the best thing for the likes of Toki. Words can't shame them; they have no shame in them." She thought a moment. "Some men thinks No means Yes. A maid like you be a challenge to them. Like as not he and that scarred Sidroc have a wager on who beds you first."

I shuddered. "Ugh! I would not even go down to the hall if that be true! And Toki even told me he had a wife!"

"Does he, now?" asked Burginde.

"Yes, and children too, at home! He said he did not like her much."

"Ha!" cried Burginde. "As if that be the excuse to prey upon a fatherless maid!"

I wiped my face and began to unbraid my hair. My arm hurt where Toki had held it, and the hem of my gown was filthy with mud. I wanted to bathe and change my clothing, and put everything out of my mind.

"Sounds like it was more than just him testing you," said Burginde. "The Dane should know of it, and from your lips."

I looked up at her. "I do not want to tell Yrling! I just want Toki to leave me alone." I took my comb and drew it through my hair. "Besides, he will probably tell me that I should marry, and so end Toki's game."

"Ach! You be right there, and who could you wed in this wasteland?" She had picked up my mantle and was shaking it out. "Still," she went on, "the Dane should know; he is the closest thing to a real protector you have; and tho' Toki be his own kin he cannot allow you to be harmed." She hung the mantle on a wall peg. "And to think the sly dog has a wife and kiddies!"

I could not think about telling Yrling, and wanted only to forget the meeting on the road. "Burginde, will you bring the tub for me? I want to bathe now, even if the water is not warm."

"Just let me go down to the kitchen yard; Dobbe always has a cauldron on, and a hot bath will do so much more good than a cool one." She took up the buckets and opened the door.

"You must at least tell my Lady about this," she said, and began to go.

"I would rather tell Yrling himself," I said with warmth. "Do you not think Ælfwyn has enough to worry her without the sport of Toki?"

She shrugged her shoulders and went down the steps. I pulled off my gown and tried to brush the mud from it, and then I paced around the room myself as I had seen Ælfwyn do so many times.

"O, stop it," I said at last to myself. "It is over, and it was nothing. He will leave me alone, or the next time I will hurt him before he hurts me."

At the same time I thought of Toki's last words, when he spat upon the ground and said he did not want me. Perhaps he really would leave me alone now. Then I recalled his final words, 'Sidroc can have all.'

Could Burginde be right, that the two cousins were betting over me? I felt troubled over all this, and knew I must not give Sidroc reason to think I liked him. I thought of another thing Toki had said, about Yrling giving me to one of his warriors. Yrling too, had spoken to me about Sidroc, saying he was the better man for me. What if Sidroc should ask Yrling for me? I trembled, and trembled the more to recall Yrling's words to Ælfwyn: 'Perhaps I should give you to Sidroc.' Could he then simply give me to his nephew as he had threatened Ælfwyn?

I would not do it; I would not accept it; I would run away. Then I thought, It will never happen; Ælfwyn would not permit it; I need not fear. But the memory of what she had said earlier, that she wished I could be married too, stuck in my mind. Besides, would her voice count? I thought of how Yrling had called her to his side. It was an order, and she needs must obey.

All these thoughts tumbled in my brain, and when Burginde returned with the water I was more and not less alarmed. But this alarm was deep within me, and I spoke not of it.

The afternoon was nearly gone. I bathed, and Burginde took up my russet gown and promised to cleanse it. I dressed and rebraided my hair, and then sat at the table and lit a cresset.

"Perhaps we shall have tapers soon, if the bees have done well," said Burginde.

"Yes," I said, but I was not thinking of tapers. I looked up at her and said, "Ælfwyn has been gone a long time."

"She be in there with the rest of the treasure." Burginde sighed as she sat down on her stool. "He be enjoying it all."

I put my elbows on the table and rested my forehead in my hands. "I shall never marry," I said. "I would rather take the veil if I could find the calling, or live as a spinster."

"As I do," laughed Burginde. "Aye, there be worse lives. But do not decide to cut men off so quick as that. There be as many good men as bad; maybe more good than bad."

I did not answer, and did not raise my eyes.

"You may yet love," she went on, "when the right man comes along your path; and if you do you will not know how your life got on before him." She lifted the lid of the brazier and dropped in a few coals. "Can be a good thing to be married, a very good thing, and if you can wed the man you love, 'tis the best thing in the world."

I was thinking now not of me, but of Ælfwyn. "Do you think Ælfwyn will be happy?"

She blew out a long breath. "It may be; she has got a good head, and an even better heart. 'Twas only her sad Fate to meet someone who caught her fancy, and then have to give up the thought of him to come here."

I looked over at where she sat. "She truly loves that young man," I said.

Burginde sighed again. "Aye, but love him or not, it could not be; and she may bear that love for him all her life, but she can no more wed him than she can fly." She poked at the charcoals. "The Dane seems to like her well enough. And once she has a babe, her longing will be eased." She stood up and stretched her back. "And her young man himself may be dead soon anyway, for he is known for his daring, and travels with the King to the most perilous battles. Her job now is to make the most of the lot she has drawn, as it is for me or for you. She has health and youth and wealth and beauty, and can do much good. That ought to be enough for one person." She looked over at me. "And she has me to spin!" At this she made me smile.

DUSK GROWS TO DARK

I T was dark when we heard Ælfwyn upon the wooden steps. She came into the room quickly and went about changing her gown with little more than a simple greeting to us both. Burginde went to help her with her clothes, and watched her with a careful eye.

"Would you like a bath? There be plenty of water, and the tub's right here," she asked, shaking out Ælfwyn's gown and rolling it up.

"No, I thank you," answered Ælfwyn in a quiet voice. "I washed before I came up."

The sadness in her answer told me not to ask if she was well. I busied myself putting away a few of my things, and was glad of the dimness of the chamber. Ælfwyn put on a fresh shift and stockings and pulled a blue gown over her head. She went to the ivory casket and pulled forth her new necklace and bracelets and put them on. As she was fastening them she looked at me. "You have changed your gown," she said.

"Yes," I answered, and tried to make my voice light. "I went to walk along the village road and muddied it."

Burginde stood behind her mistress, and I saw her open her mouth to speak. I did not need to interrupt her, for Ælfwyn spoke instead. "Tomorrow we will begin our weaving, and when we cut the first length from the loom we will make another gown for you."

I began to thank her, but she went on as if thinking out loud. "There is much for us to do, and a real lack of cloth. The men need tunics and there is no linen; we will have to buy some until we can grow flax ourselves. I should make a mantle for Yrling from the cloth of purple from my mother; there are many furs here to use for trim." She stood combing her hair, and did not look at either of us, but went on in her sad and quiet voice. "We alone cannot spin and weave for so large a household. Susa and a few other serving women may be skilled at weaving; we must find out. If not, a few village women could be brought by day to weave, or could weave for us in the village if they cannot leave."

Burginde walked over to her and patted her on the arm. "No need to solve all the wants of the burh in one day!"

Ælfwyn looked at her as if roused from a stupor. "Yes," she sighed, "there will be time for all. But there is much to do, and now I am the Lady who must order and manage so that all are fed and clothed." She looked at me and then to Burginde, and smiled. "I would I had taken more care in listening to my mother and grandmother!"

Burginde laughed. "Ach! Every woman wishes that! But 'twill be fine; you were always a good help to your mother, and Burginde knows a thing or two as well."

Ælfwyn nodded her head. She came over to where I stood. "You are not yourself, for you are never so quiet," she said, touching my hand kindly.

"O, I am well," I said, and then stopped, for I could not think of what I could say that would convince her of this.

"I am glad you went for a walk," she answered. "It is hard to be indoors so much. Tomorrow we will both go out, and it will do us good, I know." She smiled at me. "Spring is nearly here, and with it, warmth and Sun. We will ride out soon together, as you have been asking."

"That will bring us both pleasure," I said, and my heartiness was real this time. "We will learn the country-side, and find favourite places to visit."

Her face darkened a moment. "I hope we must not always ride through the village," she said. "It is too hard to see." She turned her face away a little. "Somehow I feel a part of it; I mean, of what happened to the women."

This gave both Burginde and me a start. "You must never say that!" I began. "What happened to the village has nothing at all to do with you, and never will."

"And here the first day you are wed to the Dane, you give so much of your silver to the women!" scolded Burginde. "Ach! If you had only been with me to see their faces and hear their blessing your coming! You had no hand in their grief, and never can."

These words seemed to allay her doubts, and she said, "I want to believe this is true. I do not want to become part of their fear."

"Show yourself to them, then," I said. "We should go soon and often to the village, and they will see you as you truly are, and love and honour you."

"I hope you are right. I want to go and see them, even tho' it be hard. Perhaps we will also learn what they are keeping back," she agreed.

As we were speaking thus, we began to hear the coming of the men into the hall, and knew it was time for us to go down. I was not glad of it, for I did not wish to see Toki, nor to sit by Sidroc and perhaps feed any thoughts about me he may have had. And I feared that Toki might have told Sidroc about the meeting on the road, and even lied about it to make it something it was not.

There was no way to stay behind, tho', for I would not give Toki the pleasure of thinking he had frighted me so bad as that. As we turned into the hall I resolved to look calmly on Toki. But he was not at the table, nor was Yrling. Sidroc sat in his usual place, as did the other men. Ale was on the table, but the food was not yet come.

Ælfwyn hesitated a bit, but then walked to the table and sat at her place. Sidroc had stood to greet us as he always had, tho' by now we knew he was the subject of amusement from the other Danes for this courtesy. Still, he did it, but I could not tell if he did so to amuse himself, or really to honour us. He sat down, and did so almost in Yrling's place, so that Ælfwyn was at his right.

I did not wish to speak, and was relieved when he addressed Ælfwyn. "You are beautiful, Lady," he said. "The blue of your dress makes your eyes even deeper, as blue as the waters of my native coast."

His voice was serious, and it made me look at him and to Ælfwyn to hear her reply.

"You do me great honour," she said, and colour came to her cheeks so that she cast down her eyes for a moment.

He did not speak again. After a moment had passed, Ælfwyn asked, "Where is my Lord?" Her eye travelled around the hall from table to table.

"He is with Toki. They will be along soon," he answered, and he also looked out across the hall.

I wondered to myself if Toki was talking to Yrling about me. Surely there were scores of things for them to speak of, and I must be the least important. I tried to put the thought out of my mind, but could not.

As we were sitting thus, the door of the treasure room opened, and out stepped Yrling and Toki. Ælfwyn's face twisted in dismay as she saw them coming out of the room she had so lately left.

The two were still talking, and it seemed to be a grave matter. Both men were unsmiling, and when they came to the table took their seats silently. Sidroc moved over and was now very close to me. Another Dane who never spoke to me and scarcely ever looked my way sat at my left, and I slid away so far that I was nearly touching him.

"Asberg has won your favour, eh?" asked Sidroc, but so softly that only I could hear him. The other man was deep in his cup and paid no mind.

I moved a little away from the other Dane and said, "No one here has won my favour, nor I hope is anyone concerned with the winning of it."

I tried not to look at him. "You are frosty tonight," he went on. "Strange, since I saw you walk today in the Sun."

I turned to him. "You saw me on my walk?" I asked, wondering if he had somehow seen my meeting with Toki.

He shrugged. "Only when you went out."

I was glad of this, for it seemed that he had neither seen nor heard what happened. I did not have to speak more, for Yrling now addressed Sidroc in their own tongue, and they and Toki were soon deeply involved. I would not look across at Toki, but it seemed he was urging Yrling to do something. Sidroc seemed to be listing reasons not to do it, and Yrling considering the different sides, and bringing up new points.

I listened as the food was served, and glanced over to Ælfwyn. Her face wore a patient look, and she smiled faintly at me. I leaned back away from the table, and she made bold to lean back as well, and I whispered to her.

"What do you think they speak of?" I asked.

She shook her head. "It always sounds like arguing, unless they are laughing, and even then it sometimes sounds like arguing."

"Do you think we will ever learn this speech?" I hissed, beginning to enjoy myself.

She was not able to answer, for Yrling suddenly stood up, and she straightened up attentively.

Yrling called out to the men, and the voices that had filled the hall ceased. He held his arms up, and called out something that made the men respond, not in a cheer, but in answer. Then he went on, speaking at some length, and his face was grave at times, and the faces of the men watching him were grave as well. But then he would say something and grin, and the men would laugh and cheer, and raise their arms. In this way it went on for some time.

When at last he sat down, he turned to Sidroc with a set face, and spoke to him almost harshly. Sidroc said nothing, only nodded his head.

I glanced at Yrling and saw Toki grinning and speaking into his ear. Ælfwyn looked over at me, and then at the platter in front of her, and pushed her food about without lifting it to her mouth. I felt in that moment that she disliked Toki even more than I did.

Sidroc gave a low sigh, and I turned to him. A short laugh came from his lips. "At least now you are looking at me," he said. "Perhaps it takes my defeat to catch your eye."

"Your defeat?"

"Yes, a small one, but any defeat is hard to take," he said, and his eyes went from me to Yrling and Toki.

"I do not understand," I began. "Tell me what happened, and what Yrling spoke of."

"Some of our brothers have been at battle in the South, and lost, and Yrling has decided we must send aid to them," he said, and he looked at me rather closely.

"At battle in Wessex?" I asked.

"Yes, in Wessex, but do not fear, it is not at your Lady's home. This battle was far to the South of that place."

"Even farther South?" I asked, and tried not to sound alarmed.

He smiled. "Yes, they have struck deep into the heart of the Kingdom of Wessex. I think it will soon fall."

"But you say this battle was lost."

"Yes, for every battle cannot be won, even by us. But mistakes were made afterwards, and that is what concerns me."

"What kind of mistakes?" I asked, and looked straight at him. He smiled, and the scar went crooked.

"It does not matter, for now Yrling has decided to try to make right what should never have been done." He looked once again over to Yrling, still speaking and listening to Toki. "It does not concern you, and women and war do not mix."

I thought of the village women. "No, Sidroc, you are wrong, for war affects women as much or more than men." I spoke very seriously, and was aware that this was the first time I had used his name.

He studied my face before he spoke. "I am glad you speak my name. It has been long since a woman used it."

I looked down at the table. "Have you also then a wife at home?"

"No," he said, "no wife waits for me, or me for her." Then he said, "How do you know that Toki has a wife? Did Yrling tell you, so you would beware?"

"I do not need Yrling to tell me to beware of Toki. Everything about Toki makes me wary. But it was he himself who told me he was wed."

"He must want you very much if he was honest with you," Sidroc said, and he almost laughed.

"He does not want me at all, and told me so, and I do not want him," I said with some warmth.

"Then who do you want?" asked Sidroc, and his face had grown quiet.

"I do not want anyone. I am here to serve the Lady Ælfwyn, not to be wed."

"But surely she expects and wants you to marry," he said. "All new brides want their friends to marry."

Here I thought of what Ælfwyn had said to me in the morning, and had to smile. But I could not share that with him, and said, "Why are you always telling me what women want, and how they talk to each other? Do you listen at doors? Or have you known so many women that you know all about us?"

"No, to both," he laughed. "But unlike some men I like to think, and one of the things I think about is women."

I must have blushed, for he went on. "Not just in the way Toki or Yrling thinks of women. I mean, think of what you might be thinking."

"That is what makes you so clever," I said, but I did not smile.

"I have need of cleverness, for if I were not clever, men like Toki would take all."

I did not speak, and he took up his cup and drank. I drank also, and began to eat again. After a while I resolved to speak, for I wished to learn more of what Yrling would set to rights, and more if I could about the battle in Wessex.

"You said that you think Wessex would fall."

"Yes, for they have won a few battles against us, but they can be worn down. Either we kill them and take what they have, or they flee the field and then pay us rich tribute to leave them alone. So we will win in the end."

"They are good warriors, I hear," I said, and then hoped this was not the wrong thing to say. "I am from Mercia, and we were not always at peace with Wessex," I added.

"Mercia or Wessex, Angle or Saxon, it is all the same to us," he said. He looked at me and began to smile. "You will have divided loyalties, then? Not only between us and the Saxons, but between Mercia and Wessex?"

I felt confused and did not wish to answer.

"It is all right," he said. "I will answer your question anyway. Æthelred of Wessex is a good warrior, which is why he has had victory over us. But he is running out of gold, both to feed and arm his men, and to purchase peace when he has the chance. We, on the other hand, have endless gold."

"Then why do you want more?" I asked, hoping that it was not a foolish question.

"Because gold is never truly endless; there is always the lust for more. Besides, we want more than gold."

"What more is there?" I asked, hoping that I would not be shamed by the answer.

He did laugh, but not unkindly. "Not what you might think of. What we want is land. We want the one thing you Angles and Saxons will not give up so easily, and that is land that we might settle here."

"But is that not what Yrling and you are doing? Do you not intend to stay?"

"Yes, we do, but there are many more of us that want the same thing, and so we need more land."

I did not want to ask more; it was clear that the Fate of Four Stones would be the Fate of many burhs if the Danes had their way. I looked over at Yrling, and began to wonder about him. Sidroc watched my looking, and I turned back to him. "Tell me about Yrling," I said. "Is he an atheling as well as a Lord?" He looked uncertain. "Is he the kinsman of your King?"

"O, no, he is not. He has become jarl through his prowess in fighting, and through the wealth he has captured, or bargained for."

His eyes went to Ælfwyn, and I thought too of the rich tribute she had brought, and thought too of the gold Dobbe had told us that the first bride of Yrling's had brought.

I began again. "Around his neck Yrling wears an ornament of silver, shaped like a blunted spear tip. It is the one jewel he wears every day. Is it a sign of rank?"

Sidroc glanced down the table to where Yrling sat, still speaking to Toki. The silver ornament hung about Yrling's neck and gleamed in the firelight as he moved.

"No, all warriors may wear it. It is the hammer of Thor, the thunder God," answered Sidroc. "It confers great strength, or so some believe."

So Thor was Thunor. I recalled my own father and kinsman, and thought of how they had worshipped Thunor the Thunderer as well. It felt strange to remember this likeness between my own people and the Danes. But the hammer was new to me; I could not remember seeing any such ornament before.

I thought of how Yrling had taken it from his own neck and placed it upon Ælfwyn's. "When they Hand-fasted, Yrling hung it upon Ælfwyn," I said.

Sidroc nodded. "It is one of the hammer's uses, to consecrate, and to bless a bride."

I looked back at Yrling, and felt the better of him, to hear that he had blest Ælfwyn in this way.

"You do not honour our Gods, yet you do not seem displeased," began Sidroc.

I looked at him, wondering how I should answer. I could not speak amiss of the Gods, tho' it be the error the Prior had told me of. But I did not have to speak, for he went on.

"Your God seems a sad fellow, and good only for peace." He said these words slowly, as if he had given it much thought.

"He is called the Bringer of Peace," I answered, but I was hesitant to press on, and so finished, "War cannot be all you seek."

"No," he smiled, "we look for peace as well, when we have won what we want and need. But we have Gods for war and for peace, and Goddesses too, to honour our warriors and to bring plenty and pleasure. These Gods were yours as well, but your peoples have largely forgotten them, and speak their names no longer. Now you have only a man hung like a thief."

I could not counter this, and did not try. I did not know where to begin. I felt only ignorant and confused.

He looked down the table at Ælfwyn, and then back at me. "Your Lady is not as the one who proceeded her, always in prayer with a holy man. Yet she is Christian, as you are?"

I nodded, but felt amiss, as if ashamed. I had prayed little since I had left the Priory, and without a priest nearby, had given up observing even the Sabbath. Ælfwyn rarely seemed to pray, or if she did, did so in private; and never spoke of God unless in anger. Yet I remembered all that was good about my years with the Prior: how he gave freely to all who were needy, how he purchased slaves from cruel masters that they might be free, how he had given me the art of writing and that of sums. All of these things were good, and all, he said, were done in His name.

Then I recalled Cedd, and the laughter of his timber hall, and the grove of oaks into which he carried me with ewers of honey and sheep's milk, that I might pour out sweetness for the Goddess Ceridwen, whose name I bore. And I recalled also the sacrifices of pig and cock and sure iron that Cedd himself made to Thunor and to Woden, that he might have victory in battle and at the hunt.

I looked at Sidroc and at his leathern shirt and his silver armlets and the rings upon his fingers, and in the glinting torchlight thought for one moment I was back in my kinsman's hall. A great joy took hold of me, for I said to myself, Here is life indeed, and tho' there be war, there is peace now in this hall, and pleasure. And feeling this, my heart flushed, and Sidroc looked at me without comprehending, but smiled at me a smile I had never seen him give.

Then did I beat back my joy, for I would not wrong Sidroc and let him think he himself was the source of it. But it was too late, and he touched my hand with his own, and whispered to me.

"I want you, shield-maiden," he murmured, and his hand closed over mine.

I tried to draw back, but tho' he did not hurt me, his hand held me. I glanced around to see if anyone was watching us, and felt my face flame. He brought his head closer to my own, and spoke so softly that he breathed the words.

"I want you," he said again. "I want you for my own."

I would have tried to rise but did not wish the eyes of the hall to be upon us. Instead I shrank back as much as I could on the bench, and pulled my hand. He did not resist, but let it slide from his, and I leaned back and took a deep breath. I wanted to leave but did not dare, fearing that he might try to stop me.

He made no move to take my hand, but said quietly, "I do not want you as Toki wants you; I want you for my wife."

Now I opened my mouth to speak, but he went on.

"Do not speak yet. Hear me first." He glanced down for a moment, and then looked back to me. "We are much alike, you and I. More alike than you can know, for you are younger and a woman and have not seen the world as I. In one thing only we differ. You are as beautiful as Freyja, and I as ugly as the Trickster. But in all other things we are as one. You said I was a better man than Toki, and I can see that for all her virtues you are a better woman than your Lady. Yet just as you are second to her in this place, so am I second to Toki. But it will not always be so. One day soon I shall be first, and someday surpass Yrling himself. This I know."

He paused, and I thought again to speak, but he silenced me with a check of his head and went on. "With me you will lack nothing. I am richer even than Toki. Only Yrling has more treasure than I. One day I will command more than even he. I will have a greater hall, more men to fill it, and greater fame. You will have all you desire."

Now he leaned forward again, and lowered his voice to a whisper, and there was an urgency in it which frightened me. "I will be good to you, shield-maiden. Never before have I wanted a woman as I want you."

Finally he stopped. I felt helpless and unable to speak. A hundred things turned in my brain at once. I only wanted to get away.

"I must go now," I said hurriedly, as I pushed myself up from the table. I walked as quickly as I could across the floor, trying not to break into a run as I headed for the passageway that led to the stairs. I felt all eyes must be on me but I could not raise my head to look.

CHAPTER THE TWENTY-SIXTH

THE WORK OF EACH

THE chamber never seemed as small to me as it did that night. I paced from one end to the other as the noise of the hall below rose up and filled my unwilling ears. The day had held too much; Toki had tried to snatch me on the road and now Sidroc had said he wanted me for his wife. I knew that at least at this I should feel honoured; a man of high rank had chosen me. But instead of feeling honoured I felt merely preyed upon.

Burginde came up, full of gossip from the kitchen, and took no note of all this. "Dobbe said they would be up all this night, roasting and baking," she said as she locked the door. "Something be going on, but we know not what. And the Lady asks if you be well. She saw you leave the hall and feared something had made you ill. But Sidroc told her you were weary and felt you must lie down."

"Yes, he was right," I mumbled.

In the morning Ælfwyn did not come up to us. As Burginde and I dressed we heard by the great commotion beneath us that the hall was filling with men, and decided we should go down.

The door of the hall was open, and men were passing in and out. Before us three Danes shouldered bulging hide packs which they lowered onto the trestle tables that now filled the centre of the hall. Upon the tables was piled a vast array of packs, sheepskins, and hides. On these lay leathern tunics, and some too of hammered rings, swords sheathed and unsheathed, spear shafts and spear points, saddles and bridles, knives and helmets. Amongst all this I saw for the first time the broad-bladed axe, the skeggox, which the Danes alone used in their warfare. We regarded all this, and those who moved amongst these things. Perhaps twenty men were there, opening packs, looking at swords, tightening buckles and straps, polishing the dull iron of their helmets. They all called and laughed to each other as they went about this, and paid us no mind.

A look told us that the table we normally sat at was not in place, and that neither Ælfwyn nor Yrling was in the hall. The door to the treasure room was shut.

I turned to Burginde, but she spoke first. "Dobbe will have us some broth and a bite to eat; 'twill be but a moment to fetch it, and you can up to the chamber again and eat in peace until my Lady appears." She turned and skirted the tables and went through the kitchen passage.

I took a few steps toward the stair, but then stopped and watched the Danes. Each man was sorting and sifting through his weapons and war-kit, and doing it with the cheerful talk and laughter which men about to face death use. It was not strange to me; again I saw the timber hall of Cedd, and the open faces of his ceorls as they thus equipped themselves. What was strange was this: that each ring tunic, each spear, each saddle, each sword, that each and all of them before me now was of far greater make and worth than that my kinsman's ceorls or Cedd himself had known.

I looked at the men themselves, young and tall and hale. Very few had lost fingers; fewer still bore any limp or haltness from injury. The scarred arms or chipped ears amongst them were worn well, as the signs of fierce battle; they were all strong, and proud in their strength. I remembered the thegns of Ælfsige, Ælfwyn's father, who had brought us to Four Stones, and that they were fine men, the finest I had then seen. Now a veil had dropped from my eyes and I thought with a tremble that the power in those thegns of Wessex could not withstand the power of these Northmen who aimed to conquer for themselves all which they saw.

I closed my eyes for one moment, and the noise and bustle before me grew distant. Then a sound behind me made me turn, and there was Sidroc, walking with Toki through the open door, both laden with hide packs and laughing with each other in their own flat-sounding tongue.

Toki made a mocking gesture of respect to me and passed on and dumped his pack on the joined tables. Sidroc stopped before me, and lowered his pack to his feet. Over his arm was hung a baldric of red-dyed leather, worked all over with silver bosses. From it a black wood and leathern sheath held a long sword with broad iron guard. The only decoration was on the grip of wood, deeply and skilfully carved.

The laughter was gone from his face, and he spoke to me easily, even kindly.

"I will not make you run from the hall again," he said, and the directness of this made me look down. His voice was light, and I could not tell if he had given up his pursuit of me. I felt confused, almost as much as I had when I had fled the hall.

A long moment passed, and I could find no words to meet his. I simply nodded. He turned towards the activity of the hall.

"I must go now," he said, and started to lift his pack.

"Wait," I said, and laughed a little, for it seemed bold of me to so stop him. "I only mean, can you tell me what is happening? You are preparing for a siege?"

"A siege?" He laughed too. "No, not a siege, or anything like it."

His easy manner gave me great relief. "Then what is all this?" I asked.

"Nothing of concern. Yrling will take a few men, fifteen or twenty, and go to meet our brothers of whom I spoke last night."

I nodded. "And fix the mistakes that were made," I said.

"Yes, but you should not call it that, since only I believe that they were mistakes." He looked around. "It no longer matters."

Again I knew not of what he spoke. "Will the men go far into Wessex?" I asked. "All are arming as if for battle."

"We do not expect any battle at all, but only fools leave their swords sheathed. We control lands for only the distance of a three days' ride." He paused for a moment. "Also, one always finds opportunities on the road."

I knew by this he meant they would take whatever they could along the way. But I did not dwell on it; a new thought came into my mind. "If you all three go, who will command Four Stones?"

"We will not all go. Yrling will choose whether Toki or I will stay. But he will not tell us until the last moment."

I thought of this. "Why?" was all I could ask. "Surely he trusts you."

He looked at me, and gave a little snort. "Of course he does not trust us."

"O," I said, feeling more stupid than ever I had.

"We will not leave until tomorrow night, so I will see you again," said Sidroc, and then he turned and joined the others.

I walked slowly back to the stairs, turning all this over in my mind. Nothing surprised me more than Sidroc saying that Yrling did not trust him. He had said it with real impatience, as if a small child had asked the question.

Still, I was glad to learn that there would not be a siege, or even, if all went well, a battle. I was not long in our room when Burginde came up with a bronze platter and ewer.

"The kitchen be upside down. Eomer says the Danes are taking a waggon and going off somewhere. Dobbe had already sent food into my Lady and the Dane, and had this all ready for you," she said, setting it down before me.

There were several newly baked wheaten loaves, and some hen's eggs, broken open and boiled in broth. I fell to and Burginde pulled up her stool.

"I saw Sidroc downstairs, and he said fifteen or twenty men would leave tomorrow for Wessex," I said.

Burginde clucked her tongue. "Ach! What if they fight in Cirenceaster, and break so soon the Peace Ælfsige made!" She shook her head. "I do not know if my lamb could bear that, having sacrificed so much."

"I do not think Yrling is that bold. Sidroc said they sought other Danes who had lost a battle far from Cirenceaster." I thought about what Sidroc had told me. "I do not believe they will seek a battle with anyone. At least if Yrling is only taking twenty men he will not."

We heard a woman's step on the stair outside, and both rose and went to the door. It was Ælfwyn, wearing her yellow gown, but with her hair tied back in her silk head-dress in a way I had never seen before.

She greeted us and said, "Burginde, I would bathe now. Do you go and draw me water." Burginde took both our large buckets and went down the stairs with them.

"Your hair," I said to Ælfwyn.

She went to the wall where we had hung a large bronze mirror. She regarded herself in it for a moment, and touched the way her head-dress was tied about her head. "I do not like it, do you?" she asked, turning to me. "Yrling says it is the way married women tie their hair in his homeland."

"Hmmm," I said.

"He must have got it wrong," she said, turning this way and that in the mirror. "This makes me look like a cottar's daughter."

"You could never look like a cottar's daughter," I said in protest.

"I do with my hair tied up like this. I cannot think that the wife of a jarl would wear a wrap in so crude a way."

"Their tastes are different from ours, perhaps." I remembered the coloured designs on Yrling's bare arms. "Yrling has blue and red serpents pricked into the skin of his arms."

"Yes," agreed Ælfwyn, and she began to loosen her clothes. "But that is different; he is a man, and he told me they honour the strength of He who fought the world serpent."

"Yes, Thor, whose hammer he wears," I said.

"That is right," she answered, "for he told me about it."
She untied her head-dress and shook out her hair. "Even
tho' it be the style of his homeland, I do not think I will
wrap my hair this way."

I brought out our large brass tub and took linen towels
from chests. "Burginde said the kitchen is busy; it may be
a bit until she can come with the water."

She stopped undressing and we both sat down. "I am
glad Yrling told you of the hammer he wears," I said, eager
to hear more.

"He wears it all the time," she said, "even when he –
wears nothing else." She was blushing, but her voice was
steady. "Last night I asked him about it, for I wanted to
know why he had placed it around my neck when we
Hand-fasted." She swallowed and looked down, but she
was smiling. "He said it was to make rich my womb, so
that we might have many children."

She went on, but no longer smiled. "He said the
hammer was a powerful protection to both men and
women. Then he raised it to his lips and kissed it, and held
it to me, and I – kissed it too. I suppose it was a dreadful
sin, but just then it did not seem so. And it made Yrling
more pleased than I have ever seen."

She looked up at me. "You were raised by the Black
Monks. Do you think I will go to Hell for that?"

I tried to think before I spoke, yet I wished to speak
quickly, for I could see she was in some distress. "No," I
said, "although I do not know what the Prior might say."

Here I began falsely, for I knew most exactly what the
Prior would say, that it was all sin and error to honour the
Gods in this way, for he thought all that was of the Gods

should be not honoured but destroyed. But this I could not say, perhaps because this I could not believe.

"No," I went on, "I do not think there was real error in this, for you only meant to please your husband, which the Black Monks say always is the first duty of the married woman, so if by this small honouring of his God you have pleased your pledged husband, then who could find it amiss?"

Her face was hopeful. "Good," she said, "I am easier now in my mind about this. It did trouble me, yet as I said it made Yrling more pleased with me than I have yet seen." She combed her fingers through her hair and went on. "He said he does not care if I am a Christian, and that I might even have a priest come live here, as long as I do not pray and cry to make him and his men get baptised." She smiled as if at the memory of this.

"A priest? Then there might be learning, and books, and sums, and many other good things at Four Stones," I began.

"Yes," she laughed, "and think how Sidroc and Toki would enjoy teasing him! We will have to find a special priest, one who was once a warrior, to stand up well in this place."

I thought of the watery-eyed Watcher, unlettered, ignorant, but devout, who had been rounded up by Sidroc to bless Ælfwyn. Such as he would bring no learning nor letters to Four Stones.

We heard Burginde at the bottom of the stair, and I went down to help her, and we filled up the brass tub with the two buckets of hot water and Ælfwyn bathed with lavender oil in her water.

"So you two know all that's going on?" asked Burginde, as she dried her mistress off.

Ælfwyn laughed, and I did too. "We have not yet spoken about it," she said.

"What?" asked Burginde in real surprise. "Not spoken about it, when the whole keep's torn up with preparation, and the hall be filled with blood thirsty Danes sharpening their swords, and Dobbe cooking for three days' worth of adventuring?"

"Calm down, nurse, and let me tell you what I know. I tried to speak to Yrling; it is not easy, for we often times barely say anything to each other. He seemed glad to hear me speak, and tho' at times it was hard, he spoke to me as well."

She paused so long that Burginde urged her on. "I am remembering what he said, that is all. He is angry at some Danes for fighting a battle. I think he is angry because they broke an agreement with other Danes. They also broke a treaty with an ealdorman of Wessex, which one I do not know, but this does not seem to trouble Yrling much. When I saw this, I questioned him, for I said, You have made a Peace with my father and grandsire, and I want to think that you will honour their pledges to you. And he saw how grave it was to me, and he said he did and would honour the Peace as long as my father and grandsire did; but I felt fearful that he said that only because he would be good to me last night."

She stopped, and both Burginde and I were silent, waiting for her to go on. I had been braiding her hair, and brought her my small mirror so that she might see my work. "That is good, for he admires our braids. Now he will not miss the jarl's wife's head wrap." And she smiled at me.

"There is not much else. He said he was sorry to leave me so soon, but that he would return within two weeks or so."

She looked troubled. We were silent for a time, thinking of these things. Then she said, "I do not know how to feel. I am angry and upset that some Danes have been at battle, and I wish soundly for their defeat. But my own husband is a Dane who is, I think, going to aid these same men. And he is a warrior and has done many cruel things to my grandsire's people and to the folk of Lindisse. For this a part of me hates him. And he has cost my father and mother great worry and great wealth. Now they feel in some degree secure that their lands will be left in peace. They wish me joy in this marriage." She sighed and looked down at her hands. "And Yrling himself is not cruel to me, but kind, and has given me great treasure in jewels."

Ælfwyn finished speaking and sat quietly. I looked at her, and my heart was filled with love for her courage, and love too of her great goodness, for she did not once speak of what this marriage had cost her in grief, but was resolute in her desire to fulfil her parent's bidding and do all she could for the good of her people.

She turned to me. "What would happen if Wessex fell? It would become as Lindisse."

She shook her head as if to drive this thought away. But it would not be banished so easily, for it was the thought of all three of us.

Burginde spoke now, and as often, brought good counsel with her words. "And such a one as you," she scolded, turning from the clothes chests to her mistress, "brought up in the finest hall, with the wisest father and most sensible mother, would be believing the boasts of a tribe as bluster-ing and noisy and lying as the Danes? Goose!"

Ælfwyn nodded and smiled a bit. "Mother used to say that the men who boasted loudest had the most need of it," she remembered.

But I do not think any of the three of us thought the Dane's boasts to be empty.

We sat at the table for a time, and then Ælfwyn said, "I suppose we should begin the weaving today," but she did not go to the looms, nor even look at them.

The noise of the men in the hall rose up to us, and as we women sat there it was easy to guess what they were about. We heard the rhythmic pounding as the spear points were hammered onto shafts of ash wood. We heard too the hollow thud of the alder shields, as the men tried them with mock blows to see if they were sound. Beneath all this we heard the steady scraping hiss of the whetstone as the men drew their blades over it.

Burginde regarded us for a moment, but did not speak. Instead she walked to the large weaving chest, opened the lid, and brought forth three spindles. Then she brought forth a sack of carded wool, and three distaffs, and brought this all over to where we sat.

"Spinning's best at a time like this, and we have just as much need to spin as to weave," she said firmly, and handled both Ælfwyn and me a spindle and distaff.

"You are right, Burginde," answered the Lady, taking up the spindle, "and we shall need stockings soon. Let us spin for stockings so that Ceridwen may see the fineness of your thread."

"Your thread could be as fine, if you put your mind to it," replied Burginde with a mild reproach.

"You know I have tried," said Ælfwyn. "No one can spin as finely as you, not even my dear mother."

"Ach! 'Tis always the same, you praise my work, and I end up with all the fine spinning," sauced back Burginde, but it was clear she was proud to be praised in this way.

So we set to work, each wrapping our distaff with a loose coil of the wool, teasing it out with our fingers and letting the weight of the steadily dropping spindles before us twist the soft staple into thread that crept up the length of the spindle shaft. It was a pleasure to do; never did I think I would welcome spinning as I did that morning. But then I was with Ælfwyn and Burginde, and this chore which had always seemed so arduous at the Priory became something we three shared between us in the privacy of our chamber.

So we three women went on with the work of our hands, just as the men below went on with theirs.

LIGHTNING

AFTER we ate at noon we spun for a bit longer. Burginde had almost twice as much thread as we, and the lumps in my own made me ashamed of my little skill. Burginde held her thread differently from me, and she took time to guide my fingers.

"'Tis a smoother pull if you let the first finger droop downward, like this," she said, bending my hand, "and no thread can be even if your pull be not smooth."

I practised this a while, and Ælfwyn teased us both, and said soon she could give up spinning forever if I only could learn this craft as well as Burginde.

Then Ælfwyn began to yawn, and it was the nurse's turn to tease her, for it was clear, she said, that Ælfwyn had found something better to do during the nights than sleep.

Ælfwyn put down her spindle and threw a nearby pillow at her, and we all three laughed.

She stretched and yawned again. "I truly am sleepy. I will lie down and rest for a while. We have done enough today." She pulled off her gown, curled up on my bed and pulled a coverlet over herself. "Work no longer, Ceridwen. Or if you do, let it be something that pleases you."

I put down my spindle, but Burginde kept on with her work. "There will be thread enough for stockings by tonight," she said. "Sleep well."

Ælfwyn sighed and snuggled into the bed. "It will be good to sleep up here again. We must remember to bring up my bedding before Yrling leaves and locks the treasure room." And in just a few moments she was asleep.

I wondered what I should do. The light was not strong enough for fine handwork, and I began to weary of the room. "I think I will go into the hall," I said to Burginde.

"Good," she answered, without looking up. "Likely one of them will cut their fingers off gawking at you rather than their sharpening."

I was surprised at this. "But they almost never look at me," I said. "I do not even think most of them know I am here."

"Humph! I see them looking, and the stars above only know what they be saying in that coarse speech of theirs."

My face must have shown my alarm. She laughed at me and said, "All that's been known to you is your kinsman's hall and the monks that raised you after. Of course the brutes below gawk and speak of you; you be of marrying age and quite comely. 'Tis the way of men, and 'twould be little different if we were here or in the hall of Ælfsige."

I hesitated, and she stopped her work. "Go on," she said, with mock impatience, "you be safe enough in the very hall. Just remember what I told you yesterday about some men thinking No means Yes." She made a little gesture towards the door. "Go and see what you can see. All is well here, and anyone can see yours be a restless nature."

The hall was much quieter; perhaps half as many men were left from the morning. The tables which had been a jumble of hides and packs and weapons now were laid with order. Each shield upon the table was flanked by several spears, their tips pointing outward into the room. Two sheaths lay by each shield, one each for a knife and a sword; and those who would carry also the skeggox had laid this battle axe with their other arms. Most of the weapons lay sheathed, their owners having finished preparing them. Other men still worked at the whetstone, or sat polishing their blades.

I stood some little distance watching all this. Then a man who worked alone at the end of one of the tables turned and saw me. It was Sidroc, and he nodded at me as if he would have me come over. I crossed to where he stood, one foot up on a bench, polishing the blade of his sword with a wooden buffer covered with leather. The long blacked iron guard between the blade and hilt ended in two iron balls that gleamed dully. He did not speak, and I silently regarded his work. His movement was smooth and light, but he attended on each stroke, and when he took the grip in his hand to turn the blade his fingers closed around it with the sureness of the practised warrior.

At last I spoke. "Your swords are different from the swords of my kinsman's men, and those of the thegns of Ælfsige."

"Yes," he replied, going on with his polishing. "Ours are longer by a handspan, sometimes a hand's length. Theirs are a bit broader at the hilt."

I considered this, and asked, "Which is better?"

He held the blade up to his face so he could look along the length of it. "Either one will kill a man," he said simply.

I nodded my head mutely and looked away, aware of the foolishness of my question. After a moment he went on.

"Our longer blade extends a man's reach, and that is nearly always a good thing. But if you are fighting in close quarters, a shorter blade can be brought to bear easier. So they each have their place."

I looked at his height. "You are so tall that your reach must already be greater than most men's."

He nodded. "Yes, but a fast short man can undercut a tall one if he be bold enough."

"Like the tale of David and Goliath," I said.

"I do not know the saga you speak of," he answered.

"It is a story in the Holy Book of Christians, about a young boy who slayed a powerful giant because the giant was over-proud of his force. David was the boy, and he threw a rock that hit the giant in the head and killed him."

"Foolish not to have worn a helmet," replied Sidroc.

I did not try to explain that this was not the point of the story, but that David had prevailed because of his goodness.

So we were quiet again for a while, and I studied the things that lay upon the tables. Perhaps Sidroc's mention of a helmet made me realise that by each and every shield there sat an iron helmet. Some were plain, but many were decorated with inlay of bronze, or covered over with copper foil.

"Every man has a helmet," I said, almost to myself.

At my kinsman's hall only Cedd himself and two or three of his richest ceorls had helmets. The rest of the ceorls wore only leathern caps, strapped over with thin bars of iron.

"Of course," Sidroc answered. "All of Yrling's men have helmets, not only those going with him tomorrow. Many of them have ring-shirts, and each has the finest swords and knives that can be made or captured." His tone was serious, and he looked at me as he said this. I hoped my face did not betray the trouble I felt.

"That is how we have won Lindisse, and how we will continue to win," he finished, and then returned to his work.

I watched him for some little time, and then made bold to speak again. "Are all Danes so well armed? Are all so tall and strong as you men here?" I tried to make the question light, but I felt my voice quaver.

He laughed. "No, we are better warriors than most, and Yrling spends much treasure in arming us, tho' we often capture what we need, as well."

He looked over the war-kits before him, and then back to me. "When we took Lindisse we fought against peasants swinging ploughs. Even the warriors were poor fighters and poorly armed. Only here at Four Stones did we find a real fight. Merewala and his men were seasoned, and well equipped."

He did not need to tell me that despite this, they all were slain.

"Even against the best that we meet, we almost always win. Every man in this hall is worth two men of Lindisse or Wessex; some are worth more."

He stopped and looked at me again. "I myself have seen Yrling kill three men almost at one time, and twice I have killed more than ten men in one battle." There was no boasting in his voice; he was stating a fact.

I must have swallowed hard, for he smiled. "Do not be troubled. You are safe here."

I realised how odd it was that he was right; that Four Stones under the control of Yrling was now one of the safest places we could be. But my thoughts went on, and I spoke them.

"I would not be safe, and I would not be here, if I were my own brother," I said, looking him full in the face.

He seemed startled at this thought, and I went on. "If I were my own brother, you would be preparing to kill me right now."

At first he smiled, but then said quietly, "Yes, I would kill your brother." He looked down for a moment. "Especially if it meant capturing you."

Tears of anger and of some unknown grief were starting in my eyes. "You would not capture me," I managed to say. "I would die by my own hand before you touched me."

I could no longer see clearly, and could not trust my voice. I turned to go. He made a quick motion with his hand as if to bid me stay.

"This morning I said I would not drive you from this hall again, and now I have nearly done it. I did not mean to frighten you. I meant only to show you the worth you have in my eyes."

I stood there before him, and he slipped his sword into its sheath, and sat down on the bench with the sword over his lap. I did not raise my eyes, tho' I could feel that he was looking at me. Finally I sat down next to him.

It seemed like a long time passed. He said, "You have all the advantage."

I did not understand this, and remained quiet.

"I want you, and you know it, but you do not yet want me," he explained. "So you have all the advantage." His voice was mild. "Women very often do," he finished.

I thought of what Toki had said to me on the road, that sometimes men had no choice. Yet Sidroc had chosen me in the first place.

"I am sorry that you want me," I managed to stammer.

He laughed. "Every man at Four Stones wants you. You can have your pick."

"The other men never even look at me," I ventured.

"That is only because you came with your Lady. You are seen as part of the tribute, and the tribute belongs to Yrling."

My face must have twisted in dismay, for he laughed and said quickly, "Do not be upset." Then he said gravely, "It is a great protection to you to be seen in this way. Nothing else but marriage to Toki or me could provide you with such protection."

I said nothing to this, but I felt my anger conquering every other emotion within me. I spoke not, but just tossed my head and looked straight before me.

Sidroc also looked ahead, and when he spoke his voice was quiet. "You are beautiful, shield-maiden, but it is your proud spirit that makes me want you." He paused, and went on. "Now I will say something that will make that proud spirit flame. I say it not to anger you, but to show you how well I regard you. It is this: Yrling would give you to me in a moment. I have only to ask him, and you would be forced to be my wife."

He reached his hand in front of me as if to stop me from rising, but did not touch me. I bit my lip but looked straight ahead. He went on. "What you must know is that I will never ask Yrling for you. I ask only you for you."

He put his hand down on his sword again, and said, "I am used to taking what I want. But I can also wait. I want to be your choice, as you are mine. I want you willingly. That is all I will say."

My anger was gone, and I felt almost numb. I believed he spoke the truth when he said he would not ask Yrling for me. Yet tho' he had meant to honour me by telling me this, in it was still a terrible threat. If I did not say Yes at some point he could in fact grow tired of waiting and ask Yrling. Ælfwyn had been forced to be Yrling's wife; why should not a dowerless maid be forced to wed Sidroc?

No other man had ever spoken to me like this; no other man had ever wanted me like this. I had scarcely seen the two ceorls whom the Prior had chosen for me to pick from. I felt the honour in Sidroc's desire for me, but I could feel nothing else.

He did not seem to expect a reply from me, and indeed asked a question which awoke me from my numbness. "How old are you?"

"I have fifteen Summers."

"You are older than you look," he replied. "I thought you might be fourteen."

I did not know what to say to this; many girls married at thirteen, tho' Ælfwyn was nearly seventeen.

"I am three-and-twenty," he said, as if he had expected me to ask the question in return. "Toki and I were born the same Spring. Yrling is only seven years older than us."

He went on, as if thinking about this. "I am already three-and-twenty, and have never been married. For a long time I did not want to marry; when I was still at home I wanted only to come here and fight, and since I have been here I have been too busy. Also I have not seen any women with whom I have wanted to spend more than a night."

All the time he was talking this way I felt as if I could barely rouse myself. It felt as if something important had happened between us; that he had somehow decided that he would have me as his wife and that there was nothing I could do about it.

I looked at his sword as it lay across his lap. The plain iron of the hilt gave off a dull gleam. The designs carved into the wooden grip were of two men facing each other with intertwined legs and arms.

I found my voice and asked, "Your sword bears a name?"

He touched the hilt and nodded, and said something that sounded like 'Thruma'. "Lightning in your speech."

I nodded my head. I thought of Cedd and the sword he was burnt with.

"You are like us," he said quietly.

I did not answer. I did not want to. Instead I turned my head and looked around the hall. It was nearly empty; it must be late, and I wanted to go back to our chamber.

Sidroc leaned forward and looked into my eyes. "Tonight we will go and make Offering to the Gods for the success of our journey. Come with us, shield-maiden. Odin will listen to us. It will be as if Freyja herself asked."

I looked back at him. I opened my mouth, but words would not come.

"Come with us tonight," he urged. "We will go at dusk. If you wish, ask your Lady to come with you. It will give Yrling great joy if she does."

Tho' I sat there still, I was no longer in the hall. My eyes were filled with sudden torch light in the darkness of a grove I knew well as my kinsman and his men held aloft flaming brands. I heard the clanking of iron as the men moved about the ash tree, chanting their call to Woden in the night. I heard the squeal of the piglet as my kinsman slit its throat and watered the roots of the ash tree with its blood. I heard again the glad cry of the men.

"I will come," I said. I got up and walked across the floor to the passage leading to the stair. The coloured pavement seemed to move under my feet.

THE OFFERING

I was halfway up the stair when the door of our room opened and Burginde came out on the landing.

"I be fetching ale for Ælfwyn. Do you want a bite to eat as well?" she asked as she passed me.

"No," I answered, "but I am thirsty."

She stopped on the stair and squinted at me in the dim light. "You should have napped yourself. You look all worn out."

She continued on her way, and I went in and found Ælfwyn pulling on her gown.

"It was good to sleep," she said. "Where have you been?"

"Only in the hall," I said.

"Are the men done with their preparations? Did you see Yrling?"

"I did not see Yrling. The men are mostly done." I walked over to the window and closed it against the gathering dark.

"Sidroc asks if you and I will come out and make Offering with them." I said this slowly, and there was a long pause before Ælfwyn answered.

233

"Make Offering? You mean sacrifice to their Gods?" She did not seem to be judging this, but merely considering it in surprise.

I looked down at the floor for a moment. "Yes, they will make sacrifices to their Gods for their safety and success."

Then I recalled Sidroc's words. "Sidroc said it would give Yrling great joy if you came."

"I am a Christian; I cannot sacrifice to the Gods. To do so is the worst blasphemy." There was no fear in her voice as she said this, only a kind of wonder.

I nodded my head but said nothing. She walked across the room to me, and her eyes searched my face. "Yrling must think that I am willing to forsake my faith after what I did last night."

"Yrling has nothing to do with this; he does not expect you. It was Sidroc who expects me to come. It is just that he said it would give Yrling joy if you were there as well."

"Sidroc expects you to come?" she asked in amazement. "Why?"

She answered herself before I could speak. "Is it because you were heathen before you went to live at the Priory?"

"Yes," I began, "I suppose so. But he expects me because I told him I would be there."

"You told him you would come?" She pulled a chair from the table and sat down. "To make sacrifice to their Gods?" Again there was no judgement in her voice, only wonder.

I felt I must say something. "They are the Gods of my father and kinsman," I finally said. "For half my life they were my Gods."

Ælfwyn's face softened, and her voice was kind. "What of your mother? Were they her Gods as well?"

"No," I said, "not her Gods; but she was heathen just the same, and worshipped the Gods of the Old People."

"Ceridwen, who bears the cauldron of life," she answered with a nod. She stood up. "And you want to go and do this thing?"

I waited a moment and searched my heart. "Yes, I feel that I want to."

"What will happen there? What will you do? I did not even think women were allowed."

"Women are important in offerings to Woden, or Odin as they call him; men believe the Gods listen best to a woman."

"They believe that? Our priest at home teaches that women must work hard to have their prayers answered, since it is by woman's fault that we are all born in sin."

"Yes, I know." I looked straight at her. "The Gods are not like that; the Gods honour women, whether they be Goddesses or mortals. And in their offerings, men honour women too. It is the shield-maidens that choose who is to die in glory, and who carry up the souls of the dead warriors to the hall of the Gods."

"Is that why Sidroc calls you that? I thought he just meant a fierce woman by it."

"They have another name as well, but most men call them the shield-maidens. Also Freyja, the Goddess of love and beauty, is a powerful warrior. Many men make sacrifice to her."

Burginde now came in with the ale, and as she filled our cups said, "They be gathering below, dressed to go out, and slinging on their swords."

Ælfwyn lifted her cup to her lips and drank. Then she said to me, "Let us go, and watch."

So we two wrapped our mantles about us and headed down the stairs.

About twenty men were in the hall, strapping on their baldrics and pinning on their wool cloaks. Several of them, including Toki, were lighting torches from the firepit, and lining them up ready to be carried out into the night. Yrling was there with Sidroc, and they turned and saw us dressed to go out. Yrling's face lit up at the sight of Ælfwyn. She went towards him, and Sidroc walked over to me. He spoke not, but only looked at me. He wore the slightest of smiles, so slight that his scar almost did not move.

Yrling called to the men, and they picked up the torches, and we walked down the stone steps and out of the hall. The night was clearer than the day had been; already the brightest stars, the wanderers, shone out above.

I had not been out in the keep yard at dark. Now I saw the canvas awnings pulled down over the armourer's workshop, the storehouses shut up to keep the goods from damp, the great oak doors of the stable closed. Along the top of the palisade watchmen stood, and oil lamps mounted next to them on the ridge of the walls flared away. We walked singly or in twos, and the torches cast a strong light and made huge our shadows. Yrling led the way with Ælfwyn beside him. We heard a creaking noise and a side door in the palisade opened, and a Dane struggled through it carrying a large wicker cage holding two cocks. He was greeted by many of the men, and he fell in with the rest of us.

We walked on, and soon the ground began dropping away, and we passed a clump of trees, and walked through them and on. All this time Sidroc said nothing, and I also spoke not.

Ælfwyn had taken hold of Yrling's arm, for the ground was growing rougher. We were no longer on a path but walking through trampled grasses. The ground grew soft, and softer still, and the torch light shone on the remnants of horsetail and bishop's mitre and other plants that love the wet. We stopped, and just before us I could see a dark slash in the clay, as if a trench or ditch had been dug. As the torches grew closer to it, the glint of metal within the trench told me that weapons and other such things had been offered here. A wooden post, taller than a man, rose up out of the pit, and as the men moved about enough torch light fell to show that it bore the carved image of Odin.

Yrling moved before it, and Ælfwyn came and stood by me and Sidroc. She did not speak, but slipped her hand into mine, and tho' it was not a cold night, she shivered in her thick mantle of marten fur. We now all stood close together in a single curved line, and Yrling stood facing us with his back to the pit of clay and the image of his God.

He raised his arms to the men, but it was clear he did not address them, for when he spoke he kept his eyes upon the starry heavens. His voice was different from any I had heard him use, smooth and rhythmic; and his words rose and fell as if reciting a saga. He went on, his words a chant, and I closed my eyes and only listened. The flatness of his tongue and the strange words began to yield some secrets up to me: I heard the names of the Gods. I heard the names of Odin and Thor and Tyr and Freyr and Freyja and Loki. And as I heard him speak these names in his own accents, I realised that these were the first words he had so spoken that I recognised.

I opened my eyes and looked about me. Ælfwyn still gripped my hand. She was watching Yrling with wide eyes, but there was no fear in them. Sidroc stood on my other side, and when I glanced at him I saw his eyes too were closed. Yrling went on with his chant, and some one of the men, perhaps Toki, began another chant which wound in and around the chant of Yrling. Other men joined in with this second man, slowly at first, but with gathering voice. Then a third chant began, started by Sidroc; and men joined with him, so that all three chants were intertwined. It was as if three forces met and were speaking, and I knew it to be the Answer of the Gods, in which the men tried through their voices to engage the Gods in their requests.

Then Yrling fell silent, and the second chant dropped away, and the third as well, and there was only a low sound, almost like a growl, coming from the throats of the men.

The man who had the two cocks in the cage drew them out feet first, and the flapping and squawking of the cocks were the only other sounds. He stepped before Yrling, and squatted down so that the frantic wings of the birds brushed the damp Earth. Then the growling noise rose up loud in the throats of the men, and in one motion Yrling dropped down on his knees and pulled his sword from his baldric. He held it just a moment above the cocks, and then the blade flashed through the night and in a single movement struck off both bird's heads. Then the Dane holding their feet let go and Yrling speared both birds on his sword blade at once, and with a cry cast the still-flapping bodies into the clay pit.

The men cried out, and I knew at this moment they would all draw their swords as one, and salute the Gods; and this they did. And Ælfwyn and I stood there, clasping hands, as Yrling held his sword aloft, and each man held also their sword aloft behind him and cried out in joy and in hope that the Gods had listened well.

Then with this joy on their lips each man strode to the pit, and plunged the tip of his sword into the soft clay, and so took part in the slaying of the sacrifice. Yrling turned back at us, and saw Ælfwyn, and looked at her with light in his eyes, and held out his sword to her. I said in her ear, "He wishes you to pierce the Earth with it for him; the Gods will honour him if you do."

She stepped forward and took the heavy gold hilt in her hand, and moved to the edge of the pit and raised the sword and plunged it with good force into the Holy Earth, and Yrling's eyes filled with pleasure. We all stood a moment under the cloak of night, the wanderers bright above us. The only sound was the soft rustle of the men wiping clean their blades. I looked up into the heavens and felt as if a bright star had fallen into my breast; as if my dead father and kinsman and lost mother stood with me.

Yrling spoke, in a clear glad voice, and we began to move away from the place of sacrifice, back up through the moist ground and dry grasses and towards the palisade of Four Stones. And tho' the men spoke around me, I heard not, for my ears were full with what Sidroc had said, 'You are like us.' He walked at my side the whole way, and never spoke. He had no need to, for those words of his were ever in my ears.

We gained the palisade walls and walked through the keep yard and down the broad stone steps into the hall. The men went each to their war kits on the tables, and moved them onto benches along the walls, and began to set up the tables for the meal.

Ælfwyn and I headed up the stairs. Her face was flushed from laughter with Yrling, and when we were inside the room her colour deepened.

"Well," she said, and almost seemed to hide her face as she took off her mantle, "now I suppose I really will go straight to Hell."

That night sleep took a long time to come. I looked up into the dimness of the roof rafters above me, and imagined the stars bright in their paths overhead. I closed my eyes and the hall below seemed far away. I saw again the torchlight under the night sky and heard the chanting call of the Danes at the place of sacrifice. I saw Ælfwyn raise the sword and saw again the face of Yrling, hot with pleasure and love for her action. I thought of what they were doing right now; that he was going away for many days, and going into danger, and even in my ignorance I knew that his embrace would be the stronger and his touch more urgent because of this.

I did not want to think these things, but just then my thoughts were not mine to command. My mind ran from one thing to another. At times Toki's face came before me, laughing and sneering. Most of all I seemed to see Sidroc, and to remember his words. If he really wanted me so badly, he must esteem me very much. Yet how could Sidroc ever be my choice?

Then I would think of Ælfwyn, and that she never in a thousand Summers would have chosen Yrling, and yet she seemed to be content. Perhaps she would one day even love him. At least he was kind to her, and she tried to be kind to him in return. So all of these things kept tumbling about in my head, and beyond it all I knew that she and I would tomorrow night be alone with either Sidroc or Toki, and could not decide which was the better and which the worse.

As I was pulling on my boots next morning Ælfwyn came into the room with her beautiful hair loose over her shoulders. She wore last night's gown and sash, but looped into the sash was a huge ring of iron and bronze keys. They jingled as she came into the room and she burst out laughing when she saw us.

"He has given me all the keys," she said, and laughed again as if she could not believe it.

"Too bad all the rooms they opened be burnt down," answered Burginde.

"They are not all burnt down. Besides, most of these are to chests in the treasure room. And he has given me the key to the room itself!"

"To the treasure room itself?" I asked. It hardly seemed possible that a Dane would entrust his new wife, a woman of Wessex, to hold the keys to such riches in his absence. I did not have to say this; I knew all three of us were thinking it.

Burginde gave a little whistle. "'Tis hard to believe," she finally said.

Ælfwyn stood before us and laughed again. "I know; I can scarce believe it myself. I was surprised that he did not give me any keys the day we were married, as is the right of every bride in Wessex. Then I thought how foolish it was to expect this from him. And then this morning Yrling gave me this whole ring. He said it was a custom that on the third day of marriage the woman receives the keys."

"So she's had three days to prove her worth, eh?" asked Burginde warily.

"You are so hard, Burginde," answered Ælfwyn. "We do not know their customs."

She untied her sash and let the heavy ring slip out into her hand. Even Burginde could not resist the temptation to look closely at the keys as Ælfwyn fingered them. "There is another set, of at least some of these, and Yrling said that either Sidroc or Toki would hold them while he was gone."

Burginde sniffed at this, and Ælfwyn gave her a little shove towards the door. "Go on, Grumpy, and fetch me hot water," she said.

When she was gone Ælfwyn turned to me as she was undressing. "You know Ceridwen, I begin to think he is not so different from our own people." She looked about as if searching for words. "In some ways he is very different, his speech and his Gods, and of course he is a Dane, and all of that is so strange. But he is good to me; better than I ever thought possible." Her voice grew soft, and she stood looking at the cluster of bright keys upon the table. "When he is with the other men, he is something fearsome; he looks just like what I had most feared. But when he is alone with me, he is . . . good to me. He is always very – eager, but he touches me gently afterwards."

She looked down and her cheeks flushed. "He wants very much to have children."

"Perhaps you will soon," I said.

She only nodded, and Burginde came bumping up the stairs with the bath water.

DEPARTURE

IN the hall Yrling sat alone with Sidroc and Toki. Food and drink were before them, but he spoke to them earnestly and they touched it not. As we walked by I saw Yrling's and Toki's war-kits, for they were easy to discern by the fineness of the helmets and the gilt upon the bosses of their shields. Next to these I recognised the shield and helmet and plain iron-worked sword of Sidroc. Even then they did not know which of them was to go and which would stay.

Ælfwyn and I went to the table, and the men moved over to make room for us, but barely looked at either one of us. Yrling went on talking in the same low voice. I felt him more formidable than ever, and just at that moment imagined him sitting at table with Ælfsige, bargaining for the tribute and the hand of Ælfwyn.

Ælfwyn and I began to eat, and slowly the three men joined us. Yrling stopped speaking, and both Sidroc and Toki asked questions. As he answered them he seemed to notice Ælfwyn for the first time, and took her hand as it lay upon the table. He smiled at her with real pleasure and went on talking.

Afterwards they walked out of the hall and into the keep yard. Ælfwyn and I watched them go, and then went over to the firepit. We looked down silently on all the ready war kits of the Danes, and each thought our own thoughts.

Up in the chamber we found Burginde spinning. She looked at Ælfwyn and shook her head.

"How he can leave such a one as you so soon to resume his killing and plundering is beyond the likes of me."

"He is not killing and plundering," answered Ælfwyn. "At least," she hesitated, "it is not his intent as he leaves."

I could only think of what Sidroc had said about opportunities along the road. "Here," I said, taking up our spindles and trying to make cheerful my voice, "let us catch up with Burginde so we truly will have enough for stockings."

Just before noon we heard a man's step on the stair.

"It must be Yrling," said Ælfwyn, quickly setting down her spinning. "He said this morning he would come for me." She gave me a quick, shy look and then went down the stairs.

Burginde and I continued to spin in silence. At last I said, "I think he cares for her, and that it is hard for him to leave her so soon."

"Well, he be having his full of her right now. At least he be not indifferent to her beauty." Her spindle reached the floor and she stopped in her work for a moment. "Nor should he be, for he could not find a woman as good and as beautiful as she. And of course right now he be kind to her; all new husbands are. The sooner she can be gotten with a babe, the better."

"You do not seem to like him very much," I said.

She went back to her spinning. "I like him as much as I need to; 'tis only what Ælfwyn herself is doing."

In the afternoon I went down to the keep yard. I could tell by the whinnying of horses that they were being brought out from the stable, and I wanted to see them, and perhaps visit Shagg.

Outside the hall a waggon was being loaded, and in it I could see shields and spears and several chests of provisions. From the great stable the horses were being led to a leathern tie stretched between two sheds, and their neck ropes fastened to it so they could be saddled and bridled. I stopped and looked at them long, for they all of them were splendid beasts, firm-necked, long-limbed, and tightly muscled.

The horses stamped and tossed their heads, and the yard was filled with their whinnying and the laughing and calling of the men. I saw the young stable boy Mul, Ecgwald's cousin, holding the head of one horse who was trying to rear, and watched in dismay as a Dane cuffed him for his efforts.

Sidroc came out of the stable, leading a bay with a wonderfully long black mane and tail. He tied it far from a prancing red horse, and came over and stood by me. "They will fight if I do not keep them apart," he said, indicating with his head the two animals.

"Is the bay yours?" I asked.

He nodded his head. "He is my favourite; I have five others."

I thought of the wealth this represented, to have six horses of such quality.

Now Toki came up, leading his grey horse, and stopped before us. He slapped the loose end of his rein in his open hand and looked at us both, but did not smile or sneer. He spoke to Sidroc in their own tongue.

Sidroc answered him in a short voice and Toki laughed and led his horse away.

Sidroc stood and watched him. "He said if I am the one to go that you will be his woman by the time I return," he said, still looking after Toki.

I began to speak, but he went on. "He knows you do not like him. He only says this to try to torment me, so whether I go or not I am troubled." He turned to look at me. "This is one reason Toki will never be powerful. He will always be a boy, playing the games of boys."

At that moment I hoped that Toki and not Sidroc would be going with Yrling, but I could not bring myself to speak openly this wish of mine. I wished they would all go, or none of them go.

Another Dane came up and said something to Sidroc, and he said to me, "Yrling wants me in the hall."

So we both turned and walked to the hall.

Toki was before the firepit, shouldering his pack and shield. He grinned at Sidroc and spoke to him, and Sidroc answered. I could sense no anger in their voices or their faces. Toki walked past us and out into the yard, and we saw Yrling and Ælfwyn through the open door of the treasure room. She raised her hand, so I followed Sidroc across the hall and through the treasure room door.

Yrling was lacing his ring shirt over his leathern tunic, and already wore his leathern leg wrappings. Upon the bench his black baldric lay ready. Ælfwyn was dressed as she had been when she went down, with her new keys looped onto her sash. She smiled at me as she stood before the bed.

Yrling spoke to Sidroc, and Sidroc nodded his head and answered, and I saw no disappointment or surprise or other emotion in Sidroc's face.

Then Yrling spoke in our own speech to Ælfwyn. "Until I return Sidroc commands. You must obey him and keep all in good order. I will return as soon as I can."

His voice was firm and his face serious. He looked at Ælfwyn and said no more, and Ælfwyn answered, "I understand," in a clear grave voice.

He smiled and pulled her close with his arm. He did not kiss her or speak more to her, but turned to his baldric and sword. Beneath it sat a ring of keys, which he tossed to Sidroc. Then he lifted the baldric over his head, and strode out of the room.

We followed him, and passed the shield and baldric of Sidroc, alone at the firepit. I wondered how he really felt as he walked by it.

Outside the door Osred was harnessing two horses to the waggon. Danes carried bridles and saddles to their tied mounts. The horses stamped and tossed their heads, and the yard was filled with the whinnying of the horses and the laughing and calling of the men. We saw Toki mount his beautiful grey horse and force him to prance about so he jostled the other horses, which made the Danes near by curse him. Toki laughed and sped forward as if he would be the first out the huge gate, now standing open for the horsemen.

Then Yrling swung himself into the saddle of his red stallion, and all the men were horsed. Yrling spoke out loud to Sidroc, and Sidroc replied, and Yrling turned his horse and looked down on Ælfwyn, and raised his hand in salute. She raised her own, and a slight smile crossed her face, and he called out and the horsemen moved across the yard and out the great doors of the wooden palisade. The waggon creaked behind it, and then it too passed through the palisade gate, and the doors were slowly shut.

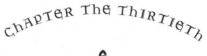

TO BEAR THE TRUTH

WHEN darkness fell we began to hear the men fill the hall below.

"Sounds as loud as if they all were there," said Burginde, as we prepared to go down. "They be wanting to make up for their smaller numbers with louder noise."

Burginde was right. The men sprawled over the tables and benches as if it was the first day of a holiday. As I looked them over a new thought came to me, that perhaps Yrling had had Sidroc stay because he could keep them in better order than Toki.

Sidroc sat at the main table. Only two other men sat there; the rest had been chosen by Yrling to go with him. Sidroc rose as we approached, and to my delight he took the place where Yrling always sat, and placed Ælfwyn at his left hand, and me next to her. This was the first time we had sat thus, and I felt glad for it, for it meant she and I could really speak to each other during the meal.

We three laughed and jested together as we never had before, and then Ælfwyn asked him, "How is it that you speak our tongue so well? For you speak much better than Yrling."

He nodded. "It is only because of Yrling that I do. When Toki and I were still young, and Yrling first began coming to these lands each Summer, he brought back many slaves from Northumbria and Lindisse. These became part of our household, and because Toki and I were young and always near them, we learnt their speech. We knew we soon would sail for the rich lands from which they were captured."

He paused. "Yrling was older, and away, and so did not learn as we did. But he will soon catch up, since he has taken a wife from Wessex, and one who is not afraid to speak to him."

Ælfwyn did not seem to notice this praise, and it was clear she thought about the folk carried off in raids so many years before. Then she asked, "You knew then you too would come here?"

"O, yes," he answered, "for there is little for us at home. We are too many with too little land, and it is poor and stony. Here there is much land, and few people, and Winters as mild as our Spring. So we knew we too would soon sail, and make our fortunes here."

She only nodded her head. Some little time passed, and the mood of the table had changed. Then she asked, quite earnestly, "If you intend to stay here, why have you not brought wives?"

"We have been at war for almost two whole years. Those of us who have wives at home thought we could bring them before this. But not until this Summer will they come."

She went on. "So your wives, and sweethearts, will come this Summer, and the men will begin to farm?" There was a note of intent in her voice, and she did not take her eyes from Sidroc's face.

"Yes," he answered, shrugging, "the women will come this Summer, when the seas are calm."

"And the men will farm?" she persisted.

"Crops will be raised," he replied. "Also animals."

"And there will be no more raids?" she asked, and once again I wondered at her courage and boldness.

At last impatience shown on his brow. He looked at her long, and then spoke as if well choosing his words. "We do not all have what we want. Those who are tired of battle will farm."

She thought of this, and tried another way. "And Yrling will divide the land between you, so that each man has so much, as we do here?"

"Yes," he said, "I think he will."

She was again quiet, and then looked at him. "And what of the village women? How will they survive?"

He shrugged, and she went on. "Their husbands are all dead. Why do not the men here take up with them?"

"I do not know," he answered. "I myself never visit them. It is said they will have nothing to do with those who want to marry them, tho' some of them will meet with the men in return for food."

"They are hungry, and have hungry children," said Ælfwyn, and her voice was on the verge of anger. "You have already despoiled all of them, and their daughters too. Why should you wonder that they will not marry you?"

"Because in other places the women will wed us, if only as you say, to keep themselves alive." His voice bore no anger, but the words were terrible just the same.

Ælfwyn did not speak; her eyes were lowered and I felt her trembling at my side. I could think of nothing I could say to drive out these awful truths.

Sidroc looked over to us, and shook his head. "You do not understand these things," he began, and he looked about him as if searching for words. "It is the nature of war that men are killed and women are taken."

Ælfwyn lifted her head, and there was fire in her blue eyes. "Is that what you said to the daughter of Merewala when you killed her father and ravished her?"

Sidroc clapped his hand upon the table so that the platter jumped. "I did not ravish the girl. Yrling and I were fighting Merewala and his men when it happened. Some of us broke into the hall and found where the women were hiding. It never should have happened. Yrling was very angry. He wanted to wed her."

"Wed her?" asked Ælfwyn, in a voice without colour.

"Yes. He had never seen her, but she was a princess of Lindisse, and so he wanted to wed her. He was very angry."

Ælfwyn shook her head as if trying to accept all this. "Did Yrling punish those who had despoiled her?"

Sidroc thought for a moment. "No, he did not," he conceded. "But as it turned out, they did not live long, for they were amongst the men carried off in the fever we had last Winter."

There was nothing more to say. Ælfwyn and I sat silently, and Sidroc picked up his goblet and drank. He said to us, "It is hard to hear such things. I will speak of them no longer."

Ælfwyn shook her head and said, "No Sidroc, do not say that. I am glad that you speak to me thus." And it was clear by her voice that this was so.

He leaned forward a little with his reply. "I am glad you can bear the truth. Most women, and many men, cannot."

"I hope I can always bear the truth," answered Ælfwyn. She sipped from her golden goblet, and it felt as if all was right between them.

We ate a bit more, and drank, and then she asked him, "You told us that those who were content would settle down. Tell me if you will be one of those?"

Here a smile spread across his face, and tho' he did not look at me my face burned and I looked down. "No," he answered slowly, "I am not yet content."

THERE WILL BE LINEN

"**L**ET us find Dobbe," suggested Ælfwyn in the morning. "She was once seamstress here, and will know all about the growing of flax and the making of linen at Four Stones."

I was eager to go anywhere, and so we two went down into the kitchen yard. The bread ovens were being stoked by two men, and on the massive table Eomer was dressing a pig. He looked up at us, and dipped his head, and called out for Dobbe. The old woman came forward from one of the sheds, her hands all over flour from her bread baking. "My Ladies," she croaked, and her eyes watered so she looked as tho' she forever wept.

"We have come to ask you about the making of linen at this place," began Ælfwyn. "I do not see a retting pond, nor any flax in the fields."

"Aye, there be precious little of anything in the fields," answered Dobbe. "But a pond we have, or had; the Danes let it dry up. 'Tis the hollow yonder before the great wall, to the left of the gate."

Neither one of us remembered noticing such a hollow. Ælfwyn asked, "What about flax? Or did you buy it?"

Dobbe smiled faintly. "Buy it we never did, nor grow it either, for we were so blest with it growing wild in the vale that we gathered it at will, and it grew as thick as parsley, so that we never wanted for it."

"And now it too is gone?" questioned Ælfwyn.

"I hear tell it is gone, all trampled by the Dane's horses, for the vale is now naught to them but a pasture ground for their beasts."

Ælfwyn nodded her head. "Another thing, Dobbe. We want women to spin and weave. What village women could come here?"

"Here?" echoed Dobbe. "None will come here."

Ælfwyn tried again. "Then will the women spin for a wage in their village?"

Dobbe looked as if she could not comprehend. "There be nothing to spin, and no one to spin it for," she said at last.

"You do not understand. There will once again be sheep and flax. Therefore there will be fleece and linen, and we will need many women to spin and weave, and they will weave for this hall and also for their own families." There was great firmness in Ælfwyn's voice.

Dobbe trembled the more, and the tears flowed fast down her withered cheeks. "If you make such things come to pass, then you are an angel sent from God."

Ælfwyn laughed aloud, but she spoke with gentleness to the old woman. "I am no angel, only a woman who must provide clothes for her household." She took a step nearer to her. "You will help me, Dobbe? You will tell the women not to fear me?"

Dobbe nodded her head. "No one living could fear you, Lady. I will do all I can."

"Then I thank you," smiled Ælfwyn.

As we were walking past the great stable I saw the boy Mul moving within, and we went in after him. He bobbed his head but was speechless.

"Mul, this is your new Lady," I began, raising my hand to Ælfwyn. He bobbed his head again, and I felt it best to go on with my talking rather than try to get a word out of him.

"We are going to ride out today, and I want you to ride my mare first so she is tame again." I spoke slowly and tried to make my words kind. Ælfwyn and I began to walk to the end of the stable where I knew Shagg was.

"I ride her every day, Lady," Mul finally choked out. "Each morning we take all the stabled horses out, and run them, and yours along with them. She be fit to ride."

We three stood before Shagg. "I am glad to hear that," I said, scratching her ears as she pressed forward to greet me. "We will come back later then," I said, still rubbing her ear.

Mul reached out his hand and she nibbled at his fingers. I began to laugh, but then saw how thin was the hand and arm that Mul extended. He was at the age when boys begin to shoot up to young men, and are often gawky; but it was more than this; he looked as tho' he were starving.

I turned to Ælfwyn and read the same thought in her eyes. Mul still held his hand out, generous with affection. His rags barely served to cover his thin body, and there was an ulcer on his leg above his naked foot. Over his right eye was a brown and purple bruise that extended to his ear, and a bit of dried blood sat in the hollow of the ear. I remembered how a Dane had cuffed him across the head in the keep yard.

I stood looking at him, and then Ælfwyn did something. I do not know who was more surprised, Mul or me,
but I think it was the boy, for what she did was this: She
touched his face. She reached out her beautiful white fingers and gently touched the bruise above his bloody ear.

He almost jumped, but did not; only took a gasping
breath.

She drew back her hand, and looked straight ahead
for a moment and then to me. "Go to the kitchen," she said
calmly. "Bring eggs and bread and whatever you can."

I turned and left, walking as fast as I could. The whole
way my eyes were burning at the memory of how he had
flinched at the touch of a gentle hand.

In the kitchen yard I saw Susa and had her take a scrap
of cloth. Into this she tied boiled eggs and loaves and half
a roast fowl and two cold boiled turnips. As I watched her
tie this small bundle, I knew that this was more food than
Mul had eaten or even seen for many days. I knew he would
never have bread made from wheat; if he had bread at all it
was from barley or oats. I wondered how long it had been
since he had had any fowl. I tucked the bundle under my
arm and started back for the stable, aware of all the meat and
drink that was set before me each day in the hall, and that I
ate without thought. I remembered how we had eaten our
first meal in the chamber, and praised the food, and Burginde
had simply said, We must thank the wretches thither for it.
Mul was the wretch who went hungry while we ate.

When I entered the stable I saw Ælfwyn still standing with Mul. I went to them, and Ælfwyn pointed that I
should give the bundle to him. He took it, trembling, and
backed into the corner.

Ælfwyn looked at his hunted face and said quietly, "Eat it now before anyone sees you."

She turned away, and she and I walked slowly up past the row of stalls. We could just hear the rip of the cloth being pulled apart, and a then a gasping, gnawing rush of sound as he fell upon the food.

We walked on without turning, and stopped in the stable doorway until we were sure Mul had enough time to eat in safety. Then we went on, straight into the hall and up the stair to our room.

Burginde was not there, and the room was quiet. I did not want to speak; I could not read Ælfwyn's mood and was fearful of saying the wrong words.

"Now I understand why Dobbe does not believe we can once again make linen." She looked at me, and her eye was bright and her voice steady. "There will be linen, and wool, and these people will be fed."

I took Ælfwyn's arm and squeezed it. "How wonderful you are," I said.

She laughed. "Please not to say that. I have no idea how I am going to do all this." She sighed, and then said, "I only know that I will."

"Yes," I said, "I know that you will."

Burginde came clumping up the stair. "There you be," she said, huffing as if she had been running. "That Scarface be looking for you. Something about horses."

"We are going to ride out," said Ælfwyn. "Do you wish to come? We could find a very mild horse for you."

"'Twould have to be dead to be mild enough for me," answered Burginde. "No, there be plenty to be doing here. Laundry and spinning be my choice over riding."

"As you wish, since I know I hardly work you at all," said Ælfwyn.

"I did not say that," protested Burginde.

"No, I did," answered the Lady, which made both she and me laugh.

We took our mantles and gloves and headed downstairs. Sidroc was in the hall in front of the firepit. Under his leathern tunic he wore one of linen. Leathern wrappings strapped his leggings. He did not wear his baldric and sword, only his knife on his belt. He was pulling on a pair of gloves.

He nodded at us, but said nothing, and we were quiet too. We walked out into the yard and back towards the stable. Outside it were two stablemen, holding the halter ties of three beautiful mares: a black, a chestnut, and a grey. We stopped before them.

"These are three mares of Yrling's," he said to Ælfwyn. "Choose one."

She regarded them all. "Since it is just for the day, I choose the chestnut," she said.

"It is not for the day, but to be yours each day," Sidroc said.

She looked at him, and he nodded his head. "It is true. He told me to bring you these three that you might have your choice."

She laughed. "Then I still choose the chestnut; I think it the most beautiful."

"I think you have chosen well," answered Sidroc. He looked at me, and then walked into the stable. He came back leading a bay mare. He stopped and said to me with a smile, "You do not have a choice. This mare is for you."

It was a beautiful animal, with a delicate tapering head and the same long black mane and tail I had admired on the bay stallion.

"Thank you, but I will not ride Yrling's mare but rather my own," I said.

"It is not Yrling's, but mine; and it is now your own, for I give it to you," he answered.

I looked at Ælfwyn, and then back at Sidroc. I shook my head and said, "I cannot accept such a gift."

I looked again to Ælfwyn for help, but she gave me none. She glanced at Sidroc, and then at the bay mare. "You cannot ride Shagg, Ceridwen; she will never keep up with us."

I looked at her, speechless, but she went on. "I want to ride fast, and it will not be fair to me if you are poking along on that pony."

Finally I shook my head again, and looked back at Sidroc. "No, no," I said. "I cannot accept this from you."

He stood there, looking back at me, and then said quietly, "Then I give this mare to your Lady," and passed the lead to her.

She took the lead and said, "I thank you." Then she looked at me and said, "Now I have two mares, and I can only ride one. So I choose to give one to my friend." And with this she placed the lead rope in my hand.

I knew my face was flaming, but I did not know what to do. Ælfwyn did not wait, but simply kissed me on the cheek, and the two mares were led away to be saddled and bridled. She whispered in my ear. "Do not be silly. There is no harm in taking such a gift; he is now my kinsman." She smiled and said, "Tho' he wants to be your kinsman."

When the mares were saddled Sidroc went off, and
came back mounted on a handsome roan horse. As we
moved off, Ælfwyn said to him, "You are not riding your
magnificent bay?"

He answered with a little laugh, "No, for we would
not have a good ride if I took him along with your mares.
This horse is gelded, and will leave us all in peace."

The bay mare felt big beneath me; certainly she was
far taller than Shagg. She had a beautiful way of lifting her
feet which made her almost prance. Her long mane spilled
over her neck in a shimmering wave of black.

I looked over at Ælfwyn, sitting so gracefully upon
her new mare. Its mane and tail were nearly the colour of
her own hair. She glanced at me, and tho' I felt a bit uneasy
about this gift from Sidroc, I could only smile back for the
sheer pleasure of the beauty of these two mares.

Once outside the gate Ælfwyn turned and pointed
across the roadway. "That must be the retting pond," she
said, for the hollow there was still wet and boggy. "Not too
close to our windows, as you wished," she said to me, and
I could but laugh.

Sidroc rode a bit before us, and now stayed his horse.
As we came up to him she asked, "This was once the retting pond, where the flax stalks were soaked?"

He looked back at the hollow. "There was a pond there;
for what reason I do not know. We watered our horses at it
until we carried the spring that fed it into the yard."

She nodded. "It is a retting pond, and we must allow
it to fill again so that we might have linen."

He did not respond to this, but she did not seem to expect an answer. She was now looking ahead along the road.

We went slowly, tho' the road was fairly good. We neared women working outside their tumbled huts or digging in the wet Earth of their tiny crofts. Never was I more aware of the difference between those who can ride, and those who must walk. The beauty and value of our horses, and the height it gave us as we looked down upon the villagers made great the gulf that distanced us. They looked at us mutely, and some of them seemed to raise their hands in a sort of greeting to us, but just as many scowled as they saw who rode with us. I felt sorry that Ælfwyn should see this; she wanted so much to help them, and had given so freely of the secret silver to show them this. But one silver coin could not remove the grief from the hearts of these women, nor could all the gold in the world give them back the life of peace they had lost.

I tried to smile down at the women, but could not; and when I looked at Ælfwyn I saw her face was frozen too in a kind of quiet sorrow. She did not hurry through, as many would have done faced with such misery, but rode even more slowly.

One woman who was working at a tub outside her hut was bolder than the rest. She rose from her work, and stood at the broken wattles of her croft gate, her eyes fixed on Ælfwyn. She called out in a clear voice, "I bless your coming, Lady."

And at this Ælfwyn reined her horse, and bent over and put out her hand that the woman might touch her, and the woman reached up and touched the soft gloved

266 OCTAVIA RANDOLPH

hand as if it were a holy thing. Ælfwyn spoke no word, but her eyes were full of the speech of pity and goodness.

All this time Sidroc rode slowly and quietly behind us. I could not tell his thoughts, or even see his face, but I felt grateful that he did not curse the village women or try to hurry us along the road. Few men like him, I thought, would have had this patience. Yet he was one of the men who had reduced these women to their misery.

When we had gone some way along the trail, we began a slow canter. Sidroc moved his horse forward and said, "This is a good place for speed; the ground is smooth."

Ælfwyn looked over to me and asked, "Are you ready?" and I twisted my fingers into the mare's mane as I grasped the reins more firmly.

"Yes," I answered.

"Good," she said, and then was gone, for she had of a sudden kicked the chestnut mare and was off.

Sidroc waited not an instant but was after her at once. I too, had no choice, for my mare fairly bolted after them, and I held on as hard as I could. Ælfwyn was far ahead, but Sidroc had the advantage, for the longer legs of his horse ate up the distance between them in a moment. They went neck and neck, and I could just hear Ælfwyn laughing and the laughter too of Sidroc.

I urged my mare forward and loosened my grip on the reins. She dashed to catch them, but the trail was too narrow to join them at full speed, so we ran a little outside and behind them. Sidroc began to pull ahead of Ælfwyn, and she kicked the mare forward even faster. But Sidroc began to slow, reining his horse down, and we all three began to canter again.

He turned to Ælfwyn. "You do not like to be beaten," he said with admiration.

She was breathless and laughing. "Nor do you, or you would not have stopped," she replied.

He laughed too, and we rode on at an easy pace, resting ourselves and the horses. Sidroc fell in next to me, but did not speak.

I felt I must say something to him, so I said, "This mare is wonderful. But you should not have given her to me."

He was quiet, and then said, "I did not give her to you. You refused my gift, so I gave her to your Lady."

Now I felt that I had truly acted amiss. "I am sorry if I have slighted such a noble gift," I began. "It is just that . . ." I could not finish; I did not think I could make him understand that I did not want to be bound to him in gratitude for a gift of such value. So I only said again, "I am sorry."

"It is all right," he said lightly. "At least you are once again speaking to me. Since Yrling left you have hardly said a word to me, or looked at me."

"It is only proper that you should speak with Ælfwyn," I began uncertainly. "You are now her kinsman, and she has no one of her rank here."

He looked as if he had not thought of it quite this way before. "Yes," he only said.

The meadow was now giving way to slender trees and spreading bushes. The trail remained broad and smooth, and we three rode together along it.

Many thoughts were turning in my head as we went along. The Sun shone brightly down upon us, and the air was warming up. Our horses were beautiful, and it was a great pleasure to be out of the keep yard at last. Yet it was hard to feel any real happiness.

The trail began to rise beneath us, and the low hills that could be seen from the window of our day chamber were before us. We went on, and Sidroc stood up in his stirrups and called out a long loud whistle of many notes. Ælfwyn and I looked all around the hills, and saw no man, but the whistle was returned none the less. The trail dipped down, and we rounded a clump of trees and looked across the wide expanse of a sheltered valley. The first thing I saw was a great timber longhouse, freshly made, large and of good and sturdy build. The roof was of sod, but other than this it looked very like the timber hall of my kinsman.

Beyond the longhouse were many paddocks, large and small, and in them were the horses that made up the great treasure of the valley. Perhaps two hundred horses were there; far more than the number of Yrling's men.

The men by the longhouse were calling to Sidroc, and he said, "I will be back soon. Then we will ride up to see the horses."

He cantered off, and Ælfwyn and I turned our mares. The horses in the paddocks were whinnying and nickering, and our mares called out in response. Mine wanted to join the others, and I had to pull her hard to turn her away.

"How beautiful your mare is," commented Ælfwyn as I urged the bay forward.

"Sidroc says I should thank you for her," I said, and then had to laugh a little. It was impossible to feel angry at Ælfwyn for helping me gain such a wonderful horse. Still, I said, "I wish you did not give her to me. I do not want Sidroc to think that I like him."

She lifted her eyebrows. "You do like him," she said.

"Well," I said, feeling flustered, "he is much better than Toki, but I do not like him; not in the way he wishes I would."

Of a sudden she was serious. "I am sorry. I will not tease you about him. He is easy to like, despite his scar and all. He treats both of us well, and I believe I can trust him." Her voice began to trail off. "But he is still a Dane . . ."

She went on in a quiet voice, "I do not even know what I say anymore. I am wed to a Dane. I am now a part of his life, and there are none about us but Danes, at least amongst men of rank."

She sighed, and lowered her head. I looked down also, and began to notice the stubble through which we had been walking.

"Flax," I said. "Ælfwyn, here is the flax. We are walking on it."

She looked across the ground. "Yes," she agreed, squinting at the shrivelled stems. "It is all over."

We traced the perimeter of the trees, all the time looking down. "It is here," she said, peering over her horse's mane, "and here, and here also." There was gladness in her voice, and we moved our horses forward at a trot.

"And more here, and here," I called out, as our mares crossed the moist Earth. Everywhere was the Winter-dried stubble of flax.

"'As thick as parsley,' that is what Dobbe said," she answered.

"If they do not move the horses, this will grow up well this Spring," I said. "Do you think there is enough here?"

She looked across the unfenced portion of the valley. "I think so, at least for this first year. It will take awhile to get the pond ready, and to find women enough for the

pounding and hackling of the stems. But we will not be
able to harvest the flax until Hlafmessetide anyway, so we
have time, and if all this field here remains untrampled, I
think we will have enough." She looked at me and beamed.
"How glad I am that we rode out today!"

"Yes," I answered. "First we are given beautiful mares
to ride, then we find both pond and flax. It is a lucky day."

Sidroc now rode up to us. He was smiling as he came,
and we could not help but smile back at him. "What have
you found?" he asked, looking down. "Gold upon the
ground?"

Ælfwyn laughed. "Not quite gold, but something
valuable just the same. This plant we walk upon is flax,
from which linen is made. In August we shall keep many
people busy with retting and hackling, and by late September have much linen thread to spin. Then we will weave,
and so have cloth for all the men, and new tunics can be
cut and sewn."

Sidroc looked doubtful. "This is where we keep our
horses. We need this as new pasture land."

Ælfwyn still smiled, but her voice was steady. "And
you also need linen." She paused and said, "How else will
the men of the hall be clothed? We will save a great deal of
silver if we grow and make our own."

He thought about this. "It will be easier, perhaps, if we
have our own supply," he agreed.

"Good," she replied. "I will tell Yrling about it as soon
as he returns." With this she rode ahead of us.

My mare now turned her head and nibbled at the
neck of the roan horse Sidroc rode. He laughed and said,
"She is wise, and picks her company well."

"Thank you for this beautiful mare," I said, feeling that I must at last say so with the gratitude I felt.

He moved his hand as if to dismiss my words. "It is not my gift," he said again, but his voice was without anger. He added, looking down at the mare, "She is about four years old, and this Spring should be bred for the first time. Choose well your stallion, and you will increase your riches quickly."

These words, true as they were, made me blush, for I felt he spoke about me as well. Finally I stammered out, "Perhaps I will not breed her this first year."

He turned in his saddle to look at me, but I kept my eyes down on the mare's neck. "So she will not have a mate, just as you will not?" he asked. His voice sounded playful, but I did not want to look at him.

I did not answer, and he went on. "In my country every woman marries," he said, as if to tease me with this.

"Every woman?" I had to ask. It did not seem possible. Of course I realised no woman there would be taking up the Holy Path, as they did here, but even so, it seemed hard to believe that every woman could find a husband.

"Yes," he said, and I looked at him and he began to smile. "At home a man can have as many wives as he can support. Therefore there are no unmarried women."

My mouth must have dropped open, because he laughed. "It is true," he said, and I knew I must believe him. "Each wife is treated as an equal, and all children are equal too."

I looked ahead at Ælfwyn and had a sudden thought. "Does this mean –" I began, but he answered before I could end.

"No, no," he said, still smiling but speaking in earnest. "Yrling wants only one wife. When we came to this land we found your women would not accept this custom of ours. So since we are to settle here we too will take only one wife."

He stopped talking, but I could not answer; I was still too surprised.

He spoke again. "Therefore it is more important than ever that the wife I choose be the right one."

Again I did not speak. We went on, and nearly caught up with Ælfwyn. Then he said in a low voice, "You will be mine, shield-maiden. That is all I will say."

As we rode by the longhouse Ælfwyn said to Sidroc, "Since you can build so fine a building, why do you not repair Four Stones?"

"It is not mine to repair," he answered, but then went on. "We did some work on it, but when the fever came many men died. Other things became more important."

Ælfwyn regarded the timber hall a long time. "If you can build as well as this, I hope it will not be long before Four Stones is rebuilt."

"Yes, we can build such things well," he returned. "You should go to Jorvik and see."

I knew Jorvik was the fallen city of Eoforwic, the chief place in Northumbria. It had been taken by the Danes, and rebuilt, since so much had been destroyed in the battle. It was an old place, and had been a great city under the Cæsars, and had been ruled until just a few years ago by the Northumbrian king Osbert. Now it was wholly Dane, tho' they had in name only a Northumbrian king of the Danes' choosing.

She did not reply. We began to cross the field of flax stubble and head to the trail. When we reached it Ælfwyn looked down at the hard clay under our horse's hooves and said, "You have done a great deal in a short time." She said this quietly, as if thinking aloud.

"Yes," agreed Sidroc, "but we have just begun. Next Summer, and the Summer after, this land will ring with the hoofbeats of our horses, and many more cities like Jorvik will be ours."

Ælfwyn said carefully, "You speak as if soon all here will be Dane."

"Most will be, yes. Northumbria and Lindisse already are ours, and Wessex will soon fall. Mercia has little defence, and will follow."

Ælfwyn waited a long time to respond. "If Wessex falls, what will happen to the Peace that was made with my father and grandsire?"

"I cannot say; I do not know. Yrling will honour the Peace he made, but he is a jarl, not a King. He cannot keep others from your home."

It was simply said, but the words were terrible. Ælfwyn pulled up the reins of her mare, and turned her horse so that she faced Sidroc. She looked at him and said, "My father made this Peace on the belief that Yrling was a great jarl, powerful enough to keep his word by his own men, and to keep other Danes from Cirenceaster. Now you are saying this is not so?"

"Yrling will honour the Peace he has made. This is all I know."

Ælfwyn took a breath, and I could see there was a war within her breast. But she did not flare up, and instead looked long at Sidroc. She only said, "I must and will believe this."

She turned the head of her horse, and moved ahead of us down the trail.

I was greatly troubled by all this, first by the calm words of Sidroc, and then by the question of Ælfwyn which he could not answer. We rode on, with me thinking about this all the time, and then I said to Sidroc, "You think Mercia also will fall?"

"Yes, for it has fewer defences than Wessex, and cannot stand long against us once we turn our efforts there."

I thought about this and said, "King Burgred has ruled a long time, and in peace."

"Now he is old, and can no longer command as he once did."

I thought of his wife, the good queen. "Æthelswith, his wife, is the sister to King Æthelred of Wessex."

"I know. But Æthelred does not have enough men to divide his forces across two borders. He can no longer aid Mercia when his own Kingdom is falling."

I thought of my small village, and the timber hall of my kinsman, and the life I had known there by the marshy banks of the river Dee. My father and kinsman were dead, and no ceorls remained to fight. My thoughts turned to the Priory, and the monks who lived in peace and poverty there. Who would defend them?

"What are you thinking?" asked Sidroc.

"Of my dead kinsmen, and of the Holy Men who raised me when I was alone."

"The Christian priests always have much treasure," said Sidroc, as if he was remembering this.

I felt close to tears. "These men do not. They are poor, and gentle, and have but little gold, and that for the Glory of God."

"Their God is not glorious. He is not a warrior, and does not even take a wife."

"I do not mean glory in that sense. I mean that the few treasures they keep are to honour God."

"Gold is for men, and the pleasure it brings us and our women." His voice softened. "You yourself remark on the many good things we have. Gold and silver and fine horses and rich stuffs are for those strong enough to win them. You and your Lady now are part of us, and many such things will be yours." He stopped, and then went on. "And you, shield-maiden, are not as the other women of this land. You are like us."

I did not want to hear this, and I could not find words to answer any of it. I began to move my mare ahead to join Ælfwyn. Some impatience I was feeling stopped me, and I turned to Sidroc. "Why do you not use my name?" I asked.

I did not know if he would laugh, but he did not. "I want to, but it is hard for me to say," he answered. "I like to hear your Lady call you by it," he finished.

I felt suddenly abashed that I had made him speak thus. "It is the name of a Goddess of the people of Gwynedd," he said, after we had ridden on in silence for awhile.

"How do you know that?" I asked, amazed that he had this knowledge of a folk so distant, and of their Gods.

"I asked. Your Lady told me," he replied. After a time he said, "How came you to have such a name? The Welsh are your enemies."

"We have often fought them, yes. But we have lived on their borders a long time, and some of them live amongst us." I remembered the small bones and dark hair of the Artful One, and decided to tell him. "Tho' I do not look it, my mother is of their people."

He nodded. "Your father captured her and did not sell her because she was beautiful."

This thought startled me. "I do not know," is all I answered.

He glanced at me and asked, "Tell me of the Goddess you are named for. Is she the shield-maiden of those people?"

"No," I said. "She is more the bringer of good things."

"Like Freyja," he said. "Love and pleasure and glory."

"No," I said slowly. "Not just the same. It is more like abundance. Ceridwen bears the Cauldron of Life."

"Ah," he answered, and sounded thoughtful. "Life." He added simply, "Then you will bear many children. That is good."

HARD QUESTIONS

WE went into our room and took off our mantles and gloves and smoothed our tousled hair. Ælfwyn went over to the wicker cage and looked in at the linnet. The little bird was silent, and Ælfwyn also spoke not. I wondered if I should speak to her, or perhaps just fetch our spindles so we might work.

I began to move towards the spindles when she said, "I do not know what I will do if Cirenceaster is attacked." She looked at me and raised her hands in a helpless gesture. "It is too hard to believe Sidroc's words, yet I must believe them. What will happen if another, more powerful Dane decides to fight my father?"

I had no answer, but she sought none. "My father cannot pay another tribute such as he sent to Yrling. He is rich, but he has many people to care for." She crossed to the table and sunk down in her chair. "Perhaps the next Dane will not be content with only treasure, but want as well the hall and lands and sheep and slaves that make up my home."

I yearned to speak some comfort to her, but knew none. I sat next to her and said, "Yrling will honour the Peace he made. Sidroc said that you can bear the truth, and he honoured you in saying this. I do not think he would lie to you." Now I began to cast around for words of my own. "And Yrling is powerful. I do not think he would let any other Dane take Cirenceaster."

She lifted her head and asked, "Then he himself might take it?" She turned this thought over in her mind. "My father would never relinquish his lands. He would die defending them."

I began to say that surely Yrling would not kill her own father, but these words died in my throat. There was no reason for me to think that he would not. I felt certain that she held the same thought, and neither one of us spoke.

In the afternoon Burginde rummaged amongst our wool sacks, feeling with her hands how much carded fleece was left.

"And what will we be doing for wool when this fleece we brought with us is gone?" she asked, to no one in particular. "Shear the heads of the Danes and spin that?"

But Ælfwyn took the question seriously. "Yes," she said, "That is our next task, to find wool. Flax and retting pond we have. Sheep must be got somehow; I do not know how."

"Dobbe said the sheep here be all eaten," said Burginde.

"And gone wild into the woods," remembered Ælfwyn. "I wonder if they could be gathered up again. The wolves could not have eaten them all."

"It is worth a try," I said, and tho' I was ignorant of the ways of sheep, I well knew that Ælfwyn was not.

"Even if we recovered ten ewes, it would be ten less we need to buy," she said with decision.

Burginde stood with her arms on her hips and laughed. "Never did I think the day would come that you should question the need to buy anything! 'Twould do your dear mother good to hear you speak thus; she was always a great one to manage and despaired at her careless daughter!"

Ælfwyn took it in good humour. "That was before I myself was charged with providing for the needs of a household." She eyed the sacks of fleece along the wall. "Besides, this should have been my first concern all along. I am scheming for linen, that we might have that smoothness next to our skins, when wool, which drives away the cold and will clothe even the poorest amongst us, is a hundred times more important."

I could but smile at her. "Since you plan for both, there will be both."

"I pray that may be." The softness faded from her voice. "The better that I manage, the less lack there will be, and the more content Yrling and his men."

⁂⁂⁂⁂⁂⁂⁂⁂⁂

As we drank our broth next morning Ælfwyn was quiet and thoughtful. She tossed a few crumbs to the linnet, and looked at it for a long time.

"My bird is not well," she said. "I think it will die if it is kept here much longer."

The tone of her voice made Burginde and I look at each other. It was as if Ælfwyn spoke of herself and not the linnet.

She turned to me and said, "Do you go after you eat and let it free."

"Yes, of course I will," I said, as kindly as I could. "Do you want to go with me?"

She shook her head. "No, it is of Cirenceaster; I have lost too much of what I brought."

"Perhaps it will fly home," I said, trying to sound cheerful.

"We have more need of the sweetness of its song here in this wasteland," said Burginde.

Ælfwyn nodded to all this and sat back down. "Where will you take it?" she asked.

I thought about this. "I do not know. Somewhere outside the keep yard, where there are trees and shrubs, and it can shelter and be safe while it learns freedom again."

"That is good," she said quietly. "Please be careful. I do not like to send you alone; perhaps Burginde should go with you."

"No, no; I am fine," I answered, "and will welcome the chance to walk, and especially to do some slight service for you."

In the yard I headed for the small door by the gate. Once outside I walked a few paces, and then paused to look about. Ahead were the clumps of trees we had passed on our way to the place of sacrifice. Surely there I would find a good place to free the bird. I looked down at it in the wicker cage. It seemed to know it was away from the confines of our chamber, for it fluttered about and beat its wings.

I went on past the trees, to the wooden post rising out of the sacrifice pit. A glistening black wing flapped from within the shallow pit, and a raven cawed and rose from the remains of the Offering, beating its great glossy wings and complaining at my presence. It flew into the branches of a beech not far away, and looked down upon me the whole time I was there.

The pit was littered with bits of metal. Broken knives and bent swords and shattered helmets glinted as they lay half covered in the soft clay. Bones of many small animals, some with hide still clinging to them, were strewn about. Feathers drifted and swirled in the slight wind, and a clot of them were caught up against the base of the wooden post. I raised my eyes to the post. The image carved upon it was crude and simple, but it had in it a force that held my eyes long as I gazed upon it. It was Odin, one-eyed, all-seeing; and in each fist clutched close to his chest was gripped an unsheathed sword.

It was much like the image of Woden before the timber hall of my kinsman Cedd. It was one of many carved images of the Gods, strong with magic, before which he and his ceorls would worship. I recalled those posts, and seemed to see them more clearly now than ever. My kinsman was now dust, and the magical images too. The Prior had pulled them down and had them burnt when he took over the hall.

I looked again into the shallow pit. I saw in it many stories of battle and gain and loss. There was death there, in the bones and skins of the sacrificed, and there too was life. There was pride, and boasting, and thank-offerings and cries to the God for prowess and deliverance. Bare and open to the merciless view of the afternoon sky, silent and unwatched by all save the ravens, the pit revealed its truths of the men who had gathered there.

And I gazed upon this, and stood thus clutching the linnet's cage to my chest; and the tears started down my cheeks and dripped from my chin. I set down the wicker cage and dropped to my knees in the soft Earth, and I sobbed.

I wept for what I had known, and what I had not known, and what had been lost. I wept for my dead father, whose face I could not remember, and for his dead brother who had raised me. I wept for the lost hall of timber, and the burnt images of the Gods. I wept for the Prior, and for the arts he had taken such pains to give me.

I wept for Ælfwyn, for her beauty and courage, and wept, too, for the young man she had loved and would never see again. And I wept for these Danes amongst whom we now dwelt, and of whose lives we were a part. In them was cruelty and lust, and also goodness and love, and I wept the more to think of this.

My tears fell from my eyes and watered the quickening Earth, and I stumbled to the beech tree, and lifted my wet eyes to its branches scratching the face of the sky, and called out loud and long the name of She whose name I bore. And no one's face came before me; not my kinsman nor the Prior; no one condoned or condemned. I was alone with Her, and at that moment She was in the beech; and for that moment I felt a great lightness and joy, as if a stone had been plucked from my heart.

I hung the cage from the lowest bough, and pried open the little door, and the linnet hopped from perch to perch and at last leapt into the air.

And I took my sash from around my waist, the sash with the pheasants in thread-work upon it, and tied it on the bough and so made Offering; and I kissed the grey bark of that tree, and felt joy.

Then I walked on, up the path, around the shrubs and budding trees, and back towards the keep of Four Stones.

CHAPTER The THIRTY-Third

THE VILLAGE
AND ITS SECRET

NEXT day Burginde brought up food from the kitchen. As we ate she of a sudden jumped up and flung her iron warp beater at the corner.

"Mouse!" she cried out. "They be getting so bold they come as soon as our food does."

We had before this heard mice rustling in the night, and once Burginde had surprised one in the very act of escaping from our larder chest; but this was the first time one had been so bold as to enter the room in plain sight of us all.

"We need a cat," I said.

"Ach!" answered Burginde, retrieving her beater from the floor. "Spooky yowling things. Near as bad as the mice."

"I think we should get a cat, now that the linnet is not here to suffer from it," said Ælfwyn. "You recall the yellow one we had, Burginde, she was gentle and pleasant to stroke."

"And as good as catching a mouse as me," said Burginde.

Ælfwyn only laughed.

283

"There must be cats in the stable," I offered. "Shall we go and get one?"

"You go and choose one," said Ælfwyn. "I picked the yellow one, and as Grumpy says, she was no mouser."

So I took up my mantle and went off to the stable. I was glad to see Mul outside, holding a horse as the smith finished shoeing it. He led the horse around a few times, and the smith spoke to Mul in the tongue of the Danes, and seemed to tell him that the shoe was a good one, for Mul led the horse inside the stable.

I followed him in. "You speak the speech of the Danes?" I asked in some wonder.

"No Lady, not speak it, but I know now enough of it to understand what they say to me." He paused, and shifted awkwardly. "Be you looking for your mare? I will fetch her up."

"No, but I am looking for something – a cat. We have mice aplenty in our chamber, and they are growing bold."

"Ah," he said. "That is bad. If they are bold that means there are many, and soon you will have a swarm."

"Ugh. Well, we do not want that. Do you have any cats we might take?"

"Yes, Lady, and you might have your pick, for we have a nest of kittens in the loft, and they be all yours for the taking."

"We will start with one, and see how it works," I laughed. "I hope we do not need all of them."

He shook his head. "Swarms be bad." He climbed the ladder and vanished into the hay loft.

I heard scuffling, and Mul appeared, clinging to the rungs with one hand and trying to stay the furious claws of a tiny kitten with the other. It was a strange coloured little creature, speckled brown like tortoiseshell.

"'Twill be the best mouser of them," Mul assured me.

"How can you tell?" I asked.

"It be the only one that looks like its mother, and she be the best mouser in the yard." He kicked at a pile of rough cloth upon the stable floor. "I will put it in a sack, so you can take it without fear. 'Twill soon tame, with you Ladies."

I returned to our chamber holding the sack out at arm's length. I spilled it open unto my bed, and the kitten leapt out, spitting and dancing sideways. We three laughed so hard that we could scarcely talk, and Ælfwyn seemed pleased with my choice. She took a fragment of roast fowl and tossed it upon the floor. The kitten pounced upon the meat at once, perhaps because it seemed to fly into its view, and then finding it so savoury, devoured it.

Ælfwyn tossed another piece to it, and said, "Well, little Browny, I feed you now to tame you, but you must work hard in clearing out mice to get more."

In the hall that night Ælfwyn said to Sidroc, "On the morrow we will ride out to the village so that I might speak to the women about spinning and weaving for us. We will not be gone long, but I want you to know that we will go."

He nodded his head and I wondered if the way Ælfwyn said this made him smile. She did not ask him for permission to go, but she was careful to tell him that she wanted to and would go. I felt how clever she was about this; she did not want to claim too much freedom and anger Sidroc, nor did she want to lower herself to the estate of a younger sister with no freedoms at all.

And ride out we did. First we had to put Burginde on Shagg, which was not easy, for the nurse fairly balked at having to do so, but Ælfwyn said she would not let Burginde walk while we rode, so ride she must.

When we three women came down, Mul had our horses tied by the mounting block.

"Mul," Ælfwyn said, "Does your mother still live? Is she amongst the village women?"

He stammered, "Aye, my Lady, she be still alive, and living there."

"I am glad to know that, Mul, for I have need of her help, and hope in return to help her as well," she replied. "Tell me her name, and I will seek her out."

"Meryth is her name, Lady," he said, "and her croft be the one closest to the walls of Four Stones." "Good," answered Ælfwyn. "Then perhaps I shall speak to her first of all."

Mul nodded his head, and Ælfwyn took the stirrup he offered and climbed into the saddle. Mul helped me, and then Burginde up, and we set off, at a slow walk to please the nurse, through the yard.

The morning was a fine one. Winter's back was truly broken, and now nothing could stay the coming Spring. "Burginde," said Ælfwyn, trying to get the nurse to ride even with her, "you will remember which women seemed the most sensible and trusting, and which could speak for the others with some authority, and so I will count on you to help me."

Burginde's elbows were jostling up around her shoulders. She swayed from side to side upon Shagg's broad back, and her ruddy face was redder than usual with the effort of keeping her seat. "Ach!" she complained. "You might count on me more if I knew my brains would not be knocked out of my head by this jolting beast!"

But there was no time to tease her back, for we were nearly before the first of the huts. As we reined up, a woman who had been behind the hut appeared, struggling under the weight of a wooden tub which she held in her arms. A baby was strapped upon her back, and as she came upon us she nearly dropped the tub in her surprise. She was, like all the villagers, thin and ragged, and her face was pinched and faded. A few wisps of colourless hair escaped her dirty head wrap and rested on her brow. Still, she had a vigour and erectness about her, and I was glad to see that a smile of welcome and interest began to play about her face.

"Greetings," began Ælfwyn, with great courtesy. "Are you Meryth, mother of Mul?"

"Aye, Lady, that I am," replied the woman, and dipped her head low, "and you be the new Lady of Four Stones, the one who has fed my poor boy, and been so good to us here."

Ælfwyn only nodded at the mention of these kindnesses. "We have come for your help, Meryth. I want to speak to the women here, as many as is possible, for I want truly to help rebuild your village. And as surely as I stand before you I need your help as well, for since I am now Lady of Four Stones I have a large household to care for, and we want both linen and wool, and the women to spin and weave it."

Meryth took this all in, and nodded her head gravely.

Meryth answered, "If you Ladies please to ride on to the last huts, we could all gather in the croft of Wilfrida the Dyer. I will follow and bring the women to you."

We rode on slowly down the road as Meryth went from croft to croft, gathering women and their children to join us. As we reached the hut of Wilfrida, Burginde said, "Be ready now for the mistletoe on the tongue," but I think Ælfwyn was too much in her own thoughts to hear or answer.

The door to the hut opened, and an old woman peered out. Her hands, stained a sort of blackish blue colour, proclaimed her calling, and we knew we had found Wilfrida.

She saluted Ælfwyn with her hand, and bobbed her head. She was chewing something, what I could not tell, and tho' she did not speak she did smile in a cracked way.

Ælfwyn looked down at her from her mare and said, "Greetings, Wilfrida. I am Ælfwyn, the Lady of Four Stones, and I have come to speak to you and all the women. Meryth is bringing them, and we will meet here in your croft."

Wilfrida pulled wide the door and croaked out, "Be ye welcome, Lady."

I tied our horses, and we passed through the low croft gate. We did not stand there long, for soon we heard the sounds of the approaching women. There were perhaps thirty or forty women gathering. I looked at Ælfwyn, wondering how she would speak to so many. She gave me a little glance and then drew a quick breath.

Wilfrida opened the croft gate, and the women filed in, one by one before us, and stood on the unploughed plots of the croft. They stared, wide-eyed, at us, and some smiled a bit, but all, save Wilfrida and Meryth, who tried to hurry them in, seemed ill at ease.

I looked about and found a wash tub, and turned it over, so that Ælfwyn might stand upon it and be seen and heard the better. She stepped up on it, and looked across at the worn and unwashed faces of the women before her.

Again she spoke with courtesy and kindness. No woman of her rank, I thought, spoke thus to cottars; yet speak she did, and hearing her I thought no woman nor man could hold any fear of her.

"Greetings, good women. I, Ælfwyn, thank you for your welcome, and come to show myself to you in peace. I am now mistress here, and your distress and want sorrows me, and I begin by pledging to you my aid and help, so that you and your children might live and grow strong."

Many of the women's faces softened, and I thought I saw several of them clutch at their bosoms where they might be hiding the silver coin they had received as token of Ælfwyn's concern for them.

"I know that you have suffered greatly, and nothing can restore to you the life that was yours under your old Lord and Lady;" she went on, and the women stirred at these words, "but I desire to help you feed yourselves and your children. I do not yet know how this will be done, for we need seed, and tools, and most of all help in sowing. But I will try."

Now the women were turning to each other and whispering, some of them with fear, but others with hope on their faces. Ælfwyn paused and regarded this well. After a few moments she went on.

"Perhaps you have no reason to trust me, and I do not fault you if you are fearful. But I came from my home to help spare it from the sufferings you now know, and so will do all I can to help you."

"In fact," continued Ælfwyn, "I have need of your help, and that is one reason I speak to you today. I have great need of spinners and weavers, for the household I must supply is a great one." She spoke slowly now, as if grasping for the right words, and for the first time began to falter. "Since so many of you are now . . .alone, perhaps some of you would be content to spin and weave for me . . ."

The buzzing amongst the women now became open speech. I did not understand why they were so agitated, and it was clear that Ælfwyn did not either. I looked at Burginde, but she was looking hard at Wilfrida.

Meryth pushed forward. "Forgive me, Lady, but we must speak to you, for you may be our last hope," she began in a low and urgent voice, but several other women began to shriek and call out against Meryth's speech.

"Be still! Be still!" cried out Wilfrida, and the women were silent, save for some sniffling.

We all turned and regarded the withered face of the old woman. She glared at the village women and began, "Here be goodness, and life, and help, and ye be deaf and dumb to it," Wilfrida cried, gesturing to we three. "What proofs do you want? Did ever the first Lady of the Dane ride out to see us, and she be even a Lady of Lindisse? And here be a Lady who blesses us with silver and stands before us, and asks our help, and pledges hers, and ye be only gawking."

Wilfrida cast her sharp eye at Meryth, and Meryth once more began to speak. But Meryth turned and addressed the women. "My loss be not less than the rest of yours, for my eldest son is dead, and my risk is as great as any of yours, for it be the return of my husband we speak about, and my new babe is not his, but of the Danes. And I say, if we ever hope to bring those still living back to us, let this good Lady help us do so, for she be our best hope."

This speech amazed us, and we did not understand, but we did not have to wait long for light.

Meryth turned to Ælfwyn and said, "Lady, some of our husbands still live, tho' like wild animals, foraging in the forests, and we be fearful to bring them back, for the Dane may sell them off as slaves far from us. So if you can bring them back, and we can farm again, we will live."

I think Ælfwyn was too astonished to speak, and Wilfrida went on. "'Tis true, Lady, some of our husbands and sons escaped the slaughter of the Danes, and once the fighting was over should have returned; but for fear of capture and slavery in a distant land they live roaming the forests North of here. If the Dane will not sell them they will return, but most say they would rather starve in the forest than be shipped off in chains."

Ælfwyn found voice and asked, "They have lived in the forests for two years?"

Meryth answered, "Yea, Lady, for nigh onto two years now."

"Do they ever show themselves? How do you know they still live?" she asked, trying to grasp it all.

"They send word; by one way or another we hear of them. The monk who came here not long ago carried a message from them. Sometimes they try to send us meat they snare, but it be dangerous."

Ælfwyn looked at me, shaking her head. She turned back to Meryth and the women. Now that she knew their sacred secret, they looked at her with even more fear and awe. When she spoke, her voice was full of warmth. "It is amazing that they live. I am glad for it, and I will do what-ever I can to make certain they can return in safety. Until then I swear a solemn oath that this knowledge lives and dies in our breasts."

Each woman sighed out in release. They pressed forward, murmuring thanks and prayers.

We mounted and left, but not before Wilfrida thrust into Burginde's hands a basket of dried ferny leaves.

We slowly moved off, the women around us raising hands in Fare-well. Meryth bowed her head before Ælfwyn in gratitude.

Burginde was the first to speak. "So if the Dane will neither slaughter nor sell the men, we will have farming, and food again."

I said, "No wonder the women would not marry the Danes. Their own husbands still live, or some of them, at least."

"Yes," answered Ælfwyn, thinking it all through, "and I cannot believe that Yrling would think it anything but good that these men still live, for the labour it will bring and the money it will save."

"Still," questioned Burginde, "how can you be certain the Dane will not sell the men? 'Twould be most awful to tell him and then have him round them up and send them off for the silver they would bring."

Ælfwyn's answer was simple. "He must be made to understand that they will do more good here, farming." She looked down the road to the looming palisade of Four Stones, and spoke almost to herself. "Flax and wool and these village men returning home, that is all I must asked him for." And she gave a little laugh, as if it was too great a task.

"I want to get off this beast and walk," complained Burginde.

We went slowly back to the keep, for Burginde walked behind us as I held Shagg's rein in my hand. We talked along the way, but as we got closer we fell silent. The watchful Mul took our horses and we walked through the yard and rounded the corner to enter the hall. As we did we saw Sidroc coming up the stone steps. He had a slight smile on his lips, as he wore so often, but as he came closer I saw he was looking at me in a fixed way.

He did not greet us other than stopping before us and nodding his head. Ælfwyn returned the nod and went on, with Burginde behind her, but the way in which Sidroc looked at me made me stop.

We stood there silently, watching Ælfwyn and Burginde disappear down the steps into the hall. Then he turned to look at me again.

All he said was, "On my ride today I passed by the place of Offering."

There was some light in his eye, but I could not read his face. I did not know what to say, but I felt my cheeks begin to burn. He had seen the sash which hung as an Offering to Her, and knew, or guessed it, to be mine.

Without speaking I moved away and walked down the steps into the hall. I went straight up the stairs to our chamber, and there found Ælfwyn washing her hands and Burginde busy with fetching a towel. Upon the table lay my sash, neatly folded.

I picked up the sash and as calmly as I could laid it with the rest of my clothes. Then I turned and went back down into the hall, and saw Sidroc standing alone at the firepit.

I walked over to him and stood by his side. His eyes were narrow as he gazed into the glowing coals.

He began to speak, but kept looking at the fire. "Do not be angry that I returned it to you. When I saw it I felt that you would not like Yrling and the other men to see it."

In fact, I only then began to think of this; but I felt at once that I did not want the other Danes to know that I had made Offering in this way.

"You think of everything," I said, but so softly that he had to move his head closer to hear me.

"If that were true you would be mine tonight, and every night," he answered. "And do not fear the wrath of your Goddess for taking your Offering. I left Her something of my own in its place."

"Then I thank you even more," I whispered.

I did not know what would happen next, and I did not expect what did happen. Sidroc gave a little cry, almost like a groan, and reached his arm around my waist and pulled me close to him. He pressed me hard against his body, and I felt the strength in his arm across my back and the hardness of his chest against mine, and smelt the savour of his mingled smell of man and leather from his leathern tunic. He did not try to kiss me, or even lift my face to his, and he did not speak more, but just crushed me to him, as if by his strength he would make me part of him.

My heart was beating very fast, and I could feel his heart beat too, and I was full of fright for what he might say or do. Yet I could not believe he would harm me, but rather felt that it was I who did all the harm to him.

Then of a sudden he released me, and I could draw breath again. He looked at me with burning eyes and said, "I do not want any part of you until I can have all of you."

The way he said these words made me feel as if a war went on in him, and I saw I truly should fear him, and his desire for me. I felt myself tremble, and tears started from my eyes.

"Go now," he said, and I turned and walked away.

THE DANISH RIDER

THAT night at table I was not alone in being more quiet than usual. Sidroc scarcely spoke, and Ælfwyn too was deep in her own thoughts. Perhaps the men seemed noisier to me because we were the quieter. A few times quarrels broke out, and Sidroc rose and called out to the men as they sprawled over the tables and pushed each other. They waved off his words, but stopped just the same. It was not hard to see that they, and Sidroc too, were restless.

The morning was easier, for it brought light and activity. Ælfwyn and I began the day by sorting through linens in the treasure room. We found a chest she had never before looked in, and she lifted the lid. Inside was a man's green dyed mantle, richly embellished with gold wire sewn onto the border, and lined with miniver fur. It was not in the style of the Danes, and she spoke my thoughts.

"Merewala's mantle," she said. "It must be, for it is of a worth befitting a great Lord such as he."

Beneath it lay more men's clothes, including linen tunics of fine weave and workmanship. "Woven by the Lady Elspeth herself, and sewn by old Dobbe," wondered Ælfwyn. She looked at the tunics and said, "Yrling needs these, as well as Sidroc, I am sure. I should ask him when he returns. He may have forgotten they are here."

She folded them up with a sigh and laid them in the trunk. "Clothes should be worn by the living," she said softly, and I could not help but recall the words of Sidroc, 'Gold is for men, and the pleasure it brings us and our women.'

We locked the door and started back to our chamber. Ælfwyn had another thought. "Meryth said her new babe was of the Danes. If her husband returns, what if he abuse her for this, or kills the child? That would be cruel indeed, after all she has suffered."

She went on, "In Wessex there are laws forbidding the death of such a child, but if the woman herself kills it, no one brings her to judgement."

We went up the wooden stair and she finished by saying, "But if Meryth did not slay the babe at its birth, she must regard it. Besides, these are Christian folk, and we must trust that the men, if they return, will grow to accept such things."

"One thing I will not accept is mouse heads in my bed," answered Burginde as we entered the room. She was shaking the coverlet of her bed and the kitten's latest trophies fell to the floor.

"Better heads than the whole mouse, running," replied Ælfwyn with a laugh.

"Who be Christian?" asked Burginde, picking up again on our words as we entered.

"The village," answered Ælfwyn, taking up her spindle. "But they have had no holy man here since the fall of the keep, only visits from lay-wanderers like the one who came to bless me. We should get a priest, or monk, or someone, to come here to live. Even Yrling said I might, and if we do not, the village will lapse, perhaps, and it will be on my head."

"Pish," answered Burginde. "You be having enough on your head without the salvation of the whole village."

"Still, I should provide for it, and it would be good to hear prayers again, as we did each day at home," she remembered.

She turned to me. "And you would welcome it very much, would you not? For then you could continue with your writing and reading, and sums, and all the things you have pledged to teach me."

I was uncertain, and slow to answer. "Yes," I said at last, "if one schooled in all these things could come, it would be good for our learning," I admitted.

But within my own mind I said: Any such priest who comes will want to destroy the place of Offering, or will at least forbid us women to go there. And this thought lay on my heart like a stone.

Burginde chimed in. "The feasts we could keep ourselves, just as you might be saying your own prayers as your dear mother does."

"But it is different at home," protested Ælfwyn.

"It be different everywhere," answered Burginde. "Your mother would say her prayers whether she had a holy man or no."

"Well, it would be easier at least to have help," grudged the Lady.

"And do not be pressing so much on the Dane. When he returns he will hear no end of changes you wish to make, and tho' they be all for the good of the keep, 'twill be hard for it to seem so to him. Let him be a heathen a bit longer, and in peace, without the harrying of priests about." Burginde said this with so much firmness that it was impossible not to heed her words.

Ælfwyn nodded her head as she turned this over in her mind. "You are right, nurse," she said. "I would not anger him now, when there is so much work to be done. All in good time."

We spent the afternoon spinning, and because we had been speaking about letters and learning, we began to plan on how I would teach Ælfwyn to write and read.

"We can use my wax tablet to begin, for in it I learnt myself, so it is clever wax and already knows its letters," I smiled. "Next Spring when we have lambs we will prepare parchment, and by then you will handle the stylus so well that a quill will come easy to you," I told her.

"I hope we will have lambs," she answered.

"Lambs or not, you will learn to write, and soon be able to sign your own name and much else too," I promised.

"Imagine what my parents will say when they are read a letter I wrote myself!" she asked.

"Imagine what Fall will be like with no stockings," answered Burginde, gesturing to the spindle Ælfwyn had set down.

As we were laughing over this, we heard a loud, shrill whistle coming from the yard below. We stood up and went to the windows, and could see several Danes hurrying through the yard towards the hall. We heard more whistling, and loud calling, and men calling back.

We three women looked at each other, and then out to where the Danes hurried below. "What is it?" I asked.

"Could it be?" asked Ælfwyn. "Is Yrling come?"

"We needs must find out, and cannot do so here," answered Burginde.

So we put down our work and went down the stair and into the hall. It was empty, but the outside door was open, and we saw Sidroc standing on the steps, looking across the yard.

Through the gate a lone rider, a Dane, came galloping up, on a horse so lathered and spent that it heaved as it drew breath. The Dane leapt from the saddle and stood, barely able to hold himself up, before Sidroc. His face was covered with grime and he looked as spent as his mount.

He spoke rapidly to Sidroc, and one of the Danes who had gathered to listen handed him a dipper of water, which he gulped down in one swallow. He went on, more slowly, and Sidroc spoke back to him, and the Dane answered. Then Sidroc uttered a cry like one of great anger, and with his booted foot kicked a barrel that stood at the base of the steps so that it toppled and rolled away. He called out, but it all seemed to be words of wrath. The Dane moved off, his message delivered, but Sidroc stood on the step in a rage. It was awful to see him thus, and more than awful as we did not know the cause of it.

"What is it?" cried Ælfwyn, coming up to him and speaking the alarm we all felt.

He ignored her plea, and she grasped his arm with both her hands. "Sidroc, tell me, what is wrong?" she cried, pulling on his arm and trying to look into his face.

Still he would not answer. "Is it Yrling?" she begged. "Has something befallen him?"

At last he spoke, but his voice was full of wrath. "No. Nothing has befallen him. But they have failed in what they had meant to do, and now things are worse than before."

He breathed out a long and angry breath. "I must ride, now, and go to them." He looked at Ælfwyn and me and said, "Do not ride out, or leave the yard, when I am gone."

"When will you be back?" asked Ælfwyn.

"Soon," he said.

"And Yrling is well?" she asked again.

"Yes," he said, but the impatience grew in his voice.

"And may we not go even to the village?" she asked.

"If you take one of Yrling's men with you, you may go."

"But who will command when you are gone?"

"I will tell you before I go. I have much to do." And he strode off to the great stable and left us there.

There was nothing for us to do but to go up to our room.

Ælfwyn and I sat at the table, our spindles quiet before us. Burginde took hers up and stood by the window. We watched the rhythmic spinning of the spindle whorl as it dropped slowly towards the floor.

I looked at Ælfwyn, but she remained quiet. "You must be glad that Yrling is well," I offered, after many minutes had passed.

Her brows knit together. "In truth," she said slowly, "I do not know. I was aware as I asked Sidroc about him, that if he told me that Yrling was dead, I could go home."

My mouth opened, but I said nothing, and she lowered her face in her hands. I looked at Burginde, but her eyes followed the movement of her yarn, and her face held no expression.

Ælfwyn raised her head and looked at me. "I am afraid there will be war," she said.

"There be already war, and plenty of it," replied Burginde.

"I mean at home, in Cirenceaster. Sidroc has told us that many more Danes will be coming this Summer. They cannot all stay here, in the North. And if there is war throughout Wessex, and even at Cirenceaster, what will be the good of the Peace my father made? The tribute would have been paid for nothing."

I thought of the lands of her home, how rich and verdant they must be; and thought of them laid waste by the Danes the way Lindisse was. I thought too of the Fate of the women of Lindisse, and of Merewala's daughter.

"At least you live, and are well," I answered.

She turned on me. "What of my mother, and two young sisters? What of my father, and grandsire, and all the lands they have held for time out of mind? What of his thegns, and their wives and children, and all the cottars and all the slaves?"

"Hush," said Burginde, stopping in her spinning. "Will you be raving at us, when we be all as one in this life with you? The Lady is right: you live, and are well, and are wed to a powerful Lord, and through him can perchance stay the hand of the Danes against your father. At home you could do nothing; nothing but weave the burial sheets that will wrap the men."

The thought of this grim task made us all quiet. Ælfwyn leaned back in her chair and looked limp. "Forgive me my sharp words," she said. "My work is here, to provide for my new people. And if I should please Yrling, it may fall that I may protect and serve my family in Cirenceaster as well."

"But do not put all that on your brow," warned Burginde. "Things may not be as bleak as our speech. King Æthelred will in no wise give up. Think first of the tasks at hand, of the care of your husband and household, and the getting of a babe."

Ælfwyn seemed not to hear this, and went on with her thinking. "But how can I care for Yrling, or ever please him, if the Danes make war at my home? If he does not honour the Peace, I could never honour him."

Here I spoke. "Sidroc told us that Yrling would honour it, and try to see that other Danes did as well."

But saying this, I thought again: Far better to have war at Cirenceaster with Yrling than some strange Dane. At least then Ælfwyn's family might be spared.

We heard movement beneath us in the hall, and then a man's tread on the lowest of our wooden steps. We did not need to be told that it was Sidroc, and rose at once and went down to meet him.

His anger still shown on his face. He was dressed as if for battle, and it was an awesome sight. Beneath his wool mantle he wore his ring tunic, covered all over with iron rings so close upon the next that no spear could pierce it. His legs were wrapped in leathern wrappings, and his red baldric slung across his chest held his sword, and his belt, his long knife. He pulled on his gloves as he began to speak.

"Do not ride out when I am gone," he repeated. He spoke to us as if we were children.

"We will not," answered Ælfwyn, and she could not hide the sulkiness in her voice.

"Do not look for us in less than a week. Until we return, Jari will command."

"Jari," said Ælfwyn, in a way that made it clear that the name held no meaning for her.

"Red hair. Three fingers on his sword hand," replied Sidroc. He began moving away, down the steps leading to the yard.

"Yes, I know him now," answered Ælfwyn, and tried the name out again. "Jari."

Before the steps a Dane held the bridle of Sidroc's bay stallion. Across the saddle front was lashed a spear, and Sidroc's helmet was tied next to his bedroll and pack at the back of the saddle. The horse danced and pawed the ground. He too seemed eager to be off.

Sidroc swung up in the saddle and took the reins. He looked down at us, and Ælfwyn said in a quiet voice, "Be well."

He nodded, and said, "And you, Lady."

Then he looked at me and spoke again, perhaps words of parting; but it was of his own tongue, so I knew not. I raised my hand, but could not smile. He kicked his horse and was gone.

⁂

Then followed the hardest week we had ever known, for we were like unto prisoners in our own home. We could not ride out, and so were deprived the pleasure of the warming Spring weather. We did not go down to the hall at night, but took all our meals in our chamber, for we would not sit alone at table with all the Danes gawking at us, or worse, by sitting by ourselves seem to invite the brutish Jari to join us. We could not walk to the village, for Ælfwyn would not take one of the Danes with us, and who could blame her? – for to take one of them into the midst of the village women was too cruel. Besides all this, we did not know what went wrong with Yrling, or why they failed, or how things were now worse. All we knew was that Sidroc was very angry, angry enough to go himself to join them, leaving us and the rest of Four Stones to the command of another.

When the week had passed, we began to look for return of the men, and to expect them by the hour. But another day passed, and another, and then a third, and Burginde grew so weary of our expectation that she teased us about our eagerness.

THE RETURN

ANOTHER day came; eleven had passed since the message from the lone horseman. The morning had been a dull one, not good for fine work, so we sat or stood with our spindles until we took our meat at noon. Burginde went back to spinning, standing by the open windows, and Ælfwyn and I sat and worked over the alphabet in my wax tablet.

The afternoon was far gone when we heard the first of the whistles from the men posted on the palisade. We all peered out our windows, straining to see and hear, and just waited. There were more whistles, and shouts, and calls of all kinds, and as we left the windows and hurried down the wooden stair we heard the sounds of many horses trampling outside the hall. So they were come.

The door of the hall was open. We stood well inside, near to our stair, for we did not want to be in the way of the men as they came in. We could see outside several of the horses, dusty with travel, and some men moving about them, and hear above the jangling of the horse's trappings and stamping of their feet much talk in the speech of the Danes, calls of welcome and such, no doubt.

And then the men began to come in, and Ælfwyn stepped forward, clasping her white hands together and twisting one of her rings as she waited.

The first to come in was Yrling himself, and Ælfwyn cried out a little gasp when she saw him, for tho' he was talking and even laughing to the man next to him, his left arm was wrapped up close to his body as if it were broken, and the left side of his face was covered with a bloody scab from his forehead to his chin, and the eye swollen shut.

Then everything seemed to happen at once. Ælfwyn ran to him, and he looked at her and grinned and called out to her, but when he tried to put his good arm about her he grimaced in pain. Burginde went to her, and I saw them question him, but could not hear his answer, for the room was now filling with the rest of the party. But since he was on his feet, and talking, his hurt was not a bad one. It was not clear what had befallen, accident or battle.

The men were all very grimy, and their weariness shown in their filthy faces. Still they laughed and called to each other at the joy of returning home, and chaffed one another in loud voices. I saw Toki, his yellow hair streaming back loose over his shoulders. His swagger was not so great as I had recalled, and he was almost quiet and scarcely joined in the noise of the men about him. Some of the men carried or dragged hide sacks with them, and then laughing held up the contents to show them off. This I knew at once to be battle-gain, and that they had in fact joined in warfare on their trip, for the fact that some brandished newly captured swords and seaxs told me this.

Then I saw Sidroc come in, walking slowly, and dragging a pack behind him. He was not wearing his sword, and I saw the red leather of his baldric stuffed into the top of the pack he dragged. He looked at me, and his face was white.

Burginde came by, rushing on her way upstairs. "The Dane be not bad; 'tis his shoulder. 'Twas put out of joint when his horse stumbled."

That explained the scab on his face as well; he must have scraped it badly when he fell.

Ælfwyn ran to me and said, "Burginde is going to get the Simples and some clean linen. He is not badly hurt, thank God, and only laughs about it." In her voice was some agitation, but also true relief.

"They have been at battle?" I asked.

"They were ambushed, from what I can understand. Yrling says Sidroc saved his life."

Sidroc stood a few feet away from us, and lifted his pack with effort to one of the tables the other men were setting up.

Ælfwyn and I looked at each other, and together crossed over to him.

He smiled at us, but his face was so pale that the scar which he had borne for many years upon his cheek looked fresh again.

Ælfwyn lifted her hand to his face and lay it on his forehead. "Sidroc, you are not well; you burn with fever," she said, drawing back her hand.

"I am all right," he said, but it was clear from the slowness of his speech that this was not true.

Finally I spoke. "What is wrong? Was there fever where you were?"

"No," he said, and his voice was dull. "I took a spear cut, under my arm, and it is hot now." He leaned back on the table, as if for support.

Ælfwyn said, "It must have festered. It should be searched and dressed. It is too easy to die from such wounds."

She began to say more, but Burginde came back, and she looked across the hall to where Yrling now leaned against the wall. His face looked pinched and very tired.

"Burginde," she said, "come and help me get Yrling to the treasure room, and then come back with more linen so that Sidroc's wound might be washed."

She turned to me and said, "You must search it carefully, and wash it well. It must have started to seal up with the fester inside, or he would not have so great a fever." She spoke with firmness, but with calmness as well, despite the noise about her and the hurt to Yrling. "I will come and help you when I can."

"Yes," I said, feeling real alarm as I watched her hurry off with Burginde. I had never searched a wound, but only seen it done. Sidroc was sick with fever, and if I did not do well, he could die of it.

He stood before me, leaning against the table. His eyes were closed, and I lifted my hand to his face and touched it. "You are so hot," I breathed aloud. He opened his eyes and looked at me.

"When did this happen?" I asked, and reached across his chest to unpin his mantle.

"Four days past. No, five," he answered slowly. I drew the mantle off and dropped it on his pack. As I did I saw beneath his left arm a dark stain, the colour of rust, which showed even through the leathern tunic he wore, and clotted around the linked iron of his ring shirt.

"We have to take off your ring shirt, and I will try to do it as gently as I can," I began, and my fingers fumbled at the leathern lacings that ran up the front. He moved his right hand up to help, and together we pulled the lacings through. With each pull I saw him fight off a wince.

"You must drink much water and ale," I said, knowing that this would help stave off the fever. "I will go and get you some."

I ran to the kitchen yard, and brought back an ewer filled with weak ale and a bronze cup. "Drink this now," I said.

He lifted the cup to his lips and laughed a little. "You command well, shield-maiden," he said. "I will leave you, and not Jari, in my place next time."

I was glad to hear him tease me, hoping that it meant that he was in not too great danger. "I am going to pull off your ring shirt now," I said, and took hold of it and pulled it back off his shoulders.

Luckily the leather beneath did not stick where the blood stain was, but moved off easily. As I pulled the shirt I saw something drop out of the front of it. It was small and silver and Sidroc caught it quickly in his right hand as it fell. Some talisman, I thought, since it fell from his breast.

The linen tunic he wore beneath was begrimed and streaked with dirt. It would not be easy to take it off, for the wound had bled into it, and a jagged circle of dried blood, as large around as two man's hand-spans, marked where the spear had hit. It was on the curve of the back by the ribs, just beneath the armpit. The spear must have been driven so that it ran in the arm opening of the ring tunic.

As I was considering all this two Danes were watching us with interest. They were talking and laughing, and sometimes spoke to Sidroc, so that he opened his eyes for a moment and spoke back to them. I turned to face them, and they silently regarded me. I surprised myself by saying, "Go away," in a loud voice to them.

This made Sidroc laugh, and he spoke to the men, and they laughed, but they did move away.

Burginde came up to me, carrying a small copper basin and an ewer. Behind her was Susa, who held a wad of linen sheeting and one of the sewing kits from our room. They put this down on the table by me, and Burginde peered closely into Sidroc's face. She touched his forehead, and said, "Ach!", and then touched his cheek. He tossed his head a bit; I think he grew weary of us measuring his fever. She ignored this and turned her attention to the bloody spot on his tunic.

She picked at it a bit, and Sidroc flinched, and she said, "'Twill have to be cut off. I hate to cut such a tunic, but I can sew it up as well as cut it off."

She opened the sewing kit and took out a pair of shears, and made a cut up the very front to the neck so that the shirt came off the right side of him. Upon his bare chest was a design pricked in blue, such as I had seen on Yrling's arms. It was a dragon, or a bird of some sort. Wrapped around his chest was a narrow band of cloth, and Burginde cut through it too, tho' it was stuck fast over the wound. "Field dressing," she said.

"Now soak it off with warm water," she said, gesturing to the bloody linen. "I will come back in a while to see how you do."

She moved off, with Susa, towards the treasure room. The door of it was open, and I caught a glimpse of Ælfwyn moving within.

I looked back at Sidroc and said, "I think you had better lie down so I can work better."

I moved the packs along the table to make a space where he could lie. I took his mantle and spread it on the rough wood surface, and with some difficulty he stretched out upon it, face down.

I poured out warm water into the basin and dipped some onto the stained tunic. At once the water released the dried blood, and the bloodied water began to run all over. I had to catch up the cleaner ends of the linen tunic to catch it all. Soon the whole piece was stained red.

I lifted it as gently as I could, but it still stuck in places. Though Sidroc had his face turned away from me I knew it must have cost him some pain. I added more and more water, trying to soften it so I could lift it. At last it came off, and with it the bandage beneath, so that I now looked at the wound itself. I poured some water onto a fresh piece of linen and dabbed at it. The wound was long, as long as my hand, and had a curving shape. It was almost like a flap of skin. Bits of some dried matter that did not dissolve in the water stuck out of it. It was very ugly.

"It does not look deep," I said, trying to sound confident.

He turned his head so it faced the table edge. "If it were deep, I would be dead now," he answered.

I leaned forward to look at it more closely. The edges of the wound were blue, and it gave off an awful rotting smell. I picked at one of the bits of dried matter. "There is something like straw in it. Did you use anything to staunch the blood?"

"Yes," he answered. "I do not know the name in your speech. We find it here growing as it does at home."

"I think it must be yarrow," I said. "That is what we use, but it works best when it is green. This is Winter-dried, and old."

"One cannot always fight in Summer," he replied.

"You are sure there is no metal left in the wound?"

"I cannot see into the wound, nor did I see the spear, but I think the point did not break."

I took a breath. "I am going to have to open the wound, and search it, and so cleanse it," I said.

He said nothing.

"It will hurt, very greatly," I went on.

"I have had wounds searched before."

"I will do it as quickly as I can, but I will do as well as I can," I said.

He turned his head to look at me, tho' it made him grimace to do so. "I know you will do well," he said.

I went to the pack he had dragged in and took his knife from his belt. The grip was of wood. I went to his face and held the handle before him. "Take this in your teeth," I said, and he did.

I moved back and looked again at the ugly wound. My heart was beating so fast that I thought it would burst from my chest. Tho' we were not far from the firepit, my whole body felt cold. I tried to calm myself by drawing a deep breath, and I shook my hands in the air to feel them again.

I dipped a piece of linen in the water, and pressed it hard over the wound. Sidroc did not move, even tho' I pushed with force. I drew back the cloth. The wound had begun to bleed again, which was good. I covered it once more, and pressed again, and I could hear Sidroc stifle a groan. The wound now bled freely, and I soaked it up and with my fingers tried to lift the flap of skin. I could not grasp it, and looked in the sewing kit and found a narrow warp beater, almost like a dull knife, that I could slip inside the wound. It caught in some places where it had begun to heal, and I had almost to rip at it to open it. I did so, and for an instant caught the gleam of white rib bones before the blood flowed and obscured my view. I knew Sidroc bit down hard on his knife grip as I did this, but I did not take my eyes from the wound. I poured a bit of water into my cupped hand and thence into the wound which I held open with the warp beater. I did it again, and a third time, hoping that I was flushing all the dried bits of yarrow from it. I lifted it a final time. I could smell nothing but blood, and could not tell if all the fester was gone.

"I think it is clean now," I said. I felt weak and light-headed, as if I would retch.

Sidroc opened his mouth and the knife dropped with a clatter to the stone floor. He gave a great exhalation of breath. For a moment he was quiet.

"Spit in it," he said.

I was so startled that I stood dumb. "What?" I finally asked.

"Spit in it," he repeated, and closed his eyes. "Spit in the wound."

I stood still and did not move. I did not want to do such a thing; it seemed like a magical binding of some sort.

"If a maid spits in your wound, it heals twice as fast," he said.

"O," I said. I still did not want to do it. Then I thought that if I refused to do it, he might think I was not still a maid. I was a maid, and did not want him to think other-wise, and then I felt anger at all this. Why should I care whether he thought I was a maid or not?

But I leaned forward just the same and spat in it.

He did not say Thank you, or anything at all, but just nodded his head.

Now I began to bandage the wound, and cut many squares from the linen sheeting, and folded them carefully, so that they would lie smoothly. I ripped a long narrow piece, and wrapped it over the squares, and Sidroc raised himself up off the table enough for me to thread it across his chest. I wrapped it three times about, using two pieces, so that the linen over the wound was secure.

Sidroc sat up, slowly. His face was no longer white, but I knew the flush on his cheek was due to the pain I had caused him. His hair was damp, and his face looked wet.

I put my hand up against his brow, and he did not flinch under it.

"You must drink again," I said, and handed him the cup.

But instead of taking it he pressed into my left hand the object he had been holding in his right. "This is yours," he said.

I lifted my hand and looked at it. It was a curved silver disk, worked all over with a pierced interlace design which knotted all along its border. On either side of the disk was a silver arm, wrapped with short but heavy black silk cord, and with a silver toggle on one end and a loop in the cord on the other. It was a bracelet, wonderfully worked, and the pureness of the silver was such that it shone like the full Moon.

"I cannot accept this," I said, and tried to pass it back to him. "It is of great worth."

He smiled slightly. "You are right, for it cost a man his life."

Now I wanted it in my keeping even less, and my face must have shown this.

"Do not worry," he said. "I would have killed him anyway. But the brightness of the bracelet caught my eye, so I went for him first."

"No," I said again. "Please to take it back."

His voice was grave now. "I cannot take it back, no more than you can take back the service you have rendered to me."

"It was no special service," I protested. "Ælfwyn would have done it, or Burginde."

He shook his head. "You do not understand." He waited, and found the words. "I do not want to be in your debt. If you do not take this bracelet, then I will be."

There was no way out. "Yes," I said at last. "I see." I looked at the bracelet again. "Only pledge me one thing," I said.

He looked at me with eyes that said, I will pledge anything to you.

"Pledge me that if I ever have need to return it to you, that this bracelet will remind you of my slight service."

His voice was almost rough as he answered. "You will never have need to return it. It is yours, no matter what may come."

"Then only remember what I have said," I finished.

He nodded his head, but I do not think he understood my words, just as I did not; for I did not possess the dragon's egg that grants forward sight. I could not tell how or why I might need his help.

I took the bracelet, and fastened it upon my wrist. He took up the cup and drank of the ale, and gave it to me, and I drank as well.

I looked down at my gown. It was the russet one, and it was spotted with blood and bloody water. He looked at the blood upon it, and I wondered as he looked if he thought it gave me power over him.

"I will wash my gown in a running stream," I said, repeating the remedy that would make null the power of another's blood on your clothing.

I did not know if he understood this, and I did not want to explain. I did not have to, for Burginde came by.

"You be looking well," she said to Sidroc, regarding him closely. "I am hotting ale with feverfew in it, and will bring you a cup of it."

He nodded, and she went off and returned not with a cup but a clean linen tunic. This she cut up the centre, and Sidroc slipped it on, for he could not raise his left arm over his head without pain.

"Ach, what a day for the spoiling of linen," she complained, but seemed cheerful enough. "I will be doing nothing but mending."

When she was gone he turned to the table where his ring shirt lay. He began to lift it and I said, "Do not put it on. It is so heavy. You have no need of it here, and it will disturb the wound."

He shook his head at these words, and said, "Help me put it on."

So I did, and laced it up. He turned back to the table and spoke. "I must go and kill my sword, since it failed me."

He drew it out of the hide pack, still in its sheath.

I stepped in front of him. "You cannot go anywhere. You are badly hurt, and hot with fever, and must rest now."

"I am not badly hurt," he answered. "I have fever, but it will pass."

I put my hand on his arm. "Please do not go, Sidroc," I asked.

He stopped and looked at me and I let go his arm. "Come with me then."

"No. I do not want you to go at all. It can be done in the morning."

"I am going. Come with me."

It was nothing but foolishness for him to go; he looked as if he could barely stand. But I saw he would not be stayed, and I did not want him to go alone.

I picked up his mantle but he shook his head. "I am warm enough," he said, making light of his burning fever. "You wear it."

I fastened it around my shoulders, and he straightened himself and started slowly towards the steps leading to the door. In his right hand he grasped his sheathed sword, and his left arm he held close to his body. I shook my head, feeling angry with myself for not stopping him, but I followed him out of the noisy hall into the yard.

Night was approaching fast, but there was still light enough to see. He crossed over the yard to the smith's shed, and called out, for tho' the awning was not yet rolled down, no one was to be seen.

"Weland," he called, and I knew he jested here, for the name he called was the name of the weapon-smith to the Gods.

A Dane appeared from a door out the back of the shed, his face wreathed in a grin. His eyes went from Sidroc to me as he listened to Sidroc's words. Then he brought forth three iron hammers, and lay them on the anvil before Sidroc. Sidroc looked at all three, and then choose one. He tried to lift it with his left hand, and I saw the effort it cost.

I stepped forward and spoke as I lifted the hammer. "Let me take it. You cannot carry both sword and hammer."

The hammer was heavy, and cold. I held it with both hands.

The smith looked at me again and spoke to Sidroc. I could not imagine what he must be saying, and I did not want to know it. Sidroc answered back, and then we walked away, me cradling the heavy hammer against my body.

We turned not towards the main gate, but towards the kitchen yard, and came to the small door that led through the palisade. It had not yet been fastened for the night, and Sidroc pushed it open with his arm and we stepped through it and onto the path leading to the place of Offering.

The sky was clearing as the Sun set, so that bright colours began to show in it; streaks of dark red and yellow. I wished that we had brought a torch, as we should surely need it soon, but it was too late to go back. The wind, which had been still all day, began to lift, and I felt cold even in the warm mantle I wore.

Sidroc walked a little ahead of me; the path was narrow and I did not want to jostle him. I could not see his face and was glad of it, for he must have been in great pain. He walked slowly, but was very straight.

We passed the grove of young trees and clumps of shrubs, and came to the place where the ground began to fall away. Ahead were the beech trees, and just beyond that, the Offering pit. Some last rays of the dying Sun struck the image of Odin as we neared it.

Sidroc made straight for the pit, and stood before the carved wooden post. He drew his sword from the black wood scabbard, and the scabbard fell to the clay at his feet. He raised the sword before him, as if in salute to Odin, and I saw again the fineness of the metal that he held. Then he plunged the tip of the sword into the wet clay of the pit, and with his foot bent back the blade so that the hilt with its carved grip rested upon one of the round stones that outlined the pit. He put his hand out, and I placed the hammer in it, and he raised it over his head. With a blow of great violence he swung the hammer down upon the bent blade. As he did he cried out one word, what I do not know, but his face told me how the effort of the blow had hurt his wound. And as one with the hammer blow and the cry from Sidroc, the hilt of the sword flew high into the air as it snapped from the blade. I raised my eyes to watch it, and for one moment it glinted in the last light of the Sun. Then it dropped, a dead and useless thing, into the pit.

Sidroc bent down and picked up the empty scabbard and held it with the hammer in his right hand. He turned away from the pit and made ready to move off. But I could not move, and only lifted his mantle which I wore to my face. No tears fell from my eyes, but I felt that I wept inside my breast.

I knew he came closer to me, and I turned so he would not see my face. As I did, I saw a slender silver chain glitter upon the bough on which I had hung my sash.

I did not wish to stay in the place of Offering any longer. My eyes were filled with the sight of the death of the fine sword, and the sight of the wound that Sidroc bore. I felt the silver bracelet upon my wrist, heavy and beautiful, and thought of him that Sidroc had killed who had worn it before me.

Sidroc did not speak, but came up beside me as I walked. His face was white again, and I felt sure his wound must have bled afresh. The sky was dark now and it was hard to see the path. I reached out and tried to take the hammer from his hand, but he would not let me have it. We went slowly, but even then he stumbled several times.

We stopped for a moment at the smith's shed. The canvas was down but Sidroc lifted it and lay the hammer upon the anvil. We walked across to the hall.

The fire was burning high and all the men were there. Food had been brought, and drink, and some of the tables had been set up as usual, but few men were sitting at them. It was easy to tell which men had returned with Yrling. They roamed around the hall, talking and eating and drinking as they went, stopping to see what booty this one or that one of their fellows had captured, and showing off to those who had not gone what they had themselves won.

The head table was set up, and food and drink was upon it, but Yrling was not there. I saw him across the hall, talking to several of his men. His face had been bathed, and looked much better. His hair was combed, and he wore a new tunic. His arm was wrapped close to his body with a cloth woven in blue and gold wool. In his hand was a seax, which he was holding out to the men. Even from a distance I could see it was of fine make, for the hilt glittered with silver as he held it up. The Danes did not use the angle-bladed seax; they preferred the straight blades of their own knives. Still, they would not shun a fine weapon when they had won it.

As I was looking thus at Yrling he saw us, and came over to where we stood. He spoke to Sidroc, and Sidroc answered back, and Yrling seemed to jest with him, for he patted Sidroc on the shoulder. I began to move away. Ælfwyn came around the corner into the hall; she must have been up in our chamber. She spoke first to Sidroc.

"I am glad you are back. Burginde will bring you some feverfew ale," she began. Her voice was kind and her face held real concern. "And you should eat something, as well."

"I do not want to eat, but only to sleep," answered Sidroc.

"Then we will make up a bed for you right now," said Ælfwyn, and gestured to the treasure room.

He shook his head. "I will sleep here," answered Sidroc, and made as if he would lie upon the table again. "I will not have to move much."

I unpinned his mantle from my neck and spread it upon the boards. He began to unlace his ring shirt. His fingers moved slowly, and I wanted Yrling to help him, but he did not. So I stepped before Sidroc and drew the leathern laces out. I pulled the heavy shirt back and off his shoulders. Luckily no blood showed on his linen tunic, and he lay down on the table.

"That is well," said Yrling. "The table is high and will trouble less the hurt you have."

We could all see the wisdom in this. Sidroc closed his eyes almost at once. We stood watching him, and Ælfwyn looked at me and then down at my bloodied gown.

It was not her, but Yrling that spoke. "You have done well, shield-maiden," he said. "You are worthy in every way."

I do not know if I blushed at this; I do not think so. There was nothing in it to shame me; he meant only praise. I nodded my head, and Ælfwyn squeezed my arm. "Do you go and change your gown," she said, "and come down and eat with us." She and Yrling moved off.

I stood before the table on which Sidroc lay. His face was turned towards me and he was breathing quietly. He was already asleep. As I regarded him, Burginde came up, a bronze cup in her hand.

"There you be," she said, with some little edge in her voice. She thrust out the cup to me. "'Twas hot and cooled three times since you left. Fine time for a stroll."

I took the cup from her, and she brought her face down close to Sidroc's. "Hmmm," she said. "He sleeps, but I would wake him for this," she said, pointing to the cup. "His weariness is so great that it overtakes his pain, but soon he will awake from it, and he will wish he had drunk it."

"I will stay then, and make certain he drinks it when he awakes," I said.

"It must be drunk hot," Burginde insisted.

"I will hot it with a poker," I answered.

For reply she simply dropped her hands and said, "Ach!," and moved away.

I stood before him, and then one of the other Danes dragged a bench over behind me. He pointed at it as if to say, Sit.

I mumbled my thanks and sat down. None of the men had ever done me a service before, even one as slight as this. I held the warm cup in my hands and sat alone before the sleeping Sidroc. My hand lay on my lap, reddened with his blood. I looked again at the silver disk on my wrist. I wondered what woman grieved over the man who had worn it. Perhaps she herself had come to the place of battle and took his body home, and had sat before it, watching it in death as I watched Sidroc, that he might live.

The ale in the cup looked dark, and a bitter smell came from it. I held it until it cooled, and kept on holding it, breathing in its sharp bitterness. Then Burginde came, with a platter of food and my silver goblet, and placed them next to me on the bench. I turned and saw that the table that Yrling and Ælfwyn sat at was empty, and they were gone.

"Eat now," she urged, "and then come to bed. He'll not be alone, surrounded by these brutes as he is."

I felt numb, but put the bronze cup down next to the platter, and stood up. "I will leave this here, lest he awake and be able to drink or eat," I answered. It was only when I rose that I found how weary I was.

"Good, good," encouraged Burginde. She gave me a little push towards the stair. "I will fetch water; we will soak your gown."

"No," I answered. "Tomorrow I must wash it myself in a flowing stream."

"Ach!" she chided. "That will never leave him go from your grip." But she said no more of it just the same.

OF THE AMBUSH

I T was mid morning before I saw Ælfwyn in our chamber. She looked a bit tired but also slightly flushed. "There you are," she said, kissing me warmly.

"Forgive me," I began. "I went to wash my gown."

She looked puzzled. "That is Burginde's work," she said.

"She is busy enough."

"Yes," she nodded. "She is down with Sidroc now." She touched my hand and said, "It is not right that you should tend to him all the time."

I could not help but ask, "By 'not right' do you mean 'not just' or 'not seemly'?"

"Both. You are not his wife or sweetheart, or even sister; therefore it is not right that you must tend to him after all that you have already done."

"I did nothing more than you yourself would have done," I said.

"That is not true. I admire you so much for searching and dressing his wound. Burginde said it was bad. I am sure I would have been sick."

"I almost was sick," I answered.

327

"Yrling is still asleep," she went on, and gestured to the table. "Come and eat, and let us talk before I go down again."

There was an ewer each of broth and ale, bowls of boiled eggs, bean porridge, and dried apples. I was very hungry and fell to.

She took up a cup of broth and said, "Yrling is well, only worn from lack of sleep. His shoulder will be sore for some days, but there was no real hurt beyond that."

I looked into her face. "I think you must need sleep as well," I said.

"O, I am fine," she answered. "And I did sleep, but tried to be so careful not to bump him that I lost some rest."

"Perhaps you should sleep here until he is better, then," I suggested.

"No," she answered quickly. "That would not be right. He needs me, and I want to be with him."

She lowered her eyes, and spoke softly. "Yesterday, when you and I stood together in the hall, waiting for the men to come in, I was of a sudden fearful that he would not return. When I saw him, I felt glad – glad that he lived."

Her voice was earnest, and she looked me full in the face. "I know now that I want him to live, and be well," she said.

I took her hand in mine. "I am sure that you do, and am happy to know it," I answered. "He is blest to have such a wife as you. I will not forget the look on his face when he saw you last night."

She smiled and said, "And I too am fortunate, for I begin to care for him." She took up her cup again, as I did. Then she recalled something else.

"One man did not return," she said gravely. "He was killed in the ambush."

"How did it happen?" I asked, realising I still knew nothing about it. "Was it when they went to fix things?"

"No, it was not, and I myself know little about the first part of their trip. I think they had done what they could, and then, five or six days ago, were ambushed."

"Who ambushed them?" I asked.

"Thegns of Æthelred, and some common ceorls as well," she started. We heard footsteps on the stair, and I rose and went to the landing. It was Burginde, wiping her hands on her apron as she climbed the heavy wooden treads. She came into the room, and Ælfwyn asked, "How is Sidroc? Is he improved?"

"Aye, somewhat, but the fever still be greater than it should be. He will neither drink nor eat, for it pains him too greatly to move. If he were on his back he could be given some drink from mouth to mouth; but he must lie on his belly, off the wound."

I felt troubled by all this, and thought to rise. Burginde finished by saying, "I think I will be off to the dyer and see what she says. She be the closest there is to a leech."

"Stay a moment and eat something before you go," invited Ælfwyn. Burginde drew her stool up to the table and sat with us.

"I am telling Ceridwen of the ambush in which Yrling and Sidroc were hurt," continued Ælfwyn. "Also one man was killed."

"More than one man was killed, by the looks of all the booty," replied Burginde with her mouth full.

Ælfwyn paused. "Yes," she said quietly. "I mean one Dane was killed."

The nurse shrugged her shoulders. Ælfwyn went on with her tale. "They were not far from the borders on their way back when they were attacked by thegns of King Æthelred. I asked Yrling why it happened, but he would say little."

"Why it happened?" echoed Burginde, and her eyebrows rose so high they nearly touched. "The Danes be ranging over the lands of the King, raping and pillaging on their way home, and you wonder why they be attacked?"

Ælfwyn did not answer at once, but pressed her hand to her forehead. "I did not say they were raping and pillaging," she started. "Yrling did not say that . . ."

"Of course they were taking food along the way," I said, trying to sound calm about it. "All warriors do that."

"It is that Toki's fault, I know it," blurted Ælfwyn. "Since Yrling returned Toki has been slinking about like a whipped dog. Even Yrling said something about it to me, that Toki had been too greedy."

Burginde spoke again, and spoke firmly. "Like as not he ravished the wrong woman, one of the wives or daughters of the thegns. Or just drove off too many cattle, or trampled too many cottars under the hooves of that great beast of his."

"Perhaps the thegns attacked only because the Danes were in Wessex, and they did not want them there," said Ælfwyn.

"Yes," I agreed, and tried to put some heart into it.

We were all quiet for a moment, and then I asked, "How did Yrling get hurt? Burginde said his horse fell."

"That is right," said Ælfwyn. "He was riding in advance through a woodland trail. They were going quickly to get out of the woods as soon as could be. The thegns had stretched a line across the path, and hid amongst the shrubs and trees. When Yrling's horse stumbled, they rushed out on the men from all sides."

"Clever," nodded Burginde. "They had the brains but not the brawn to outmatch the Danes."

"Yrling was lucky not to have been killed at once. He rolled off to one side, and was trying to rise, but his arm had been put out of joint at the shoulder in the fall. Sidroc came up behind him and fought off the two men who went for Yrling."

"And killed them," said Burginde.

"Yes, I suppose he killed them," admitted Ælfwyn. She looked at me. "They were being attacked."

"Yes," I said, and tried to make steady my voice. "Any group of men would have done the same. They had to defend themselves."

"And they killed them all?" questioned Burginde. She had finished eating and was putting on her mantle to go out.

"Yes, all," said Ælfwyn, in a faint voice.

"They had to defend themselves," I said again, and felt anger at the nurse for the bluntness of her speech. She beyond all women should know how painful it was for Ælfwyn to repeat this.

"'Twill not be gone long," said Burginde, as she started for the door. "All be well with you both?"

"Yes, go ahead, we want nothing. If Wilfrida can help, have her come herself, with you," answered Ælfwyn.

Burginde left, and we returned to our meal. I passed more apples to Ælfwyn, and she saw my wrist for the first time.

"It is beautiful," she said, fingering the shiny disk. "How fine is the interlace! Is it from Sidroc?"

"Yes," I said. The beauty of it made me smile, but not with any real gladness. "It is part of the battle-gain he won."

"O," she said.

"I did not want to take it, but he made me by saying he did not want to be in my debt."

She thought about this. "Then I think you did well to accept it," was all she said.

"You have not told me how Sidroc was injured," I went on.

"I do not know exactly. Perhaps when he was fighting for himself and Yrling, too. Either way I owe him great thanks." She looked at me. "Did he himself not tell you of it?"

"No, nor did I ask. I only know, as you do, that he was wounded by a spear thrust. It was skilfully driven, for it went in the arm opening of his ring tunic."

"One man was killed, and Yrling nearly so, and Sidroc truly hurt. And Toki was not injured at all," she said, with bitterness in her voice.

"And some thegns and many ceorls of your King are now dead; we do not even know how many," I added, and placed my hand over the silver bracelet on my wrist. "And now I wear this, which a man of Wessex was killed for."

So we were silent.

"Where did you two go last night?" she asked.

"Sidroc wanted to go to the place of Offering, and destroy his sword. I could not keep him from going so I walked with him."

She nodded. "A few of my father's thegns still do such things, tho' they be baptised." She rose and said, "I will go now to the treasure room and see if Yrling be awake. You can stay here if you like."

I said, "I will sit with Sidroc until you need me. I do not think he should be left unwatched."

"That is good of you," she said. "I will not let you stay there long."

I picked up the ewer of broth; perhaps Sidroc might drink of it. We went downstairs together, and Ælfwyn crossed to the treasure room door and went in. I stood in the hall and looked it over. The hide packs of the returned men had still not been cleared away, and around each I saw the booty they had pulled out the night before: swords, seaxs, leathern tunics, linen tunics, even shoes, all stripped from the bodies of the dead and dying. The only pack unopened was that of Sidroc.

On the bench before him was fresh food and drink, untouched. I walked over and stood before him. A wool coverlet was pulled around his shoulders. His face was turned towards me, and his lips were parted. I could just hear his breathing. His hair was damp and I could see the fever was still strong upon him. I did not want to touch his face and so disturb him, but sat down before him as quietly as I could. I began to feel real fear that I had not cleaned all the fester from his wound, and that it would need to be opened again.

"You do not have to sit here," he said, without opening his eyes.

"You are awake," I said in surprise.

"Yes. You do not have to sit with me." He spoke slowly, but clearly enough to see the fever had not gone to his brains.

"I sit with you because I want to," I said, and then added, "The Lady Ælfwyn would sit with you herself if Yrling did not need her."

It took a long time for him to answer, and he still did not open his eyes. "So you sit with me as a service to her?"

"No," I said, in some little anger. I recalled Ælfwyn's words. "I sit here because I want you to live, and be well."

He laughed, but feebly. "I am in no danger of Death." He opened his eyes and looked at me. "You wear the bracelet," he said.

"Yes," I said more calmly. "This and every day I will wear it. It is precious."

He was quiet, and closed his eyes again.

I reached over and touched his face. "You are still so hot, Sidroc."

I pulled back the coverlet and looked at his tunic. A pale yellow stain showed on the clean linen above the wound, but no blood was there. The tunic was damp from his sweat.

"You must try to drink, and eat," I said, trying not to sound frightened. "Try to sit up."

He opened his eyes. "It is hard. My side and arm is stiff."

"Try to stand then," I urged.

I pulled the coverlet back and off him. He pushed himself up with his good arm until he sat on the edge on the table. Then he stood upon the floor.

I picked up the cup on the bench and held it to him. By the smell I knew it was the ale made bitter with feverfew. "Drink this; it is bitter, but then drink this broth after it."

He drank it down, and then I filled the cup with broth, and he drank this as well. Some colour came into his cheeks.

"Will you eat something now? I do not want the bitterness of the ale to make you sick," I said, and looked at the platter. There were eggs and loaves and roast fowl. I tore one of the loaves and handed it to him. He took it and ate, and ate also of the fowl.

As I watched him I thought of Ælfwyn, and her belief that the ambush had been in some way caused by Toki.

"Was it Toki's fault, that you were attacked?" I asked of a sudden.

He looked at me. "Toki is often too greedy, and often at the wrong times," he answered.

I looked around the hall, convinced that this meant Yes.

"Why then does Yrling keep him with him?"

"Toki is a good warrior," he said, "better than most. Also the men like him, for he is always bold. Even when it is stupid to be bold," he ended.

"You could have been killed. Yrling could have been killed."

"Each day I fight I could die in battle, or Yrling."

"Ælfwyn says you saved his life."

"I killed those trying to kill him, but in truth no man can save another. The shield-maidens choose you or not."

I stood silently, thinking of all this. Sidroc leaned back against the edge of the table, and closed his eyes.

"I am sorry to make you speak so much," I began. "It must be hard, with your wound."

"Today all things are hard," he said. "I will lie down again now." He lowered himself onto the table. In a few moments he was breathing deeply and again slept.

I felt heartened that he seemed so much improved; at least the fever had lessened and he could rise and stand. I thought of how weary he must be, and of how long the ride home must have been for him and Yrling, in pain and unable to stop and truly rest.

I sat before him as he slept. The hall was empty and felt chilly; the smallest of fires burned in the firepit. As I was waiting thus a shadow fell before me from the doorway. I turned and glimpsed Toki, and cursed Fate for being found here alone by him watching over Sidroc. I did not look at Toki, but resolutely kept my face away from him. He came into view at last, walking with mock quietness so as not to rouse Sidroc. He stood a few paces behind the table on which Sidroc lay, and grinned at me in silence.

I had decided to leave when the tortoiseshell kitten scampered in from the yard. She lifted her tail in greeting and picked her way over to me. She disappeared under the skirt of my gown and wrapped herself around my ankles, and then came out again. At this I blushed greatly, and knew that Toki watched it all. I bent down to push the kitten away so she would not do it again, and my eyes met Toki's as he leered at me from where he stood. I hated him at that moment more than I had even on the village road, for he tried to shame me for a silly thing when Sidroc, who was hurt due to Toki's greed and probably cruelty, lay injured before him.

I heard noises from the doorway, and turned and saw Burginde coming in with her basket. Toki moved off and lounged about by the fire as she came to me. I rose to meet her, and she set down her basket and spoke.

"Sorry I be so tardy. Wilfrida was out a-gathering and I had to go after her. My legs be as tired as pups."

I looked in the basket. A few of the plants and roots within I recognised, but many I did not. There were the young and fresh leaves of dragonwort, and comfrey, and something like Lady's mantle.

"We can make a poultice from the comfrey, and lay it over the wound to help it draw," I decided. "There was a monk skilled at leech-craft at the Priory, and I saw him do that on a ceorl who had been slashed by a boar's tusks."

"Good, good," muttered Burginde. "Then I will leave you in charge of the basket." She lifted her head and looked across the hall. "Is the Lady out yet?"

"No, but I am sure that Yrling still sleeps, as does Sidroc. I think she only sits by him so that he will not wake alone."

"Then I be going up to start my laundry. Do you want work? I could bring your spindle; 'tis light enough for that."

"No, I will go with you now." I did not want to leave Sidroc alone, but even less did I desire to be left in the hall with Toki as well.

VALUABLE FOR RANSOM

IN the morning when I went down Sidroc was standing before the table. He wore a clean linen tunic and I could see that the wound beneath it had been wrapped. He had his hide pack open and was sorting through his battle-gain. I saw a leathern tunic, leg wrappings, clothing that looked like mantles, a set of bronze shoulder clasps, and a small opened pouch in which several silver rings sat. Off to one side were two swords, both sheathed in fine scabbards. He moved slowly and with care, and regarded each item well as he set it out.

I came up to him and said, "I am glad you are so much better."

He turned and grimaced as he did. I moved over to his left side so he would not have to turn so much.

"Yes, I slept well at last." His voice was steady and strong, and his colour was returned.

I suddenly felt that now that he was better I would not make so bold as to touch his face to check his fever. It was strange, for a day ago I had touched him without fear or shame. Now tho', he was growing well, and strong, and so all between us must be as it had been before.

"Who wrapped your wound?" I asked.

"Your Lady did."

I looked across the hall. The door to the treasure room was still closed.

"They are out in the yard. Yrling is choosing his new horse. His red stallion broke its front legs when it fell so we killed it in the woods. It was a very good horse, as good or better than my bay."

"I am sorry it was lost," I said. Sidroc went on with his pack, and drew out something that looked like a baldric.

I regarded the things before us, and asked, "What will you do with this?"

"Those things I do not want I will trade or sell for that I do."

I thought of the costly bracelet I wore. I did not think much on the table could compare in value to it, save for the swords. He now picked up the swords, and drew them out of their sheaths, and examined them closely. One sword had a grip covered in ivory or bone, into which were carved many small figures. The hilt was polished steel, cut all over with grooves into which was set bright copper wire in spiralling designs. He lifted this sword for a moment, and then set it down.

The second was longer, like onto the swords of most of the Danes, and had a long and massive hilt. The pommel of the hilt had coils of silver and some darker metal, coloured bronze perhaps, set into the steel.

This sword he lifted and held for a long time. Then he took up the shorter sword, and laid it flat in the air so its tip just rested on the table. He took the larger sword and laid it, just where the blade shot forth from the hilt, upon the flat blade of the one beneath. He released his hand, and the large sword lay still upon the other without falling.

He regarded this well, and caught up the sword and tossed the smaller aside. He glanced at me. "It is large, but will never grow heavy in the hand, for the blade and hilt balance each other." He held the blade closer to his eyes and ran his fingers over the carvings on the blade.

"This one had good things," he said, as if to himself. I wondered if the thegn he spoke of also had worn the silver bracelet.

"I will take this sword as my next," he decided. He squinted at the figures and letters carved into the blade. "This is your speech," he said, and held the sword before me.

"Yes," I agreed, looking at the lettering. The sword carried both runes and lettering. The runes were crooked and hard to read, but the lettering was clear.

"This is the sword of a Christian," I told him. Just beneath the hilt, carved into the steel of the blade, were the words 'Agnus Dei', the Lamb of God.

He shrugged. "Tyr does not care, nor do I. I will have the smith mark it for me. Besides, most of your people are Christian, so we have much that is marked by them." He took his own scabbard and slid the new sword into it.

"Do you want to sit down? You should not get too tired at first," I reminded him.

"It is easier to stand than sit. I am not tired."

I sat down on the bench and looked up at him. He leaned back against the edge of the table and regarded me steadily. The pain and fever had left his face, but it looked thin and worn beyond his years. Yet he smiled, so slightly that his scar did not move.

"Will you tell me what happened in the South, and why you rode to Yrling?" I asked, feeling very bold.

His eyes narrowed, but he did not take them from me. At length he said, "Yes, I will tell you." He shifted his position and began. "There were two amongst us, two brothers, who were not long ago Yrling's men. Last year they left together, and sailed North up the coast to set up for themselves. They found little but gathered more men on the way. Then they sailed South, to Anglia, and had much success on raids. Their numbers grew, and the brothers quarrelled and split up. One of them, Svein, sailed to join his father in the Kingdom of the Franks. The other, Hingvar, drove deeper into Britain, into Wessex, and after some good fights made peace with the reeve of that place, who gave him much gold.

"Then Svein, who had sailed, returned, for he had heard of the riches of Wessex. He attacked the reeve who had made peace with his brother Hingvar, and killed him. The brothers fought again, and their men against each other as well. Then Æthelred of Wessex and his men came and fought against both brothers together, killing many of their men and capturing much booty.

"This was bad, but in the battle one of the brothers had captured some of Æthelred's closest men, those who were his own kin. These are valuable for ransom, and also a way of escape, for we have learnt the chiefs here will pay to have their men restored, and will not risk the lives of those captured. That is why Yrling went, not only to see what should be done next, but also to help make the trade, for he is skilled in this and has gained much by it."

He shifted his position and went on. "But when Yrling arrived he learnt that in anger Hingvar had killed or maimed the men his brother Svein had captured, so that their price would now be nothing. This he did to punish his brother, but to do so was stupid and costly, for no one can now gain, and the anger of Æthelred when he learns of it will be great."

He paused, and I asked, "Why did you ride to Yrling? To give him counsel in this?"

"Yes, I rode to him to argue that he should come away quick. It was not our battle, and we had little to gain once the men he meant to sell back were dead."

"And he did heed your advice?"

"Yes. Toki argued the other way, but Yrling had seen enough."

"So you left to return here, and all went well until the ambush?" I asked.

"Yes. All went well. Toki took too much upon the road, and so we walked into a trap."

I thought about what this truly meant. They were a small band of men, riding fast, taking food and whatever else they saw along the way. After Burginde's speech that morning it was not hard to imagine what excesses Toki or any of them had committed. I did not want to ask, and looked away from him.

He spoke after a while. "I think now you are angry. I should not have told you this."

I felt sick and sorry about everything. "Please do not say that, Sidroc. I do feel anger, yes; but many other things as well. Perhaps because of the worry and the long wait and your own anger when you rode; and we were left alone and shut up in our room, and did not know what was happening; and then you returned at last, and you and Yrling were hurt, and I – feared for you."

He laughed and said, "Then I am glad I was not the one killed."

"Do not laugh at me," I said, feeling close to tears at all I had heard and was feeling.

"I do not laugh at you. You show no fear in your speech, and this I admire."

We were both quiet, and I composed myself. "What will happen now?" I asked him.

"Nothing soon, for us. We heard that Æthelred was injured in another battle, a great one. But we will not strike against Wessex until Summer."

"You mean, Yrling will not strike?"

"Yes, Yrling."

I asked my next question carefully, and with as much calm as I could. "Do you think then Cirenceaster will be attacked? If not by Yrling, then by another Dane?"

He came close to not answering, and took a long time before he replied. "Yes. I think that if Yrling does not move quickly he will lose Cirenceaster to another."

"Cirenceaster belongs to Ælfsige," I said, and felt my voice was very small. "Yrling made Peace with him so it would remain so."

"Sometimes it is better to be given things than to have to take them," he began. "A gift arrives in good condition. Booty often times does not."

My lips could scarcely form my words. "And Ælfwyn and the tribute were the gifts. Now that Yrling has them, he will attack and take the rest . . ."

"I do not say that," he countered. "Only that if Yrling does not move, he will lose much."

"Ælfwyn said her father would die before he surrendered his lands," I recalled.

He nodded his head. "Then he will die."

Then Ælfwyn and Yrling walked, smiling and talking, into the hall, and we were silent.

THE GOLDEN FLEECE

THAT night the hall looked again as it did of a normal night. The fire blazed up, crackling, in the pit, and the torches shed their dancing light from their iron holders on the walls. Sheafs of ash-handled spears rested upright in the corners, and the heavy tables were set on trestles in the middle of the hall. Most of the Danes were already inside, standing before the tables or talking in groups. A hoot of laughter made us turn our heads. Toki was jesting, cup in hand, with another man standing by the kitchen passageway, and being very loud about it.

We saw Yrling, standing in speech with Sidroc near the head table. Sidroc was leaning against the wall as they spoke. I wondered if it was due to his wound; he had said it was easier to stand than sit. Both wore leathern tunics over their linen shirts, tho' Yrling's arm was still wrapped close to his body with a wool shawl.

We approached the table, but they did not join us. It was clear from their faces that their talk was of serious concerns. We sat down, and since no man was there between us, turned to each other.

"From tonight I am going to try to speak more at table, so that you and I can speak not only to each other, but to Yrling and Sidroc as well," Ælfwyn began.

"Too bad Toki understands our speech," I said, eyeing him as he downed another cup of ale.

The serving men began to bring out platters of food, and the men drifted to their places. Yrling sat down next to Ælfwyn, and I looked up at Sidroc.

"Would you rather stand?" I asked. "I can break your food for you, and hand it to you, if it would pain you less."

He smiled a little at this notion. "I will sit now, until I must stand again," he answered, and slowly swung his long legs over the bench.

"How much better you look," I could not help but say.

"Yes, because of you," he replied simply. "I told you it would heal twice as fast."

I lifted my cup to hide the flush on my cheek.

More platters were set before us, and I watched Ælfwyn choose and break up food for Yrling, since he could not use his hurt arm.

Yrling did not stand and speak to the men that night, and I guessed it was because the trip had not been a successful one. Still, neither Yrling nor any of the men seemed in bad spirits. Perhaps the pleasure of arriving home dulled the disappointments of the journey.

After a little time had passed, and we were mostly finished with our meal, Ælfwyn turned to Yrling and spoke in a way that we might all hear.

"While you were gone we warped the looms," she began. Yrling nodded at this, and she went on. "We have been busy spinning, and it is good that I brought with me sacks of carded fleece from Cirenceaster, for I was sorry to learn that the flocks that once belonged to Four Stones are now almost gone."

Yrling looked at her in a way that showed his doubt of where her speech was headed. I sat forward, trying to show my interest, and Sidroc shifted on the bench and rested his chin in his hand, watching her. Toki was leaning back from the table, cup in hand, staring at nothing on the hall ceiling.

She took a breath and went on. "The fleece I have brought will not last long, and the wants of the hall are great. We all will need wool, and even more so when those you expect come this Summer with their wives."

Yrling did not say anything, either to stay her speech or bid her go on. Toki now was listening, and grinning as he did so.

"It is important that we build up our flocks again," she said boldly. "Lindisse was once good sheep country, and must be again, for without our own sheep we must barter or buy fleece, which is very dear."

Toki held his cup in his hand and bleated, "Baaa."

Ælfwyn glanced at him but went on. "Sheep bring everything good, and many things that we now lack. With sheep there is milk, and cheese, and tallow." She stopped and looked about at us. "And fleece to line the scabbards of swords," she said, looking from Yrling to Sidroc, "and parchment from lambs," she went on, with a nod at me, "but most of all the wool itself, which we can spin and weave and so meet our own wants for cloth, and sell what we do not need."

"Baa, baaa," bleated Toki again. The other men at the table who could not understand Ælfwyn's speech laughed along with Toki.

She rose from the bench and turned on him. "Wool is the whole wealth of my people," she said fiercely.

Before her sat a small dish of pure gold. It had come as part of the treasure she brought. She lifted it in her hand and asked, "Where do you think this came from?"

Toki rolled his eyes, but was silent. She turned back to Yrling. A smile played about Yrling's lips, but it was one of admiration. She set the golden dish before him.

"This is only fleece, changed to gold," she said softly. She sat down again, and was still.

Yrling fingered the dish. "Sheep are costly, and must be cared for," he said.

"Cloth is more costly, and we can raise and spin wool of greater fineness than we can buy," she answered.

Toki snorted at this. She kept her eyes upon Yrling and spoke calmly and with authority. "Besides, we have a few sheep to begin with; it is a start. There are nearly thirty in the yard, and the village women have seven. We must stop killing the ewes for food, and instead breed them up with the best of the rams."

For answer, Toki swung his feet up so they hit the table with a bang. Ælfwyn turned to him and said, "If this one thing had been done last year there would be more meat and wool too, today."

She turned back to Yrling, and her voice was more gentle. "And as for care, the villagers will do it. We must give them a share in the success of the flock, and then they will care for them well, for their own gain depends on it."

Yrling nearly laughed. "You have thought much on these things," he said.

Her answer was serious. "It is only my birthright. Do not forget where I was raised," she murmured.

Yrling narrowed his eyes at the golden dish and said, "That I never forget."

Then Yrling said no more. Lost in thought, he gazed at the dish. Toki began talking to the man next to him. The moment seemed to be slipping away. Ælfwyn looked over to Sidroc with a plea in her eyes. He rose from the table slowly; it was clear he was sore and stiff from the careful way in which he moved. He faced Yrling and spoke.

"If the Lady can spin wool into gold, perhaps you should let her," he began.

Yrling jerked his head up to look at Sidroc. Ælfwyn smiled at them both, and took heart.

"Not into gold, perhaps," she answered, "but into much silver; silver that will be saved and silver we will soon earn from the sale of our extra fleece."

"Where will the sheep come from?" asked Yrling.

Ælfwyn was quick with her answer. "I think that more may be found in the forests, left from those that went wild. They could be driven out, and the best of them added to the flock. The others we can slaughter for meat and hides, so we will gain both ways."

Sidroc looked at Ælfwyn and then to Yrling. "It is clear she has a head for profit," said Sidroc. "I think your Lady will save you much silver, if you let her. She has also a plan for the making of linen."

And Sidroc touched the sleeve of his own shirt and spoke in their shared tongue to Yrling.

Ælfwyn grasped Yrling's arm and said, "Yes, and it will cost nothing at all, for flax and pond are already here. You have only to keep the horses in the valley from trampling the flax and we can cut it at Lammastide."

She looked pleased to have had the chance to bring this up as well, but did not forget her goal. "But tho' linen is good next to the skin, nothing is more important than our sheep."

Yrling considered this. "And to eat in the meantime –?"

Ælfwyn did not have this answer, but Sidroc did. "We have time now to hunt. There is deer and boar in the woods." He smiled at Ælfwyn. "We will be hunting out ewes and rams there anyway."

"We could lay snares for hares," I ventured. "There are many about, breeding, as it is Spring."

"Yes, hares; and wild birds such as pheasant and woodcocks and partridges, which would be good on the table," agreed Ælfwyn.

Yrling listened to all this, and finally spoke; and it was with decision. "If it will save silver, we will do this thing." He looked at Ælfwyn as he touched the small golden dish. In his voice was now a challenge. "And if, by your sheep, you bring me more gold, I will be made glad."

Ælfwyn smiled at him, a smile of triumph, and grasped his hand.

※※※※※※※※※※※

When we finally rose from the table that night Ælfwyn motioned that she would go up with me for a moment. Yrling and Sidroc were talking together, with Sidroc still standing. Toki sprawled at another table, watching the gaming and calling out advice to those who played. He had never stopped drinking all evening and looked as if he barely kept from sliding off the bench he sat upon.

On the way up the stairs I took Ælfwyn's hand. "How proud your parents would be of you," I said, with all the warmth I felt.

She laughed, and it was clear she too was pleased with her success. "Yes," she said, as we gained the room, "but I am not out of the woods yet."

"Woods," repeated Ælfwyn slowly, and looked at me. "Ah!"

I looked back at her, searching her face for a clue to her sudden distress. Then my own light dawned, and I remembered.

"The village men are in the woods, too," I said. "Hiding."

"What if Yrling sends men tomorrow to start looking for the sheep?" she asked herself. "I did not mean to have to tell him about them so soon."

"Perhaps he will not start tomorrow," I suggested. I had another thought. "Perhaps the village men have caught the sheep, or at least some of them, and live off them in the forest. If so there may be more sheep than we think, for they would have bred them up."

"And Yrling could get both sheep and men back at the same time," said Ælfwyn, "so that shepherds we would not lack."

"And Meryth and the other women would have their husbands back."

"And the fields will be planted. So it could be a good thing all round. I will just need to speak to Yrling before he sends anyone out."

Burginde came up the steps, bumping two wooden buckets of water. Her face was furrowed and she was muttering under her breath as she came in. Her apron was splashed over with wet.

"Oafs and louts!" she huffed as she set down the buckets. "That Yellowhair tried to fright me in the kitchen passage."

"Toki is drunk," said Ælfwyn in disgust. "He is just childish enough to do such things."

Burginde changed her apron, and set about helping Ælfwyn select clothing to take downstairs. I slipped off my shoes and stockings and was about to pull off my gown when I heard the mewing of a cat. The landing was dim, and I could not see if Browny was there. I stepped out and listened, and thought I heard her cry again, but it was a strange, muffled cry.

I walked down the first few steps. "Browny?" I called.

I moved down a little farther and then heard her cry, much clearer and closer.

A figure moved out of the shadows along the wall below, and I saw Toki, holding the kitten by its tail and smothering its cries with his other hand. Toki was grinning and said something in his own speech.

"You are too bad, chasing Burginde and now hurting a kitten," I scolded him. His grin looked frozen on his face; I do not think he heard anything I said. I reached out my hand, wanting him to give the kitten to me, and he took a step closer. I was halfway up the stairs and so leaned forward towards him.

Of a sudden he dropped the struggling kitten, and lurched instead at me. His two hands shot under my skirts and grasped me around my bare ankles. I fell back on the steps, and called out, "Toki! Stop it!"

I twisted to try to kick him in the chest, and as I did saw Ælfwyn appear on the landing above me. Then Burginde stood by her, lifting a bucket and shouting as she flung it at Toki's head. It glanced off his forehead, dumping water all over him, and he staggered back against the wall, gasping, at the force of it.

Men were now come into the space, drawn by the noise we made.

Ælfwyn looked down and spoke to Toki, and she was in a rage. "To touch her is to touch me!"

"Aye, and that be the second time he grabbed her," sputtered Burginde.

I began to stand up upon the stairs, wanting to get into our room. Then Sidroc pushed through the circle of Danes who stood watching and went to where Toki leaned, half-sitting, against the wall.

He bent down and picked Toki up by grasping the collar of his leathern tunic. Toki stood, but barely, and Sidroc drew back his fist and slammed it into Toki's face. He crumpled upon the floor, and Sidroc kicked him with great violence as he lay there. Toki groaned and made no attempt to stand or even crawl away.

"Sidroc, he is drunk," I said, coming down the stairs towards them. He did not look at me, only glared down at Toki as he kicked him again. None of the men made a move, and regarded this all in silence. I looked back at Ælfwyn. In her face was anger and disgust and now concern as well.

"Stop now, Sidroc," she said, and came down the steps herself. "You will kill him."

He did not regard her, but only stood over Toki as if he would kick him again. Ælfwyn came to him and said, "You will open your wound and bleed again. Stop."

She scanned the faces of the men around her. There in the back stood Yrling, watching with hawk-like eyes.

He inclined his head, as if to say to her, Come. She looked once more at Sidroc as he stood over Toki, and then dropped her hands and passed through the men to Yrling. They turned and went into the hall together, and slowly the other men turned also and walked away.

Toki groaned again and made some gesture to pull himself away. Blood flowed as a rivulet from his mouth and nose, and he choked as he tried to breathe. His yellow hair was clotted with red.

Sidroc kept his face down, glaring at Toki as he tried to crawl along the wet floor. I did not want to leave them alone. I had often hated Toki, but I did not want to see him die; not by Sidroc's anger; not when he was drunk and could not defend himself; and most of all not, as it seemed, over me.

I went to Sidroc and made him look at me. "Please," I said.

I looked in Sidroc's face, with the scar showing sharply against his cheek. I thought of all that had been, good and bad, between Sidroc and Toki; more than I could ever know, reaching back to when they were boys together. Sidroc's anger now was only a small part of what he bore for Toki, and the reasons he forbore from killing him must be equally deep and old.

Sidroc did not kick Toki again. He stepped back from him, and gestured to three men who still stood and watched. His voice was hoarse as he spoke to them, and in response they lifted Toki and carried him away. I went up the stairs without looking back.

That night, in the dark, Burginde spoke before she went to sleep. "Men be queer beasts. They will kill their kin for a maid, and let him live for her, too . . ."

NO BARGAINS

THEN followed two days of quiet; and we were all glad for it. Ælfwyn and Burginde and I worked at our spinning and weaving, and the life of Four Stones went on about us. Sidroc was about the hall, resting as he let his wound heal. Toki was nowhere to be seen, and Ælfwyn told me that he was mending at the camp in the valley of horses.

As for Yrling, on the second day he unwrapped his arm, and had no need to tie it up, for the soreness had left his shoulder. The scrape on his face was healing well, and would leave no mark upon him.

The next morning was fine, and Ælfwyn had asked Yrling if he might ride with us to the vale of flax, as we now called it between ourselves. It was a pleasure to be out, and it was clear that Yrling took pleasure, too, in seeing Ælfwyn on the chestnut mare he had given in his absence.

As we rode along Ælfwyn spoke to him of those things she hoped to do, pointing out the retting pond and telling how easy it would be to allow it to fill again. Through the village she was silent, except to say that the women needed seed, for their store was very low.

We neared the entry to the vale, and Yrling whistled our approach, and a whistle answered back. We rode in, and Ælfwyn and I turned to each other in gladness, for the flax shown bright green and thick everywhere upon the ground. We rode through it awhile, and Ælfwyn stressed that all that was needed was for it to be kept untrampled until high Summer. Yrling listened to all this, nodding his head, but saying little.

We three got off our horses and walked, and then Ælfwyn gave me a little nudge as she said, "Yrling, it would be a good thing, would it not, if the village could produce more?"

He did not answer, but shrugged his shoulders.

"What I mean is that the village women are nearly starving –" she went on; but he cut her off.

"That is their own fault," he said. "They will not take up with the men."

Ælfwyn took a breath and tried again. "Yes, I know, and I think I know why." Yrling looked at her sharply, and she went on at a rapid pace. "What I want to say first is that it would be good for us all if the village could produce more. It should be able to feed itself and us too, but we must help."

She went on more slowly. "We must provide seed, for wheat and barley and oats, and also give them a share in the flocks we will build, as I have already said; and try to help them build up their livestock."

"There is more to this bargain," said Yrling, looking at her closely.

She tried to smile and make light of it, but it was clear she was worried. "Yes," she went on, "there is more to this bargain, and it is good. The reason the women will not take up with your men is that some of their husbands still live. If they could come back safely, without fear of hurt or of slavery, the village could once again prosper. And I think then the single women will wed your men."

Now it was out, and she stood back and looked at him with fear and hope mixed on her face.

"They live?" he asked in some amaze. "Where? Why do they not come back?"

"They do not come back because they fear being sold to distant lands." Ælfwyn searched his face. "Is it not true that you have sold many of the people of Lindisse this way?"

He nodded.

"That is why they fear returning. But they are much more valuable to us here in the village, raising grain and tending our flocks." She grasped upon this idea. "They will bring us more silver here than abroad; for once they are sold they can never bring you profit again. If they stay here, and work and farm, they feed themselves and us and bring us silver every year from the excess we can sell."

"Where are they?" he asked slowly, but the smile he wore was not unkind.

She nearly gulped. "I will tell you; I want to tell you; but please to tell me first they have nothing to fear; and that they may come home."

He shook his head, and his answer was firm. "No. I will make no such bargain with my own wife."

She cast about, looking desperate at what she had done.

He changed everything with his next words. "You do not have to bargain with me. That is what you do not understand."

Her face coloured from white to red as she asked, "Then they may come home?"

"Yes," he said, but his voice was stern. "And never again try to bargain with me. A wife should not play such games with her husband."

The blush of shame was upon her cheek, and she hung her head.

"I am truly sorry," she began. "I did not know what to expect, and tried only to protect the secret that the village women gave me in trust."

He nodded his head. His voice was softer when he spoke again. "You want to change much, and that is good, for I wish to see this place as it was once. But you must not go behind my back."

She lifted her head and said in a steady voice, "I promise I will not." She lowered her eyes for just a moment and said, "The men are living in the forest North of here."

"They should come back," is what he answered. "Tell the women tomorrow."

He smiled at her, and just touched her chin. Then he turned and looked at me. "And you, Lady, should marry soon. There is trouble enough in my hall."

His voice was light, but I swallowed just the same. We had stopped walking, and now began again.

"But I need her," said Ælfwyn, in a playful tone. She took Yrling's arm. "She will help me more in my work if she does not wed, at least for a little while."

"Yes, but Sidroc will take her away when he goes," he answered.

"Sidroc is going?" asked Ælfwyn.

"He will go sometime. I do not know when. But when he does, he will take his woman with him." He looked now at me, and added, "He spoke for you, long ago."

"But why will he go?" she asked. "He is your nephew; will he not stay with you?"

"He will go when he has enough treasure to do what he wants to do; or when he can gather enough men to go with him."

A rider came towards us from the timber hall, and Yrling got on his horse and rode to meet him. We stood, watching him ride off, thinking of all we had just heard.

Ælfwyn turned to me. "I do not want you to go, ever," she said.

I found my voice and said, "I will not go. These men may not pledge to each other, but I am pledged to you, and in your service; and I will never go, lest you yourself send me away."

"Which will never happen," she answered with decision. She breathed out a long sigh. "Things are better now than I had any right to expect. The village men may come home; at least that worked out right."

"You were very brave to speak to him as you did," I said. "Few women would have taken the part of the village as well as you have."

"Do not say that; I am really ashamed. Yrling is right, there should be no bargains between husband and wife." Then she said what I myself was thinking. "It is true I barely know him, and that he did awful things to Lindisse. But he has been nothing but good to me."

We climbed on our horses and walked slowly until Yrling returned to join us.

"Toki is well," he told us as we started out of the vale. "His face is not yet pretty again, and he says he recalls no part of the night; but he is well." He seemed to be laughing to himself over this.

"I recall the night well, and that he touched my friend," said Ælfwyn seriously. "He must never do it again."

"I think he will remember that much," laughed Yrling.

⚬⚬⚬⚬⚬⚬⚬⚬⚬⚬⚬

The village men returned two days hence, but we did not see their coming. They came under cover of dark, and found their broken huts and unplanted crofts, and found too their wives and children who had been without them so long; and their homecoming was private to each of them. It was Burginde who told us they had come, and she had it from Dobbe, so we knew it was true. At noon we thought to go to the village, and rode out into an afternoon of warm Sun and soft breezes.

We saw at once the presence of the men, for they were afield already, and walked the unploughed ground of the great common plots. Some women walked with them, and small children too. As we came closer we saw that the men were dressed wholly in the skins of animals, and wore no other clothing than the sheepskins and deer hides which wrapped their bodies. Women at their huts stopped in their work and raised their hands to us, their faces light with hope, and maybe, happiness; they nodded towards the field in which the men walked. One man, newly returned, and not far from the road, laughingly carried his children on his back and swung them through the air in sport. Outside another hut a young woman, great with child, worked at her meal-trough as if it were any other day; but what was different was the man who silently and sternly regarded her as she did.

Then we saw Mul. He looked somehow older, and held a stick up for Ælfwyn to see as he spoke.

"Ladies, the sheep are at Wilfrida's croft, and there are these many, and I have numbered them four times."

Ælfwyn looked down at the stick and counted its small notches. "Forty-seven! That is very good, Mul. This then will be the first accounting of the flock."

Mul seemed proud, and grinned.

"All is well at home?" Ælfwyn inquired. "Your father has returned?"

"Aye, Lady, all is well," he answered, and shuffled his feet. "Only he scarce knew me in the forest; I had grown so, he says."

"And your mother is well, and baby sister?" asked Ælfwyn pointedly.

"Aye, aye, they all be well, and my mother today looks happier than I have seen her in my memory," he answered.

"Then all is truly well," she said, and I myself felt her sigh of relief.

CHAPTER THE FORTIETH

UNREST WITHIN

T HE next day came four riders, Danes; and rode into the yard and spoke to Yrling. They brought a great number of horses, fifty or more, which they drove in a restless herd. That night these four Danes sat at meat with us at the head table, and the following morning were off again, driving their horses before them.

Nor was this the only visit, for more such men followed a few days later. Again they drove horses, heading South. These men had also many waggons with them, pulled by oxen, containing what I did not know. That night Yrling spoke long with them, and his face and voice told me that what he heard did not please him.

Sidroc listened to all that was spoken, but said little himself. Before I left to go upstairs I turned to him and asked, "Why do these men bring so many horses with them, when they themselves are so few? Are they going to sell them in Anglia?"

He turned to me as if I had roused him, and answered, "No. They take the horses overland to meet those who sail from the North."

"From near Jorvik?"

"From beyond Jorvik. It is faster to sail down the coast than to ride."

His eyes went back to Yrling and the strange Danes.

"Why are they sailing?" I asked, afraid of the answer.

"They sail to war," he said, and looked at me for a moment. "It is starting."

"O," was all I could say. I looked over to where Yrling sat, clutching his cup as he listened to the riders. His piercing eyes were hooded by his brows, but no expression moved upon his face. Ælfwyn sat with downcast eyes by his side, gazing at the golden dish before her. She scarcely moved. I did not think she needed Sidroc or anyone else to tell her what I had just heard.

"It is far from Summer," I said, and Sidroc again turned and looked at me.

"Yes, too far, and we have not enough men to do what Yrling wants." His eyes were steady as he looked at me. "Do not be alarmed. Nothing will happen yet."

I mutely nodded and left the table.

I did not see Ælfwyn until the morning, when Burginde prepared her bath. Her first words were, "I have told him that my family is as dear to me as my own life, and that if they were harmed I could find no happiness on this Earth."

She shook loose her hair from her head-dress, and pushed it away from her pale face. "I spoke to him half the night, boldly, and asked – begged – that he protect them." She looked down at the floor. "I did not even ask for the protection of their property, only for the sparing of them."

"Did you say that, if it must fall, you would rather see him take Cirenceaster than another?"

She nodded her head, and tears rolled from her closed eyes. "Yes," she whispered. "And tho' he spoke not, his face showed his amaze at this. Yet he took me into his arms and held me close, as if . . . he were pleased with me."

Burginde had been busy readying the tub. Now she lifted her head and spoke. "'Tis the understanding you have shown," she said simply, and said no more.

I thought about this, and said, "If Cirenceaster must fall, you accept it, and want the least harm done; and this he respects." I recalled Sidroc's words. "Yrling also wants the least harm done. He would not want Cirenceaster to end like Lindisse, for your sake and his own."

We were all quiet.

"There are many other places than Cirenceaster. This he reminded me," said Ælfwyn. Her voice held a note of hope, but her face showed it was not strong within her.

She ended, "I do not want to help my husband to take over my own family's home; but even this I would do to keep them from destruction."

Later that day we heard news from Burginde. "Toki is here, and down in the hall. He be the same as ever, on the outside at least," she said, and then chortled, "but 'tis not likely he'll be grabbing at any cats, great or small."

"I wish he had never come back," answered Ælfwyn, speaking for us both.

When we went down into the hall that night we saw Toki by the firepit. Near him stood Sidroc, his foot up on one of the smooth hearth stones, looking into the fire. They appeared to be talking, but I did not study them to find out. Perhaps there was now peace between them.

Toki took his place at the table as before, and we ate and drank as if he had never been away. One thing only was different, and it was this: Toki would not look at me. If he spoke to Sidroc or looked in our direction, his eyes never rested on me. It was as if I were not there, and I was very glad not to have the roving blue eyes of this man upon me. There was a change, too, in Sidroc. He looked differently upon me, and once I saw him scan the face of Toki, to see, I think, if Toki looked at me.

Yrling spoke, and put this out of my mind, for what he said made us all listen.

"I will not go to Jorvik," he announced, and then gestured to Sidroc and to Toki, "but you, and you, will go, and leave tomorrow; and bring us those things as we want."

Ælfwyn was all interest at this, and asked, "And sheep too?"

"Yes, sheep and other things we have need of. Everything can be found in Jorvik."

I looked at Sidroc to see how he received this news. I knew he wanted to again see Jorvik, and had often spoken of it, but I did not think he expected now to be sent with Toki to do so. His eyes opened wide for a moment, and then narrowed, but aside from this his face showed little sign of his feelings.

Toki, however, was quick to show his gladness at being sent on this mission, and tho' his mouth twisted in disdain at the mention of sheep, he called across the tables to some other Danes in a boasting way.

I wondered why Yrling was sending them together, and watched his face as he spoke to them about the trip. He told them of the route they should take, the waggon they would need, and who to speak to when in Jorvik. Ælfwyn listened carefully to all that was said, as carefully as if she herself were going.

When I went up to our chamber, Ælfwyn went with me, and told Burginde and I that we might ask for a few things, not too great in size, that might be brought back. Burginde had her answer ready at once, "Cheese"; and tho' both Ælfwyn and I laughed, we agreed it would be good to taste cheese again, and she said she would ask for it.

"I will ask for another large copper tub, so that I might bathe more easily downstairs," thought Ælfwyn. "What would you like?" she asked me.

"Bee's wax," I answered, "so that we might make you a true wax tablet, like mine."

"Very good," Ælfwyn agreed, "and perhaps they could bring some candles as well."

She returned in the morning saying that Yrling would add our requests to those things he wanted brought from Jorvik. As we were dressing she added, "He is wise, in his own way, and I begin to learn from him. I asked why he is sending them together, since Sidroc had nearly killed Toki. He laughed and said that was why he sent them."

"Because they will have to work together on the road?" I asked.

"Yes, just that."

Burginde was not impressed by this. "If only one comes back, the other's word will be as naught as to what happened," she warned.

"They will come back," said Ælfwyn. "Tho' I would be happy if Toki would decide to stay in Jorvik."

We had our broth and bread, and then went down into the hall, where we found Sidroc and Toki preparing to leave. They had their bed-rolls and hide bags at their feet, and on the table before them sat their war-kits. Sidroc's new sword, heavy and magnificent, hung from his red leathern baldric.

Yrling was speaking to them as we came up, and we stood silently until he finished. Then Ælfwyn spoke, to both Sidroc and Toki. "Have you ever bought sheep before?" she inquired.

Toki rolled his eyes, but said nothing. Sidroc smiled so that he nearly laughed. "No, never before have I bought sheep," he answered.

"There are important things to look for," began Ælfwyn, earnestly. "Our greatest need is for good rams. Choose at least two, of the best you can find. Take a curly horn over the straighter kind, and choose those which have a deep chest and short legs. Sheep for sale would not have been shorn yet, so you will see them in full fleece. Take your hand and drive it gently into the fleece by the ram's back hocks. The fleece should cover your hand at least from fingertip to knuckle; the longer the better. And look for a long tuft on the chest, between the front legs; that is also a good sign."

All three men were looking at her as she went through these instructions, and all I think were amused; but Yrling's eyes were lit with pleasure as well.

"Get as many ewes as you can, and as young as you can," she went on. "The age of the rams does not matter; a good old ram can be got cheaply and will save silver. We will have young rams enough if those you now choose be good ones."

I thought how strange and wonderful it was, that this young woman should stand before these men and thus instruct them. I looked at Toki as he looked away, and recalled the curl of his lip as he had tossed the pouch containing the great pearl at Ælfwyn upon the journey here; and most of all I remembered the first night we had seen Yrling, and the real fear these men had brought us as they nearly broke into our chamber. All of this had passed, and the unknown was now known. I looked at Ælfwyn, and felt great pride, and great gratitude for the distance travelled.

She thought of another thing. "Who is driving the waggon? It should be a man who knows the ways of sheep, and can help herd them."

Sidroc answered, "The ox-drover you brought with you."

"Osred," she said. "Good. He will be a great help."

The men shouldered their packs, and Yrling took up some of their things as well. We walked to the steps and out into the yard. The waggon stood ready, and Osred scratched the ears of one of the yoked oxen as he waited. Sidroc's bay stallion was there, saddled, as was Toki's grey. They fixed their packs and weapons upon them, and Toki swung up into his saddle.

Sidroc turned to me. I mumbled, "I wish you a good journey," and looked down at the ground. He spoke, but softly, and in his own tongue. He mounted his horse, and turned to raise his hand to Yrling. The waggon creaked forward, and they moved away.

DEATH OF A KING

A full week passed, and it was a peaceful and good one. No more strange Danes came to Four Stones, and the sentries on the palisade were quiet. In the village the fields were being turned, and men and women worked in the damp soil from light to dusk. Tumbled huts were straightened and rebuilt, and the crofts once again protected by low fences of woven wattles. The rhythm of the village seemed nearly restored, and as no woman came to Ælfwyn to seek protection, we hoped none were abused.

At night we sat with Yrling in the hall, and he spoke to us, and we to him, and I felt his strangeness grow less. Tho' he was often stern, his eyes were kinder when he looked upon Ælfwyn, and he listened when she spoke. It was clear, too, that his desire for her was great, for tho' he rarely took her hand or touched her before others, he often called her to him during the day, and the treasure room door would close behind them.

One morning a messenger rode into the keep yard. The past two days had been wet, and the ground was naught but mud. We stood in the drizzle in our clogs and watched as Yrling spoke to the man, a young and haggard Dane with dripping wet yellow hair. Yrling gestured that the man should come in, and Dobbe was sent to bring him food and drink and refill his hide pack for the road. The messenger stood by the firepit drying himself as Yrling questioned him. We two women waited for news.

At last he left, and Ælfwyn did not have to ask, for Yrling turned to her and spoke. "Æthelred of Wessex is dead," were his words, and his eyes were bright.

"The King is dead," Ælfwyn repeated, but in a toneless voice.

"He died from wounds he took at the battle of Meredune. All will be easier now, for his young brother is named King."

"Ælfred," said Ælfwyn. "The Witan has chosen him as King?"

Yrling nodded, and then smiled. "I have not seen him fight, but I do not think he will last long. The Raven will pick the bones of the Dragon."

Ælfwyn did not reply, but nodded her head and walked wordlessly away and up the stairs. I followed her and she told Burginde of the tidings.

"King Æthelred is dead, and the Witan met and chose Ælfred as King," she said, and then slumped down in her chair at the table.

"Ælfred?" asked Burginde. "He be a fierce fighter, when he be well, but he is often not."

I looked my question to Ælfwyn, and she said, "He is the youngest of our great King Æthelwulf's sons, and was never meant to be King; and never, I am sure, expected to, for he had four brothers before him. But all four have ruled, and now, all four died, and so the son that Æthelwulf had meant as a scholar is now our King."

"Burginde says he is not well?"

"It is sad, but true, for he is plagued by an illness that saps his strength and gives him great distress. His bowel, I think." She looked about her, and only shook her head. "The council must feel needy to have chosen him, for as Yrling says, I do not think he can last long."

"How old is he?" I asked.

Ælfwyn thought for a moment. "He has twenty-two Summers," she said, "the same as . . . the same as one who rides with him." Now she lay her head down on her hands. This was the first time since we had come to this place that I had heard her speak of her lost love, and she could not hide the pain of thinking of him.

"If your Witan chose him, they must believe he can win," I said, "even if he be young and unwell. Many good men must have pledged to him, and he must be very rich, and can supply them with all manner of arms and horses."

"The best men are now sworn to him," answered Ælfwyn in an empty voice, "and he has great riches." She looked up at Burginde and said, "It is the end."

For once Burginde did not deny this, but sat lost in thoughts of her own. I wanted to rouse them, to bring some word of courage or of hope, but words failed me. All I could think of was the day that Sidroc had told us that Wessex and Mercia would fall. Nothing and no one would be out of their grasp. The bracelet on my wrist glinted as I moved my hand, and felt at that moment to be the heaviest lead and not purest silver.

Burginde got up from her stool, and slowly went about her work, but Ælfwyn and I remained, she sitting, and me standing, mired in these thoughts.

We heard a footfall upon the wooden tread of our stairs, and the thought that Yrling might be wanting her

then was too terrible to bear. But it was only Susa, and
she came into our room and told us that some sacks of
wool Ælfwyn had sent to the village women to be spun
had come, and were in the yard.

We went with Burginde down into the yard. Before
the hall stood Meryth, and a man of the village who pulled
a simple wain. Upon it sat two large baskets, brimful with
balls of newly spun wool thread. Meryth came forward to
us, and bowed, and we saw her babe tied to her back. The
man behind her dipped his head with an uncertain look
upon his grizzled face. He still wore the animal hides he
had come home in, and his feet were bare.

"Here is our spinning work, my Lady," she said, "and
this man, my husband, Arsuf."

Burginde picked up one of the balls and unravelled an
arm's length of it. "Fair work," she said, running her fingers
along it.

She passed the ball to Ælfwyn, who took it up and
said, "It is good work indeed." She could not smile as she
said this; her grief was still strong upon her.

They stood looking at Ælfwyn, and she said in a
strong and grave voice, "More sheep are coming, from
Jorvik, and they will be ready for shearing. Do you shear
those brought from the forests, and those to come, and
from that fleece spin for yourselves enough to weave gar-
ments for your returned men."

This was bold of her, for she gave away the fleece to
the villagers as tho' it were hers alone, and not hers and
Yrling's. She raised her hand to dismiss them, and turned
her back and walked away. In the hall she saw Yrling,
coming out of the treasure room, and went straight to him.

"The village men have no clothes," she said, and in her voice was both fear and a challenge. "I have ordered that they shear the sheep and their wives spin and weave for them."

Yrling seemed not to comprehend, but nodded his head. "The sheep are for you, to make gold from. I do not question how you do it."

We heard these words, and knew again the freedom this strange man granted her, and the respect that he showed her. I knew with what gratitude Ælfwyn listened, for in reply she took Yrling's hand and touched it for a moment to her heart.

Several noons later we sat as usual weaving in our chamber. The good light was fading when the sounds of whistles made us all three turn our heads to the windows.

"They must be come back from Jorvik, unless it be another messenger," mused Burginde, craning her neck to see.

It seemed too much noise for a simple messenger, so we went down into the yard and there saw Yrling, standing and waiting as we did.

The first rider we saw was Sidroc, and Toki behind him, both they and their horses dusty with travel. We knew they had brought sheep with them, for they could be heard, baaing and jingling their bells, tho' see them we could not. Sidroc called out to us, and his face wore a smile, and I smiled too at him. He swung down from his horse and crossed to Yrling.

"We heard on the road," were his first words. "Æthelred is dead."

We did not hear more, for then we were near engulfed by a flock of sheep, trotting and tumbling around the corner at us. Walking amongst them, crook in hand, came Osred, and behind him were three strange Danes, mounted on horseback and leading a pack horse. The waggon we saw last of all, driven by another strange Dane who walked beside it.

The sheep swirled around us, and Ælfwyn's face shone as she regarded them. There were three unhappy old rams, glaring balefully at everything about them. There were two score at least of ewes, and many of them were followed by lambs which ducked their snowy heads against their mother's round sides for protection.

Ælfwyn waded into their midst, and Osred grinned with pride.

"These are beautiful sheep," she said, beaming.

"They be fair; they be fair, Lady," nodded Osred. He looked up for a moment to where Sidroc and Toki now stood with Yrling. "'Tis a good thing I was sent too, or you might be standing amongst goats now," he chuckled. "But when it came time to bargain, they were very close; none better," he added, in fairness; and he rubbed his thumb against his forefinger to show how well they had bargained for the lot.

"Good," said Ælfwyn, bending down and catching an ewe up by its neck. She pulled the creature's ears and stroked its bony face as it bleated. "Keep them here in the old cattle pens tonight, so that I may look further at them, and count them myself, and tomorrow take them to the village shepherds."

We went to where Yrling stood, speaking now to the strange Danes. He made a gesture of welcome to them, and they dismounted. The waggon was now pulled up closer to the hall steps, and Osred returned and unyoked the oxen and led them away.

Sidroc jumped upon the waggon board and unlaced the awning, and within we could see basket after basket of goods. First he brought forward several sacks, one of which he pulled open at the top and thrust his hand into. Grains of yellow wheat sifted through his fingers.

"There is wheat, and barley, and oats," he said, and if it had been sacks of gold and silver it could scarce have been more important, for here was the seed for the empty and waiting fields around us.

Burginde was already at work at another basket, and I guessed by the wetness that showed about its base that she had found the cheeses. She pulled back a handful of dark rushes, and brought forth a small round cheese, white as a goose egg. She raised it to her nose and smiled. "And plenty of them," she said, feeling about in the recesses of the basket.

In the front of the waggon winked a great gleam of copper, and Ælfwyn clapped her hands together and cried, "My tub," and Sidroc climbed into the waggon and brought it out, huge and beautiful, into the Sunlight. It was no ordinary wash-tub, but had upon it designs, impressed in the copper, of grapes and vines.

Sidroc and Toki carried in the tub, and the baskets and barrels, and set up the tables on their trestles, that we might look at everything in its turn. There was all manner of useful things: Lumps of salt, and polishing stones, and bronze and copper goods; and also things that gave gladness. Sidroc unrolled a strip of cloth upon the table, and within lay twelve pair of candles; tapers so beautiful they must have been dipped for a church. He opened before me a small cask of pale yellowy stuff, and I touched and smelt it, and knew it to be beeswax.

"These things are not easily had," he said in a mild voice, and we knew he was proud to set them before us.

Ælfwyn held the candles in her arms and said, "I thank you for all your work. Soon we will have bees kept, and we will have this precious stuff as we need it." She sniffed at the candles and closed her eyes in pleasure.

She then looked across the room to where Yrling stood with Toki and the strangers. "Who are the men you brought?" she asked.

"Some who would join with us. I know one of them, and think they will be worth the feeding," he answered, looking also at them.

She looked then at Toki, standing in the background behind Yrling. "Toki looks as sullen as ever," she noted, and then looked back at Sidroc. "You did not quarrel on the road?"

He shook his head and laughed. "He is angry, for he lost his helmet," he answered.

"Lost it? That which he was so proud of?" she asked, and I knew from the twist of her lip that she recalled our first sight of Toki and his helmet, with the setting Sun glinting off the gold of it.

"Given it away, I should say," he replied, tho' it was hard to imagine Toki giving any thing of value away. "I saw him lose it once, fording a stream, and he stayed behind and dived and dived until he found it." He regarded Toki as he said this. "This time it is gone for good, for he lost it in a wager at Jorvik, to one of Jarl Healfdene's men."

We could hardly believe this, and showed it.

Sidroc only smiled. "We were gaming, and winning, and winning makes you bold. Then the Gods turned away, and the fall of the bones gave his helmet to another. He tried to buy it back next morning, but Healfdene had moved on." Sidroc glanced over to where Toki stood. "Toki never knows when to stop," he finished.

I could not tell if he shared some regret in the loss of something so wonderful.

"He will have another made," he shrugged.

He turned now to his own bed roll, and the pack tied onto it. He smoothed out a tanned hide, and drew out of the pack a number of small things wrapped in cloth or in leathern pouches, and laid them upon the hide. He took up a folded square of blue-dyed leather, so small it would fit in the palm of your hand. He opened it and set two tiny vials of glass, stopped with wood plugs, upon the hide before us. One was of green glass swirled with gold, and the other of blue glass swirled with silver. He was watching our faces as he said to Ælfwyn and me, "These are for you."

Ælfwyn laughed and said, "I will guess that the blue one is for me, and the green for Ceridwen; and that you have matched our eyes."

He nodded, and handed the vials to us, and I could not keep my joy secret. I pulled open the stopper and lifted the vial to my nose. A scent like all the roses of Summer came forth, so powerful and strong that I gasped.

"They are from far, far to the East, and the oil more costly than gold," he told us, but he did not say it in a boasting way.

I put the stopper back on and held the vial up to see the light through it. It was as if an emerald had been melted and cast with gold.

"It is fitting that the vessel for such precious stuff be a treasure itself," I told him. "I thank you more than I can say."

Ælfwyn too held hers up and marvelled over it, and she took his hand in hers and said, "How good you are to us, Sidroc," with real warmth.

"The world is full of good things, and Jorvik has many of them," is what he answered.

He stood watching our pleasure, and I was glad to show it to him. His eyes met mine, and he glanced down at the hide, and at the things he had not yet unwrapped. Then I knew he had more treasures which he had brought, and brought for me; and I felt the warmth of colour on my cheek and realised I should go before he tried to give them to me.

Ælfwyn read this too, and seemed to hesitate, and then said, "I must go and find Dobbe," which let me say in return, "I will go with you."

So we thanked him again, and held our beautiful vials close in our fists, and went and told Dobbe of the cheeses.

※※※※※※※※※※

That night I lay awake until the stars faded, feeling at times troubled and almost angry with myself. I thought of Sidroc, and of Yrling, and of their strangeness, and their true goodness; for they were good men, at least to us; and lived, I tried to tell myself, to their own lights, as all men do. I saw Ælfwyn, grown content and even happy in her life with Yrling, knowing the freedoms he gave her and how much he esteemed her. If Yrling lived, she could, in her own goodness and wisdom, rebuild Four Stones and make happy the lives of the folk of Lindisse.

I thought of Sidroc, and his desire for me, and felt for the first time how wrong it was to turn from such desire from a good man; and I believed him to be good. Perhaps he might stay here, with Yrling, and Ælfwyn and I could be together, as she had once wanted. I thought of the women who would come from his homeland in the Summer, and wondered how I might feel if Sidroc grew weary of waiting for me and turned to one of them. I would be relieved, I felt; I would be free; and then I thought I lied to myself, for I knew I must feel the loss of regard such as he bore for me.

Then I thought of the conquest of Wessex, and that of Mercia, and of Kent, and of all other Kingdoms of this land; that they might all fall at the hands of the Danes, just as Northumbria and Deira and Anglia and Lindisse already had. I thought of the brutality of their taking, and that I lay safe in the hall where the daughter of Merewala was ravished, and Merewala bled, protecting what was his. I thought of the village women, and their cruel usage; and of all those slain, men and women, here at Four Stones, thegn or cottar; of poor Dobbe's son; and of the holy man who once lived here and was cut down with no regard to his calling.

But beyond these sad thoughts rose this simple truth: I am with these men now, and live amongst them, and accept their gifts; why should I not wed one, and one who regards me so well? I saw Sidroc, and his scarred face, and his dark eyes looking into mine. I recalled the day he had held me hard against his body, and I knew again his desire for me. I recalled his voice, steady and low, telling me he would wait for me. I recalled, too, our times at the place of Offering, and heard his voice repeat, 'You are like us.'

Yet the thought of these things, and my love of Ælfwyn, too, could not make me easy about this. Some thing inside me could not open to Sidroc, and I nearly cried in my anger as I tried to convince myself that I should.

※※※※※※※※※

I finally slept that night, but then was roused again by some noise in the yard. The sleep was so heavy on my eyes that I could hardly move, but then Burginde arose, muttering, and lit a cresset from the brazier. We could not tell what it was, and could see nothing but a few torches moving in the yard, but the noise of creaking waggons and men talking told us that some other Danes must have come without warning. We pulled on our shifts and mantles and crept down the stairs, listening. The hall was dark, yet I heard Yrling's voice, questioning and harsh, as he spoke to some men in the open doorway. I did not see Ælfwyn, and wondered if she had come out of the treasure room. Yrling stopped speaking, and moved away into the yard with the other voices, and we heard more talk. We went upstairs again, and into our room, and looked out our small windows into the dim yard. We seemed to hear noises around the side of the hall, as if men were going through the animal pens to the kitchen yard.

"'Tis nothing but late night visitors, looking to be fed," grudged Burginde as she crawled back into bed. I too felt tired, and slept with the sound of a waggon filling my ears with its creaking as it moved off.

In the morning when Ælfwyn came up Burginde greeted her with, "More mouths to feed," and jerked her thumb in the direction of the yard.

"I do not think so," answered Ælfwyn. She looked distracted. "At least they are not here any longer. They were Danes, and I do not know what they wanted, but Yrling was very angry when he came back."

"He would not tell you why he was angered?" I asked.

"No, and he is still angry now. He was going to take a few men hunting today, but now because of whatever happened he will not leave until tomorrow." She pulled a tangle from her hair with some little force. "I feel fearful, and afraid of knowing; yet I wish he would tell me."

"Perhaps it is better you do not know," I found myself saying.

She looked truly troubled, and only nodded her head.

"'Tis probably nothing bad in your eyes; or even something meaning good to Wessex," suggested Burginde, and we all tried to hold to this thought.

CHAPTER THE FORTY-SECOND

EVERYTHING CHANGES

THAT night we had ewers of special ale on the hall tables, and Yrling spoke to the men of the hunt to come, and we drank to their success.

"I will not go, this time," said Sidroc to me. "I will be moving the horses to their new pasturage."

My interest showed, and he went on, "It is not too far from the valley, on the way to the forests. There is good ground there, well-drained."

"We are so glad that there will be flax," I said, and tried to show in my voice the gratitude I felt for his help. "And if you are over that way, perhaps you will see Yrling and his group on the way back."

"And carry in the kill," he nodded. "The stags will all be gone to higher ground, but there might be pig for the taking."

The meal was a noisy and a good one, for the men going with Yrling looked forward to the hunt, and the rest of them to the bounty they might bring back. Yrling too seemed at ease again, and to have set aside what had angered him during the night.

In the morning Yrling and Toki and a few others left so early that when Ælfwyn came up to our chamber she told us they had already ridden. Sidroc was about, she said, and had told her that tomorrow he would be gone for most of the day or perhaps over the night when they moved the horses. The morning was a quiet one for us, but we welcomed it, and spent the good light it gave at our looms. About noon we heard a slow tread on the wooden stair outside our room, and guessed that Susa was come with our supper. Burginde went to the door and opened it and there found Dobbe herself grasping the tray.

She had never before come into our room, and so we were surprised, but what surprised us the more was the look on her withered face. Burginde took the tray from her and placed it upon the table, and Dobbe stood in the doorway, gazing upon us, her arms shaking from the palsy, and perhaps, I thought, fear. We rose from our looms and took a step nearer to her, since it was clear she did not intend to move.

"Dobbe?" asked Ælfwyn in a kind way.

Dobbe's eyes watered as they latched on to Ælfwyn's face, and she shook the more. "Lady," she croaked out, "I have ill tidings, and I am afeard."

None of us questioned, but all of us must have stiffened as we waited for her next words. She took a step into the room, turned and closed the door behind her, and then came forward to within a few feet of us.

"There be a man, a prisoner, below the hall in the kitchen yard, and he be a man of Wessex." Dobbe jabbed her finger at the floor as she said this, but never took her eyes from our faces.

"A man of Wessex? Here? Where is he? Who is he?" gasped out Ælfwyn.

"Who I do not know, for when the Dane – the Lord, that is – had him brought in, he ordered all of us back to our beds, and made it clear that it should be as tho' we saw nothing." She started openly to weep, and Burginde came to her and placed her stool before her that she might sit. But she stayed upon her feet, and wiped her face with her apron, and went on. "Where, I can answer, for he is in the remains of the old cellars beneath the hall. They open only to the kitchen yard, and there be a Dane there now to keep us away and the prisoner in."

"The men who came in the middle of the night must have brought him," I said. "I recall we heard noises around the side by the animal pens."

Dobbe nodded her head in agreement.

"Have you fed him? Is there any way to learn who he is?" asked Ælfwyn, still shaking her head in the amazement we all felt.

"I have ladled up food for two, but last night the Dane who watched the cellar entry only laughed, and ate both platter's worth. And I have not heard any noises from the prisoner, but the cellar, tho' it be tumbled into in places, runs a long way, so perchance he be too far away to be heard."

Ælfwyn turned to me, her eyes glowing. "We must help this man," she said, and tho' it was spoken in a whisper, it was a whisper full of defiance. She turned back to Dobbe and asked, "Who can help us help him? Do you know? Is there anyone?"

Dobbe put her hand to her forehead and said, "Mul, the stable boy, brought him in."

Ælfwyn whirled to Burginde and ordered, "Bring Mul at once," and Burginde was gone.

Then Ælfwyn crossed to her huge weaving chest, and pushed open the top, and with speed brought forth the small casket that housed her secret silver. She dipped her hand inside, and then went to Dobbe and pressed a silver coin into the shaking hand.

"You have done well by me, Dobbe. It took great courage to come. Go now, before you hear more. Tell no one that you have told us these things."

"Eomer knows I have come to you. We have been man and wife for forty years, and have shared all between us," replied Dobbe.

"Of course," Ælfwyn granted. "Eomer is different."

Dobbe kissed the white hands that had pressed the silver into hers, and wiped her face again, and went down the stairs, leaving us alone to wait for Burginde and Mul.

They were not long in coming, and the quick light step of Mul was followed by the slow tread of Burginde. I closed the door behind them, and stood near to it that I might hear anyone's approach.

Mul's gawky face did not wear the quick grin it always showed to Ælfwyn, and he stood before us as if he already knew what we would ask. He pulled at his straw-coloured forelock and bowed his head to us.

"Mul," began Ælfwyn, without any word of greeting, "I know there is a prisoner below us, and that he is a man of Wessex, my own country. Do you tell me what you know, for I must help him if I can."

Mul looked around the room, and swallowed hard. "Aye, Lady," he choked out, "I will tell you all I know. He was brought by the visitors of two night's ago, who asked your Lord to keep him. He be a man of Wessex, and the King's own kin, and rode with the new King Ælfred; for he be the son of the ealdorman of Kilton."

All colour fell from Ælfwyn's cheek, and she dropped her hands like stones at her sides. She breathed out one word, "Gyric."

A sound like a low wail came forth from Burginde's throat, and I myself gasped to hear the name of Ælfwyn's love spoken as the prisoner. Ælfwyn said nothing more, but stood and stared at Mul in unbelief.

I spurred myself and asked him, "Did you speak to him? Are you certain it is him?"

"Speak to him I did not, Lady, for the Danes were all about us, and it was dark; and he was bound, and I think, gagged and hooded too as they carried him in. I could not see well, and was kept away, and they only wanted me because I know the cellars."

"So you led them into the cellar?" I asked.

"Aye, and then was chased out of it. But I heard them talking, and they forget or do not care that I know so much of their speech."

Ælfwyn now spoke as if awaking from a dream. "I must see him. I must see him now," she said, and made almost as if she would fly down the stairs that moment.

Burginde took her arm and pulled on it. "Stop, Lady," she said, in a voice as urgent as her mistresses'.

Mul too stepped forward and said, "Lady, he be guarded by a Dane as we stand here, and no one is to know that he be even here."

"Yes, Ælfwyn," I said, seeing the real fear Mul had, "we must not risk those who are innocent."

Ælfwyn stayed herself, but her words tumbled out. "What will I do? I must get him a horse so he can escape."

She took a step toward Mul and asked, "You will help me, Mul, will you not? If I have need of you, and can promise you will not suffer for the aid you give me?"

This time Mul was quick with his answer. "I will do anything to aid you, and will suffer for you, too, if I must."

She drew a deep and calming breath. "I will not make you suffer, Mul, I swear it." She looked at me, and I saw in her face all the questions that circled her mind. She turned her eyes back to Mul. "Go now, and wait to hear from me. I will need a horse," she said slowly, and then her eyes caught flame, "at least one, so think you how you might help me in this way."

He nodded his head and asked, "Will it be tonight?"

"Yes," she answered. "Tonight or tomorrow night; I do not know." Her eyes moved quickly around the room, but she was not seeing. "Perhaps two horses," she whispered.

"Go, Mul," I said, and nearly pushed him out the door. I did not want him to hear any more of this.

"Gyric is here, he is here," she breathed aloud when we were alone. "I will see him; I must see him soon."

"Ælfwyn, you are mad, and talking treason," I implored. "You cannot see him. What if you were caught?"

"I will not be caught. I must see him again, and must allow him to escape."

I sat down at the table, unable to stand any longer. "How will we do it? He is under guard. The Danes will never let us in. And even to show we know that he is there is to endanger Dobbe and Mul."

Ælfwyn paced around the room, and said firmly, "I do not know yet. We must think, think, of how best to free him."

"Drug the Dane that guards him," said Burginde. She sat down upon her stool and looked up at us with a sharp eye. "If only one be guarding him, he can be drugged, and a horse be made handy outside the wall."

"Yes," answered Ælfwyn, "my chestnut mare."

I turned on her. "It must not be your horse," I argued. "Any horse but yours. How will it look when it is found missing? Will you have Yrling know that you set him free? I tell you, you are speaking treason against your own husband."

"Why should I care? Gyric is held prisoner here, and I can help him. There is war everywhere, and more is coming. I will not pretend any more that Yrling will honour the Peace he made. Why then should I not free the man I love?"

"Hush!" ordered Burginde. "Helping him to freedom is one thing; speaking so another. The Lady be right; 'tis much too dangerous for you to see him." Ælfwyn cried out in anger at this, but Burginde went on in a firm and steady voice. "And seeing him serves no purpose, except mischief. Do not speak of two horses; he will go on one, and go alone."

"You are wrong, nurse," she answered, and nearly spat out the words. "I will see him, if only for one moment. If I do not, I will die."

She paced around the room, and her mood of anger quickly passed. "What blessed Fate that Yrling is gone!" she said. "We must act now, and make the most of it."

I still sat at the table, and she came up to me. She touched my hand and said, "You will help me, Ceridwen, will you not? I do not think I can free him without your good thinking."

"Of course I will help you," I said, and tried not to sound sulky. "But it is dangerous, and I am afraid, for myself; and even more for you." I chose my words carefully. "Yrling cares for you – loves you – and trusts you. We must be careful to make it seem as tho' you had nothing to do with Gyric's escape."

She lowered her eyes and slowly nodded her head. "Yes, I must protect all of us. It must seem as tho' he escapes by his own powers." She looked over to Burginde, who sat with head cast down. "Burginde, no one knows me as you do; and so I beg you to forgive my rash words." She stood up, and looked at both of us. "I will not make treason against Yrling, I swear to both of you; but I must help Gyric to escape. Wessex needs him. Ælfred needs him. He may even help save my own family. If by doing this I make treason against Yrling, then I will be guilty."

"You must not get caught, that is all," nodded Burginde.

"I will not," murmured Ælfwyn, but her thoughts galloped on. "You spoke wisdom when you spoke of drugging the guard. We must do it." She turned to Burginde. "How do we do it?"

Burginde scratched her chin. "Your own dear mother did it once, I recall; not like this, of course, but to make a sick man sleep long so he would heal."

Ælfwyn raised her eyebrows and asked, "She did? How did she do it? What did she use?"

"I do not remember," admitted Burginde. "'Twas long ago."

"Wilfrida will know," I thought aloud.

"Aye, Wilfrida; she be a healer," agreed Burginde. "She has all matter of herbs hanging."

I crossed to the door, stopping to pick up a basket on the way. In it lay the dried ferny leaves Wilfrida had once given us. I reached instead for my leathern satchel, but tucked the leaves inside it. "I will go now, and see her." I went to Ælfwyn and kissed her cheek. "Promise me that you will do nothing until I return. I will ride rather than walk so I may be quick."

"I promise," she answered.

"And make your ride seem as tho' all is just as usual," advised Burginde.

"I will, as much as I can," I returned.

Mul was not about the yard, so I had to point out my mare to the Dane I found in the stable. He brought her forth, and as he saddled her I thought he looked more closely at me than at other times. But then, I was alone, and not with Ælfwyn, and so his eye might be more bold. I calmed myself and acted as if I went on any simple errand to the village, and was glad that I need not speak to him.

I headed out along the village road, trying to walk my mare slowly as if I enjoyed the Spring Sun. Perhaps my mare felt my fear, for she whinnied and side-stepped and tossed her head noisily as we went.

As I neared Wilfrida's croft I began to look for her across the fields, or by the stream, for I knew she often worked there as well. But Fate blest me, and as I rode up to her hut I saw steam rising from her iron cauldrons. The stuff she stirred was inky black and smelt very foul.

I slid off my mare, clutching my hide bag, and she came forward and regarded me. Her jaw moved; she seemed always to be chewing something. She nodded her head and said, "Lady," as a greeting.

"Wilfrida," I began, and tried to slow my words and not show the fear I felt, "I have need of your wort cunning."

"Aye," she answered, chewing still, and regarding me even more sharply. She glanced at the bag I held, laid down the dark paddle, and then said, "Come in, and tell me of it."

The hut was dark inside, tho' she left the door open as we went in, and for a moment I just stood until I could again see. My eyes went to the single rafter overhead, and the bunches of herbs and bundles of peeled bark and dried roots that hung there.

"I need something to make a man sleep," I said, getting it all out at once.

She regarded me for a moment and then asked, "Sleep ever?"

"No," I answered quickly. "I do not want to kill him, only to make him sleep deeply for a few hours."

"Hmmm," she replied. "To sleep sound for one night?"

"Yes, that is it; he must sleep sound for one night, and not awaken until morning."

"And you have his feeding in your command?"

"Yes, food and drink both," I answered.

She nodded as if this were a good thing, and scanned the rafter above her, considering each bundle in its turn. She reached up and brought down a cluster of gnarled, greyish roots. She lay these upon a stool and then turned to a pile of red pottery bowls, each covered with round wooden plugs. She opened one and brought out a fistful of dried stems and leaves with prickly withered pods.

She held up one of the grey roots in her hand. "Peel this, and grind it, and boil it with his ale, and let it cool, and then strain it fine. 'Twill give a slight bitter taste, so strong ale, like ivy, or rough beer, be best."

"Cook his meal with this," she went on, holding out the dried leaves and pods, "porridge of some sort, or browis; and when it is cooked, pull out the pods and slice them open and scrape out the sticky part within, and stir it back into his food. 'Twill leave no taste. Give him both ale and porridge together, and he will sleep long and very deep."

"But he will not die?" I asked in fear.

"No, he will not die, but only wake in the morning with a bad head."

"What are they?" I asked, as I could not name either one.

"The root be cowslip, and the pods, thornapple."

"I need enough for two night's worth," I said.

"You may take a month's worth if you want, but do not give too much each night, or he will retch on it and wake rather than sleep."

"Please to show me once more how much I should use," I asked.

She went over it again, and then I opened my leathern bag to take them. I saw the ferns within and pulled them out. "This you gave to us when we first spoke to you, but we know not what use it has."

Her wrinkled lips cracked into a smile, and she said, "'Tis for your Lady, to get a child faster. She should steep it in ale or broth and drink it for three nights before the half Moon."

"I thank you, Wilfrida," I said. "I have nothing to repay your kindness with, but –"

She spoke over me. "I will take no payment to make a Dane sleep. The other is a gift to your Lady."

When I started up the stairs to our chamber Ælfwyn
came out on the landing to meet me. Her face said that
each moment I was gone had been hard to bear. I pulled
open my satchel and showed her the roots and leaves, and
told her how they must be prepared.

"I will go now, to Dobbe, and give her these," I said.
"Will it be tonight? Do you think we can have a horse
ready so soon?"

"I have been thinking on it; I do not know," she
answered.

"Also, he will need arms," I remembered. "They would
have taken his sword and everything. He will need whatever we can find."

"And kit of some kind," chimed in Burginde. "Some
food, and tinder, and so forth."

Ælfwyn put her hand to her brow. "He may scarcely
be clothed. And he will need silver for the journey South;
at least I have much silver to give him." She turned to us
and asked, "He is three day's ride from a border. How will
he ever make it?"

"Not to think of that; that be his riddle to solve. Think
instead of the horse, for that is most important," counselled Burginde.

I thought then that he would have only a few hours
before it was discovered he was gone, and the Danes gave
chase. At least Yrling would not be back for three or four
nights, so the pursuit would be led by others, probably
Sidroc.

Ælfwyn must have had like thoughts, for she said,
"Sidroc told me he might spend tomorrow night with the

drovers moving the horses. If he does, both he and Yrling will be gone, at least for a short time."

"Then that be better still, and we should work to free him for tomorrow night," said Burginde.

"Yes, and we will have another day to find the horse and kit," I answered. I had another thought, and turned to Ælfwyn with it. "I will go to Gyric tonight, and tell him of our plan, so he can counsel us, and so that he knows of it and can prepare himself."

"Yes, we will drug the guard tonight, and we will go, and I will see his face again," murmured Ælfwyn.

All my strength was in my answer. "You must not go; you must not be seen with him, for what if we be caught? It is one thing for me to be caught with him, but life or death perhaps, for you."

"What of your life?" she asked.

"Do not worry about that; I know I am right. If I should be caught helping Gyric, Sidroc will be my judge, for Yrling is away; and Sidroc will not harm me. This I know. And if Gyric escapes, and suspicion falls on us, I will openly take the blame, for if Sidroc feels Yrling will punish me, he will run off with me, and so save me from danger."

She opened her mouth and looked at me. "You will do this for me?" she asked.

"I am pledged to you, and will do anything for you; but I do it feeling my life is not in danger, but yours surely might be if you were caught."

For answer she embraced me, and kissed my cheek. "Only you must let me see Gyric, just one time, after you have told him of our plans. Please."

I could not refuse this plea; the tears were in both our eyes. "Yes," I nodded, and then sat down and tried to think. "I will have Dobbe drug the guard tonight, and tonight I will stay in the kitchen yard and hide until the hall goes to sleep. Then I will find Gyric, and tell him, and then send some sign to you and you can come down and see him while I am certain the guard still sleeps."

Ælfwyn listened hard to this. "What signal will you send?"

Burginde had the answer. "Take one of the balls of wool yarn, and cast it out the window before you go, so that we have the other end here. 'Twill fall near the side gate if it be cast from our farthest window. Then tie it to something below, and pull upon it when she may come down."

"You are too clever, nurse; that is a good and quiet signal," said Ælfwyn. "Now we must find him a horse, and kit, and have all ready for tomorrow night."

"We have many things for a kit right here; for we had so much in the waggon we came in," I remembered.

The three of us went around the room, gathering things that would be needful. Hide bags we had many of, and took the best amongst them and into it put a brass box filled with lye-soaked tinder, several flints and two good irons, two small bronze pots, bronze spoons and a spit fork, a folded deer skin that might serve as ground sheet or cover, and such like items. Ælfwyn went again to her secret silver, and drew out handfuls and handfuls of coins, and dropped them into a black leathern drawstring purse, and then went to her jewellery caskets and began plucking out rings and bracelets and pins of silver and gold. These she dropped into a pouch of red-dyed leather, and we knew it to be the one her great pearl had come in.

Burginde watched all this, and spoke the concern I felt as well. "Do not be over-rash, for the Dane might miss some of your jewels, and be most careful not to give any of those he himself gave you."

"I give those I came with; that is all," answered the Lady, but it seemed that she gave every jewel she owned. "Gyric will need them far more than me. They may buy his life on the road."

She paused and said, "I would never give him that which Yrling had touched." And when she said this we hung our heads and looked away, for at that moment all the distaste she had ever felt for the Dane was new and strong within her.

She lowered her voice and said, "Yrling will miss nothing. He does not care what I wear, as long as I am willing to take it off when he wishes."

CHAPTER THE FORTY-THIRD

A MAN OF WESSEX

I found Dobbe in the kitchen yard and went straight to her. We stepped behind one of the large domed ovens, and I passed the herbs into her apron and told her how they must be prepared.

"But how can we be certain the prisoner is not drugged too?" I asked her.

"I will serve up only one platter, and one ewer of ale, to the Dane, and doubt he will ask on behalf of another," she answered.

I nodded. "Tonight at the end of our meal, I will slip into the yard here, and wait until the guard sleeps. Have a smock in the passageway, so that if the guard sees me, I will look as one of the kitchen women."

She nodded her head. "You can wait in the grain shed, 'tis close to the cellar. I will leave food and drink there to take with you, for the poor man has had aught to eat, methinks, in days."

"That is good, Dobbe. Is it safe to take me there now, that I might have some idea of where I am going tonight?"

"Aye, 'tis a good notion, and you will see too the cellar opening and the place where the guard sits. It be a new man each night, and he stretches out and sleeps by the steps going down."

We moved from behind the oven, and started slowly across the yard. "Turn the loaves, Susa," Dobbe croaked as we passed the young woman feeding the oven's fire.

Beyond the long work tables sat a number of small sheds, some of which I knew housed the kitchen staff, and some supplies. My eyes went to the stone base of the hall, and I saw a Dane seated on a stool, leaning back and wearing the tedium of his charge on his face. He wore no arms but his dagger-like knife, but resting behind him on the wall stood his iron-tipped ash spear. Near him lay a ramped opening leading down under the outside wall of the hall. It must have been nearly beneath the treasure room, I guessed, by looking up at the small window high in the timbers of the upper wall.

Just across from this Dane was a small shed, and Dobbe gestured to it, and said to me in a loud and quavering voice, "That be the shed, Lady, and please to ask the Lord for timber for it; for it be ready to fall down if we do not shore it soon; 'tis not fit to house even the rats."

I did not think the Dane could understand our speech, but it was wise of Dobbe nonetheless to speak so, and she stood with me outside the shed, as if she was pointing out to me all that must be done, and so I had a good chance to look about me. She pushed open the door, and we both winced at the loud creaking it made. I saw sacks of meal and sieves and worn quern stones within.

We came out again, and for one instant my eyes met the eyes of the Dane, but he only crossed his legs and leaned back farther on his stool. I could not see much of the cellar opening, only that it was a ramp. The rest was hidden in dimness.

Dobbe and I parted, and I headed upstairs feeling some relief that this first part of our task was underway. Ælfwyn met me on the stairs, and touched the key ring on her sash without speaking, and we went down and crossed to the door of the treasure room and she unlocked it.

I told her of all that I had seen, and she dropped to her knees and pressed her hands against the wide floorboards she knelt upon.

"Gyric is here," she whispered. "So close to me, and I will see him tonight."

She closed her eyes, and the look that crossed her face was of purest joy. I saw her joy, but felt only fear for what it might make her do. What if Gyric asked her to ride off with him? It would be certain death for them both, I thought; for Sidroc would follow at once, and send word to Yrling in the forest, and the Danes would hunt for them until they found them; and I did not think Yrling would show mercy to his young wife, but slay her on the spot.

Then I recalled that Gyric had acted with reason and calm before, and had not run off with her when they had first met and loved each other, and that he must love her still and would not take her into such danger. I tried to hold to this thought, but it was hard, watching her; for the power and force of her love and desire for this man was so great that I thought that at one word from him she might gladly forfeit her life.

She rose, and went to a chest that held the clothes of dead Merewala, and pulled forth the fine things that lay there. "Yrling will never miss these," she said, and she set aside a mantle, and linen tunics, and leggings, and leathern leg wrappings.

She turned and faced a long chest that held captured swords. She took up her keys as if she would open it, but I said, "You cannot touch the swords, Ælfwyn; Yrling surely has each one counted and valued; and since you hold the keys will know you took one."

This speech stayed her, and I went on. "It must look as much as can be that he escaped on his own, so that no one here will suffer." I tried to say this with all the urgency that I felt, for I knew fear; where she, only love and desire.

She nodded her head. "Yes," she agreed, and turned from the chest. "He will have to take whatever weapons the guard has, and make do with those."

We locked the room, and carried the clothes upstairs. I looked upon her face as she touched all that we prepared for Gyric, and wondered how things would ever be right between her and Yrling again.

We heard Mul's voice call out Halloo from below, and I went out on the landing and motioned him to come up. His narrow face was still solemn, but his eyes were bright as he bowed to us.

"Have you found a way to get a horse?" asked Ælfwyn eagerly.

"Not for certain, Lady, but I think we are close," he answered. "I bethought me that the Danes be moving their horses tomorrow, and we will take most of those in the stable and turn them to pasture, and bring others in their place; and I will ride with them."

"So you think you could somehow hide a horse where it could be found later by the prisoner?" I asked.

"Aye; perchance; if I be driving some late, near dusk, or taking some to water, over to the pond; and all the Danes be busy, I might tie one in the clump of trees yonder."

"On the way to the place of Offering," I said.

"Aye, along the path to that place."

Ælfwyn pressed her hands together. "Good," she answered. "If you take several horses, and there is much confusion, they will not notice if one less returns with you." She thought a moment. "Choose a good horse, a fast one, but not one that will be missed right away."

"Aye, Lady, 'twould not think of touching one belonging to the Dane or his kin," he answered.

"We have no trappings for it," I remembered, not knowing how we had forgotten this most important point. "Without a saddle he will never be able to ride fast."

"That be one thing that is ready," grinned Mul. "There be many saddles and bridles we be working on in the great stable, for they come in to be mended of broken girths or worn reins. I have what we need in a sack, ready to go to my father's tonight."

"To your father?" asked Ælfwyn. "Why? I do not want him to know of this; it is too dangerous."

"Know he must, Lady, unless you can figure how to get the saddle to the horse; for the ones I lead wear only a neck-rope. My father can take the sack at dusk to where the horse is tied, and no one be the wiser."

We could find no answer to this, so must agree. The circle of those who aided us in this thing grew, and so did the danger to all of us; but without help it could not be done.

"Then we will plan for tomorrow night," ended Ælfwyn. "Come to us in the morning, Mul, before you leave with the men, so that we may speak one last time." Mul nodded his head, and she added, "And I, Ælfwyn, thank you with all my heart for your help."

When we three were alone in the room Burginde went over to the table where sat the untouched platter of food. It had been hours since Dobbe had brought it, but it seemed days. She went down the stairs with it, and Ælfwyn sat at the table. Of a sudden she looked tired, and I too felt so weary that I could sleep. Before her, where I had left them, lay the ferny leaves from Wilfrida. Ælfwyn picked them up and said, "I recall these. Did you find out what they are for?"

"They are a gift from Wilfrida. She says if you steep them in broth or ale, and drink it three nights running before the half Moon, you will get a babe." As I said this, I knew it was the last thing she wanted to think on.

The afternoon was far gone, and soon we must prepare to go to the hall. I unwound a ball of wool out the last window, and then went down into the kitchen yard and caught it up and tied it where it could scarcely be seen to a broken piece of gate post.

"You will be certain not to come down until I pull hard on the yarn?" I asked Ælfwyn back in our room. "It may be a long time, half the night, before I go to Gyric."

"Yes, I will be certain," she promised me, "and both Burginde and I will wait on the wool, so that we are sure it is you pulling and not the wind."

So we went down.

The meal was the hardest I have ever known, for we wanted only for it to be over, and needs must act that all was well. I felt shaky and weak, and the ale went to my head at once, and tho' my mouth was dry I forced myself to eat instead to steady myself. With each mouthful I thought of the Dane in the kitchen yard, and of the food and drink he lifted to his lips.

I found it hard to speak, and hard to sit next to Sidroc after what I had said about him to Ælfwyn. I was about to do that which might force me to run off with him; and he sat at my side knowing none of it.

Ælfwyn kept her part well, for she talked and jested with Sidroc, but her jests wore a false brightness, like a thin sheen of gold over copper. But Sidroc did not seem to notice, and talked of the moving of the horses, and the game that might be brought back by Yrling, and of hunting hawks that would come in the Summer.

At last it ended, and we lingered long, and the tables began to be broken down, and then Ælfwyn recalled she must speak to Dobbe; so it began. She walked into the kitchen passageway with me, and stood there while I found the smock Dobbe had left. I pulled it on, and Ælfwyn went through the door into the yard and came back with Burginde. They stayed a moment in the passageway, and then Ælfwyn kissed me and turned and walked back into the hall with Burginde.

I pushed open the door and walked through the yard, lit now by torch light, and stopped for one moment by the washing pot near where Dobbe stood. She nodded to me, and I made some pretence of straightening up around the yard as the others went about their work. One by one the torches were rubbed out in sand until only the cooking pit gave light. I walked to the grain shed, and as I passed the cellar opening heard the snores of the guard within. The door to the shed was open, and I slipped inside and stood there in the dark. There was only the thinnest sliver of Moon, and I stood still and wished I had some source of light. I felt around and found a platter with an ewer and a bowl of food. There were odd rustlings about me; the shed was old and creaky and doubtless full of rats as Dobbe had said. My eyes grew stronger in the dim light and I settled upon some grain sacks to wait.

I do not know how long passed. I had no way to gauge the time, with either candle or lamp, and inside the shed I could not see the movement of the stars as they circled over my head. I strained my ears as I listened to the snoring of the Dane, and wondered how deeply he was asleep. At times I thought only a few moments passed, and at others was fearful that I had waited too long and it would soon be dawn.

I did not know how I would find Gyric in the dark of the cellars, and as I recalled Dobbe telling me the cellar was tumbled in, I wished over and over for a candle or a cresset. This need drove all other thoughts from my mind, and I resolved to go to the cooking pit and relight a torch, or at least bring a burning brand of some kind to give me light. If the guard were drugged, he would no more wake to light than to noise. Without light I thought I would never reach Gyric, and the fear of being caught was made far worse by the dark.

I went out as quietly as I could to the firepit, and found a rush torch, and split it in my hands to make it smaller, and held the oily tip of it to the embers. It caught at once, and I tried to shelter the light with my smock as I hurried back to the shed. The light danced about the little room, and I took heart.

Now I resolved that it must be time to approach the Dane, for his snoring grew faint so I thought the drug must be at its height. I took the torch in one hand and the ewer in the other and left the shed. I held my breath as I stepped through the opening and down the ramp, not knowing what I should do if he suddenly awakened. But awaken he did not, tho' he lay on his back and the light from my torch fell full on his face. Against the wall behind him was his spear, and by his side lay his belt and knife. I wondered if I should move his weapons, but thought best not to touch them, for if I should need a knife, I could come back and take it.

I walked farther into the space, and almost lost my footing. There were three stone steps, and they were slippery, as if they were wet or slimy with growth. I went down them and tried to cast the light about. There were walls and pillars of stone, and passageways, and piles of rubble beyond. The floor was wet and of beaten clay, and I heard a trickle of water from somewhere. The whole place had a damp and evil smell, and as I moved my torch a rat scuttled across the floor.

I wanted to call out, that Gyric might hear me and guide me to him, but I could think only of the Dane behind me and the many Danes above. I moved forward, and chose the central passage as it was largest, and walked slowly down it, casting my light from side to side. There were tiny rooms, as small as monk's cells, lining either side, and some of them were filled with rubble from their own broken walls, and some were empty save dust and cobwebs, but none held a man. The passage ended in a cave-in, and I turned back. I looked at the maze of passages before me, and chose the one nearest. I did not have far to go, for one of the rooms had a low wooden door affixed to it, and an iron bar shot across it. I put down the ewer and pressed my eye close to the tiny opening in the door. I could see nothing, but found my voice and hissed out, "Gyric, Gyric of Kilton?"

There was no reply, and I set the torch against the stone wall and took the bar in both my hands and slid it in its bracket. I pushed open the door and stepped in.

The room was low, so low that I must stoop as I entered. It was as small as the other rooms, and against one wall lay the form of a slight man. He lay with his back towards me, and his arm cast over the top of his head. He wore only a ragged tunic and leggings, and his feet were bare, and the awful smell of the place told me he was lying in his own filth. I reached for the torch and propped it against a stone, and then took a step closer.

"Gyric," I whispered. "Are you Gyric of Kilton? I am a friend." He did not answer, and for a terrible moment I feared he was dead. "Gyric of Kilton," I repeated.

At last he moaned, and stirred slightly, and I said again, "Gyric, Gyric," and he uttered one faint word, "Yes."

"You have friends here, and I have brought you food and drink, and we will help you get away," I said, and hurried to fetch the ewer.

I went to his head, and knelt down and put my hand on his shoulder to turn him. His long hair was tangled and matted, and I brushed it off his forehead as I cradled his head in my hand. The torch light flickered across his face, and then my mouth opened in a scream that did not come forth from my throat; for he had no eyes. Where they had been were two blackened sockets, void and empty, and showing the mark of fire upon them.

I let his head fall back in my lap as I covered my face with my hands. At that moment the world seemed mute, struck dumb by my horror. He moaned again, and I somehow lifted my hands from my eyes and looked again at him.

"Are you Gyric?" I asked through my tears.

His answer was more moan than word, but it was "Yes."

"I am a friend," I said, and my whole body trembled. I reached for the ewer and knocked it over, but caught it up again. "Drink this," I whispered, and held his head up and lifted the mouth of the ewer to his lips. He drank, slowly and painfully, and it ran down his chin onto his filthy tunic. He turned his face and retched it up again. I wiped his face with my smock as my tears fell down and wetted his cheek.

I laid his head down as gently as I could and took the torch up and cast it over his body to see if there were blood spots from open wounds. I could see nothing but the ghastly maiming.

I knelt there by his side, looking at his profile in the guttering torchlight. His face was covered with many week's growth of beard, but his nose was fine and straight, and the line of his brow smooth and broad. He scarcely breathed, and I watched his lips, gentle and almost delicately curved, as they parted slightly. I looked upon this, and kept my eyes fixed upon his lips so they would not rest upon the hideous holes beneath his pale brow.

"I will come back," I breathed to him. He did not answer or move, and I looked upon him once more as I gathered the ewer and torch.

I edged out of the cell and slid the bolt in place, and made my way back to the ramp. My heart was racing within my breast, and I could not feel my legs beneath me. I reached the sleeping Dane and passed him, and then stood again under the stars in the kitchen yard. I snuffed out the torch in the dirt, and laid it by the cooking pit, and left the ewer on the table. Then I drew a breath and stepped through the doorway into the passage, and pulled off the smock and left it where I had found it.

I rubbed my wet palms against my gown, and entered the hall. It was too dark to make out any of the sleeping men, and I made my way as quickly as I could, gained the wooden stairs, and flew up them. Ælfwyn herself opened the door, her eyes wild with distraction. As she shut the door the tears began flowing down my face. Burginde still stood by the window, waiting for the sign that did not come.

"Why did you not signal? Did you see him? Is it Gyric?" implored Ælfwyn, all her fear in her voice.

"Yes, I saw him; and it is Gyric," I answered. "But they have maimed him – grievously."

A look of terror came to her face, and Burginde crossed over to her and put her arms about her. Ælfwyn stood silent and unmoving, and then asked in a voice hardly above a whisper, "Is he still a man?"

I shook my head, trembling. "It is not that. He has suffered the poker. They have put out his eyes."

Ælfwyn opened her mouth, and lifted her hands to her face as she gasped, "Put out his eyes?" Then, tho' Burginde be there about her, she fell upon her knees in her horror and disbelief. "No, no, no," she wailed, "no . . ."

I went to her and took her hands. She twisted her head up and away as if she would escape this horrible truth, and tears fell fast from beneath her closed eyelids.

"We will go tomorrow," I said, "and take him from there."

She could not hear in her grief, and I said again, "Tomorrow we will take him from there."

"Take him?" she breathed. I stood back as her tears overcame her in a great spasm of grief.

"Take him to safety, so that he might live," I said with some force.

She shook her head, and pulled at her hair. "He will not want to live," she said.

"We do not know that," I replied, and anger rose up and joined my grief.

For answer she had only tears, and I too held my face in my hands and wept.

"Who did this thing?" she wailed, clenching and unclenching her white hands in fury.

I looked up, and thought of this. "Not Yrling; the wound is not fresh." Then I knew. "Yrling rode to two Danes, brothers, who had quarrelled over war one of them had made with a reeve of South Wessex. Out of spite one brother maimed or killed the prisoners taken in the battle, so that the other could get no ransom for them."

She listened to this, but held her hands out before her as if she could fend off the truth. She dropped her arms and said, "And Gyric was one of them."

I wanted to turn our speech from what had been to what could be. "He is dying," I said.

"He is better off dead," she choked out.

"He is alive now," I answered in real anger. "I will take him away, tomorrow."

She shook her head, disbelieving. "Take him away?" she asked. "How will you take him? Where will you go? You would not get beyond the keep walls."

"I do not know. Mul will get a horse for Gyric and bring my mare too."

"I will not let you; I forbid it," she answered.

I looked at her steadily. "You cannot do such a thing. I will take him away tomorrow."

"Where will you go? You do not know the country around here."

"Neither does Gyric, and we thought he could make his way. I must do the same."

"But you say he is – dying."

"He is very weak, yes; and I must take him someplace safe where he can rest and grow well."

"He will never be well!" cried Ælfwyn, and her voice rose in fury. It ended in sobs, and she asked, "What if he dies? What will you do?"

"I do not know. I will come back, I guess."

Now she crossed over to me, and took my hand. "Swear you will come back if he dies. Swear it," she pleaded.

"I swear it," I said, weeping openly with her, and feeling what little chance I had of getting Gyric away from Four Stones, and of keeping him alive for long if I did.

"He cannot die; he cannot die," she went on, and burst into fresh tears. "I will lose my mind with worry for you. You will send me word somehow if you make it to safety with him; swear it."

"I swear; I will find some way to send a message to you, even if it be a token which will carry meaning between us."

"Yes," she said, "yes," and looked almost feverish. She let go my hand and clapped her own to her forehead. "It will never work," she groaned. "Sidroc . . . Sidroc will hunt for you, and find you, and after he kills Gyric will bring you back."

I could not find an answer for this, for I felt what she said was true. I looked down at the heavy silver disk gleaming on my wrist. I unfastened it, and held it to her.

"When he learns I am gone, give him this. Beg him, for me, that he not follow."

She did not take it, and only shook her head. "That will not stop him," she whispered.

"You must fix it so it does. Tell him anything you need to, but give him this and say I, Ceridwen, beg him not to follow."

"What if Yrling wants to follow?"

"Perhaps he will not want to. He did not want to take Gyric in the first place, and is content to let him die here so he might not be troubled by him. He can earn no gold from Gyric now, and may think he will die soon anyway."

We talked back and forth, trying to make sense of that which was senseless; and Ælfwyn wept and cursed in her grief and rage. At last Burginde brought forth cups of ale, and we drank, and she warned us that we should sleep soon. I bathed my face and hands, and pulled off my clothes and fell into my bed. For a long time I heard Ælfwyn's muffled sobs as she lay weeping, weeping.

THE LAST DAY

BURGINDE awoke me. It was after dawn, and light streamed through the windows.

"Mul be here," she urged us, "and has not much time."

She brought us shifts and gowns and we slipped into them, groggy from grief and lack of sleep. She opened the door and Mul stepped inside and bowed to us.

"We be near ready to ride out, Lady," he said to Ælfwyn. "Is all still as it was? A horse in the grove yonder?"

I came up to him and answered. "Mul, the prisoner is wounded, and cannot ride alone. I will go with him. Can you somehow bring my bay mare to the grove as well?"

His thin earnest face looked into mine in wonder. "You be going, Lady?" he asked.

"Yes," I responded, but said no more.

"Your mare be not one that we be moving," he thought aloud. "She is to stay here in the yard. Can it not be another horse?"

"I would rather not take a second horse," I answered. "The bay mare is mine, rightfully, for she was a gift; and so at least I do no wrong in taking her."

He looked doubtful, and he cast his eyes about the room. Then he lifted his head and said to me, "She be ready to be bred, these last few days; and her calling and whinnying be driving the stallions mad. If you could ask that she might be bred, I would have cause to take her out with the other horses."

"That is good," I answered with relief. "Will you take her then and tell them that I desire this?"

He shifted from foot to foot and finally answered. "It be better if you do the telling, Lady." He swallowed and said, "The tall one, that Sidroc, he be in charge. He be down in the yard now."

I nodded. "I will go then and speak to him." I thought of another service Mul might render. "You know the land about here, Mul. Is there a village or trev where I might take the prisoner? Some place safe where he could rest?" I bit my lip and spoke my fears. "I do not think I can keep him alive on the road."

Mul let out a long exhalation of breath. "There were trevs with huts aplenty from here to the coast before the Danes," he began. "But the folk in them are all killed, or driven off." He jerked his head and added, "There be my mother's sister."

"Where does she live?" I questioned, heartened at this one hope.

"'Tis the problem; she and my cousin live no where and every where, and roam all about these parts."

I did not understand, and he went on, "If you speak to my mother, she can help you."

"Thank you, Mul, I will," I answered.

Ælfwyn had said nothing this whole time, but was delving in the weaving chest. She came up to Mul and gave him two silver pieces, and said, "Then you will have two horses ready late tonight." He nodded his head. "I will not let you suffer if you are caught, Mul. Do not fear that," she ended as he left, with a strength that, for that moment, overcame all our fears.

I combed my hair quickly, and as there was no time to plait it, only covered it with a head-dress. Burginde came up to me and searched my face. "You be so pale," she scolded gently, "and your eyes all red from weeping." She pinched my cheeks to bring colour to them.

I fastened on my bracelet and said to them both, "After I speak to Sidroc I will go on to Meryth's. I will try not to be long."

Ælfwyn once again lay upon her bed. She nodded wordlessly, and I left.

The yard was busier than I had ever seen, as the great stable was being cleaned with the change of horses. Osred stood at the head of a yoke of lowing oxen who dragged a wain piled with clean straw. A knot of horses circled outside the stable, straining at their neck ropes and pawing the ground and whinnying. I saw Mul, mounted on a horse and holding several others by their lead ropes.

Sidroc walked out of the stable with another man, and I raised my hand to him. He came over, glancing at the silver disk on my wrist. I tried to smile at him as he came, but as he drew nearer could only think that if all went well, I was looking on his face for what must be the last time.

I did not wait for a word of greeting. "Mul has told me that my bay mare is ready to be bred. I have come to ask that you take her and breed her to a horse of your choosing."

I think this surprised him more than anything I could
have said, and as he looked at me I forced myself to look
also into his face. He smiled, but it was a smile I had never
seen before, serious and searching. He took a step closer
to me.

"My bay is at the camp right now," he answered. "I will
take her to him this noon."

I wondered if the colour came into my cheeks. I only
knew that the gladness his face showed came from a false
belief; and I felt ashamed. Then I did what I had never done.
I reached out my hand, the one that bore his bracelet, and
touched his hand. "I thank you, Sidroc," I whispered.

My eyes felt sore and dry, and for that I was grateful,
for I feared I might weep. I drew back my hand before he
could take it, and tho' I dropped my eyes he looked at me
carefully.

"You are well?" he asked, more gently than I had ever
heard him speak.

I did not trust my voice, and only nodded. A Dane
called out to him, and he turned his head for a moment
to answer him. "Do not fear for your mare," he went on. "I
will make sure she is not hurt."

Again I nodded, and he said, "We will be away tonight,
settling the horses, but I will see you tomorrow." He moved
closer to me, and I held my breath. "Your choice is a good
one," he said softly. "You will not regret it."

I walked so rapidly to Meryth's hut that I was near out
of breath when I reached it. Her husband sat on a bench
nearby, working with an adze fashioning a plough handle
from a tree bough. I did not expect him to be there, but

since he would take the trappings to the horses he was an important part of my plan. I needs must trust him and speak freely before him.

Meryth handed me a dipper of water, and I drank. "Meryth," I began, "I will leave with the prisoner tonight, for he is sorely wounded and cannot ride without help. Mul told me that your sister might afford us shelter. Is this true?"

"Lady?" she asked in wonder. "You will go?

"Yes," I said firmly.

"And he is sore hurt?" asked Meryth, sorrow settling on her brow.

"Yes, and I do not even know if he will live," I answered. "Is it true your sister might help us?"

She nodded her head, uncertain, and her husband rose up behind her. "Gwenyth be a good healer," she said, "a powerful one, but –"

"Gwenyth be turned a black witch," said her husband in a hard voice, "and be as ready to kill a man as cure him."

"Arsuf, I ask you," pleaded Meryth. He grumbled, but sat back down again at his bench.

"She be hard to find; she has no fixed place to live, but she and her son wander about," explained Meryth. "She is a very good healer, perchance the best, it used to be said, that ever lived here, but . . . she be . . . strange."

I gestured to her that I did not understand, and she went on. "The priest, God rest his soul, who was here at Four Stones, was cruel to her, and after a while she went . . . wild. She left, and never came back." She thought for a moment. "She has a son; it is the son of Merewala, for when Gwenyth was young she was fine looking, and a favourite of the Lord's. She bore him a son, but when it had reached two

Summers in age, it became clear that it was an Idiot. Mere-wala would have no more to do with her, for he planned to marry again, and was fearful of it catching." Her mouth twisted in pain as she spoke. "The priest made much of it, saying it was God's mark upon a whore."

I could not see how this strange and fearsome woman could help me, nor how she could be found, but I asked. "If I could find her, do you think she might shelter us?"

Meryth again shook her head, but then looked uncertain. "Perchance, Lady; I do not know. Perchance if you ask for my sake. I have always loved her, and she, I think, me, through it all."

"How could I ever find her?" I asked, more to myself than to Meryth.

She disappeared into her hut and emerged with a brass bell. "Take this with you; 'tis the way I find her; or she finds me, I should say. At this time of year she may be just South, along the glades that skirt the woods. Sometimes I have gone there and walked and rung this bell, and if she is within earshot, she comes."

I took the bell, and Meryth smiled down upon it and said, "'Twas the bell of an old cow we had, when Gwenyth and I were but girls."

"You say she may be just South?" I questioned. "I will be circling around from the pond; will I find the glades you speak of?"

"That you will, for the village stream splits, and one branch of it feeds the pond. Follow it. It grows wide in parts, with open glades on both sides, and thick woods beyond it. You can shelter in the woods when you need to."

"I thank you, Meryth, and if I find your sister will tell her of your goodness to me." I turned to her husband, who still sat in grudging silence. "Arsuf, you have my great gratitude for your help."

He nodded his head, but shrugged at the same time. Meryth came forward and said, "May God bless and protect you, Lady."

I went back to the hall and up to our chamber. Ælfwyn lay still upon her bed; I do not think she moved since I left. Burginde sat upon my own bed, and had my leathern satchel before her, next to a pile of clothes.

"Mul should be able to bring my mare tonight," I told them, and tried to make my voice sound strong. "And Meryth has given me this bell to ring to help me find her sister."

"A bell to ring?" asked Ælfwyn faintly, and then turned her face away.

I looked at the clothing Burginde was packing for me. Some of them were mine, but many of them were Ælfwyn's.

"I cannot take these things," I began, pointing to the pile.

Ælfwyn spoke from her bed, and her voice was dull. "You must take all that you can carry; for it may be all that you have for a long time. Also my things are fine, and can be sold or traded along the road."

I saw the wisdom in her words, and nodded my head. I stood there by my bed, watching Burginde roll the clothes and neatly fill the bag. Sun poured in from the windows, and cast all in a new brightness. Ælfwyn lay still, as if she were asleep. The Browny was curled into a ball on Burginde's

bed, safe and content. I brushed a tear off my cheek and
went to the wall where my father's seax hung. I placed it
with the clothes, and brought forth my comb and mirror,
and suchlike things, and set them on the bed in readiness.
I thought again of Sidroc's scarred face, and the look in his
eyes when he said I would not regret my choice.

Then I pictured Sidroc overtaking me and the dying
Gyric in the fields or forests, and the single spear-thrust
that would end Gyric's suffering; and I saw Sidroc before
me, his dark eyes flashing as he faced me.

"How will you bring the young man up?" asked
Burginde. "He may be too weak to walk."

I lifted my eyes to the rafters. I had not thought of
this, but now I must; I could never carry him. How, too,
would we get beyond the palisade wall? The small door by
the kitchen yard was always bolted at dark.

"I must have help," I conceded. "A man, a strong one."
It must be some one already in the kitchen yard: Eomer. "I
will go now and speak to Eomer," I said.

I found him at the grindstone, turning it with one
hand as he held a butchery knife to it with the other.
Sparks flew and it screamed as he sharpened it. His back
was bent with age and his head was bald, but his arms and
shoulders were still broad and strong. He did not stop in
his work, but after a nod to me went on. I glanced about
and saw a Dane across the yard at the cellar opening. It
was yet again a different man.

I turned back to Eomer and said, "Tonight there will
be two horses hidden in the trees near where the Danes

sacrifice. The prisoner is wounded, and I seek a man who will help him out of this place and to the horses."

Eomer kept his eyes upon his work, but said, "You have your man, Lady."

"The guard will be drugged again, but there still will be danger, perhaps great danger," I warned him.

"He be a man of Wessex, be he not?" asked Eomer slowly as he went on with his grinding. "I too be a man of Wessex, and Dobbe a woman thereof, and so our boy was of Wessex, tho' he saw it never."

"Thank you," I said.

"Who be the second rider?"

"I will be," I replied.

He stopped now, and turned to me. "A maid like you?" he asked. He shook his head, but turned again to his stone.

"There be a way out of this yard, that the Danes know not," he told me. "'Tis there by the stream; the panel above it slides open. We will get wet, and there is a sharp drop beneath it, but 'tis not longer than a man's height."

I looked over to where the kitchen stream flowed out of a small opening in the timber palisade. "That is good," I said gratefully. "I do not know when I will come tonight, but it will not be too long after the hall sleeps. Ask Dobbe to again feed the guard as she did last night."

He nodded, and I left.

Back in our chamber I sat down upon Burginde's bed and stroked the tortoiseshell kitten in silence. She purred and curled her paws up over her little brown head in response. I looked down upon her, content and free from fear, and at that moment I could know nothing except my wish that everything be as it had been before the strange Danes came in the night with their tragic cargo.

"Do not touch the weapons of the Dane who guards him," said Ælfwyn from her bed. Her voice was quiet. "If he awakens and they are disturbed, he will sound the alarm at once. But if all seems normal, it may be many more hours before it is known that Gyric is gone."

"You are right," I said, turning to her. She still lay without moving, facing the roof rafters above, and with her eyes closed. "I will have my seax; that will be enough."

She did not say more, but silently extended her hand to me. I rose and went to her, and sat upon her bed and held her hand. Both of us spoke not, for our fear and sorrow was too great for words.

Burginde came in with a platter, and looked at us as she set it upon the table. "You must eat, both of you, and drink this good broth, too," she gently scolded. She filled two cups and brought them to us.

I took mine and drank, and rose up to go to the table, for I felt thirst and hunger and weariness all at once. But Ælfwyn moved not, tho' Burginde stood over her with her cup.

"You must eat and drink, and so stay strong," she urged her, "for you will have need of strength these next few days."

Ælfwyn sat up at last and took the cup of broth, but would touch no food.

I ate, and Burginde sat upon her stool and ate with me in silence. Then she said to me, "Lady, you must lie down and rest, and sleep if you can; for tonight there will be no rest for you."

I nodded, and pulled off my gown and lay down on my bed in my shift. The room was quiet. I heard Burginde take up her drop spindle and begin spinning, and that was all. I kept my eyes closed and tried to sleep, but fearsome images came to me: I saw Gyric dying on the road, from the hardship of our travels; or saw us being hunted like animals through the forest. The worst image of all was this: That I went that night to free him, and that he had died, alone and uncared for, in that miserable hole beneath us.

I slept at last, and when I awoke the room was growing dim. Ælfwyn stood at the window, looking out at the darkening sky. Burginde brought water, and I bathed, and then she and Susa brought up our meal. Susa turned to me and said, "Dobbe says to tell you, All is well."

Susa looked uncomprehending, but I nodded my head and said simply, "I thank you."

Ælfwyn sat with me, and ate a little, but this time it was hard for me to eat, for my throat felt tight and dry. I drank broth and ale and sat listening as Burginde reviewed where my satchel was; and that Dobbe had made up food and drink for us; and that Eomer would be ready for me.

Then there was nothing to do but wait. Time crept along, and we heard the noise of the hall reach its height and then begin to lessen. We heard the tables being broken down, then the dragging and scraping of the trestles against the stone floor. It grew still.

As the quiet grew beneath us, so too did the urge to speak. I said to Ælfwyn, "I will do all I can to find Meryth's sister, and all I can to care for Gyric."

She raised her downcast eyes to mine, and answered, "Promise me that you will return . . . if . . ."

"I will return, I swear it," I said, so she would not have to finish.

"I will keep Yrling from coming after you," she said. "And I will beg Sidroc not to follow. But if anyone should hunt for you, I hope it will be he who finds you; for he will not be cruel to you." Her words seemed strong, but there was fear in her eyes as she said this, and fear too in my breast.

I could not answer this. I did not want to speak of what Sidroc might do. I unclasped his silver bracelet from my wrist for the last time, and pressed it into her hands. "Fare-well," I said.

"Fare-well," she answered.

I went to Burginde, and she took me into her arms and kissed me, and said, "Be well, Lady. I pray you be blest and protected."

Ælfwyn was before me, and we were in each other's arms, and the tears we wept were for ourselves and for the leaving of the other and for the Fate of Gyric.

"You will send a message," she finally said.

"I swear I will," I answered. "Fare-well."

I tore myself away from her, and went to the door and opened it to the darkness below.

DARKNESS INTO DAWN

I made my way through the dark hall and past the sleeping men, quaking as one of them snored loud or tossed on his pallet. I groped through the passageway, and pushed open the worn door out into the kitchen yard. By the large cooking pit, illumined by its embers, sat the hunched form of Eomer, who rose to greet me. He had a stout length of hempen rope coiled about one shoulder, and two large packs and my satchel were at his feet.

"He be deep in his cups, and near dead to this world," he whispered, jerking his thumb in the direction of the Dane in the cellar opening.

"We will need a torch," I whispered back, and tried to steady my voice so that Eomer would not hear my fear. He picked up a short bundle of oiled rushes, and cast it into the coals to light it. I took it from him and gestured, Come.

We gained the opening, and walked down the ramp to where the Dane lay. He did not stir, but breathed in a shallow, gasping hiss of a snore. A cup, near filled with ale, was beside him, as was an ewer, and I could only hope he had drunk enough. At his side lay a long dagger, sheathed, and along the wall, his spear.

We went down the few steps and into the first passage. As we reached the low wooden door my heart pounded so that my hand trembled, causing the torch flame to dance and flicker as if we stood in open wind. Eomer moved in front of me, and slid open the iron bar and pulled open the door. I moved into the cell, and saw Gyric lying much as I had left him.

I could not find voice to speak his name, and was terrified to touch him lest he be dead. But I moved closer, and knelt down by his head, holding the torch above him. Eomer came into the space and looked down upon us. "Ah," he cried out as he saw Gyric's face. "Those cursed gits! What they have done to him."

Gyric moaned, and moved one of his hands as if he would cover his face, and by this told us he lived still.

"Gyric," I whispered. "We are friends, come to take you out of this place." He did not answer, or seem to hear me, but I went on, "We have horses waiting, and now we must go to them."

For answer he had only a moan. Eomer stooped down and half-dragged, half-carried Gyric out through the door. In the passageway he lifted him upon his shoulders, and I shut the door and set the iron bar that served as bolt.

Gyric spoke not, and lay as a dead man across Eomer's shoulders, and tho' the old man bent under his burden, his step was firm as he followed me out of the passage and past the unknowing guard.

We walked as rapidly as we could across the yard to the place where the kitchen stream flowed out. Eomer dropped down upon his knees and lowered Gyric to the ground. Gyric said nothing, and moved not, but I knew he breathed.

Eomer returned and pressed himself against the base of the palisade wall, and with all the force in his body strained against a panel there. It slid back upon itself and the opening where the stream flowed out was doubled and more than doubled in size.

"'Tis for the Spring flood time. The stream grew large each Spring before the Danes took it underground, and this way 'twould flow out without flooding the yard," he explained to me, and uncoiled the rope from his shoulder. "You go first, Lady, holding onto this rope as you go, and then I will lower the bags to you, and finally the man."

I took firm hold of the knotted end he passed to me, and stepped into the stream and knelt in its cold waters. I crawled backwards through the opening. I could not see where I was going, the stones were sharp through my gown and thin boots, and the water soaked me through. The stream fell away beneath me, and I clambered and groped my way down a wet and slippery rock face, nearly falling. I stood at the bottom, and Eomer's face appeared through the palisade.

"Now the packs," he hissed, and he drew up the rope, and lowered them one by one. I untied them and carried each out of the stream bed, and stood waiting, trembling with wet and fear.

It seemed many minutes passed, and I heard much splashing and movement above me. I saw the legs of a man as Gyric was lowered feet first by Eomer. He let him down slowly, by a rope tied criss-cross around his chest, but still Gyric bumped against the sharp rock as he came.

When he reached the bottom I worked to untie the wet knot. I tried to keep Gyric leaning against the rock face, but he crumpled into the few inches of water we stood in. I dragged him from it, and tugged upon the freed rope. Eomer pulled it up, and in a moment stood by my side.

He spoke not a word, but lifted Gyric once again. I gathered up the three packs, straining under their weight, and followed Eomer in the darkness. We both stumbled, and once I had to lower the packs and take them up again to better carry them. My gown was dripping and bound against my legs and made my walking harder.

Now the ground rose up beneath us, and again I stopped, my arms aching, to rearrange the packs I carried. Eomer went on, and beyond him I saw the clumps of trees, just coming into full leaf, which I hoped hid our horses.

As if to answer my hope we heard a horse nicker, and Eomer went straight to it. It was my bay mare, saddled and bridled, and tied by a neck rope to a young tree. As we approached her we heard rustlings, and found another horse, dark in colour, tied not far away. This one too was both saddled and bridled, and I spoke aloud my thanks to the bravery of Mul and his father.

I dropped the packs and brought the second horse over. It was a good sized animal, larger than my bay, and Eomer said, "This one for the young man; the mare for you."

I stood at the horse's head, stroking its neck and trying to keep it calm. "We will have to tie him on," pronounced Eomer, "'tis clear he cannot ride without it."

I moved to one side of the horse, and Eomer came to the other, and heaved Gyric on to the saddle. I braced his leg as it came over and tried to steady him, and Eomer fitted Gyric's feet into the stirrups and then pulled his arms about the horse's neck.

"Give me strips of cloth of some kind, that I might tie his hands and feet without hurt to him," whispered Eomer. I dropped to my knees and sorted through my satchel, and found a sash and a head wrap. Eomer tied the stirrups and Gyric's ankles under the horse's belly with the long sash, and then his wrists loosely around the horse's neck with the wrap. Gyric's face rested against the animal's mane, and I moved his head to the other side so that he could breath more freely. He moaned, and seemed almost to whisper, but scarcely moved, and allowed us to position him as best we could.

I stood at the horse's head, and Eomer tied one pack onto its saddle rings, and then tied my satchel and the second pack to the saddle of my mare.

"'Tis ready, Lady," he said, and he took up the reins of the horse that bore Gyric. I went to my mare and pulled myself up on her, and Eomer handed me the reins and neck rope of Gyric's horse. Then he thrust his roughened old hand into mine and said, "God speed you, Lady."

I took his hand, and pressed it hard as I looked down into his weathered face. "I will never forget you, Eomer," was all I could say.

I touched my mare's flanks with my heels, and she moved off, the head of Gyric's horse just even with my saddle. I turned once to look, and saw Eomer making haste back to the palisade wall. I was out of sight of the wall, but not, I thought, out of earshot, and I did not want either of the horses to neigh loudly. We moved on, past the place of Offering, and the pit littered with weapons and the bones of sacrificed animals; and the beech bough across the clearing soughed in the gentle wind and I saw the silver chain glitter upon it.

Beyond that was grassland, and the ground fairly smooth, and I knew I should quicken our pace. I moved my mare into a canter, and the second horse tossed its head and whinnied in irritation at the feel of Gyric's weight against its neck. I slowed, and drew the second horse closer, and spoke to Gyric, but he answered not. I placed my hand on his back, and felt him breathe, and so resolved I must go on at a canter and so make distance between us and Four Stones.

We gained the pond, which looked a dark well now that the Moon had set. I slowed our pace as we circled around it, for the ground was soft and our horses liable to stumble. I found the stream that Meryth spoke of, and we picked our way along it. Open land lay on either side, and I moved away from the stream bed to gain firmer ground. We went on, and whenever it seemed safe I urged the horses into a canter.

I must believe, I told myself, that Eomer would get back safe, and that the Dane that guarded the cellar would not wake until morning, and that no one would check on Gyric until sometime after that. But as I repeated these thoughts to myself, I saw that any one of them might not be true; that Eomer might at that moment be forced, under pain of death, to tell how and where he had left us; and that Danes now were saddling their horses to ride after us. Sidroc and Yrling would not be leading them; what would happen to me when they found us? I knew the answer too well, and did not think that Sidroc's claim to me would carry weight with such men at that moment, for to them I would be a renegade and a thief, guilty of treason. This thought chilled me so that I stopped our horses, and with trembling fingers opened my satchel and searched until I found my seax, and tied it firm about my waist. Not that I thought I could in any way repel the Danes, armed with their spears and swords, but that I might thrust it in my own breast before they caught me. Then I thought: What further torment might they put Gyric to? Or would they end his life at once?

These thoughts were pure anguish, and I forced myself to turn from them. I drew forth the bell Meryth had given me, and gently let the clapper fall against the bronze wall of it. It made only the slightest tinkle, and I held it and with good force shook it, and its metal voice rang out, bright and loud.

I rang it again, and again, and then urged my mare into a canter. We went so fast that no one on foot could catch us, but if Gwenyth and her son heard it, they might call out to us, and stop us that way.

We made our way through the grasslands, skirting the marsh, and keeping within easy distance of the stream. I stopped many times to speak to Gyric, calling his name and placing my hand on his back or brow to see if he still lived.

I went as fast as I thought safe for him, for to carry him out alive and deliver him to some safety was the whole goal of my leaving, so nothing would be accomplished if I killed him by hard usage upon the road. We went on and on, walking and cantering as we could, and with me ringing the bell often as we went.

The sky above grew darker, and the stars were obscured by a thin haze of cloud, and we must only walk for fear of our horses stumbling. Then the first birds sang out, and the sky paled from its inky darkness, and I knew that dawn was come.

It came fast, and the grey of first light gave way to yellow and then pink streaks in the heavens. Gyric's horse grew clearer to me; it was a big black gelding. I looked around us and for the first time saw the stream, still dark in its grassy path, and the bold dark line of thick trees across the plain from us.

I was tired, and clammy, and growing cold from my wet clothes, which had dried but little; and Gyric was soaked through. Yet as I turned back to look along the stream bed I felt we must not stop so soon, but try to add to the miles between us and Four Stones. I came up even to Gyric's head, and placed my hand upon his back, and said, "Gyric, we must go on, for one hour more. Then we will find shelter and rest."

And I spoke thus as much to hear my own voice as to tell him this, for he answered not. I urged our horses into a canter, ringing the bell the whole time. The Sun was shining down on us now, and on the grasslands dry and wide between stream and forest. We would be easy to see if anyone, friend or foe, searched for us.

"We will stop now, Gyric," I said, and tied the bell to my sash. I swung down from my mare and nearly fell, so wobbly were my legs. I led both horses to the stream, and with my hands braced Gyric upon his saddle, and the horses bent their necks and drank long. I remounted, and turned our horses across the grass to the forest.

The trees stood up thickly, all come into the freshness of their first leaf; but for the dense growth there was no good place for horses to enter. We went along, and I saw a narrow path, like a deer track, leading into the trees. I knew that wherever we stopped we might be there a long time, for I could not think how I might get Gyric upon his horse again until he was well enough to mount alone.

I tied the horses to a low hanging bough, and slipped amongst the undergrowth along the track. It came into a small clearing, where an ash tree grew alone, as is their wont, upon a mossy ground.

I looked about the space, and thought it safe from view, and so turned and made my way back. I tied the reins of Gyric's horse to the saddle rings of my mare, and then took her bridle at the cheekpiece and coaxed her in. She did not like it, but she came, and with her the gelding.

"Gyric, I am going to take you off your horse now," I said, and tied the gelding's neck rope to the trunk of the ash. The knots Eomer had made had grown tight around the stirrup irons, but at last I picked them apart. When his feet were free I loosed his hands from the silk scarf which bound them about the gelding's neck. I reached up, and put my arms around Gyric's waist, and pulled so that he tumbled off the saddle and onto the packs I had piled to break his fall.

He groaned, the loudest I had heard him make, and lay in a heap at my feet. I made haste to spread the deer hide, and then threw the sheep skin over it, and rolled him upon it, face up. There was fresh blood upon his face, and I saw his lip had split from hitting against the neck of his horse as we rode.

He was damp and filthy and his little clothing hung half off him, but I could see nothing but the ghastly maiming to his eyes. The morning light fell upon him, dappled as it was by the trees that overarched us, and revealed the full horror of what he had suffered. His brow was smooth and perfect, and the pale cheeks beneath bore no scar; but the burning poker had been driven into each eye socket, searing off the eyelids, leaving aught but empty pits. These were blackened from char, and there was glimpses of white, such as bone, and glimpses too of a waxy substance like onto tallow. On one temple, extending from the socket to the ear, was a deep burn mark, and I thought of the fiery poker missing its mark as he struggled against it.

I looked long upon the brand his temple bore from that struggle. I looked upon him, lying before me in exhaustion and pain, having known such torture; and looked upon the nobility of his face, so horribly scarred; and saw the gentle movement of his parted lips as he breathed. I looked upon him, and tears of a grief such as I had never known fell upon his face from my own wide green eyes. I wept for what he had been, and who had loved him, and what Life, if it did not desert him now, would hold for him, maimed as he was.

The horses moved, and I rose and went to them, tying them with neck ropes where they could browse on the young growth of the forest floor. I went back to where Gyric lay, and pulled open the kit bag, and took out the warm mantle that Ælfwyn had packed. I covered him with it, and then thought he must surely take some nourishment or die from hunger. I opened the food pack, and on the very top found a black leathern weapon-belt, dressed all about with silver bosses. I drew it out, and found hanging from it a long seax in a black wooden sheath.

"Ah, Ælfwyn," I said aloud, "why did you do this? Yrling will surely punish you when he finds it is gone."

Nonetheless I held the belt and its precious knife to my breast as my tears fell. I set it aside, and searched around in the pack. There were two jugs, sealed with wooden stoppers. I opened the first and found it held ale. I pulled the stopper on the second, and held it to my nose. It was broth, and must have been poured in very hot, for the pottery in my hand still held some warmth. I shook it to mix the fat in it, and tasted it.

I went to Gyric, and knelt by him, and took his head in my lap, and bent over him and held the mouth of the jug to his lips. "Try to drink this broth, Gyric," I whispered. "I will go slow."

I poured a little into his mouth and he swallowed it, or seemed to try. I lifted his head more, and braced it with my arm, and poured more of the broth past his lips. He swallowed, and I drew the jug back, not wanting to make him retch with too much.

He moved his head, and I again gave him more broth, which he swallowed. I set the jug down, and wiped his face. His hair was tangled and matted with straw and filth. I sat back looking at him. I drew a linen head wrap out of my satchel, and folded it and lay it gently over his empty eyes.

I pulled the mantle up around him, and said, "Sleep now, Gyric, and when you awake I will give you more broth."

I almost thought he tried to answer; his lips moved, and I brought my ear close to his face, but could make out nothing.

I found roast fowl and boiled eggs and bread and cheeses in the food pack, and ate a bit of cheese and bread. I looked again at the seax. It had a hilt embossed with silver, and a grip of horn, and into the blade was carved spiralling designs. It was a fine piece; the seax of a thegn of wealth.

I looked at Gyric, lying sightless and still, his hands and wrists bare of rings or bracelets, his gold pins and necklets wrenched from him, his spear and sword taken, his swift horse branded by another. I took the seax and lay it by his side. It was meant for Gyric, and tho' he knew not it was there, he should have it still.

Then my own weariness overcame me. I pulled a wool coverlet from my bag and wrapped it around myself and slept.

〰〰〰〰〰〰

I woke to the sound of our horses as they tore at the leaves and tender branches within their reach. It was still bright, but the Sun had passed its highest point, and it was now afternoon.

I felt stiff and achy as I sat up, and took a long drink from the ale jug to lessen my thirst. Gyric lay as before, and I went to him. He lay very still, and there was no way for me to know if he slept or not. I touched his arm and asked, "Gyric, will you try to drink?"

I lifted his head and held the broth to his lips, and he again drank a few swallows of it. He turned his face away, as if he would take no more.

I sat back on my heels and looked about me. The horses would be growing thirsty soon, and would need to be taken to the stream to drink. Also they must be allowed to graze on the grass during the night; the leaves of the forest could never sustain them. I feared too that in the woods they might eat something poisonous to them.

Gyric must be made more comfortable, with dry, clean clothes; and I must build a fire so that we could have warm food and protection from wolves.

I decided first to go to the stream and fetch water. I took the basin, and took also the bell, determined to ring it if it seemed safe. As I stepped into the grassland all was still before me; a few birds swooped and darted in pursuit of each other, but nothing else moved. I took the bell and rang it loudly, but just once, for the loudness of it startled me; so I held it silent in my hand.

I moved across the greensward to the bank of the stream, and knelt down, and splashed my face with the cold water. The water was slow moving, but not deep. I watched the ripples settle, and saw my reflection form. Of a sudden two faces appeared in the water over mine, that of a man and a woman, and I jumped up and turned to face them.

"Who are you, and how came you by that bell?" demanded the woman in a clear voice.

She was slight, and tall, and dressed in the coarsest of clothing, but her high voice was full of command. She had golden hair, full of curls, and cut short like a boy's, and a thin pointed face, just growing pinched. Her eyes were narrow and brilliant blue and full of distrust. I thought at once she was fey, for she had about her an odd beauty, like a little child who has suddenly grown old.

"Meryth gave it to me, that I might find you," I answered, and bent to pick up the bell which had tumbled out of my lap when I jumped up.

She was quick to answer. "Meryth is well?"

"Yes," I assured her. "She is well, and asks that you might help me as a favour to her, for I have great need of help."

She eyed me carefully, looking me up and down. "You? Have need of my help? You are rich. How can I help you?"

She did not let me answer, but went on, "Are you gotten with a child that needs ridding? Do not tell me you came all this way for that! Any woman in the village could help you. Wilfrida the Dyer will give you the herbs."

"No, no," I answered. "It is not that. I travel with a young man of Wessex, who was greatly wounded by the Danes."

The look of distrust she wore grew even stronger. "Who are you?" she asked, but her voice was steady. I scarce knew how to speak to her; she had been a cottar in the village, yet she treated me as proudly as if she had been a Lady, and me, a shepherd's lass.

"I am Ceridwen, daughter of the dead Cerd, an ealdorman of Mercia, but lately I am of Four Stones. It is there I met your sister, and she said you were a powerful healer, who would help us."

Again she eyed my gown, my sash, my silver pins. "You live amongst the Danes," she said, and there was contempt in her face.

My fear and surprise was now mingling with anger. "Yes, for the Lady I serve is of Cirenceaster in Wessex, and was sold by her father to the jarl Yrling to secure peace for her homeland. The match was not her choice, but since she has been Lady there she has done many good things for the women of the village. Meryth will tell you when you see her."

Here she stepped forward and took the bell from my hands. She was silent, and closed her eyes briefly as she held it. She stood next to the man and I regarded them both. He was huge, like a giant, yet had a round head with the face of a little boy, with eyes and nose so small that they seemed lost on his face. Above his brown eyes was a shock of dark hair. Despite his great size I do not think he was more than fifteen or sixteen. He stood back a bit from the woman, but never took his tiny eyes from her. Like her he was dressed in the coarsest of undyed wool, rough with fringe at the edges, and was shod in shoes made from deer hide or pig hide, with the hair still upon it. Each wore a knife, tied around the waist by a strip of plain leather, and sheathed in a simple sheath of the same brown leather. Each wore mantles of undyed wool, but instead of being knotted around their necks, both were pinned with silver brooches, hers set with garnets, and his with blue stones of some kind. On her hands also were two silver rings, and as I looked on these things she drew herself up and regarded me with amusement.

I looked at her and recalled her sister Meryth, and wished with all my heart she were there to ask for us. Yet I was alone, and must ask for myself, and for Gyric, who lay dying perhaps as we spoke. "Please help us, Gwenyth," I asked, and thought her look softened. "I have much silver to give you," I offered.

She laughed. "What is your silver to me? I do not go amongst men. Holt and I live where we want. We trap our food, and carry all that we own with us."

I thought again. "I have other things of value to offer. Clothing, and bronze goods, and pins and brooches and rings."

Her face told me that these things, as well, meant nothing to her; and I said, "I do not ask for myself, but for the man who lies dying and needs your help."

"Take me to him," she said at last.

Then I realised I had not told her that she might be in danger if she aided us. "I have stolen this man away from the keep of Four Stones," I began, "and have stolen a horse, and other things, and when the Danes discover this they will hunt for me."

She looked at me for one moment, and a strange smile lit her face. "Where I take you they will never find you," she answered, but her voice and manner filled me with foreboding.

She and her giant son turned, and shouldered packs made of basketry, brimful; and we made our way to the line of trees.

We reached the deer track, and I went in, and then Holt came crashing behind me, and then Gwenyth. We stood in the clearing together, and Gyric lay before us.

"He is the son of the ealdorman of Kilton, and kin to the King himself," I told her.

She did not take her eyes from him, but simply answered, "He is a killer, like all the rest."

She went to him, and bent over and drew off the linen wrap from his head. I saw her start, but she only muttered, "Ha! He will kill no more."

I turned my face from her, but when I looked back she was touching his brow and wrists, and then laid her head upon his chest. She rose, and spoke not to me, but to her son, who was all this time stroking the head of my bay mare and patting the black gelding.

"Holt," she said, and in her voice was suddenly much gentleness. "Tie these packs and our baskets to the horses, for I want you to carry this man." She spoke slowly to him, and he stopped in what he was doing and smiled, and set to work.

I gathered up that which I had opened, and knelt down by Gyric and brought my face close to his. "Gyric," I said, "we will have help now, but first we must go to safety."

His lips moved slightly, and I folded up the linen wrap and tied it gently around his head so that it covered his eyes.

I turned to see Gwenyth watching me. There was no look of compassion or pity on her face, nothing save the cool gaze of her narrow eyes.

Holt lifted the saddles upon the horses for me, and tied on the packs and baskets. He went about this work slowly and carefully, with hands strong and skilful.

Gwenyth called to him, and he lumbered over and stood before her. She pointed to Gyric, and Holt bent over and picked him up. Gyric was slight and not tall, and Holt carried him in his huge arms as if he were a child. We set off along the deer track and out to the stream, Gwenyth leading, then Holt, and then me and the horses.

On the grass Gwenyth said, "Holt, we are going to our high home."

"High home, high home," he echoed, and nodded his head. We walked through the stream and out across the meadowlands beyond.

Gwenyth began to hum an odd tune, and held her hands down at her sides and a little behind her as she walked. She waved her fingers as she went, each in its turn, and kept on with her humming.

We were heading for the woods before us, and had walked some little way when I began to turn to check that no one followed us.

"Do not turn around," instructed Gwenyth in a quiet voice.

"Why?" I asked, wanting to turn even more.

"Because," she answered, and her voice was now a sing-song, "I am closing the door behind us, and your look will open it."

I did not say anything, and I did not look back.

I WANT YOU TO LIVE

WE followed a creek into the woods, walking in its thin skim of water. The bed of it was sandy and we left no tracks.

We went on and on. The creek rose up with the land, and still we walked for what seemed a long time. It was dim the moment we entered the forest, for on this side were many dark fir trees rising up on either side of the water.

The creek widened, and grew stony, and it was harder walking. We came to a place where bright green moss grew as the thickest carpet on one side of the creek, and at this place Holt turned and came out of the water. Up a narrow path we went, and then we were at an open place, but bordered all around by heaps of rounded rock. In it were a few things of wood: a table, a bench, a rude shelter of split logs, covered over with cut rushes. There was a small firepit, and a bronze cauldron hung over it from a tripod of rusted iron.

Holt went and stood in the centre of this place, and turned to us and said, "High home," in a singing voice, and smiled a foolish and happy smile.

Gwenyth walked to the table and gestured that Holt should put down Gyric upon it. He did, very gently, and Gwenyth turned to me and said, "The creek flows here too; the horses can drink now."

She filled a bucket and carried it to the cauldron. I went to where Gyric lay, and pulled his mantle closer around him. It was a green mantle from the dead Mere-wala, embellished all over with spirals of gold wire, and thickly trimmed with miniver fur. I had fastened it with a large silver pin from the pouch I carried, and the richness of the cloak was a bitter jest on the battered body of him who it enfolded.

"I will only undo what you do," said Gwenyth in a quiet voice.

I looked at her, not understanding.

"The mantle," she explained. "I am only going to take it off."

Gwenyth motioned me to the firepit, and went to the little shelter and came back with an armful of split wood. I laid the fire, glad that I could do something useful, and struck out sparks onto my lye-soaked shavings. They caught almost at once, and I fed the smouldering flame. She moved back to Gyric, and I went and stood on the other side of him. The first thing she did was draw off the wrap over his eyes, and as she did so I know I flinched. She looked long into the blackened sockets, and even pressed her fingers along the sides of them, which made Gyric twist his head and utter a low wail. She took her hands away, and then drew off his mantle. "Help me pull his clothes off," she said. She lifted one arm over his head, so we could pull his linen tunic off, but he groaned so loudly that she stopped and placed her arms along the sides of his chest.

"It must be done quick," she said, and she slipped her arms under his waist and lifted him slightly, and I grasped the hem of his tunic and pulled it off as smoothly as I could.

His bare chest and shoulders and belly bore a number of dark purplish welts. She ran her hands down his body from under his arms to his waist, and he groaned again.

"They broke his ribs when they beat him," she said, and then stood back and considered this. "If he bleeds inside he will die for sure."

I bit my lip at this new sign of the cruel usage of the Danes. Why beat a man they had already blinded?

Now she was pulling at his filthy leggings, and I turned my head and mumbled, "I have clean things for him," and made as if I would go fetch them.

But Gwenyth saw my blush, and said in a mocking tone, "O, you tender maid, that never saw a man."

Tears stung my cheeks as I moved towards the packs. As I dug in them, pulling out the clothes of Merewala, I looked up to see Gwenyth standing before me.

"Take this," she said, thrusting a small basket at me, "and fill it with the smallest birch leaves you can pick."

The basket was quickly filled, and I returned to find Gwenyth squatting by the fire, working over a basin. Gyric was lying under a wool coverlet; the new tunic and leggings lay on the bench nearby.

I held out the basket of leaves, and Gwenyth glanced up from what she was doing. "Crush them," she said, indicating a small mortar amongst the things that surrounded her. "We will boil them for a drink for him."

"I have both broth and ale, if they are useful," I said.

She thought a moment, then said, "Boil them in your broth."

She went back to her work, which was peeling a number of roots into small shavings. I added handfuls of the bruised birch leaves to the pot, and set it on the edge of the firepit stones to heat.

Gwenyth ladled steaming water out of the cauldron and into the basin that held the peeled roots. "'Tis betony; 'twill be a rinse for his wound," she said as she stirred it around. "The wound is clean; the poker seared it so the flesh does not rot around it, and there is no maggot to be plucked out, tho' he was uncared for. Still, the rinse may help it."

I made bold to ask her, "You said it would be bad if he bled inside. Do you think he does?"

She did not look at me but went on with her stirring. "That I do not know. He may; he was badly beaten." She turned and regarded him as he lay upon the table. "This may be why he speaks not. He suffered pain from the poker, great pain; but tho' he has no fever, 'tis as if he has been out of his head."

I rose and went to him, and stood silently by his side.

"He is all over lice, but I will do nothing about it now. First we will see if he lives through the night," she said.

"He is so pale," I said.

"Could be from his great weakness, and he will mend of it when he drinks; or because he bleeds inside and is dying now as you watch him," said Gwenyth, without lifting her eyes.

I swallowed hard, and went to the packs and drew forth the sheepskin and coverlets we had lest Gwenyth want them. I came back with them, and saw Gyric's old clothing on the ground.

"They are crawling," said Gwenyth. "Better boil them now."

I picked them up and dropped them into the cauldron. Gwenyth rose and stood by Gyric with the basin in one hand and a strip of cloth in another. She dipped the cloth into the basin and dabbed at the charred holes beneath his brow with it. It was hard for me to look on Gyric, but harder still to bear the moaning and muffled cries which came from him as she did this. I went to his other side, and took his hand in mine and said, "Gyric, we seek only to help you." The warm water from the cloth dribbled down into his blackened eye sockets. He moaned, and I grasped his hand harder and said to him, "We will not hurt you, Gyric." Tears were in my eyes; I felt one tiny part of his terror and pain; and that tiny part made me feel as tho' my heart would break for him.

She finished and said, "Bring the broth."

It was beginning to simmer, and the birch leaves floated on the top of it in a solid green skim. I brought it and a small wooden spoon to Gwenyth.

She tasted it and nodded. I went to Gyric's head and raised it in my hands, and she held the spoon to his mouth. He did not take it, but she let it drip in slowly, and he swallowed. We gave him many spoonfuls this way, and finally laid his head down.

The Sun was dropping fast now, and the shadows grew long in the little camp. We built up the fire again, and as we did Holt came over and began looking through the basket packs.

My body was sore from riding all night and from lack of sleep. My shoes were still wet and I unlaced them and laid them near the fire to dry. I was hungry and thirsty, and Holt and Gwenyth must be too. I went and brought my food bag and opened it. I said, "I have roast fowl, and eggs, and bread," and began taking these things out of the pack and setting them upon the bench.

Gwenyth emptied a small pouch next to mine. There was some roast meat, what I could not tell, and as if in answer she said, "'Tis hare; we set many snares and they feed us well." She also set down a few small wrinkled apples, which surprised me. She must keep a cool root cellar somewhere to have apples this late in Spring.

Both she and Holt went first for the bread, which they fairly devoured. I thought it must be one of the things they would truly miss, living as they did. Since they must eat hare all the time, I ate of it, and let them eat the roast fowl I had brought. The eggs too, they enjoyed, and ate with relish. They must gather wild eggs on their travels, but such a supply could not be depended upon. The look on Gwenyth's face as she ate her egg told me a long time had passed since she had lived near tame hens.

I ate an apple, cutting it in sections with my seax. It was still sweet and even juicy inside. I opened the jug that held the ale and passed it to Gwenyth. She took one swallow, and then passed it back to me, saying, "'Tis good stuff; but save it for him," meaning Gyric.

Ale, too, the common drink of all, would be something they would never have in their wandering lives, and her refusing it for the sake of Gyric was a kindness I did not expect. I watched her as she ate. She wore a sharp look upon her face, and her clothes were coarse, and years had passed since her first youth; but anyone could see why she would have caught the eye of Merewala. I looked again upon the large silver pin which held her wool mantle. She had this, and the pin set with blue stones which her son wore, and the two rings of silver upon her hands. This was all that remained, save the boy himself, of the days when she was the Lord's favourite. And as I thought of this, and the hardship she must have known, I thought how great was her pride to keep these four jewels which adorned their rags unsold after all these years.

As I thought these things she lifted her eyes to me, and I found myself lowering my own under her searching gaze.

She rose and went to Gyric and gestured to me to bring more of the birch broth. We fed him again, but this time he would not take so much of it.

After we had done, she said, "Now time will tell its tale."

I nodded my head. It was growing dark, and the fire from the pit showed more and more brightly every moment. Holt was now under the open-walled shelter; perhaps he already slept. I looked down at Gyric as he lay still upon the table. I thought of the damage which our ride of the night before had done to him. Then I thought that he would have surely died in the cellar of Four Stones if he had not been taken from there. I turned to Gwenyth as she stood beside me.

"I thank you for all your help," I said.

Her voice was low, but it held no gentleness. "He will not thank me," was all she answered.

I turned away, stung by her words. I stumbled to my kit pack and took out my mantle. I spread out a coverlet, and wrapped myself in it upon the hard and cold ground.

I do not know why I awoke; I think the fire crackled loudly and startled me. The waxing Moon hung low
in the sky, and no night bird sang out. I looked around as
I remembered where I was, and in the firelight made out
the form of Gwenyth as she stood by Gyric.

I rose and went to her. She was pressing something to
his lips. It was not a cup, and I could not tell what it was.
A chill ran through me as I recalled the words of Meryth's
husband saying that Gwenyth would as soon kill a man as
cure him. Gyric meant nothing to her; and I recalled what
she had said when she first saw him: 'He is a killer like all
the rest.'

I thought of these things, but beat back my fear as I
came up to her. I stood silently by her side, waiting for her
to speak. At last she did. She drew back her hand from his
mouth, and said, "'Tis speed-well; I steeped it in your ale.
I got a few drops of its juice into him."

She stepped back and sighed, and rolled her shoulders as if they ached. I was ashamed at my thought that
she might harm him; she may have been up all night. She
looked at Gyric and said in a low voice, "I do not think he
will live."

"He must live," I said in return, and her quiet way
filled me with more fear than her earlier fierceness did.

She shrugged her shoulders. "I have done all I can for
him. If you desire him to live, you must call him back."

"Call him?" I asked, fear knotting my throat.

"Yes," she answered. "If he truly knows what has happened to him, he will not wish to live. None of his kind
would choose a life without sight. But you may still keep
him from the Lands of the Dead, if you call him back."

She moved by me, and in the flickering light I saw her go to the shed and lie down. I stood by Gyric and looked down upon his still form. Only the slightest movement of his chest told me that he breathed.

I sat upon the bench and brought my face close to his ear. In the dark I could not see the cruel burn on his temple; I could not even see the dark hollows which were once his eyes. What I could see was the line of his brow, and nose, and lips, and chin, and I kept my gaze fixed upon this.

I looked upon him for a long time, and then words formed within me.

"Gyric," I whispered. "I want you to live."

He did not move; he did not moan; his lips were still.

"Gyric, I want you to live," I said.

I leaned closer to him, and took his hand in both of mine. "I want you to live," I said again.

I sat there in the dark, his hand in mine, my face close to his ear, whispering his name and saying, I want you to live.

I did not weep as I spoke to him thus; nor, do I think, I prayed. I did not think of Ælfwyn, and her lost love for this man, or of her grief over losing him, only to find him again thus maimed; and I did not think of Gyric himself, perhaps desiring to die as he lay before me; I could not have thought of these things that night and borne it.

Perhaps I did not think at all, as I sat there by him, but only willed; for all I knew were the six words I said over and over again: Gyric, I want you to live.

I awoke to a hand on my shoulder. It was dawn, and Gwenyth stood next to me. My head lay on my arms on the edge of the table, my hand still covering Gyric's. I straightened, and stood up, and Gwenyth bent over to hear Gyric breathe. He stirred slightly, but did not make a sound.

She did not speak to me, but went about the tasks of drawing water and stoking the fire. I went to the creek, and washed my face and hands and found my comb. I brought forth food from my pack, and Holt and Gwenyth and I sat and ate, nearly in silence.

Then Holt wandered off to the creek, and Gwenyth and I sat together without talking. She rose, and heated more of the birch broth, and I helped her feed it to Gyric. He took many swallows of it, and when he was done we covered him warmly.

Gwenyth stood, bowl in hand, looking at Gyric as I folded a coverlet under his head to serve as a pillow. Without taking her eyes from him she said to me, "He will live."

I raised my hand to my face, and uttered aloud my thanks.

She said, "Do not thank me. He lives because of you."

I wanted to tell her this was not true; that it was her craft, but she spoke before I could begin.

"He lives, because of you," she said again. "One part of him will never forgive you."

AWAKE IN THE DARK

GYRIC did not speak that day, but he moved more. Once when we held his head to feed him broth he put one arm behind him as if to hold himself up. Gwenyth spoke little to me, and said nothing to him. She sent Holt to take the horses to graze in the small meadow where the birches grew, and he was gone all the day long with them.

The day was filled with Sun, and even the little camp, ringed by stone as it was, grew warm. In the afternoon we heated a full cauldron of water, and Gwenyth floated henbane in it, and she bathed Gyric with it. I took a basin full of it and soaked his hair, combing it out carefully, and thus we rid him of lice. I dried his hair with a linen towel, and it was soft and bright and fell nearly to his shoulders in a wave of coppery gold. So he was clean again, and I felt, must know more comfort.

I bathed too, and changed my gown and washed my shift and stockings, which I had worn since the night we had left Four Stones. Looking through my bag I found another pair of shoes, made of green leather. They were ones Ælfwyn had brought with her from Cirenceaster and never yet worn. I had three of Ælfwyn's fine wool gowns in addition to my russet and green ones. Four of her silk gowns also lay there, one blue, one green, one dark red, and one pale yellow: she had given me almost all of her best clothing. In my satchel I had a black leathern pouch stuffed with silver pieces, and the tiny red one, full of rings and pins and brooches and chains. There was something too in the bottom of my satchel which I could not recognise by feel. It was long and slender and heavy, and wrapped in a piece of scrap leather and tied with a cord. I took it out and unwrapped it, and again knew the lengths Ælfwyn and Burginde had gone to provide for us, for within lay a spear point, very sharp, and only wanting a shaft. I wondered where they had found it. Perhaps Burginde had taken it from the weapon smith's stall. I would cut a sapling later and see if I could carve a shaft for it.

I went alone down the trail to the birch grove, and plucked more fresh leaves for Gyric, for I had used all I had gathered earlier. I showed them to Gwenyth when I returned, but she nodded and made no comment. I longed for her to be kinder to me, and did not understand why she was not. I sat looking at her, and she seemed to read my thought, for she suddenly turned on me and demanded, "What?"

"Nothing," I said, looking away, "I said nothing." But then I turned to her and asked, "Why are you not kind to me?"

"Why do you expect my kindness?" she asked in return.

I looked around the barren little camp and shrugged my shoulders. "Only because I have tried to be kind to you, and have, I think, done you no harm. And you have helped me greatly, and so I wish you were kinder that I might be able to thank you."

"Would kindness make my help greater?" she asked.

"I do not know," I answered, confused. "You are not like Meryth," I said, and added, "She loves and defends you still."

Her narrow blue eyes shot back to me. "My sinful ways are still not forgotten, or forgiven, eh?"

"You are not forgotten, at least by her," I answered, "and all must miss your healing skills. Besides, you did nothing more than any village girl might."

"I bore a cursed child," she said, and tho' her voice was light it was full of mockery. "A child that was gotten by a Lord. And he loved me, too, that Lord; but proved his cowardice, for because of Holt he put me away from him." She stood up and walked a few feet away, and then turned.

"As for my craft, 'tis a bane as well as a blessing. The priest at Four Stones hated me for my skill, for I could heal when he failed. I was first brought to Merewala because of it. His little daughter had fever, and I cured her. Merewala gave me a ring, this one," she said, thrusting up her right hand, "a silver ring to a cottar's daughter! He did not forget me then; the next week was the first time he brought me to his bed. I had twelve Winters, and was scarce more than a child myself. I pleased him, and he gave me many gifts, and my father's croft grew crowded with sheep and goats, and upon my breast I wore this pin I wear today. When Holt was born Merewala was full of joy, and I think nearly took me to the hall to live with him and his daughter and his older sons. But he forsook us when he saw that Holt was odd, and so I forsook him."

I did not know what to respond to all this. "Are you happy here?" I asked, looking about.

"I am free," she answered. "Free of the village, and its troubles, and its comforts too, when it had comforts. I lived two lives there; one as healer, and another as the bedmate of Merewala, and in both of them I was damned."

When the Sun grew low in the sky Holt returned, leading the horses. He had over his shoulder several dead starlings and one partridge. Around his neck hung the thin gut sling with which he caught up the bird's legs and so snared them. Gwenyth praised him for his skill, and set to work skinning the birds for our dinner. We roasted the starlings on spits of green wood, but the partridge she boiled, to make more broth for Gyric.

We simmered the birch leaves in the broth as before, and fed Gyric spoonfuls of it; and tho' he did not speak he seemed more aware of us.

Holt was busy working with his knife and a piece of hide. Gwenyth regarded him and said to me, "He is making boots for your friend."

I was surprised at this; tho' he had carried him a long way Holt scarcely seemed to notice Gyric.

"That is good of you, Holt," I said. He stopped in his work and looked up at me with a grin.

Gwenyth said, "All hand work he does, and does with skill. He makes our shoes, and wove the baskets that carry our goods."

Holt did not look up, but nodded and gurgled at this praise. As I looked at Holt I remembered that he was Merewala's son, and that all of his other sons were dead, and that he too had crossed the shore of Life. Holt lived, and knew pleasure, because his father had cast him off.

When it was time to sleep I set up my bed roll near the table, and before I lay down I went to Gyric and again spoke to him, saying his name and telling him he was with friends.

I awoke in the dark to the sound of a fretful calling, and jumped up and went to Gyric. He was tossing his head from side to side, and pushing his arms out as if to keep something away. He called loudly, and his wailing told me he rode the night-mare. I took his hands and grasped them hard and tried to wake him, saying his name again and again.

I left him for a moment and shoved a few sticks of wood into the failing fire. By its light I saw Gwenyth rise and step out of the little shelter. She looked at me but did not come forward.

"Gyric," I said, again taking up his arms and holding him, "awaken. It is a dream. You are safe now."

He called out again, and then there was a gasp, as if he truly did awaken. I let go his arms and placed my hand on his brow to try to calm him. "You are safe, Gyric," I repeated. "You are safe now."

He drew a deep breath, the first deep breath I had known him to draw; and cried out a little at the pain of his ribs. The next breath was slower and his body relaxed against the table. He lay back and was quiet, but moved his hands as if he were awake.

I touched them with my own, and said, "Gyric."

His lips moved, as they had many times before, but now they formed words. He asked in a whisper, "Who are you?"

I tightened my grasp on his hands, and found my own voice, and answered, "I am Ceridwen. My father was Cerd, an ealdorman of Mercia."

He was quiet a long time, and I did not know if he heard me.

"Mercia," he repeated, in some wonder. "What place is this, where we are now?"

"We are in Lindisse, in the forests surrounding the keep of Four Stones," I answered.

"Lindisse?" he asked back, and raised his head a little.

"Yes, but we are safe from the Danes. We are with a woman of Lindisse and her son. They live in these forests and have sheltered us."

His head dropped back, and I said, "You are weak from your wound, and from the journey here. You must try to rest."

"How did I come here?" he asked, slowly.

"I took you from the cellar of Four Stones," I said. The tears in my eyes were now rolling down my cheek. "I am so glad that you live," I said, and tried not to sob.

For answer he pulled his hands away and lifted them to his face and pressed them over the wrap covering his wound. His fingers groped beneath it for an instant. His mouth opened, but no cry came forth. He did not scream; he did not wail, or curse; but only kept his hands clenched over his empty eyes so tightly that his whole body trembled.

"Gyric," I pleaded, and placed my hands on his.

"It is true," he gasped.

"Yes," I wept, "it is true. But you live; you live."

He turned as if he would bury his head in his arms. He howled a long, bitter wail of grief, and I placed my hands on his shoulders. I could not speak; my tears came too fast.

He did not say more, but only hid his head and shuddered. I began to fear that he might go mad from the shock of it.

"Gwenyth," I called, "help him, please."

She came forward and looked not at him but at me. "There is no help for him but the truth, and now he knows it." The words seemed cruel, but her voice was mild as she said it.

I turned my face from her, but she walked to the table and then spoke to Gyric. "You will see no more, and the world as you knew it is lost to you. Yet you have cheated Death. He has left your side empty-handed. This is also the truth."

She moved away, back to the shelter. Gyric was trembling and I pulled his mantle closer about his shoulders. His breath came in low rasping gasps as he began to sob. His face was buried in his hands. I sat down on the bench and placed my hand upon his arm.

He spoke again, in a hoarse whisper, and I had to bend over him to hear it. "I would wake, but not know if I dreamt. Only the pain I felt told me I still lived," he said. His voice was so low that it was as if he spoke only to himself.

He rolled onto his back, but still kept one arm flung over his face. "Each time I woke, I woke in this darkness; and I would remember all, but not believe it, tho' my fingers told me."

I said nothing, and suddenly he asked, "Are you there?" with a kind of panic in his voice.

I pressed his arm and said, "Yes, yes, I am here."

He felt for and took my hand in his own and grasped it. "Do not go," he said with strength.

I closed my other hand over his and answered, "I will not go."

He moaned, and pressed my hand so tightly that I thought it would surely break. Then of a sudden he let it go, and flailed against the empty air around him.

"Why did they not kill me?" he demanded in anguish. "I am worse than dead. Why did they . . ."

He did not finish, and I asked him, "Were you captured in a battle by the men of Svein?"

He started and answered in a whisper, "You know this? Yes; and we knew we would be held to ransom. But then we were separated from each other, and one night, for no reason, they . . . this – happened . . ."

"It was Hingvar," I said, scarcely able to say the word.

"Yes! Hingvar," he answered, and his anguish turned to rage.

The words tumbled from my mouth. "They did not want your ransom price. That is why they did this. Hingvar slayed or maimed all the captives to spite his brother Svein."

He lay back, silent in his amazement, and then asked, "How is it you know all this?"

"I have been amongst the Danes at Four Stones," I answered, and each word felt like an admission of guilt.

In reply he gave only a low cursing wail. I bent over him and touched his arm. "Gyric, you are still weak, and this is much to hear. Will you take some broth or ale, and then try to sleep?"

He did not answer me, and lay before me panting out his grief and anguish, gripping his hands and sobbing.

It was terrible to see, and worse to hear, and I felt help-less and sick and weary. Beyond this I felt the foolishness of trying to comfort him with offers of sleep, or a cup of ale. Yet I did not want him to surrender completely to his grief; I feared for him. I sat back down on the bench and waited until his breath calmed, and then spoke again.

"I am going to warm ale, and have some," I began, and as I said this I knew my voice began to tremble with my tears. "Will you have some too?"

He was silent, and I rose and took the ale jug and pushed it into the ashes and glowing coals of the fire. I looked up at the sky. The stars stood out brightly and alone. "It is hours until dawn, Gyric," I whispered. "You should try to sleep."

I found a cup and poured out some of the ale, and drank of it, and then went to him. "Here is ale," I said. "Please try to drink some."

He raised himself on one elbow, and took the cup in his hand and drank. He passed it back to me and groaned as he lowered himself.

"It is your ribs," I said. For answer he only winced. "Will you sleep now?" I asked, not expecting an answer. "It is many hours until dawn."

He nodded his head, and I sat down by him. I could not know if he slept, but I waited until my own weariness overcame me before I went and lay down myself. I pulled the coverlet over my head, too tired even for tears.

WE TELL OUR TALES

DAYLIGHT awoke me, and I rose and looked about. Holt and Gwenyth were gone; they must be already afield.

I went to where Gyric lay. He was still, but did not breathe as if he slept. I sat down on the bench, wondering if I should speak to him, and wondering further what the day would bring. To free him from Four Stones so that he might live had been my only thought. Now that he did live I must think of his growing stronger that we might travel. I could not know if any Danes searched for us, or how long it was safe to stay in the camp, or if we endangered Gwenyth by keeping her and Holt here while Gyric mended.

As I sat there, thinking on all this, he moved his hand to his chest, and fingered the silver pin that held his mantle.

"This is not mine," he said softly.

"No," I answered. "But it is yours now."

"Tell me again who you are," he said, and his voice was quiet.

I was glad that he spoke, and glad too for the calmness in his voice. I moved closer to him and said, "My name is Ceridwen, and I am of Mercia."

467

"You said your father is an ealdorman?" he asked, in the same low tone.

"That is true. His name was Cerd, and his lands were at the Western borders of Mercia, by the river Dee. But he died before my birth, and his brother Cedd raised me until he died as well." He listened to this without moving.

"We are in Lindisse now?" was his next question.

"Yes, not far from the keep of Four Stones."

"And you took me from there?" he asked.

"Yes," I answered.

"By yourself? Alone?"

"Yes, alone, but many there helped me free you."

His thoughts now circled back, and he asked, "Which Dane now rules at Four Stones?"

I squeezed my hands together as I answered. "The same as that who conquered it: the jarl Yrling."

"Yrling?" he asked, and there was in his voice disbelief and wonder. "The same that has wed a Lady of Cirenceaster?"

So he knew, and I must now tell him the rest. "Yes," I began, watching his face as I spoke. "I was in the service of the Lady Ælfwyn there."

His voice held no colour as he answered. "I heard last month that Ælfsige had made Peace with Yrling, with her as part of the prize." He spoke as if all of this had happened long, long ago, in a distant past.

"It near broke her heart to go," I said, recalling her journey to Four Stones.

He turned his head away, and was silent. Then he asked, "Did she see me? See me like this, at Four Stones?"

"No, no," I reassured him. "When we first heard you were captive there, she thought only of a way to help you escape. It was before we – knew you were hurt. She wanted very much to see you, but the danger to her was too great. I went down to the cellar alone, four nights ago, and found you." I slowed myself, wanting to speak carefully. "I saw you could not ride by yourself, and so planned to ride with you to safety."

He was quiet a long time. "This was your choice, to leave with me?" he finally asked.

"Yes, my own; and I would not let any one stop me."

"Why?" he asked. "Why did you do this?"

I could scarcely answer, my throat was so tight with tears. "I feared you might die."

"You stole horses from the Danes?"

"One," I answered. "The second horse was mine, a gift."

"From . . . her?"

"No," I said, biting my lip. "From one of the Danes. A nephew to Yrling."

"O."

I felt some urgency to go on. "Many at Four Stones helped me. The stable boy tied our horses in a safe place; his father had them ready saddled for us. The cook drugged the Dane that guarded you, and her husband carried you out of the cellar and to where our horses waited."

He turned his head back to me, but did not speak. "We rode all night long, do you remember it?" I asked.

He shook his head. "I think I was cold," he answered.

"Yes, I am sorry. You were wet, for we had to go down a stream bed to get out of the keep yard. Two days ago we found Gwenyth. She and her son live in the forest, and she is a powerful healer."

"What day is this?" he asked.

I thought, and replied, "It is the thirteenth day of April."

"Then it is Good Friday?" he asked.

"Yes," I remembered. "Sunday is Easter Day."

"How long was I at Four Stones?" he asked.

"Not long. You were brought only two days before I first saw you, and the next night we left."

His voice was very low. "My family will think I am dead."

I was quiet, thinking of the grief and uncertainty they must feel.

He spoke again, in the same low tone. "The prince saw me captured, but it was so long ago that all will think I am dead."

"Do you mean Ælfred?" I questioned. "He is now King."

"King? Æthelred is dead?"

"Yes, of wounds he took at a battle near Meredune. The Witan chose Ælfred to succeed him."

This was much to take in. I tried to turn away from all this by saying, "I hope you will eat now. We have good provisions, and you must be very hungry."

He raised himself on his elbow and said, "I want to stand up."

"Yes," I said. "Holt, Gwenyth's son, is making you shoes. Until they are ready you must walk carefully."

As he straightened himself the wrap around his empty eyes loosened and began to fall. He caught it up quickly and tied it around his head.

He swung his legs onto the ground and stood. His twisted mouth and furrowed brow told me that every part of his body must be sore. Now that he stood, I did not know where he wanted to go or what he wanted to do.

"I need to – to relieve myself," he said, and lowered his head.

"O," I said hastily, "yes. There is a trench; we are close to it." I touched his arm. "Can you walk? It is not far."

I led him across the clearing to the trench beyond the line of fir trees. He walked slowly, hesitating at each step. When we got to the trench, I stood, my face burning, next to him. I did not want to leave him, but I did not want to shame him.

"Here it is," I said. "I will come back."

I went to the fire and began to warm the broth, and took out bread and some cheese from the food pack. I went to the stream to draw water and filled the cauldron. I had been gone many minutes when I passed through the fir trees. Gyric stood close to where I had left him, only he faced another way.

"Gyric," I said softly, so as not to startle him. He nodded his head, and turned towards me. He did not move, and I went up to him and touched his arm. I led him back to the clearing, and brought him to the bench. I filled a basin with warm water, and he washed his hands and wiped his face.

I laid the food out on the table before him and said, "Here is cheese and bread, and also broth."

He put his hand out and found the bread. I sliced the cheese into thin cuts and placed them in his hand. He was, as I knew he must be, hungry, as his thin frame showed. Despite his hunger he did not eat quickly, but stopped often to take a sip of broth. I knew this was good, and that eating thus, he would keep his food down.

Trees crackled near us, and he started and began to rise. "It is Holt, and Gwenyth," I said, and placed my hand on his arm.

Holt bore last night's catch, a hare, over his shoulder, and in Gwenyth's hands were bunches of wild cress. They came to the table but did not speak, and I felt awkward. Gwenyth kept her cool blue eyes upon Gyric, but I could not read her thoughts.

"Gwenyth and her son took us in and sheltered us," I said to Gyric.

He was silent for a moment, and then said, "I thank you for your help." He held his head down, and his voice was so low that I just heard him.

"I did little," Gwenyth answered at last. She looked from me to him, and then walked into the shelter. Holt had moved away from the table and had returned clutching a piece of hide. His face wore his lopsided grin, and he crouched down near the fire and set to work upon the other shoe for Gyric.

We sat alone at the table while Gwenyth skinned the hare and boiled water. Gyric had stopped eating, and I tried to get him to take more, but he shook his head.

"Are you weary? Will you lie down again?" I asked, not knowing what to do next.

He moved his head slightly, but I could not tell what he meant by it.

"Your ribs are still sore. You need rest while they mend," I went on, feeling like I was babbling.

He did not answer, and his head was sunk so low that his chin almost touched his chest.

I looked around the little camp for light which did not come. "Perhaps you would like to be by yourself," I ventured. I began to rise. "I will go and check the horses," I said.

For answer he put his hand out in the air as if he would catch my arm. "Do not go," he said, in a voice barely above a whisper.

I moved my hand to where his still reached, outstretched, towards me.

"I will not go," I said quietly, and sat down. He touched my hand with his own for a moment.

We sat in silence for a long time. Gyric was still, with his head lowered. The morning Sun glanced through the trees and struck his back, and the red-gold waves of his hair shone on his shoulders. There was a lightness and spareness about him, as if boy and man were mixed within him. I sat mutely by his side and regarded him, and for a time he too spoke not.

"What will you do now?" asked Gyric in a low voice.

The question surprised me, so deep was I in my own thoughts.

"Do?" I responded. "When you are well enough, we will quit this place and begin our journey to Wessex."

He did not answer, so I went on. "Gwenyth has sheltered us, but soon she and her son will wish to be off. When you are strong enough we will begin our journey. We have two good horses, and a full kit to travel with. Also we have much gold and silver jewellery, and many silver coins, all from Ælfwyn."

Finally he spoke. "You will travel with me, all the way from Lindisse to Wessex?"

"Of course," I answered. "You must get home to Kilton, to your people."

He moved his head a little, but did not turn to me. "We are a very long way from Kilton, and there is nothing but danger upon the roads."

"There is danger everywhere now. But what else can we do?"

He shook his head slowly. "Why – why did you do this? Why did you take me from Four Stones?"

I thought for a moment. "It is as I told you last night. When Ælfwyn found you were a prisoner, all she could think about was helping you escape. Then I found you could not ride alone, so that is why I am here."

"You are risking your life for me, every moment." I did not answer right away, and he went on. "You left Ælfwyn, and the life you had in her service, to do this."

"Yes," I answered, "and I love her, and will miss her." I tried to keep my voice steady. "When we are safe in Wessex I will send her a message; she begged that I might do so."

He kept his face in profile to me, and his next words were a whisper. "Is she well?"

"She is well," I said softly. "She went to Four Stones for the good of her people, and she went loving you." Tears were now come into my eyes, and I brushed them away. "Since she has been at Four Stones she has done many good works for the folk there, and has relieved them greatly. She is building up flocks of sheep, and having the fields sown, and has shown her wisdom again and again to the Danes."

Gyric did not move or respond to any of this, but sat as still as if he were deaf and mute. When he spoke, his voice was hoarse. "And she is wed to Yrling?"

"Yes," I said. I cast around for what to say next, and the truth came forward. "Tho' he is a Dane, he is good to her, and esteems her greatly."

He moved his head, as if he nodded. "And you," he finally said, "how did you come to know her? I never met you at Cirenceaster."

"No, I have never seen that place, or any part of Wessex. I was raised by the river Dee, and travelled upon the Northly Road, and there met Ælfwyn and her train as they went to Four Stones."

"How came you to travel there?" he asked, and turned slightly to me.

"I left the Priory to seek a station. It was Winter, and I met bad weather upon the road. Ælfwyn kindly took me in and offered me a place with her in her new life."

I saw Gyric's brow furrow as he formed his next question. "You left a Priory?"

"Yes," I said quickly. "But I did no wrong. I had come of age, and did not wish to wed the men the Prior had chosen for me, nor did I have a calling for the veil."

"How old are you?"

"I will have sixteen years this Summer."

"You are a maid of sixteen?" he asked, his brow furrowing more.

"Yes," I answered, as simply and as firmly as I could.

He shrugged. He put his hand up as if he would rest his brow in his palm, but when his fingers touched the wrap that covered his wound he stiffened and put his hand down again.

I did not have a chance to say more, for suddenly Holt was before us, holding out his huge hands. "Shoes," he sang out, and grinned.

"They are very good, Holt," I praised, looking at them. They were cut from the thickest part of the deer hide, and stitched with leathern cords, and had a leathern lacing up the side by the ankle to fit them.

Gyric turned towards Holt but said nothing. I took the shoes and placed them in Gyric's hands.

"Thank you," he said, but in his quiet voice there was a note of frustration.

He began to bend over to put one on. He winced from the effort, and I asked, "Shall I do it?"

He straightened, and I knelt down and placed his foot in the shoe and laced it up, and did the same to the other.

"Now you can walk more freely," I said, and thought at once what a stupid thing it was to say. Gyric said nothing, and Holt still stood before us, grinning. I remembered the iron spear point in my satchel.

"Holt," I asked, rising to fetch the bag, "do you think you could make a shaft for this point?"

I drew the spear tip out and passed it into his giant hands. He held it up and looked at the hollow for the shaft. He turned it around and around in his hands; I thought he had no idea what it was.

"Spear," he said.

"Yes, a spear," I answered. "Could you fit a shaft to it?"

He nodded his head, and once again drew his knife from his belt.

I went on, "Make it as tall as you."

Gyric sat silent through this all, and Holt lumbered away with the spear point.

"You have a spear point?" he asked when I sat back down.

"Yes, a good one, and very sharp. I found it in my bag. Ælfwyn or her nurse must have put it there." He said nothing, and I went on, "It will be useful, as a walking staff."

I went to my other bag and returned with the black belt and seax. "We have this, too," I said, pressing it into his hands. "It is, I think, a gift from Dobbe, the cook. She is a woman of Wessex, and drugged the Dane who guarded you."

His fingers moved slowly over the belt and rested on the leathern scabbard. He touched the silver hilt of the seax, and his fingers closed around the carved bone grip and drew it forth. With his other hand he cautiously followed the curve of the polished blade.

He did not speak, and I went on. "It must be the seax of Merewala himself. I have never seen one of such worth. It is by far the most valuable thing we carry with us."

He fitted the blade back into the scabbard, and then lifted the belt to me.

"No, it is for you," I said. "I have a knife, my father's old seax."

He paused, but then stood and found the buckle ends and strapped the belt around his waist so that the weapon lay across his belly. His right hand moved to position the scabbard, and he slowly drew the seax forth again. He held it a moment, and then guided it back into the sheath.

This simple act filled me with something like gladness, tho' my throat caught.

He sat back down again, and rested his hands on his knees. "You said Ælfred is now King," he said quietly.

"Yes, we heard it just a few days ago. Æthelred died from his battle wounds, from a place called Meredune. Your Witan met and chose his young brother as King."

He was silent, and I went on, "You are his kin, are you not? Ælfwyn once told me that your father and Ælfred's father were as brothers."

"We are kin, but closer in our hearts than we are in blood."

I almost said how glad Ælfred would be to learn that Gyric was alive, but stopped myself. "Ælfwyn says your father is a great chieftain, and ealdorman of Kilton."

For answer he nodded. "What else do you know?" he asked in a low voice. "You must have seen and heard much from a jarl as crafty as Yrling."

"Not, perhaps, as much as you think; for the Danes used to speak their own tongue before us, except for Yrling himself, and his nephews, who spoke our language as well." I thought of what I could tell him that would have meaning. "I know that many more Danes are coming this Summer, when the seas are calm, to join Yrling. They think they will rule Wessex and Mercia as they do Lindisse and Northumbria."

After a while he said, "You have seen them. What do you think?"

I thought before I answered. "They are very good warriors," I began, "but they are strange. They do not value the things we value. They do not pledge to each other, and even tho' Yrling feeds and arms his men they leave whenever they find a richer Lord to serve or a fatter land to take." Then in fairness I went on, "But the same things that give us joy gladden them too: gold and horses and song and fine things, and good food, and the hope for glory."

"And beautiful women," muttered Gyric.

I thought to myself: They are men, like any other; but this I did not say.

"They are cursed heathens," said Gyric with something like heat. He ended with an awful oath. "Christ blind them."

"They are heathen, and worship the old Gods," I answered softly.

He said nothing; I do not think he heard me, for his anger was come upon him again. He clenched his hands into fists upon his lap, and his brow creased deeply.

"Do you want to walk?" I asked, feeling helpless. "Or perhaps you are weary and wish to sleep?"

"I will lie down," he said. I shook out the sheep skin to fluff it, and he stretched out on his back on the table, his hand on the hilt of his seax. He winced as he lay down.

"Your ribs must pain you very much."

"I tried to escape, before I was brought to Four Stones," he answered. "Hingvar's men caught me and kicked me until I knew no more."

"You tried to escape after . . . after they wounded you?"

"Yes," he answered shortly. "I must have been out of my head. I was like a blind dog crawling along the ground, looking for a way out. It was good sport for those who found me."

I said nothing, for I could think of nothing fit to say. I lay his green mantle over him and said, "Try to rest."

The Sun was now high overhead, filling the camp with needed warmth. Gwenyth was nowhere to be seen, and all was quiet. I felt my own weariness, and went and lay down on my bedroll and slept.

LEAVE-TAKING

IT took a long time for me to fall asleep that night, and I lay awake gazing at the waxing Moon. I did not know how Gyric and I would find our way out of Lindisse. It would not be safe to use any roads we might find, so we must go overland, which would be slow. Even then we might be seen by Danes, or brigands. If our horses could not outrun danger we would be lost, for I could not defend us. I did not know how long our food would last, or how we could find more. All these thoughts kept tumbling in my head, and I had answers for none of them.

In the morning I brought warm water and a linen towel to Gyric so he might wash. He turned away from me and untied the wrap around his wound, so that he might wipe his face. He reached again for the wrap, but his fingers missed it where it lay upon the table. I silently pushed it within his reach, and he found it and tied it over his empty eyes. I walked away from him, that he might wash more fully, wishing that he knew he need not hide his wound from me.

He walked now with the spear that Holt had fitted as his staff, and in my heart I praised Ælfwyn and her cleverness for providing it. It was tall and stout, and a good

481

support for him as he walked, for he could place it before him and so be sure of his next step. But greater than this, it was a weapon, and a worthy one for a King's atheling, wounded as he was. The seax, too, he wore at all times, and oftimes rested his hand upon its hilt as he sat.

That noon Gwenyth began to gather up kindling and place it under the little shelter. I went to the fir trees and began pulling out the dried twigs and branches beneath them, and laid them next to what she herself gathered. After a while she said to me, "Holt and I leave tonight."

"Tonight?"

She answered me without stopping in her work. "The Moon will be near full, and give us light to travel."

She guessed at my thought and said, "Stay as you need to."

I thought of the debt I owed her. "I cannot repay your help to us, but only hope that you will take some silver for yourself, and Holt, and for Meryth, too; for she helped me greatly and I could not reward her."

"It will be long before I see Meryth."

"Silver does not go bad, and she would welcome it greatly," I urged. I went to my satchel and drew forth the black pouch. I counted out ten new pieces of silver, and went to Gwenyth and pressed them into her hand. "Take them for the sake of your son, and your sister, if you will not take them for yourself."

She did not look at the wealth in her hand, but regarded me closely. For answer she closed her fingers over the silver.

I went over to where Gyric sat at the table, knowing he must have heard this. As I sat next to him he said, "I will be ready to ride on the morrow."

"There is no rush," I said. "Gwenyth says we are safe here, and it is better that your ribs be more healed."

There were indeed many comforts in the camp that we would soon do without. Here we had water, and a good firepit, much kindling, and the big iron cauldron. There was even the little roofed shelter should it rain.

"I will be ready tomorrow," he said. "It is a long way to travel. We should begin soon."

I knew he was right, for as the weather grew warmer, the Danes would be more likely to grow in numbers as they moved across the countryside.

"Then we will start tomorrow, if you feel well," I conceded.

ΧΣΧΣΧΣΧΣΧΣ

Gwenyth and Holt gathered their basket packs and took their leave of us just after dark. Gyric and I sat together at the table as the night deepened. It was a still night, and without Gwenyth and Holt the camp seemed silent and empty. After a while I rose and poked a few more sticks into the fire. It crackled in a welcoming way, and I stood near it for both its light and warmth.

"Are you there?" asked Gyric, of a sudden.

"Yes, yes, I am here," I answered, coming towards him. I stood near him, wondering what more to do.

He lowered his head and said, "You do not say much." The way in which he said this told me that he wished I would speak more.

I sat down on the bench next to him. "I am sorry. You are very quiet yourself, and I do not want to chatter while you are trying to mend."

He moved his head slightly. "You do not chatter," he replied. His voice was so low that it was if he questioned himself. "What will happen to Ælfwyn, and the rest of the Saxons who helped you, when they find I am gone?"

I took a breath and said, "By now they know you are gone; it has been three days. Yrling was away hunting, but he must be back by now. We did not think he would care much. Yrling did not want to accept you from Hingvar's men and was very angry about – about what happened to you. So if he does not care about losing you, all he might care about is the black horse, and he has a valley full of good horses. One might not be enough to really hunt for us for."

"What about you? You are gone as well."

I did not answer at first, but then said, "Ælfwyn is clever, and I feel certain she would persuade him not to hunt for us." I tried to give my voice a confidence I did not feel. "And I did all I could to make it seem as tho' it was all my doing, alone and apart from Ælfwyn. I would not let her give us anything that made it look as tho' she betrayed Yrling in helping you escape."

He listened to all this, and then said quietly, "You are a good friend to her."

It was easy to answer this, and I did so with real warmth. "She is the best and brightest of women to me, and like the sister I never had."

"Yet you only met in February."

"Yes, but much befell us since the day we met." I looked into the fire. "I do not think the number of days matter when you share as much as we did."

Now he turned his head away, and murmured, "I know what you speak of."

When I awoke in the morning the sky was grey and low with clouds. I stood up, stiff and achy from my night upon the ground. The sheepskin beneath me was warm, but after sleeping so long on the feather beds of our chamber, the ground felt hard indeed.

Gyric was already up, or at least standing by the table. The spear, which he kept propped up at one end of it, had fallen to the ground, and he reached out with his bare foot to feel where it lay. I crossed over to him and picked it up and placed it in his hand.

He nodded his head for reply, and I said, "I will warm some water so we might wash, and boil some broth out of the partridges while I start to pack." It was Easter morning, but I could not speak any word of glad resurrection to one as sorrowful as Gyric.

He put out his hand and found the bench and touched the shoes he had left there the night before. I knew it was painful for him to bend. I dropped down and gently took them from him and laced them upon his feet. For thanks he only nodded again. He rose and began picking his way across the camp. He could find his way beyond the circle of trees, and also to the tiny upper creek where we filled the cauldron.

I wanted to bathe before we started our journey, for with the large cauldron in the camp it was easy to heat much water. I felt foolish as I looked around to see where I might undress and wash myself. I could just stand by the cauldron, but felt shy to do so. I had never been naked before any man, and Gyric might guess by the splashing of water what I was doing before him.

I took a basin of hot water to the creek and mixed it with some cold, and quickly stripped off my gown and shift. I wetted my whole body down with the warm water of the little basin, and rubbed myself hard with the towel to get both dry and warm.

I dressed myself and came back into the camp. Gyric was by the firepit, and I stood near him as I combed out my wet hair. I said, "I will begin to pack now, and then we will eat."

He took a step forward and then stopped. I felt he wanted to help me, and I cast about in my mind for something he could do.

"Will you count out our silver?" I asked him, fetching the black leathern pouch. "It will be good to know how many pieces we have."

He sat down again, and pulled open the pouch which I set before him. I watched him lift a piece and place it before him upon the broad table face.

I began gathering up all those things which lay about. I shook out and rolled up our hides and sheepskins, and tied them secure with leathern cords. The partridges Gwenyth had left us began to boil, and I fished them out and dropped a loaf of wheaten bread into the broth. I took it from the fire to let it cool, and then came over to Gyric. All the silver was back in the pouch.

"You are done," I said.

"There are eighty four whole pieces, and four cut quarter pieces."

"That is a lot of coin," I said. I turned to my satchel and drew out the red pouch. "Here is much more silver, and some gold, too," I said, emptying it before him.

He did not reach out to feel it, and I picked up one of the silver pins and touched his hand with it. "Here is a silver pin set with garnets," I explained. "Here are three more, plain, but with good silver work, each."

He slowly rubbed his fingers against these things as I spoke about them. "This is a wide bracelet of silver set with blue stones," I said.

"Dark blue?"

"Yes," I answered, glad he showed some interest.

"It must be lapis," he said.

"Here are two gold rings," I went on, and threaded one each of them on his littlest fingers. They fit, and as I looked on his slender hands thus glinting with gold, I was moved to say, "Wear these yourself, and also the silver bracelet. They are meant to be yours anyway."

He did not answer, but reached out and found the bracelet again. He fingered the silver, tracing the bezels that held the three blue stones upon it.

"It is very beautiful," I remarked.

He took it in his hand and pressed it over his right wrist. He gave a small sound, like a sigh, and lay his hands upon the table.

"I have had both pouches in my satchel," I told him, "but perhaps it is best if we each carry one. You take the jewellery; it is small, and you can wear it on your belt."

I scooped the rest of the jewellery into the pouch and pulled it tightly shut. Gyric unbuckled his belt and threaded the drawstrings through it. I was glad to see him wear the rings and bracelet, and to have him take the pouch into his keeping. Other than the small amount he had eaten it was the first sign he had given me that he had any interest in living.

"That is good," I said, regarding now the large pouch of silver. "I think I will keep only a few coins in the pouch on my sash, and put the rest into my satchel for safe-keeping."

He nodded his head, and I turned now to our food. The broth was cool enough to eat, and the bread had thickened it and given it savour. I sprinkled a tiny pinch of salt on the bowl we shared. For the first time since I had left with Gyric I felt some lightness in my heart.

"I am grateful for this day, and this food," I said by way of blessing.

CHAPTER THE FIFTIETH

FOLLOWING THE SUN

I did not have an easy time saddling our horses, for they were both taller by far than Shagg and their saddles much heavier. Gyric tried to lift one of the saddles for me, but his face showed at once the pain it cost him to lift anything. I did not do a very good job, and tho' Gyric held their heads firm, the horses skittered and neighed their displeasure at me.

This was how we set out: I tied the reins of the black gelding to the saddle of my mare, and I walked at her head, leading her. Gyric placed one hand on the saddle of his gelding, and used his spear as a staff before him. We left the clearing behind and started down the trail past the birch glade that led to the creek.

"We can ride now, if you think you are able," I said, looking down the length of the creek as far as I could.

He nodded his head, and I held the stirrup as he lifted his foot into it. He took hold of the glossy black mane and swung himself into the saddle. He groaned as he did so, and his face twisted.

We went on a little way, with me turning in my saddle to look back at Gyric every few feet. I felt sure he was in pain from his ribs, but that was not the reason for the grief he wore upon his face. His head hung low, with his chin nearly touching his chest. The long dark mane of his horse spilled over his tightly gripped fingers. I thought he was miserable, and tho' he said nothing, his misery showed in every part of him. I could not speak comfort to him, for I felt I had none to give, and the only sound was our horses splashing through the water of the little creek.

After a while the creek widened a bit, and the grassy space surrounding it opened. "Here are green branches before us; duck down," I warned Gyric.

I watched him flatten himself over his horse's neck, and then straighten as I called, All clear.

So we went on like this, picking our way through the little creek, sometimes coming up to walk upon the grass, but mostly staying in the water, for the passage was easy and we left no track on its sandy bottom. Gyric said nothing, and tho' I looked back at him again and again, he never changed in the way he sat upon his black horse: rigidly upright, but with his face cast down.

We went on all afternoon, sometimes crossing larger streams, but always keeping in our Southerly path. We saw not a soul, and heard nothing but the song of birds busy with their Spring nest-building. Many hours had passed when I stopped my mare and turned back to speak to Gyric. "Are you hungry? Would you like to stop and rest?"

He shook his head slightly, and then answered, "I am not hungry."

I looked at his face, and at his fingers, still twisted tightly in his horse's mane. "Well, I am hungry and tired too," I said, deciding we should stop.

As I finished saying this a doe with her fawn crossed the creek not a horse length in front of us and flashed into the woods. My mare tossed her head and snorted and I let out a gasp of surprise as they did.

"What?" called Gyric in a sharp voice.

I turned back to find him sitting up anxiously in his saddle, his drawn seax grasped in his hand.

"Nothing," I answered. "I am sorry. It was a deer and her fawn. They ran in front of us, and startled me."

"O." He slid the seax back into the black scabbard.

"The Sun will set soon. Do you want to stop now and make camp?" I asked again. I looked around us. "There is room about us, just here, for the horses to graze all night."

For answer he nodded.

I guided our horses unto the grass and slipped out of the saddle. The ground seemed to rise up very fast under my wobbly legs. Gyric swung down from his gelding and began untying his spear. As I loosened his horse's reins from my mare's saddle I said lightly, "I feel I can scarce walk. I am not used to riding all day as you are."

He stopped in his work and turned his head to me. I wished he would say something; it was hard to try to speak to him when all day he had not spoken in return.

"You must be tired, then," he said, and there was concern in his voice.

"No, I am fine," I countered, not wanting him to worry about anything so silly as my tired legs.

"Our horses are good ones, as you said," he went on. "Your mare is steady too, if she did not shy at the deer."

"She is a good animal, and beautiful too," I replied, glad to engage him thus. "She was bred for the first time a few days ago," I recalled aloud.

He now had his spear before him in his hand. "Then you will have two horses next Spring," he answered.

I had somehow not considered this fact before. It was hard for me to think of next Spring; to think of where I might be or what I might be doing so far from now. I did not want to think of it, and just said, "Yes, you are right."

I untied the packs from the saddles as Gyric held the horse's heads. He moved forward next to his own horse, running his hand down the animal's neck to his chest. His fingers found the saddle, and he reached beneath to find the girth buckle, and unfastened it. He pulled the saddle off, and set it upon the ground. I watched his face as he did this, to see how much pain this caused him.

"Is the soreness in your ribs better?" I wanted to know.

"They are growing better," he said quietly.

I tied the horses by neck ropes where they could browse, and drink too. I went to work to gather up stones from the creek bed to rim our fire, and find dead wood dry enough to burn. We had much good tinder in the brass box, and mixed with the dried last year's grasses I found, caught easily as I struck out sparks with flint and iron.

The last light was fading from the sky now. Gyric sat by the fire as I heated some of the partridge meat and some cheese on one of the stones. I looked up into the sky and said, "The Sun is setting, and I have not seen it all day."

He raised his face a little, as if to look up. It seemed then to have been a stupid thing for me to have said, to complain of not having seen the Sun that day. I was quiet, and we ate as it grew dark around us.

We had a few day's rations left, if we were careful. I recalled the deer that had crossed our path, and the birds that flew before us as we travelled, none of which I could catch. I hoped we would soon meet with folk from whom we could buy food, for soon we would be hungry.

Gyric said nothing, and I looked at him a long time as he sat facing the warmth of the fire. The line of his brow and nose and lips caught my eye and held it. He sat still, his lips just slightly parted. His face held much beauty, in the fineness of his features and the delicate curve of his mouth, and I gazed long upon it.

The wrap around his wound was smooth and white in the golden light. He had not had it off for one moment since he had awakened in Gwenyth's camp. I wondered how the wound was, and how much more the charred holes would heal, and if the burn mark upon his temple would fade; but tho' I wanted to, I could not bring myself to ask to check it. And this was not for the horror of it, for that horror was passed in me; but because I knew he did not want me, or anyone, to see it. This gave me a sudden pang that made me lower my own face and look away.

"We need to travel West as well as South," he said, and I turned to his quiet voice.

"Why is that?" I asked, so glad he was speaking that tears had sprung into my eyes.

"We must head West for Mercia, and cross from it into Wessex. If we ride due South we will reach Anglia first, and it is now held by the Danes. It will be slower, but safer, if we ride West to Mercia."

"We will do it then," I said, ready to agree to anything that would help ensure our safety.

I thought of something else. "And is your home not far West in Wessex as well?"

"Yes," he answered, "so if we make it as far as Mercia we will have lost nothing, for we can head almost straight South through Wessex."

These last words chilled me. "Do you not think we will reach Mercia?" I found courage to ask.

He moved his head. "We will reach there," he said, as if to reassure me. There was no heartiness in his voice, and we were both quiet.

"Gyric," I began, eager to ask his counsel, "what shall we do when we meet up with people? For we must see or be seen by someone soon, and we will need to seek food, too."

He did not answer right away. "You will have to make a quick judgement, each time you see someone. Cottars and bordars and suchlike folk will be glad to have your silver in exchange for food. But even they should be treated carefully. Folk are desperate, and might try to take what you have by force."

"We will be together," I said. "If you are at a distance behind me, they will not see your wound, and would not try anything while I went to bargain with them."

He was silent at this, and tho' I wondered at the wisdom of my saying it, I saw that there was truth in it. But he did not have a helmet to hide his wound, and anyone suspecting he was blinded might seize upon us both.

"As for warriors, if you spot any, stay well away. They are as likely to be Danes as Saxons."

I knew this was true, for they dressed much alike, especially in their war-gear. "The Danes I have seen are very tall and strong," I recalled aloud.

"Yes. Many of them are taller than we are, but I have killed my share of them."

I said with some firmness, "I know you were a great warrior, for you fought at the side of the new King."

He turned his head away from me at this. "I was a good fighter," he answered softly.

I wanted to touch his arm, but I did not. Instead we sat again in silence.

"You have a seax," he said in a low voice. "Do you know how to use it?"

"Use it?" Of course I used it all the time, to cut leather into strips, to punch holes, to cut small branches; but I knew this was not what he was asking.

"Use it against an opponent," he went on.

I shook my head. Before I could answer he said, "There is no reason you should know; you are a woman, and one raised by churchmen, too. What is important is this: when you are smaller than your enemy you must use his strength to help you."

I did not understand, and he slowly stood up. I stood too, and faced him. "Are you wearing it now?" he asked.

"Yes, I wear it; I have since we started," I said, pulling it out of the sheath on my sash.

"Good. Have it with you, always. Now act as if you are going to attack me."

I stepped back a bit and raised my arm over my head. He put his hand up and I feared he would find the naked blade. Instead he grasped my wrist.

"That is what you must not do," he instructed, pushing my hand back with force. The seax dropped out of my fist onto the ground behind me. The strength in his hand and arm surprised me; he was almost hurting me. He let go my wrist and dropped his own hand.

"Do not raise your hand high. Any man can wrench your weapon away from you. He will not use spear or sword on you, for he will want you alive. If you are attacked from the front, let your enemy come close to you, and keep your seax low, at your waist. He will lunge at you, and use his own force to drive himself upon your blade. If he is wearing a leathern shirt, or a ring tunic, do not even try to pierce it. A wound to the thigh will disable him, and you can break and run."

I was quiet during all this, taking it in. "Do you understand?" he asked.

"Yes, yes," I answered, and bent to retrieve my knife.

He sat down again and I sat by him. "If you are grabbed from behind, do not try to pull away. Instead throw yourself with all your weight back against the chest of your attacker. He may lose his balance and fall to the ground, giving you your chance to run. Even tho' you are a maid, you can outrun many men, especially if they be in battle-gear. Think of escape first, and not of killing your enemy. If he is wounded only a little you can oftentimes get away."

He thought a while, and then spoke again. "If we are pursued on horseback, cut the reins to my gelding. Your mare will run faster unfettered."

"I would never do that," I said. "If we are pursued we will stay together."

He turned his head away from me and said quietly, "You do not know what they will do to you. Me, they will simply kill."

"I do know what they will do," I answered. "The same as they do to all women."

I could only remember the village women, and the daughter of Merewala. I stabbed a piece of wood into the fire.

I felt angry now, angry and sad; and we sat in silence. I did not want our conversation to end this way, nor did I think I could sleep. My eye fell upon our food pack, and I was moved to speak. "We have food for only three days or so," I began. Gyric turned his head towards me, and I went on, "I know we must look for folk from whom we can buy food, but what if we find no one? Can we catch something?"

He considered this. "We could fish, where the water is deep enough. We would need to make a hook."

"I have iron needles; perhaps a hook could be fashioned from one of them."

"Good. A hook we can leave overnight while we sleep."

"What about hares, and larger things?" I wanted to know. "The woods on either side of us must be running with game. Could we snare them? Gwenyth and Holt did."

He thought on this a moment, and then shook his head. "It would be hard. Snares work best when you set many of them, and then check them each morning. They are not suited for those who camp each night in a new place. Also, they must be made and set with care, and placed where animals run. It takes time, which we do not have."

"Then we will try to fish when we can, and look for farming folk too," I answered. I felt much better talking about all these things; to know that Gyric thought about how we should travel and how we might find food made me feel not so alone. Just to have him speak to me was important.

I EXPLAIN MYSELF

IN the morning the sky was still clouded over, and the slight breeze smelt like rain to come. We ate, and saddled the horses, and set out to follow the creek bed once more. Gyric was again quiet. It was, I think, easier for him to speak when night had fallen, and tho' I did not know why, I felt this to be true.

About us were woods of larch, maple, and oak. We were always cautious, and quiet, too, as we rode along, but I felt my caution had changed within me. I no longer feared being followed from Four Stones. Many days and many miles had freed me from this fear, and Four Stones seemed in my mind far away indeed. Now I felt cautious about what strangers we might meet ahead. I hoped we would come upon some wood-cutters or charcoal-makers, and so be able to procure food and perhaps even shelter, and was thus heartened by the signs of cut trees we passed. But we could also stumble across Danes, and as we went along I wished I had more knowledge of trail-craft, and could read the story that each bent twig and trampled bit of forest floor might be telling. Gyric would know all this, I knew, for he showed by what he said that he had skill in these things; and showed too that he knew much of the birds and beasts that roamed the forests. When we stopped to walk our horses through a part that was too low with young maples for us to ride, a bird called out sharply in the forest stillness, and I asked aloud what it might be.

"A calling chaffinch," he answered. "That is the male."

"How many things you know about the woods," I praised.

"Many hours of my boyhood were spent in the forests of Kilton; there and on the water," he replied.

This was the first time he had spoken of his home, so I went on, "There are lakes there, too?"

"The biggest lake of all: the sea is there. Our hall is built hard up against it, for it sits upon a cliff, and its waters foam far beneath us."

I looked around at the dark greens and browns of the forest and tried to picture this. "I have never seen the sea," I admitted. The moment I said this I realised that he would never see it again, either, and I felt abashed at my careless words. But he did not remark at this, or show by any sign what he might be thinking.

For supper we ate the last of our boiled eggs and the partridges. Now we had naught but bread and cheeses and a few dried apples. I found something that looked like lamb's lettuce, for the horses went to it at once and tore it by the roots to enjoy all of it. I nibbled on a leaf and added a handful of it to the water I boiled the partridges in.

As we ate a few rain drops began to fall, and as they gained in strength we moved away from the fire circle I had built to the shelter of the trees. We sat cross-legged upon our sheepskins under hides we had laced to the tree boughs, and between the overhanging leaves and the hides themselves were safe from all wet.

The fire sputtered and spat as it was pelted by the rain, but our food was hot and I had poured the morning's broth into the jugs already. The smell of the damp wood smoke mingled with the rising smells of the wet trees and forest floor, and it was rich and pleasant to the nose, full of Spring and new life.

"Tell me of your father," said Gyric, when we had finished with our meal and sat listening to the pattering of the rain through the leaves above us.

His question surprised me; my thoughts were far from my home. "His name was Cerd. He was ealdorman of the shire of Dee, from the river's border to the Northly Road," I began.

"So he was one of Burgred's picked men," replied Gyric.

I had not really thought of my father like this, but it must be true. "Yes, tho' I myself have never seen the King," I answered. "My father died before I was born, defending the hall he had built in the Kingdom of Gwynedd. His brother Cedd became ealdorman, and due to the fierceness of the Welsh he did not try to reclaim my father's lands, but contented himself with his own holdings East of the river."

"And you had no brother or sister?"

"That is right. I was alone, and Cedd had no children, so he took me as his daughter, and I lived with him in his timber hall." This brought a smile of pleasure to my lips, and I think, into my voice.

"So Cedd took you as his own. How did you come then to live with churchmen?"

"Cedd died, and his lands were taken by the Priory to be Bookland," I answered simply.

"Bookland? How could that happen when he had left you as his heir?"

I felt confused, and answered, "I do not know, but the Prior appealed to the King and had the lands made Bookland for the upkeep of the Priory."

"And this was not the wish of your kinsman?"

"I am sure it was not Cedd's wish; it was the wish of the Prior."

"That is wrong. Without a brother or other kinsmen, the hall and land should have fallen to you. Your father and his brother both were ealdorman, and you their only issue. You were cheated out of your inheritance." He said this with something like heat in his voice, and I could only blink my surprise.

"What happened to the ceorls and your slaves, and the hall?" he asked next.

"I do not remember. The ceorls and slaves went away, somehow. The hall," I recalled with real sorrow, "was turned into a granary by the Prior."

"That is bad, very bad. The men were left Lordless, which should never happen. And all the wealth in the slaves went to someone else." He was silent, as if thinking on all this, and then said, "If there is peace again perhaps you can appeal to Burgred." He shook his head. "It will be hard to have your land made Folkland again, and given back to you; but since you will pay far more taxes on it than the Prior does as Bookland Burgred may be ready to listen. He needs all the tribute he can gather."

He thought a moment longer and then added, "At least the Prior should be made to pay you for what he took from you."

I knew not what to say. "Our shire is a poor one," I said at last, "and the Priory poor also. The Prior always seemed to give his silver away, to the relief of the poor, or in buying and freeing slaves. I do not know how he could pay me."

"He has no right to do good works with moneys he has stolen from a maid," Gyric countered. He turned his head to me and asked, "You were a child when this happened?"

"Yes. I lived then at the Priory, and was baptised."

"Baptised? You were heathen?" His voice held real surprise.

"Yes. Me, and Cedd, and Cerd, too."

"No wonder he took your lands. He felt he had the right to."

I thought of all this, and then said, "If it was wrong to do it if I was Christian, it was wrong to do it with my being heathen too."

He gave a sound almost like a snort, and nodded his head. "Yes, that is just, but that is not the way things work. You had no standing, or property to protect, in the eyes of the Church."

I was not going to say the Church was wrong, so I said nothing.

Gyric went on to something else. "What did you do at the Priory? You did not take the veil, and you are well old enough to have wed."

"That is right. Since I wanted neither there was no place for me, so I left to seek a station with a noble family."

"The daughter of an ealdorman should not need to seek such a station, unless it is out of love."

"It was out of love, for when I met Ælfwyn she treated me with naught but goodness, like her own sister." I felt a rush of sadness, remembering all this. Gyric too turned his face down.

His voice was low. "What did you do together?"

"We would spin, and weave, and all the common things such as that; and ride out for pleasure, and talk, and sing together. Also I was teaching her to write, so that she might send her own letter to her parents."

He lifted his head to me. "You yourself can write?"

"Yes, and read, too, both of our own tongue, and some of Latin. It is the great gift that the Prior gave me." I began to ask a stupid question, but stopped myself in time.

"I know of few women, other than my mother, who read and write," continued Gyric.

This interested me greatly, for the only women I had heard of who had these arts were those of high rank who had taken the veil. "Your own mother reads, and writes, too?" I began to think of how much I should like to meet this woman.

"Yes. She taught us both – my brother and I."

Gyric's voice had changed; the tone had lowered, and I knew he thought again of what he had lost. I did not want him to sink in despair after all we had spoken of. He held a short stick in his hand, and with it traced a random design in the fleece he sat upon.

I decided to say something bold, and try to continue our speech on this topic. "Have you then books of your own? It is good even to be read to."

"At Kilton we have many books," he said, but with no gladness in the owning of them.

"Many?" I could not help echoing. I almost added, 'I should like to see them,' but it was too bold a thing to ask. It made me remember that I did not know exactly how he expected to return home. I wondered if when we got to Wessex he might find some man to travel the rest of the way with him. After all, he had never really agreed to my going the whole journey with him. Perhaps he might even ask me to leave him when we were safely past the border and into Mercia, since it was my home country. These thoughts flooded into my breast and troubled me greatly.

He said no more, and I sat alone with my uncertainty. The rain had lessened a bit, and after a time I roused myself and thought to stand up and stretch before I lay down for the night.

"Are you going far?" asked Gyric, raising his face to me.

"Only to check on the horses. They are quite close to us, but the rain makes it dark." I thought he might need to relieve himself and said, "Do you want to walk with me?"

He nodded his head and scrambled to his feet. The roof of our hide shelter was low and he had trouble clearing it. I took his hand and we stepped into the small grassy clearing. I led him to a few trees on the other side of it. The ground was sopping wet and I felt it almost at once through my thin boots.

I put his hand on a tree trunk and said, "I will be back when you call for me."

I went over to the dark forms of our horses, speaking to them as I approached. They were standing together, dozing, and my mare had her head nestled up against the mane of the gelding.

As I stood there looking at the horses I heard the cracking of branches and a low, angry cry. I turned and hurried to where I had left Gyric, and found him a few feet away, on one knee, grasping his other shin in his clasped hands. He had tripped over a low-laying tangle of shrubby growth, and one foot still lay caught in it.

"Are you all right?" I cried out. I knelt down next to him, and tried to lift his hands from his leg.

He pushed me away. In the set of his mouth there was frustration and anger beyond whatever hurt his leg had received. His chin was held low. He was wet from his fall, and the linen wrap about his wound was twisted up to show the burn upon his temple. I said nothing more, but just knelt there next to him. He made a sound, and then I saw his shoulders begin to tremble. He let his hands fall from his shin and his whole body shook as a strangled sob broke from his lips.

He put both his hands on his face and choked out, "I cannot even cry anymore." He made a terrible sound, almost like laughter, but the laughter of the mad, or the damned.

And hearing him say this, that with his lost eyes were also lost his tears, made my own eyes well up.

I could speak no words of comfort, except to say his name. I touched his shoulder, and tho' he did not pull away, I felt I was unwelcome, and drew back. He needs must grieve, and I must let him.

He moved, and tried to stand again, and I was quick to pull his foot free from the tangle which had tripped him. He put his hand out, and I placed it on my arm, and guided him back to our hide shelter. He lay down without a word, and pulled his mantle about him; and I too lay down in the wet darkness, waiting for sleep which took a long time to come.

WHAT WE HAD TO DO

THE morning was bleak, within and without. Gyric was sunk in despair. He scarce spoke a word to me and my own fears and worries about what would happen to us grew silently in my breast. To add to the discomfort we felt from the wet, I could not get our fire started again, for a drizzle fell steadily upon us.

It made no good sense to try and travel when the skies were obscured with thick clouds and the Sun could not guide us. So we sat silent and damp beneath our hide shelter. I began to really wonder if Gyric would not dismiss me if and when we reached the borders of Mercia. I had no idea what I would do if he did. I did not believe I could find my way safely back to Four Stones alone, even with the fast mare I now rode, for too many Danes would be abroad. Perhaps he would counsel me to return to my first home. But I did not want to return to the small village by the marshes of the Dee: I felt no call to the land there. Such were my thoughts as I sat hunched under my deer hide, trying as best as I could to stay dry.

Only our horses seemed to welcome the rest. My mare rolled over and over in the wet grass and was playful with the gelding, nipping at his hocks and tempting him to chase her. Watching them I marvelled at how blest animals were to be free from the concerns that troubled our own heads. I recalled the Browny, curled up snug and happy upon Burginde's bed and purring, as we three women suffered with our fears around her.

And this thought – of my lost life with Ælfwyn and Burginde, and of the comforts and concerns we had shared in our narrow chamber – broke through my silent sorrow at last. It seemed that our lives then had been happy indeed, or at least, full of hope and content. The threat of war had troubled us, and the usage of the folk of Lindisse at the hands of the Danes was a constant reminder of the cruelty that might soon visit other parts; but I could say in truth that Yrling was a far better man than we had hoped. Ælfwyn had reason to care for him, and these reasons went beyond the gold and silver treasure he had given her. Just a few days ago I had thought I would spend my life with Ælfwyn, at Four Stones or wherever Yrling might take her, and this thought troubled me not; for I felt that Ælfwyn might have some great and good effect on him. She had already accomplished much, and was growing, day by day, in wisdom and in cleverness, so that she might procure the most bounty for her new people.

So much had changed when old Dobbe haltingly told us of the prisoner below the hall. The image of me in the damp cellar turning Gyric's face toward the flickering torch rose up in my eyes. Beyond my first horror was my desire, far stronger than all else, that he might be delivered from that place. Now Gyric lived, and I had not tried to see beyond this first goal when I carried him from Four Stones. Gyric lived, but he lived in misery.

I sat hunched under the sopping deer hide, and as the rain redoubled its fall above us, I began to weep. I folded my arms around my knees and lay my head upon my damp sleeves, and my tears rolled down from my cheeks and slipped through my fingers into the wet wool of my gown.

"Why do you cry?" asked Gyric in a low voice.

I did not turn my head to look at him, but sobbed out my answer. "Because you are so miserable."

He did not answer, but his question stopped my weeping. I wiped my face and turned to look at him. He was sitting just an arm's length away from me, but it seemed a gulf of a thousand miles. He was cross-legged, and his right hand rested on the hilt of the shining seax. "I am not what I was," he said, and tho' his face looked set and steady, his words came haltingly.

"Many men are wounded in battle," I said, trying not to snuffle.

His answer was swift and violent. "This was not battle. I was taken, bound, from a tent in the middle of the night to the cook fire, where a poker was rammed into my eyes!"

This recollection, vivid in its horror, brought fresh tears to my eyes. Gyric sat rigid and taut as I watched his knuckles grow white gripping his seax hilt.

"It was an act of treachery," I choked out.

"Why did they not kill me?" he asked, raising his face to the wet heavens. "They have left me worse than dead. That is what they wanted. To make me a loathsome, creeping thing, a worm upon the ground. That is all I am now!"

"Do not say that!" I answered. "I did not bring you out of that hole at Four Stones for that! You are a man. You have been wounded, cruelly, but you will always be a man. You are alive; that is what matters."

"You did not know me before. All you can see is this – crippled thing that I am now."

"You are right, I did not know you. I can only know you from the first time I saw you, and that was at Four Stones. When I saw what they had done to you my whole heart moved within me, but not for one moment did I have any thought but to carry you away from that place that you might live."

He jerked his head and gave a snort. "Yes, a maid of sixteen carries me away!"

I nearly spat out my next words. "Should I have left you to die?"

The anger in this question made him stop, and then he slowly turned his face to me.

When he spoke again, his voice was low. "You risked your life to save mine."

"Yes, and I would do it again. But to hear you regard your own life so low is to regard mine as nothing."

He gave a sudden exhalation of breath, and his shoulders slumped. He let go of his seax and touched both hands to his brow. "I owe you everything. That is what is so hard for me. From now on I must only take."

My heart was full, and I tried to speak all I felt within me. "That is not true. I know you were a warrior, but a man is more than his sword. Your father and mother, and your brother, they will rejoice to hear that you live. It will be as if you returned from the grave to them. They will sorrow at your wound, but will rejoice that you still walk the Earth."

He gave a small cry of anguish which showed me again how hard it was for him to think on his homecoming. This gave rise to a new thought, and he uttered the next words as an oath. "They will be made to pay! Far beyond my wer-gild, they will be made to pay. My father and brother will not rest until they slit the throat of he who did this."

There was nothing to say to this, for I knew it was true. The lust for vengeance would be strong indeed, for Gyric was not only the son of a powerful Lord but an atheling to the King. I gave a sigh, wondering silently how many men would die as a result of Hingvar's act of spite against his brother.

Gyric's thought had moved on, and he spoke with new force. "It was stupid of me to have been captured. I almost let them."

"Let them?" I asked. He had never before spoken of the battle.

"Yes. Ælfred and I were fighting shield-to-shield. He was not strong that day, but weak from loss of blood from his illness. The fighting had gotten too hot, and I seized the dragon banner from Ælfred, so that the Danes would think I was the brother of Æthelred. He is my size and there is a likeness between us. I broke off from him, and it worked: the Danes pursued me, and Ælfred's other men closed up around him. So I was captured with some com-panions, and the Danes thought for two days that they had Ælfred himself."

"So because of your likeness, the Danes mistook you?"

I knew also that Gyric was very rich, and that the arms and ring tunic and jewellery and clothes of him would be of equal fineness to that a prince would wear.

"Yes, that and because I carried the dragon standard of Wessex. Ælfred always carried it for his brother." The next question was asked softly, as to himself. "Who will carry it for Ælfred now that he himself is King?"

I thought on all this, and then said, "It is likely you saved the life of Ælfred." He did not answer, but my thoughts continued to their end. "And since Æthelred was soon to die, in saving Ælfred you saved the life of a King."

He shrugged. "No man can predict how any battle will turn."

He was quiet for a moment, remembering, for he went on, "We fought shield-to-shield many times since we were boys, and many times shared the battle-gain. Now I am useless to him."

I saw the anger rising again in him, and he went on, "Christ blind Hingvar! He and his men will be made to pay."

His anger was hard for me to watch, as just as it was. But since it was his due, I would not try to turn him from it. "Hingvar has many enemies, both Saxon and Dane," I said.

Gyric spoke through gritted teeth. "I pray it is the hand of a man of Kilton who robs him of his life."

There was nothing I could say. He too, was still, and we sat with only the sounds of the dripping trees as answer.

Then he turned his head to me and asked, "You know all these things because Yrling told them to you?"

"Yes," I slowly said, "not Yrling so much, for he was away much of the time and does not speak our tongue as well as – his nephews."

He gave a snort and tossed his head. "So the young bucks were clustered around you, filled with stories, boasting of their skills."

"Not quite like that," I stammered. "One of them I did not like at all, and scarcely ever spoke to; and by the end he did not like me either."

He inclined his head, and his voice was low, and I thought, tinged with disgust. "And the other? The one who gave you your mare?"

I was surprised he recalled where my mare had come from, for it was amongst the first things we spoke of when he awakened in Gwenyth's camp. It made me slightly uneasy that his memory was so sharp, and that such a thing would stick in his mind.

"The other would speak to me," I admitted. "We tried to learn things from him, Ælfwyn and I, because he was easy to speak to and treated us well." I felt as if I was defending myself, and I did not know why I should.

"And he gave you gifts."

"Yes," I answered slowly. "The mare was, of course, the greatest of them."

"What is his name?" he asked, steadily.

I did not want to answer, but I did. "His name is Sidroc." I took a long breath and added, "He counselled Yrling against getting involved with Hingvar or his brother." I thought to add, "And Yrling had no part in what Hingvar did. He was, as I have said, very angry."

His voice was reckless with his own anger. "You do not have to defend them to me. If I could I would kill either one of them in an instant."

Perhaps he said this because they were Danes, and more so because Yrling had accepted him and thrust him into the cellars of Four Stones to die. And perhaps he said it also because Yrling had taken the woman he loved from him.

"I am not defending them," I replied, but I knew there was no strength in my voice. "But I chose to be with Ælfwyn, and she had no choice but to go to Four Stones."

I felt some sense of injustice stirring within me. "It is not our fault," I began, not feeling really clear myself of what I was speaking of. "I mean what they – the Danes – do. Ælfwyn has given up so much to try and save her people at Cirenceaster." I did not think I needed to remind Gyric that the chiefest thing she surrendered was her hopes of being wed to him. "And she has worked hard to help the folk of Lindisse. Her father and grandsire ordained this thing. It was in no way her desire; you above all should know this. Having made this sacrifice to go, what should she do? Treat the Dane and his kin with disdain?" I felt close to tears now. "You do not know what she suffered."

He did not answer. It must be hard for him to hear me speak of suffering, I thought. But I said to end, "She did what she had to do."

Perhaps my earnest tone made him turn his face to me. He nodded his head wordlessly.

YOU HAVE
NOT SEEN US

T HE Sun dawned upon us, streaming its rays across the little clearing in which we were camped. We ate, and I began to pack up. Gyric spent some time smoothing and rolling up our sheepskins, and securing them with leathern cords. He moved slowly and cautiously in doing these things. I felt real gladness in watching him, and I wanted to praise him; but I made as little comment as if he were whole and did these things, for I did not wish to embarrass him.

We were nearly packed, and I was over saddling my mare when a sound from the trees before me made me stop. I caught a glimpse of a small, dark animal, and then a much larger, lighter form. My mare whinnied as a squat black piglet darted from the edges of the trees. Just behind it was an old woman, bearing a stick and a limp tie which had clearly slipped from the iron ring in the piglet's nose.

The woman started in fear as she caught sight of me, and flailed at the piglet in an attempt to drive it away. "Dame," I called out. "I will not harm you." I turned to look at Gyric. He was standing by the trees we had slept under, grasping his spear in one hand and his drawn seax in another.

The piglet had frozen when it had reached the open grass, and the woman bent down and slipped her rope through the creature's nose ring. Her eyes went uneasily from me to where Gyric stood. I spoke again, as much to reassure him as the old woman. "Do not fear us, woman," I repeated. Her watery eyes looked strangely wide in her thin and wrinkled face. "We will not harm you. We are seeking to purchase food, if you have any to spare."

She did not answer, and I said, "Is your home near here?"

Again she did not respond. "We will not harm you. We will pay you for food," I said once more.

"In silver?" she asked. Tho' her form was slight, her voice was harsh.

"Yes, in silver," I answered, glad for any response.

"We have food," she said, just as harshly.

I grew cautious, and wondered who she spoke of. "Where do you live, and with whom?" I asked, trying to make my question a command.

She blinked but answered readily enough. "Only at the next stream branch; 'tis a short walk. I bide with my husband, and my son's wife, and my son's children."

I nodded my head, and thought to go and ask counsel of Gyric. "Stay here while I speak to my brother," I said to her.

I approached Gyric, and he shifted uneasily from foot to foot as I came up to him.

"Gyric," I began in a low voice, "Did you hear all? This is an old woman, a wood-cutter's wife perhaps."

"I heard," he replied. He said no more.

"Shall I go with her and buy food? She says it is not far." I looked back to where she stood, gaping squint-eyed at us. "I think she can be trusted."

"Yes, go," he answered. Of a sudden he said, "Do not leave me here."

I touched his wrist. I saw at once how terrible it would be to be left alone, waiting for me to return.

Before I could speak he said, "We will go together."

"Yes, yes," I agreed. "The horses are nearly ready."

He put away his seax and then said, "Say no more than you need to. Do not go too near her dwelling place, or get far from your mare. If anything happens, recall what I told you. Try to get away. Your mare is fast."

"Nothing will happen," I said, fearful at his fear. The woman watched us without speaking as we finished preparing our packs. She drew the tattered tie which held her piglet closer to her. She had much more to fear from us, I thought, than we did from her.

"Lead on," I said to her, trying to sound like Ælfwyn speaking to a village woman.

She walked quickly out of the clearing, staying close to the creek bed, pulling the piglet behind her. I walked our horses in the water, looking ahead as far as I could. The creek led past an open space, showing signs of having been but recently cleared. In it was a large but rude hut, surrounded by a wall of river stones rolled into place and topped with stakes of wood. Working in the croft were two figures, as shabby as the old woman herself. One was an old man, her husband, no doubt; and the other a woman.

They stopped their hoeing as they saw us, and the old woman went to them, pushing through a wattle gate and tying the piglet to the open door of the hut. I reined our horses in and spoke to Gyric in a low voice, telling him all that was before us. As we waited there, two girl children came around from the back of the hut and stared at us across the low fence.

The second woman came forward, wiping her hands on her apron. She was young and rather comely, but her eyes had a quick roving quality that made me look about us. I moved my mare so that I was well in front of Gyric. The woman did not speak, but nodded at me in greeting.

"We are seeking food," I began, trying to keep my voice steady and calm. "We will pay in silver for what you can spare."

"We have grain, wheat and barley both," she answered. Her eyes were everywhere: on my gown, my mantle, our horses, and most of all, I thought, resting on the face of Gyric, with its linen wrap over the eyes.

"That is good," I said. I looked at a few hens scratching in the grit at the hut's door. "And have you also eggs?"

"We have many eggs, Lady," she answered.

"And have you any meat?"

Her eyes darted back to mine, and then she admitted, "Stag meat, smoked."

"Good. Do you go and boil a score of eggs, and we will take them, and a haunch or equal of your smoked deer, and a measure of wheat, and a measure of barley."

"As you wish, Lady," she replied. She turned her back on us, and went about gathering that which I had asked for. I edged my mare back to Gyric and spoke to him.

"They live here alone, one hut only. They are not charcoal-burners or wood-cutters, from the looks of things. I do not understand it," I told him, looking at the tiny farmstead.

"Likely they are outlaws," replied Gyric. I started a bit, but he went on, "The son she did not mention may live, and the whole family of them be in hiding here."

I looked again at the hut. "That would explain the newness of things. The hut and wall look fresh."

"Like as not the son is about; be wary," warned Gyric in a low voice.

I turned and scanned the circle of stone again. The old man worked alone in his row of beans. The woman had disappeared into the hut. Now she came forth carrying a large chunk of dried meat, through which the bone rose. The old woman stood at the cooking pot, and the two children were running to her from around the back of the hut, their little hands clutching eggs.

"I see no sign of a man, save the old one," I told Gyric. "But I will watch the hut door carefully."

My eyes roamed from the door to the crops rising from the dark soil of the croft. "Peas," I said, not able to quell my excitement.

I called over to the young woman, "Have you peas to spare? We will have them if you do."

She nodded her head and set the two girls to work gathering the pods.

"Gyric, we will have fresh peas," I breathed, my mouth watering at the thought.

For answer he said, "Keep wary."

I drew myself up and watched all around us with care. The young woman came to us and took up the smoked stag haunch, a knife in her hand. She shaved off a sliver which she handed to me. I tasted it, rich and smoky and savoury, and said, "It is good."

I unlashed our empty food bag and gave it to her, and she knelt upon the ground and fitted the huge joint into it. The old woman came forth with two small sacks with drawstring ties. She pulled them open before me that I might look within. One held kernels of golden wheat, and the second tiny pearls of winter barley.

The eggs were cooked and fished out of the cauldron and tied into a rope net. The young woman held the eggs before me, that I might see them, and then lowered them into our food bag.

Lastly the children came forth, their aprons overflowing with bright green pea pods. These they dropped into the bag, and the young and old women both lifted it, and with them holding it steady I turned in my saddle and tied it through the iron saddle rings.

"I thank you for your help," I said. I reached in the black pouch at my waist and drew forth a piece of silver.

The old woman came to me, eyes glinting, and I handed the coin to her. She clasped it tightly in her brown fist, and grinned in satisfaction.

I looked down upon them and in parting said, "You have not seen us."

The young woman looked up at me and returned, "You have not seen us, Lady."

I nodded at her, and turned our horses back along the stream bed to our creek.

"You did well," Gyric said to me when we were away.

This praise made me blush; I felt the warmth on my cheek. I recalled the way the younger woman and I had eyed each other. "You must have been right about them being outlaws. Each of us wanted to know the other's story, but neither of us would ask."

"No one must know our story," said Gyric.

"Of course not," I returned.

He gave a sound almost like a laugh. "You said I was your brother. You think quickly."

"I did not want to say your name, and it was the first thing I could think of," I explained

The morning Sun felt delicious against my back, and now that we had provisions for many days the fear of our going hungry vanished like the dew drops on the grasses we walked through. We rounded a bend in the creek, and in a clearing to one side grew a copper beech, alone and majestic, standing out in front of the larch and maple trees like a queen before her court. Her unfolding leaves were tinged with gold and green and seemed to beckon to me.

"I want to stop a moment," I said to Gyric.

I slipped off my mare and dug in the food bag until my hand touched the netting which held the eggs. They were still hot to the touch, and I pulled one of them through the mesh. I went to the base of the copper beech and lay the egg in the great swelling fingers of its roots. I touched my lips to the silvery bark of the trunk.

I turned back to our horses. Gyric was sitting attentively on his gelding, his face turned directly towards me. I wondered for one moment if I would have done this thing if he were sighted. I wondered next if I should tell him what I had done. I thought I could guess what he thought of the worshipers of the Old Gods: That heathens were savages. He might feel shock or surprise or perhaps amusement, and I did not want my gift to give rise to any of these thoughts in him.

Then I felt a twinge for having given as an Offering one of our precious eggs. They belonged to both of us, and I should not surrender one without Gyric knowing of it. I shook my head to myself, and said inwardly, That is my egg for today. So in the end I said nothing.

We rode on, and the day was kind to us, filled with light breezes and true warmth. Along the way we stopped as I spotted dock and sorrel and the broad leaves of plantain beneath our horse's hooves. I gathered their fresh new leaves, remarking more than once to Gyric, "We shall feast today!"

My heart felt light as we travelled on. We had had no sign of anyone following us; we had safely procured food in abundance; and we made, I thought, good progress on our way. These things seemed much to be grateful for, but as I spoke to him of all this he made but little answer.

That night when we camped I worked up the feast I had promised. I boiled the peas and we ate them first, sweet as honey. The dock and sorrel and plantain leaves I stewed with shreds of the smoked stag, and made broth which I bottled in our jugs for the morrow. I added barley to what remained and boiled it until we had a thick browis. I sprinkled upon it a bit of salt from my twist, and it made a dish fit for those in a timber hall.

Gyric ate of all this, and had an egg also, so he ate more that night than he had ever before on our journeying; but tho' he praised the food, he did not eat with relish. I watched him as he ate, and saw that the sadness in him made the savour of all good things pale.

THE WORK
OF MY HANDS

THE next day the creek that we were following dipped down into a sort of ravine. We reached the bottom, and found that it vanished in a boggy pool. We climbed the side of the ravine and stepped out of a line of scrubby trees.

"O," I said, all in surprise. A road, empty of all travellers, lay before us in the narrow clearing. "Here is a Cæsar's Road, Gyric, for it is made of cut stones, dressed so they fit together."

"Cross it, quick," he directed.

I took another look up and down and then pulled him and the horses across. We entered the trees on the other side, and went not far before we heard our creek burble up again. We stopped and stood side by side on the mossy edge of it.

"I wonder if that is the same road that Ælfwyn's waggons travelled," I said. "I did not recognise it, but the trees were thick about it, with no landmarks."

"This is the fifth day since we started," he recalled. "As slow as we have travelled, we could not have gone far South. Likely it is the same road."

"Do you think we are still in Lindisse?" I asked. It was strange, looking around at the trees, to think we were anywhere other than a peaceful woods.

"I think we are, yes."

I had a new thought. "How will we know when we reach Mercia?"

"We will have to ask, when we find someone safe. The borders will not be patrolled. Besides," he added, "they keep changing."

"So you think there is war right now?" I asked. The Sun was dappling through the branches over our heads, and the air was sweet with bird song. War was hard to think of.

"I know it. We must expect war all along the Eastern edges of Mercia, and the Northern edges of Wessex."

"I know it, too," I admitted, remembering the streams of horsemen who had passed through Four Stones on their way South. The faces that filled the hall each night at Four Stones came before my eyes. "They think they will win, Gyric," I began, "and all of Wessex and Mercia be taken by them, just as they have taken Lindisse and Northumbria and Anglia."

He considered this for a moment, then spoke with a grim voice. "All warriors think they will win. You cannot fight if you do not."

"Burgred's army is great, is it not?" I asked. "And the army of Ælfred, it is greater still?"

"King Burgred has troubles within his own country, just as Ælfred has them in his. Ealdormen and rich thegns try to make a separate peace with one Dane or another, and do not answer the call of the King. Or they themselves wish to be King, and grudge that the Witan chose another."

"A separate peace – that is what Ælfsige did," I murmured. "He tried to make a peace with Yrling, and sent some of his thegns in place of himself and his best men to Æthelred."

"Yes," answered Gyric with bitterness. "He sold away what was most dear to him; gave away his greatest treasures, and now the Danes will raven at what remains."

He fell quiet, and I stood by his side as our horses snapped off tender branch tips in their reach. When Gyric spoke again, his voice was clear. "I heard the treasure he sent was great. Yrling will only use it to arm his men against us."

"It was a great treasure," I answered softly. "But the riches Yrling keeps in his hall is greater still. Swords and spears and fur pelts of splendid beasts, and ring shirts and helmets."

"Saxon booty," snorted Gyric.

"Yes, Saxon; and stuffs from the lands of the Franks, and silks and oils from the farthest points of the East, and gold and silver arm-rings and bracelets and rings and pins from every land."

"And are they generous with it?" he wanted to know. His voice was filled with disdain.

"Yes," I answered, feeling ashamed to have had any part of it. "They are generous."

I felt badly now, and said nothing more. He must have sensed my thought, for he said, "Their generosity gave you a good horse, and you have used it against them. That is what matters."

I felt even worse now, for I saw again the face of Sidroc as he drew close to me in the bustling keep yard when I asked him to take my mare and breed her to his stallion. I had deceived him – betrayed him, in a way – leaving only the bracelet of heavy silver to ask pardon for me. My hand closed over my bare wrist which had borne that bracelet, and I know I sighed in my shame.

Gyric moved his head, and asked in a low voice, "What troubles you?"

"Nothing," I lied. His mouth moved, and I knew this answer would not suffice. "I am only remembering, that is all."

"Did he love you?" he asked. "Yrling's kinsman, Sidroc?" The words were simply spoken, but they jolted me.

"I do not know."

"But he wanted you."

"He wished to wed me," was all I could answer.

"Would you, if you had stayed?"

"I did not stay."

My mare came up beside me and bumped me on the shoulder. I cupped my hand on her downy muzzle and moved a little away with her. I did not want to speak of these things, and I did not want to hear Gyric ask of them. There was an edge in his voice, an edge of anger or of bitterness.

"Does Ælfwyn know happiness?" he asked. His voice was barely above a whisper.

I turned on him. "No, she is not happy. She was forced by her father to leave her home and travel far to marry a man who is a great enemy to her people. She did this loving another man – you. None of this was her choice, but she went, for the good of Cirenceaster. Now she knows there will be war anyway, and she thinks the Peace her father made will be worthless. Then to add to her trouble, she finds that you are held a prisoner at Four Stones. She risked her life, far more than I did, in every way that she helped you; for her husband would have rightly slayed her if she had been caught. Then I had to tell her that you had been wounded. I thought her grief would kill her. Now she has had to stay behind, begging the men of Four Stones not to pursue us. She has to protect not only herself, but all those who aided us in our escape, lest their part be found out. She does not know how we fare, or even if you live, and we cannot imagine the sorrow or danger she herself may be in. No, I do not think she is happy."

I felt each of my words must have fallen like blows upon Gyric's head, but I spoke the truth, and he must hear it.

At last he answered, with another question. "Yet you said Yrling is good to her?"

"Yes, he is. He has been kind to her, has given her many freedoms and listens to her speech at table. He is a far better man than he could be."

I thought of how the lot of the folk of Lindisse had improved since Ælfwyn's coming. "She is raising the villagers from wretchedness to hope again. She has brought back the men of the village who were in hiding, has had seed grain brought from Jorvik so that the fields are again being tilled, and has started up a flock of sheep so that both hall and village might be clothed. She has done all of this for a place she never wished to see."

He did not say more, tho' from the way he held his head I felt he listened well. We had stood still for many

minutes, and were not far from the road; we must go
deeper into the trees.

I looked about us, gauging what we should do. The
creek on this side of the ridge was narrower and more
twisted, and the ground more uneven.

"I think you should ride, while I lead our horses. The
way is rough with tree roots and stones," I told him.

He swung his head as if roused from a dream. "I want
to walk," he answered.

"It is hard walking, even for me," I reasoned. "Riding
will be faster; and safer, too, if you duck down when I tell
you to."

I knew he did not like to ride while I led our horses;
he wanted either to walk with me or for both of us to ride.
I could only guess that being led while I walked made him
feel more helpless than when we both rode, even tho' in
both instances the reins of his gelding were tied to the
saddle rings of my mare.

He turned and felt for the ties on his saddle, and
began with no further word to lash his spear. He pulled
himself up upon his horse.

We did not make fast progress that afternoon, for the
creek led us through ground that heaved with stones. I
began to look for a place to spend the night earlier than
usual, for I wanted to use what daylight we still had to sew.
Also, the slow speed of our advance was wearing on both
of us. My feet were sore through my thin-soled boots, and
Gyric was tired of being told to lean over his horse's neck
to avoid being hit by a leafy bough.

I found a bit of a glade, with enough grass in it to support our horses for the night, and with an alcove of rock
hard by the creek to hold our fire. When we had unsaddled

the horses and unpacked our kit I began gathering dead wood so I might have plenty for our fire. The sky above the trees was clear and just beginning to fade of its colour.

I set and lit our fire, and filled our small cauldron with water. Then I rummaged in my satchel and pulled out my sewing kit, the beautiful pair of shears Ælfwyn had put in, and one of my fine linen head wraps.

Gyric lay back upon the ground, bolstered by his saddle, and I sat cross-legged upon my sheepskin nearby. I fingered the wrap I had taken out, knowing by the fineness of the thread that it must be one that Burginde had spun for. The thought of her plump plain face and ready humour brought a smile to my lips, and a twinge of loss within my breast. I smoothed the head wrap before me, and picked up the sharp shears and cut it in thirds. I threaded up a needle with linen thread, and took one of the new-cut pieces of fabric and folded back a hem, and began my work.

"Is it dark yet?" Gyric asked, as I pulled my needle through the fine linen cloth. He lay tracing the designs on the hilt of his seax with his fingers.

"No, it is far from dark. I wanted to stop because I have things to do which want light. I am sewing now."

"I cannot tell how much time passes," he said slowly. "I thought we had not gone far today."

"I do not think we did, either. Once we crossed the road we went slowly, for the way by the creek was narrow and rooty." I glanced over to the tiny stream of water. "The creek is growing very small, Gyric."

"We have had rare Fortune to follow it so far. Still, we should not want for water, for all courses run at their full now."

I finished my hemming and stood and came over to him. He sat up, and raised his face to me. I knelt by him, hoping I would say the right things. "Gyric," I began, "I have a clean wrap for your wound. It will be less bulky and heavy to wear."

I stopped, for he had stiffened. "Is that what you were working on?" he asked.

"Yes. I think it will give more comfort, and the one you are wearing is now quite soiled."

He put his hand out, and then said, "Thank you. I will use it in the morning."

I did not place it in his hand but went on gently, "Will you not let me look at your wound, Gyric? I would like to know that the flesh is healing."

He put his hand down and pulled his head back. "It is all right," he answered in a short voice.

I sighed, and started again. "I would like to know that it is all right. Please let me check."

He lowered his head, but spoke not.

"You do not have to hide your wound from me," I told him. "I have seen it many times. I was the one who wrapped it first."

His lips parted, and I thought he would at last speak, but he was quiet. He reached up and slowly untied the wrap. It fell into his lap, the barrier gone. He sat with his hands limp at his sides.

"I thank you," I breathed. "I am going to touch your face." I placed my hand on his cheek and gently turned his face towards me. The light was still strong enough for the wound to reveal itself fully to my gaze. I was biting my lip so hard that I feared it would bleed, but I made no sound as I looked upon his empty eyes. The blackened recesses of the sockets were flaking, showing a dark red tissue beneath. Web-like strands of dark matter now shrouded the waxy areas I had first seen. The wound had no odour, nor did it ooze in any place. There was no maggot or louse amongst the scabbing tissue. The burn mark upon his right temple had seared up, and its colour was changing from the black of burnt flesh to that of a flat reddened scar.

I looked long upon his face, and upon that wound, and felt a great steadiness within me as I did. It did not take courage to look upon it, for my fear of it was gone. I saw only his own courage looking back at me as he sat with his unwrapped face lifted to mine.

"The flesh heals well," I finally said. "It does not pain you?"

For reply he shook his head. I took up the new wrap and held it over the wound, tying it in back. When I had done he reached up and re-tied it.

I sat back on my heels. It was not an ordinary wound, which would heal and leave the bearer scarred but no less able. I could not comment that the mass of raw and name-less tissue in the empty sockets was beginning to knit itself together, tho' it was; for what had been the most precious of the senses was now fated to be only a pit of scarred flesh. But still, the wound healed, in its way; and that was solace, at least to me.

"It heals well," I said again. I added, in an uncertain way, "Thank you."

"Why do you thank me?"

"Only because you did not wish to let me see, yet you did."

His voice was so low I could scarce hear him. "How could you bear to look at me?"

This surprised me, for it was so different from my own thoughts. "I look at you all the time. This time, I looked also at your wound. You are not your wound."

He was silent, but a movement of his shoulders told me he listened.

"I will get our supper now," I said, making my voice light.

THICK WOODS
AND LITTLE COMFORT

T HE next two days were a great challenge, for our little creek dove underground and did not come up again where I could find it. This meant that it no longer served as our pathway through the forest, and we needs must walk slowly, zigzagging through the birches and alders. The forest was thick in places, with much under-growth, and our horses could not make their way; and we must circle round to find spots of thinner growth where they could walk through.

Gyric had to spend much of this time on his horse, being slapped by branches as they brushed by him. As for me, my stockings were in tatters, and my hands and wrists covered with scratches from trying to forge a way before us. The russet gown I wore these two days was pulled and snagged so that it aged two years in that time. My head-wrap was pulled off so many times that I at last went bare-headed, with my hair trailing in a braid down my back, rather than let it be torn to shreds by the twigs and brambles that clutched at us from all sides. And my Moonflow came as well, and tho' I was not crampy I felt tired and dull. Burginde had packed for me several wool-filled linen pads and a pair of short drawers, and her foresight in caring for me made me weepy in missing her.

To add to this, to keep close to a southwesterly course was hard for me, for I could scarce see the Sun glinting through the heavy growth of trees. I feared at times that I was leading us in circles, knowing at best that our progress was slow and uneven due to the roughness of the way. I began to yearn to get out of the thick forest.

The following day the ground rose up beneath us, and the fir trees thinned to larches, and there was more Sun and open glades with grass for our horses to graze upon. We stopped for a long time at midday that they might eat. This break refreshed all of us, for Gyric and I sat in the warm Sun as our horses grazed. After we had eaten Gyric lay down in the grass, and I think, even slept.

For the rest of that day the ground rose steadily, as if we were climbing a long, low hill. The welcome Sun was hot upon us, and we rode without our mantles for the first time. A stream, noisy with its Spring fullness, rushed by us as we climbed, so we had much water for our thirsty horses.

We came to a crest on this hill, and after seeing so little of what lay ahead it was a pleasure indeed to stand next my mare and look out. Because I was looking for both of us, I spoke at once, and described to Gyric all that I saw as my eye fell upon it. "There is a plain below, which rolls, with many trees edging it, but not as thick a forest as that we have just passed through."

"What happens to the hill we are on?" Gyric wanted to know.

"It ends. When we ride down to the plain it will be much flatter."

"And the stream?"

I craned my neck to see if I could follow its path. As I looked, a movement far below caught my eye. I caught my breath and quickly turned our horses a few paces back into the shelter of the trees.

Gyric was still mounted, and asked, "What is it?"

I walked back to my vantage point and squatted down upon the ground. "Riders. A whole group of them, on a road I did not see before." I stopped and counted them. "Fifteen, sixteen. Sixteen of them. They are moving away from us, across the plain."

"Danes?"

I strained my eyes, but could learn nothing; they were too far off. "I cannot say . . . they carry no banner." I scanned them again, trying to find some clue. "Now there is a waggon – no, two waggons – just coming into view, behind them."

As I squinted at the waggons, trying to learn more, Gyric asked, "Where is the Sun?"

"To your right."

"And the riders?"

I looked at them as they grew smaller. "They go South," I answered.

Gyric's voice was flat. "Danes."

I stood looking out, watching the mounted figures weaving over the plain on the road below. At times they vanished from view behind trees, to reappear, smaller still, in the distance. The waggons were the last I saw of them. The light tarpaulins shone in the afternoon light for a long time. Two things only were going through my mind: that we had been that close to discovery and death, if they were Danes, or that close to real help, if they had been Saxons.

Gyric did not seem to be thinking of this; or if so, he had dismissed it already and gone on. "There is a road below; now we know that much. We must be wary. Others will be travelling upon it."

I did not like the idea of drawing close to the road, but knew we must. And we would near it at the safest time, for by then others upon it might be stopping for the night. Fortune had been with us to make the riders pass when they did, and warn us of their presence.

We headed down, keeping well within cover of the trees. We were able to stay mounted the whole time, which heartened me, for if anything should happen, I wanted us both to be on horseback so we might flee as quickly as possible. Still, our mood was very different than when we had climbed the hill enjoying the warm Sun on our faces. Gyric rode with his hand upon his seax hilt, and I too could not keep my hand from touching the knife strapped to my own waist.

"We are at the bottom now, Gyric, but I do not know which way lies the road." I said this in a quiet tone, afraid even then we might be near new horsemen.

"Head West. We will cross the road at some point; it does not matter where." His own voice was low, and it had a confidence I welcomed.

The Sun was well behind the trees when I saw a clearing. "It is the road," I told Gyric. "It is not a Cæsar's Road, for it is only of dirt. We will disappear quickly on the other side."

"Be certain we leave no prints," he cautioned. "Drag a leafy branch behind us to be sure."

"I will take you and the horses over first. That way I can do a good job."

We crossed the road and passed into the trees. I slipped off my horse and tied her reins to a bough and cut a small oak branch. I ran over to where we had crossed, and dusted the leaves upon the slight track we had left in the hard clay.

I felt a great sense of relief when I returned to Gyric. The act of finding and crossing the road freed me from some of my fear. One look at Gyric's face told me he did not share my relief. His white brow was furrowed, and his hand still rested upon his sheathed seax.

"It is all right now," I told him, and tried to make cheerful my voice. "We have crossed safely and have left no track."

The tone of his voice told me he was of a sudden sunk in despair. "I am worse than useless," he said.

"Do not say that," I protested, recalling how I relied on his counsel. "It is you who are doing so much of our thinking. You said to head West and we would find the road. We did, and we are across it and safer. And I would not have thought to hide our tracks."

"I am like a piece of baggage," was his reply.

"You are not," I answered, feeling impatient. "You are no more baggage than I."

"You are doing everything."

"I am doing what I can, just as you are."

He did not answer, but turned his face away. I did not know what more I could say. I felt relief at crossing the road, but he felt only grief at what he could no longer do. At that moment I was so unhappy that I nearly began to cry. I did not, for I knew my tears would bring no release, but only make me feel more alone.

We rode on, but did not go far, for the Sun was almost set. I could find no water, but our horses had drunk much during the day, and we had filled both our crockery jugs. We camped where there was much new grass for our horses, but we did not eat as well as they, for I did not build a fire, fearing we were too close to the road.

DANGER MET,
AND BOLDNESS SHOWN

I N the morning a bird awoke me, calling loudly from a
tree above us. I sat up, and heard the bird again, and then
looked over to where Gyric lay. The second call was he himself, for he whistled back to the bird, mimicking its cry perfectly. The bird called again, and then fluttered off.

"Very good," I said, and felt truly glad to see him thus.
"You whistled just like him."

"That is the problem," he answered. "He would not
have flown away if I sounded more like his mate."

So the morning started, and started well, for Gyric
and I spoke of suchlike things as we broke our fast and
readied our horses. Our progress was good in setting out,
for the trees made it possible for us to ride.

Late in the day we came upon another road, or track,
really, for it was so narrow that a large waggon would have
a hard time of it. It was old, and deeply rutted, as tho'
wains had been pulled over it for years and years without
repair. I described this all to Gyric, and since it looked
deserted we decided to ride upon it for awhile, and spare

ourselves and horses the trouble of always going amongst the forest trees.

We had ridden on some good distance and had rounded a bend when two figures suddenly stood up in the road ahead of us.

I reined my mare in at once and turned her slightly so that the gelding would not walk into her. Gyric knew I was startled; he had his hand on the instant upon his seax and bent his head towards me.

"Gyric, there are two men ahead, cottars perhaps. They are very ragged. They stood up in the road when they saw us."

I tried to keep the fear from my voice as I said this, but my fear was real. The men stood staring at us with unblinking eyes. They were in rags, but young, I thought, and able-bodied. At their bare feet lay lumpy sacks the contents of which I could not guess. They might be poor cottars, about to beg food of us; but the way they eyed us and our horses told me they were prepared to take and not to ask.

His voice was low as he asked, "How far away are they?"

I gauged the distance as best I could, not wanting to meet the challenging gaze of the two. "Fifty or sixty paces only. They are staring at us, but not moving."

"Have they weapons of any sort?"

"One has a staff," I breathed back to him.

His words were quick and urgent. "You must pass them so that they are on our right. Do what ever you must, including trampling them, to make certain you pass them on our right. Ride at a fast canter. Do not stop or rein your mare in for any reason. Do you understand?"

"Yes," I whispered, feeling nearly frozen with fear.

"On our right," he repeated. "Now."

I turned the head of my mare back to face the ragged men, shortened her reins in my hand and kicked her sides with both my heels as hard as I had ever done. She took off, and I turned my head for one instant to look back at Gyric. His gelding was nearly over-running my mare, and I caught a glimpse of the unsheathed seax as it gleamed in Gyric's hand, held low and straight out.

Then we were upon the men. They stood to face us squarely in the road, trying to block the way, and both gave a grinning yell as I bore down upon them. I held my mare as well as I could to the far left of the track. The one with the staff was raising it in the air as the other lunged at my mare's bridle. I saw a flash of hands and teeth and then heard a cry and curses; and we were past them, galloping down the track. I turned and saw one of the men on his knees, holding his arm where Gyric had slashed it with his seax. The other stood, shaking his staff at us and uttering oaths, but we galloped on until they were out of sight.

I slowed my mare, and then stopped her, and my chest was heaving in an echo of her own hard breathing. I turned to Gyric as he sat upon his black gelding, his left hand twisted hard into the depths of that glossy mane, his right clutching the bared seax.

I was trembling and light-headed and unable to speak. My throat was choked and bone-dry. A smear of blood filmed the edge of the shining blade of Gyric's seax, and my eyes rested upon it.

"Take us into the woods," he ordered.

"Yes," I answered, scarcely able to form the word. I guided our horses into the trees, and went on a little way until we came to a place large enough to dismount. I slid off my mare. Gyric swung down from his horse and stood, resting one hand on his saddle for balance. The other still held the seax, and I saw his own hand was shaking.

"Are you hurt?" he asked.

"No; one put his hand on my bridle, but then let go."

"That was the one I got."

"Yes, the one that grabbed my bridle; you cut him in the arm or shoulder." Tears started to fill my eyes as I went on, "There is blood on your seax."

He bent to the ground and wiped the blade clean, then stood and slid the seax back into its sheath.

"You are not hurt?" I asked.

He shook his head. "We took a risk riding on the road. It was stupid to take it. I am sorry for it."

I had never heard any man speak like this before. "Do not be sorry," I countered. "I wanted to take the road, too. You kept us from falling into trouble."

"You did your part. You did not flinch or hesitate. Did you almost run them down?"

"Yes, I almost did. They would not move, and then at the last moment they tried to grab the bridle."

"Good. You were very steady."

"I am just thankful my mare did not shy or rear."

"She is steady, too."

I pulled out one of our crockery jugs and pulled the stopper. "Here is water, if you like to drink," I offered.

He took it from my hands and lifted it to his lips. I watched him, remembering his words of praise for my actions, and remembering too his own shaking hand. How difficult and fearful it must be to try to fight an enemy you could not see.

"We are a good team," he said, and handed the jug back. His words were light, but hearing them gave me a great and sudden gladness. I drank some water, and poured a bit of it over my wrists and shook my hands hard to free myself of the last of my fear. Now that the fright was behind us, and we had faced and overcome danger, I felt safe again, and even a bit reckless.

"We are a very good team," I echoed, and almost laughed.

We went on our way picking our path through the trees for what remained of the afternoon. Before the Sun dropped too low we camped where we had both pasturage and plenty of water, for we came upon a little dell with a free flowing stream running through the bottom of it. There was a wealth of dead-wood about, and I collected a huge pile of it, for I wished to take advantage of the warm weather by washing as many of our dirty clothes as I could.

I felt a sense of cheerfulness as I set about this task, laying the fire and filling our small cauldron. The dell was a spot of quiet beauty, bright with the flat green spears of nodding vale-lily. The final rays of the Sun were still lingering in the glade where our horses grazed. Gyric lay back upon his sheepskin, leaning against his saddle.

I plucked a stem of vale-lily and held its tiny white bells to my nose, inhaling the sweet fragrance. "'Where dragons bleed, maidens weep,'" I remembered aloud. Gyric turned his head, and I went to him and lifted the little blossoms to his face.

"Vale-lily," he said, breathing in the scent.

"Yes," I answered. "The whole dell is full of it. Once a dragon bled here."

I looked around us at the mossy rocks, and the slender black birches leading to the stream. The stream was shallow. No dragon could live there, and I could see no cave; but still it was not hard to think that a small dragon would have chosen such a place to live, for they, like men, loved beauty in all things made and natural.

"Do you think dragons still live?" I asked Gyric.

He thought for a moment before he answered. "I do not know. It has been a long time since any one has seen them; at least since my grandsire's day. If they still walk the Earth they must do so in secret."

"Perhaps there is not enough treasure left," I suggested. "So they have gone deep underground with it all, and do not come up so often as they did."

"They will have to hide deep indeed to keep it from the grasp of the Danes," answered Gyric.

This mention of the Danes changed the mood for both of us. Gyric tossed away the stem he held, and I was left remembering the pricked-in design of a dragon that Sidroc bore. The Danes must have dragons in their homeland, too, but I thought about this in silence and said nothing more about it.

The water in the cauldron was beginning to boil. "It is washing-day," I said, trying to reclaim my former good spirits. "The sky is still clear, and I think it will stay so, and be dry. I will wash all your linen tunics, if you will be warm enough in your mantle for the night."

He nodded, and pulled his tunic from over his head. It was the first time I had seen his naked chest and arms since we had left Gwenyth's camp. His skin was very fair, and I saw that all the welts had faded. His red-gold hair fell down upon his bare white shoulders. I could not help but look at him, tho' my cheek flamed; the slenderness and fineness of his body caught and held my eye. Then he pulled his fur-lined mantle around him, and hugged himself as if he were chilled.

"Are you cold?" I asked. He never liked to be very close to the fire, but I went on, "The fire is a good one. Will you sit nearer it?"

"I am not cold," he said.

So he sat there as I gathered up our clothing to be washed. Soon I had fresh cut stakes festooned with leggings, stockings, tunics, shifts, and gowns. These surrounded our fire like dancing wraiths, swaying under their own wet weight.

I re-boiled water to make our morning's broth, and cut slabs of the smoked deer haunch, and brought out eggs, and we ate of this as the darkness began to fall. For drink we had, as always, dippersful of cold water.

"It will be good to have ale again," I said, remembering and missing this staple. I passed the dipper to Gyric and he took it and drank. Then he made me glad by saying, "Kilton is famed for its ale. My mother brought with her a recipe from her family, and from that time our ale has been the best in Wessex, even exceeding that of her home."

He had never boasted of anything before, or even spoken much on any everyday topic. I had been trying to form a picture of the woman who was Gyric's mother; a woman who read and wrote, and provided for the wants of a large and populous hall. And too, she must be beautiful in face and form, or Gyric himself would not possess such beauty.

"I am sure all she does, she does well," I said.

"Yes, that is her; she does all things well, and all men respect her for it."

"Tell me of her," I asked, moving closer, for who would not wish to hear more of a woman who is spoken of in this way? "What is her name, and where did she come from, and tell me of the other things she does well."

"Her name is Modwynn. She is the daughter of Maerwine, who was bailiff of Sceaftesburh. She owns much land in her own right, and brought with her many hundred head of sheep. She is much younger than my father, by nearly a score of years."

"What does she look like?"

He thought a moment. "She is tall, near as tall as my father. She is still straight and slender. She has fine hands."

"Like you," I murmured.

"I have her hands," he admitted with a little shrug.

"And she taught you letters?"

"Yes, me and my brother, and one Summer, Ælfred too."

"She taught the King?"

I thought he almost laughed. "He was not the King then; he was only a boy, as I was."

"So Ælfred lived with you?"

"He stayed with us often, as his father Æthelwulf was King then, and so they travelled about Wessex. He was so much younger than his brothers that he spent much time with us, for his mother Osburh was a friend to my mother as well."

I thought back to what I had heard of Ælfred. "I have heard that the new King is a great scholar."

"That is right. He has been to Rome twice, and would have joined the Church had his brothers lived, and won peace."

"They say he is a fierce fighter, but that he is not well."

"He has an illness that troubles him; it makes him bleed within, and no leech has cured him. When he is ill with it they are certain he is going to die; he can keep no food nor drink within him. Then it will pass, and he is able to rise and even to fight within a day or two."

"He must have great will," I thought aloud.

"Yes; great will, and great faith in God." He added in a sombre voice, "And a great task before him."

We sat, each to our own thoughts. My mind turned back to Kilton.

"Tell me of your father, and of your brother."

"Godwulf is my father. He is ealdorman, and was made such many years ago by Æthelwulf. They fought shield-to-shield for many years, and were brothers to each other in their love. Years ago Godwulf himself could have swayed the Witan and become King, but he had no sons behind him. He had not yet wed my mother, and his first wife had died without issue. He called for Æthelwulf as King, always supporting his claim, for Godwulf knew the work of strengthening Wessex would take more than one man's lifetime. That is the most important thing I can say of Godwulf."

"And your brother?"

"His name is Godwin. He is four years older than I, but some say we are so alike as to be twinned. He is bigger than me, tho'; and a little taller."

I saw that he had real love for this man; there was a softness about his lips that told me so, and his voice spoke also of his love, for it was full of pride. "He is the best fighter I have ever seen; that anyone has seen." Here he stopped, and seemed lost in thought.

"He must be very skilful," I said, hoping to hear more.

"He is, skilful and strong; but most of all he is smart. He is the smartest fighter I have ever seen."

"Did he too fight alongside Ælfred?"

"No; he fought with Æthelred. Æthelred was King, so Godwin fought alongside him; for Godwin will be ealdorman after my father."

"Rank-to-rank," I mused. "So you fought with Ælfred when he was prince, and your brother with the King."

"That is right; for it is fit that men of the first rank fight with the King, and those just behind them with the prince."

"Will he be with Ælfred now?" I wondered.

"I cannot say. Kilton is large and rich, and he and my father have many thegns to command. Godwin may be home now if Ælfred does not need him elsewhere in Wessex."

I sat thinking of all this, and then asked, "Godwin is four years older than you?"

"Yes," he answered, and the gentleness in his voice returned. "But he never treated me like a boy. We were always equals in everything."

"He must be a good man," I said softly.

He nodded his head. "The best. And he is happy in everything. His only grief is that he has no children."

"Surely he has wed by this time?"

"Yes, he has been married for six years, but his wife, tho' a good woman, has given him no son or daughter."

"Perhaps it is not her fault," I offered.

Here Gyric shook his head. "No, for he had a son once, with a village woman; and if she and the babe had not died long ago I know he would have by now brought the boy to the hall to be his son." He shook his head again. "His wife cannot bring forth a live child. They are all born dead, and they have given up trying."

"That is very sad," I answered. "Sad for all of them." I thought of the long lost child, and his dead mother, and asked, "How did his little son die? Of the fever?"

Gyric lowered his face. "Godwin does not even know. He curses himself each day for not caring better for it when it was born. One day he rode through the village and saw the mother and child being laid out for burial. A cottar told him the child caught sick, and then the mother after."

He added, in his brother's defence, "He was young; he did not know enough to care." I said nothing, but he went on. "She was just a village woman. He did not think anything of it."

"Perhaps she loved your brother," I said, making bold to speak for her. "Surely she loved their son."

A shrug of his shoulders was his only answer. He said, "It does not matter now. She was just a village woman, and he gave her silver in exchange for a few nights."

I thought to myself: She paid with her life for those nights, just as Godwin pays with his regrets; but this I did not say. I looked at Gyric and spoke to him very boldly, tho' my voice was soft. "Did you too give silver to village women?"

He turned his face to me, and his mouth opened. I did not know if he was angered by my boldness, but he answered me with something like a laugh. "Yes; once or twice. There were a few who always welcomed the coin."

There was no reason for me to be shamed, but my cheeks were hot. "O," was all I said.

"You are different from other maids," he went on. "You are a surprise in what you say and do. I do not think I have ever met anyone just like you."

"I am too bold," I answered. "I am sorry."

"Your words are sometimes bold, but it is not that." His voice was not unkind, nor did he seem to complain of this fact. "Besides," he went on, "if you were not bold . . ."

His words trailed off, and he did not finish; but I could guess that he meant it was my boldness that had plucked him from the cellars of Four Stones.

FLOWING WATERS

I did not like to leave the mossy dell in the morning. I felt that here a little window had been opened into this silent young man for me. Hearing him speak of his home in Kilton, and of his parents, and most especially of his brother Godwin, made me feel as tho' I could know him, and that he might want to be known. Part of this, I thought, grew out of the fright we had faced on the road. There was now a bond between us, and Gyric's words, "We are a good team," were always in my head. But there was something else about him, and it took me until this morning to know what it was. It was as simple as this: I did not fear Gyric as I feared other men.

I thought about this as I packed up our camp. I had never been treated harshly by any man; but at the same time, the men of equal rank I had known expected me, and all other women, to obey them; and behind that expectation was the threat of harm if you did not. I had never lived as close to any men as I had the Danes, and never had any man desired me as Sidroc had. I had no choice in this; he desired me and had told me many times that I would be his. If I had stayed and wed him, he would have been good to me, better I think than Yrling was to

Ælfwyn. Many times when I had been near Sidroc I felt I was the one who caused him hurt; yet I knew he had no fear of me, while I had much fear of him, despite or because of his desire for me.

With Gyric all this was different; and I searched myself carefully to see if I did not fear him because of his wound, and the limits it put upon him. But it was not his wound, I was sure; nor was it that it had been me who had taken him from Four Stones and perhaps saved his life. It was something else, but I could not easily name it. He said I was different from any other maid, and I thought him to be different from any other man. There was a thoughtfulness about him, and something like real gentleness within him, notwithstanding his flashes of fierce anger and grief. I wondered if the closeness I felt to him was akin to the closeness I would have known with a brother, for even in his anger and grief, there was an ease I felt in being near him.

I had stopped in my work to look at him. He had, as he did each morning, shaken out our sheepskins, and rolled them tightly with the deer hides we used as ground sheets. Now he tied them with leathern cords to our saddles as they lay upon the ground, feeling with his fingers the difference in our two saddles, for the one my mare wore was plain, while his had tooled designs cut into the leather of it. Then he straightened himself and rose, and with his spear in his hand took a few steps.

"Ceridwen? Are you here?"

"Yes, I am here," I answered at once, and I think I startled him by how near I was. I felt a sense of shame to have been watching him as I did, but I could not help it; it gave me pleasure to regard him.

"You are so quiet. I thought you had walked away."

"I am just finishing with our kit," I lied, stuffing things noisily into the bag. "We are ready to saddle the horses now." So we set out, tho' I turned and looked back into the little dell as we rode away.

The Sun was not yet overhead when the trees grew thinner about us. There was no road or track in sight, nor yet sign of settlement, but we stuck close to the line of trees for safety, until there were few indeed to shelter us. Riding in the open gave its own pleasure, tho'; and the noon Sun was hot upon us, and the grass as high as our horses' knees and brilliant green.

"There are no tree stumps. Perhaps it has been pasture land," I said to Gyric, describing the meadow-like plain we walked through.

As soon as I had finished these words I saw where we truly were, for as we rose up upon a little knoll there before us flowed the dark green body of a river, cutting through the bright grass like a huge serpent.

"It is a river, Gyric, a great one, wider far than the Dee," I said, looking up and down its length as it revealed itself.

"How wide is it?" he asked, sitting forward on his horse as if to close the distance.

"Let us get nearer to it, then I can gauge better."

We drew closer, but lost the vantage point in doing so. "I think it is about twenty paces wide," I said, doubtfully.

Our horses were now at the banks of it, and the ground was wet beneath their hooves.

"It must be the Trent. Mercia is on the other side."

I looked, wide-eyed, across the river to the grassland on the other side. "Then we are that close to safety?" I asked.

"We do not know if the border still holds," answered Gyric.

I considered this, but his thoughts were going on. "Does it flow fast?" he asked. "Can you see a current?"

I scanned the flowing waters. "It does not look fast. At least, I see no ripples upon the surface."

"And it is quiet," he thought aloud. "We are at the very banks, and cannot hear it. A good sign."

I looked up and down the banks. It would be easy for our horses to get into the water, and to climb out again. I only hoped that the current was not strong.

"Find me a stone," directed Gyric, as he swung down from his horse. I climbed down too and found a few round rocks. He selected one and then said, "Watch it carefully."

He drew back his arm and threw it with force over the water. It plopped, splashing, a ways from the other bank.

"It fell into the water, about two horse-lengths from the far shore," I said, hoping I was close in my estimate.

He shook his head and gave a little laugh. "The river is far wider than twenty paces," he said.

He palmed another stone and threw it again, with more force. It too fell into the water.

"It went farther, but did not touch the shore," I reported.

"It is forty or fifty paces wide here. Does it narrow? Can you tell?"

"It looks the same, in both directions. The banks are gradual here, but firm. It grows marshy to our right."

Gyric stood facing out towards the river, fingering a final stone in his hand. "I am sure it is the Trent. We have done well. If it is still Mercian territory on the other side, we will have done very well."

"I pray that it is," I said, but my heart was in my throat, for many reasons.

"We could try to find a ford, but it could take days, and lead us into more danger, since Danes will be looking for the easiest ways to move their supply waggons. Since the entry is easy here, and the current probably weak, I think we should cross where we are."

"Yes, I agree," I answered, honoured that he seemed to be asking my opinion.

"Are you all right?" he asked, turning to me. "Our horses should have no trouble with the swim."

"Yes, I am fine," I answered, but my knees were buckling beneath me. I could not swim, and the thought of clinging to my mare as she attempted to cross the wide river made me feel weak. What if she should buck me off, or I somehow slipped off with the whole saddle?

Gyric was already turning and pulling on the girth straps to check them. "And to think you just dried all of our clothes, too," he said lightly.

Together we retied our packs so everything was as high as we could make it. Then he felt for the reins of his gelding, and untied them from my mare's saddle. I did not want to be separated from him, or for him to become separated from me, but I bit my tongue and spoke not.

"Our horses will swim better apart," he said, and I nodded my head mutely.

He mounted, and asked, "Are you ready?"

"I am ready," I managed, and pulled myself up.

"Just urge her into the water, and let the reins go slack. If she tries to turn back, kick her forward. Once she starts swimming, let her alone, and just hold on. When she starts to climb out, it might be slippery, so hold tight."

I was already holding so tight that my hands were trembling. But I moved her to the water's edge, and the black gelding came up beside us. Gyric held the reins in his hands for the first time, and used his heels to urge his horse forward. He had no look of concern upon his brow. If he felt any, he hid it well.

My mare paused, and lowered her head and tried to drink, but I gave her a little kick instead. She stepped into the water, and I kicked again, and she took a bound and suddenly I was splashed as she plunged chest-deep into the green waters. Almost at once she was swimming; the river bottom must drop off quickly. She held her head high and her ears pointed straight back at me. I think she enjoyed it as little as me. The cold water swirled around my legs, soaking my gown, but everything, including me, seemed secure. Gyric was just next to me; his gelding was pulling away and even passing my mare.

The river bank looked far off, but my mare kept her head pointed straight at it. Now the black gelding was in front of us, and I beat back the fear that he might pull away from my mare. She kept swimming steadily. It was an odd feeling, for at times I felt myself almost lifted from her saddle.

Gyric reached the bank first, and I had a moment to watch his gelding gain its footing and struggle out of the water before my mare touched bottom. Then we were out, with the same little bound with which we had entered. She was tossing her head, and her nostrils were flaring, and I only wanted to get down off her.

Gyric was already standing on the ground by his horse's head, and he gave the shiny wet neck a pat. I came up to him, catching up my gown and wringing its hem of water.

"It was a long swim, and they were heavy loaded," he said.

"It was very long," I agreed, and tried to laugh.

"Did everything make it across?" he asked, as his hands swept over the pack on his saddle.

"Yes, and not everything is soaked," I answered. "The tip of my nose is dry."

He gave a smile, and it was wonderful to see, and wonderful to think I made it happen.

"We are in Mercia," he said, and got ready to mount again. "Let us hope it is still ruled by Burgred."

He handed me his reins, and I again looped them through my saddle rings. Our first goal was the trees before us, for we needed to unload our horses and dry out and re-pack our gear. I looked at everything on this side of the great river with real interest. It looked just the same as the other side, yet we were now in my home country, and not a land ruled by the Danes. Or at least, these were the things we hoped.

"I do not want to stop, but we will regret it if we do not," he said to me, as we approached the woods. "It cannot be long before we find a bailiff, or some shire man of rank."

I wanted to ask what we would do then, but the question stuck in my throat, for I dreaded the answer. I feared that Gyric would arrange for some man to escort me back to my village, and he himself find some thegn or ceorl to ride back to Kilton with. He was rich and from a famed family; any man of Mercia would readily go with him if he could. Now that he was well enough, why should Gyric wish to have me continue on with him? I would likely be a burden, and slow him down, compared to the speed with which he and another young man could ride. Then too, what would he do with me once we reached Kilton? Where would I go? I would be truly far from my Western village then, and his family would have the trouble of sending me back with an escort. Such were my thoughts upon setting foot in Mercia again.

I found an open place, not too far within the line of trees, and we freed our horses and spread out our things to dry in the noon Sun. I had not said anything for a long time, and Gyric too was quiet next to me.

"You are less than a week from your home," he said at last.

I did not answer, tho' I always tried to speak soon after he spoke to me. "Yes," I finally said.

"You should take as much as the silver as you want, and all the jewellery," he went on. "I will not need much to get back to Kilton."

Tears were flooding into my eyes, but I made steady my voice. "All of that is for you," I said through clenched teeth.

"I do not need it now," he answered. He turned his face away from me, and lowered his head. "Soon we will find a man to ride with me; he will do it on the promise of gold at Kilton. You need it far more than me."

My heart was swelling in my breast as if an unseen hand had gripped it. "I do not want to go back to my village. I left it just a few months ago. I do not want to go back. It was my choice to leave."

He moved his face so I could see it, but I could not read his expression. It took a while before he asked, "What will you do? You cannot wander around; there is war."

The tears were flowing fast down my face, but still I kept my voice from breaking. He could not know or understand why I wanted to stay with him. I did not know myself. All I could think of was the night I had found him in his cell, and that, kneeling beside him, I had looked at his face and vowed I would come back for him. Everything grew from that moment.

"I do not want to wander around. I want to ride to Kilton with you. We are not very far, now, are we?"

He inclined his head towards me, but did not raise it. "You will come all that way with me?"

"Yes," I answered, and my words tumbled out. "It is my wish to do that. I want to see the hall on the cliff – and meet your mother who reads and writes – and see the books you told me of –" I stopped to wipe the tears from my eyes. "And see the hunting hawks – and the waters of the sea crashing on the rocks . . ."

"You want to see all that?" he asked.

"Yes," I stammered out, "and meet your people, especially your mother."

As I said this last a terrible thought struck me: that perhaps he thought that I sought a reward for bringing him home. "I do not want anything, or any of the silver; I only want to ride to Kilton with you." I said this so firmly that it stopped my own tears from flowing.

He dropped his hands and said, "My father will give you much gold. Even crippled as I am, he will pay for me."

"You are not crippled, and I will not take a grain of gold. I only want to – see Kilton." I wept again, and I stood up to hide it from him.

When he spoke again his voice was calm and steady. "There is still danger, even tho' we are in Mercia. We may find more trouble here than in Lindisse."

"We have always been in danger, from the first," I answered back. I looked around the clearing to where our horses nosed together in the grass. "We are a good team," I reminded him.

Now it was his turn to echo me. "Yes," he granted. "We are a very good team." He nodded his head and ended, "Since you really want to, you will ride to Kilton with me."

BLOOD

W E went on our way, and I at least had a light heart within my breast. Now I knew I should continue on with Gyric to Kilton. It was true that he had not said that he wished me to go there; rather, that I could since I wished it, but this troubled me not. What mattered was that I should see him to his home, where he would be safe and cared for. I did not and could not think about what came next.

"If we find a road, shall we take it?" I asked, when we had started out. The riding was easy, for the rolling grass-land gave way to a light woods, and we could make good time through it.

"I would rather find a track, and take it to a trev or hamlet, so we could question the folk," he answered. "If troops are moving, they will be on the roads."

"Then we could buy more food, too," I agreed.

"Pay attention to the sky. Look for fires that might signal a settlement," he went on. "Sometimes you can see or smell village cook-fires before you find their ploughed fields."

But look as I might, we found no trace of fields or folk all afternoon. We made camp that night in the same

open woodlands we had travelled in day. It was a beautiful night, warm and clear, the darkening sky already twinkling with the first stars. I sat close to the fire, gazing into
the glowing heart of it, and then lifting my eyes to the
brightening stars.

"It is Walpurga's night," I remembered of a sudden.
Walpurga was the Goddess of Fertility to our people of
old, and this her night. "Tomorrow is May Day."

Gyric touched his spear shaft as it lay beside him,
running his fingers slowly over the ash wood by the iron
tip. We had not wished to lose track of the time, and so he
had been careful to number the days as they passed.

"Yes," he answered, as he counted the notches he had
cut, one for each evening. He released his hold on the
spear. "At Kilton there will be big fires tonight," he recalled.

"And there will be much feasting and drinking," I
added, remembering the way my kinsman kept this night,
and the way it was kept also in my village, tho' the Prior
tried to shame the folk for their behaviour. At dark men
and women would go into the fields and give themselves
to each other on the freshly ploughed Earth; it made fer-
tile the fields and ensured a rich harvest. And too, any
woman who wished would conceive a child on this night
as she lay on the Earth with the man of her choice.

I did not speak of this, but I guessed he was thinking of it too. "The folk will crowd the fields tonight, and
tomorrow crowd the village church, asking forgiveness,"
he said, and I wondered if he scoffed.

It was the same way at my village, and probably too, at
the village at Four Stones while the priest still lived.

"It is an important night," I ventured.

He did not answer me, and I wondered if by saying this I had lowered myself to the level of a cottar. Then I recalled my father's brother, ealdorman of my shire, the richest man there, who also honoured Walpurga and all things of the old Gods.

"Yes, as even our chantry-priest says, it serves the need of the folk. It is important to them."

He said this so lightly that I felt ashamed. I thought of the grove at my kinsman's timber hall, and thought, too of the place of Offering at Four Stones. I wondered what the men there would do to honour this night, and if Yrling would bring Ælfwyn out, and embrace her upon the warming brown Earth, joining those of the village in this sacred rite.

"Of what do you think?" asked Gyric, rousing me from my distant thoughts.

"Nothing much," I answered, not wanting to bring up Ælfwyn.

"Perhaps you were still thinking of the fires of Walpurga, and the cottars in the fields," he said in a light voice.

"No," I replied, and chose to be honest with him. "I was thinking of Ælfwyn, and hoping that all goes well for her and her new people."

He turned his head away, and I regretted having mentioned her name. "Her new people are my enemies, and I cannot wish any of them anything but damnation."

"I was not thinking of the Danes," I answered quickly. "I thought of the folk of Lindisse who she is trying to feed and clothe."

He nodded his head, but muttered, "If they prosper, the Danes prosper."

There was no answer for this, for he was right. At first Ælfwyn thought that the better she managed the affairs of Four Stones, the more content Yrling would be, but it soon became clear that growing fields of wheat and grazing cattle would not content him. If these things could be had as well as gold and silver plunder, so much the better; that was the way Yrling thought.

"How much food do we have?" he asked next. I was becoming used to him changing the topic of a sudden.

I pulled our food pack over and drew everything out, and examined it with care in the fire light. "There is a good deal of the haunch; two day's worth. A few handfuls of barley. A handful or two of wheat."

He listened to all this, and said, "We need to go on half-rations until we come to a settlement. It is better to be slightly hungered for a few days than to exhaust all our provisions and starve."

"Yes," I agreed, not looking forward to this at all. I put everything away and consoled myself by saying, "At least I am finding things to gather." In the last week, the Earth had been generous in sending forth dock and succory and starwort and lamb's quarters. Boiled down, they were tender and delicious, and relieved many of our cravings for fresh green things.

"Yes, but they alone cannot keep us travelling; not for long."

"You are right," I conceded, thinking of how hungry I was every night when we made our camp. "How welcome bread will be," I thought aloud.

"Yes; bread – and ale," he agreed. "Will you give me your needle case?" he asked now, jumping, I thought, from one thing to the next.

"Here it is," I answered, pulling it from my satchel. "Do you have a splinter?"

"I want to see if we can form a fish hook," he answered, and promptly pricked himself as he tried to pull a long needle from the leathern quill.

I began to reach to him, but then stayed my hand. I sat back on my heels as he bit his bleeding finger tip.

"Do you want help?" I offered.

He shook his head, and returned to touching the needles. "Is this the longest?" he asked, pulling it out for me to see.

"It is," I assured him.

He held it carefully out towards me. "Put it in the fire where you can pull it out again when it begins to glow," he instructed. "Use whatever way you can to pull it out, and I will bend it in a piece of leather to make the hook."

That is just what we did, for when the needle grew red I plucked it from the fire using tweezers, and dropped it into a scrap of thick leather. Gyric folded the hot needle around it, and it did not snap, so for the cost of a precious needle we had an even more precious fish hook.

"When we are next by water we will fish over-night," he said, fingering the cooled hook. "The streams are full of fish this time of year."

"I will never be so glad to dig for worms," I returned. And so in this way we tried to make light of our fear of coming hunger.

In the morning we ate the last bit of barley, and so the fear of lack was not far from my thoughts. The day echoed my mood, for the Sun was veiled with overcast, and a mist like the finest fog rose up from the Earth.

At times the Sun burned through the mist, and at others the mist grew thick about us, but it was not cold, only damp. We stopped at midday, and I gave Gyric a slice of the smoked haunch, and I took a nibble of it myself, but kept from eating more. As it began to grow dim we crossed what looked like an animal path in the low growth.

"Gyric, here is a trackway, perhaps made by deer or wild pig. We will follow it and see if it leads to water."

Within a few horse length's the track opened, and became wider, and I saw what looked like wheel ruts in the soft reddish soil. At one place the track narrowed, and then turned and opened up, leading along the edge of a large ploughed field. There, across the straight furrows, rose a cluster of huts.

"Gyric, here it is, a little trev. There are six or seven huts, centred in a big field."

"Who is about?" he wanted to know. "We must still be wary."

I looked at each hut carefully. "There is no one I can see." The Sun's setting rays cast sharp shadows across the furrowed field. "Strange, since it is far from dark." I eyed the scene again. "There is not even one fire burning."

Gyric shook his head, and a little motion of his body made his gelding try to back up. "This is not good. Go around it; do not move close. We will get at a distance, and you can watch from there."

I turned our horses, and then stopped, for I had heard a strange sound. Gyric's face showed he had heard it too.

"Was that a child?" I asked him.

He held up his hand, and we were both quiet, waiting for the sound again. It did not come, and I began to move our horses. Then we heard it, louder than the first time.

"It is a child, crying," I said, and turned to look over the fields to the huts. "Someone is there, that we know."

"Get at a distance, where we cannot be seen," said Gyric again.

I turned back up the track we had taken, and we rode a little way through the elders. We sat on our horses, and I watched the huts as the creeping shadows slanted across them. We sat for many minutes, and then heard the child wail again.

"Perhaps there is some trouble there; sickness, perhaps," I said.

"It could be fever," warned Gyric.

"Yes, or just a child left alone for some reason, while the others are out gathering, or at some other task."

I looked across at the surrounding fields. There were peas, and beans, and rows of young turnips, and carrots, and parsnips, I thought; all bordered by long straight rows of wheat.

"The crops do well; there is plenty here," I said, and recited all that I saw. The mist in the air made the light look soft, more like dawn than dusk.

"We will ride down," Gyric decided. He began unlashing his spear from his saddle. He gripped it upright in his right hand, and we rode down through the scrub.

Ahead was a low wattle fence, and as we walked by it I started and gasped. My mare shied and took a little half-step to the side, and Gyric's gelding bumped into us and whinnied, and Gyric reached out and caught my arm with his left hand and hissed, "What?"

My eyes were held at what lay just a few paces before us, for there in the faltering, misted light lay the form of a woman, dead. She lay upon her back, her round eyes rolled open to the setting Sun, a dark smear of blood crusted on her temple. Her legs were spread apart, and her simple gown was pushed up over her hips.

Gyric said again, "What?" and gripped my arm with such force that I awoke from my silent horror.

"It is a woman, dead before us. She has been ravished," I choked out.

I tore my eyes from her and looked beyond to find another form, marked with a throwing spear thrust upright from his body, lying not far from the open doors of the huts. "There is a man, dead, with a spear in him," I went on.

"How long dead are they? Are the bodies swollen?" asked Gyric in an urgent voice.

My face was covered with my hands. "No. Not long, I think," was all I could answer.

We heard the child cry again, and I looked across the field. A little boy of two or three years toddled out of one of the huts, grasping at the open door and wailing. He was dressed in a ragged shirt, far too large for him, a cast off perhaps, of his now-dead father's.

"A boy is crying at us from the door of a hut," I told Gyric.

"What else is there?" he wanted to know. "Do you see fresh tracks? Many horses? Find where the intruders came and left."

I tried to look around at the ground, but my eyes could scarce see. I slipped off my horse and walked, trembling, to the dead woman. The furrow she lay upon was broken and trampled, but I did not see the print of horse's hooves. I came up beside her and quickly snatched at one end of her gown and pulled it down to her bare ankles. I looked at her open eyes as I did this; they were blue. Her hair was fair, and lay in a knot of yellow behind her head. Her head wrap, a mere scrap of rag, lay in the brown soil where it had fallen during the struggle.

"Ceridwen," said Gyric.

I turned to him, and each word was a sob. "She – has been – killed by a blow to the head; there – are – many footprints by her, but I – cannot tell how – many – men. There – are – no hoof prints here."

"Come on, we are going," he said.

The child wailed again. "The boy," I sobbed, looking across at him clutching at the door.

"Leave it," Gyric ordered. "The rest will come back soon enough."

I looked up at him, speechless.

"There are six or seven huts, you said. You see only two dead; the other folk have fled, and will be back soon enough. The boy will be all right."

I was walking past the woman now, straight to the child, and tried to keep my eyes fixed on his ragged little shape as I passed the man. He was face down, and the light spear had caught him in the centre of his back as he had tried to run towards the woman.

I reached the huts, and saw now where the invaders had come, for the ground there was churned up with hoof prints. I glanced at them, and went to the child and reached my arm about him and carried him off. I pulled his shirt over his head as I passed the two silent forms in the field.

The boy was whimpering in my arms as I came to our horses. Gyric sat forward, his spear end planted in the ground, and spoke to me as I tried to place the boy on my saddle. "Ceridwen, we cannot take this child with us. Believe me, the other folk will come back."

"How do you know? And what if – they come back instead, the riders?"

"Did you find prints?"

"Yes, many of them."

Gyric snorted, and his lip twisted. "They never come back. But we must ourselves go, for others may be following, taking the same route." His brow furrowed deeper, and he went on, "There are no animals, you said. They carried off the livestock for food. They came from the other side of the fields; there must be a road there."

"Yes."

The boy was really crying now, and I could not get him to hold on to my saddle so I could mount behind him. I was crying, too, and wondering if he had watched his parents be slaughtered. "Gyric, will you take hold of this child? We cannot leave him here to die."

"I tell you, he will not die; the cottars will return."

"What if they have been rounded up, to be sold as slaves?"

He shook his head. "No. They are not slaving now, only taking supplies. The dead were worth silver; they would have taken them if they had been slaving."

I did not want to argue. I wanted to get away from the place of death, but I could not leave the boy behind, sobbing, and terrified. "Can we not just go somewhere safe and watch until they return?" I pleaded. The child was limp and heavy in my arms, his little legs dangling against me.

"Yes," he finally said. "We will go back up to the ridge and make camp. The cottars may come back by cover of dark." He reached out one of his arms and said less grudgingly, "Let me take him."

I lifted the boy up to Gyric's saddle, and he closed his arm about him, which occasioned fresh screams from the boy. I made haste to mount, and then reached back and took the child onto my own saddle, trying to calm it and myself at the same time.

We picked our way up one side of the ridge, and I found a spot where we could spend the long night ahead of us. I did not make a fire for fear of being seen, but only tried my best to comfort the child and keep him quiet. At last he fell asleep on my sheepskin, sucking his thumb and still breathing tiny hiccoughing cries.

Gyric sat beside me in the dark as I waited for any sign of life moving about the huts below us. The Moon rose up, casting his soft glow upon the fields, and I was grateful his light was too dim for me to see the dead who lay there.

"What if they do not come?" I asked, troubled that I was now putting us in extra danger on the hope of their return.

"They will come," Gyric answered, and his voice was kind, tho' tired. "If they do not, we will carry the boy with us until we reach the next trev, and can give it to the cottars there." He seemed to read my thoughts, for his next words were, "They cannot all have suffered like this."

Tears began flowing from my eyes, and I tried to stop them.

"I am sorry for what you have seen," he went on, quietly.

Images of the dead woman, of the dead man, of the riders bearing down on them flooded into my mind. I could almost feel the terror of the woman as she fled; the men pursuing her, catching her up; her struggle; the man, perhaps her husband, running to her, only to meet his own death. I pressed my hands over my face, but could not stop seeing her staring eyes, bloodied head, her open and exposed thighs.

"It is part of war," he said, gravely.

Something like anger now mixed with my tears, and I stammered out, "That is the excuse we always hear."

I took a breath, and my anger came to the forefront. "If they wanted and needed food, that is one thing. But to ravish and murder her –"

I felt him shrug in the darkness. "It happens a lot. Not just the Danes, either." His voice grew low. "Even good men sometimes do it, in war."

"Ravish women? Murder them?" I asked in disbelief.

"Yes," he answered slowly. "Something happens in battle; when you are going into battle. Something inside of you. I cannot explain it to you. Sometimes even good men do it."

"Do you do it?" I asked, in my anger.

"No. I have never done it," he said firmly. "I would not do such a thing; at least, I cannot ever imagine doing it."

I felt helpless to say anything. His voice was pained, and honest; he was being truthful to me about something lesser men would boast of doing. In peace-time the penalty for ravishing women was exacted in silver; but in war-time all men went unpunished, and I knew well that no one brings charges against the victor of a battle.

My eyes ached from crying, and I felt weak and sick. "I do not mean to be angry at you," I whispered. "I am just angry at it all."

He nodded his head, and made a small sound of assent. The Moon was high; it would start to set soon. I looked down at the sleeping child by my side, and drew a coverlet up over him.

"We should rest now," offered Gyric. "Whether the cottars return or not, we must ride tomorrow."

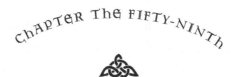

THE GIFTS
OF THE HOUSE

I was wakened at dawn by the wailing of a woman, and thought for a moment it was part of my own troubled sleep. But Gyric was touching my arm, and I sat up and blinked in the grey light as I heard the wail again. "They are come," he said in a low voice.

I stood and peered down on the trev below. Four or five people were there. One stood over the body of the man, and I watched as he pulled the spear from it. In the foreground the wailing figure knelt by the form of the dead woman.

"Should I go down?" I asked Gyric. "I do not want them to think the boy is lost, too."

"We will all go," he answered, and so we gathered up our kit.

We started through the scrub, the boy on my saddle before me. I stopped our horses at the edge of the field. The folk were now by the huts, laying out the bodies; and then one of them turned and saw us. I raised my arm, and tried to make strong my voice. I spoke no word of greeting, but only called, "The boy is here, and safe."

I urged our horses ahead at a walk, and one of the men pushed out of the knot they formed and came straight to us. The woman, who I now saw was old, recognised the shabby little shape before me and came almost at a run. I passed the boy, who was crying again, down to the thin arms of the old woman, who clutched him and kissed the little head without ceasing.

The men, of all ages, and all of a cottar's estate, stood speechless looking at us. I did not know what to say to them, and wished Gyric would speak. I turned to Gyric, but now a group of folk, clustered around a single rider, were approaching the huts from the other side. The men left us at once and went to them, and I said to Gyric, "Here is a new group of folk; women mostly, and many children; and in the middle of them is a rider carrying a spear."

"The bailiff, or a reeve," answered Gyric.

"He is coming right to us," I had time to say.

The group of folk were in tumult. Women and children were crying over the dead, and rejoicing too, as they saw each other and the lost child; and the mounted man drew his horse away from them and continued to us. He was stoutly built, not yet of middle age, and riding a horse, who like himself, had seen brighter days. He wore no sword, only a plain-hilted seax in a worn leathern sheath across his belly, and the spear he carried had a crude point forged by a black-smith, and no weapon-smith.

As he drew nearer his eyes travelled from me to Gyric and back again. He stopped his horse before us, and bobbed his head in greeting. "Sir," he said, and took his eyes from Gyric's face and said to me, "Lady."

Gyric spoke now, in a way and tone I had never heard. "I am Gyric, son of Godwulf of Kilton in Wessex. We came here yesterday and found the boy, and stayed in hopes his folk would appear. The Danes, I think, had not been gone long when we came. Tell me the name of this shire, and who you yourself are."

Through this speech the rider had never taken his eyes from Gyric, and they scanned his green mantle and the silver pin that held it, rested on the hilt of his fine seax, gauged the worth of the big black horse he rode. Each time his eyes returned to the slender wrap of white linen tied around Gyric's eyes.

Gyric sat straight on his horse, his voice and manner full of command, and waited for the man's answer.

The man bobbed his head again and said, "Sir, I am Wilfric, and I am bailiff of this place, Hreopadun by name. If you have been on the road you know the Danes have engaged our King Burgred; they have forded the Trent and ride freely now, tho' we are mustering a force against them." He stopped, and glanced at me, and then went on, "You are right, Sir, that your paths nearly crossed. These folk who fetched me tell that the Danes were here just yesterday morn." He kept looking at Gyric, but now his tone changed. "You are truly the son of Godwulf?"

"I am," answered Gyric in a low voice. "I was captured in battle. I ride now from Lindisse."

"Lindisse?" asked the bailiff, his voice full of amaze. "No Saxon comes live from Lindisse."

"We did," responded Gyric quietly. "This Lady is a country-woman of yours. Her dead father was ealdorman by the river Dee."

The bailiff faced me, wonder in his eyes, but he again bobbed his head. "Lady," he said once more.

"I am Ceridwen, daughter of Cerd," I told him.

He took this in, and then looked back at us both. "You travel then to the Dee?"

"No," answered Gyric. "We go to Kilton."

He shook his head. "A long way to go, Sir, even in peace."

Gyric was quick with his reply. "There is war then, through Wessex?"

"Aye," nodded the bailiff. "There was a great battle at Lundenwic, and another last week at Bedanford. The Danes are everywhere now; they come from all sides. Ælfred has all he can do to raise the muster."

"The King is well?" asked Gyric. "Ælfred is well?"

"Aye, Sir, from what little we hear, he still rules."

We were all quiet, and the sounds of the cottars behind us became the louder to us for our own silence. I looked over to them, and the bailiff's eyes followed me.

Gyric was the one who spoke, and his voice was hard. "The Danes who came, do you know who they were?"

"We know nothing but that they are abroad. The folk were too frighted to recall aught but they were Danes." The bailiff shrugged and ended, "To such as these, the Danes are all alike."

He looked back at the huts, and turned to us and said, "Sir, if you will wait but a moment, I will take you and your Lady to my home. We will be there by noon, and our house would be honoured by your presence." My face must have shown my gratitude, for he added, "You can rest there, Lady. My wife and daughters will care well for you."

Gyric nodded his head in agreement. "We have travelled far, and without shelter. We thank you for your offer."

I dug into my black pouch as we neared the huts, and held three silver coins tight in my hand. I searched the faces of the cottars until I saw the old woman who had been weeping. A small movement of my hand drew her close to me, and I stopped my mare for one moment to thrust the coins into her shrivelled fist. She did not speak, and I was glad of it, for her tears said enough. A few of the others raised their hands in silent Fare-well, and I nodded to them and moved my mare forward across the fields.

We gained the road on the other side of the field. I saw at once the marks of many horses in the soil, but saw no other trace of the violence that had been wrought by those who rode them. The morning was again misty, and lightly damp, but for once I had no need to always check the Sun in its course overhead, for we were now with one friendly to us, who led us with confidence over his native shire. Perhaps because of this, or because too of the weary and sorrowful nature of the night, I felt great relief to be led, and especially to be led away from the little trev.

Wilfric's house, when we came to it, was a whole collection of buildings, large and small, and edged about with a wooden palisade taller than a man. All the household seemed to be out in front of this fence, from Wilfric's wife and young sons and daughters to his slaves.

A pleasant-faced woman in a good blue gown came forward and bowed to us, her hands clasped before her. "I am Hildfleda, wife to Wilfric," she greeted us, and the kindness of her smile and good sense upon her brow filled me with a lightness I had not known in many days.

Wilfric gestured at the open door of his hall, and I touched Gyric's hand, which he placed on my arm, and we went first through the door. The hall was snug and stout, the timber walls white-washed and pocketed all around with small alcoves. The sunken firepit, full ablaze, was in the very centre. It was not a large hall, and there was no grandness about it, but to me it looked like every comfort we had missed now lay at our feet.

"Sit you by the fire, Sir and Lady, and take ale," Hildfleda invited.

A bench stood ready by the firepit, and at once a man bearing a tray crowded with brass cups was before us. A second man carried a bronze ewer, which Hildfleda took up. She herself poured out the ale for us, and placed the cups in our hands, as a sign of honour.

Wilfric offered, "Bide here as long as you wish. Our roof is honoured by your stay."

Gyric nodded his head and answered, "Tomorrow we will take our leave, but today we accept the gifts of this house."

I felt glad at this, and touched the arm of Gyric that he might know it. We lifted the cups and drank of the sweet, nutty brew.

The savour was exquisite, and for the peace and comfort and safety of it all I think I nearly laughed, a laughter close to tears.

Hildfleda watched me, and said gently, "Lady, you are travel-weary. Will you not come with me, before we sit at meat?"

"Gladly, good woman," I answered. I turned to Gyric and said softly, "I will not be long."

He sat on a bench for the first time in weeks, drinking good ale, safe amongst those who could be counted as friends. When he answered me his voice showed all of this. "I will drink another cup of this fine ale," he returned.

Hildfleda led me from the hall to a squat timber washing hut. Outside burned a fire over which hung an iron cauldron, ready simmering. I bathed, and washed my hair, and Hildfleda treated me with every kindness. I combed my wet hair until it dried somewhat, and wrapped it in a clean head-wrap, and so arrayed I went back to the hall with her.

Gyric was there, sitting in silence with Wilfric. I came up beside him and touched his hand to let him know I was returned. Hildfleda filled our cups again, and excused herself to her kitchen yard, leaving the three of us alone by the fire. It was quiet, and the speech of the crackling logs was the only sound in the white-washed timber hall. I sipped my ale, and wondered what if anything the two men had spoken of while I jested with Hildfleda. Perhaps without me there Wilfric had found it more difficult to speak; he looked upon Gyric with some unease.

"Sir," he started, and cleared his throat. "I see you bear a hurt to your eyes. We have a skilled leech here who might help."

Gyric turned his face to the man, and his answer was short. "They are not hurt. They are gone. A Dane called Hingvar burnt them out with a flaming iron."

Wilfric lowered his own face, but Gyric did not move. The older man pulled a bronze cross from around his neck, and touched it to his lips. "Christ blind him," he swore under his breath.

"He will be worse than blind before he is dead," returned Gyric. His voice was colder, and quieter, than ice.

I reached out and placed my hand over Gyric's own as it gripped his cup. At that moment I did not feel bold in touching his hand this way. A sister would have done it, or anyone who cared for him, and the pain he bore.

The tables were set up, and benches carried in. All the household came into the hall, and we sat at meat together, with Gyric and I at the centre of the head table, seated between Wilfric and Hildfleda. We ate a meal that I had not had since a high feast day at the Priory, for there was two kinds of browis, and roast kid, and fishes stuffed with dried pears, and sheep's cheese and goat's cheese and many, many loaves of good bread. All of these things were put before Gyric and I on a brass platter, the best in the house, for we alone did not eat from wood. I broke Gyric's food for him, and told him of each thing I set before him, and he ate well and with relish for the first time. There was more of the dark brown ale, and we drank many cups, and Wilfric spoke to Gyric solemnly and with respect; and the eyes of the household folk seemed fastened upon us during it all.

I felt a strange sense sitting there, a sort of quiet joy in the very centre of me. I had been in danger, now I was safe; I had been hungry, now I feasted; I had seen great cruelty, now I knew kindness; the folk about me all spoke my tongue, and with my own accents, for I was back in Mercia; and all of these things gave me content. But my gladness did not spring from them, grateful tho' I was. The deep pleasure – the joy I felt – was sharing all this with Gyric, sitting by his side, watching him eat and drink, rendering him small services to make lighter his sorrow.

He did not say much; he did not speak at all of our tale, except that part pertaining to the trev; but his voice when he spoke to Wilfric was strong and full of authority. In that small hall I was allowed to know a different part of him, and he, another part of me. For the first time we had others about us like onto our own kind. Here we were not renegades, fleeing capture and death. Wilfric and

Hildfleda regarded us with courtesy and honour, and to see Gyric treated with such dignity seemed to return one tiny part of all that had been snatched from him, tho' it be as if one pebble remained from a whole mountain.

The fire burned low in the glowing pit, and the last cups of ale were poured out, and the folk all about the hall yawned and stretched and began to take themselves off to their final duties of the day. Hildfleda rose and smiled upon me, and gestured to an alcove that her daughters were making ready for me. And tho' sleep was heavy upon me from the rigours of the day, and I was drowsy, too, from all the rich ale, I did not wish to be parted from Gyric, nor let him be parted from me. But Wilfric rose too, and spoke in Gyric's ear, and made ready to lead him off that he might prepare for sleep to come. So we all four stood, and I slipped my hand into Gyric's for one moment. I said to him, "Bide well through the night"; and then I made myself turn and go with Hildfleda. I stopped one moment as Gyric placed his hand upon the arm of Wilfric to be led away to one of the waiting alcoves.

When I turned back to Hildfleda, I lowered my eyes, which were brimful; and her own eyes were moist as she searched my face. What she thought of us I could not tell, for she spoke not her thoughts, but only smiled on me kindly.

The alcove was next to that where Wilfric and Hildfleda slept, and I knew that her young daughters gave it up to me, that I might sleep in a place of comfort and honour. I pulled off my gown and snuggled beneath the wool coverlets, and the rush mattress let off a faint sweet odour of dried lavender. I murmured one word of prayer, that all be well with Gyric, and fell into the arms of sleep.

ALONE AND TOGETHER

WHEN I finally pulled back the curtain in the morning, I was abashed to see that everyone else was gone from their alcoves. Outside my own, on a bench, sat Hildfleda's daughters, patiently waiting to attend me. A low fire burned in the pit, but the hall was otherwise empty.

My eyes searched the alcove where I thought he had slept, and at last I said, "Where is my Lord Gyric?"

"He is with my father, and the leech is with them," answered the eldest with a curtsey.

She had no sooner spoken thus, that Wilfric appeared through the main door of the hall. At his side, with his hand on Wilfric's arm, walked Gyric. He was freshly dressed, with a clean linen wrap tied about his wound, and his copper-gold hair flowed in waves to his shoulders; but what caught my eye and held it was his face, for he had shaved, or been shaved; and the clean smooth line of his bare face set off his manly beauty as I had never before seen.

I knew my eyes showed my gladness at seeing him, for after Wilfric's greeting, he left Gyric alone with me. I touched Gyric's arm, and we sat together on a bench before the fire. "How well you look!" I could not keep from saying.

He smiled and touched his hand to his chin. "At least I am not so shaggy now." He settled on the bench and added, "The leech did it, and gave me razor and oil to have upon the road."

"This house is full of goodness," I answered, full in earnest.

He nodded his head. "Wilfric has cared for us and our horses, and we will carry away much provander when we ride. I will make him take silver for all his trouble."

"Gyric, please to give me the jewellery pouch. I should like to give Hildfleda a ring for what she has done."

He pulled the red pouch from his belt and passed it to me, and I chose a wide silver ring, edged with granules of silver bead, as her gift. As he threaded the pouch back onto his belt he asked, "Are you ready to ride?"

I looked around at all the comforts about us, savouring the safety and goodness of the place. I thought briefly of this, and then thought of the freedoms of the road.

"Yes, I am ready," I answered, and felt of a sudden eager to be off.

"Good. After we have supped we will take our leave."

※※※※※※※※※※※

We rode through grasslands all day, and that night made camp just within a woods. When I had built our fire I drew out some of what Hildfleda had packed for us.

"Roasted goose eggs, and boiled hen's eggs, and sheep's cheese in tansy leaves, and loaves of brown bread, and loaves of wheaten bread, and kid, and bunches of cress, and sacks of new peas, and beans and barley, and dried pears and apples and cherries, and much more, too, Gyric," I recited, looking at all this bounty at our feet. A crumpled bit of waxed cloth caught my eye, and I unfolded it. "And salt – another twist of salt, too. How generous she was!"

All of these good things made me feel almost gay, as if we were on an afternoon's outing. "What will you have, Gyric? A little of each?"

"Whatever you choose. It does not matter."

I stopped in my treasure-hunt and looked at him, sitting across from me. "Of course it matters," I said, recalling that just last night, in Wilfric's hall, I had taken pleasure in seeing him eat with some relish for the first time. "We have many good things here. I want you to have what you like most."

"It does not matter. Some kid or cheese, and a loaf."

The hollowness of his voice told me it truly did not matter. "Here is ale," I said, and guided a cup to his lifted hand. He took it, and drank. For that at least I was grateful, and resolved to drink none of it myself so that he might enjoy it the longer.

"We should hobble the horses," he said. "Wilfric gave us a pair. Can you help me do it?"

"Hobble them?" This surprised me, for they had never wandered.

"If we lose them, we lose much, for a horse triples its value in a land at war. We must guard them well against theft."

"Yes, of course," I said, glancing around me. The horses were grazing nearby, tied loosely by neck ropes.

"They cannot be driven off quickly if they are hobbled, and your mare is sure to whinny if anyone strange
tries to touch her."

I rose. "Shall we do it now?"

We found the leathern hobbles in our kit bag. He held
the horse's heads as I slipped the slender straps over the
front legs of both horses. They did not seem to be worried
by them, and resumed their browsing.

We sat down again, and I tried to engage Gyric in our
food. He ate some kid, and a bit of cheese, and a small loaf.
I tried to fill his cup again, but he would drink no more.

Still, I was not troubled as I sat beside him in the flickering firelight. I knew he was sorrowed. No one had more
reason to be, and this I accepted with my whole being. I
did not want to try to change his sadness; I did not presume to think I could. I only bore within me that same
feeling, alive and growing, that I had felt in the hall the
night before: that deep and quiet content of sitting near
him, watching his face, doing some small service for him
that might light a candle in his darkness.

And too, I was once again alone with him. With all the
dangers and discomforts of the road, I knew that I chose
it over the safety and comfort that a hall afforded; for the
road we shared alone, and together, and we knew each
other first and foremost in this way. I thought then of the
rich timber hall at Kilton, and the greatness and wealth of
his people. I could not know or guess what would become
of me after we arrived there, and I did not allow myself to
dwell upon it when so many other uncertainties faced us.

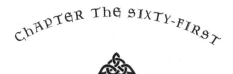

THE WELL

AT dawn the skies cleared as the Sun rose up in the East. Most of the morning was spent in the same woods, and not until we stopped at noon did the trees begin to thin about us. We leaned against a broad oak trunk and nibbled at some loaves and roasted eggs. As we rested there, a faint acrid smell wafted to my nose, and I gave a quick sniff and then a much deeper one. "Charcoal-burners," I said. "Perhaps we are near their huts."

Gyric smelt it too, and inhaled deeply.

"Charcoal-burners?" he asked, raising his face to the forest sky. "At work burning in May?"

Of course he was right; the charcoal makers did not begin their burning until the Feast of Peter and Paul, and late June was six weeks away.

We remounted, and the oaks gave way to alders and maples, and between these were many trackways, showing signs of old and constant use. "It cannot be long before we are at a trev, Gyric. The pathways are well-worn, and all begin to run together."

Now a smudge of smoke appeared behind the trees before us, and the smell grew strong indeed. Before I could tell Gyric of the smoke, he said, "That is no smith's forge; nor burning of coke either."

The edge in his voice made me slow our horses even more. "There is smoke now," I told him. "I see it clearly, rising above the maples before us." Drifts of it now floated by us. It was sharp, and made of many smells, and held none of the sweetness of the charcoal-burner's art in it.

His face was uncertain, and I reined our horses to a stop. Without reply he pulled his long seax from his sheath, and held it low and flat against his gelding's neck. "Be wary," he said, as he had so many times before.

"Shall we go on?" I asked, not knowing what we might find, but fearing the worst.

"Yes, but tell me all as you find it."

I made my mare quicken her pace. "There are fields ahead. I see an edge of a furrow beyond the trees."

As we gained it, the wind shifted, and a cloud of smoke, black and acrid, stung my eyes and made me cough. I stopped our horses at the edge of the furrow, and with watering eyes looked across the field.

I made myself speak slowly. We were a long way from what I gazed upon, and the distance made the scene seem less than real. "There are ploughed fields before us. Beyond the fields is a little burh, like onto the size of Wilfric's, or larger; I cannot tell its size from what is left. Most of it is burnt, and there are a score or two of huts before it, burning too. The palisade is nearly down. There are many small timber buildings within the burh still smouldering. A few folk are moving about the fields close to the huts. There are no horseman. There is no fighting."

"Can we be seen?" was his one question.

I scanned the scene again. The few figures moving about were far from us, and kept close to the heaps that were once huts. "No one looks this way."

"Take us back within the trees so that we pass without being seen."

"We are going on?" I asked dumbly, still blinking at the destruction before us.

"Yes. There is nothing but misery there. We cannot help them, and may ourselves be harmed. Go."

"Yes," I mumbled, and kicked my mare to turn her head.

We entered the line of trees again, and picked our way past the fields that edged the despoiled burh. I did not speak to Gyric, and he did not say more. A few curls of smoke drifted through the trees, but I could no longer see their source. All was still. Perhaps the smoke drove the birds away. I was grateful I could not hear the wailing of those who remained alive in the burnt settlement. Thinking this, I cursed my cowardice, so great that I wished to spare myself the sound of others' suffering.

We went on, slowly and steadily, and in silence. The Sun began to lower in the sky, telling me that we should soon make camp. I did not wish to stop, but to travel as far as we could before nightfall.

We came to a stream, wide and full-throated in its Spring flow, and my mare nickered as she smelt it. I slipped off her back, and went and plunged my hands into the cool water. Gyric's gelding nosed his way to the stream's edge, and I untied his rein so it might freely drink.

"Since it is already dusk, and there is water here, we should stop," said Gyric from his saddle. He swung himself down, and his gelding moved forward to the water. It was nearly dusk, for amidst the forest trees it came on quickly; but I felt much surprise that Gyric knew this.

"You are right," I said, and my voice must have showed my wonderment.

"A nightjar sang, not long ago. They never call until the Sun is gone."

I did not recall the birdsong, but my thoughts were so heavy that I might have been deaf to much. Gyric heard and remembered everything; his knowledge of woodcraft was great.

He put out his hand and found his gelding's flank, and then unlaced his spear from the horse's side. "Is there fodder enough here for the horses?" he asked me.

I looked around the small clearing where we stood. "There is a bit of grass on both sides of the stream. It will be enough," I decided.

We freed the horses from their trappings, and I went about setting up our camp. We were both quiet. Gyric sat upon his sheepskin, leaning back against his saddle. After I had got the fire lit he spoke. "I am trying to think which way they are riding," he began.

I did not need to ask who he spoke of; the graveness of his voice told me it was the Danes.

"You do not think they will stay here in Mercia?"

"If that is their goal, they will turn East, and attack the larger and richer burhs closer to Burgred. The places they have destroyed here provide provisions, but little treasure in the form of silver or arms. I think their goal lies in Wessex."

"It is a rich land," I breathed aloud, recalling all that Ælfwyn had told me.

"Yes, it is a rich and fat land; and it is but imperfectly defended. The Danes must be ready to engage the nobles of Wessex on a scale that we have not yet seen."

I watched him as he sat, tracing over and over again with his fingers the carved design in the hilt of his seax. When he again spoke, his voice was low.

"We won at the Vale of the White Horse. It was the first real contest we won against them. I wonder if we have ever won again."

I wanted to say, Surely, yes; or remind him that the battle he had been captured at had finally been won by Ælfred's forces; I wanted to say any word of hope or comfort, but no word came. I thought instead of sword-less Wilfric, and of the folk of the destroyed burh; and thought of any Dane at Four Stones with his ring shirt and gleaming sword and battle-axe; and this thought made me close my eyes.

The smell of our little cook-fire made me speak. "What of those they meet in their path? Will every settlement suffer as the trev and burh did?"

"By now runners have been sent by the reeves and bailiffs. The folk will be warned, and at least have time to shelter their livestock. Burgred himself may give chase if he is not far. The Danes move swiftly, but the ealdormen of Mercia have good forces. The Danes will not always find the taking so easy."

"And us?"

"Nothing is changed. We must keep overland as often as we can."

We did not speak of much else, and the night closed up around us.

The next afternoon we came upon a well-rutted track, old but too narrow for swift travelling by many riders, so we thought it safe to take it since it went South. We were wary in doing so, but we made good time upon it. The Sun and warmth gave its own comfort, and to my delight I saw whole sheafs of May roses, full in bud and ready to bloom, along the track as we went on.

At one point we found a stone well, with a pail and dipper ready to be lowered by thirsty travellers. Nothing else was about, save for the pile of small stones heaped by the grateful as a thank-offering to the ancient water spirit of the place.

"How well ordered King Burgred keeps this part of his land," I remarked, after we and our horses had drunk our fill. "It is like the stories of times past, when a woman and new-born child could walk alone the breadth of Northumbria, from sea to sea, and do so in peace and with water and a brass dipper at every stream put there by the King."

"That King is long dead, and Northumbria taken by the Danes, and no man or woman walks in peace now."

I did not answer this truth; there was no need to. I looked about for a stone to add to the pile. All the near ones had already been gathered up, and I had to walk down the track a long way to find one. When I added it it made a little clinking sound.

"What are you doing?" asked Gyric, turning toward me and the sound.

"Thanking the well-spirit," I answered without shyness.

I thought he might laugh, but he did not. "Is there a pile for Offering?"

"Yes, and it is old and very tall." I hoped I did not sound a fool. He said nothing more.

We sat for a while longer, and our horses browsed amongst the tender growth fringing the track. Gyric was always the first to rise whenever we rested; it was always he who said it was time we should move on. Today he did not speak of going onward, but only sat quietly, leaning against the cool stones of the well-head. The Sun was shining full upon us, and I thought I could almost see the May roses unfurl as I gazed upon them.

I too was content to sit in the peace and solitude of the place, and only my mare straying too far down the track made me rise. "I am going to fetch my mare. She is wandering," I told Gyric.

He took his spear in his hand at once, and stood up.

"We do not have to go," I said, returning with my mare.

"It is late, and we have stayed long. We must ride." There was no strength in his words, and it was easy to see he did not wish to leave.

"Are you weary? We can stop now and camp the night, and make a fresh start after a good long rest," I offered.

"I am not weary." His gelding had stayed close to him, and now Gyric was fumbling with the horse's saddle ties, lashing his spear against the animal's flank. He stopped what he was doing, and lowered his head. "I was thinking of my return home," he said at last.

All our speech was of the Danes and their destruction; the threat of coming war must weigh heavy on his mind. Perhaps he feared that Kilton would be soon attacked.

"Because of . . . what you may find?"

"Because of how they will find me."

We had spoke thus once before, when he was hot with rage over what had been done to him. Today there was no anger in his voice, only sorrow; and I knew it to be the foreshadow of the sorrow his people would know when they found him alive but so maimed.

I thought carefully before I spoke. "They think you are dead by now."

He nodded. "They must. It has been too long without word, or call for ransom."

"Then they are grieving your death. When you return, they will rejoice in your life."

He shook his head, and lifted one hand toward his face. "Rejoice? When they see . . . this? All that I was, I am no more."

"You are still what you were," I began weakly. I heard Gwenyth's caustic words in my ears, 'He will kill no more.'

"I will be worse than dead to them. I am fit for nothing; not even the Church. I am nothing but a loathsome cripple, and a burden to all."

Tears pricked my eyes, but I made steady my voice. "You are not a cripple, and you will never be loathsome. Even in times of war more is needed than just another sword. I know this; how much more should you know it, who are older and have lived so much? I sat at your side in Wilfric's hall and heard him ask your counsel, and watched him regard well all you told him, for you have wisdom and cunning with or without your sight. All that you have told me of your family says that they are brave, generous-hearted, and wise. They will greet you with love and honour."

I thought of one more thing. "And what of the robber you slashed upon the road? You saved us from theft and worse with your seax, even as you are; and it was your courage and craft that did it."

He was listening to all I said, but tho' his lips were parted, he did not speak. I felt the warmth in my cheeks and felt ashamed of my words. "Please to forgive my boldness; I am too hot. But please never speak of yourself like this. It is too hard for me to hear."

This was even bolder of me, and I surprised myself by saying it. Why should he care how I felt about his words? There was no reason he should try to please me with them. To hide my boldness, I set to work with my mare, checking her packs and getting ready to ride.

Gyric stood by his gelding, and lifted his hand as if he wished me to take it. I did at once, and hoped it was steady in his own.

"Forgive me, Ceridwen. It is hard not to think of myself. All that is left to me is to think."

He folded his fingers over my hand for a moment.

To find my voice I said, "Thought is our greatest gift. That is what the Prior said."

He nodded and made ready to mount. "Yes. The Church gives harbour to even such as I."

A little racing fear shot through me, and I asked, "Have you then ever thought of the Church?"

He shook his head. "I never thought of it, no. I never felt the calling. Now . . ."

He did not go on, and I did not want him to.

"Gyric, Kilton will be safe?"

He drew a long breath, as tho' he had given much thought to this question. "I think all will be well there, at least for now. The Danes strike at the least defended places first, not at the strongholds. The hall at Kilton has its back to the sea, and tho' the Danes be expert with their boats the channel is treacherous to all who know not its tides. The plains before the hall drop down, so that all the land about can be seen for many rods. No troops could advance without warning. Our storehouse and granaries are great, and a siege would take many months before we lacked for grain or meat."

"Then we have no need to fear for your people."

"No. All we must do is to get to them."

THE SOIL OF WESSEX

WE followed the trackway all the next day, and met no one. The weather continued fine, and we made good time at a fast walk. The next morning we came upon a posting, for we found a tall stone dolmen that marked the crossing of a second, larger road.

Gyric considered this. "We must always be wary about meeting others, but in a day or two we must find folk to speak to. We will be nearing the border of Wessex, and I will want to learn the shire we are in, so I can fix where we are. Also, how is our provander?"

"We have some beans and barley, and a few eggs, and some dried cherries and pears. Enough for . . . O, for two days," I gauged, reviewing in my mind what remained of good Hildfleda's generosity. The first few days with all her bounty we had feasted, eating up quickly all that would not keep.

"Then let us hope that tomorrow or the next we will come upon those who can reprovision us and give us the news."

Remembering the comforts of Wilfric's hall made me hope for more to come. Perhaps once in Wessex we would meet a bailiff or reeve, or even be taken to an ealdorman's hall, and Gyric would once again be honoured as was his due. I looked forward very much to seeing that. But even the humblest hut would welcome us, I knew, for we had silver in plenty.

"We have spent little of our silver since we started, and have all of our jewels save the ring I gave Hildfleda."

"The silver and jewellery is yours. I want you to have it all, so it is good we have spent little." He touched the bracelet he wore, and then lowered his voice. "This, and the rings I wear, I would like to keep, as they are gifts from you."

My heart sunk at this, for it seemed he spoke of our soon parting, and that the silver cuff and gold rings would serve as a reminder of my little service to him. "They were Ælfwyn's things," I managed to say. "Take them to recall us both."

Now I knew I said the wrong thing, for his face fell. "We should be on our way," he answered, and I moved our horses out of the road and into the trees before us.

In the night owls hooted and awakened me, and I sat up on my bedroll and poked at the embers of our fire. Across from me Gyric lay on his back, asleep. I thought of the first night I had seen him, filthy and near death, and of the night I had held his hand and whispered that I wanted him to live. I stood up, clutching my mantle about me, and knelt down at his side. His right hand was on his chest, and the blue stones were like black holes on the wide band of silver he wore on his wrist. I wondered what keepsake of his he would give me when it was time for me to leave Kilton. The tears began to come into my eyes

at this thought, but I would not let them, and I stood and
went back to my sheepskin.

⁂

At noon the land began to rise a bit, and the larches
gave way to shrubby things like elders. We went up and
over a rise, and I looked out upon a plain, with three high
mounds green with grass before us. Between two of the
mounds was a huge wooden pole, rising from the Earth
and taller than any of the mounds.

"This is a place of burial, Gyric. The chieftains who lie
in these barrows must be great, for the mounds are huge.
Woden is carved upon a tree trunk, and looks down upon
them."

"Are there three mounds?"

"Yes, three."

"And the carving lies between two of them?"

"Yes. Do you know this place?"

"I know it well. We are in Wessex! This shire is ruled
by Ceolfrith, who is known to my father. I have been here
three or four times. We are farther South than I thought,
and a little East. We will be at Kilton in four or five days."

We approached the burial mounds. They were identi-
cal in size and length, and carpeted over with the growth
of fresh grass looked like the hulls of three huge green
overturned boats.

I stopped our horses before the image of Woden. It was
old, and no longer cared for, for the paint had worn away
from the shaft, and a part of the God's arm had been eaten
away by insects or dry rot. No one left Offering here, for the
pit beneath the figure was choked with years of old growth

of grass and weeds. The bottom of the shaft was marred with the names of many men who had stopped to carve their names into it before they continued on their travels.

"Why do we stop?" asked Gyric, and I moved my mare hurriedly onward.

"I was looking at the image of the God."

"Of Woden?"

"Yes, of Woden."

"I am surprised it still stands. It would have been pulled down long ago, but for the mounds."

To destroy an image of the Gods protecting a burial site was to evoke the wrath not only of the God, but of the dead entombed there. I knew few in Wessex would fear Woden, but the haunting of the ghost of an ancient chieftain would be something no man would tempt.

"Is it like those you recall as a child?" he asked. He did not seem to be teasing me. "All images of Woden look alike to me."

"Yes. They are all much alike, in the way that images of the hung Christ are."

"In the chapel at Kilton there are many carvings, both of Christ and of the Saints. We have no images of Woden, tho' he is still sung of in the hall." He thought of this, and ended, "We sing of Woden and Thunor, but never pray to them, and pray to Christ but never sing of him."

"He is not glorious, not in the same way the Gods were," I found myself saying.

He did not seem shocked at my words; for answer he only nodded his head. I thought of how few people I would have said such a thing to, for fear of being misunderstood; and felt again the freedom and ease that his presence gave me.

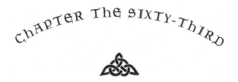

I KNOW LOVE

THE next morning was warm, with a golden mist in the air. Birds flitted overhead, calling as they darted, and on the rolling grasslands I saw fat brown hares hopping away, startled by our coming.

Then the pasturage grew rougher, and there was naught but trees before us. This wood was a great one, full of oaks of mighty stature, so great that nothing grew in their shadow. The forest floor was still brown with their lately fallen leaves, and the reaching boughs so full of their new growth that the very air seemed green above our heads.

The going was not easy at times, but I was glad to be in the forest again, and could not help but feel cheerful as we went. A creek we followed opened up to a little clearing, with grass and Sun; and tho' there was still an hour or more of good light we stopped and pitched our camp, for here was even ground, grass for our horses, and water for us all.

I gave some thought as to which gown I might wear as we approached Kilton, for both my green and russet were travel worn, and as through Ælfwyn's great kindness I had the choice, I would appear before Gyric's people in clothing that suited his own high estate. I went over all of Gyric's things, and gave thanks again for the ancient oak chest that held the dead Merewala's clothing, for beyond the magnificent green mantle he had fine linen tunics, woollen leggings, and leathern leg wrappings. Only Gyric's shoes were odd, for they were the rough deer skin pair made by Gwenyth's son Holt in their camp. Yet they fitted Gyric well, and he never complained of them, tho' he felt the deer hair still upon them each morning as he fitted them on his feet.

"What are you doing?" asked Gyric. He was sitting cross-legged upon his sheepskin, not too close to the fire which I had already started.

"Just sorting through our clothing, to make certain that all is in order for our arrival in Kilton."

He turned his head a little away, so I thought it best not to dwell on this.

"Tomorrow or the next day I hope we come to a good place for laundry, as I need to wash some things," I went on.

He did not say anything, and I once again felt that I was chattering away. But he seemed to brood more when I was quiet, so even when I myself was unhappy I tried to keep speaking to him, and to sound cheerful.

It was a wonderfully mild evening, and I kept the fire small, just enough to warm our food and to give light to my movements around our camp. The outlines of our browsing horses grew dim in the gathering night. The beautiful Moon rose, a tender young sliver in the darkening sky. As I lay on my sheepskin, welcoming sleep, I uttered a silent prayer of thanks for his company.

We awoke to a dawn that was like unto a Summer's morning, for the stillness and mildness of the night gave way to a pink sky and the gentlest of breezes. When the Sun was overhead we stopped to eat, but went on our way almost at once, for it was quite warm and there was no water for our horses. The woods began to thicken and so it made spotting any creek or spring more difficult. Most of the time I had to walk, and lead our horses. After we had gone on for awhile I thought it seemed to be growing brighter, and hoped this meant that ahead of us the trees were thinning and we would find a clearing. My hope was rewarded beyond measure, for of a sudden the trees began to fall away to shrubby growth, and the blue sky appeared over our heads in all its fullness, and we stepped out on a greensward bright with new grass.

"Gyric, here is a lake before us, beautiful and blue, with grass running down to it."

I could hardly contain my pleasure at seeing it. Here was water, and washing, and gladness to the eye as well. On our travels we had come to few water courses other than the streams we depended on or the rivers we had crossed. Now before us lay this small lake, as blue as the stones in the bracelet Gyric wore.

I stilled my gladness for a moment as I carefully scanned the edges of the lake.

"There is no hut or sign of folk here," I began, wanting to describe everything with care to Gyric. "The grass runs down to the edge of the water before us, and around the opposite edge there is some marshy growth and willows. The lake is small, perhaps at its widest thrice as broad as the Trent, and nearly round."

As I finished saying this my mare tossed her head and whinnied as if impatient to drink.

"Shall we stop here, Gyric? The horses could drink their full, and I could do our washing, and . . . and . . . it is just so beautiful," I ended, feeling eager and hopeful that he might agree. There were still many hours left to the day, but as he himself was no longer urging us to hurry, I hoped he might consent to our stopping.

He nodded as his gelding too, began to toss its head. "Yes, we should not turn away from a good thing," he answered, patting the animal's neck.

So we went out upon the bright greensward, and near to the circling trees we pulled off our horses' trapps and set our campsite. We hobbled the horses, and they browsed along the grassy bank, drinking freely from the lake water. I started a fire, and began hotting water, and pulled out all our soiled clothes, and made ready to wash them. As I was doing this Gyric went walking cautiously up and down along the edges of the lake, carrying his spear as his walking staff. After a while he came back and sat down near to where I was hanging our wet things. He stroked his face in a thoughtful way. His beard had begun to grow back, and he fingered it for awhile.

"I think I will try to shave," he said at last.

I turned from the shrub I was hanging a wet tunic on. "O," was all I could think to say. I did not want to show my concern. Wilfric's leech had given him a razor, which of course would be very sharp.

Gyric turned and began feeling around for his hide pack. I pulled it to him and sat down before him, watching his hands run over the contents within. "Is this it?" he asked, pulling out a small wood box tightly wrapped with a leathern cord.

"Yes, I think so."

His fingers pulled at the cord and untied it, and he carefully separated the two halves of the box. Inside was the razor, a slender piece of glinting steel as long as my little finger. A handle of bone ran the length of it on one side. The edge of the blade was so fine and sharp that it made me wince to look at it.

He put his fingers cautiously into the box, and touched the bone handle, and picked the razor up. He held it for a moment as if deciding something. "Is there oil?'

"Yes," I said, pulling a little crockery vial from the box. "Here is that which the leech gave you; also, I have oil as well."

"I will use this."

He turned his head to me. "Is there some warm water?"

"I will bring it," I answered, and came back with a bronze basin. He had set the razor down in front of him.

He looked uncertain, and I wondered if I should offer to help in some way or if I should just go. To my relief, he smiled a bit and then said, "I hope I do not cut my nose off."

He splashed his face with the hot water, and then dried it, and then rubbed the oil upon his beard. He took up the razor and held it against his cheek as I held my breath. The first few strokes were very small and cautious, but he seemed to grow in confidence as he held the blade. "How am I doing?" he asked, after he had scraped away almost all the growth on one side of his face.

"Very well."

"I am not bleeding to death?"

"Only in a few spots," I joked back to him.

The hardest part was near his mouth, and he nicked his upper lip, and there were a few skipped places here and there, but in all I could scarce believe how well he did. I think he too took some pleasure in the finishing of this task, for his mood was now much lighter.

I brought him fresh water, and he rinsed and dried his face. The afternoon Sun was hot and bright above us, and even tho' my gown was still wet from my washing duties I felt warm.

"I think now I will swim, since you say this lake is so fair," said Gyric.

"Swim?"

Since I did not know how to swim, I did not think I wanted him to swim, either. How would he know where he was going? What if he should get into some trouble?

He began unlacing his shoes and pulled them off, and then stood up. "Do you mind if I take off my tunic? I will swim better without it."

"Of course not," I mumbled, still not wanting him to go but feeling glad at his desire to do so.

He stripped the white tunic off, and I knew I blushed. I touched his arm, and he took my hand, and I led him to the edge of the water. "There is grass all the way here. At the other end there are reeds." I looked down at my wet gown. "While you swim, I will stay here and wash my hair."

The water touched his feet and wet the wool of his leggings. "Just call to me, and I will know which way to swim back," he said.

He let go my hand and stepped onto the soft margin of the lake. A few more steps and the water was up to his knees. I stood there on the bank, watching him with clasped hands. He moved slowly, but with steadiness; and with a few more steps he struck out and cast himself full length into the blue waters. He swam strongly away from me. I was amazed to see how quickly he moved, and amazed too to see the grace with which he did it. On land he must always go slow, and with caution, and even then often tripped or bruised himself by hitting something. Here in the water he moved unfettered, and seeing him so made my eyes grow wet with tears.

When he had gone some ways he turned and faced back to me, and I called out, "How well you swim!" and in reply he raised his hand before striking out again.

I turned and fetched my comb, and feeling foolish, pulled off my gown and stockings but not my shift. Then I came back to the water's edge, and waded in up to my knees, and knelt in the soft soil, and wetted myself and my hair all over, and all the time took pleasure in watching Gyric as he swam back and forth in the deep water. I stood up, and wrung out my hair, and went to my satchel and pulled off the shift that was clinging to me, and rubbed myself dry and put on a fresh shift.

Gyric was still swimming about far from shore. I called his name, and he began to swim towards me. I stood at the edge of the water with a linen towel, and he came steadily closer to shore. Then the water was shallow enough to stand up in, and he waded in towards land, his dark wool leggings streaming with water and the linen wrap about his wound wet through.

"How well you swim!" I praised him as I handed him the towel. "I wish I could do it."

"You cannot?"

"No. The waters of the Dee were marshy, and the Prior never allowed me to go in the fish pond."

"Godwin and I learnt when we were young, in the sea. Lakes are simple compared to swimming in our swift channel."

"I admire you so much," I said, and I think there was so much meaning in my voice that I tried to temper this by going on, "Let me get you dry things."

He had no dry leggings; they were all wet; but his linen tunic was so long that it covered him decently, and he made no comment of it. I went and brought out one of our blankets, and lay it upon the grassy shore, and fetched my comb, for I had not finished combing my wet hair.

When I had hung Gyric's things up to dry I told him, "I have spread a blanket, if you like to sit down," and he put out his hand and took my arm.

We sat down on the blanket facing the blue of the shimmering lake, and I combed my hair, and oiled it with a bit of the lavender oil I had, and sat with pleasure in the golden Sun. It warmed my bare arms and ankles, for I still wore aught but my shift; and Gyric leaned back on his elbows next to me and stretched his slender bare legs out before him.

We sat thus in silence, with me combing my hair dry, and a slight movement from Gyric made me turn my head to him. A lock of my hair had fallen against his arm, and he had closed his fingers around it, and held it quietly in his hand. I put down my comb, and he spoke in a soft voice.

"Ceridwen . . . what colour is your hair?"

I thought a moment of how best to tell him. "It is almost like yours, gold; but yours is more red-gold, and mine like the colour of chestnuts."

He did not release his hold on the lock of hair, but now asked, in a voice even softer, "What colour are your eyes?"

"They are green, dark green, like moss."

Now he dropped the hair and lifted himself on one elbow, and raised his hand before him. "I want to . . . touch your face," he said, almost breathing the words.

He reached forward and gently touched my cheek with one finger. Then he stroked it with his whole hand, and then slipped his fingers over the line of my brow, my nose, and then around my mouth. His finger rested for a moment on my lips, and I knew I moved not, for I could scarcely breathe. He leaned towards me, still touching my lips, and then his own lips were touching my face, and he pressed them to my forehead, and to my cheeks, and then he kissed my mouth; and never had I been kissed by man before.

He kissed my lips very gently, and then held my face with his hands and pressed his lips against mine, and slipped his tongue into my mouth and tasted me deeply. I clasped my arms around his neck and felt the smoothness of his face and the ripples of his soft red-gold hair as I grasped it, and most of all the long sweet pressure of his tongue inside my mouth.

And then one of his hands moved along my shift, and I felt his fingers slide up my naked leg, and caress my thigh. He pushed my shift up and cupped my breast in his hand, and drew his mouth away from mine, and took my nipple into his lips. I knew I gasped for breath; my heart was beating so that I felt it might burst beneath his tender lips. He said my name, Ceridwen; but did not so much say it as breathe it; and then he said it again and again as he brushed his lips over my breasts and throat and fastened on my mouth.

I could not speak; my only answer was in my kiss. He pressed his thigh between mine, and groaned as he panted out my name. And within me everything opened to him, everything; and every part of my being was his; and the smallest part of what I wanted to give him was my body. I felt no fear, there was no room in me for anything but the bliss that his kiss awakened; and I moved my legs and he seemed to fall into me, hard and urgent. There was pain for a moment; sharp and hot, but nothing could mar my joy as he buried himself deep within me; even that pain brought me joy. His lips kept kissing my face and panting out my name, and he moved within me with great power-ful strokes. I felt as part of the Earth beneath us, and part of the sky that blanketed us, and part of every living thing; I felt for an instant that I was him and me too. Then he shud-dered, and made a sound almost like a groan, and clasped me even tighter to him; and then he lay still on top of me.

He shifted a little, but kept his face close to mine, and with one hand pressed against my cheek. His breathing slowed, and became regular, and I did not know if he slept. After a little while he moved again, but did not speak. The way in which his arm still held me said everything to me, and I only hoped that my arms about him spoke my heart to him.

His face was buried in my hair; I could not look at him. He sighed, and pulled himself away from me, and just lay face down by my side. He still did not speak, tho' now with all my heart I wished he would, for the sigh troubled me greatly.

I turned to him, and he moved a little farther from me, and I began to tremble so hard that no power at my command could make me stop. But he would not turn to me, or speak either; and now my heart, so full and joyous before, was shot through with fear. I yearned to speak his name, to touch him, but I thought he shrank from me.

The Sun was still bright above us, the sky as blue, the air as warm, but the fear that took control of my heart was as the icy hand of Winter. I lay there, trembling alone beside him, and as I watched him his shoulders began to move, and I wondered if he wept.

"Gyric?"

For answer he thrust out his hand, and I grasped it, and he pressed my hand hard to his lips, and then released it. He spoke, and his voice was hoarse. "We should go on. I want to find someone to ask news of."

Numbly I rose, too miserable for speech or even tears. I smoothed my shift, and roughly braided my hair. Gyric rose too, and found his way to our packs, and I picked up the blanket and folded it. I walked to him, and felt the tenderness of my broken maidenhead.

I plucked our damp clothes from the shrubs, and handed the driest pair of leggings to Gyric. I pulled on a gown and stockings, and mutely began packing our kit up. I felt I moved in a dream. Nothing I touched seemed real, even our horses as I caught them and saddled them were like shadows.

We tied the packs onto the saddle-rings, and through it all Gyric never spoke. We climbed onto our horses, and left the lake and the greensward of grass behind us.

Perhaps an hour passed. We walked through scrub growth, the lowering Sun to our right. Once or twice we crossed trackways, small and unworn. A few birds sang in the afternoon light, and the tall grasses brushed against our horses' legs and made a swishing sound. The rest was silence.

I felt as if I sat upon my mare in a stupor, but even in my dullness I saw a movement in the brush ahead of us. I lost sight of it, but as we went on saw it again. I was loath to speak, but knew I must. "Gyric, there is a man, a wood-gatherer, I think, walking before us. He is trying to hide from us."

His answer was quick. "Stop him. I must speak to him."

I looked at the set of his lips as he said this, and urged my mare forward. I glimpsed the man again, looking over his shoulder as he darted amongst the shrubs. "Stay, fellow," I called out, wanting him to know I was a woman and he need have no fear of me. I lost sight of him, but as we approached where he had last been I called again, "Fellow, do not fear us. We will not harm you."

We stopped, and a rustling to one side told us he was near. "Come out," Gyric commanded.

The man came out, bent under the cloth sack of fallen branches strapped upon his back. He was old, and his face full of fear. Perhaps he was gathering in woods forbidden to him. He stood before us, speaking not, and perhaps gauging if we were of his shire.

"There is coin for your answer," began Gyric, in a voice so sharp that the man's legs nearly looked to crumple in fear beneath him, despite this promise.

"Yes, my Lord," stammered the gatherer.

"Where is there a Holy House near here?" demanded Gyric.

The man blinked his surprise. "Near here, my Lord? We are near nothing."

"There is no Abbey or Priory near?"

The man blinked again, and shook his head, fearful that his coin was at stake by this answer. "No, my Lord, I would there was for your sake." The man jerked his head and recalled, "There be a monk not far. He be a watcher, and a fierce one, too. But 'tis no Holy House, only his hut."

"Where is he?" demanded Gyric.

"Not far, my Lord, not far," answered the gatherer, and he brightened, for now his reward seemed secure. "Go on until you find an ash as great as they ever grow, and turn West, and then there be a brook, and then the path to the watcher's. 'Tis not far; your horses will take you there before dark."

Gyric was pulling at the red pouch at his waist. He flung something bright down on the ground, and the man pounced upon the quarter piece of silver.

"All blessings to you, Lord," he cried.

But Gyric turned in his saddle and said to me, "Let us go."

I urged my mare forward, and only one thought was in my mind: That Gyric sought a Holy House so that he might leave me there. From a Priory I had come, and that is where he meant to leave me, for he was ashamed of me and what had happened.

I found the ash tree, for it was indeed as great a one as ever I had seen, and as I looked upon it remembered it was the tree of all learning and truth, and my truth now was of my misery.

We turned West, into the lowering Sun, and went on through the woods, tho' I had as little desire to find the holy man as to meet my own death. I saw the brook, and then just by it, a pathway that turned off, and knew it must be the one leading to the watcher's hut.

"Here is the path," I told Gyric, and my voice caught so that I could scarce form the words. "We will have to walk the horses. It is too low to ride."

He swung down from his horse at once, and I got off mine, and he put his hand on his gelding's saddle and was led by him as I walked at the head of my mare. The Sun was going down, and it was darker still as we went farther into the trees.

My legs felt so weak that I could not keep going forward. I stopped, and at last my throat opened, and I sobbed out my misery. "O, Gyric, do not put me away. Please just let me go with you to Kilton. I will leave you before we reach your hall; I only want to be sure you are safe."

His mouth opened, but he did not speak. He reached his hand out through the space that divided us and found my shoulder. He pulled me to him, and then both of his arms were around my waist. He pressed his cheek against mine and his voice was tight. "Put you away? I do not want to put you away from me. I cannot; you are my wife."

"Your wife?"

"Yes, you are my wife, if you will have me as I am."

Now I think he also wept. He clung to me, and I to him, and all the joy I had felt and all the pain were as one within me; and I felt as one with his joy, and his pain.

He kissed my wet face and whispered, "I made you my wife in my heart there by the lake, but was too cowardly to ask you. I only wanted to find a priest so that I could ask you before a witness."

"Your wife?" I asked again, when I could find my breath.

"Yes, if you will take me as I am now."

For answer I pressed my lips to his brow, and to his lips. But even in my joy I still did not understand, and must ask him, "But why did you turn from me at the lake? I thought you were angry at me, or ashamed."

"I was, angry and ashamed both, but not with you; never with you. I was angry at myself. I did not really mean to . . . do what I did, but I wanted you so much, and once I began to touch your face I could not help the rest. Then I felt shame because I had not spoken for you in any way, nor told you that I wanted you for my wife. I was afraid to ask, but could not keep myself from acting."

He took my hands in his and kissed them, and held them folded in his, to his face. "I felt I did not have the right to ask," he went on. "I could not tell what you wanted. You only spoke of getting to Kilton; and since I could not see you I never could guess if you might think of me."

"Think of you?" I echoed, and some laughter mingled itself with my tears. "I have thought of nothing else since the first time I saw you. From that night nothing else mattered. I only wanted to free you, to see you grow strong again, to be with you."

He laughed, too, and endlessly kissed my hands. "Then you are my wife?"

"Yes, yes, Gyric, I am your wife, and I make you my husband. From the moment you kissed me you were my husband."

"I want to find this watcher and say these things in front of him."

"Yes," I said, laughing and wiping away my tears, "I want to hear them again, and forever."

So we started down the path again, and this time my body felt as light as a wind-blown thistle, and my feet scarce seemed to tread upon the ground. The little brook was once again before us, and we crossed it in two steps, and beyond I saw a clearing with a tiny timber hut centred in it, and the hut was so thatched with straw that it looked a haystack with a door. Before the hut was a cookfire, with an iron cauldron hung above it, and dinner ready cooking within, for steam rose out of it.

I stopped our horses at the edge of the clearing, and told Gyric, "Here is the monk's house."

Almost as I said this a figure emerged from the timber hut, and so filled the doorway as it came out that I wondered how it ever had gotten in. It was a man, large and powerfully built, and with a dark curling beard that nearly covered his face. His eyes were narrow and bright, for even in the setting Sun they twinkled as they regarded us. His clothes were of the simplest make, a dark brown surplice of coarse wool; and a cross of iron or some other black metal hung on a cord about his neck. He moved slowly, and stood before his camp fire, and regarded us not unkindly. He moved his right hand in welcome to us, and I saw the tips of two of his fingers were missing.

I remembered myself, and bowed my head to him, and said to Gyric, "Here is the monk."

Gyric reached out for my hand, and I took it, and he stepped ahead as if he would go to the man. "Good Brother, I would have you witness my pledge of marriage to this Lady, for I have made her my wife in Nature, and wish our union to be blest by the Church as well."

The monk's twinkling eyes were fast upon Gyric as he said this, tho' he looked a moment at me to see if I assented. I felt the warmth upon my cheek, and smiled at the monk and nodded my head, and he turned his eyes back to Gyric and studied him with some interest.

"I will be your witness," agreed the monk, and his voice was as deep as he was strongly-made.

"Good," said Gyric, and then he turned to me and took both my hands in his so that we faced each other. He paused a moment, and began. "I, Gyric of Kilton, second son of Godwulf, proclaim this woman Ceridwen to be my wife. I pledge to honour her in word and deed, to protect her with my own body, and to care for her wants. I swear to fight her battles, and to accept her debts as my own. Nor do I make claim on any goods which are hers. All that she brings with her is rightfully and truly her own possession."

He stopped then, and drew me closer to him, and pressed our clasped hands to his chest. "Ceridwen, you are the woman I choose as my wife. I want no other. I seal these vows with my kiss."

He kissed my lips, and then I took breath and kissed the hands I held, and I pledged to him.

"I, Ceridwen, daughter of Cerd, proclaim this man Gyric to be my husband. I swear to honour him in every way, and to be a blessing in his life, and give him no cause for sorrow."

My heart was brimful as I said this, and I spoke with all the fervency of my being. "Gyric, you are my husband. I want no other. And this vow I seal with my kiss."

We kissed again, and he held me as if he would never let go; nor did I ever wish our embrace to be broken. And as I was pressed thus against his heart, having heard him pledge, and having pledged to him, I said within myself: This is my supreme moment; the time that I shall cling to in all that comes ahead. Never shall I know happiness as great as this.

The monk spoke, and his voice was low and kind. We turned to him, and I saw he stood with arms upraised above us.

"I witness the pledging of this man and woman, that they have joined hands and sworn to each other. And I bless their union in the Name of the Father, and the Son, and the Holy Ghost."

We bent our heads to receive this blessing.

"Thank you, Brother," said Gyric, and reached for the pouch of silver he wore. He began to pull it open to reward the monk.

"So it is you, Gyric," replied the monk, regarding Gyric with great solemnness.

Gyric stopped and took a small step nearer to the monk. He cocked his head as if he might hear the huge man's words better. "How do you know me?" he asked in wonder.

"I have known you since you were a lad, but I have not seen you for many Winters," answered the monk.

"Cadmar?" asked Gyric, and again moved a little closer to the monk.

The monk's answer was mild, and his eyes, too, seemed full of tenderness. "That was my name in the world, yes. It mattered little then, and nothing now."

"Cadmar," said Gyric, and put out his hands.

The monk took them for a moment, and with a sudden gesture enfolded Gyric in his massive arms. They embraced, and laughed together, and held each other out at arm's length. Gyric spoke, and in his voice was awe. "My uncle has never gotten over your loss. When you left his hall, and the world, he told my mother he should never see your like again. You were always the best of his warriors."

Cadmar shook his shaggy head. "All that is of the world, and all that I leave gladly behind," he answered, but I felt I saw in his bright eye some glint of pleasure that his fame in the world still lived.

Gyric turned his face slightly, and said, "Ceridwen, you recall that my mother Modwynn was the daughter of a rich bailiff in her home shire? Her brother is now bailiff there, and keeps a fine hall, and Cadmar was amongst his thegns, and always his favourite."

Again the big man shook off this praise. He held Gyric by the shoulders, and peered down searchingly at his face, and the narrow linen wrap about his eyes. Then Cadmar spoke. "How come you to be here, and not with Ælfred?"

Gyric sighed, and dropped his arms. "I was captured by Svein at Englafeld. While I awaited ransom his brother Hingvar came and burnt out my eyes."

Cadmar lifted his own hand to his brow, and I think ground his teeth in dismay.

"Then I was taken to Lindisse, and would have died there had not this Lady carried me off with her."

Cadmar looked at me with new interest. I came up to Gyric and touched his arm, and he took my hand in his.

"Then you are doubly blest," answered Cadmar, "for your new wife is not only beautiful but brave."

No one had ever called me beautiful in front of Gyric, and the hearing of it gave me great pleasure, for Gyric turned to me of a sudden as if he had never before thought of this; and indeed, how could he? And Cadmar had said these words of praise with great strength and heartiness, so that I blushed.

"Yes," said Gyric; and that is all he said, but it was enough.

Cadmar looked at both of us, and then around the little clearing. "Well," he said with cheer, "we must make a wedding-feast, and you must stay and accept what humble comforts I can provide. Each night I spend awake in the forest, but I will return at dawn."

"Right willingly," answered Gyric, and I too nodded my assent.

"We have eggs, and loaves and other good things, Brother," I told him. "There is no need to diminish your store."

He gestured to the cauldron, now bubbling at the full, and proclaiming by its odour what was inside. "And I have fish aplenty, so let us make a feast of it."

Cadmar brought forth from within his hut a bench and table-slab and trestle, and since it was so mild, we set up for our feast under the starry heavens. From our own packs we put out eggs, and bread, and dried apples and pears. Cadmar ladled up the fish he had boiled with new onions and cress, and so we ate. Gyric and I sat together, so close upon the bench that our bodies touched, and his arm was always around my waist. Such was our wedding-feast, in the forest hermitage of the warrior-monk, and if we had sat in the hall of the King himself, and dined from golden plates, it would not have brought me more pleasure.

The two men spoke of many things. Cadmar did not know that Æthelred had died, and that Ælfred now reigned as King of Wessex. Indeed, he knew almost nothing of the world since he had left it, and he listened to all Gyric had to say with sober attention. Gyric spoke not only of the present, but of the past, and I learnt more of Cadmar's fame as a fighter when he was still in the world, for Gyric recounted it from all that he had himself seen and heard. And I learnt too, what had made Cadmar turn from the world, and its glories and pains: He had fought a battle with his own two sons at his side, and watched them be killed.

"One moment they were next to me, flanking me as we fought, and the next moment I stood ankle-deep in their blood. Gold and glory meant nothing to me from that hour, for I had lost that which cannot be reclaimed."

"They were young," recalled Gyric.

"Yes, too young. Caradoc knew sixteen Summers, and Barden, seventeen. They were hot-headed and hasty as their father, and in my pride I would take them into the thick of any battle. And at the end my pride won me their blood."

We were silent. As I gripped Gyric's hand I wondered if he thought that he too had been punished for his pride. Gyric had let himself be captured to help protect Ælfred. He had always assumed that he would be ransomed; all Danes knew an atheling brought a high price. But the gold Gyric would bring meant nothing to Hingvar, who only meant to punish his own brother by spoiling the ransom on Gyric's safe return.

"Things do not turn out as we expect," murmured Gyric.

Cadmar roused himself from his thoughts and answered, "That is truth, and well spoken. So much the greater then to seize that which is true and lasting."

I knew Cadmar spoke of the joys of the Spirit, and not of this world, but Gyric nodded his head and pressed his lips into the palm of my hand.

I BIND MYSELF TO YOU

W E sat there talking under the stars until the Moon slipped beneath the circle of trees.

"It is time that I am off," Cadmar told us. "The nights I spend within the forest, and in prayer. All that you find here, humble as it is, is yours. I will return at Sunrise, and now bid you Good-night." He disappeared into the hut for a moment, and came out with a simple mantle over his arm, and with this little preparation for the coming night, set off.

Gyric and I sat at the rough table, his arm still about my waist, and my hand clasped over his.

I looked over the little clearing and said, "To think here we should find an old friend!"

Gyric nodded. "Yes. And that such a man as he should be the one to witness our pledging. A man known to me, a man who has changed his estate so greatly. How strange life is."

"It does not trouble you, does it, that Cadmar has seen you?"

He shook his head slowly. "No. He is like me, some-how. His life is not what it once was, just as my life is not. And he has my respect, and the respect of all men. I am glad, very glad, that he and not a stranger witnessed our pledges."

This speech filled my heart. It was the first time Gyric had spoken of his new life without cursing it.

"Ceridwen," he asked suddenly, and with a pained voice. "Do you know what you have done today?"

"I know I have wed the man I desire; and I know I have never desired man before. I know that I have passed from maiden to wife, and that the passage gave me great joy; greater joy than I ever knew."

"I hear you say these things, and I believe them, yet I do not know why you feel them. Not about me. Not now."

I put my fingers to his lips. "Hush, Gyric, do not say this. Do not wound me when I am so full of happiness. Just as I am as you find me, so are you. We can do nothing to change that, but only give thanks that Fate has cast our lot together. At least, I give thanks, and always will. There is nothing else I want."

He grasped my hand and pulled me to him, and kissed my lips and whispered, "I want to feel you, naked under me, again."

I gasped, and shivered in his arms, and he held me close and kissed me.

I did not wish to go into Cadmar's hut; it did not seem right. So we spread our bedrolls by the fire, just as if it were our own camp, only on this night we laid the sheepskins side by side. We knelt together upon them, and Gyric pulled off his tunic, and grasped at my gown, and I untied the sash from around my waist.

"Give me your hand," I whispered, and he did. I took his hand in my own, and I wrapped my sash about our wrists with my other hand. So I made fast our hands for a moment, and did so with the sash upon which I had worked the pheasants; the sash which was my finest work, and which I had given, in another lifetime, at the place of Offering.

Although I spoke not he knew what I was doing, for he said softly, "I have nothing to give to you to hold; no true token of my livelihood, for I no longer know what that will be. And as for my possessions, I have nothing here but what you have given to me."

All my heart was in my answer. "I too hold nothing, and give you naught but myself."

"You have given me everything; even restored me to life," he breathed.

"I bind myself to you, Gyric."

"I bind myself to you, Ceridwen, forever."

Now I only kissed him, and thus sealed our Handfasting. I drew off the sash from our wrists and tucked it beneath our sheepskins.

We pulled off the rest of our clothes. Our bodies shone together in the white Moonlight, and the linen wrap around Gyric's head seemed almost to glow. He lay me down, very gently, next to him, and began to kiss my mouth, and his hand glided over the skin of my arm and throat and breasts. Then he touched my belly and rested his hand for a moment over its soft roundness, and then his fingers touched the furry place between my thighs.

"I do not want to hurt you," he whispered.

"You will not hurt me."

"I did, today, by the lake, because you were a maid. I want to be gentle with you."

I put my arms around his neck and pulled him to me, and felt him, hard and hot against my thigh. He raised himself above me, and I lifted my head a little and looked down the length of our bodies.

"Will you touch me?" he breathed. "I want to be touched by you."

"Yes," I breathed back. I reached out my hand and fingered this finest of tools, smooth and iron-hard and warm and yielding all at once. "O, Gyric, how beautiful you are. Like a young stallion."

He did not laugh at this, or at any other thing I said. I stroked him, and he put his head down upon my shoulder, and then found one of my breasts with his mouth. He lowered his hips to mine, and I guided all the warmth and power in my hand to my own furry wetness. He fell into me, slowly, and groaned as he did; and I too gave a little gasp as the hardness of him found my deepest part.

"Ceridwen," he whispered. "Wife."

Tears were running from my eyes, from the sharp sweetness of his body in mine, and at his naming of me.

I clung to him, and kissed him, and as he drove into me he whispered my name over and over, and as many times as he said my name he called me Wife. Then he said, "I want to feel this forever. To move within you, to touch you like this, to give you every part of me."

And I had never before thought that in the act of Love a man gives of himself as fully as a woman does; but when Gyric said this, I saw that this was true, that it was as sacred and giving for him as it was for me.

He thrust himself more deeply within me, and shuddered and groaned and slipped his arm beneath my back and held me against him. His breathing grew quiet, and he loosed his grip on me, and kissed my face and said my name over and over.

He lay next to me, and stroked my body with long smooth strokes. He rubbed my nipples between his fingertips, and stroked my belly, and ran his hands along the inside of my thighs. Then he moved his fingers into my furry thicket, and with one finger parted the tangled hair. He ran his finger up and down the soft folds there, now slick and wet from him, and centred on the tiny warm spot in the mound above it, and touched me there where I had never touched myself. He moved away from me and slipped down my body, and suddenly his head was between my thighs and his mouth upon the tiny inflamed centre of me. He pressed his tongue against that burning dot, and nibbled with his lips around it, and tasted me completely. Then a thousand stars seemed to rain down upon me, and I felt a pleasure so great and deep that I thought I might die, and I cried aloud as hot waves of joy flowed from that tiny burning centre that Gyric held cradled with his lips and tongue.

He lifted his head, and moved, and leaned over me, and plunged his tongue into my open mouth. And I tasted us both, man and woman, every pleasure of our bodies mingled together, salt and spice.

"I love you, Ceridwen. My dearest wife, I love you."

I breathed back those words I had most longed to hear and to speak. "Gyric, I love you. I love you, I love you."

To have known with our bodies a small part of this Mystery was enough, was everything. We need say and do no more. He lay back, and I lay against him, my arm across his chest and my face against his. The linen wrap about his wound had moved so that I could just see the scar upon his right temple. I kissed the mark of fire, and in answer he stroked my face. I reached across for our blankets, and covered us, and fell asleep in his arms, my lips against his cheek.

⚜⚜⚜⚜⚜⚜⚜⚜⚜⚜⚜

I awoke to Gyric's voice in my ear. "The lark is singing, my love."

I opened my eyes. It was still dark, but it was the lark that sang out. Dawn was near. I reached up and kissed his face, and once more pressed my bare skin against his.

He held me for a moment and then asked, "Are you laughing, or weeping?"

"I am laughing, because I am so happy."

The lark sang out again, and I knew I should rise and heat water so that we might wash. Cadmar would be coming back soon, and I did not wish to be still abed when he did.

So we rose, tho' it was hard to tear ourselves apart. I warmed water that we might wash ourselves, and we dressed, and did all this laughing and kissing. I combed and braided my hair, and put the comb in Gyric's hand, and he paused for a moment; but then without turning from me he reached up and untied the wrap about his wound that he might comb his hair.

His face was pale and fair in the early light, so that the dark hollows beneath his brow seemed the darker. I watched him steadfastly, with my heart full of joy.

He finished combing, and then tied the wrap on again. "My hair is grown very long," he said, touching it as it lay on his shoulder.

"Yes," I teased, "it is near long as mine."

This made him laugh, for mine fell past my waist, but he said softly, "It is that long hair that made me start kissing you by the lake."

He put his arm out, and enfolded me against him. As he held me thus we heard Cadmar coming through the woods, singing in a lusty voice that we might be ready for his arrival. He greeted us warmly, and tho' I know I fell to blushing, his twinkling eye was kind as he looked upon me. We broke our fast together as the Sun rose warm and yellow above the hermitage.

When we had finished Cadmar said, "I will not sleep for a few more hours. It is a fine morning, and you are not far from Kilton. Will you not stay the morning and fish with me?"

Gyric thought about this, and then said, "A few more hours will not matter. We are not more than two days from Kilton now. We will stay and fish."

Cadmar smiled. "Good, for I know a spot where the fish are hasty."

This made me curious. "You mean they wish to be caught?"

"Well, they want my worms, which is much the same. I have built a weir, and trapped them in a deep part of my stream, so that they are hungry for whatever I offer. This is why I am still fed so well," ended Cadmar, and patted his belly.

Cadmar took up his basket and lines, and we followed him along the stream through the woods. The ground rose a bit and there was the place that Cadmar had built his weir, for I could see the tops of the wicker-work poking through the green water.

We sat beneath the willows, and Cadmar dug for red worms with a little spade he took from his basket, and then both he and Gyric baited the hooks, and tied the thread lines to willow wands which Cadmar cut fresh.

Sure enough, the fish were both hungry and hasty. One of the lines began to move at once, and Gyric drew it up; but as the fish upon it was small, Cadmar cast it back in again. But we did not wait long, for soon the line Cadmar held was tugged, and he grasped it and pulled up a fine fat bream. This went into the basket, and then I felt a strong tug on the wand I held, and drew it up with a shining bream flapping and spraying droplets of water on the still surface of the pool. I was so happy I laughed, and as Cadmar caught up my line and guided the fish to him, Gyric also had one fast on his line, and in this way quickly had ten or twelve fine bream.

The basket was filled, but we did not rise and leave, for it was pleasant sitting together on the mossy bank. The Sun fell down upon us, and broke through the slender arms of the willows and dappled us with light. The sweetness of Summer seemed full upon us, tho' it be but the middle of May.

We sat quietly, each in our own thoughts, and perhaps it was the sweetness and safety of the place that made Gyric say what he did. "Cadmar," he asked, and turned a little to him. "If my uncle needed you, would you come?"

The monk had been leaning back on the moss. Now he sat up, and looked hard at Gyric. His answer was a question, and very slow. "Come? Come as what? As what I was in the world, or what I am now? Come to fight, or to pray?"

"To fight."

"I am done with all that."

"You have been gone from the world for three years. You do not know how grave the danger is. When you fought for my uncle, the Danes would come in Summer and raid, and then be gone again. Now they do not go, but Winter here as well, and each month more sail the Northern Sea and come to our shores. But they do not come only to plunder and sail off, but to plunder and then to stay. Four Kingdoms have fallen already, and Wessex and Mercia will be sore pressed this Summer."

This was much the same news Gyric had told Cadmar the night before, but today Gyric spoke of Cadmar as being a part of it. Cadmar listened with the grave attention he had shown last night, but shook his head slowly in response to Gyric's words.

"I have forsaken the world. Your uncle released me from my pledges to him. I will fight no more."

"Would you not fight even for my father?"

Cadmar thought on this, and then said, "Godwulf is the greatest ealdorman in Wessex. His thegns have greater glory than any save the King's."

"Yes, and Godwulf keeps all his thegns with such an open hand that they all praise him. He is ever generous with silver and arms and horses and food and drink, and every thegn in his hall wears a silver arm-ring given by his hand, and the men who sit at Godwulf's own table wear a golden arm-ring given by him. Every man of his will gladly die for him. But all his many thegns are not now enough, and my father now arms and trains the best of the young ceorls in Kilton, and soon, too, I think, will arm even the cottars, for he knows every man will be needed. He spoke of these things to me and my brother before I left. This is how grave our need is."

"I will not kill again," uttered Cadmar, but as he said this he ground his teeth.

But Gyric would not relent. "Would you not fight for me, who was crippled by the Danes?"

For answer Cadmar clapped his hand to his brow, and groaned. Still Gyric went on. "Cadmar, the loss of one such arm as yours is great, and becomes greater day by day. There are priests that fight; and Abbots too who take up arms, as you well know."

"I am no trained priest, strong in holiness; only a simple watcher."

"You are one of the best warriors in the Kingdom."

"No. I am grown old, and have lost my taste for war."

Gyric tried one more time. "Your sons were killed by jarl Healfdene's men. Healfdene will be back in Wessex soon."

Cadmar's answer was silence. It was hard to sit there and listen to all this; hard because of the pain in Cadmar's face as he protested the charge that Gyric would have him take up; and hard too to think of what might befall all of Wessex before long.

Cadmar was still quiet, and at last Gyric spoke. "I am sorry, old friend. This is the path you have chosen, and I must honour you for it."

And Gyric lifted his hand in friendship into the space between them, and Cadmar grasped it at once. The monk did not speak, but wore his trouble on his face, where he could not hide it from me. Gyric, too, seemed troubled, perhaps because he had caused Cadmar pain, but also because he thought much of what lay before us all.

When we finally rose and headed back to the hermit-age the Sun was nearly overhead in the sky. I looked about the tiny clearing. Cadmar lived here, wanting nothing, in peace and safety. It was not hard for me to see why he should wish to remain.

Cadmar bid us stay and dine with him before we set off. I brought out loaves and Cadmar flayed open the fish and cleaned them and ran them through with green sticks. These he roasted over the fire. We sat at his table and ate, and the sad words of the morning seemed forgotten.

The Sun was truly over our heads, and Gyric and I began to pack for our leavetaking. Our horses had had a good rest, and the grass all about the clearing was cropped short as proof of it. Cadmar helped us as we saddled them, and he looked them over carefully and said, "These are fine beasts."

Gyric was pulling tight his gelding's girth strap. "They are taken from the Danes," he said, and this was the only reminder of their solemn speech of the morning.

Cadmar nodded his head, and looked again lost in his own thoughts.

We lashed our packs upon our saddles, and as Cadmar had forced all the rest of the roasted fish upon us our food pack was no less full than it had been when we had arrived. The monk would take no silver, even when Gyric asked him to, as a wedding-boon. They clasped hands again, and Gyric and I called out Fare-well one last time, and turned away from the monk and his solitude. We retraced our steps down the path, and as I walked I thought of what had happened there just the day before. The narrow pathway had not led to misery and abandonment, but to the joy of my wedding Gyric, of hearing him pledge to me, and of pledging to him. Everything had changed in a moment on that pathway, and all because I at last spoke my heart to him, and he answered.

We came out to the edge of the trees to where the stream ran, and before we mounted our horses Gyric held me close. And as we kissed there the Sun shone full on our faces, and I knew that Gyric felt its warmth upon his cheek, for he lifted his face to it.

I whispered "Life is sweet, is it not?" and for answer he kissed me again.

"If we do not stop this, we will never go far today," he said at last, and in truth I did not care if we stayed right there and went no farther.

But stop we did, and swung onto our horses, and set out.

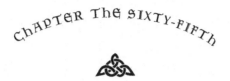

CHAPTER THE SIXTY-FIFTH

TREASURE LIKE THIS

GYRIC felt it was now safe to ride upon the road we found, and so we did, with the Sun at our right shoulders. This road was a good one, of hard and smooth clay, well-made and well-kept. We could have cantered if we had wanted, for there was no danger of our horses catching their hooves, but I did not suggest it, nor did Gyric. After a while he said, "Ceridwen, I do not want to meet anyone before we reach Kilton."

"You mean, if I see folk upon the road, we should not come upon them?"

"Yes. It is safer that way; but it is not only that." He twisted his fingers in his gelding's black mane. "I do not want to be seen by someone who knows me. They would want to go ahead to Kilton, and tell my family I still live, and tho' it may seem unkind, I do not want this. I want to go to my parent's hall in my own way, and time."

"I understand, of course I do."

He nodded his head. "I knew you would."

He reached out his hand for mine, and when he had it pressed it to his lips. "Is there a place here to stop?" he surprised me by asking. "Or is it all woods on both sides?"

"I think there is a little clearing beyond the trees, just to one side of us."

"I want to stop, just for a while," he said, and squeezed my hand.

"Yes," was all I answered, and we got down from our horses. I led them through the scrub-trees, Gyric walking by his gelding's side. I tied the horses, and then I was in Gyric's arms, and he was kissing me so that I could not catch my breath, nor did I wish to.

"I want to kiss you all over," he whispered.

I pulled out our sheepskins and we fell upon them. And he did kiss me everywhere, and I too was bold, and stroked and touched every part of his beautiful body.

I knew I was clumsy as I did this, and thought I should feel shy of what I did, but did not; for the joy of being with him in this way, and the sheer beauty of him, and the way in which he gave his body to me left no room in me for shyness or fear. He was gentle with me in every way, even when his desire for me was greatest, and when at last we lay quiet he pressed my hand over his heart with great tenderness. We dozed for a while, and when the Sun was slanting to the West finally dressed and came out upon the road again.

We travelled upon the good clay road, and no one saw us, for when we heard someone before or behind we went into the trees until they passed out of sight. But this only happened twice, so it was not a hardship. At dusk we came to a cross-roads, marked by a huge stone dolmen. As I built our fire that night Gyric said, "We are on my father's lands. This is Kilton."

"It is?"

I looked around me, expecting something different. The forest was much like all we had ridden through in Wessex.

"Yes. As soon as we crossed the road by the dolmen, we were in Kilton."

"Then you know this place well."

"Yes. I have hunted many times in this very forest."

It grew dark as we sat there side by side, and I looked up into the heavens. "The Swan is flying across the sky, and the Bear is chasing it," I told Gyric, looking at the star patterns above us. One of the wanderers was bright, and looked blue in the warm night.

"Why do the wanderers not travel with the rest of the stars?" I asked him.

"I do not know," he answered, and raised his own face to the sky. "They are so much larger than the other stars."

"They are leaders, not followers," I decided. I leaned my head against his shoulder. "You are a leader too, Gyric. Your speech is such that would inspire any man. When you spoke to Cadmar, I saw that he struggled within him, for your words struck him to the core."

"Men do not lead only with words. Action is what is most needed."

"'Words inspire action,'" I remembered.

"Is that from the Holy Book?"

"No. It is something Woden said after he gave the gift of rune-writing to his people."

"I do not recall that," he mused. "You know more sagas than I. But," he went on, "it is a good saying: 'Words inspire action.' And it is true."

I sat quietly next to him, not wanting or needing to speak more. The time for sleep grew near, and we undressed and lay down together. Just feeling his naked skin against mine was pleasure enough.

At dawn I sensed he was already awake, tho' he lay still beside me. I touched his cheek, and he took my hand at once. "Is it light?" he asked.

"It is just dawning now," I told him.

He pressed his warm body against mine and I put both my arms around him. He began to kiss my face and lips, and with his slender fingers to stroke my breasts. But he stopped, and lowered his face next to mine. His hands were still and he did not move.

I stroked his back and touched his hair, and wondered what was wrong. His shoulders began to shake, as if he wept, and I held him fast in my arms. He pulled away from me, but kept his hand upon my face.

"Gyric," I whispered.

He shook his head and laid his face against mine, but pulled back again. "I want to see you," he cried out. "I will never see you. Cadmar said you were beautiful. I want to see you!"

He fell back upon his sheepskin, facing the lightening sky, the wrap about his wound as blank as what it hid. There were no words within me that could answer him. I fell upon him and began to kiss his white brow, and his cheeks and chin and lips, and the tears that streamed from my eyes wet his face and hair. I wept the tears that he could not, and wept them for us both, for we both were denied through the loss of his eyes.

Suddenly he was full of anger. "Why did you not let me die?" he asked, and each word fell as if he had struck me.

But I could not pull back from him, and buried my face in his chest and sobbed. The image of Gwenyth rose up in my mind, and I heard her terrible words, warning me that a part of Gyric would never forgive me.

My own anger stirred within me, and I was able to make steady my voice. "I wanted you to live, that is why. I risked everything for that."

"O, God," he groaned, and put both of his hands over his wrap. "Forgive me. O Ceridwen, forgive me."

I put my hands over his. "I do not need to forgive you. I know your anger is not meant for me. Your anger is just. But do not let it come between us, Gyric. That I could not bear, after all we have suffered together."

He let me move his hands, and then he enfolded mine, and pulled my face to his. "No man ever had treasure like this," he said. "No man ever had a wife so courageous or true."

He kissed my lips, and kissed also all the tears from my wet face. "And I know you are beautiful," he whispered. "I feel it when I touch you."

"I do not think I am as beautiful as you," I whispered back. "You are the most beautiful man I ever saw."

"Even . . . as I am?"

"Yes. Your lips and mouth, the line of your nose and chin, the smoothness of your brow, your hair, your fingers, so long and slender; your arms and legs . . ." I trailed off, too shy to say more. "Every part of you. You are so beautiful."

I laughed a little as I went on. "And we are the right size for each other."

"Yes," he agreed, and began to kiss me. "Our bodies fit together well. Very well."

"We should dress," said Gyric at last, but he did not take his lips from off my throat. "I do not want some wood-gatherer to come upon us, rutting like two cottars under a haystack." I had to blush and laugh at the same time; and so we rose and set off.

We took a small trail, in places not much more than a deer track. The growth was thick about us, and we were noisy, for our horses trampled upon small branches that snapped beneath their hooves. We paused for a moment on the trail, and heard the crashing of some other creature coming near. I held my mare's head, and Gyric, who was mounted, quietly said my name. I put my hand upon his knee so that he knew I was alert, and tried to keep both our horses from moving.

It was too late. The noise came closer, and a moment later a gruff voice rang out.

"Stay!"

I saw the swaying of branches before us, and a glimpse of brown, and then a burly yellow-haired man carrying a hide pack upon his back stepped into the path before us. "Stay," he bellowed again, but in truth there was no place for us to go, as he blocked the way ahead. He was armed with a short sword at his side, but made no move to draw it. "Who tempts trespass on my Lord Godwulf's lands?"

"Godwulf's son, Gyric," answered he in a calm voice.

The man's amaze could have been no greater. His jaw dropped open, and he took a step back to get a better vantage point at which to stare at Gyric as he sat upon his horse.

His eyes fastened upon Gyric's face, but he said no more. Gyric slipped off his horse and came and stood in front of me.

"Is it you, my Lord? You are returned?"

"I am Gyric."

The man fell upon one knee in the trail before us, and sputtered, "Forgive me, my Lord. The hall is lamenting your death."

"I am not dead."

The man was studying Gyric's person, and convinced himself that no ghost stood before him. "No, my Lord." The man looked about the walls of green that surrounded us. "But how come you here, my Lord? We are only an hour from the road. Let me take you to it. We will be at my Lord's hall before dark."

"No. Who are you? What is your name?"

"I am Cort, your Lord, one of the gamesmen. I am setting snares for your Lord's table."

"I recall you. I want no one to know that I am arrived. Do not return to the burh tonight, and tell no one you meet that you have seen me."

The gamesman nodded his head, his mouth still open. Gyric pulled out a silver piece and held it in front of him, but it was nowhere near the man. The gamesman took a few steps and touched Gyric's hand, and the coin dropped from one to the other.

"Thank you, my Lord. All will be as you command."

"Go on your way now," answered Gyric.

The gamesman began backing away, and then Gyric called to him. "Stay, fellow. You are about the burh. Is all well there?"

The man blinked at Gyric. "I think all is well, my Lord, save that all be grieving you. My Lord Godwin was gone for weeks, trying to bargain for your return. All he heard was that you were dead. It was said amongst us gamesmen that he took a whole casket of gold with him, to buy back your life with."

"My Lord Godwulf is well? And my mother?"

"They be well, my Lord, but – but pardon me, my Lord, your father's hair is grown more white than ever."

"Go on your way now."

"Yes, my Lord. Yes."

So the man went.

When we could hear the fellow no more, I touched Gyric's hand. "What joy there will be when they all see you."

His answer was short, and sad. "They will see me – yes."

We went on, crossing from one trail to another, heading steadily South. We paused in a clearing late in the afternoon, and a breeze came up as it often does at that time of day. There was a smell in it that made me sniff.

"It is the sea, Ceridwen. Do you smell it? That is how near we are."

"The sea? It can be smelt?"

I took another sniff. It was tangy and fresh and not like any other thing my nose had met.

"Yes, not only smelt, but tasted. It is salt, and fishes, and sea-weeds, and everything else that dwells there," he said. "Tomorrow you will see it," but his voice was quiet as he told me this.

We stood together for a few moments longer, and he said, "In the morning we will come to the hall. There is a place I know that will be good to spend tonight at, a glade with a spring. From there we will be only an hour or so from the burh."

Near dusk we found the glade. We loosed the horses and unpacked our things as we had always done, and I built our fire and warmed our food as I had each night; but tonight we both knew that this was the last time we should live this way. Tomorrow we would enter the comforts and joys and sorrows of the hall, and our life together on the road be over, forever.

And as I did every task that night, I held this knowledge within me, so that I think I touched my brass tinderbox in a different way; and regarded our little bronze cauldron with real affection. I recalled when Ælfwyn and Burginde and I had arrived at Four Stones, and the waggons were unpacked and the chests and baskets brought into our chamber, and thinking then that the waggon in which we had lived, and which had been shelter and a home to us upon the road, was now again only a common waggon. So now our tinderbox, and cauldron, and roasting fork, and bowls – all of these needful and precious things for our journeying – would lose their importance and become no more than what they were.

Our meal was a quiet one. I did not try to rouse Gyric from his thoughts, for I knew much crowded upon his brow. He ate little, and spoke almost not at all, but I could not feel troubled, for always his hand was in mine, or his arm around my waist.

We lay together that night without coupling, but only held each other, simply and sweetly. He stroked my face and hair for a long time, and I fell asleep upon his chest. Later in the dark I woke to his cry as he tossed in his sleep,

and knew he rode the night-mare. I woke him with words
and kisses, and he slept again, and tho' he told me not of
his dream, it was not hard to guess that it was of the night
he was maimed.

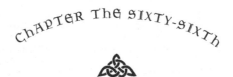

THE WELCOMING

THE morning dawned, and I touched Gyric's cheek. He took my hand at once and kissed my finger-tips. I felt then that he might have been lying awake by my side for hours.

A breeze blew to us from the West, and on it was again the smell of the sea, telling us which way we must ride. I sat before our hide packs and drew out those clothes that I thought most fitting for us to wear that day. Amongst the silk gowns that Ælfwyn had given me was one of a watery green colour, and I chose that, and wrapped my pheasant sash around my waist. And I wore for the first time the green leathern shoes that she had packed for me as well, and put on at my throat the silver disc pin set with green stones she had given me the day she was wed to Yrling. And so thanks to Ælfwyn's great kindness I would appear before Gyric's people splendidly arrayed, with a gown and jewel of great worth.

For Gyric I chose the best of the linen tunics from Merewala's chest, and a pair of dark blue wool leggings, and the leg-wrappings of brown leather. He had no light-weight mantle, only the green one trimmed with gold wire and lined with miniver. But it was magnificent, and worthy of a King's kinsmen, and he pinned it around his shoulders with the huge spiral silver pin that had been amongst the treasure that Ælfwyn had given us. On his right wrist he wore the silver bracelet set with lapis stones, and on each of his little fingers, the gold rings. Beyond all treasure that he carried was the silver and gold-hilted seax that he wore at his waist.

We packed our camp for the last time, and I took a little effort to make our horses as trim as I could. I combed their manes and tails with my own comb, and as Gyric sat quietly by the spring, I plucked a rose for each and threaded its stem in close to the horse's ears. Even they should be bedecked, I thought, for they had served us long and well upon our journey.

We tied our packs upon their saddles, and I looked about the glade a final time, to be certain that we left no thing behind. Gyric stood by his gelding, and after he had lashed his spear against the animal's flank turned to me.

"I am ready," is all he said.

We set out into the beautiful morning, and I gave thanks for its fairness. We passed out of the glade into the trees, and one look told me that they were often trimmed and cut for wood. Here too were broad paths rutted from the wheels of heavy-laden carts. We travelled on the broadest of these, and the trees began to thin to grassland.

To one side of us I spied a low wooden tower, of simple make, upon which was a platform of wood. From it a man turned and screwed up his eyes at us. About his shoulder he wore a leathern strap from which hung a brass horn.

"Gyric, there is a sentry ahead of us, in a tower."

"He is one of the ward-corns. Stop your mare."

The man now was scrambling down the tower, and ran to us with his horn held in his fist. He stopped before Gyric's horse and knelt. "My Lord, you are back," he gulped, not taking his eyes for one moment from his master.

"Yes, I am back. I go now to my father. Do not sound your horn, or leave your post. I know that you have seen me, and have been watchful."

The ward-corn was too astonished to say more than, "Yes, my Lord. As you wish it."

We left the man, gaping in the grass after us.

The trees fell away as we rode up a slight knoll, and upon the top of it I reined my mare, for below and before us was all our goal.

My eyes swept over the whole plain. Just before us were groves of trees planted in rows, with cottars working amongst them. To one side was a rolling expanse of pasture land, clustered with flocks of sheep so thick that hundreds must graze there. More were crowded into wooden pens, which I guessed might be the milking pens, for now that Summer was near upon us and the lambs weaned the cheeses would be made. Beyond the milking pens was a fenced pasture which held four score or more of spotted cattle, more than I had ever seen together in my life.

Beyond this was the village of Kilton, with huts so many that I could not guess their number. Each had a large croft, and I saw many cattle biers and pig-houses and fowl coops within the crofts. A broad smooth road ran through the centre of the village; and my eye followed it, a dull red ribband, as it wound to the palisade of the burh of Kilton. There my eye rested long. The burh stood thrusting up upon a cliff of rock. Beyond it lay the brilliant blue waters of the sea.

From our vantage I could see beyond the palisade and into the yard, and knew at once that I stood before the largest buildings, of the finest make, that I had ever seen or imagined. The hall itself was easy to mark, for tho' it was set well back in the yard beyond the palisade wall, it was so tall and large that it proclaimed itself at once.

There were many other buildings in the yard, of all sizes, and a chapel built of stone; but my eyes were fixed upon the tall white timber walls of the hall.

"It is like the halls of the Gods," I finally said.

"There are orchards before us," Gyric replied. "Let us take the road that runs through them."

I turned my mare down the grassy slope and we gained the road that would bring us to the trees. There were medlars, and apples, and quinces, and cherries, and I think many more that I could not name by their bark or tiny fruit. Folk bent amongst the trees, weeding or trimming sucker-growth, and as we approached they stopped in their work and looked at Gyric. Some of them ran out to us, and some of them ran away, and others crossed themselves. None of them spoke to us, or called out to Gyric, for they were too humble to approach a Lord; and since none of them looked to run ahead to tell others, I did not tell Gyric that they watched us.

We passed out of the trees, and walked upon smooth grass. I looked back and saw a few of the orchard-workers trailing behind us at a distance, their faces filled with amaze.

The burh was before us, and now I could see a great number of men at one end of the palisade fence, hard at work in the morning Sun. "There are many labourers digging a big trench before the wall, starting at the left," I told Gyric.

He turned his face as if he looked at the place. "That was Godwin's idea. I am glad my father allowed it. It will help in the defence should we be besieged."

We were not far from the wall now, and my eyes were fastened upon the open gate. A movement above caught my eye, and I looked up to see the figure of a woman walking along a parapet on the top of the palisade. Her back was to us, and we were far below her and many paces away, but I knew at once it must be Modwynn, the mother of Gyric. She was tall and slender, and wearing a mourning-mantle of cream-coloured wool.

I stopped our horses, and said softly, "Gyric, your mother walks the ramparts above us."

Then my eye was caught by a man who walked along the top of the gate arch. He looked at us and raised a shining horn to his lips and sounded a long low note.

Modwynn turned, and looked down upon us where we sat on our horses, and she moved not. I raised my hand to her, and tried to smile, but I think she saw me not; her eyes were fast upon Gyric. Her hands went to her heart, and she stood without moving. Suddenly she turned and vanished from the parapet; and all the time the sentry upon the wall blew out the long note from his brass horn.

Men dressed in the way of warriors started to rush out from the gate to meet us, but then stopped, their faces joyful and grave and wondering; and then Modwynn and a man in a cream-coloured mantle trimmed with gold thread-work hurried through them and came fast to us.

"Here is your father and mother, Gyric," I told him, for the man, white-haired and aged, carried the dignity of his estate upon him.

I turned away from his parents to Gyric, and his face was pale. He took a deep breath, and swung himself down from his horse, and I slipped off my mare. Now his parents were nearly upon us, their eyes full of tears and joy.

Gyric took a step forward and held out his hand, not in welcome, but to stay their movement towards him. They both stopped and stood speechless and wondering.

"I beg you to stay father, until I speak to you," began Gyric, and his whole body trembled as he asked this.

He fell upon his knees and began to speak. "I have come back, and know you have grieved for me, and beg your pardon for it. I have come back, but nothing shall be as it was, and now I shall be only a burden and never a blessing to you. I am alive, but the Dane Hingvar has burnt out my eyes."

Godwulf gave a howl, and raised his clenched fists towards the heavens, and Modwynn pressed her hands against her face and wept. Then she took a step towards Gyric, but he raised his hand again as if to fend them off.

A man, young and vigourous, now ran across the field to us from the farthest end of the palisade. He ran straight to us, and with such boldness that Gyric too turned his face towards his approach. The man ran up to us, and I looked him in the face, and my heart turned within my breast, for before me stood the face and form of Gyric, but whole and unmaimed, for his eyes of golden-green flashed as he looked upon his kneeling brother.

"Gyric!"

"Are you here, Godwin?"

"I am here, brother," he answered, and the horror in his father's face told Godwin everything about the linen wrap that Gyric wore.

Gyric turned his face back to his parents, and went on. "Now that I am back, maimed as I am, I beg you to accept me. And if in any way you welcome my return, then I beg you to accept this Lady with me, for without her I would have been dead many weeks. At great risk to herself she carried me from the keep of Four Stones in Lindisse, and kept me alive when I was near death, and has travelled all these many weeks with me, in hardship and danger, and has shown nothing but courage and faith. She is the sole reason I live, and return to you; and I have made her my wife."

During this speech the eyes that had been fast upon Gyric turned to me, and looked at me with wonder. Tears were running from my own eyes as Gyric spoke, not only from the horror and pity and love in the faces of his parents and brother, but to hear now his great praise of me.

Now Gyric, still kneeling, pressed his two hands together before him, as a thegn does to vow to his Lord. His words were scarce above a whisper. "Do you accept me into your hall, father?"

Godwulf waited not an instant, but crossed the grass between he and his son in one stride, and clasped the upraised hands between his own. I did not hear what he said in return, nor did I see what happened next, for suddenly Modwynn was before me. She caught me up and embraced me, and the tears upon our faces mingled as she kissed me and spoke. "My dearest daughter. You have brought my son back from the dead to me."

Her face, lined with years and ravaged by grief, was full of beauty and nobility beyond any I had seen in woman. I had no answer for her but my kiss, for her words choked me.

She turned to her youngest son, and clung to him and wept in his arms, and Godwulf kept one arm about them both. I lifted my head and saw Godwin there, and again felt my heart move within my breast; and I could only stare at him as he stood before me.

He was taller and broader than Gyric; he had more of his father in him. But the hair was the same coppery-gold, and the face had the same smooth brow, straight nose, and beautiful mouth. It was Gyric; it was him in every particular; but it was as if Gyric were whole again. I stood staring at him as if elf-shot. His eyes were truly golden-green, and he stepped closer to me and a voice within my soul whispered, This is Gyric, whole.

Then Godwin spoke, and his voice was his own, and not Gyric's. "Who are you?" he asked, but not unkindly. "You did what none of us could do."

"I am of Mercia. I am Ceridwen, daughter of Cerd. My father was an ealdorman by the river Dee."

I said these words as I had so many times before, but now they seemed without meaning, or at least not to answer his question.

He just looked at me, and then he turned to his brother, and the two of them embraced, and I could not tell if they were laughing or weeping.

Gyric called my name, and I was in his arms, and he embraced both me and Godwin at the same time. And there was such strength in this embrace that I could not breathe, so strong was it; and in the arms about me I felt that all the strength and health of Godwin and I flowed willingly and joyfully into my beloved Gyric.

Then Godwulf started to shout out commands; and Modwynn came up beside us, and we were all walking towards the gate. I was aware that a large number of folk were now gathered about us, and that there was much noise and tumult; and that men were leading our horses behind us; and I even saw that the orchard workers still stood, a long way off, watching us. Now we were going through the gate, and there were so many men about us that it seemed a whole army dwelt there, for they were all dressed in leathern tunics and wore seaxs strapped cross their bellies.

Everyone was talking at once, and some of us were still crying, and folk who knew not what had happened were coming out of this or that work-shed or stable in the yard, and seeing for the first time the returned Gyric; and all of this was on top of the ordinary noise of a great hall's yard, for there were penned cattle lowing, and sheep baaing, and pigeons cooing and fluttering in and out of a big dove-cote, and roosters crowing for no reason.

Now we were before the great hall itself, and I looked up at timber walls made of slabs of oak four times my height. The huge oak door stood open on iron hinges as thick as a strong man's wrist. Godwulf walked in first, with Gyric's hand upon his arm, and me holding Gyric's other hand.

I had nothing to compare it to; it was twice as large as the ruins of Four Stones. Like all timber halls, it had a firepit, and trestle tables ready to be set around the walls; but nothing else was like the hall of my kinsman or the hall at Four Stones. Firstly, it was light inside, almost bright; and it was not the smoke hole above the firepit that made it so. At the centre of each of the two long walls there were set two wooden frames with iron casements, and these iron casements held many score of small pieces of glass, so clear that the Sun streamed through and made sharp shadows on the floor. The walls, too, were painted white, but not only white; for there were coloured designs of all sorts upon them, birds and dragons and flowers and trees and running harts and hinds. There were several doors cut into the walls, leading to where I knew not; and one of the long walls had many sleeping alcoves cut into it. The floor beneath our feet was of creamy stone with grey veins in it, and it too seemed to give off light. At the far narrow end of the hall the stone floor stepped up to form a low platform. It was there we all went to, and serving men came running out before us and set up a broad table on its trestles before we reached it.

Godwulf still held his son's arm, and I his hand, and when we came to this step Gyric seemed to be waiting for it, so that Godwulf had only to say a word and Gyric stepped up upon it without tripping.

There were thirteen of us who came and stepped upon this stone platform. There was Godwulf, and Modwynn, and Gyric, and me, and Godwin, and eight men, all dressed as warriors, save one, who I just noticed, a young man with dark hair who wore the surplice and beads of a priest. The men who were warriors were of all ages; two of them looked as young as Gyric, three of them looked to have thirty years or so; and the last two were older still, with streaks of grey in their hair and eyes lined with years. And all of them, even the youngest, looked battle-hard and grim, and all watched well the faces of Godwulf and Godwin.

Another man was there upon the stone step with us, but I could not tell his estate by looking at him. He was not a thegn, and he was not a churchman, and he was not a serving man. He did not sit with us, but rather perched upon a tall stool at one end of the table, saying nothing, but listening to all. He was a man above middle-age, with a sharp and wizened face, and he held his head canted so that he seemed to be ear-first as he faced you.

Serving men were everywhere. They carried forth two great carved oak chairs from against the wall and set them side by side; and in these great chairs sat Godwulf and Modwynn. They set benches on either side of these chairs for the rest of us, while others carried basins with water that we might wash our hands, and linen towels to dry them. Even the serving men were different from those I had ever seen before. Their tunics were clean, their hair neatly trimmed, and they worked quietly and quickly at their jobs. Modwynn spoke to one of them.

"Bring the mead that is in the smallest cask in the black chest."

Gyric spoke in return. "Mother, I have been longing for your good ale. Could we not drink that first?"

Modwynn's face creased in pleasure. "Go to the ale-house, and bring the last cask in the line there," she now told the serving man.

A silver tray as round as the full Moon was carried out, and upon it sat two goblets of pure gold, and these were set before Godwulf and Modwynn. A second silver tray came, crowded with cups of silver, and silver trimmed with gold, each different from the next. One each was set before us, and I saw that Gyric's cup had his name carved into the golden rim of it.

The ale came, and Modwynn rose, and herself took
up the ewer, and as a sign of great honour poured first
for her returned son, and then for me. Then she poured
out into Godwulf's cup of gold, and then into Godwin's of
silver and gold. Lastly she poured for the young priest, and
then for herself; and the chief serving man, who was like
unto a steward, poured for the rest.

Gyric moved his hand to feel the stem of his goblet,
and as he touched it and took it up all eyes were upon him.
He reached for my hand and held it fast as we lifted our
cups.

The ale was the kind known as bright ale, for by long
standing it becomes pure and clear, so that it looks bright
as it is poured. The savour of it was delicious, like walnuts
and toasted loaves and cream and spice; it was none of
those things, but tasted a part of all of them.

We had one cup, and then a second, and then it was
time to tell the tale.

I sat quietly at Gyric's side, holding his hand as he
told the story. He began by telling of the last battles he
fought with Ælfred while Æthelred still lived and ruled
as King. There had been three battles since he had left
Kilton, and each, except for the first at Æscedune, the Vale
of the White Horse, had been won by the Danes. These
things they had heard from others, for the battles were
great ones. He told of the battle at Englafeld where he had
been captured, and how he had taken the dragon banner
from Ælfred, and that the Danes led by Svein had thought
that he was the prince.

I watched the faces of the others as he said this, and
knew that they had heard this already, perhaps I thought,
from Ælfred himself.

Then he told, as simply as he had told me, the story of his maiming: that while he was awaiting ransom, Svein's brother Hingvar had come and taken him in the middle of the night and put out his eyes with a flaming poker.

His voice was quiet during all of this. Godwulf clenched his fists and looked as if he would howl again, but did not. Modwynn covered her face with her hands and sobbed. Godwin leaned forward on the table and grasped the stem of his goblet so tight that his knuckles went white. The priest held the cross he wore about his neck in his hand, and his lips moved in silent prayer. The other men sat rigid and still, turning their eyes from Gyric to Godwulf to Godwin.

"I do not remember much more. I tried to escape later by crawling away, and was kicked until I was senseless. Then I remember nothing until I awoke in the forests of Lindisse."

He stopped, and turned his face to me, and all there at the table did as well.

"My wife is Ceridwen, the daughter of a dead ealdorman of Mercia, by the Dee. She must tell you how she came to be at Lindisse, and how she carried me off."

I took a breath, and did not know if I could keep steady my voice. Gyric pressed my hand, and I gained calmness and courage.

I told them of my earliest life, and of how I had come to meet Ælfwyn upon the Northly Road. They all knew of Ælfsige, and of the Peace he had tried to forge. The name of the Dane Yrling seemed to mean little to them; but then Lindisse was far from Kilton. I said that we had learnt that a man of Wessex was held captive in the cellars below the hall at Four Stones, and that as Ælfwyn was a woman of Wessex she wanted very much to help, tho' she risked great harm from her own husband if she was found out. And the rest I told exactly as it happened, and praised at every chance Ælfwyn's bravery and generosity, and the great courage of those who had helped us escape.

Gyric took up the story then, and told of our adventures upon the road, and all that we had done, and all who we had met, good and bad. The last and best of these, he said, was Cadmar, who lived not two day's ride from Kilton, and who had witnessed our pledging.

"When were you wed?" asked Modwynn.

"Three days ago," answered Gyric.

"Tonight will be a wedding-feast, as well as a thank-offering," smiled Modwynn.

We all sat and were quiet. Godwulf was gazing up at the roof rafters. His jaw was still clenched in anger and in grief. Godwin too had not moved, and leaned across the table, staring steadfastly at Gyric. The young priest had his head lowered. The other men sat still, watching Godwulf as if for a sign.

Godwulf lowered his head to look at us, and began to speak. His manner was gruff, and I could see his eyes were wet.

"Ælfred sent a rider to us the day you were captured. He did not wait for our gold, tho', but offered his own to the Danes for your return. Godwin rode at once to Ælfred, carrying a great store of treasure with him for your wergild. But Ælfred's own gold had been refused, and your brother could learn nothing of where you were. At last a message came to them, saying that you and your companions had been killed while trying to escape."

"And Ealhelm and Eadwold and Wistan and Ælfric? They have not returned?" asked Gyric. He turned his head from side to side, as if hoping one of them sat near him now, and would call out to him.

"None of them," answered Godwulf.

Gyric let go the stem of his cup and sunk his forehead into his upraised hand. All were silent, looking at him, wondering if he would speak more, but he did not.

The steward who had been standing behind Modwynn came up and whispered to her. Modwynn rose and touched her husband's shoulder and said softly, "There is much to prepare. I will be back soon."

She moved away, and the steward and other serving men who had been standing nearby followed her out a rear door.

As soon as she was gone, the table drew closer, and the air about it was tight with tension. Godwin rose and came over and stood before Gyric, the narrow table between them. Godwin had his hand on the hilt of his sword, and he gripped it so his fingers had no colour left.

"Gyric," he began, in a voice raw with anger. "In the morning we will come and pledge your revenge."

Gyric reached out with his right hand to Godwin, and Godwin stepped forward and took it, and Gyric pressed the entwined hands to his own breast, and in this way showed his assent.

And no man at that table did aught but grimly nod their heads, and stamp their feet upon the stone floor to show they wanted blood; none save Godwulf and the priest. Godwulf howled as if he would with his bare teeth destroy the man who had maimed his son; and the priest was mouthing prayers over and over as if they might deliver all of us.

The hall rang with this noise, for it was near empty save for the men who stood clustered by the door, waiting. Gyric and Godwin let drop their hands, and Godwin stood before his father and drew a long breath. Godwulf nodded to his elder son, and I saw all the eyes of the thegns upon Godwin. Godwin motioned with his hand, and the thegns got up as one man and followed him across the stone floor and out of the hall. The young priest too rose, and went away, and the strange man upon the stool slipped off as well; and Gyric and I were alone in the vast hall with Godwulf.

THIS BELONGS TO YOU

I felt fear at that moment of this mighty Lord, and felt over bold as I looked at him; but look I must, for I needs must be Gyric's eyes as well as my own. He sat in his great oak chair gazing on Gyric, and his pale blue eyes were again wet as he did so.

He rose and left his great chair, and came and sat upon the bench next to his son. Gyric put his hand out, the one which Godwin had just taken in pledge, and asked in a soft voice, "Father?"

And Godwulf took Gyric's fine hand in his own scarred and callused one and said, "Yes, my boy."

I thought surely they would want to be alone. As I began to rise, Gyric stayed my hand from slipping from his.

Now Godwulf spoke to his son, and each word was heavy and slow. "My boy, why did you come upon us as you did? The shock was great, to all of us."

"Forgive me father, I never meant to give you further hurt. We were stopped in the forest by one of your snares-men, and then again by a ward-corn, but I ordered both to silence. I wanted to speak to you first, to come before you myself and tell you what had befallen me. Forgive me if I have done wrong."

Godwulf pondered this for a moment as he turned his son's hand over in his own. "I understand. It was your tale to tell. A man must be the first to tell his own story."

Gyric nodded his head, and Godwulf turned his eyes from his son to me. I tried not to flinch under his gaze; but as I looked upon him I was most aware that he was powerful and rich and a renowned warrior.

"And your story, Lady, is also one of wonder and amaze."

I mutely nodded my head, but could not smile, try as I might.

"None of your kinsmen, father or uncle, live? All at the river Dee have passed from the Earth?"

My throat tightened, for I saw he could not be pleased that his son had taken a woman such as me for his wife: I was from an unknown shire in another land, my father long-dead and of little importance, and I brought nothing to Gyric as far as lands or sheep or cattle.

"My mother lives, my Lord. But she is not of the world," I managed to say.

"There is no relation to whom I could send a bride-price?"

"A bride-price?"

I could scarce believe it. He did not complain that I brought no riches with me; he thought instead to send treasure to my own folk.

"You are an ealdorman's daughter. I expect to pay well for you for my son, tho' I can never match what you have brought me."

"I am only sorry that I bring so few goods into this hall," I murmured.

"None of that matters. You have brought my son alive to me again."

He touched the green mantle that Gyric wore and asked, "How came you by this fine mantle?"

"My wife provided it, like all else."

"Well, rather the Lady Ælfwyn I served at Four Stones did," I told him. "It was part of the clothing she gave for Gyric from the chest of the dead Lord of Four Stones. She was very generous in outfitting us," I ended, wanting to give her far more credit than I could.

"Ælfsige's daughter," muttered Godwulf, shaking his head. "It is a bad business."

He looked down at the seax that Gyric had strapped across his waist. "And this fine seax? Was this also from the trove of Four Stones?"

"Yes," answered Gyric, and pulled it out so that his father might examine it. "We think it was Merewala's, and that one of the serving women hid it after his death. At least Ceridwen found it in a food bag, which had been packed for us by such a woman."

"You had true friends there," nodded Godwulf, and held the hilt in his hand. "It is better than my own."

"Then I give it to you, father," Gyric said at once.

"No, no," replied Godwulf, and guided Gyric's hand to the hilt. "It shall remain yours. You have worn it these many weeks, and already drawn blood with it."

Wood creaked on wood, and Modwynn came through a door behind us. She left it open, and I heard a faint booming sound from outside. I whispered to Gyric, and he stood up. I too stood with him, and Modwynn's face was full of love and sorrow and joy as she came up to Gyric. She clasped him to her, and then made him sit down again while she stood behind him, her hands upon his shoulders.

"We have not enough time to kill an ox, but we shall have a milk-calf for our table tonight, and as many other good things as Kilton yields," she told us, and her voice was low and mild and full of gentle pride.

She stroked Gyric's hair with her white hands, slender and beautiful like his own. She looked down at me and smiled. "What an ornament we have in you, daughter," she said, and my whole heart went out to her, not for her praise, but for the kindness in her tone, and for the ready way she named me daughter. She turned to her husband and said, "It is a long time since we have had such a beauty at our table."

Godwulf looked at me and nodded, and then looked back to Modwynn. "A beauty sits by my side each night," was his answer.

She laughed, a sound wonderful to hear, for I knew it must have been many long weeks since any laughter had crossed her lips.

Godwulf stood up now, and Gyric felt him move and rose too in respect.

"I speak now to Godwin," was what Godwulf said to us all. "Keep well until I see you."

He walked the length of the hall and went out the main door, and the group of fighting men who had been standing there the whole time parted and then followed him out.

Modwynn took my hand, and gave it a little squeeze. She turned to Gyric.

"Godwin has given you the bower-house, Gyric. I am having your things brought to it now. Would you like to go there and rest?"

"The bower-house? Where will he and Edgyth sleep?"

Modwynn's voice was gentle. "Edgyth has gone home, Gyric. She has been gone for four months, since Candlemas." She turned to me. "Are you weary, Ceridwen? Perhaps just to rest would be welcome."

"You are so kind, my Lady," I told her.

"Please to call me Modwynn," she smiled.

Gyric seemed lost in thought, and now said, "Yes, I would like to be quiet for a while. And Ceridwen wants to look at the sea. Let us go out into your garden, and from there to the bower-house."

Modwynn began to take his arm, but Gyric stopped and asked, "Can you have my spear brought to me? The one tied to my saddle?"

"Of course," answered Modwynn, and clapped her hands. When it was brought Gyric stepped forward, free from my hand and that of his mother.

"I know the way well," he told us in a low voice, and so we set off.

We crossed the stone floor, moving slowly, and drew closer to the open door. The booming sound grew louder as we did.

We stepped over a threshold and into a pleasure garden such as the singers of songs tell of, for it was hedged on one side by fruit trees, and screened by a fence to keep beasts away, and it had within all manner of blooming plants and vines, so that the air was thick with their perfume. At one end there was a kind of pavilion, with benches and a table, and vines growing up and around the sheltering walls. And behind the pavilion was a walkway of stone, built upon the very edge of the rock; for this was the utmost face of the cliff upon which the keep sat.

Gyric reached out and took my hand and said to me, "Now you will see the waves crashing against the rocks," and we walked, arm in arm to the pavilion, Modwynn at our side.

And we went and stood there at the edge, and I looked a long way down at red and brown cliffs, raw and bare and full of beauty, and watched the green waters crash and swirl below; and the salt water was running from my eyes as I looked at this. Gyric held my hand and I knew he recalled all the hundreds of times he had stood there as boy and man looking out upon this beauty; and I knew he trembled for what he had lost.

I made myself speak. "How beautiful it all is," I told him, and kissed his cheek.

I looked at Modwynn, and saw that she wept and turned away.

The salt smell rose up and mixed with the scent of the roses in the garden, and some sea spray too was carried up to us by the wind and wet our faces. I looked long upon the churning waters of the sea, crashing and sucking and tossing its white mane against the rock below.

Then we turned our backs on its call, and faced into the sweetness and safety of the pleasure garden, and walked amongst its trees to its end. There stood a round timber building, the door of which was open. We stepped inside, and I saw two serving men at work, pulling chests into place.

The bower-house was not large, but it had many things of worth in it. Firstly, it too had an iron casement, set with many small pieces of glass, so that the light streamed into it. There was a firepit for warmth in Winter, and brackets on the white-painted walls which held oil lamps. There were three chairs and a good sized table, handsome and well-made, and many good wooden chests. Above all was a beautiful wooden bed, carved so that the bedposts that rose at the corners looked like the heads of dragons.

"How wonderful this is," I said.

"I hope you will be happy here," answered Modwynn. "There is more work to be done, but for now I will have some cakes and ale sent to you."

She gestured to the workmen to follow her, but I stopped her with my hand. I wanted very much to give her something rare and precious and worthy of her great kindness.

"Please, Modwynn, are my packs from my mare here?"

"Here in the blue chest," she said, and went and lifted the cover for me.

I reached in and pulled out my leathern satchel. In the bottom lay the tiny scrap of linen in which I had wrapped the green and gold glass vial filled with rose oil from Sidroc. It was, I thought, the finest and rarest thing I possessed. Sidroc had said that it was far costlier than gold. My hand touched the pouch, but I could not draw it forth. I could not give this gift to Modwynn; it was the gift of a Dane, and a Dane had robbed her son of his sight. And I could not give it for the memory of the

Dane who had given it to me, desiring that it would give me pleasure.

Instead I drew forth the wool pouch into which were rolled the silks. I shook out the gown of dark red silk and the gown of blue silk, and held them up, gorgeous and shimmering. I pressed them into Modwynn's arms. "Please to take these. They are the best I can offer you, and little enough."

"How beautiful. I rarely see such fine silk. Thank you, daughter. I will wear them in memory of this most happy day."

"It is you who have made me happy," I told her, as we embraced.

She crossed to where Gyric stood, and stroked his hand lightly. "Rest now. We will not meet in the hall until dusk."

She left, and we sat down upon the bed. It was covered with a blanket of blue-dyed wool, so dark that it was as midnight. The wool was soft, and the feather mattress under it softer still.

I took Gyric's hand, and lifted it to my lips, but could not speak. My heart was too full.

As we sat there I saw a movement outside the open door, and Godwin stood in the opening.

"Godwin," I said, and stood up.

"Come in," said Gyric, and Godwin crossed over to us. Gyric still held the spear, and Godwin looked at it and understood why Gyric carried it.

He touched the shaft of it and asked Gyric, "Do you want this?"

"I just want it close," answered Gyric.

Godwin sat down next to him, and Gyric turned his head towards him. "It is good of you to give us the bower-house," he said.

Godwin shrugged. "I do not need it anymore. It is only right that I sleep in the hall with the rest of the men."

He looked at me, and said by way of explanation, "My wife has gone to her home shire, but there is no trouble between us. She is a good woman."

I did not know how to respond to this, so just said, "I am sure she is a very good woman. I hope she will come back soon so I can meet her."

He looked at me for a little while before he answered. "Yes. She would like you."

He kept looking at me, and I felt the warmth come into my cheeks. Then he seemed to realise he was being bold, and looked away himself.

It felt awkward in the room, and I wondered once again if I should go. In the hall Godwin had told Gyric that on the morrow he would pledge to avenge the harm done to his brother. There must be much he wanted to say.

I glanced at Godwin, and saw he fingered a heavy gold bracelet on his wrist. It was made of braided bands of yellow gold and red gold, and his finger traced the pattern of the braid.

Of a sudden he stood and began to pull it off. It fitted tightly about his wrist, an unbroken circle.

He looked at me as he drew it off. "This belongs to you," he said, and took up my right hand and pressed the gold bracelet, warm and heavy, over it.

Before I could speak he said, "Gyric, I give your wife my bracelet."

"Your gold bracelet?"

"Yes," he said, but he spoke now to me. "It was only one part of the treasure we wanted to offer for Gyric's life. So it is rightfully yours."

I touched Gyric's hand, trusting he would speak. "You must accept it," he told me.

Godwin looked at the ring of bright metal I now wore. It moved freely upon my wrist, but would not slide off.

"The gold-smith will fit it for you," he said.

"I would never cut such a piece of gold," I told him.

"Then you accept it."

"Yes, since Gyric bids me to."

I did not smile, nor did he. The bracelet was magnificent, perhaps the most costly thing Godwin possessed, yet he gave it away more than willingly, almost forcing it upon me. His first words to me came to mind: 'Who are you? You have done what no one here could do.' I wondered what he thought of me. I even wondered for a moment if he resented me, or resented that I had not somehow brought back Gyric unmaimed.

We stood looking at each other, and then a serving woman came in with a tray with ale and cakes. Godwin touched Gyric on the arm and said, "I will see you tonight at the hall."

OF MY FIRST
NIGHT IN THE HALL

GYRIC and I sat alone at the table, and I poured out ale for us. The door was still open, and the Sun and light of the garden outside entered the little bower-house. I could hear birds twittering as they flew from branch to branch, and under it all the low roaring boom of the sea.

Gyric said almost nothing, and put down his cup and lowered his head. All about us was beauty and comfort, and most of all, safety; and those who loved him now knew he lived, and as we sat there were preparing a feast for his return; and his parents had showed naught but kindness and regard for me. I wanted to speak of these things, for they mattered greatly to me, and I valued them beyond measure; but I was silent, for I saw that he was sunk in his own thoughts.

He took my hand, and his fingers fell upon the gold bracelet, and he traced the braided design of it with his finger tip. "I too had a gold bracelet that you would wear now, if it had not been wrenched off by the Danes."

For answer I lifted his own hand to my lips.

"Will you lie down with me?" he asked. "I just want to hold you."

I crossed to the door and closed it and we walked to the carved wooden bed. We lay down together on the top of the soft wool blanket, our arms about each other.

The bed posts with their dragon heads curved up over us. Their mouths were open and a flame of carved red-painted wood shot out from each. But they did not look angry or fearsome; it seemed that they were only guarding their own treasure. Then I realised that those lying upon the bed were the treasure they guarded, and how clever this was.

"This dragon bed is very magical," I told Gyric.

"Yes, dragons. You will like it. But it was not magical for Godwin. He had it built when he married."

"It will be magical for us. We will be happy with each other all our lives. I know I will be happy with you."

He did not answer, and I wished with all my heart that he would. But I did not press him, but only lay in his arms, stroking his face.

We fell asleep like this, for when I woke the light had faded in the room. I heard a slight tapping at the door and rose and opened it to a young girl who smiled and curt-seyed to me. She passed me a basin of warm water, and then left us.

The time was thus near for us to go into the hall, and Gyric and I washed our hands and smoothed our clothes.

Gyric said, "Modwynn told me she had my things brought here. There should be a small bronze casket amongst them."

We went together from chest to chest, and found the little casket. Gyric put it on the table and lifted up the lid.

From the top he drew out a narrow circlet of gold and placed it about his brow. Then he dug about and found a tiny leathern pouch, the contents of which he emptied into his palm. They were gemstones, of all colours and sizes. He fingered one, and held it up to me. "Is this the emerald? I will have it set in a ring, as my morning gift to you."

"Yes, and it is most beautiful."

He pressed it into my hand, and we kissed, a kiss of passion and love. He took the emerald stone and laid it back in the jewel casket. As I began to pinch out the cressets we heard footsteps outside, and a strong rap at the door.

"Enter," called Gyric, as I went to open it.

It was Godwulf and Modwynn. Both had put off their mourning clothes and were gorgeously arrayed. Modwynn wore the blue silk gown I had just given her, with a yellow head-dress. Godwulf wore a tunic of cloth of purple, very rich, and trimmed all over with silver thread-work. And each of them wore, about their brow, the same thin fillet of gold which Gyric had put on.

Even tho' I myself wore silk, I felt I stood before a King and queen, and felt abashed as I gaped at them. Modwynn came to me, and without a word lifted a circlet of shining metal she had in her hand and set it upon my brow; so that I too was crowned with gold.

I took Gyric's hand and guided it to my brow, and he felt the thin fillet which his mother had just bestowed upon me, and he kissed the golden circlet I wore. And every night we wore these golden circlets when we sat at table in the hall.

This first night the four of us walked together into the great timber hall, a hall crowded with men and women

and the clatter of plates and the rich savour of good food
in the air. And there was music, too, for the wizened-faced
man who had sat near us before was now walking, brightly
clad, amongst the throngs, striking a small harp, and he
was followed by a young woman who beat upon a little
drum to keep time, and next to her a boy held a cymbal.

And all the folk within wore their best and gayest
clothing, like a true wedding-feast; and save for the fact
that all the many thegns wore their seaxs strapped at their
waists and never took them off, one might think that only
peace and joy reigned here.

One thing also was different; for silence fell when we
four walked in, and the new husband was not greeted with
a wedding-cheer from his companions. Every torch was
lit, and cast its dancing light over the faces of those who
stood and looked upon us, and they each wore the look of
sorrow and wonder and tempered gladness.

Serving men stood ready behind the chairs of Godwulf and Modwynn, and we four came to the head table
on the stone platform. Godwin was already there, wearing
too a circlet of gold upon his brow; and the dark priest,
Dunnere by name, was there; and the same thegns who
had sat with us in the morning. Godwulf sat down, and we
too, and all the rest of the hall took their places.

Godwulf gestured to the harper, and he began to play
again, and the serving men came in great numbers to
every table and began to pour out drink and bring great
trays of food; and so the noise of the hall was restored.

The steward began to pour out mead for us, for its
sweet smell proclaimed itself even before it touched the
lips. I looked at the cup which had been set before me
and saw that it was the match of Gyric's in every way,

silver with a golden rim. It only lacked the lettering which named Gyric's as his own.

"Gyric, my silver cup is the same as yours," I told him.

He reached out and I put the cup in his hands. He fingered it and touched the plain rim. "It is my wife's cup," he said, and his voice held real pleasure. "My parents gave me two silver cups when I was fifteen. The second has been wrapped away all these years, waiting for the woman I wed to drink from it."

Gyric pressed the cup in my hands and said, "Tomorrow I will have the gold-smith cut your name into it."

I looked over to Modwynn, who was watching this with joy in her eyes.

Our beautiful cups were filled with mead, and Godwulf stood and lifted his gold goblet in the air, and for a moment the hall again was silent, and each man and woman took up their cup. Godwulf turned to his youngest son, and raised the cup to him, and in a voice hoarse with love and grief gave the simplest and most ancient of toasts: Wes Hal; Be Whole.

I looked at Godwulf's face as he so blest his son, and could see nothing else. We drank, and I took Gyric's hand as we did, and when we put down our cups they were filled again, and my heart was brimful of love and joy in him and his folk.

Food began to come, and Gyric and I ate from a silver salver and a silver bowl that night and every night since, and used spoons of silver; and Godwin too ate from silver, and Godwulf and Modwynn from a salver of pure gold. And what we ate was this: Roast salmon, and boiled eels, and funny sea creatures I had never seen before which Gyric told me were winkles and whelks; and a sweet frumenty made of white wheat boiled with sheep's milk; and thick browis of new and dried peas; and then trays of cracknels, like onto the cakes we had eaten in the bower-house, but hard and fried and dripping with honey; and then the milk-calf, which was roasted whole, and of a wonderful savour. And we drank first the mead, and then many cups of the bright ale brewed by Modwynn.

I looked about the hall, crowded with the thegns of Godwulf. At some of the tables women sat amongst them, the wives or sweethearts of the men. They looked back at me shyly and dipped their heads and smiled. In the very back was a long table, thick with the thegn's children who were old enough to have earned the privilege of eating in the Lord's hall.

When the serving men had cleared away the last of the good things to eat, and we sat with our cups being ever filled and refilled, the harper came and sat upon his stool at the very end of our table, and took up the little harp into his hands, and held it close against his breast.

He struck the harp so that the sound rang out into hall. All turned and looked at him, but he looked at no one and no thing save the strings which trembled under his fingers. All eyes were upon him, so I knew he was no common harper, but a true scop, a keeper of the word-hoard, skilled in all manner of saga telling. The first song was of his own making, the story of Gyric, for the saga he sang was of the return of a beloved lost son to his father's hall. And I was in the saga, too, for the scop sang in his song much of what both Gyric and I had told in the hall that morning, and changed little. The song ended at the wedding-feast of the returned son, but the last lines warned of blood to come, and Fate unrealised.

When the scop first started this saga, none of us knew of what he would sing, and when line by line he revealed his story, those who sat at Godwulf's table could not turn from the harper's voice. Gyric sat rigid next to me, scarce breathing as he listened, and I put my arm around his waist and held tight to him. The scop praised the courage of Gyric, and damned the treachery of the Danes, and praised too the courage and fairness of the maid who fled with him out of danger to face more danger upon the road. And tho' all in that vast hall knew by then that the scop spoke of me, I did not blush nor lower my eyes, but listened as if I did not know the end to our story, now turned by this harper to song.

When the scop finished, he struck hard upon the strings of his harp, and at last raised his eyes to Godwulf. Godwulf stared at the man, and I thought his eyes burned. Then Godwulf plucked off a small golden pin from his tunic, and threw it to the scop in answer to his work. And after the scop had caught up this rich prize, he bowed low and long to his Lord.

The scop sat again upon his stool, and again opened his word-hoard, and sang snatches of the sagas that all in the hall had heard before, for he sang of the hero Widsith, and of Weland, the artificer of the Gods; but this night he had added a new song to their store.

The torches had burnt themselves out and been renewed many times when at last Godwulf rose and gave the sign that the night had come to an end. Some thegns began to take down the tables, and others to bring out pallets on which to sleep.

Modwynn took Gyric and I each by the hand, and spoke to us. "Your father and I will come and bless your union tonight," she said.

She sent a serving man with a torch to light our way. The night air was warm and still and the pleasure garden full of the sweetness of night-blooming blossoms. When I opened the door of our bower-house, the roar of the sea followed us in. I left the door open and lit the cressets. In the flickering light I saw the loving work of Modwynn before us, for upon the dragon bed was a mound of rose blossoms, pink, white, and red, heaped in sweet profusion. I lifted an armful of them to Gyric's face, and kissed him, and he grasped me about the waist and pressed me and the blossoms to him.

We heard Godwulf and Modwynn as they walked along the stone path to the door. Gyric and I stood before the bed, and I held the beautiful roses in my arm.

They came in, and Modwynn's eyes were filled with love and tenderness as she looked upon us, and upon the roses on our marriage bed. I took Gyric's hand, and his parents raised their arms above our heads.

Godwulf spoke first, in his low and gruff voice.

"I acknowledge the union between my son Gyric and this woman Ceridwen, and that she is truly his wife. Welcome, daughter."

Modwynn lowered her arms, and touched each of us on the golden circlet we wore. "I bless you, my son, and bless and welcome this woman as your wife into our hall, and into our hearts."

They took our hands, and I tried to praise and thank them for their great goodness; and Gyric too began to praise them for all the love they had shown us. They would hear none of it, and with many tender embraces they bid us Good-night.

That night I lay long awake in my husband's arms as he clasped me hard to him; and we gave our bodies to each other with kisses mingled with sighs, for all that we had said and heard that day. And the carved dragons looked down upon us, guarding us as treasure.

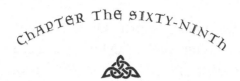

THE OATH
OF VENGEANCE

A serving woman came to the door in the morning, and brought us hot water and a brass tub. As we made ready for the day I thought that it was the first morning in so many when I did not rise and build a fire, and pack and saddle horses.

We went into the hall. Godwin was there, and his golden-green eyes fell upon Gyric and followed him. A door opened, and Godwulf and Modwynn came out of the room that must be their chamber. They sat in their carved chairs, and we ate slices of wheaten bread and toasted cheeses and drank weak ale.

No one said much at this meal. All knew what was to come, but Modwynn smiled upon Gyric and I, and made the silence easier to bear.

Godwulf raised his hand to Godwin, and Godwin stood and followed him out of the main door of the hall.

Modwynn leaned forward, and put her white hand to her brow, but said nothing. The three of us sat there, alone and waiting.

We heard them return. Godwulf came first, and behind him in single file walked five thegns, all with their hands upon the hilts of their sheathed swords. Then walked Godwin, and behind him too were five thegns, also with their hands upon the hilts of their swords.

Gyric rose and stood as he heard them come in, and I stood too, but Modwynn sat, her hands folded tightly before her, and her eyes upon her husband.

The thegns came before the table, and took two benches, and set them in a single line before us. Each of them drew his sword and sat down. And each man of them lay the naked blade upon their lap, and by doing this signified that they would pledge to everything that their Lords might say, and would without stint accept any charge their Lord might lay upon them. As long as they kept their swords upon their laps this would be so, but if any man there heard some charge which he was not willing to take up, he might without dishonour rise and sheath his sword, and so be dismissed; and no blame would come to him.

Godwulf sat down in his chair, and lay his sword upon the table before him. Godwin drew his sword out of his sheath, and lay the naked blade on the table before his brother, and stood before Gyric and looked long at his brother's face before he spoke.

"My sword is before you, brother."

Gyric reached out and touched the glinting metal, and answered in a low voice, "I accept the works of your sword."

Godwulf spoke, in his slow gruff voice. "The Dane Hingvar has treacherously maimed my son Gyric, and I proclaim that Hingvar's life is forfeit. His blood shall be on my hands. I do not ride myself to wreak vengeance, but charge my son Godwin to carry the warrant of death with him. And I pledge also my five best thegns, who will ride with Godwin, and seek the blood of Hingvar as Godwin himself will."

Now Godwin spoke, his words thrilled with anger. "I ride to wreak vengeance for my brother Gyric, and will not rest until I have plunged my hands in Hingvar's blood. And I pledge not only my own life, but the lives of my five best thegns, who will follow me and seek revenge as I do."

Then Godwin put out his hand to his brother, and touched him, and Gyric once again enfolded Godwin's hand against his own breast. As they stood thus facing each other with locked hands, Godwin turned his head and saw that no man behind him had sheathed his sword; so all pledged to follow in this charge unto death. Godwin nodded at the men, and they all cried out as one, and pounded their feet upon the floor.

Godwin and Gyric released their hands, and Godwin looked again into his brother's face. "Last night we sent riders to Ælfred, to Sibyrht, to Ceolfrith, and to Ælfsige, telling all of them of your return and asking them for news of Hingvar. As soon as we learn where Hingvar is I will be off."

Gyric nodded, and Godwin lowered his voice and said, "I have never seen Hingvar. Tell me how I will know him."

"Once seen, you cannot mistake him. He has a long red beard which he wears in a braid. In battle he wears an iron helmet painted red."

"And his companions? How will I know them?'

"If he has made peace with his brother Svein, then they may be together. Svein has red hair too, but not so bright as Hingvar, and he wears no beard."

Godwin was listening to each word with great intent, and never moved his eyes from Gyric's face. "And the other Dane – the one that would let you die beneath his hall – tell me again of him."

Gyric raised his hand and shrugged slightly. "His name is Yrling."

"Yrling," Godwin repeated. "He is a dead man. But Hingvar first; first Hingvar. And when I find him, I will not be quick about it, brother. I will make him suffer worse than you did. He will beg me for death before I am through with him!"

These words were so terrible, and Godwin's voice so full of wrath, and his hatred of Hingvar so just, that I covered my face with my hands. As I did I knew that Mod-wynn wept silent tears where she sat with her head in her hands. I looked up to see Godwin's bright eyes upon me.

"Sister, you sat at Yrling's table. Tell me of him."

It took me a moment to find my voice; my throat was so clenched it ached. At last I was able to breath out, "He is . . . perhaps as tall as you . . . he has light brown hair, worn long . . ."

"What of his companions?"

Gyric spoke for me. "He has two nephews with him. They must always fight at his side."

I could not keep my voice from shaking. "Yes . . . one is easy to mark; he has bright yellow hair . . ."

"What is his name?" Godwin demanded.

"Toki."

"And the second?"

"He is tall, and dark. He . . . has a scar that runs from under his left eye to his chin."

"What is his name?"

"Sidroc."

As I spoke this name, I sat down upon the bench, and hid my face in my hands. I felt to my core the wretchedness of betraying one who I knew loved me, and who, tho' a Dane, was innocent of any part of Gyric's wound.

Somehow I found strength to rise again, and to open my mouth. "Godwin, Yrling's nephews had no part of this. And Yrling himself did not want to accept Gyric at Four Stones, and was very angry with the Danes who had wounded him; and angry with those who had brought him to Four Stones . . ."

"I do not care about his anger. He is a Dane, and part of this, for he thrust my brother into a cellar to die. I tell you, his life is forfeit. I only pray I live long enough to kill him too. But my desire for his blood does not compare to my lust to catch Hingvar. Hingvar is far more important."

I slumped down again on the bench. Gyric still stood, and one hand still rested on the naked blade of Godwin's sword.

Godwin put his hand over Gyric's, and swore, "I will not die before I have killed Hingvar."

Then Godwin took his brother's hand away from the blade, and Godwin picked up the sword and slid it back into his sheath.

Godwulf stood and bellowed, "The pledging is done. Vengeance will be had."

And Godwin turned and walked from the hall, and the thegns all rose and followed him.

Godwulf touched Modwynn on her shoulder, and she rose, her face white and her lips thin. One son who she thought dead was returned to her, tho' maimed. Now her other son pledged his life to avenge the act. Her face was not wet with tears, as I knew mine was, and she walked away with Godwulf with a steady step; but I knew her heart must be near to breaking within her. I touched Gyric on the hand, and he took mine and held it hard, and I led him out into the morning Sun.

MORE LIKE A WOMAN

TWO days passed, days spent in welcome rest and comfort. Gyric took me about the great expanse of the burh, like onto a whole village within the palisade walls. My awe was great, not only for the richness that was Kilton, but for the justness of his people, for all, even the many slaves, were decently fed and clothed.

Modwynn came to me one afternoon as Gyric and I sat in the pleasure garden. She had a ring of keys in her hand, such as she always wore at her waist, only those she held were not so many. She took my hand and pressed the ring of keys she carried into it, and spoke to me. "These are yours, Ceridwen, as you are Lady after me now. Will you come and I will show you what they open?"

I kissed her for this great honour which she now gave me, and Gyric urged me to go with her, and so I left with Modwynn. First we went into the kitchen yard, and we opened together, she and I, all the store houses, filled with fresh-made cheeses and smoked meats and roasted eggs and sack upon sack of barley and wheat and oats and peas. And we looked at houses which held naught but cask after cask of mead, or of ale, ready standing and waiting to be tapped.

She took me into the pantry and opened the chests which held the gold and silver that graced the table; and the chests which held the bronze and copper; and lastly she took me into the chamber which was her own, and in which she had slept with Godwulf for so many years. It was the treasure room of Kilton, filled with rich stuffs. But what most caught my eye was an upright loom which held a piece of fine linen, upon half of which was worked in coloured threads many beautiful designs of linked spirals and twisting lines, and the skilfully worked forms of running stags and flying birds.

I stood before it, almost unable to praise it, and she came up beside me and touched a needle stuck in it, ready charged with coloured linen thread.

"This is Godwulf's winding sheet," she told me, simply and quietly, and with love in her voice. "He asked me to begin it when he reached his sixtieth year, and I am still at work upon it."

And she touched with her white hand the shroud that she had woven for her husband, and which with its gorgeous thread work would wrap his body as it was lowered into the grave.

I did not presume to try to answer her, or to praise a work of such love and art; and I felt awe at this woman, and awe, too for the many years she had spent at Godwulf's side.

At last I said, "Gyric told me when we were upon our travels that all that you did, you did well, and that all men respected you. I never forgot those words, and now that I am here with you I see how just they are."

She laughed to hear this praise from her son, but her eyes shone with pride. She turned away from the loom to a large plain chest on the floor. She lifted the lid and began taking up what lay within. "I have many more linens for your bed, and also new towels woven last Winter. We will take them to the bower-house so you will have a good store."

We each took up armfuls of the snowy linens, and made our way through the empty hall and into the pleasure garden. As we walked along the path, we saw Godwin and Gyric standing together in the pavilion, talking and laughing.

Modwynn and I did not disturb them, but went on our way to the bower-house. Once inside we put down the linens, and then stopped a moment in the door to look back at the two men. We could still see them, partially screened by the vines that grew up the sheltering walls of the pavilion.

"How alike they are," I said, almost to myself, as I looked at Godwin standing near Gyric.

Modwynn nodded, and then smiled slowly. "Yes, in the face they are alike; tho' now Godwin begins to show his age. A few years ago they were truly as twins. But Godwin has always been serious. He knew from a little boy that one day he would be ealdorman of Kilton, and it made him Fateful. Gyric was the light-hearted one, always laughing and jesting."

This mention of Gyric brought sudden tears into my eyes. He was so often silent, and wrapped in his own pain and thoughts; to think of him as light-hearted and jesting was hard indeed, tho' I longed to see him so.

For reply Modwynn simply put her arm about my shoulders. "You go now and join them," she told me. "I will see you tonight in the hall." She walked along the line of trees back through the garden.

I began to walk to the pavilion. I could hear Godwin speak, but could not make out his words. As I went down the path the hem of my sleeve was snagged by the thorns of a rose-bush. As I worked to free myself, the breeze shifted slightly, and Godwin's voice came clearly to my ears.

"No; she is not like that, either. She is more beautiful. She is – she is like the statue of St Ninnoc, the one on the North wall of the chapel. She is just like that, only – Cerid-wen looks more like a woman than a saint. She is more pleasing, if you know what I mean. And her eyes . . . she has the greenest eyes I have ever seen; like a cat's. But they are not yellow-green, they are like . . . a new leaf of mint."

"She told me once they were the colour of moss."

"Yes. Moss; they are just like moss."

Gyric's words were slow. "I recall that statue well. She truly is like it?"

"Yes; very much like it. Only more like a woman. And the eyes of the statue are painted blue."

The wind shifted again, and their words faded. With a tug I pulled my sleeve from the rose thorns, and I snapped off a white blossom and cradled it to my breast. I turned and hurried past the bower-house and out of the garden. I was almost running, but trying not to; and my cheeks burned from what I had heard Godwin say; and I felt some tiny seed of shame to have stood so long overhearing him.

I reached the stone chapel, and pushed open the heavy oak door, and stood blinking in the dimness looking for the North wall, and the statue. There was only one it could be, and I walked to it and fastened my gaze upon it, my heart beating so that it near filled the space. The statue was large, almost half life-size, and it showed the young St Ninnoc. It was brightly painted; the saint wore a gown of brilliant red; but it was her face I studied. She had a smooth broad brow, arched eyebrows over large, wide-set eyes, and deeply curving lips set in a smile. There was a sameness there, I saw, and if the bright blue-painted eyes had been turned deep green, it could have almost been my likeness.

I again heard Gyric telling Godwin, "I recall that statue well," and felt a thrill of joy that this gift had been made to both of us. I stepped to the base of the statue, and kissing the rose I still clutched, lay it at the feet of the saint.

That night in the hall we ate and drank and the scop struck his harp and sang out tales of loyalty and love. I sat at Gyric's side, wearing as he did a narrow circlet of gold upon my brow, listening to those who thought of me as part of their family speak a tongue which I knew fully. I felt a part of all of them, and a deep and quiet joy filled me.

Later in bed Gyric stroked my face with his finger tips. He always touched me so, touched every part of me; but this night he stroked my face with great tenderness and care.

"Wife," he breathed into my ear. "I know what you look like now; I know. Godwin told me. I can . . . I can see you, in my mind."

And as he touched me, he felt a tear running from the tail of my eye, a tear of joy; and he kissed it.

Two days later, at mid-day, a messenger came, riding hard into the keep yard. We answered the summoning horn by gathering in the hall. A serving man came forward with a cup for the rider, and he drank from it and wiped his dusty face. Gyric and I stood together, and several of the chief thegns who had followed us in stood behind us. The messenger knelt briefly before Godwulf, and rose and began his message.

"I have been to Witanceaster, and have there seen Ælfred, King; and he spoke to me himself. He has heard nothing of Hingvar or of Hingvar's brother Svein, but sent from that hour riders of his own to seek word. He swears he will send to us if he or anyone in Wessex learns where Hingvar is."

The faces of both Godwulf and Godwin showed their thwarting at this news, tho' neither man spoke. Godwulf moved his hand to dismiss the man, and the messenger spoke again.

"My Lord, I have a message from Ælfred, King, to my Lord Gyric."

"Deliver," said Godwulf in his gruff way.

The rider turned to Gyric, touched one knee to the floor, stepped nearer him. Gyric moved forward, and waited.

"My Lord, the King rejoices to hear that you live. He will come to Kilton as he may to see you, and until then sends you this token as the gift of his heart."

Here the messenger reached into the breast of his tunic, and took out a pouch of leather and drew from it a piece of glinting metal. He reached forward with it, and gently touched Gyric's hand, and Gyric found the gift, and his fingers closed around it. The messenger bowed, and stepped back, and left us.

I put my hand on Gyric's shoulder, and Godwulf and Godwin crossed over to him; and Gyric opened his hand and we looked down on what lay in his palm.

No one spoke but Gyric; it was he who told us of the preciousness of what Ælfred had sent. "It is the gold cross he wears ever, the one his father King Æthelwulf and he brought back from Rome when Ælfred was a boy."

He took the cross by its gold chain and lifted it over his head, and put it around his neck. As he did so his lips moved slightly, as if in some silent prayer, or vow; or thanks perhaps, for Ælfred's love. And never did Gyric take the gold cross off, but wore it thenceforth.

WHAT I BEGAN

THE hall did not have long to wait to hear where Hingvar might be found, for the next night as we all sat at table the horn was sounded again, and another road-weary rider was brought in. It was one who had been sent to an ealdorman named Sibyrht, who ruled a shire in the East of Wessex; and the word he sent was this: That Hingvar and his men were moving East and North, perhaps back to Anglia, and that Sibyrht himself would engage Hingvar if he came too close to his own shire.

For eleven men in the hall the meal came to an end right then; for Godwin called the chosen thegns about him, and they began to pack at once, so that they might be ready to ride at first light. We all looked upon Godwin and his thegns as they moved about us, going from alcove to alcove, spreading out their hide packs upon a table made ready. We watched them with perhaps different thoughts, but the same hopes. The thegns who would not ride looked on, and in some of their faces I saw awe, and the restlessness of envy. Three of the thegns who would ride were married, and I saw the faces of their wives, proud, fearful, and hopeful, as they watched their men prepare; and watched the pale eyes of Modwynn, filled with love and sorrow, as they followed Godwin all around the hall. Godwulf too, watched his son, but as often as he looked at Godwin he turned and looked at Gyric. I knew his anger was fresh upon him, for I thought he cursed as he clenched his golden goblet.

At last Godwin and the thegns did as much as they could, and Godwulf signalled that the night should come to a close. Everyone rose, the serving men carried off the last of the cups, the thegns throughout the hall began to knock down the tables from their trestles, and Gyric said to me, "Take me to Godwin."

I took his arm, and we crossed the hall floor to the firepit, where Godwin and the chosen thegns had laid their packs. The fire had burnt low, but the torches about the walls were still lit. Godwin stopped what he was doing and came to us, and touched Gyric. "I am here," he told him.

I thought Gyric would speak, but he did not, and only stood before his brother, silent. The linen wrap about his wound gleamed white in the fire light. Godwin raised his hand, and reached to touch Gyric's face, and for one moment I thought he would lift the wrap from off his brother's face and look at the terrible maiming that he rode to avenge. I held my breath; but Godwin did not do this. He only touched the wrap with his fingers, and then lowered his hand.

I thought Gyric trembled. I shook so that I feared that I might fall. Godwin embraced his brother, and I heard Gyric rasp, "I will come at dawn before you ride."

Gyric turned, and walked a little away, and I looked at Godwin and yearned to say: You must come back, you must come back for Gyric's sake, for the sake of all at Kilton.

But no words fell from my lips, tho' tears formed in my eyes. Godwin turned his golden-green eyes on me, and all the light and movement and keenness that had been burnt out of Gyric's countenance was before me, and my heart moved within my breast as it had the first moment I had seen Godwin.

And with his eyes he read my thought, for he answered me, "I do not wish to die." His words were quiet and low. "There is too much I have not yet lived to do. I have seen twenty-six Summers, and want many more. I have still no son, or any child behind me. Godwulf is old, and if I die Gyric cannot now rule Kilton. I want to live, but more than life I want revenge for Gyric, and I will die winning it, if I must."

Then he stepped forward and kissed me on my forehead, just where the golden circlet lay upon my brow. I put my arms about him, and he held me fast in his embrace. "I will finish what you began," he whispered.

The strangeness of his words did not keep me from speaking this time. "You will come back," I said, and commanded that this might be so with every particle of strength in me.

But for answer he gently pushed me away from him, and I went to Gyric and clutched his arm. Blind with my own tears, I led him from the hall.

We scarcely slept that night, nor do I think did anyone within the palisade wall. The garden was still in shadow as

we dressed, only far to the East could be seen the first grey
streaks of morning. All the doors to the hall were opened,
all the torches ablaze, and from out in the yard through
the great main door could be heard the stamping of horses
and jingling of bridles as the packs were tied on to the
saddles. Now I saw the chosen thegns of Godwulf attired
in all their war-gear. Godwin I saw first, for he stood in the
centre of the hall, speaking to his father, his light copper-
gold hair looking near as bright as his father's swan-white
head. Godwin listened to the old man, and then quietly
spoke; his face was resolute but not grave. He wore a dark
leathern tunic, and over it one of iron rings, blackened so
that no light shone off the fire from it; and under his arm
he held an iron helmet, also coloured black. He wore dark
leggings and leg wrappings over them of black leather,
and from his black leathern baldric hung his silver-hilted
sword, and beneath this across his belly, his seax. Nothing glinted from him; whatever gold or silver he wore
was hidden, save for the hilts of his weapons; there was
no showiness about him, only the sober gear of a trained
warrior who fights to kill: and the sight of him was more
awe-ful for it. The ten who went with him looked much
the same, dark and grim, with no glitter about them, and
all of them bore also a black shield of alder wood, studded with iron bosses. The priest Dunnere was there, and
he went amongst each of the men, speaking in the Holy
Tongue; and he blest each of them in turn.

Modwynn came to her eldest son, bearing in her
hands a large silver tray crowded with cups, and Godwin
took one, and each of the thegns took one as well. Then
the eleven of them stood together in their battle gear, and

Godwin raised his cup, and the ten pledged thegns raised theirs, and so they saluted each other, and drank.

Godwin came to us, and again embraced Gyric, and said, "I will not die before I have killed Hingvar."

That is all he said. He turned and called out to the men, and they swept through the door. Modwynn had her arms about Gyric and I, and the three of us walked with all the others into the yard. I saw Godwin and his men swing up upon their horses, and lash their spears across their saddles.

And in front of all of us stood Godwulf, quiet in his lordly power, his white hair falling to his shoulders. Godwin turned in his saddle and raised his arm and saluted him, and Godwulf lifted his arm to his son. Then Godwin and his men were gone, and the still-rising Sun shed no warmth upon us left in the echoing yard.

The days that followed went by so slowly that it seemed mid-Summer instead of May. The light and warmth of the lengthening days, the comforts and safety of being at Kilton, the great kindness Modwynn showed me, the deepening joys of my love for Gyric; as precious and valued as this was to me, nothing could dispel the shadow across my happiness. For Gyric and Godwulf and Modwynn it was even worse, and I thought real gloom settled into their hearts.

The movement of the hall went on endlessly about us, but it was quieter, I knew, without Godwin, and each night all looked at his empty place. The scop took up his harp and sang songs of war and love and honour; but he did not sing again the song he had made of Gyric, nor would he, I thought, until some end came of it.

Gyric did all I asked, listened, walked with me, would do everything I wished except ride out; but all that he did he did with little relish. Only in the dragon bed did he seem fully alive to me, and only there could I find real happiness, for there his passion was undimmed, and I could taste again the bliss that I had known with him from our first day of love. But those hours were too few, and even they often ended with his sigh, as he closed his hand about the gold cross on his bare chest.

A week passed, and then two, and it was June, and every fullness and beauty of Summer was about us. And since seven Sundays had passed since Easter, it was now Whitsuntide, the greatest festival of the Church next to Easter itself, and so it must be celebrated, sorrow or no. There was a procession through the village, and a feast given for all the folk as a gift of the hand of Godwulf. On Whitsunday all Kilton crowded behind us into the little chapel and saw the wooden statues wearing real mantles of bright wool for the day; and I tried not to look too long at St Ninnoc.

Soon after this Modwynn and I and some of the younger women in the hall went riding together. We spent the morning riding the hard clay roads of Kilton, viewing the fields in their first harvest, and flock after flock of fat sheep. All of this put me in mind of Ælfwyn, and of a sudden my heart cried out for her.

As we rode into the yard Modwynn and I were alone, and I said to her, "I want so much to honour my pledge to the Lady Ælfwyn at Four Stones. I promised her that when Gyric and I reached safety I would send some word to her, that she might not worry. But I can think of no way to send word to Lindisse, not even a token."

Modwynn listened to this plea, and thought aloud. "Lindisse is very far, but messengers travel even the greatest distances. But what messenger would be safe going there? It is wholly of the Danes."

I had no answer; it was the same stopping point I had always reached. Then she answered herself. "A churchman will go," she said.

"A churchman? Go to Lindisse?"

"Yes. They have need of them enough. A bishop should be asked to send churchmen, since it is the first task of the Church to convert the heathen, and no one is more heathen than the Danes." She smiled at me. "I know what we will do. Ælfred will come soon. Write out your message, and have it ready for his coming, and I will ask him to have it given to the Lady. Surely some priest or monk will be bold enough to try to take God's word to Lindisse."

The thought of what I might say in this letter gave me a sudden unwelcome chill. But I shook it out of myself, and with many thanks left Modwynn at the hall door.

I found Gyric in the garden where I had left him. I went to him and he raised his face to me, and I kissed his lips. I thought of the nights and mornings spent in his arms, and of the touch and taste of him; and wondered what Ælfwyn might think when she learnt that I lived with and loved Gyric, and was the wife to him that she had once longed to be. I did not think I could write any letter which could explain this aright; and the thought of a strange monk reading my words to her made my throat dry. No letter would give me all the space I needed and wanted to tell the story as I wished to.

I said to Gyric, "This afternoon I will write my letter to Ælfwyn, since your mother feels sure that the King will send a churchman to deliver it."

This is what I told him. What was left unasked was what he might desire me to say to her for his sake.

He did not answer me. I touched his hand and asked, "Is there . . . any one thing I should tell her?"

He shook his head, and only said, "Tell her the truth."

This was my truth, and how I wrote it to her:

TO THE NOBLE LADY ÆLFWYN,

Mistress of Four Stones in Lindisse, and begging the good and prudent judgement of the Holy Servant of God who reads these words to her; that she may hear them in private. Lady, know that she who you took in and treated as your own sister is well, and sends you by the work of her hands this greeting. Gyric of Kilton lives, and has grown strong amongst his people here at Kilton, for we journeyed here together, arriving the 18th day of May. Tho' his hurt be grievous, his folk rejoice in his life, and have received me with great kindness. And now I reach out and embrace you as my true sister, and hold you to my breast as I tell you that Gyric is my husband, and I his wife, and that we know true joy together. And this happened upon our journeying here. I send my kiss to you, with every thought for your safe and happy life. I will send again to you as I can, and beg you to send to me if you might be able. Until then I am your loving

CERIDWEN

It did not say enough; it did not say half of what I wished it to say; but it was the truth, and I read it to Gyric and he solemnly nodded his head. When I was done, and all the ink had dried, I lay it away in the wood chest that held my leathern satchel.

THE FULFILLER
OF OATHS

NONE of us were too busy to count each day that Godwin had been gone, and now these days numbered twenty-four. Each of us greeted every new day with some hope, and each day that passed without his return hope fled empty from our grasp.

One mid-day Gyric and I sat alone in the pavilion. It was misty and cool, and the Sun passed slowly from cloud to cloud, hiding her face and making silver the sky. As we sat together, listening to the roar of sea against rock, the brass horn of the palisade sentry rang out. Gyric lifted his hand, as if to keep me from speaking. We heard first a short note, then a long, and then a short; and this was followed by a long blast.

"Godwin," said Gyric, and stood up at once. "Godwin is back."

Before I had a chance to take his arm the side door of the hall opened, and Godwulf strode across the path to his son.

"He is come," he told us, and these short words were all he uttered.

He took Gyric's arm and I followed them as they hurriedly crossed to the open door. The hall was being emptied of serving folk and weaving women, and the thick oak table was being set up on the stone platform. In a dark corner I saw the wizened scop standing silently, his ear cocked, waiting.

Godwulf guided Gyric to the table, and stood next to him. Modwynn was nowhere in sight; perhaps she was in the furthest part of the burh, or even in the village.

We stood there, the three of us, on the stone platform, unmoving as we faced the great open door. Now we heard some noise from the hall yard; now the thegns at the door moved onto the broad step to look; now we heard the trampling of hard-ridden horses and the jingling of metal against metal.

The waiting thegns parted, vanished. We heard the wail of a woman, then two; then a lone dark figure stepped through the door.

It was Godwin. He came first and alone, and as he approached the table a line of other men followed him in. But I saw no man but Godwin; it was he whom my eyes caught and held. He walked slowly, but seemed unhurt. He wore the same blackened ring shirt and dark clothing as when he had left, but now they and he were begrimed and streaked with dirt. His black baldric still held his sword, and his seax lay still in its sheath, but he did not rest his hand upon its hilt as he approached us, for he grasped in his right hand a small leathern hide pack. Now I saw that his right arm had been hurt, for the tunic sleeve had been cut open, and his forearm bandaged, and he bore too a wrap across the back of his right hand as it gripped the leathern pack.

I saw all this as he walked to the table, but more than these things I saw his face: for no one, I thought, could look upon it and then look away. He seemed to have aged ten years in the days he had been gone. There was a look about him, in his eyes, in the set of his mouth, that struck real fear into me, and quelled within me the joy I felt at seeing him alive and whole. The face was filthy, and tired, and worn, but the eyes and mouth spoke the tongue of sheer torment.

He stopped before us, and looked behind him at the men as they followed after. They were the pledged thegns, and I counted them as they lined up behind him. The first were two together, for one was held up by another, and bore around his thigh a blood-stained wrap that showed he had suffered great hurt. Then came another, and another; two, three, four, five. Eleven men had ridden to avenge Gyric. Six now stood before him.

All the waiting thegns who had stayed behind came into the hall, and the great door was swung shut, closing out the wailing of the women in the yard. Godwin stepped onto the stone platform before Godwulf and Gyric.

"I have fulfilled my pledge," he told them. "Hingvar is dead."

Godwin raised the leathern pack he carried in his hand and dropped it upon the table in front of his brother. It fell with a dull and clanging thud, and the thought of what might be inside made me feel of a sudden sick.

Gyric put out his hand and touched the pack, but he did not open it. He pulled back his hand, and I thought I felt him tremble at my side.

Godwin's eyes had been fixed upon his brother, but now he raised them and looked quickly all about the hall. "Dunnere!" he cried. "Where is Dunnere! Get him."

A thegn at the back pulled open one of the doors and ran out to fetch the priest.

Godwin's eyes fell upon me, and I think he saw me for the first time. "Sister, leave us," he told me. His words were low, but each was a command. "You will not want to hear what I am about to tell."

I clutched at Gyric's hand. The place was filled with horror, but I did not want to leave Gyric. But Gyric him- self bid me go, for he made the slightest movement with the hand that held mine, and so I let slip my fingers from his, and backed away from the table to the door.

A thegn pushed it open for me, and I looked back to see Godwulf and Gyric unmoving before the table, and Godwin looking with burning eyes at them both.

I stumbled out into the garden, trying to calm my racing thoughts. I walked back and forth along the paths, and the hem of my gown grew wet from brushing against the sodden grasses. At last I forced myself to sit at the table, and tried to still myself by listening the sea beneath me.

I rose and walked to the edge of the stone walk to look down upon the rocks. As I stood there I heard a noise, and turned to see Modwynn, her skirts in her hands, come rushing in a gate of the garden on her way to the hall. I raised my hand and ran to her, and we clasped each other.

"Godwin is well, he is whole," I told her, and we were both breathless. "He has suffered some small hurt to his sword arm; I do not think it is bad."

"God bless him," she murmured, and crossed herself.

"He said he had fulfilled his vow."

She put her hand to her lips, and then drew breath and nodded. "Is Dunnere with him?"

"Yes, he called for Dunnere right away."

Now the beautiful white hands rose again, and she crossed herself once more. "May God forgive him," she whispered.

She turned as if she would go into the hall, but I caught up her sleeve and stopped her. "Godwin ordered me out of the hall. He would not let me hear what he did to Hingvar."

Modwynn swallowed hard, and murmured a near-silent prayer. Pity was in her face, pity for her son, and what vengeance had driven him to wreak. "God forgive him," she said again, and this time tears welled in her eyes.

She brushed them away, and composed herself with a breath. She looked at the hall door, closed against us. "We are going in," she told me, and took up my hand in her own.

We went to the door and she took the bronze handle of it in both her hands, and pulled it open. A thegn stood just inside, but when he saw who it was he did not stay us.

The hall was quiet. A bench had been brought for the returned thegns, and the one with the wound to his thigh was now sitting upon it, his leg rigid and straight before him. His eyes were closed and I thought he gritted his teeth against the pain.

Godwin still stood before Godwulf and Gyric, but the old man now sat, his brow creased in thought. Godwin, tho' he stood, looked slack, as if he barely kept his feet. Off to one side, a few feet away from him, knelt Dunnere, his hands clasped together, his eyes closed, rocking slightly to and fro as he prayed. Gyric stood motionless at the table, his cheek pale and his head lowered. I saw that the pack had been opened before him.

I came up to Gyric, and could not keep my eyes from flitting to the opened pack. There was something like a horse's tail in it, or a hank of bright-dyed fleece; I could not make it out. When I was closer I saw the red mass for what it was, and the sight of it made me shudder, for it was the braided beard of a red-headed man. It was coarse and wavy and bright red in colour, and I tore my eyes from it as I saw that the tips of it were fused and singed from burning.

The pack held also several arm rings and bracelets of silver, and something like a buckle or shoulder pin of gold. It was hard to make out what each thing was, for they were all jumbled together, and some of them were broken or bent.

I heard Godwulf speak. He was questioning Godwin about the movement of some Danes, names I did not know. I did not listen well, for my eyes now cast over the other smaller bags that lay before Gyric. I saw a sword hilt, the blade broken off short, and the hilt embellished with silver and copper wire. There were more bracelets of silver, some just the plain ropes of metal the Danes favoured, others finely wrought; there were a few arm-rings, and also some finger rings.

Then in one pack I saw a talisman I knew, and a cry came to my lips. There lay the silver hammer of Thor that Yrling wore each night and day about his neck. The shining silver chain was broken, but the amulet itself lay perfect in its brilliance upon the dull leather.

I cried out as I saw it, and my fingers went to it, but I could not touch it. Godwin had been speaking, and now he stopped, and looked at me.

"It is the Dane Yrling's," he told me, and his voice was flat. He seemed to recall something, and said to Godwulf, "Ælfsige is dead. That is how I caught Yrling. The Dane Healfdene attacked Cirenceaster, and it was a lure too strong for Yrling to resist. He came, and fought against Healfdene, and that is how I took him."

He looked back at the thegns who shadowed him, and said, "It was there I lost Eadweard and Leofwine."

Godwulf considered this news a moment, and then asked, "And do you know the Fate of Cirenceaster?"

"No, my Lord, I do not," answered Godwin. "We were few men against many, and Ælfsige was no true friend to Æthelred or Ælfred. I was there by good chance, for after I had done with Hingvar I heard that Healfdene was moving against Ælfsige. I went only on the hope of catching Yrling there."

Now the injured thegn shifted on his bench, and stifled a groan, and Godwin turned back to him and bent low over the man.

This was a spur to Godwulf, for he rose again. "The vow has been fulfilled. Vengeance has been won."

No man answered this time; no man spoke. The fruits of the pledging laid before Gyric, and Godwulf looked down upon them. "There is good treasure here, Gyric, wrested from your bitter foes. Do you accept these proofs of vengeance?"

Gyric's voice was steady and cold. "Yes."

Godwin came forward and picked up his sword from the table, and took his brother's hand and laid it upon the hilt. He spoke no word to him, but Gyric closed his other hand over that of Godwin, so that both wielded it.

Gyric let go the sword, and Godwin slid it back into his sheath. Gyric's hands went down to the treasure, and he touched it. And I knew he had touched it before, for when his fingers met the hank of singed beard, they drew away.

"I give this treasure to the care of Dunnere the priest, to be melted down and sold to aid the poor of Kilton," he said.

Dunnere rose and came swiftly to the table. His eye scanned the silver and gold there, and he dipped his head before Gyric. "My Lord, you shall be doubly blest in heaven," he told him.

Dunnere began folding up the packs. Some sound must have escaped my lips, for Gyric turned his head slightly to me. I looked at him, and my eye fell again upon the hammer of Thor.

I touched Gyric's hand, feeling all eyes in the hall upon me. "My Lord," I stammered out, calling him thus for the first time. "Please to give me the silver amulet from Yrling."

Dunnere's dark eye flashed at me, and I said quickly, "I will pay its weight in silver coin to Dunnere, to relieve the poor."

This did not matter to Gyric; the twist of his lips showed me this. He did not understand my desire for the piece, nor could anyone else in the hall.

There was no way but the truth. "It has meaning to me," I explained. "Because of the Lady I served at Four Stones, Ælfwyn. Yrling put it around her neck the day they Hand-fasted. I was there. She . . . she had at one time some regard for him. I would like the amulet for her sake. I will send it to her."

For one moment he was silent, and moved not. "Take the amulet," he said quietly. "There is no need to replace it with your own silver. There is treasure enough here."

I reached out and plucked the silver hammer from the table. The broken chain swung from my hand like running water. The amulet was cold and heavy in my grasp.

Men were moving now about the hall. Thegns set up tables, and serving men were coming in. Godwin went back to the injured thegn and sat down next to him. Godwulf came up to Gyric, and laid his arms around his son's shoulders. Modwynn vanished into her chamber; I knew she must have gone for the Simples chest.

I saw Godwin rise, and begin to walk towards the main door. Holding the silver amulet in my hand, I stepped off the platform and hurried after him. He was almost to the door when he turned and saw me.

No one was near us. I knew many folk waited outside the door, including the widows of the dead. Perhaps he went now to speak to them. But something within me would delay him in even this pitiful task.

He turned and looked at me, and I felt his weariness was so great that only by force of will he stood before me. But his eyes told me it was not only weariness of body, and the hurt from his injured arm that afflicted him; but rather some sickness of the soul.

Now that I was so close to him, I did not know how I could trouble him with my question. Still, the words rose to my lips, and I spoke. "Godwin, the nephew of Yrling – the tall one with the scar – did you kill him?"

His eyes searched my face, and scorched me with their gaze. "Why are you crying?" he demanded.

"Because . . . because he is a friend to me."

"Well, he is an enemy to me, and to Gyric, and to Godwulf, and to all else here at Kilton."

He turned his back upon me and started moving away.

I reached out my hand but could not touch him. "Please, Godwin. Only tell me. Did you kill him? The tall one, with the scar?"

He turned, and his words were harsh. "No. I did not kill him, tho' he tried to kill us. Once I had killed Yrling, and snapped the chain from his throat, I called to my men to flee. I only wanted Yrling's life, and I had taken it. There were a handful of us, and many of them, and they were fighting also Healfdene's men. A few of them gave chase, led by the tall one. It was he who has crippled Wulfstan."

He stood before me, his arm raised towards the injured thegn.

"You are hurt yourself," I said.

"It is nothing. I must go now."

"Godwin, I am glad that you return; very glad."

He did not answer this, but turned and pushed open the door to the yard.

I went to the front of the hall. The injured thegn was lying on his belly upon a table, and Modwynn was sitting by him, the Simples chest opened before her. She was cutting the bloodied bandage off when I came up to her.

"Godwin will be back soon, and you will wish to wash his wound," I told her. "Please to let me care for Wulfstan."

She looked up at me, and her wisdom was such that she read my face even with all else which was in her care. "Are you well, daughter? I can wash and dress Wulfstan's wound."

"No, no. I want to; truly I do."

And she believed me, and rose, and I sat down by the injured Wulfstan and washed and dressed the wound that Sidroc had driven; and as I did I bit my lip to keep from weeping.

And Godwin was right, Wulfstan was crippled, for he never more could walk aright after this, but was always lame.

In the hall that night we drank to the thegns who had not returned, and I lifted my cup to them. But I could not drink to their glory without recalling the dead Yrling, nor could I have pity on the young wives of the thegns without weeping for Ælfwyn.

The scop took up his harp and sang the song he had made of Gyric and me, but now it was different, for it began and ended with Godwin, and the blood-vengeance he had won in the name of Godwulf. All listened long and hard to this song, and at its end Godwulf motioned to scop to come forward, and the old ealdorman pulled off one of the silver arm rings that he wore, a massive piece of great worth, and placed it into the scop's hands for rich reward.

I did not stay long in the hall that night. I felt sick and sad and went for the first time alone to the bower-house. I had put away the silver amulet in a scrap of linen. Now I took it out and held it. I resolved to take the chain tomorrow to the silver-smith, and have him make it whole again. Looking at the broken ends made me think of the moment of Yrling's death, and I would not send the amulet to Ælfwyn bearing such a message. I looked at the letter I had written for her and knew I must add to it some line of comfort, and felt I had none to give.

I undressed and laid in the dragon bed and waited for Gyric. I heard him come along the path, guided by a thegn, I thought, and then he stepped into the house, flushed from drink. I slipped out of bed and went to him and he caught me up in his arms and held me. I thought he trembled, but it may have been me who shivered. He had drunk much; all the men had that night, and I had left long ago; but his mood was not shaped by drink alone. Vengeance had been had, and Godwin had returned whole to tell of it himself. He had not been sacrificed in the winning of it; the people of Kilton would not be deprived of Godwin's rule once Godwulf himself was gone to the Summerlands. A pledge had been made, oaths sworn; now they were fulfilled, and tho' nothing could restore to Gyric what had been lost, payment had been exacted.

He kissed my lips, and lifted my hands and kissed them too, and pressed my hands to his face. "Ceridwen, do not be troubled by Godwin. He did not mean to be harsh to you on his return, when he sent you out of the hall."

"I understand it, my love. Is he all right?"

He did not answer at first, and I saw by the set of his mouth and the furrow in his brow that it was Gyric himself who was troubled. No strong drink or scop's song could soften the truth of how Godwin had won his vengeance. "Yes . . . It is just . . . he . . ."

"You do not have to tell me."

"No; and I would not tell you. You do not want to hear. It is just that he . . . lost his head when he caught Hingvar. He did things that . . ."

Gyric shook his head, and went on. "He did nothing that I myself would not have done," he ended, and his voice was defiant as he defended his brother.

I said nothing to this. I already had heard at the hall that Godwin had trailed Hingvar to his camp, and snatched him away from his fellows at night when Hingvar was deep in his cups. The Dane had suffered every torment as his punishment. Godwin had left no part of his body unmarked by fire or seax, and denied him even the mercy of a killing sword-thrust; the man had died slowly, and in agony. It was no more or less than he had promised at the pledging, and yet all must have expected that Godwin would have simply slayed Hingvar, as he did Yrling.

"He did what he swore to do," I answered.

"Yes. Dunnere is praying for him."

I almost wanted to laugh, but there was no mirth in me. My father Cerd and his brother Cedd had killed many men in war, and some too, I was certain, in blood-vengeance, but never, I thought, had they then asked forgiveness for the doing of it. Nor would Yrling or Sidroc or the hated Toki take a man's life and then run to the place of Offering to be absolved. Christians, I had been taught, valued life more than heathens; but they were equally willing to slay. The difference was in their eager repentance.

"Is all well with you?" Gyric asked. He ran his hands down my bare skin. "Do not get chilled."

"I am well, but only tired," I answered, and climbed back into bed. He pulled off his clothes and soon lay next to me.

"You are troubled; I can feel it," he told me.

I knew he was weary and full of ale and wished to sleep. I too wanted sleep, but felt that night that it would not come easily.

"I cannot stop thinking of Ælfwyn; that is part of it. I wonder if she has learnt of her father's death. I worry for the Fate of her mother and sisters, and the Fate of all at Cirenceaster if it has truly fallen. And Yrling is dead. What shall she do now?"

He breathed out a slow breath. "I do not have those answers," he sighed, and laid his hand on my heart. "I would that I did. Tell me what else."

I took his hand and held it in both my own. "There is Godwin. Do you think Ælfwyn will learn who killed Yrling?"

He listened to this carefully, and considered well before he spoke. "If Yrling's men were near to him when he was killed, then at least they will know why, if not who. Godwin would have called out my name as he delivered the death-blow."

This caused me to be quiet some little time, thinking on it.

"What will happen to her? What will happen to all the folk at Four Stones?"

"Difficult to guess. We only know Yrling is dead. Perhaps Healfdene won Cirenceaster; or perhaps Healfdene's men were defeated by Yrling's men, or by some other group of Danes. Ælfsige's thegns may even still hold Cirenceaster, tho' it is not likely. Yrling's men may have returned to Four Stones, or it may have been attacked by another Dane when word was spread that Yrling was killed."

I buried my head in his shoulder. I wanted to shut all of this out of my heart and mind, but to do so would be to shut Ælfwyn out; and this I would never do.

"You must sleep now," Gyric whispered, and I fell asleep holding fast to him.

I rose early, tho'; and while he was still abed went to the chantry-house and carried back more ink, and added this to the letter for Ælfwyn:

Beloved Lady, this sad talisman once adorned your neck, and that of your husband. I send it to you with tears.

Then I sewed a simple sack of white linen to hold both parchment and amulet, and so made them ready to be taken away by the coming King; and my tears fell upon the linen as I sewed it.

CHAPTER THE SEVENTY-THIRD

AS WE EXPECTED IT

I did not feel well the next day, nor the next. There was no one thing wrong with me; I did not feel strong and well and happy as I was used to. Gyric and Godwin were much together, for which I was grateful; for Gyric was always brightest when by his brother, and Godwin too recovered his strength and spirits. But looking at him I thought some one thing within him was changed forever, tho' I could not tell you what it was.

One day Godwin came to me as I was changing the linen bandage around Wulfstan's wound. He went to the thegn's head and spoke to him, and made him laugh with some jest or other, for which I was glad. Then he came and looked over my shoulder as I worked. The gash was deep and very ugly, but it did not appear to fester despite the seeping blood and yellow fluid that soaked the wrap every few hours.

Godwin spoke, almost in my ear. "Wulfstan says you care well for him. You have my thanks as well as his."

It was hard to accept thanks for this task; I felt bound by duty to care for the man. I felt too that Godwin understood why I had undertaken it.

I nodded my head, without turning to look at him. Then his hand reached out and for one moment encircled the gold bracelet which I wore as his gift. He held me thus for but an instant, and I still did not turn to look at him; but in that instant I felt all was well between us, and that no words could say more.

On the third day after Godwin's return a message came from Ælfred, and it was brought by two riders. They said that Ælfred himself would come to Kilton in a fort-night, and begged that things might be ready to receive him and his companions.

This news itself was cause for rejoicing, and cause also for much work and planning, for Ælfred would come to Kilton with at least sixty thegns, all of which would need housing and food and drink for the stay. And tho' Ælfred had spent much of his youth at Kilton, and was like unto a brother to Gyric and Godwin, he was now King, and needs must be received in especial state and comfort.

I helped as much as I could with the provisioning. Modwynn learnt that I was good with numbers, and set me to counting all the casks of ale, and to numbering every bronze cup, and to planning how much mead should be poured out each night.

On the third or fourth morning after this news I went out with Modwynn into the kitchen yard. A woman there was stirring an iron cauldron of browis, and the sharp savour of it rose to my head.

Of a sudden I felt green, and began to retch. A cook was with us, and she grabbed an empty basin and held it before me, and I lost the toasted loaf and ale I had eaten in the hall that morning. Modwynn held my shoulders and handed me a cloth to wipe my mouth. My face was hot with shame, and with, I thought, the sickness I must be coming down with. Now the cook lifted a cup of weak ale to me, but as I smelt it, I thought I should retch again, and waved it away.

"Bring water," ordered Modwynn.

I drank a bit of it, and said, "I am so sorry to retch in the kitchen yard. I do not know what happened. I have not been well, these past days. I think I am only tired."

Modwynn squeezed my shoulders and smiled. "Yes, I think you should rest. Let me walk with you to the bower-house."

She nodded to the cook that all was well, and then we went, the two of us, through the hall. It was a damp day, and Gyric and Godwin and Godwulf sat together by the fire. Godwin looked up at us as we walked by.

Modwynn and I went through the pleasure garden, and as we walked she noted, "All the roses are gone. But they will return next year."

She pushed open the door of the bower-house, and I went to the dragon bed and sat down upon it. I felt better just being away from the kitchen yard and its smells.

She sat down next to me, and placed her hand upon my brow.

"I do not think I have fever," I told her.

She laughed, very gently. "No, you do not have fever." She leaned forward and looked into my eyes. "How long has it been, Ceridwen, since you had your Moonflow?"

"I am waiting for it now. It is late, very late, but I do not always bleed right after the full Moon."

"You mean when you were a maid you did not always."

"Yes," I blushed. "That is all I can measure, because I have not bled since Gyric has been my husband."

"And that was since . . . the middle of May?"

"Yes, the fourteenth day of May."

"That is a long time."

"Yes, but my breasts are heavy and sore, the way they always are before my Moon."

She laughed and took my hand in hers, and spoke to me with love and wonder in her voice.

"My dear daughter, I think you are with child. You have not bled for many weeks, and your breasts are sore? Do you not know that often a woman's breasts are sore in just this way, when she has gotten herself a babe? And you say you have felt tired, and not yourself. You are with child, my darling daughter."

Now she was hugging me, and me her, and she was laughing and crying at the same time.

"A child! So soon! And you are so strong, so full of vigour, the babe is sure to be a strong one. How happy I am; how happy Godwulf will be! It has weighed on him so, to think no grand-child was left behind. It was sorrow enough with Godwin and Edgyth, but then when we thought Gyric was lost to us . . . Now all of that is changed, and the new year will bring new life!"

I could not help but laugh, too, for the wonder of it, and for the silly surprise of it, for now that she spoke of it I felt it to be true. I put my hand on my flat belly, and she laughed again at me, and laid her own white hand over my own.

"Shall I bring Gyric?" she wanted to know.

I felt flustered. It did not seem right for us to know and him not to, but it was all so new.

"You need time," she decided, and so answered her own question. "There is no hurry."

"I will tell him right away; I want to."

She leaned over and kissed my forehead. "That is good. It will give him such joy to hear it."

As she finished speaking someone knocked on the door, and then we heard Gyric's voice.

"Ceridwen? Is all well?"

Modwynn rose and opened the door. "Everything is well, Gyric," she told him, in a voice full of cheer. "Now I must return to the kitchen yard."

She moved past him, and I rose and came to Gyric and touched his arm.

He took my hand and said, "Godwin told me you two walked out of the hall together, and that you looked weak. Are you well?"

"Yes, I am very well. Both of us are."

He sounded uncertain at this. "You mean – you and Modwynn?"

"No, me and our child."

"Our child?"

"Yes. I have got your babe; I am with child. I did not know it until just now; but I am sure."

"A babe?"

"Yes."

He said no more, nor did I, for his arms closed around me, and he held me tight to his chest. He put his hand under my head-dress and stroked my hair, and touched my face.

Finally I whispered to him, "Are you happy, my love?"

His answer sounded as if it was coming from far away. "Yes. I do not know how to think, but I know I am happy." He shook his head and almost laughed. "I always believed that one day I would wed, and have children of course, but now that it is true –" His voice grew soft. "But nothing happened as I expected it."

"But you are happy, Gyric?"

"How could I not be? To have a wife such as you, who loves me as you do, and to have a babe with you? And so soon . . ."

"That is what your mother said," I told him, and knew my cheek was red.

He held me in his arms again and spoke low in my ear. "Of course it happened so soon. I cannot stay away from you. You are so – beautiful, and your body is so soft, and warm, and lush . . ."

His words died out, and he stiffened in my arms.

"What are you thinking of?" I asked.

"Of Godwin."

"O."

"You will give me a child soon, and he has none. And he will be the next ealdorman of Kilton, and have no son."

I had no answer for this.

His thoughts went on, for his next words were, "God-wulf will be pleased when he hears your news."

"Modwynn said that as well."

"She is right. Will she tell him now, or wait for you to tell him?"

The thought of telling Godwulf that I was with child was not an easy one. "I hope she will tell him. Or you tell him."

This made him laugh, and he kissed me.

Modwynn did tell Godwulf, and I knew it the moment I entered the hall that night, for he looked at me with an eager eye, and smiled upon me, and he did not often smile upon anyone. The smell of the food did not bother me, and I ate well; but the smell of the ale made me queasy, so Modwynn had broth brought for me instead.

As we left the table that night she told us that she and Godwulf would come to us again in the bower-house, and so Gyric knew as well that his father had been told. The Moon lit our path to the house, and I looked far up at the shining face and touched my belly and laughed, and whispered my thanks to him.

I lit all the cressets in the bower-house as we waited for them, and I thought of that first night they had come to us, to bless our marriage. Now I heard them on the path, and they came in, and Modwynn's eyes were full of love and Godwulf's full of pride.

He came to me, and took my hand, and kissed it; and then drew from his tunic a silver chain, at the bottom of which hung a lustrous pearl, almost as large as that which Ælfwyn had. He gently dropped it into my hands, and then straightened up and spoke.

"I gave this pearl to Modwynn when she was my bride. Today when she told me of your news, she offered it to you, to show you our joy in this babe."

I wanted to embrace him, and her as well, for the love shown in this gift, but he cleared his throat and went on. "I have grown old. Until lately I feared going to my grave without knowing who would inherit after Godwin. Then you came into my hall, and brought back my son to me, and now you bring his child to come as well. From today I know my name will live, and not die with this aged flesh of mine."

Now I did embrace him, and Modwynn too, and gave her great thanks for the glistening pearl. She put it around my neck, as was right as it had been worn by her for many years. The pearl looked just like an egg, and the egg is the token of fertility; and we all knew this as we stood there, but I did not blush. I felt proud to be with babe so soon, and filled with love for Gyric for his seed, and great gratitude for the endless kindnesses of Modwynn and Godwulf.

When we were alone Gyric said to me, "My father esteems you greatly. I have never heard him speak so before."

His words were slow and thoughtful, and for answer I took his hand.

"You give to him what he had begun to despair of ever having. You are precious, Ceridwen, in every degree. You have given me everything; given so much to all of us."

He reached out and found the silver chain as it hung against my breast. His fingers slipped down to the pearl, and closed gently around it.

In the morning Gyric told Godwin of our news, but I was not there with them, for I felt too queasy when I woke to go to the hall. In the afternoon when Gyric and I sat out in the pavilion, Godwin came up to us, and took my hand and embraced me.

"I am glad for you," he told us, but his voice was tight as he spoke. He turned away, joy and sorrow mingling in his face, and I was thankful that he did before Gyric felt it in him.

ÆLFRED, KING

THE day before Ælfred was expected two riders came down the clay road through Kilton, bearing each the banner of the King of Wessex. They rode quickly, so that the golden dragons upon the dark banners streamed out behind them in flight. The riders were come to say the King would arrive early on the morrow, and to be certain all was in readiness to receive him.

Modwynn received their message with pleasure. The great body of the work was done. Three oxen had been slaughtered and dressed, hundreds of loaves baked, scores of fish were being drawn up from the fish weirs, and cups, platters and bedding all gathered. Godwin and the horse-reeve had taken charge of all outside the hall, and fodder and grain for four score extra horses had been gathered.

Modwynn and I went back into the treasure room, where we had been sorting linens.

"I have never seen a King before," I told her, and I think some concern shown in my voice.

"Only watch me, and you will be fine," she counselled. "You will stand by Gyric's side as always, and I by Godwulf's. When they kneel before Ælfred, you and I will curtsey. That is all."

My face showed I could hardly believe it.

"Ælfred is like a third son to me, tho' he now be King. There is nothing to fear," she laughed.

That night in the hall everyone spoke in heightened voices, and moved more quickly than usual; all were in good cheer. Only Gyric was quiet. I knew a part of him was eager to once again be with Ælfred, and that another part, just as strong, feared the hour of their meeting, when Ælfred should once again behold him, but behold him so changed. It was always thus with Gyric, I thought, as I held him in the dragon bed that night. A war went on within him, a war without victory or truce.

In the morning we were all up and ready at first light. I dressed myself in the watery-green silk gown I had worn the first day we came to Kilton, and tied the pheasant sash with my ring of keys about my waist. I regarded myself long in my small silver mirror. I knew I was richly dressed and looked well; the mirror told me that. But much else was within me that the mirror did not show. Gyric had told me that I gave to everyone, but I felt it was me who had received so much: his love, the love of his people, and now the joy of our babe. I only wanted all to be well for Gyric, as well as it could be; and for this meeting with Ælfred to be a boon and comfort to him.

Word had come that Ælfred would soon arrive, and we stood together in the hall as we waited for the horn to sound.

When it blew, all heads lifted. The great door was swung open, and we stepped out into the warm Sun of a fair morning. All the thegns of Kilton were there, waiting, and they fell in behind us as we walked to the palisade gate. The yard folk lined the way for us. There would be no work done that day, and they stood expectantly, jostling each other slightly as they tried to be still. The horn kept sounding, and then we gained the gate and stood outside it on the hard clay road; and then before us came Ælfred, King, and all his train.

Two riders came before him, carrying each a long dark banner upon which a golden dragon flew. Then rode the King, quite alone, mounted upon a chestnut stallion. Behind him rode a line of perhaps eight nobles, ealdorman, I thought, by the richness of their dress and the worth of their horses. Behind these rode three long files of thegns, each in full war-gear. At the very end were ten or more waggons, pulled by horses.

We had now taken our places before the gate. The two riders with the dragon banners stopped, and Ælfred came towards us, and reined his horse in as well. He swung down from it, and Ælfred stepped forward and looked on us.

He was not over tall, and was slightly built, like Gyric. The hair which fell upon his shoulder was coppery-gold, like Gyric's, but far darker in colour, or perhaps it was the paleness of his skin that made it seem so. His mouth was mild, almost tender; and his eyes a bright blue; but it was in his eyes that the weight of his rule showed, for tho' I knew he was just the same age as Gyric he looked much older. He wore a tunic of blue, without any rich trim, but the gold pin which held his light mantle was studded with jewels, and he wore about each wrist a gold bracelet such as I now wore. About his brow was a circlet of gold; but it was broad and heavy-looking, and cut into it were letters which I could not see clearly to read; and the circlet was set also with gemstones of every colour. He wore a sword and seax, too, and had his left hand upon the hilt of his sword as he approached us.

Modwynn curtseyed, and so did I, with more reverence and feeling than I had ever before done. Godwulf and Godwin fell upon their knees, and Modwynn must have touched Gyric, for he too dropped down and knelt. Godwulf pressed the palms of his hands together before him, and held them out before his young King, and Ælfred at once clasped both of his hands over those of the old ealdorman, and received his homage from him.

He still held the old man's hands and pulled upon them to make him rise; and Godwulf did, and stood before Ælfred, King. Then Ælfred embraced Godwulf, and Godwulf clasped him as a son.

Ælfred stood back and turned to Godwin, and Godwin extended his hands as Godwulf had, and Ælfred took them in his own, and lifted him too to his feet; and they embraced as brothers, and Godwin's face shone with pleasure.

Then Ælfred came to where Gyric still knelt, and Gyric felt him there, and pressed his hands together and held them out to his King. And then the King did that which made tears spring to my eyes, and to the eyes of all about us, for he bent down and kissed the hands that Gyric held up to him, and then enfolded them in his own.

Gyric stood, and they embraced, and the face of the young King was pressed against that of Gyric, and I saw him close his eyes in sorrow as his brow brushed against the white linen that hid Gyric's maiming.

The King loosed his grasp upon Gyric, and went to Godwulf, and Godwulf turned to his own waiting thegns, and lifted his arm in the air, and all Godwulf's thegns sent up a cry in response, and welcomed their King with their cheers. And the watching folk of the burh joined in this cry of welcome, so that this joyous noise drowned every other.

We all turned to walk through the palisade gate, and Ælfred gestured that Gyric should come by his side. Ælfred took his arm, and the tears overflowed my eyes to see Gyric honoured thus.

All the great train that followed Ælfred came behind us, the nobles first, slowly walking their horses, and the long files of thegns; all crowded in. We gained the hall, and Ælfred stepped in first, holding still to Gyric, and then came Godwulf and the rest of us, and for a moment we were alone in the hall before it filled with ealdorman and thegns and serving men.

"I must kiss my second mother," were the first words I heard the King say, and in response Modwynn was before him in a moment, and she kissed Ælfred and he, her; and they laughed together. His voice was low and measured, pleasant to hear. Looking at and listening to him I knew why he must be so well loved, for he wore his nobility with ease, and yet with a soberness far beyond his years. All of this gave him a sort of grace which I had never yet seen in man or woman, and I was greatly struck by it.

Then the King's eye fell upon me, and Modwynn motioned me to come forward, but it was Godwulf who spoke. He came up beside me, and took my hand and that of Gyric's, and so presented us to Ælfred.

"This is the young maid that you have heard of, she who snatched my son from the jaws of Death."

Godwulf said this so gravely, and with such strength, that he might have been speaking of the deed of a great warrior; and Ælfred looked at me with eyes full of respect and even wonder.

Gyric spoke, and his voice was rich with love. "She is maid no more, for she is my wife, and even now carries my babe."

Ælfred looked at me again, and tho' I lowered my eyes for a moment, I raised them to his gaze.

"I thought I would find no woman to be Gyric's equal," he said. "Now she stands before me."

All the colour came into my cheek, but the young King went on. "Gyric saved my life, not only on that day, but many times before; and you saved his. Therefore I will honour you as a sister, just as I honour him always as a brother. And I will take special interest in your child, and do all I can to further it."

Gyric pressed my hand, and I felt his pride in me. I could say nothing to Ælfred; my heart was too full. I could but murmur, "My Lord," and I bowed to him.

When I raised my head I saw the eyes of Godwin upon me, and that the colour was fled for a moment from his face. I saw in that moment his own deep yearning for a child.

There was no time for anything more; the hall was crowded with men, and then Godwulf and Godwin were greeting the nobles; and all of them came up to Gyric and spoke to him; and around us every table in the hall was being set up, and swarms of serving folk were bringing out platters of food and ewers of drink; and the clatter of cups and calling of voices filled the hall.

A third chair was brought to the head table, one which came from the treasure room, for I had seen it there. It had a high back, and sides and arms deeply carved, and looked to be of great age. It was placed for the King between the chairs of Godwulf and Modwynn, and all the other benches set up, and so we took our places.

We stood at the table as our cups were being set out, and I saw that a thegn of the King's unwrapped a goblet and brought it forth and set it before Ælfred. It was of solid gold, and set all about with dark ruby stones. Modwynn took up one of two silver ewers, and poured out golden mead into the golden cup of Ælfred; and then she poured out for Godwulf, and then did me great honour by passing the ewer to me. So I poured out for Godwin, and for Gyric, and for Dunnere the priest, and for all of the nobles, and since I did not know their rank I chose to serve the eldest first, as a mark of respect, and so poured out for each of them, and they smiled upon me and nodded as I did.

Lastly I poured out for myself, feeling warmed through without drink.

We took our cups in hand, and then Ælfred himself raised his hand, and all fell silent, and the young King's eye was bright as he turned to Godwulf.

"The Danes have left Wessex, and have set up in Lundenwic, and have sworn on their most sacred talismans to leave us. A leader has emerged amongst them, the jarl Healfdene, and they call him their King; and he pledged to me in his own blood. And in return I gave him treasure of 12,000 pounds of silver, and this treasure I took him myself with three hundred thegns riding behind me, and behind them I had one thousand armed ceorls. This is why he accepted the treasure and left, for due to you and those others pledged to me, I was able to show him such strength in number of arms and men that the Danes resolved to fight us no more, but to be content with the treasure and warning I gave. By the mercy of God this is the news I have come to give you."

These tidings were greeted first by hushed silence, then by cries of awe and amaze. Godwulf answered in his gruff voice. "The Dragon drives the Raven from our door. God truly moves across our land, and moves in you, Ælfred, King."

And all took up this cry, Ælfred, King, so that the hall rang with it. We stood with raised cups to honour he who now led us, and who had wrought this good thing; and Gyric clasped me about my waist, and I looked at the line of his beautiful lips, now curved in a cry of joy. I glanced about me, and my eyes and heart were filled with the image of Ælfred flanked by Godwulf and Modwynn; and Godwin turned his golden-green gaze upon me as I stood there, and a true smile played on his lip and he saluted me with his cup.

And the joy that I knew from all this, from love and passion and welcome and safety, and the hope of peace, and kinsmen live and caring, was echoed deep within me by the joy I knew from my coming babe.

And every word herein is true, so I swear it.

Ceridwen, daughter of Cerd, wife to Gyric of Kilton

CALENDAR OF FEAST DAYS

MENTIONED IN THE CIRCLE OF CERIDWEN

Candlemas – 2 February

St Gregory – 12 March

High Summer – 24 June

St Peter and Paul – 29 June

Hlafmesse (Lammas) – 1 August

St Mary – 15 August

St Matthew – 21 September

All Saints – 1 November

Martinmas (St Martin's) – 11 November

Yuletide – 25 December to Twelfthnight – 6 January

ANGLO-SAXON
PLACE NAMES
WITH MODERN EQUIVALENTS

Æscesdun = Ashdown

Æthelinga = Athelney

Basingas = Basing

Caeginesham = Keynsham

Cippenham = Chippenham

Cirenceaster = Cirencester

Defenas = Devon

Englafeld = Englefield

Ethandun = Edington

Exanceaster = Exeter

Glastunburh = Glastonbury

Hamtunscir = Hampshire

Hreopedun = Repton

Jorvik (Danish name for Eoforwic) = York

Legaceaster = Chester

Lindisse = Lindsey

Lundenwic = London

Meredune = Marton

Sceaftesburh = Shaftesbury

Snotingaham = Nottingham

Sumorsaet = Somerset

Swanawic = Swanage

Wedmor = Wedmore

Witanceaster (where the Witan, the
King's advisors, met) = Winchester

GLOSSARY OF TERMS

browis: a cereal-based stew, often made with fowl or pork

ceorl: ("churl") a freeman ranking directly below a thegn, able to bear arms, own property, and improve his rank

cottar: free agricultural worker, in later eras, a peasant

cresset: stone, bronze, or iron lamp fitted with a wick that burnt oil

ealdorman: a nobleman with jurisdiction over given lands; the rank was generally appointed by the King and not necessarily inherited from generation to generation. The modern derivative *alderman* in no way conveys the esteem and power of the Anglo-Saxon term.

frumenty: cereal-based main dish pudding, boiled with milk. A version flavoured with currents, raisins and spices was ritually served on Martinmas (November 11th) to ploughmen.

seax: the angle-bladed dagger which gave its name to the Saxons; all freemen carried one.

scop: ("shope") a poet, saga-teller, or bard, responsible not only for entertainment but seen as a collective cultural historian. A talented scop would be greatly valued by his lord and receive land, gold and silver jewellery, costly clothing and other riches as his reward.

thegn: ("thane") a freeborn warrior-retainer of a lord; thegns were housed, fed and armed in exchange for complete fidelity to their sworn lord. Booty won in battle by a thegn was generally offered to their lord, and in return the lord was expected to bestow handsome gifts of arms, horses, arm-rings, and so on to his best champions.

trev: a settlement of a few huts, smaller than a village

tun: a large cask or barrel used for ale

wergild: Literally, man-gold; the amount of money each man's life was valued at. The Laws of Æthelbert, a 7th century King of Kent, for example, valued the life of a nobleman at 300 shillings (equivalent to 300 oxen), and a ceorl was valued at 100 shillings. By Ælfred's time (reigned 871–899) a nobleman was held at 1200 shillings and a ceorl at 200.

Witan: Literally, wise men; a council of ealdorman, other high-ranking lords, and bishops; their responsibilities included choosing the King from amongst their numbers.

withy: a willow or willow wand; withy-man: a figure woven from such wands

HISTORIC VERACITY

The fictional characters in this book play upon a stage of actual historical events. I have used as my framework the *Anglo-Saxon Chronicle*, a series of histories that King Ælfred (b.849–d.899) commissioned during his lifetime. The Chronicles were written in Old English save for Manuscript F, written in Old English and Latin. Unnamed scribes in various religious foundations assembled the Chronicles[1]; the dates they cover range from Year One to 1154, the final year covered in the version known as the Laud Chronicle. The *Anglo-Saxon Chronicle* itself makes fascinating reading and is a primary source for what we know of the period.

A few of the more important dates incorporated in *The Circle of Ceridwen* and *Ceridwen of Kilton* include:

871: King Æthelred of Wessex and his young brother Ælfred fight against the Danes at Basingas (modern day Basing); the Danes take the victory. Two months later Æthelred and Ælfred again face the Danes at Meredune

---

1 There are seven extant versions of the Chronicle, and a few fragments beside. The most important are known today as Manuscript A (The Parker Chronicle) Corpus Christi College, Cambridge, MS. 173; Manuscripts B and C (The Abingdon Chronicles) British Museum, Cotton MS. Tiberius A vi and Tiberius B i, respectively; Manuscript D (The Worcester Chronicle) British Museum, Cotton MS. Tiberius B iv; Manuscript E (The Laud (Peterborough) Chronicle) Bodleian MS. Laud 636; and Manuscript F (The Bilingual Canterbury Epitome) British Museum, Cotton MS. Domitian A viii.

(Marton), and after fierce fighting and great losses on both sides the Danes win. Æthelred soon dies (possibly from wounds suffered at Meredune) and his twenty-three year old brother Ælfred is named king.

874: King Burgred of Mercia driven overseas by Danes after ruling twenty-two years.

875: King Ælfred of Wessex launches naval foray in the Channel, fighting against seven Danish ships and capturing one.

877: After a battle and siege at Exanceaster (Exeter) the Danish leader Guthrum makes peace with Ælfred, and Guthrum and his picked men swear oaths of peace upon an huge silver (sometimes recorded as gold) armring, held sacred to them. One hundred and twenty Danish ships lost in bad weather at Swanawic (Swanage).

878: At Twelfthnight, while Ælfred was keeping Yule at his estate at Cippenham (Chippenham), Danes launch a surprise attack, sweeping over Wessex and driving the king into hiding, and many overseas. Seven weeks after Easter Ælfred rallies enough troops to challenge the invaders. In open battle the Danes are routed and take refuge at Cippenham where after a siege they surrender. Guthrum and his thirty closest men swear to leave Wessex and to accept baptism. The resulting treaty is known as the Peace of Wedmor (Wedmore), where the conclusion of the baptism festivities were held. The *Anglo-Saxon Chronicle* records: "Guthrum . . . was twelve days with the king, who greatly honoured him and his companions with riches."

ABOUT THE AUTHOR

Octavia Randolph has long been fascinated with the development, dominance, and decline of the Anglo-Saxon peoples. The path of her research has included disciplines as varied as the study of Anglo-Saxon and Norse runes, and learning to spin with a drop spindle. Her interests have led to extensive on-site research in England, Denmark, Sweden, and Gotland. In addition to the Circle Saga, she is the author of the novella *The Tale of Melkorka*, taken from the Icelandic Sagas; the novella *Ride*, a retelling of the story of Lady Godiva, first published in Narrative Magazine; and *Light, Descending*, a biographical novel about the great John Ruskin. She has been awarded Artistic Fellowships at the Ingmar Bergman Estate on Fårö, Gotland; MacDowell Colony; Ledig House International; and Byrdcliffe.

She answers all fan mail and loves to stay in touch with her readers. Join her mailing list and read more on Anglo-Saxon and Viking life at www.octavia.net.